Ride or Die Collection

Lauren Biel

Library of Congress Cataloging-in-Publication Data

Ride or Die/Lauren Biel 1st ed.

Cover Design: Book Love Designs by Mel

Photographer: Michelle Lancaster (www.michellelancaster.com)

Model: Chase

Back Cover Quote: Kelsey M. (@between.pages.with.kelsey)

Content Editing: Sugar Free Editing

Interior Design: Sugar Free Editing

For more information on this book and the author, visit: www.LaurenBiel.com

Please visit LaurenBiel.com for a full list of content warnings.

Hitched

M/F Dark Romance

This book is dedicated to all my readers who will never look at a hitchhiker the same way again

Chapter One

A shiver rakes my skin as the rain pelts me. My shirt sticks to me, the water pressing the fabric tight against my body. It's horrible, but it's better than where I came from. I'd walk through a hurricane as long as I was heading away from the guarded world I ran from.

Despite the rain worsening by the minute, I keep walking. Every bad decision I've ever made put me right here, on the side of the road, in the middle of the night. During a fucking storm.

Another pair of headlights washes over me and breezes by. I scoff, exhaling drops of water that cling to my lips. I can't be mad, though; I wouldn't pick up someone like me, either—a large, rugged, tattooed man, as dangerous as they come. A very real threat to society, as I've been told in front of a jury of my peers on more than one occasion. There are two types of people in this world: those who stop for a stranger on the side of the road and those who keep on driving.

If they're wise, they keep on fucking driving.

Regardless, being on the side of the road in this storm is better than prison. I'd endure a tsunami if it meant I was outside my fucking cell.

I had *just* gotten back my privileges when I escaped. I might have gone a little overboard with the newfound freedom they gave me. Took a whole fucking yard instead of an inch, but that's how I've always been. Men like me don't deserve freedom, but we sure as shit chase after it.

Another car drives by, kicking up mud and a torrential roar of water as it passes. I squeeze my eyes closed and try to center myself like they taught us in therapy. The *only* useful thing I learned in prison was how to deal with the things I can't control. But I hate losing control . . . now. Didn't mind it so much as it fueled the rampage that landed me in prison in the first place. Didn't mind it when the loss of control made me kill one inmate who was trying to fuck another. I didn't really care about the man pinned against the wall. But he had stabbed me, and it was an opportunity to catch the fucker with his pants down—literally and figuratively. He was too interested in the meal in front of him to notice me or the white t-shirt I used to strangle him. His last breath meant nothing to me because I was already a lifer.

The best part about life in prison was that it kind of became a free-for-all. They kept slapping more time onto my sentences, but I still only had one lifetime to give them. All that blood I shed in prison was essentially free. Anything I did cost me nothing. Even my little escape won't matter.

I'll enjoy it while it lasts, before they shove me back into isolation with only my fucked-up mind for company.

And fucked-up it is.

Selena

My fingers thrum against the wheel. I lean forward, trying to see for the millisecond after the wipers whoosh by before the rain obscures my windshield again. I hate driving in the rain, especially when it's a downpour like this. My wipers can't keep up, and the glare from signs and lights fucks with my eyes. It's already hard for me to see at night without the lines in the road melding with the rain-covered asphalt.

I pull over, flashing my emergency lights. I'll get myself killed at the rate I'm going, blindly driving down a highway at night. I turn off the car and sit in the near silence. Only the patter of hard rain against the car breaks the quiet. It makes different sounds as it collides with windows or the car's metal frame—almost like music.

Fog climbs from the hood, clawing at the windshield. There's a knock on the glass, and I snap my attention to the passenger-side window. That sound definitely isn't the rain. It's too loud and purposeful. My heart skips several beats and climbs into my throat.

The wind shifts and the rain changes direction, and that's when I see the shadow outside my car. The giant hand knocks on my window again. I turn off the ignition and lower the window a mere inch. Even with such a small gap, the rain finds its way down the window and onto the seat.

"Can I help you?" I call over the pounding downpour.

"Would you be willing to give me a ride to the next exit?" the shadow asks.

I look around. The road is empty, with deep pools of rainwater everywhere my eyes land. It's miserable outside. Torn between being smart or kind, I don't answer him. I'd want someone to help me if I was stuck in the rain. Thunder crashes and makes me jump.

"Miss, it's okay if you don't want to," he says with a smile. All I can see against the dark night are his white teeth and a soaked, light-colored shirt. "Sorry to waste your time. Drive safe." He pats the roof of the car and walks away.

I take a deep breath and watch him meander through the storm-cut beam of my headlights. Their weak glow gives me a little more information about him: he's a big guy. Massive, really, with flimsy, wet material hugging his muscles. I lean forward and watch him as the wipers make another pass.

Don't, I remind myself.

He doesn't even have a jacket, I argue back. *Nothing but that short-sleeved shirt, which is plastered to his body, and there haven't been any other cars on the road for a while now.*

No, Selena, don't even think about it.

He tugs at my heartstrings. *If he's so bad, he wouldn't have walked away,* I rationalize with myself. I take off my seatbelt, lean over, and prop open the door. The wind pushes back against my hand as water assaults my skin. I struggle to keep it open.

"Hey!" I call out. When he doesn't turn around, I beep my horn.

He stops, looks back, and seems to consider my invitation for what feels like forever as the cold rain soaks my skin. He heads toward my car. I'm tempted to close the door and lock it before he gets here, but I've committed. I already opened the door and invited him inside. The pressure of the wind comes off the door as he swings it open and leans down. The dome light casts a gentle glow, and I'm able to see more of him. He's maybe in his forties. Up close, his stature intimidates me more than when he was just a giant shadow leaning into the car.

He looks hesitant, maybe because I'm younger than him. If he's in his forties, I'm half his age. Maybe he doesn't like the idea of getting in the car with someone so young.

"You sure about this?" he asks.

I focus on the way his full lips hide a hint of a smirk. I swallow hard and nod. I'm not sure about anything. This isn't like me.

He sits down, saturating the passenger seat. I feel immediate regret. It's a new car, and I didn't think this through. "Sorry," he whispers when he realizes I'm staring at the now-soaked seat.

"It's fine," I say, as calmly as I can.

He smells like a storm—a wet, polluted smell that fills the small space. He flashes his blue eyes up at me as he buckles his seatbelt and waits for my move. My jaw clenches with tension over what I've done. It just feels wrong, and his good looks only make it worse. Why would someone who looks like him be walking along the highway in the middle of a storm? Where the hell did he come from?

"Are we going?" he asks, ripping me out of my panic.

I look around and struggle with the simple motions of putting the car in drive. I can't even take my foot off the brake. "I really can't see," I say. "Can we wait?"

His eyes dart as he looks behind us. "I can drive," he says, and unbuckles his seatbelt.

I shake my head. Handing control of the car to a stranger is the definition of a bad idea. I've already compromised my safety by letting him inside the car, so I'm not about to hand over the damn keys.

He blows a breath and wipes a hand through the wet hair clinging to his forehead. "God, I did *not* want to have to do this."

My heart races as soon as the words leave his lips. The hairs stand up on my neck. My peripheral vision fades to a white blur as my body panics before my brain knows what the hell is happening. He brushes a hand through his hair, exposing a tattoo of a skull with a bullet hole right beneath his hairline.

Alarm bells explode inside my head.

The man leans over and yanks something from the back of his pants. "Either you drive, or I'll drive," he says calmly. Even though I've never really seen one this close, there's no mistaking the ominous weapon in his hand, but he doesn't aim it at me until I go for the door handle. "Don't do something stupid, pretty girl." His voice is soft, almost sensual. He isn't panicking, but his calm demeanor is making me panic.

I remove my hand from the handle and put it on my lap.

"Now drive."

Chapter Two

Lex

The fear on her face makes me feel a moment of guilt about what I've done and what I'll have to do. I hoped to carjack some piece of shit and leave them on the side of the road—probably dead—but no, I ended up in the car with a sweet-faced young girl. It isn't ideal, but it is what it is. I won't let her gender affect what I plan to do. It's all in motion, and there's no turning back now.

I grip the pistol I stole from a simple B&E on the way here. I had hoped to find some money, but this would do. It'll get me money, one way or another. An armed robbery would just be another item on my lengthening list of felonies. At this rate, I'll have a scroll of them come next week, and I have no intention of actively avoiding them. It's just who I am at this point.

A felon.

Her hands tremble on the steering wheel. There's a diamond on her left ring finger. I tighten my lips. Married? Fan-fucking-tastic. Part of me hopes I won't have to make this girl's husband a widower, but the other part of me doesn't really care if I do. Everyone is a stepping stone on my path to freedom. I don't care who it is. I don't care who this girl or her goddamn husband are, for that matter.

"Where are we going?" she asks. Her voice is so small I almost don't hear it over the rain.

"Just keep driving south."

"I can't." Her eyes widen and breaths rush from her mouth. The fear on her face doesn't come from me, which makes no fucking sense. It's different.

I look at the purple rabbit's foot hanging from the rearview mirror and chuckle too low for her to hear over the rain. It sure isn't her lucky day. "You don't have a choice. What are you so afraid of, rabbit?"

Her eyes leap to mine, and I nod toward her good-luck charm.

9

"You don't understand . . ." She shakes her head as if she doesn't want to explain herself to the man with a gun on his lap, which is fair.

"Then make me understand!" My raised voice makes her tremble harder, and the car swerves on the road. When she shakes her head again, I lean over and put a hand to her throat. She squeaks as my warm skin wraps around her, but I don't squeeze. "I'm asking you once more, rabbit. What are you afraid of? Besides me." She feels so small and vulnerable in my grasp.

Her dark eyes widen, and she lets out a wavering exhale. "He'll kill me," she whispers. The words pinch past her lips, as if it hurts her to say them.

My jaw ticks. Who has this girl so damn scared? Who does she fear more than the escaped felon beside her?

I remind myself why I'm there in the first place. Her personal life doesn't matter to me. "Not my problem. You're going to drive where I tell you, then you'll be free to go."

Her throat bobs against my palm as she swallows, and she makes a point of dropping her gaze to the road in front of her.

"That's a good girl." I pull my hand away and let my fingers crawl down her neck, nearly reaching the swells of her breasts before I pull away. I can't help stealing this moment. It's been so fucking long since I touched a woman. She's lucky I have more control than I did over a decade ago. The trip would have gone much differently then. And felt a lot fucking better.

Selena

I am so exponentially fucked. I shouldn't have allowed him inside my damn car. He's running *from* something, but I need to run home *to* something. The clock on the dashboard flashes the time, ticking ominously toward nine.

My phone rings, and his name pops onto the screen. My fingers rush to ignore the call, but the man beside me grabs my wrist and hits the answer button instead. I look at him and shake my head. He squeezes my wrist harder.

"Selena?" The voice blares from the car speaker. I'm frozen in fear. The man beside me slaps my cheek hard enough to shake me back into the moment, and I can only hope my husband doesn't hear him.

"Hi . . . hello, sorry, bad reception from the rain," I say, my throat tightening.

"Why aren't you home?"

"I had to pull over because of the rain. I couldn't see anything in front of me."

"You know that's not true. I'm watching the tracker on your phone. You're going the wrong direction." Accusations lurk within his words, as if he thinks I'd run away from him. I'd never be able to.

The man's face tightens. He grabs my phone off the cradle on the dashboard, drops it on the floor, and smashes it beneath his boot. My mouth gapes as the gravity of it hits me.

"Tracking you?" he asks as he shakes his head, which is really fucking judgmental for a man who's holding me at gunpoint.

"It's complicated."

He stares at me before dropping his gaze. "Drive, rabbit." He gestures forward with the barrel of his gun.

Rabbit? I *hate* that he calls me that. I don't want a nickname from him. I want to yell at him and tell him to call me Selena or nothing at all, but when I open my mouth, the words stick in my throat. I catch a glimpse of his strong jaw and realize he probably wouldn't care if I told him I hate the name. I know nothing about him, but he doesn't seem like the understanding type. He seems like a psychopath who's judging me for my life choices, but I'm not the one carjacking a woman to escape whatever they're running from.

Chapter Three

Lex

This girl will not stop chewing on her fucking nails as we drive into the parking lot of a seedy motel about an hour south of where she picked me up. It's dark and the rain refuses to let up. The rhythmic sound of the rain and the constant click of her nails against her teeth are driving me mad. At this point, I want to cut her fingers off to end the incessant noise.

"For the love of god, stop!" I shout. She slowly draws her hand from her face and puts it back on the steering wheel.

Thank fuck.

I tuck the pistol into the back of my sweatpants and cover it beneath my t-shirt. Rain pelts us the moment we step out of the car. When we get beneath the cheap vinyl awning, I pull her into me, lean down, and whisper in her ear. "Don't do anything stupid, rabbit."

"Stop calling me that," she snaps in a harsh whisper.

"Go on, rabbit. Hop." I pinch her side, and she takes a hurried step forward with an angry blush to her cheeks. I don't want to deal with her any more than she wants to deal with me. It would be easier and quieter to kill her and take her car. By the time anyone finds her body, I'll be in Mexico.

She hasn't done anything to get me to that point yet, but it would never be entirely off the table.

We walk into the lobby, and a bell rings overhead. Wallpaper struggles to keep its grip on the walls, and what's still intact is black with mold. I look at Selena. It's clear she's never been in a dump like this before. She's wearing a slightly damp blazer and slacks, for Christ's sake. She looks clean and professional. I sure as fuck do not.

A squirrely old man waddles from the back room. His eyes jump between us. "Can I help you folks?" he asks with a furrow of his gray brow.

"We need a room for the night," I say.

"Alright. We just need a photo ID and a credit—"

"We need . . . a room." I keep my voice low and smooth as I wrap my arm around her waist. Her lips tighten at my touch, and I hope he doesn't notice that she clearly isn't here by choice. I don't need another death on my hands so soon.

A look of understanding washes across the man's face, and heat flushes his cheeks almost as much as it does hers. "Oh, *that* kind of room." He swivels his head to look toward the back room. "Eighty dollars cash will do it," he says with a flirty smile. His eyes travel down her body and overflow with hunger, and I'm tempted to gouge them out and give him something to eat that isn't her.

I clear my throat. When Selena doesn't produce her wallet, I pinch her side again. She lets out a small squeak and pulls cash from her purse.

The man cocks his head. "You okay, miss?"

I squeeze her waist closer to mine.

She flashes the man a disingenuous grin. "Yes, just nervous. It's my first time here."

"Hopefully not the last," he says with a gross smile.

I dig my nails into her side. She hasn't done anything wrong, but he's being a pig. In the broad scheme of things, I'm not much better, but at least I'm subtle about taking a moment to check out her curves.

When she brushes her dark hair back and tucks a few strands behind her ear, I notice a purplish pink hue on her newly exposed neck. Her lips are tight, and her jaw is tense. She looks so uncomfortable, which I guess is a normal response for normal people when they've been taken against their will.

The rain continues pelting the blacktop as we exit the lobby. There's an ominous silence beneath its gentle patter. A heavy quiet beneath the rain. She braces herself against the weather and hurries along, her eyes darting from one numbered door to the next, until she stops at our room for the night. 306. The six is missing, but it clearly existed at some point. I can tell by the grimy outline that remains. I unlock the door and let her inside.

Her fingers move to cover her nose, and I can't blame her. A fragrant bouquet of stale piss greets us, and the sheets look like they've been run through the same washing machine for the last ten years. The threadbare comforter has likely been there since 1963, but the television on the warped dresser looks like a newer model. The stains on the carpet bridge the gap between decades, having accumulated over the many years since this shithole was built. A roach scuttles along the baseboard. It pauses and seems to assess Selena with the same horror displayed in her rich brown eyes.

By the look on her face and the curl of her lip, she's never been in a motel room like this. I flop down on the scratchy comforter covered in horrifying floral patterns. No matter what kind of bed it is, it has to be better than the one in my cell. The mattress releases a loud squeal as I scoot back and lean against the headboard.

"What's wrong, rabbit? Not up to your standards?" I ask, but I already know. This girl has never spent a night in less than a three star, I'm certain of that. If she's really roughing it, she might have found herself in a two, but definitely not this. I'm not even sure you can give a single star to a place like this.

She sighs, slips off her jacket, and hangs it on a hook. The metal rips from the wall and drops her expensive blazer onto the filthy floor. She picks up her beloved haute couture piece with her trembling hand and holds it away from herself as if she'll catch a disease from simply looking at it. "Disgusting," she whispers.

"Fancy little show bunny," I say with a laugh.

Her eyes shoot to me and narrow. "Fuck you." As she spits out the words, her brows furrow in surprise at her outburst. It's clearly been pent up in her throat for a while now. Her frustration makes me hard in an instant. God, she looks cute when she's mad.

I adjust the front of my pants. I don't want her to see me hard, because if she gets scared . . . like that . . . I won't be able to stop myself from doing something I will *not* regret. I'm trying to behave around her, but behaving has never been my strong suit, as my record has shown. I'm not even sure why I'm trying to be good. Why does it matter?

I had fucked-up parents—a doped-up whore for a mother and an absentee sperm donor for a father. I may not have known him, but if he fucked my mother, he was probably fucked-up, too. I was in and out of the system since I could walk. I've never known anything but pain.

And I've inflicted nothing but pain.

She walks into the bathroom and squeals at something in there. I get up to see what she's fussing about and spot a used condom lying across the counter. I'll give her a pass on this one. It's pretty fucking gross, but I've also seen a man's intestines lying on a prison sink, so . . . Actually, it looks eerily similar, but instead of being filled with come, the intestines were filled with blood.

She backs into my chest, flailing the moment my body stops her motion. With a snared panic, she leaps away because going forward means confronting the menacing condom. Her eyes dart from the bathroom to me and back, as if she's trying to figure out which is more repulsive. I hook an arm around her waist to push her aside, and she jolts.

"Relax," I whisper. "Now you're hopping like an actual rabbit." I push past her and grip the thin edge of the toilet paper between my fingers. The rusty holder squeaks in protest as I pull. Once I've gotten enough to create a barrier for my fingers, I push the condom into the garbage. "All better," I say with a shake of my head as I walk away from her.

The stunned expression remains on her face. I've seen much worse shit than that in prison, and it will take more than a little condom to get me worked up.

She exits the bathroom like a surgeon who just scrubbed in, avoiding all contact with her surroundings. I rub the bridge of my nose. I'm exhausted. She has to be, too.

Even looking as weathered as she does, she still looks out of place. Like a rose growing in the middle of a landfill. Beautiful, but surrounded by trash. She perches on the rickety chair as I grab my pistol from behind my back and move it to my hip before getting into bed and drawing the stiff covers over myself. She folds her arms defiantly across her chest.

"Come on." I lift the blanket on the other side of the queen mattress and motion to her. I fold the blanket over, hoping she doesn't notice the clear come stain smack dab in the middle of one of the flower patterns, as if whoever did it aimed right for it.

She snaps her attention to me, her spine straightening until she looks twice her height. "No way," she says with a shake of her head.

"I didn't ask you. It's not a question." I raise my voice. "How else will I know if you try to leave?"

She scoffs.

"It can be hunting season if you'd like, little rabbit." I reach for the gun on my hip, but I don't need to draw it.

She lets out a long breath, stands from the chair, and climbs into bed as if she's crawling into a casket. I fight back a chuckle. She wouldn't survive a night in prison. Not one single night. She'd stroke out at intake when they made her pretty little ass strip before searching every single hole for hidden contraband. I smirk at the idea and pretend I'd be the one searching her body.

She lies as far away from me as she can, nearly falling off the side of the bed to keep from touching me. She looks up at the cracked and stained ceiling, her arms crossed over her stomach like she's rehearsing her own funeral. A tear wells and slips from the corner of her eye. I wonder what the tears are for.

Is it the room? The situation? Or whatever waits for her at home?

Selena

The room bothers me and the man beside me disgusts me, but I can't get my mind off my husband. I raise the sleeve of my blouse and rub the painful bruise on my right wrist. The stranger leans over and drapes an arm across me, and I flinch as he grazes the bruise that runs across my abdomen. I grip his wrist to push it off me, but he tugs me into him before I can. My body tenses, the hair standing up on the back of my neck. I worry for a moment that he'll try to sleep with me, but he keeps his crotch tilted away from my body.

I hate being in bed with him, but I'm not as afraid of him as I should be. The real devil waits at home. If this adventure doesn't end in a death sentence, my return home will. Bryce will fucking kill me.

At least the man beside me would make it quick, unlike my husband.

"Goodnight. Don't let the bedbugs bite," he says with a chuckle. I shiver at the thought of those creepy crawlers.

"Will you at least tell me your name?" I ask, knowing I won't fall asleep anytime soon, especially with the imaginary bugs crawling all over me now. Or real bugs. Real ones seem more plausible.

"Sure," he says. Sleep punctuates his voice. "Just not tonight. Go to sleep, Selena. We have a long drive tomorrow."

I don't know how I fell asleep or when I snuggled up to him, but when I wake up and realize the warmth against my body is his, I jump out of my skin. Panic shakes me to my core, and I rip away from the bed. Breathless, I grab my jacket and rush for the door. I have no idea what I'll do if I make it out, but I can't miss this opportunity. It might be my only chance.

A metallic sound rings out, and I stop with my hand still firmly gripping the door handle. I look back and meet his dark and dangerous gaze. His pistol is trained on me.

I was stupid to think I could get away from him. Three elephants with a sinus infection breathe quieter than I do when I panic, and they're probably stealthier when climbing out of bed, too.

My stomach churns with fear, and I let go of the door, dropping my hands lifelessly to my sides. He climbs out of bed, never letting the barrel drop from me. He steps into me and fists my hair. I whimper against his rough grasp and reach for his wrists.

"I was trying to be fucking nice to you, rabbit."

"I'm sorry." I strain to get the words out. Am I sorry, though? I'm not sorry for trying, but I should have slowed down and forced myself to be quiet like the little rabbit he thinks I am.

His nostrils flare, smelling my fear as he tugs me into his body. His hand rides up my stomach, snakes between my breasts, and stops at my throat. I strain against his touch as he squeezes and threatens to block the air from reaching my lungs. My chest heaves against his huge hand. He groans and leans over, burying his face in the crook of my neck, inhaling my scent like a certifiable creep. "You have no idea the willpower it's taken to stop myself from touching you."

"I'm married," I choke out. He doesn't seem like the type to care about the sanctity of marriage. Or laws. Or human life. It's worth trying, though. Anything is. Including my escape, I guess.

"Do you really think that fucking matters?" His breath heats my ear.

I swallow hard. "Please don't."

"Something tells me your husband doesn't deserve someone like you." His kind words contradict his harsh voice.

He's right, though.

Bryce doesn't deserve me, but I didn't have a choice. It was an unofficial arrangement between our families—a business transaction at best and my nightmare at worst. The bruises which paint my skin remind me how much he haunts my dreams. Not just my dreams, but my reality.

"Does he deserve you?" he asks as he kisses my neck. His affection chokes me more than his hand around my throat. I'd rather have his hand on my mouth than on my neck. I'd rather he kill me now than try to sleep with me.

"If you do what you're thinking of doing, I'm dead," I tell him. It's true. Even if I don't end up six feet under in some half-assed unmarked grave courtesy of this man, if I go home to my husband, I'll end up that way if this man uses me. My husband will know. He always knows everything.

"You said he'll kill you anyway," he says as he wraps a hand around my throat once more and pushes me against the wall. "So why not let me fuck you?"

My throat tightens from his words, not his touch.

"Tell me, rabbit. How many men have you been with?" His thumb grazes my jaw.

I shake my head, and he increases the pressure on my throat. "Just him," I whisper.

I was meant to be a virgin for my husband. It wasn't a religious thing. It was a business requirement.

"Do you want to be with one man for the rest of your life? What's left of it, at least."

I try to nod but his hand keeps me from moving. "Yes," I say.

But of course I don't. I haven't enjoyed sex since . . . ever. I just accepted that he'd be my shitty first and my unbearable last. I had no choice but to accept that it was my life now.

He growls, leans his weight into me, and puts his pistol behind his back. His hand rides up my thigh. My breath hitches and tears gloss my eyes.

I'm a faithful wife. I've always been faithful, despite it all. A tear slips down my cheek as I blink.

He blows a frustrated breath against my skin. "Mark my words, little rabbit, I *will* fuck you," he growls. "If not now, later. Maybe tomorrow. But for this little stunt, I *will* have you beneath me." His thumb strokes the front of my pants as his hand falls to his side.

I'm untouched. For one more day, at least.

Chapter Four

Lex

A bright sun pierces the clouds, and the car's interior is warm to the touch as we leave the motel. We start driving, and the road noise paves the way for me to get lost in my thoughts. I can't help but feel weak. I haven't had my hand on a woman in a decade. Ten long fucking years have passed without touching the delicate, addictive skin. Ten years ago, I'd have taken Selena at the motel and enjoyed every single horrifying moment of it, but I'm being fucking weak now.

Something about her seems so broken, and I don't want to break her further, which is stupid. Having always been a slave to my impulses, I've never cared about desecrating a woman before. It's taking everything in me, but I don't want to add her to my list of victims. But does it even matter? It's not like I can let her leave alive once she drops me off. I'll have no choice but to break her in the worst, most final way.

I turn my head to look at her, and every inch of her tenses. She hasn't spoken to me since I threatened to put her beneath me back at the motel. She needs to understand that it isn't just a threat, it's a promise. She had one rule, and it was for her to avoid doing anything stupid, like trying to leave. She broke that rule, so now I have to break her.

"You were a bad little bunny," I say. The more I think about her weak escape attempt, the more my frustration grows. Her lips tighten, and she refuses to look at me. "You know that, don't you?"

"Leave me alone," she snaps.

Mouthy little bitch. I take a deep breath and lean closer to her. I rub my hand up her thigh, enjoying the way her muscles tighten against my touch.

"If you keep touching me, I'll steer us into oncoming traffic."

"No you won't, sweet rabbit," I whisper. I call her bluff and run my hand across her lower stomach and slip it down the front of her slacks. As she grabs my wrist to stop me, she swerves over the center line. "Focus on the damn road," I snarl as I rip her hand off my wrist and put it on the steering wheel. Her maniacal driving is going to get us caught, which is probably what she wants. I can't allow that. "Those hands better not leave that wheel."

"Please don't," she begs. Genuine desperation pours through her strained words. It makes me hard as hell. And this is why I'm fucked up. I love how much she *wants* me to stop, *needs* me to stop.

"Please don't what?"

"Touch me," she whispers.

I smirk at her, sinking my fingers lower. "Touch you where?"

She blinks away a tear. "Down there."

I scoff. I want to hear her say it. I want her to tell me exactly what she doesn't want so I can do exactly that. "You're a grown woman, rabbit. Use your words. Tell me what you don't want me to touch and why."

She doesn't speak. I'm not in the mood for these games.

"Why don't you want me to touch your pussy?" I give her one more chance to answer before I say fuck this and make her pull over so I can take her how she doesn't want to be taken.

She takes a deep breath. "Don't touch my *pussy*"—she whispers the word—"because I'm married."

I hold my hand against the warmth of her skin beneath her waistband, just above her soft mound. I'm rabid. I want to get my hands on her, sink them lower and fuck her cunt with my fingers. Even then, I consider her statement and her desperation to preserve the sanctity of her fucked-up little marriage.

And I wholeheartedly disregard it.

I lower my hand and palm her pussy. She gasps at my touch, and not in a good way. She really expected me to stop, which is hilarious. Nothing would keep me from getting my hand on her. She had to know that.

"I'm not going to play with you, rabbit. I'm just going to hold my hand here." I try to soothe the panicked rise and fall of her chest with my words. I hold my hand against her warm pussy, with two of my fingers slipping between the closed seam of her lips and resting there. I bask in her fear as she tries to drive and ignore my hand. She gets wetter and wetter with every bump in the road. She swells beneath my fingers, and I feel the contours of her clit as her body responds to me against her will.

"How old were you when you got married?" I ask, deciding she might be more willing to talk with her swollen clit beneath my fingers.

"Eight . . . teen."

"Young little rabbit, huh?" My breaths roll over her chest, and she shivers. I feel it in my fingertips.

"Has he been the only one to make you come?"

Her lips tighten, and she refuses to answer me. But I know. Her body responds to my words so fucking well. Her slick, warm excitement coats my fingers, and I fight the urge to swirl my fingertips around her clit and make her come against my hand.

"If you don't answer me, I'll touch you," I growl. She refuses to respond, so I curl my fingers against her. She jolts.

I warned her I would play if she didn't.

"Yes, he's the only one who's made me come," she whispers with a hint of defeat.

"Don't you want someone else to make you come? Don't you want to know how it feels to have another man inside you?"

She shakes her head. "I don't want another man."

"What does he do to you?" I keep my fingers still against her clit.

"Don't make me talk about it." Her gaze cuts to the steering wheel, and she tries to pretend she's anywhere else. But she isn't anywhere else. She's in her car, with me beside her and my hand on her perfect little cunt.

Selena

His fingers remain between my legs, building heat even when they're still. His grasp is sure as his hand curves to cup me. I answered his questions. Well, I answered *enough* of his questions.

I don't want to talk about it with anyone, but especially not *him*. It's painful enough to remember the day my life changed forever. The day I learned who I was promised to. I knew what kind of person Bryce was and what his family was like. I knew I would live a regimented life under his thumb and that I would never be happy again. I expected him to watch my every move. But I hadn't anticipated the violence. He's an angry drunk, just like his father. The bruises on my body tell a story I try to hide beneath my clothes, and I'm not ready to share. I can't discuss my marriage or my husband with this stranger.

He won't even tell me his name, so no, I'm not telling him a damn thing, even as his fingers tease me.

I shake my head. "I'm not talking about it," I say, as firmly as I can with his hand palming me.

"If you don't, I'll make you come, rabbit." I know he means what he says by the harshness of his glare and the feral growl that leaves his lips as he says my nickname.

I think about it. I consider telling him something to placate him, but I can't bring myself to utter the words to describe my abuse. I haven't even come to terms with what I've been through. Before I can come up with a lie, his fingers dance against my clit, which begins to throb against my will. My stomach tightens at his touch.

"He doesn't . . . do . . . anything to me. He's just . . . controlling," I say through breaths that are becoming too sharp to control.

"You're lying to me." He leans his weight into me and rubs me faster. His thumb slides against my clit, back and forth, and I fight back each moan that rises into my throat. He doesn't deserve them.

My heart pounds against the wall of my chest. I don't want him to get me off, but I also don't want him to discuss my marriage. My hell at home. I can't tell what's worse. They're both terrible options that I don't fucking want.

I fight back the heat behind my eyes and spread my legs a little wider for him.

"You'd rather come than tell me about your marriage?" he asks with a raised eyebrow.

I drop my gaze from the road and nod, slow and unsure.

"Fair enough, rabbit," he says as I clutch the steering wheel. He rubs against my clit again before he opens me. He slips two fingers inside me, then withdraws his hand and rubs my unintended wetness over my clit. I shudder as my body responds to his touch. It feels so good, and that makes me feel so bad. So guilty.

A small moan leaves my lips, and it darkens his eyes.

"Does that feel good?" he asks, even though he knows. He can tell by the way I'm losing control of my body. My pelvis tilts against my will. I nod, but it's not enough for him. "Tell me with your words." He circles around my clit before brushing over it between every stroke of his fingers.

"It feels good," I whimper.

"I'll tell you my name if you come." He dips his fingers into me again. "Do you wanna know my name, sweet bunny?"

"Yes." I pant the word. I'm betraying my husband. I'm betraying myself. But he's going to make me come. I feel it brewing between my legs, rising into my belly. I rock my hips and grind against his palm as I leave my morals at the edge.

My body tenses, each muscle aching for release. I struggle to keep my eyes on the road with each forward scoop of my hips. He fucks me with his fingers, and I come against his hand. He growls as he feels me spasm around him, at the twitch of my clit. I shudder and try to keep hold of the wheel.

"My name's Lex," he whispers in my ear, his hot breath leaving goosebumps along my skin. He pulls his hand from my pants and puts his fingers into his mouth. Tasting me. He pushes his spit-coated fingers past my lips. My stomach tightens. I don't want to like what's happening. Everything inside me tells me not to.

But the hungry way he looks at me makes me want it to happen again.

Chapter Five

Lex

She's so mad at me. Or at herself. She liked my touch, and she hates that. But I loved making her come around my fingers. Her body reacted to me as if she hadn't experienced that touch at home. She probably hasn't. She probably hasn't had much positive touch in her life at all.

After feeling her come around my fingers, I want to get inside her even more. I want to feel her tighten around my dick. I want to fill her married pussy with my come.

I adjust the front of my pants without drawing her attention. I love knowing she's drenched, sitting in come that my fingers coaxed from her. She's so mad about it that her brows are permanently furrowed at this point. She hates the warm, sticky wetness that came from someone who isn't her husband.

It came from me.

A dark and dirty felon.

The black shadow beside her.

My eyes linger on her pants, and I smirk at the thought of how wet they probably are. We've been driving for a few hours, but we still have many more ahead of us. I should let her change, and I also don't mind the idea of getting out of these prison sweatpants.

"Stop in here," I tell her. She turns into the parking lot of a small secondhand store.

When we enter the building, an elderly woman behind a cash register looks up from a magazine and gives us a cursory glance before returning to her article. I look at Selena to make sure she doesn't try anything dumb, but she doesn't. Good girl.

I grab a pair of jeans from a long rack of clothes in the center of the store, excited by the promise of denim against my legs again. Such a simple thing I took for granted while in prison. Selena grabs a t-shirt and leggings and stands beside me.

"You'll want a little more than that," I tell her.

"Why? Where are we going? You haven't told me."

"Don't worry your pretty little head about that. Just trust me and get a few outfits."

I spot a skirt and hold it up to show Selena. The thin black material is exactly what I want to see her in. She shakes her head with a judgmental glare as she looks around. She grabs a pair of shorts and jeans and chooses a long-sleeved shirt and a cami from the next rack.

I walk over to her, put the skirt in her pile, and whisper, "For what I'm going to do to you, you'll want the skirt."

Her cheeks flame red as I leave her side to find another t-shirt for myself.

I search the rack, or I pretend to, at least. In reality, I'm watching her, waiting to see if she'll run out the door when she thinks I'm not paying attention. She looks less uptight when she walks now, like she's finally gotten a long-needed release and has more confidence because of it. I wonder if she'll feel tethered to my touch now that she's come from it.

Will it keep her from running off?

I snatch a t-shirt off the rack and head to the front of the store. She hasn't gotten up there yet, so I lean against a pillar and watch her again. She picks up a pair of panties that still have tags attached, but she puts them down with a grimace. With a sigh, she joins me at the front with her stack of clothes.

"No panties, rabbit?" I ask as we walk into the maze of a checkout line.

She scoffs. "I'm not wearing pre-purchased underwear. Can we stop somewhere else?"

"No. We need to get out of this area once you use your card. Wouldn't want your husband finding us. Maybe we can stop the next city over." I suddenly decide I don't want to push her panties aside to get inside her again. I don't want her wearing them at all. "Maybe you don't need any. You can go bare for me." My eyes move down her body, which trembles with renewed anger.

And I love it.

She tugs me away from the checkout line, cheeks flaming hot, her voice a harsh whisper. "What happened in the car is *not* happening again. We're not doing this. And we're definitely not going further. It's bad enough that I let you do what you did, and I'll have to live with that guilt, but I'm not adding to it."

"Sweet bunny," I coo, "you think you have a choice regarding what I do to you? How adorable." I brush a hand against her cheek, and she rips away from my touch. Her lips tighten and her bravado deflates in front of my eyes. "You shouldn't have let me feel you coming around my fingers, because now I want more. No, I *need* more. So when I tell you that you aren't going to wear panties or that you're going to wear that little skirt, you're going to listen. I'll make you feel better than your husband ever did."

Her eyes darken. She doesn't realize just how long it's been since I've felt the soft warmth of a woman beneath me. She doesn't understand how obsessed I am with the thought of touching her again. It's an obsession that started once I felt her, once I reveled in the warm rush as she came against my hand. She had tried to run, just like a scared little rabbit. But I would tame her.

"I'm going to shower," she says with a glance toward the bathroom. Yet another room that isn't up to my little rabbit's standards.

"Get undressed in here," I tell her with a smirk.

She clutches her clothes to her body, shaking her head in a stiff motion. I consider forcing her to strip in front of me, but her eyes well with tears. I tighten my lips. I have no idea what's wrong with that girl, but I'll find out.

"Go on, rabbit." I wave her off. I won't force her to tell me what she's been through . . . yet. Some people come out stronger when you force them to confront their pain, but others break. She seems like she'd break. She isn't strong enough to confront it on her own, and I'm not the person to make her stronger.

Selena

I breathe heavily against the cracked faux marble countertop in the bathroom. The lights flicker above my head with a low hum that grows louder with every passing moment. I've been so afraid he'll force me to undress, but not because of the infidelity. I fear seeing his expression as he becomes aware of the bruises on my body. I don't want to see the look of pity on his face.

Whenever someone catches a glimpse of my marks, they get that same look, but they don't do a goddamn thing about it. They probably think I did something to deserve it.

Bryce is a saint, and I'm the pitiful sinner.

I take a deep breath and lock the door before removing my blouse. Each unfastened button reveals more of the fresh purple bruises on my chest and stomach. When I slip the sleeves off, my eyes find the older bruise encasing my wrist. I remember the fight that caused the deep pinkish-purple mark. I remember every stupid fight. How could I forget when the proof of each one marks my skin? I touch the one on my stomach. *I wasn't home in time to make him dinner.* I graze my chest. *He forced me to fuck him because he had a bad day at work.* I grip my bruised wrist. *I took too long to get ready last week.*

I slip my slacks off, exposing a mixture of old and new bruises on my thighs. A near-perfect handprint decorates my inner thigh, almost reaching my crotch. I shudder when I remember how he fucked me to give me that mark. I flinch as I touch the yellowish bruise above my knee, where he kicked me when I was already down.

When I'm dressed, I feel like a normal wife. When I'm naked, I understand why I'm not more upset about sleeping in this scuzzy motel room instead of beneath the expensive sheets embroidered with golden threads. Those expensive sheets mean lying beside Bryce. The man out there, Lex, is on the run from something awful, and I still felt safer in bed with him last night than I ever had with my husband.

And that's fucked.

I turn on the faucet in the tub. Brown water rushes out as the pipes rattle behind the wall. It finally runs clear, albeit cold, but I get in anyway. Standing naked in the disgusting bathroom just makes me feel dirtier by the moment.

My eyes lock ahead as I clean myself, focusing on a crack that races up the wall across from me. Mold straddles it and follows its path.

A knock at the door breaks me from my trance. "I'm almost done," I call out.

When I get out of the shower, the leggings and the long-sleeved shirt I got at the store wait for me on the counter. I narrow my eyes. I'm certain I locked that door. I pick through my discarded clothes on the floor and discover that my panties have vanished.

Fucker.

"How'd you get in?" I ask as I step out of the bathroom, motioning toward the clothes I put on. He just shrugs. "And where's my underwear?" I ask.

A fierce sexual frustration shines in his eyes at the sight of me. I hate that he looks at me like that, in a way my own husband never has. I hate that I like when he bites his lower lip as he openly scans my body.

"I told you. I don't want you wearing any." His gaze leaves me and turns to the television. He knows just how to draw me into wanting his attention, wanting to be more interesting than the grainy picture on the old TV. But not so interesting that he might want to touch me.

I open my mouth to argue, but the words stick under my tongue. I close my lips, thinking better of what I want to say.

Lex's eyes leap to mine when he sees my wordless response, and the breath catches in my throat at the intensity of his stare. His expression becomes feral and animalistic, and I know I should tread lightly.

"You want your panties, rabbit?" he asks.

I nod, even though I know I shouldn't. Not when he's looking at me that way, as if a sadistic idea has just crossed his mind.

Lex gets up, reaches into a drawer, and pulls out my black underwear. He stares at me as he sits down, unzips his jeans, and tugs his cock from the spread wings of denim. A smirk crosses his face. As menacing as it is, it's wickedly attractive.

His eyes never leave my face as he strokes himself, slow and intentional. Saliva gathers under my tongue at the sight of him, but I force myself to remain stoic. Even so, he's noticed the subtle nibble of my lip, because his movements grow rougher and more determined.

"Do you like what you see?" he asks.

I want to shake my head and tell him no, but I'm frozen. I force my body to obey me enough to sit in the stiff, squeaky chair facing the bed. The TV show flashes across my peripheral vision as I watch him.

My eyes rove over the huge cords of muscles from his shoulders to his biceps, which flex with every stroke.

"Do you know what I like, rabbit? When it's not a no from you, it's a yes. Shit, even when it's a no, it's still *my* yes." He brings my panties to the head of his cock. He drops his head back and groans as he comes in my underwear, saturating the thin fabric. "We're going to have so much fun together, you and I." Lex smirks as he tosses the panties onto my lap. "Well, put them on."

I shake my head before he even finishes his sentence. Absolutely not. I will *not* put his come against my skin. "I'm not wearing those," I say, as firmly as I can muster.

"Ah, no, that's not how this works. You wanted your goddamn underwear so bad. Put them on." His smirk tightens. "I'm not asking you again." The way his jaw tenses and pulses, I know I have no choice.

He's forcing me to take what I wanted in the first place.

I swallow and stand up, taking the panties to the bathroom because I refuse to change in front of him. I can't.

I wipe off some of his come, but the wetness is too embedded in the fabric. When I slip them on, I feel his warmth against my skin. It makes me shiver. When I return to the bedroom, his eyebrow lifts as he tucks his spent cock away.

"Show me that you're wearing them," he says.

I hook the front of my leggings and lower them enough to expose the black silk. Satisfied, he relaxes and starts watching TV again.

When I sit down, the damp area is more noticeable. It's become a bit cold. As hard as I try, I can't ignore his pleasure against me. I cross my legs and cut my gaze to the stained carpet at my feet, trying to talk down the throbbing ache he's caused. Several cigarette burns surround the stain. The place is a dump, and it's easy to get lost in the mess of it. But even then, *his* mess in my panties still stays the center of my focus.

Lex's presence haunts me from across the room, and my eyes ride up to him once more, taking in every contradiction that makes him somehow attractive and disgusting at the same time. The stubble on his chin looks rough, but it still works with his otherwise sweet features. He only looks as mean as he does because he never smiles from joy. He smiles to get his way because he's a manipulator. His voice is so low and sexy, but it only masks the threats woven through his words. He isn't nice or kind. He's a bad fucking person, and he's forcing me to wear him.

Lex brushes a hand through his thick hair as he lets out a breathy laugh and stares at the TV. "I don't like when you stare at me," he says without looking away from the television.

"I don't like to wear your come," I mumble under my breath.

He puts on a smile and motions me to him. I keep myself planted in the horrible motel chair.

"Now," he commands. He has a voice he uses when I have no choice but to listen, and that word drips with his demand. I stand up and go to his side, and he rubs his hand between my legs and bites his lip. "Oh, bunny, you're going to wear those panties to sleep and then they aren't coming with us." He grazes my slit. "How does my come feel?" he growls as he fists my hair and draws me to his mouth. His lips stay far enough away from mine to accomplish little more than pissing me off. My dark hair in his grasp is still wet, and drops of cold water fall down my shoulders and make me shiver.

"It makes me feel gross."

"Get used to how I feel, because I can't wait to see you covered in my come, sweet bunny."

"We aren't doing more," I say, pushing my hands against his chest.

Lex growls—a carnal sound that makes me weak. "I love how you think I won't end up inside you. I may have to tear you apart to get there, but I will get inside. Tonight, I'll leave your vulnerable little underbelly alone. But soon, nothing will keep me from ripping you wide open."

He releases his grasp on my hair and pulls his hand from between my legs. He pats the vacant side of the bed. The swirl of arousal I feel leaves me more confused than ever.

He lifts the blanket and stares at me, but I shake my head. There's another bed this time. I don't need to sleep with him. I get up and lift the blanket on the other bed before climbing into it. When I turn over, I hear rustling, then the whoosh of cold air as the blanket lifts away from me. His warmth engulfs me as he gets into bed and lies on his back behind me.

"If you don't want to come to me, I'll come to you. I don't trust you. You might try to scurry away again, little bunny."

I won't run off, even though everything in my body tells me I should, especially the wetness between my legs.

Not only his, but mine, too.

Chapter Six

I wake up in bed, all by myself. I sit up and look for Selena, certain she's taken off. Apparently, she figured out how to be a quiet little rabbit after all. I relax when I hear the running shower. *Good girl.* She can clean herself all she wants, but it won't be the last time I cover her in my come. She may have shed her panties, but I love that she slept—at least for a while—with my come against her skin. I like that she's so torn between liking it and hating me.

She needs to learn, though. I won't allow her to have her panties unless she's wearing me, too.

After her shower, we load our things into the car and set off again. Hours later, she sits beside me, staring out the passenger-side window as the sun sets. She hasn't spoken to me since we started driving.

"Are you really still mad about your panties?"

She doesn't look at me. "It's not about *what* you did. It's *why.*"

Oh, she speaks.

"Tell me *why* it bothered you, then."

Her eyes roll and it reminds me how young she is. How naïve and innocent she is. "Because you want to own me. And I'm not someone's to own."

"You have no idea what it means to be claimed by me, sweet rabbit."

Her eyes flash to mine, fear radiating from them. "We *aren't* going further. Wishful thinking isn't going to get you inside me, Lex. There's absolutely zero chance of that, so let it go." She wants so badly to believe the words coming out of her mouth. She wants me to believe them, too.

"I don't need wishful thinking." I tap the rabbit's foot. "And I don't need luck, either. I *will* bury my cock inside you before this road trip ends. I promise you that."

Her cheeks flame red at my words. Despite reining in the side of me that would take her against her will, I will unleash that side before we reach my destination.

Even if I didn't have to kill her, I'd make sure I released her back to her husband with my come dripping from her.

We take a turn onto another back road, and then another. That's all we've been doing, and it makes the drive feel like an eternity without enough progress to make our stiff knees and numb asses worth it. I pull into a familiar-to-me parking lot. I could use a chance to stretch my legs, and I need an ID—something I can use to cross the border without suspicion. I'm too big to hide in the damn trunk.

I'd been in prison for a decade before my escape, so I don't have the connections I used to, but I know a man who makes them. He was a fairly unsavory character, even by my standards, but Rodney has the means to provide what I need. I drag us to his doorstep, hoping he still lives in the rundown apartment complex. Unless he's in prison, he should be here.

I knock on the heavy metal door, and it opens after several locks unlatch from the other side. Rodney looks at me like he's seen a ghost, his face paling in front of me. "Lexington Rowe, do my eyes deceive me? I thought you were doing life, man!"

"Don't call me that, and fuck off about my business," I snap. I hear the gasp beside me as Selena learns more of the secrets I have yet to reveal. She has to know, on some subconscious level, that I'm running from the law. She probably doesn't expect my crimes to have earned me life, though. Well, several lifetimes.

I can't deal with her feelings right now. This isn't a place to feel and look weak. Rodney will feed off that. I'll try to explain it to her later when we aren't in front of another felon. When I can answer some of the questions I'm sure she'll have. It's the sort of conversation I would never have in front of fucking Rodney.

I push past him, and he stares at Selena as if she's a steak laid out in front of him. Maybe even better than a steak. She's something so mouthwatering that he can't take his eyes off her. Admittedly, she looks fucking delicious, with her youthful innocence and prim appearance, even when she isn't dressed all proper.

I'm certain of very few things, but no one is getting a bite out of her before I do. She's my meal, and I'll slit a man's throat if he so much as sniffs her sweet scent before I can take a huge chunk out of her to fill myself with. I grab her arm and pull her into me in a protective gesture. It's not my usual way, but I feel compelled to do it. That innocence needs protecting.

"Does she need one, too?" Rodney asks, his eyes still crawling over Selena's body. He's eyeing my little rabbit like a coyote looking down at his prey. His expression relays his thoughts clearly, and he can fuck right off as far as I'm concerned.

"Just me," I tell him. "What have you been up to, anyway?" I ask, trying to draw his hungry eyes off Selena, whose cheeks have flushed under his dogged staring. It's painful for me to witness. It's like he's never seen a woman in the flesh before.

"Living the dream," he says as he wrenches his eyes away from her to finally look at me. "Served three in county for some fraud charges, but I'm back in business. My nephew stayed here and kept shit running while I was locked up."

"How much for a new ID? Or passport. Anything I can use to get my ass out of the states."

"There's time to talk business. Come with me to take a picture first." He dodges the question precisely how I expect him to. He'll keep dodging until I get too far in the process to back out, forcing me to pay whatever he asks. I push him for a price, but he just keeps avoiding the question like the expert piece of shit he's always been. He's a bottom feeder, lower than me, and I thought I was pretty fucking low.

Rodney snaps my picture and leads us into a room where he sits in front of his fancy multi-computer system. The lenses of his old glasses reflect the screens, their joints bent out to accommodate his round, wide head.

Selena and I take a seat on the couch, but she refuses to look at me. Her arms are folded across her chest like a defiant child. Which I deserve, but not here. She can't look like a child, because that's precisely what a dude like Rodney would like. When I say he's unsavory, I mean . . . fucking vile. I'd have left Selena in the car if I wasn't worried she'd be hunted in the parking lot by one of the many violent sex offenders in this complex. Honestly, if you pull up the predator map, you wouldn't even know there's a building here beneath all the red dots. Rodney's big, stupid mug would be buried somewhere in all those warnings.

I'm being real judgmental of a fellow felon, but at least I have a line I won't cross.

That reminds me of the questions I'll have to answer later. I should have let Selena hear my past from my own mouth. That would have been the mature thing to do, but I didn't want to give her more information to use against me if she somehow got away from me. She'd probably try to run once I told her, because that's how a normal person would respond. They'd run.

Despite what she thinks, I'm as happy to be in this situation as Selena is. It would be much easier if I killed her and took her car. I wouldn't have another human being to worry about while on the run. Things would be a lot less complicated if I wasn't always thinking about finding ways to get inside her.

"Earth to Lex?" Rodney snaps his fingers in front of my face before shoving an ID into my hand. "How's this?"

It looks and feels legit, and my scowl is pretty accurate.

"You failed to tell me how much," I say, putting pressure on the card between my thumb and forefinger. Rodney is a sneaky fuck, and I intended to stop him from printing shit before I got the price. I was too busy lost in thoughts of Selena to notice the sound of the printer firing up. This is what I mean. Less complicated.

"I told you, but you were staring off in la la land," he says with a dry laugh. I missed some of the shit he'd said, sure, but I would have noticed that. "It's one grand for you."

My mouth falls open. *Sneaky fuck.* "Since when has it ever been near that price?"

"Since New York switched their ID format and you became desperate enough to pay for it." A gross smile crosses his face. Oh, fuck him. Even someone like her wouldn't have that kind of money on hand. But he's right. Desperation always costs extra. That's the way the game is played.

"We don't have that, Rodney, and you know it," I say as I stand.

He meets my stance but hardly reaches my chest. He brushes a hand through his balding hair. "You have something I could take as payment." His hungry gaze drops to Selena.

Her eyes widen as mine narrow. I fucking knew those words would come out of his mouth. As soon as I saw him drooling over her, I knew he'd try to order her off the menu. He knows we have to work off the cost somehow, and he sure as shit wouldn't want to fuck *me*.

I'm torn. I don't want to give her away like that, even for a quick fuck, but I also *need* that fucking ID. There's no way around this. I'm not going back to prison. Giving her away for my freedom seems like a small sacrifice. It's one I have to make.

I cut my gaze and sit on the couch with a harsh exhale. Selena's eyes fill with betrayal. I can't look at her, but I feel the desperation as she fights against his grasp when he reaches for her. He finally gets his hands around her wrists and drags her to her feet, pinning them behind her.

"Fuck you, Lex!" she screams. Hatred radiates from her with the heat of a thousand suns.

I deserve it.

He puts his palm around her mouth, muffling her screams, and I drop my head to my hands. Does he have to do it right here? Does he have to dangle her fear and desperation in front of me?

"Shh, honey, I'll be quick," he whispers in her ear as his free hand works down his jeans. Once he gets the denim past his ass, he works down hers. My eyes leap to the pale skin of her ass as he pushes her against the wall and pins his weight into her. I swear I see the haze of a bruise on her skin, but it might have been the light from the computer screen.

I force myself to look away from her ass, and my eyes rise to her eyes. They're swollen and red with fear, the glaze of her tears coating them. I shake my head, trying to keep my hand away from my pistol.

I have to let it happen.

It needs to happen.

There is no freedom without it.

This has never bothered me before. In fact, I like glimpsing fear on the face of a beautiful girl. I always have. But this is bugging me. Really gnawing at my nerves. The burn beneath my skin is a foreign feeling for me, and I don't like it.

My muscles twitch and I struggle to keep them still. Her muffled screams wiggle between my ears and gnaw at me like sharp little rabbit teeth. I reach back for my pistol, but I can't bring myself to grab the grip. It would be too loud and messy, and the cops keep their eyes on this shady complex. They practically live on the premises at this point. Instead, I leap up while he's too busy prodding between her legs with his tiny dick and panting like he might come before he even gets inside her.

That'd be convenient, actually.

I wrap my arm around his neck, and he releases Selena the moment I grab him, his hard dick softening as I choke him. His hands claw at my wrists, and he flails against me. It's eerily similar to how she struggled against him. My lips purse as I keep a steadfast grasp on his neck, refusing to let him get half a breath.

Selena pulls up her pants, her chest heaving as she runs for the door.

"Don't you dare, rabbit. There'd be another one just like him waiting for you." My words come out strained as I struggle against the weight of a man fighting to live.

She stops, her hand on the doorknob. She has to know that darkness just veils monsters—monsters like me and definitely like him.

I get sick of the struggle. I release Rodney enough to get a grip on his head and snap his neck. The familiar crack rides up my spine, and I lower his body to the ground, wiping at the blood on my arms from him clawing at me. I look at Selena. Her eyes are full of deserved mistrust. I put something up for sale that didn't belong to me. She snatches open the door and bolts from the apartment. With a shake of my head, I grab the ID off the floor and follow her.

"Rabbit!" I call after her as she races to the car. I quicken my pace to catch up with her. When I'm close enough to grab her, I slam her against the car, turning her to face me. Forcing her to look into my eyes.

"Fuck you," she cries. Her body trembles, and fear courses through her. She's still trapped in that moment with him, even away from the apartment. Her hard glare bites at me. I deserve to be bitten like that, but her words still piss me off. I'll meet her bite with a stronger one, and she knows me enough to know that.

I lean into her, putting a hand to her delicate throat. The whites of her eyes are all I can see in the dark parking lot. She saw what I'd done in one swift motion, and here I am, with my hand around her fragile little neck. "Don't be so fucking mouthy, rabbit," I say. I feel the throb of her heartbeat beneath my fingers. Nervous sweat coats her skin.

"You tried to sell me!" she says with a strained voice.

"More like . . . loan you." I'm trying to rationalize with myself as much as her. What I did was fucked, yes, but sometimes there's no changing who you are, even in the face of something so different from what has molded you.

Her skin is hot, heated by anger and . . . something else. It courses through her veins. She inhales sharply, looking up at me with an emotion I've never seen from a person.

It's the look of someone who has just cracked.

"Kill me." Her voice comes out small and weak, but somehow still sure.

I raise my eyebrow, but I doubt she can see it in the darkness. "What?"

She lets another warm breath wash over me. "I said . . . kill me." Her voice wavers this time.

I lower my hand from her throat and rest it on her clavicle. She's taken the fun out of preying on her. Her fear has mutated into surrender in front of my eyes, an overwhelming feeling of brokenness that washes over us both. It's contagious. And I can't say that I've ever felt such sadness, even as I was beaten half to death as a child or when I knew my life was over as I stood before a judge. This feeling is foreign and uncomfortable, and I can't imagine living in that eternal state like she must. I understand why she wants to die.

If she dies, that emptiness dies with her.

"Is that really what you want, bunny?" I ask, letting my free hand move her sweaty, dark hair from her cheek.

"I'm as good as dead either way. I don't want to play this game anymore. Take the car. Do whatever. Just . . . I can't . . . do this." Her world is collapsing around her, crushing her. And it's all my fault. Well, not totally my fault. Clearly, her husband is a fucking cunt. He broke her before I took her, but I created the final crack that split her wide open.

I lean into her, putting my forehead against hers as I drop my hand from her chest. "Get in the car, little rabbit," I whisper. "The backseat."

She hesitates before she grips the handle and crawls into the backseat. I scoot her over and sit beside her. "Are you sure that's what you want?" I ask as I lean into her and rest my hand on the curve of her neck. She has such a fragile throat. I hardly noticed that before tonight, and suddenly it's all I can think about. How she's like glass in my grasp. But if she really wants this, she picked the right person to ask. I'm the only one who can do it without thinking twice. Without losing sleep. It is and always has been too easy for me to take a life.

The dome light cuts off, blanketing us in darkness, and I feel the warmth of a tear trail over my hand. Except for some soft sniffles, it's sickeningly silent. She nods her head, and I feel the motion within my grasp. She seems so certain, leaving me to think about it. My muscles twitch, and I yearn to give her the release she wants.

I lean in and whisper, "If it's what you want, I'll do it for you." My voice wavers, which is uncharacteristic of me. I feel doubt in my gut, some nagging discomfort I've never felt with any murder I've committed. And it *is* murder, even if she wants to die.

My hands ride higher to grip both sides of her head. She relaxes into my touch, as if I'm giving her a gift. To her it is. To me, it feels like a burden I don't want to bear. But I will.

I take a deep breath.

It's what she wants. It's for her. It's all for her.

Selena

I feel the heat of his hands on either side of my head, but his touch doesn't burn me like it should. I don't dare take a breath as I wait for the sharp twitch of his muscles before nothingness. It isn't that I *want* to die, but I'm just so fucking done. So tired from it all. Bryce *will* kill me when I get home. He'll end me in the worst, most painful way he can muster in his sadistic mind. It seems better this way.

As crazy as it sounds, it feels safer.

With closed eyes, I bathe in the blackness behind my eyelids. I need to sleep. I need to rest. And I'll never get that from the life I have, even before Lex took me. There's only one ending for me. There has always only been one way it could end, and it's this way: death at the hands of a man. I'm just choosing whose hands it will be.

His hands fall from my face, and he leans in to kiss me. I draw away from him, catching his breath on my inhale. He tastes like sin.

"Lex," I whisper as I push at his chest.

"If you still want to die after I fuck you, I'll do it for you." His voice is low and desperate. "Let me inside you, rabbit."

How much lower can I go? Past the six feet under I hoped for? Sleeping with him will send me on a free fall to hell, but does it really matter at this point? How important is the sanctity of a marriage that leaves me covered in bruises?

I drop my shoulders as he leans in again. The moon peeks through the windshield, offering mere glimpses of weak light. He won't be able to see my marks. He can't pity me. I can pretend to be an unmarked woman for once in my life. I can pretend I'm a normal twenty-two-year-old. I might even find a few moments of happiness.

His lips meet mine again, and I accept his kiss. I spread my mouth to let him inside. His chest rises heavily as he leans over me, pushing me against the door as he crawls between my legs. His hand wraps around my neck and rises to grip my hair. He tugs my shirt off, letting a heavy hand slip over the swells of my bare breasts. I fight the flinch of pain as his touch runs over the bruises near my waistband. I'd never let him do this if he could see me. I don't want anyone to see just how damaged I am. He tugs down my pants with the hunger of an animal at the end of its leash, and it's about to break.

I hear his zipper fall.

It's becoming real.

It *is* real.

I gasp as I feel the warmth of his cock against my pussy. I want to stop him. I reach out and push against his broad chest, but he's so strong. So *much* stronger when he's above me. "Lex," I pant, the hesitation woven through the word. It feels like it's too late. The leash is hardly holding him back now, especially when he's so close to slipping inside me.

"Shh, sweet bunny," he whispers before kissing me again. "Let me in." He growls and deepens the kiss. His firm hand explores between my legs, and I lurch into him as the touch sends electricity through my body and awakens things that have long been asleep. Maybe these parts of me had never been awakened at all.

His fingers push inside me, a touch that my body remembers. I curl my hips against his hand. He draws his hand away, and I hear him spit. He touches me again, sinking his fingers inside me. I can't see his cock, but I feel its heat against my skin. I remember how it looked at the motel. Like the rest of Lex, it's huge. I wish it wasn't so damn dark so I could see him. But if I could see him, he could see me, too.

And that can't happen.

When he pushes inside me, stretching me in ways I've never felt, I scream out, partly from the shock, but also from the realization that someone besides my husband is inside me. Ripping through me. Making me everything my husband says I am.

A whore.

A slut.

"God," he groans as he pushes deeper. "Your husband is so fucking stupid." He whispers these words before drawing back to the tip and pushing into me again. My nails dig into his sides as he fucks me, slow and sweet, in ways I don't expect. It doesn't seem like he'd fuck me this way. "Don't worry, sweet bunny. If you let me keep you alive, I'll show you how I truly fuck. I'll give you a reason to take that next breath for me," he growls, as if he senses what I'm thinking.

I melt against the door, the armrest stabbing my back in the cramped space. It doesn't matter, though. I close my eyes and allow myself to focus on the friction between my legs as he thrusts in and out of me. I listen to his deep, desperate breaths as his hips drive into mine. He shows me only a fraction of his strength, and it frightens me as much as it excites me.

He pulls out and sits down, pushing my legs out of the way. "Get on my lap," he commands in a breathy voice that makes my legs weak for a moment. I feel for him in the darkness and straddle his waist, my head nearly hitting the roof of the car. He twitches against my pussy. "I want to see you," he whispers.

His hand moves toward the dome light, but I grab his wrist and place his palm on my ass instead.

"Leave it off," I say as I put him inside me. I don't want him to see the bruises now, after his hands have raced over every sore part of me.

"I'm going to get my eyes on your body, little rabbit," he growls against my mouth as I lower myself on his cock. My heat rides down to his pelvis, and the groan that leaves his lips makes me throb. My moan breaks through the static silence.

"Not now," I whisper, my lips hovering in front of his.

"What are you hiding from me?" He bucks his hips into mine, and his huge arms wrap around my body. I feel so small in his grasp. "What don't you want me to see?"

"Leave it alone, Lex," I say as I slow my movement on his lap, nearly stopping as he forces me to confront what I refuse to. Not now. Not when this moment is so perfect.

"It's going to piss me off, isn't it?" He pulls me into him until my naked, sweaty chest presses against his. My hips stall their motion, the weight of his questions bearing down on me. "Don't think about it right now," he says. "It's something for another day." He kisses me, and it's sweet. I'm surprised he's capable of that. Being sweet.

The recently formed memory of him giving me away to that man—and then killing him—rushes to the front of my mind and contradicts every bit of this sweetness.

"You were going to let him fuck me," I whisper as I drop my head into the crook of his neck.

"I know, rabbit." He lifts his hips to meet mine. "When I saw him about to take what I've wanted . . ." He releases a frustrated growl. "There was no way I could leave him breathing. No way I could let him feel you around his dick before I felt you around mine." He kisses me so hard that it makes me whimper. "But now that I've been inside you, no one else will ever be, including your fucking husband."

With his possessive words in my ears, I ride his cock and inch toward an orgasm. It's been so long since I came during sex. Before he made me come with his hand, it'd been so long since I felt that kind of pleasure at all.

"You're tightening around me," he says, and I know. My entire body is tight and tense. My moans lengthen, becoming longer the closer I get. "Where does your husband come?"

"On my belly," I whisper.

"Have you ever been filled up?" he asks.

I swallow hard and shake my head. When Bryce fucked me, he didn't seem to savor being inside me. It was a place to push his frustration before dumping it onto my skin.

As Lex's pelvis grinds against my clit, with his cock deep inside me, I come. His hands travel down the curve of my spine and grip my ass.

"You're going to make me come, bunny." He fists my hair and cranes my neck so he can bite the skin of my throat. "I'm going to fill your pussy and then you're going to tell me if you want to live or die as my come drips from you."

I throb at his words, and it forces the pleasure from his cock. He comes inside me, the twitch of him deep in my gut. He stays within me instead of rushing away like Bryce. He basks in the pleasure I released from him, the pleasure he drew from me.

His hands ride up my sweaty body and grab both sides of my head once more. His touch makes me shiver. "What do you want?" he asks, his voice still laced with pleasure.

I had wanted to die, and even though that part of me still calls, another part has woken up and muffled its voice. I grab his hands and drag them away from my head. I wrap them within mine as I drop my chest into him, suddenly feeling twice as heavy. An exhausted pleasure weighs me down, but the weight of my sins also crushes me.

"Tell me what you want," he says.

"You," I whisper, accepting my sin.

And wanting more of it.

Chapter Seven

Lex

My mind remains on Selena as I drive us toward the next motel. We didn't get many miles under our belt because it was already late by the time I finished fucking her. It was everything I imagined, and I stayed inside her for as long as I could. As long as my dick cooperated. I had her hot, sweaty body pressed against mine, letting her cry into my chest until well past midnight. I wasn't the snuggling type—not in my nature—but I could have stayed there like that forever.

Once we get to the motel, I have no idea how she'll act toward me. She broke in front of my eyes, had asked me to do the unthinkable to her, and then came on my dick afterward. But on our drive to the motel, she hadn't given me any indication of how she felt. Was the sex only a moment in time where she felt empty and let me fill that void? Possibly.

Not that it can be anything more than that, anyway. I'm a dangerous hunter, and she's a sweet little rabbit.

I open the door to our room and go in before her. I flip on the light, and it flickers above our heads. She looks around with much less disgust than before. I think she's getting used to being ripped from her luxury lifestyle and transplanted into motel rooms from hell. There's still no communication between us. It's a stale static that I'm sick of listening to.

She pushes past me to go into the bathroom, but I grab her arm and pull her back to me. Confusion muddies her eyes when she looks up at me. Her expression is racked with guilt, and it pisses me off more than it probably should.

"Why are you beating yourself up over what we did?" I ask as I shake her arm. She flinches from my touch. I'm not trying to hurt her, but I'll never understand why she cares so much about what we've done. People have had affairs in far less dire circumstances and never beat themselves up like this.

"Because I wasn't faithful to my husband." She's filled with regret and saturated in guilt.

"Get over it, rabbit." Her regret isn't my problem or responsibility. She knew what I would do to her, and she knows I won't feel bad about it. Not now. Not ever. I'm not sorry for fucking her, and I sure as hell don't regret giving her the strength to climb into that passenger seat and keep going.

"You don't understand," she whispers with a shake of her head.

I fist her hair. "I do understand. I've done a lot of shit I should regret. And maybe I even did for a minute. Don't tell me I don't understand the gravity of doing things I shouldn't. What do you think I'm running from?"

Tears gloss her eyes. "What are you serving life for?" she asks.

I nearly release her hair at that question. I didn't expect it. I should have, but I forgot what she'd heard between Rodney and me. She found out more about me than she should have.

"Which life?" I say.

Her lip trembles. Yes, I'm serving multiple life sentences. My soul will be in prison for the next two lifetimes after this one. She has no idea what she let inside her, no idea who she let make her come. Twice.

"If you already regret fucking around on your piece of shit husband, don't ask me something like that when you know the answer will make you feel worse. Way fucking worse."

"I want to know. I deserve to know," she says with a defiant lift of her chin.

Who the hell does she think she is? She's out of her mind if she thinks she deserves anything more than the time she has left before we reach the end of the line.

She's lucky to get my cock in the interim.

I laugh, which makes her puff her chest. "Go on, rabbit." I push her toward the bathroom, but she digs her heels into the shitty carpet. "You keep your secrets, and I'll keep mine."

She flashes her eyes up at me. "Tell me yours, and I'll tell you mine."

Stupid girl. Yeah, her husband sounds like a controlling piece of shit, but she doesn't know what it's like to let the man who makes the devil blush sink into her pussy. When she hears what I've done, she'll just try to escape again. She'll probably puke from disgust when she finds out what kind of man she let inside her.

She swallows hard, and I stare at her throat as it bobs. "My husband beats me," she whispers.

"I know." I figured as much. I've seen glimpses of discoloration on her body. She isn't telling me some secret I didn't already piece together from her behavior. The things she's said. The fear on her face. The fact that he tracked her, for fuck's sake.

"No . . ." She shakes her head. Her gaze cuts away from mine as she raises her right sleeve, exposing bruises that are beginning to fade. It's hardly much to get upset about. It's not hard to bruise up a girl like her if you're rough enough, and it's easy to lose control. It's hard for *me* to avoid leaving marks on her.

Her lip trembles as she lifts the hem of her shirt, exposing some of the worst bruises I've ever seen on a living person. Her stomach and sides are shades of purple and pink. A yellow haze outlines anything that has begun to heal. *This* makes my heart quicken. Marks like that would have caused her a lot of pain. My mouth hangs open. I can't believe what I'm looking at. I can't believe how much it bothers me. It shouldn't. I shouldn't care.

But I do.

She has a way about her that makes me want to rip her away from all that hurt her so I can shield her under my own tattered wings.

"Goddamn it, Selena," I say through gritted teeth. I step into her and run my hand along her bruises. "How the fuck do you feel an ounce of guilt over what we did when he does *that* to you?"

She keeps her gaze locked on the floor and doesn't answer me. I force her to look at me by raising her chin. She looks ashamed.

"Don't pity me," she whispers, which is a really weird thing to fucking say, but not the weirdest thing she's said tonight.

"I don't pity you. I'm fucking pissed, though."

She trembles at the sharp rise in my voice. She looks like she fears I might hit her. I *am* mad, but not at her. I'm pissed at her piece of shit husband. I'm a bad fucking person, the worst of the worst, but I would never hurt her like this. I could never lay my hands on her like that, even if I've done worse to others.

I don't need to pity her, and she doesn't need anything from me. She'll gain her own wings, and then she won't need mine.

Against my better judgment, I decide to spill my guts to her, expose my underbelly and let her inside, even while knowing she won't like what she discovers within and that it will only push her away. She needs to know who she slept with.

I lean into her and get close to her ear. "Rabbit," I begin, "I'm a murderer. More than what you've seen tonight. I've killed innocent people. I killed my foster parents. I went to prison and killed fellow inmates. I'm a killer. It's what I've always been."

Her gasp pulls cool air over my skin. She fights the realization that she's let me inside her, a person so much worse than she imagined. Worse than anything she deserves.

A tear falls down her cheek and when I go to wipe it away, she rips away from my touch and runs into the bathroom, locking the door behind her. It's a fair response to finding out you came on the dick of a heartless killer.

Selena

Oh god. Oh my fucking god. I pant against the door in a panic. In my heart I knew he was a killer when I saw him so casually choke out and then kill that man. As calm as watching a commercial on TV or mailing a letter. But I had no idea how much of a monster he was. Or that he'd killed so many. He's sick and twisted. A fucking psychopath.

And I'm stuck with him.

No wonder he was so willing to kill me. He's a seasoned killer. Realization pulls me under when I get the sick feeling that he plans to kill me at the end of this.

He has to. He can't let me go. I know his name. I know too much.

I get in the shower and let the hot water run over me, listening to the heavy tick of the invisible clock above my head. I should feel more fear and less acceptance about what I've realized, but if my time is limited, I'll make the best of what little is left. No matter which way the pendulum swings, death waits at both ends.

I wash up and get out of the shower. I slip the stiff towel around me, trying to hide the bruises beneath the rough terry cloth. When I step out of the bathroom, steam follows me. I carry my clothes in my hands. My eyes catch sight of my blouse and slacks folded on the dresser. I pick them up and sniff them. He must have washed them in the motel laundromat. Probably at the last shitty one.

He doesn't look at me as he walks past and goes into the bathroom to shower. I slip on my blouse and slacks, but then I remember what happened with my underwear. I curl my lip when I recall wearing my panties after he jerked off into them. He made me keep the saturated fabric against my pussy all night. He loved that little show of ownership and control. But he doesn't own me.

Asshole, I think as I pick up my clothes.

I'm not a fan of his, but I hate myself more for liking what I see when I look at him. For what I feel when I'm around him. I hate him for bringing out these feelings that rip me in two. One side tugs me toward being the good wife I was told to be in front of a room of people I hardly knew. The other side yanks me toward letting myself play with the lawless, and that side, like Lex, is stronger.

I get dressed and lie in the single bed. I push the stained cover toward my feet. The sheet beneath it looks clean enough, at least. I curl up in bed, my dark, wet hair soaking the off-white pillowcase beneath my head. I stare straight ahead at the peeling paint on the wall . . . until I hear the bathroom door slam.

Lex is naked. I pretend to be asleep, but I peek at the cords of muscles in his arms. He has a prisoner's body—the type of physique a convict attains when there is nothing else to do but work out. His damp hair is brushed back. His taut back muscles connect to one of the most perfect asses I've ever seen on a man. I wish I had gotten to see how a body that perfect would have merged with mine. Perfect versus the most imperfect. Regret at that longing immediately fills me.

He's a killer, I remind myself.

I squeeze my eyes closed as he turns around. I'm not in the right frame of mind to talk about anything more tonight. I'm drained, overwhelmed, and more tired than I've ever been in my life.

Lex gets into bed beside me, tugging up the disgusting blanket I'd kicked away. When he turns over and backs into me, I realize his back and ass are bare. And against me. I can't believe he got into bed naked with me. I try to scoot over an inch, but I meet the edge of the mattress. My eyes clench shut, and I hope he doesn't notice the change in my breathing. I'm worried he'll feel the discomfort radiating from me as I draw my arms against my body.

"It's just nudity, rabbit. Don't get your panties in a bunch," he says without turning over.

His words infuriate me. I scoff. "I don't have panties to get in a bunch, thanks to you." I draw my legs toward my chest, making myself as small as I can.

He laughs. He fucking laughs. "Oh yeah, that's right."

His body stills as he sobers. He never tries to turn toward me. He allows the gap of space between me and his naked body. "Goodnight, bunny," he whispers before silence falls between us.

Chapter Eight

Lex

I wake up the same way I went to sleep, except now a cold sweat coats my body. The alarm clock by the bed buzzes like a hive of angry bees. The time on the clock is only a few hours later. Nothing is worse than waking up restless next to a goddamn woman like her. Actually, next to any woman at all, but she's especially difficult to just exist beside.

I turn onto my back and stare up at the dark ceiling. Every so often, headlights illuminate the room through the thin veil of the inner curtains. For a while I worried about her husband finding us, but as the days passed without him sending the goddamn army to find her, I can't help but wonder if he even cared that she was gone. Not just about being married or the marriage-centric image he portrayed, but actually cared about *her.* Is she safe? Dead? With all that generational wealth he has, why isn't he doing everything he can to get his girl back? A girl like her would make me do some real fucked-up shit to find her and bring her home.

She stirs beside me, and I hold my breath for a moment until she settles. She's making me anxious. I feel guilt and regret and something else that I can't put my finger on. I hate knowing I'll have to kill her when we get to Texas, but it's better than sending her home to the piece of shit who bruised her abdomen like that. I can't bring her with me, not that someone like her would come along anyway. Life on the run wouldn't work for a girl like her. There aren't any spas or fancy new cars on the lam.

My mind wanders to how I imagine her husband looks. Probably nothing like me. Probably well dressed and put together. Someone her parents love more than she does. All I know for sure is that he's a little-dicked piece of shit who likes to beat up on his woman.

The irony isn't lost on me. I never treated women much better, and I'd be lying if I called myself any kind of saint. She's *different*, though, and I can't wrap my mind around his inability to see that. How can he not when it's so disgustingly clear to me? With everything else good in his life, he also has her beneath him.

Fucking idiot.

My cock hardens at the thought of him fucking her. It shouldn't, but it does. I recognize the appearance of the side of me that wants to see that. A familiar to me —yet foreign to her—entity that occasionally screams in my head. At times, that side of me is hard to disregard.

I ache with an uncomfortable throb I can't ignore. My hand slips to my cock, and I bite the inside of my cheek as I wrap my fingers around the head of my dick. I circle myself with my fist as I try to be quiet and still, like I had to do when I was on the inside. I was polite about it, at least, unlike some of my roommates who jerked it loud enough to wake up the whole row.

I bite back a groan. Fuck, I want her. I *need* her. Never in my life have I wanted to rip the clothes from a woman so completely.

At this moment, with my head in all the wrong places, I turn over and scoot closer to her back. She remains motionless as I press my hard cock against her ass. There's no way she doesn't feel it. I run my hand down her side, knowing there are bruises beneath my touch. If she doesn't feel my dick pressed against her, she'll feel that.

"Don't pretend to sleep, bunny," I whisper.

She tenses and tries to fake a heavy sleep as my hand reaches the waistband of her pants and travels to the front of her slacks. I unbutton them and lower the zipper. I reach into the newly splayed fabric, rubbing the soft skin of her lower stomach and the soft hairs of her pelvis.

"There's no way you don't feel this," I say in a hushed tone as I tug her pants down. "Being asleep doesn't make it any less wrong, you know? Pretending to be asleep doesn't make it any less sinful."

I pull her pants past her ass and push my cock between her thighs. I groan at the warmth of her pussy against me. I grip my cock and guide myself into her. The muscles inside her twitch at the intrusion, and the tension rides up her entire body. She's still trying to remain faithful. It's a pathetic and sad attempt to fight what she wants and what I need. What we both need. She's too fucking wet to pretend she doesn't want it, too.

"Goddamn it, rabbit," I groan as I draw my hips back and slam them into her. It's too dark to see her face and gauge her reaction. I hope a pair of headlights will cross the window so I can see her open eyes. Because I know she's awake. "You're being childish," I say through gritted teeth. I get sick of it. I refuse to play the fucked-up game she made up to avoid the reality we're in. To avoid letting me in.

I sink my fingers into the worst of her bruises, and she yelps. Finally, a fucking reaction. I roll her onto her stomach and keep my cock deep inside her as I press her face into the pillow. Her legs clench together beneath me, and the friction is enough to make me want to bust.

"Lex . . ."

I push my hips forward, going deeper inside her. "Good morning, bunny," I say with a growl as I wipe the hair from her cheek.

"You're . . . hurting me," she whispers.

"I'm not even doing anything to hurt you . . . yet."

As she pants, pain weaves through every breath. She's wet, stretching around me just right. I'm not hurting her pussy. Not like that, at least.

"Get off me . . . please," she begs.

Despite how fucking good she feels around my cock and how much I don't want to pull out of her, I do. Self-restraint has never been a strong skill of mine, so I struggle between the bit of humanity she draws out of me versus everything I've always been.

I get out of bed, snatch the sheet around me, and flip the light switch, illuminating the room. She's pulled up her pants, but they're still undone.

"What the hell is the matter with you?" I ask, harsher than I intend, even though her wetness coating my cock makes me *almost* too hungry to stay off her.

"I—" she begins, but the rest of the words are choked off. Her lip trembles, and she cuts her gaze from mine. Her body shakes, and that broken little girl is suddenly back in front of me.

I sigh, wiping a hand through my hair. I gather my composure as best I can and walk to her side of the bed, a hand still clutching the white sheet around my waist. I lift her chin with the other, forcing her to look at me. "What was hurting you?" I ask again, more forcefully this time. "It wasn't my cock, so what was it?"

"The bruises," she whispers.

"On your stomach?" When I rolled her onto her stomach, I was careful with her. I tried to be, at least.

She shakes her head.

"There's more?" I ask, but I know the answer already. There must be more marks on her skin than what she showed me. I force her to her feet, and she flinches when I grip her bruised wrist. "Show me," I command. I leave no room for argument.

When I reach out for the buttons on the front of her blouse, she screams out a no that *almost* makes me stop. I bat her hand away and return to the buttons. She keeps wiggling and fighting me. I release my hold on the sheet, and it falls to my feet as I knock her back into the nightstand. The lamp teeters behind her. I grab her arms and pin them to her sides, and she releases a whimper.

"Stop fighting me," I seethe.

"Please don't," she begs. Her eyes widen with fear, as if she thinks I'll hate her once I see what waits beneath her clothes. Or at least think differently of her. Her hands go for my wrists again.

"If you don't keep your hands at your fucking sides, Selena, I'm going to grab my gun, put it up to your pretty little head, and force you to strip for me. Your choice." She's gnawing on my last nerve.

Her hands finally fall to her sides and remain there. I work the buttons off, one by one. She keeps her face turned away from me as the fabric spreads on her chest. More bruises. They cover her sternum and wash down her breasts. I can't even take a moment to enjoy her tits because I can't believe what I am seeing.

The front of her pants is still undone, but I ignore the brown hair between her legs and focus on another patch of purple peeking from beneath the fabric. I reach for her waistband, and she grabs my wrists with undeniable fear on her face. She's forgotten the threat I made because what I'm doing is scarier than my gun.

"Leave my pants on," she pleads.

Absolutely not.

"No, Selena. I'm going to see every inch of you. I need to know where you're hurt."

Tears fall down her cheeks, an uncontrolled overflow of her emotional pain. I slide her slacks down and my mouth gapes. More bruises. The worst is a large mark that takes up the entire length of her outer left thigh. I'm guessing that's what hurt her when I pinned her beneath my weight. My knee dug into that area, keeping her legs together as I pushed deeper inside her. Or it may have been her chest, where her hands would have been pinned beneath her breasts.

"Oh, bunny," I whisper as I rub my hand up her thigh, making her nearly jump from the pain. I wonder how I didn't hurt her in the car, but then I remembered that leg would have been cushioned against the back seat when I was over her. It all makes sense.

My erection is gone, and I hang limp between my legs. She cries as she tries to cover herself again. She looks ashamed more than anything, which rubs me in all the wrong ways. Shame isn't what she should feel. Her fucking husband should carry this burden, not her.

"I'm usually fine with pain," she rationalizes as she buttons her pants with trembling fingers. "I'm used to it. But your knee pressed right into this bruise"— she touches her left thigh—"and it was too much."

When she goes to take a breath to keep babbling on, I take the chance to pull her into my chest. She swallows the words instead of continuing. My heart breaks for her, and I don't understand how it can when I've never had one. I've never felt sympathy for anyone or anything. But my blame shifts in my selfish mind. If she hadn't tried to play Sleeping Beauty, I wouldn't have pinned her like that. I curse myself for putting the blame back on her. I'm the one who was too forceful.

"Sweet bunny," I whisper, "I'm going to fuck you, and then we're going back to New York."

She looks up at me and tries to wipe the tears from her cheeks. "But . . . why?"

I brush her hair from her face. It's sticky with the salt of her tears. "Because I'm going to kill your fucking husband."

She shakes her head. "We can't."

I fist her hair. "Which part?"

Instead of answering, she drops her jaw and allows her lower lip to tremble.

"Sweet little rabbit," I growl, "I can answer that for you. Of course I can fuck you. I was just inside you. And since I'm a murderer, I can kill your husband for putting these bruises on you." My fingers trace her chest, only partially concealed by her blouse. I drop a hand between her thighs and move upward, past the bruises that make her flinch.

"We can't kill him."

I lean closer to her mouth. "*We* aren't going to. *You* aren't doing anything. I'll take care of everything, just like I'll take care of you." I kiss her, and her breath hitches as I tug down her pants. She slips out of them, and I look at her. Fully look at her.

She's naked except for the white blouse covering her nipples. I see every bruise. Her brokenness makes me feel like I need to mend her instead of being the one who does more of the breaking. I remove the last bit of fabric hiding her body from me, and she drops her gaze.

"Don't be embarrassed about your body. These marks don't shame you. They shame *him*. Your piece of shit husband."

She flinches at the word *husband*, and my eyes narrow.

"Goddamn it, rabbit! Stop fucking caring about him. He doesn't care about you."

"But—"

"But nothing." I turn her around and pull her closer. I run a rough hand down the big bruise on her left thigh, and she jolts. "This isn't from a man who cares."

She scoffs. "Abducting a woman at gunpoint is A-okay to you, though? What do you call that?"

I bite the sensitive skin of her shoulder. My cock hardens against her ass. "Desperation? Your lucky day?" I say with a smirk as I kiss where I bit her, and I swear I see a hint of a smile cross her face.

I carefully wrap my arm around her waist, trying to avoid the bruises on her stomach as I bend her over the bed. When her elbows hit the mattress, only the mark on her wrist has pressure against it. No pain.

I run my hands down her sides, tracing the bruises that wrap around and lick at her back. Her ass somehow remains pale and perfect, without a mark on it. I want to change that so goddamn bad, but she needs to stay unmarked . . . for now. I need to give her pleasure as I show her what it's like to have a real man inside her. A man who is as angry and violent as I am, yet still wouldn't hit her.

"Lex," she whispers. There's a hint of longing in the word, a desire I've been desperate to hear.

"What do you want?" I growl. "Use your words. You know I like that."

"I want you inside me."

"Inside what? In your ass? Your pussy?"

"My . . . pussy."

"Good girl."

I fist her hair, grip my cock, and push inside her. She whimpers as she drops her head and rests it on her fists. She feels incredible. And she looks amazing. I lean over her and run my hand down her stomach until I reach the dripping excitement between her legs.

"Goddamn it, bunny," I groan as I move my fingers along the seam of her pussy. Her clit swells beneath my touch. I rub her until she backs into me to take my cock deeper. I lift her to me, wrapping my free arm around her chest. "Your husband is so fucking stupid. You know that, right?"

She hesitates for a moment before whimpering out a yes.

"I'm going to fuck you in your bed at home. Make him watch. I want him to look at what he lost until his very last breath."

Her cheeks flush. "Lex . . . don't talk about him."

I laugh. "Until he's dead, I'll mention him as I fuck you."

She tightens her lips, but they spread again as I rub circles over her clit. I caress her most sensitive area until she moans—a sound I love to hear.

"Come for me," I command as I bite her neck. "Be a good little bunny and come."

She squeezes around me, choking my dick, and I fight against her body to stay deep inside her. I rub her until she shudders against my grasp on her chest. As she spasms, her body coming down from the violent twitches of her orgasm, I thrum my thumb back and forth over her clit.

"Lexington," she whispers.

I hate my full name because it's the name on every form, every newspaper, blasted all over the internet. I hate when people call me Lexington because when they do, it calls to *him,* the person I'm trying not to be around her. It calls to the side of me I despise. The part of me who thinks about her and her husband together. The part of me I don't want to let out to play with her.

I hate that name, but when it falls from her parted lips that way, I love it.

The moment we get to Texas, I'll be off her hands—out of her hair and out of her pussy. I fully intended to kill her, eliminating any chance for her to offer information to the law regarding my whereabouts. But now?

I've decided I'll set the rabbit free.

Chapter Nine

Selena

I couldn't believe he meant what he said last night when he mentioned returning to New York. I thought he'd change his mind or that he'd said it just to sleep with me. I didn't think he'd turn around when we were so close to his freedom. I didn't expect him to go back for anything, not even to get his hands on Bryce. He isn't worth getting caught over, and if Lex gets caught, I'll end up alone with the true monster: my husband.

I watch Lex from the passenger seat as he drives. Every so often he shoots a look over at me and flashes a quick smirk.

"We should go back," I say with a nervous shake of my knee beside the center console.

He raises an eyebrow. "We *are* going back."

I scoff. "You know what I mean. Back the way we were going. Away from here."

"Rabbit, stop," he says with a stern tone that makes me shut my mouth. "If you're going to be mouthy, use it in a better way."

My jaw drops at his brazen words. He talks to me like I'm his whore, a toy to use. And now, with him, I want to be played with like that. My eyes land on the hard dick beneath the zipper of his jeans. My leg stops shaking as I stare at him.

He reaches out and grabs my hand, caressing my palm. "Did you stroke your husband's dick?"

I nod, keeping my eyes on him.

"Show me how." He brings my hand to the zipper. I consider arguing—believe me, I consider it—but an aching in my gut keeps my hand in place.

The denim scrapes against the soft pads of my fingers as I drag them toward the button. I swallow hard, lean over, and work open his pants. He isn't wearing boxers, giving me a glimpse of his cock.

"Don't be shy. You've seen it all already," he says as he fully reveals his cock, sick of me taking my time to expose him. His hand rides along his shaft before circling his head and planting itself on the steering wheel again. I stare at the bead of pre-cum on his head and feel guilt the moment it drips over the curve.

I dig my fingers into his jeans. He's already been inside me—twice. He already made me come—three times. Stroking his dick hardly seems like it'll matter at this point. I can just add it to my list of sins.

I draw a deep breath before wrapping my hand around the hot skin.

"Good girl," he groans. His fingers dig into the steering wheel as I stroke him. Despite the soft buck of his hips, he keeps the car steady on the road, which is much better than I did. "I need your mouth, bunny," he says through a groan.

I shake my head. "Wh-what? I can't. You're driving."

"So? Get on your knees and lean over my lap."

I shake my head.

"Now, rabbit! Don't make me ask you again. You can suck me off your way or my way, your choice."

I hate when he gives choices. They're never good ones.

I swallow the lump in my throat and undo my seatbelt. I swivel my head, looking at the quiet, empty road.

"Fine," I say as I climb onto my knees.

As I lean over his lap, he grabs my hair, lifting it away from my face and bunching it in his hand. I take him into my mouth. He groans in a way that shakes his whole body, like I've sent a shockwave through him. I suck him, and his hips pulse toward my mouth, forcing me to take more of him. His hand leaves my hair and plants on my ass. His fingers graze my lower back as his hand returns to my hair. He pulls me off his dick, and I look up at him.

"Does he make you suck his cock?" he asks.

I nod.

"Was he the first man you put your mouth on?"

I give him another nod, straining against his grasp. He just smirks at me as he pushes me down on his dick. He groans when my tongue meets his skin again.

"Sweet bunny, you have the best mouth I've ever felt."

His cock impales the back of my throat when he thrusts his hips upward, which makes me gag. A deep growl leaves Lex's lips. Tears slip from my eyes as I pull back enough to keep from throwing up, and I take some quick breaths through my nose before he pushes me to the base of his cock. I gag again, but he holds me there to keep me from pulling away this time. My throat tightens, and I use my lips to protect his warm skin from my teeth. My whole body shudders. He lets go so I can draw a breath without my nose buried in skin and hair.

"God, I love how you choke on my dick. Is your husband as big as me? Has he ever made you gag like this?"

I pull away from his cock and shake my head. Bryce wasn't big at all, thank God. He'd have used it as a weapon if he was as blessed as Lex.

He wipes the tears from my cheek and licks the salty evidence of what he does to me. He moans and pulls me up to kiss him, making me taste my tears as well. He fists my hair harder, and I see the glimpse of cars driving past as he pulls me back toward his lap. The other drivers can see me, ass up and doing what I'm doing, and my cheeks flush with embarrassment. The tip of his cock touches my lips.

"People can see me," I whine against him.

"Good. You're a fancy little show rabbit. You should be shown off," he growls before shoving me back down. "If you keep taking your mouth off me, I'll make you get on my lap and ride my dick. Your choice." He lifts his hips and pushes his cock to the back of my throat. I choke out air. "Good girl," he whispers. "Slip your hand down your pants and play with yourself."

I try to pull back to speak, but he holds me in place.

"Remember what I said," he tells me through a tense jaw.

I have no choice but to listen to him. My hand wanders down the front of my leggings, and I'm surprised by how wet I am. This isn't really the type of thing that gets me going, but there *is* something about the way he reacts to my touch and the feeling of my tongue riding along the perfect curve of his cock that excites me.

I rub two fingers along my slit. He controls the speed of my head as I control what happens between my legs. My moans vibrate against his cock, and the feral groan he releases vibrates against *me*. As I get closer to my edge, I feel the need to pull him from my mouth. The tense muscles in my body make it harder to keep my teeth off him.

"Is it too much for you? Having trouble keeping those teeth off my dick? You can bite, sweet bunny. You can't hurt me."

I shake my head as best I can.

"Fine. Take your mouth off me so you can come, but don't you dare stop stroking."

I pull him from my mouth and pant as I wrap my hand around him and keep stroking his cock. He's still wet from my spit. With his hand wound through my hair, he brings my face to his and kisses me, hard. His eyes watch the road as his mouth moves against mine, pushing me over the edge.

"Come for me, bunny," he groans.

And I do. I come so fucking hard, dropping my weight into him and making him swerve.

"That good?" he asks with a smirk.

"Fuck off," I say with a pleasure-laced laugh.

Lex's eyebrow rises. "I wanted to come inside you again, but I was trying to be amenable and settle for your throat. Not gonna work. I need your pussy."

My lower jaw drops, and I shake my head. Absolutely no way in hell am I riding his dick while going seventy miles per hour down the highway.

Lex leans over and hits the bar to push the seat back.

"I'm not doing that," I say.

"Rabbit," he says firmly, and the ice in his tone forces me to reconsider. "Take your pants off."

There's that voice again—the voice that makes me weak because it's so strong.

I stare at him, trying to ignore the thunder of my heart roaring in my ears. I hook my fingers into the waistband of my leggings and tug them down. I'm a sticky, wet mess from my own come.

"Climb onto my lap." He taps his thigh.

I swallow hard, surveying the road once more before carefully climbing in front of him, trying not to hit the steering wheel as I stare out the windshield. He drops one hand and helps me onto his lap. He grips my hip, sinks inside me, and lets out a growl that sends a shiver down my spine, right to the notch of the hip he's holding. He takes his other hand off the steering wheel and grabs my other hip.

"Drive," he says with a groan. "If I try to drive while buried in your perfect cunt like this, I'm liable to kill us both." His teeth scrape my shoulder before he bites into my neck. "I'm not going to last long with you. Your pussy is so fucking wet. All from my cock, huh?"

"Yes," I whimper, and try to keep my eyes on the road and my hands on the wheel as he thrusts against me. He's so fucking deep, and it makes it hard to keep the car on a straight path.

"I'm going to come," he whispers. His hips pulse before settling beneath me. I make a move to get off his lap, but he holds me in place. "Not yet, sweet bunny." He slips his hands from my hips to the wheel in front of me. "I want to feel you around me for a little while longer."

I sigh and drop back against his chest as he drives. His cock twitches inside me, and I stop caring about the occasional car that drives by as I sit on the heat of his cock. He kisses the top of my head, which almost doesn't feel real.

He doesn't seem like the sweet type. But then again, this isn't who I am, either.

Chapter Ten

Lex

I'm being incredibly fucking dumb over some woman who wouldn't have given me the time of day had I not forced her. I'm wanted. Every law enforcement agency in New York is actively seeking me out, and yet here I am, driving back into the heart of their search. I'm taking a huge risk by bringing us back here, but I can't let her go home to *him*. I have to protect her, even if she's not with me.

Especially if she's not with me.

I'm not sure how she feels about everything. If she thinks I'm kidding when I say I plan on killing her husband, she's in for a big surprise. I'll get rid of that piece of shit and when we get to Texas, I can leave while knowing she'll be safe.

When have I ever given a shit about someone's safety aside from my own? Never. Old me would have wished her good fucking luck and let her go home to that shitbag. Or I would have just killed her. Either way, this selfless behavior is very new to me.

We drive past darkness. I turn off at an exit, which piques Selena's interest.

"Where are we going?" she asks. Her voice is heavy with exhaustion. We're both tired. I can't drive anymore, and neither should she.

"I want to show you something. And besides, motels in this state would be too risky."

We drive down a road dense with trees on both sides, and I pull to the side of the asphalt, concealing the car among the overgrown bushes before I cut the engine. I get out of the car, open her door, and offer her my hand. She stares at me.

"Come on, rabbit."

She draws a sharp breath before taking my hand and getting out of the car.

Crickets chirp and break the quiet. There's little to see except for lightning bugs blinking between the trees. She wraps her arms around herself. I'm not sure if it's from fear of the dark or what. She should know by now I would protect her, even if I'm the one who drags her toward danger in the first place.

"You're okay," I tell her, though I feel her gaze burn through me.

When we get to the end of the path, I leap onto the rocks and reach down for her. She sighs and puts her hand in mine as I help her up. A sharp gasp leaves her lips the moment her feet hit the stone beneath her.

We overlook the town below. Lights on every building dot the landscape. It looks surreal. Like how I remembered, but better, because Selena is here to enjoy it with me.

"What is this place?"

I swallow hard. "Someplace I used to go when I was younger. A safe place when my foster parents were being extra shitty."

I sit at the edge of the cliff, dangling my legs over. Dirt falls from the soles of my shoes. "Come sit," I say. She walks over and squats down to brush off the grass. I cock my head at her. "Even fancy show rabbits get dirty." I tug her down beside me, and she plops onto the grass with a huff. I hate that look on her face. The judgment.

She clears her throat. "I'm not used to—"

"Getting your designer jeans dirty?" I ask with an annoyed snap in my tone.

She shakes her head. "That's not what I meant." She sighs. "I'm not used to being free."

Oh. "Me neither." I lie back, dropping my head onto my hands. My shirt rises and I feel true freedom against my skin as the wind races over us.

The moon illuminates her silhouette, and I take a deep breath. She feels so right to be around. She almost feels like a friend. It's as close to having a friend as I've ever known, anyway. But I know it's all pretend, and that makes me sort of . . . sad. I didn't get sad when I was sentenced to life, sentenced again, and then once more. I can't remember ever feeling sad like this. I turned that emotion off at a very young age. I had to. I wouldn't have survived if I let myself feel anything but anger and hatred for myself or anyone else.

"Lay with me, bunny," I whisper as I grab her shoulder and pull her into me. As if she has a choice. She tenses before relaxing into me.

Silence blankets us, except for the sound of nature. That's something I haven't listened to in over a decade. I close my eyes and bathe in it. Listening to something other than the hoot and holler of fellow inmates is fucking incredible.

Selena shivers, and I sit up enough to shimmy out of my long-sleeved shirt and offer it to her. She hesitates before she takes it and slips it on. I lie back, not giving a shit about the scratchy grass beneath my bare skin because at least I can feel it instead of the rough mattress in my cell.

She traces my tattoos, or what she can see of them under the light of the moon. I'm not proud of all of them, and I'm thankful she doesn't ask about them as her fingertips glide along my skin. I didn't hang out with the best crowds on the inside. Not that any of us could be considered the best crowd.

Her hand falls away, and soft snores come from beside me. The way she's snuggled up to me feels fucking weird. I've always been alone, especially in prison. In there, loneliness was a godsend. Growing up, I had to be okay with being alone because being lonely meant I wasn't having the shit beat out of me by the man paid to care for me.

I close my eyes. "Goodnight, bunny," I whisper as I let myself drift into sleep.

Selena

I wake up to a shiver of cold morning air racing over my cheek. Cool dew wets my skin. Birds chirp from somewhere nearby. I look around, trying to orient myself. I'm on Lex's arm, which is insane. He's shirtless and I'm wearing his shirt. He gave it to me when I was cold. He's such a walking contradiction. He looks almost . . . sweet. Serene.

"Morning," he says as he opens his blue eyes. His skin pebbles with morning chill. He leans over and wraps a strong arm around me, but I push him away. We aren't going to cuddle like this. We can't.

He takes no offense to my shrugging him off as he sits up, pulls his arm from under me, and gets to his feet. He puts his hand down and smirks. "Come, rabbit," he whispers.

I grab his hand and stand on legs that feel heavy. I'm stiff from having slept outside on the cool ground. We walk toward the car, but he pulls me to the right before it comes into view.

"Lex, the car's that way." I point back the way we came.

"Excellent observation."

"Where are we going?"

"Do you trust me?" he asks as I dig my heels into the ground.

"Not really, no."

He looks back at me and chuckles.

The trees open up and expose a large pond. The early sunlight reflects off the dark water. Ripples drift across the surface with every puff of breeze, and a small bird struts along the opposite bank, pecking here and there for its breakfast.

I stare as Lex unties his shoes and slips off his socks. He unbuttons and unzips his jeans and lets the fabric spread, exposing the soft, light hair on his pelvis. My mouth gapes as he tugs off his jeans. His cock is limp, hanging low against his thigh, but the flood of memories from him being hard rip through me, heating my body.

"Your turn," he says with a flirty grin.

"Wh-what? No. I'm not swimming in that," I tell him, as if I have any say in the matter.

"Get undressed, rabbit, or I'll come do it for you."

I pout. Childish, yes, but I do *not* want to go in that water.

When I still don't remove my clothes, he steps closer and makes good on his threat. He strips me until I'm naked in front of him. His cock is now hard and pressed against my lower belly.

"Why must you always fight me? You're the little bunny, and I'm the coyote. I'll always win."

I stare at him, my lower lip trembling in time with the rest of my body. My skin freezes, and not even the sun is enough to warm it. He grabs me, pressing his hard dick against my lower back as I flail. He carries me to the pond and throws me in. I scream until my head submerges, and I continue to scream the moment I resurface. The water isn't as cold as I expected, and it doesn't choke the air from my lungs. It's almost refreshing, but still, fuck him.

"Fuck you, Lex!"

He smirks and jumps in after me. When he surfaces, he tosses his head, his hair rushing back. Water drips from his nose and lips, and he looks so handsome at this moment. I hate how much I want to take in all his soaked and naked features and commit them to memory. He looks like he was carved by the devil himself.

I kick my feet to keep my head above water while he just stands. He's annoying like that. He moves closer and wraps me up in his arms. I steady my legs and float there as he holds me.

"Rabbits don't like to swim, huh?" he says as he curls my legs around his waist.

"Not by force."

"All of this has been by force," he says with a smirk. Lex brushes the hair away from my face. "You swam just fine so far."

My heart thrums against my chest. The sun blazes down on my pale shoulders. The world melts around us, dripping down like the water off our naked bodies.

"What do you want, sweet bunny?" he whispers. I didn't realize I was staring so hard at his lips until he spoke. His words paint the landscape again, dotting it with trees. His finger rides along my pouty lower lip. "If you want a kiss, you need to take it."

I won't kiss him. It still feels too wrong. Even though he's made me come, it wasn't initiated by *me*. I can still hold on to that stupid fact. I pretend my refusal to initiate means I've somehow negated the copious amount of infidelity we've already engaged in.

Even though my thoughts are unfaithful.

"You're so fucking stubborn," he says when I don't make a move. His hand wraps around the back of my neck and pulls me into him. He kisses me, and I let him. A frustrated groan leaves his cold, wet lips. "I'm going to take you back to the car, lay you down on the hood, and fuck you with my mouth."

No one has ever talked to me like that. It's exciting and equally terrifying. I can count on one hand the number of times Bryce has gone down on me, and I remember the stale movement of his jaw as he did. It seemed like a chore to him. I have a feeling Lex will eat me like I'm his last meal before going to his death. He'll walk to his execution with a belly full of every moment since we met. He'll leave me feeling devoured, never happy with the feasting of any other man. And he knows it as his hand rides up the back of my thighs and grabs my ass.

I push away from him and start to swim across the pond, kicking my feet as I tread water with my hands. The thought turns me on and pokes at a playful side of me I didn't know I had. I've probably always had that side, but I've never been allowed to let it surface until now, in the freedom of a serene pond with a man like Lex.

"Where are you going?" he calls.

"Catch me if you can, predator." I let out a chuckle.

He growls and takes off after me as I swim away from shore. Once the pond gets too deep, he swims toward me, his muscular body cutting through the water like a bullet. I hold my breath, dive under, and propel myself beneath the cool surface. Sounds are muffled, and a suffocating silence surrounds me. I open my eyes and take in the greens and browns on every side of me. I can't hear him or feel a change in the water, but I know he's there, hot on my trail. I feel his breath on my neck, even when I know it's not possible.

When my lungs beg for air, I pop up to take a quick and hearty breath. I can't see him. Ripples of the disrupted water roll away from me. As I turn to swim toward shore, I hear him surface behind me.

"Sneaky little prey," he says. I don't need to turn around to know his eyes have taken on a darker cast. I hear it in his voice. It's a visceral hunger lurking just below the surface that chills my veins and tells me this is no longer fun and games. When he catches me, he'll devour me.

I kick my legs and push myself toward the shore. I have to swim long after he can walk, but I still make it first. Barely. The rocky bottom scrapes my knees as I try to get to my feet and run from him. I can't look back because he's only steps behind me.

Grass cushions my bare feet, pine needles cling to my wet ankles, and I can hear his heavy, dedicated footsteps closing in. They thunder in my ears and compete with my heartbeat. I have no choice but to leave my clothes behind as I take off toward the car.

My heart nearly beats from my chest, ready to rip through my sternum. I instigated the chase and now I'm the one feeling hunted. Afraid. But I should be. I picked a true predator to chase me—to hunt me like the little rabbit he thinks I am. It's all so fucking dumb. The moment he gets his hands on me, I'm in for it. No amount of pleading will stop him from taking what he wants. What he captured. What he worked up a sweat for.

I touch my car's silver hood. It's hot from the sun's early rays. Just as my fingers land on the hot metal, strong arms grab me. He pants against my ear; it's the worst frustration I've ever seen. Like a predator who chased his prey, only to have it pivot at the last moment and escape his mighty jaws. Only . . . I didn't escape, and I won't be able to now.

He's trying to hold back and stay in control. I feel it in the tremble of the muscles in his strong body. Lex growls as he turns me around and pushes me against the hood of my car. He lifts me and lays me on my back. He has me in his grasp and doesn't look like he has any intention of letting me go. Pieces of his slicked-back hair fall over his forehead, and he brushes them back with a frustrated motion.

"That was really stupid, rabbit." He's so close to my mouth I feel every syllable against my lips.

I know it was stupid. He doesn't need to remind me. I have no clue why I did it. I just did, and now I'm in the clutches of the most dangerous predator I've ever met. He's not a coyote. He's a wolf. A majestic and beautiful creature that would happily tear me to shreds.

"I want to rip through you, take you," he groans. "But I'm trying . . . really trying . . . to make you feel good instead." The metal burns me as he yanks me toward him and lifts my thighs. I try to keep them closed, but he rips them apart with a rough touch. His fingers make the bruises on my thighs ache, and when I flinch, he ignores the pain and holds them open.

"Don't you close those legs. I told you I would lay you on this goddamn hood and fuck you with my mouth."

And he does. Oh god, he fucking does. He buries his face between my legs and licks at me like he's ripping the flesh off my bones with his tongue. It's rough enough that I raise my hips to put some space between my pussy and his mouth. He releases one of my thighs and puts a flat hand on my pelvis, pushing me against the metal.

"Don't you move away from me. Stay here and let me take what I caught." He looks up at me from between my legs. "Don't start a game you can't handle losing."

I shiver at his words, and he buries his face into me again. He keeps me firmly planted against the metal. His teeth rake the hood of my clit between him sucking on it, and it's like nothing I've ever felt—an uncomfortable pain and pleasure fighting for survival within me.

"Lex," I whisper.

He doesn't respond, just shoves three of his fingers inside me. I scream out as he stretches me. It's too sudden. I wasn't ready for it. I'm not ready for any part of him.

I never will be.

With his fingers deep inside me, he starts to lick me again. "I love it when you moan, bunny," he whispers against my clit. "It shows me you've forgotten you're married for a few minutes. Forgotten I'm the bad guy and that you let me make you come." He growls and dips his tongue inside me before pulling out and running it over my clit in a long stroke.

I bury my hand in his hair and tug him toward me, unable to resist the growing pleasure between my legs.

He pulls away from me. "I'd tell you to get your hand off me, but I want to feel you force my mouth into your pussy when you come."

I tremble at his whispered words.

His fingers push deeper inside me, and my warm wetness slips past them. He fucks me with his fingers while he works me with his tongue until I spasm around him. My chest rises, lifting my back from the hood of the car. I ride out my orgasm with a few long licks of his tongue that leave me bucking my hips against his mouth with every intense sensation.

He pulls me off the hood of my car, the metal scraping my sweat-coated skin. He turns me around, puts my hands on the hood, and drops to his knees. Before I can even get a word out, his tongue moves across my slit and keeps rising upward. I gasp as he reaches the only place on me he hasn't put his mouth.

Oh God, we are not doing *that*.

I try to pull away from him, but he grabs my hips and holds me back.

"No, Lex," I say firmly. Even as his tongue starts to feel good there. Different.

"Shh, rabbit. When I eat you, I want to devour *all* of you. Prey doesn't question how they're being eaten, they just let the predator get its fill."

He licks me and I surprise myself when a moan leaves my lips. This is wrong. It feels so damn wrong. But why does it also feel good? Dirty? Rugged? Like the man behind me.

"Every bit of you tastes like a delicacy I shouldn't get to eat. Something much too fancy for me."

"Lex," I say through a moan, and reach back to grip his hair. I surprise myself once more when it's not to pull him away but to keep him there.

He pushes his fingers inside my pussy, and I'm overwhelmed by the sensations all over again. He fucks me with his fingers and licks me until I find myself teetering on another edge I never expected.

One I've never known.

I drop my free hand back to the hood and steady myself as he brings me toward another orgasm. "Fuck," I moan, and he gives me a hard thrust in response. His fingers pull out of me to rub my clit, circling until he's over it, thrumming my hood directly. It's a sensation that instantly kicks me over the edge, like a pulse of electricity with every swipe of his thumb.

I drop both hands to the hood. My thighs tremble, and I struggle to stay on my feet. He spanks my clit as I ride the coattails of my orgasm with a whimper.

"Naughty mouth on you," he says through a laugh as he slips his tongue back in his mouth and stands up. He wipes at his chin, which is coated in my come. "I knew you'd like that, dirty little rabbit. I bet your husband has *never* eaten you like that."

I look up at him, a hint of fear crawling over me when I recognize the darkness in his gaze. He wraps his hand around the front of my throat and squeezes.

For a moment I wonder if this is it. If he's going to kill me.

"Get your clothes and get in the fucking car," he snarls, and loosens his grasp on my neck.

"What'd I do?" I ask.

"You didn't do anything wrong. Feeling that around my fingers, the clench of your tight fucking pussy, makes me want to put my cock inside you, but if I fuck you now, I *will* rip you apart." He forces me to take a step back, my thighs hitting the front bumper. "I don't want to hurt you like I've hurt others, so get your sexy fucking ass dressed and get in the car before I rip you in two and make you hate me."

Chapter Eleven

Lex

Selena stays silent beside me. I'm not sure if it's because I scared her when I showed her how much control it took to hold myself back in the woods or if she's starting to realize the gravity of where we're going the closer we get to her home. She became culpable once she gave me the directions to her house.

"What's the matter, rabbit?" I ask.

"Nothing," she whispers. But I know she's lying.

I smirk at her. "Are you mad I didn't fuck you back there? Or are you worried about what I'll do to you once I get you home?" I reach over and brush her hair from her face. "Or are you scared of what I'll do to your husband?"

She draws her face from my touch.

I drop my hand to her inner thigh, pull her legs apart, and grip the skin where her bruises are. "He sealed his fate when he put those on you and I saw them. Piece of shit like that doesn't deserve you."

I hate it but it's true. She's the first woman I've felt something for. I'm not sure what I'm feeling because I've never felt it before, but it's *something*. When I saw those bruises, I felt like I needed to protect her and get vengeance for her pain. Why else would I risk getting caught again for some pussy?

She isn't just that, though. Her pussy may be incredible, but there's so much more there. Even though we're from totally different worlds, I recognize some of her pain. I see someone who's been let down by every single person in their life, just like me. Where we differ is that she swallows it, letting it eat her away from the inside instead of becoming angry and violent. I sacrificed my freedom to make people feel some of the pain I felt.

I'm trying so hard to give her the freedom she deserves.

"Answer me," I say as I rub her thigh where I'd grabbed. "What's bothering you?"

She looks up at me, her lips drawn tight. "I feel bad for being excited."

I smile at her. "Oh, bunny, I'm rubbing off on you." My hand continues up her thigh. "But don't let too much of me inside you. You're too good for him, but also way too fucking good for me."

The way she pouts her lips at my words makes me want to pull over and rip through her in the most selfish way possible, as if she was the last woman I'd be inside before I go back to prison.

Which she probably is.

"Why didn't you sleep with me back there?" she asks. Finally.

I love that she asked me that. Fucking love it. It means she wants it. She wants me however I need to give it to her. "Remember when you said you didn't really trust me? I don't trust myself, either. I was going to hurt you back there in the woods. Not intentionally, of course, but I was just a wiggle of your hips away from being beyond the point of control."

I expect her to flinch or become scared of me, but her expression remains soft and a little curious. It slightly angers me as images of my past flash through the front of my mind. She doesn't realize what she's flirting with or what losing control really means. She's so naïve to the dangers of a man like me who has nothing to lose and absolutely everything to gain. She doesn't realize I could have shoved her face into the car's hot metal and fucked her until she begged me to stop. Her pleas would only make me savor every thrust. She doesn't grasp how little I cared about having to kill her in the beginning, or that even though I care now, I would still kill her if I had to.

She may have gotten the dirty and feral dog to lick her hand, but I'm not the sweet little pet she wants me to be. I'll still maul her, no matter how much I appreciate her kindness.

"I need you so fucking bad, bunny. I want to pull over on one of these rural roads and bring you into the backseat and—" My breath catches in my throat, silencing my voice. A cop car drives by, and the officer stares at me. I don't breathe again until I'm sure he won't turn around.

"Bad idea, huh?" she asks, though it's clear.

"In the daytime? Yeah. Seems so." I groan and rub the front of my pants.

She reaches out and replaces my hand with her own. She rubs up my length, the denim causing such pleasurable friction beneath her hand. I grab her wrist and stop her. "Not now, bunny. I want to feel this frustration for a while longer. I don't want to come in your hand. I want to be inside you."

It's odd because I almost enjoy the frustrated twitch of my cock. It's something I haven't felt in a while. I didn't wait to get my pleasure when I felt it in the past. I got instant gratification, one way or another.

The ache of staying off her almost feels . . . good. The control feels foreign.

I know I'll get to her eventually, and it will feel amazing when I spill all of myself inside her.

She looks at me with a similar longing, and I wish I could give her what she wants, but it'll have to wait.

She gestures to an exit, and I take the turn that brings us closer to her home. I pull into a fast-food parking lot just off the exit. She looks at the building with a mouth-watering stare. We've been getting quick and easy things to eat, mostly from gas stations, since the beginning. I always thought the less we were seen, the better, but I know she's hungry for a real meal when I hear her stomach growl beside me.

I park the car but instead of getting out, I lean over, grab her face, and pull her into me for a kiss. Her lips spread on mine with a similar hunger. She grabs my hair with one of her hands, as if she's remembering how it felt to pull me into her pussy with a similar grasp. I growl at her touch, struggling to control myself as I remember how she felt when she came around my fingers.

I pull away from her. I have to before I lose myself—or rather, find myself.

"Goddamn it, bunny," I whisper before giving her a final kiss, her lower lip between my teeth as I ease away. "You just wait until I can get my hands on your pussy again." My hand drifts up her thigh and I palm her, making her tremble. She's so warm and wet. Even through her leggings, I can feel it. It's addictive, and I don't ever want to pull my hand away from her. She melts into my touch, and I hope she's only thinking of how I make her feel.

I glance around the parking lot. No one is paying attention to us. I won't fuck her or let either of us expose ourselves, but she's so in need of her orgasm, and I don't want to deny her.

I move my seat back and help her onto my lap. She straddles my waist the best she can, and I pull her mouth to mine. "Grind on my dick, sweet bunny. Make yourself come."

She bites her lower lip before kissing me.

She. Kisses. Me.

She rocks her hips on my lap, and I feel her warmth through not only her pants but my own. I groan as she moves over my hardened length. It's immature, like two teenagers not ready for sex, but it feels so goddamn good. I'm not sure if it's because I'm already so frustrated, but she rubs back and forth, and it hits the head of my dick every fucking time. I wrap my arms around her waist, pulling her closer and trying to keep her from hitting the head so I don't bust. I'm much too old to come in my jeans.

She feels so good in my arms, like she's exactly where she should be. The world grows hazy until all I can see is her and the motions of her hips and chest as she chases her orgasm.

Her moans. Those goddamn moans as she gets herself closer drive me crazy. Her body tenses and the motions of her hips grow ragged.

"Come for me, bunny."

She grips my hair and grinds on me, panting in my ear. She leans into me and moves her hips in a shallow motion as she pushes herself over her edge. Aside from a subtle twitch of her pussy as she rides out her orgasm, she keeps still. Her moans and the warm throb of her on my lap almost make me come, too.

I kiss her and reach between us to feel the wet spot that soaked through her pants and into the front of my jeans. "You made such a mess," I say against her mouth. "Such a good girl. So fucking wet."

I reach down the front of her pants, feeling just how much she came. She looks down at me with the sweetest and most satiated expression I've ever seen.

She looks . . . happy.

I pull my hand from her pants and lick my fingers. She tastes incredible. She always tastes better after she comes for me. I run my wet fingers up the curve of her neck and lace both of my hands behind it. I bring her forehead to mine and hold her there. I never thought I'd be so attracted to a woman like her. She's spoiled but not spoiled rotten. There's still so much good inside her, a brokenness that keeps her from becoming what I hate. She's become something I want with every fiber of my being.

It will be so hard to leave her once I kill her husband, but living on the lam isn't for someone like her. As much as I don't *want* to leave her behind, at least I can leave the states knowing she's safe at home. She can find someone who makes her feel like I do without being me, the dog she can't trust because he can't trust himself.

Chapter Twelve

Selena

I don't realize how hungry I am until I scarf down my food. It's the first substantial meal I've had since the night Lex got in my car. My last big dinner was leftover food-truck pizza on the overtime shift from hell.

"I probably should have fed you sooner," he says through a laugh.

My cheeks heat as I realize I probably looked like a ravenous animal. I pretty much am.

"Worst captor ever," I say through a noisy sip of my nearly empty drink.

Lex smirks at me. "I'm not a captor. You're just an unwilling passenger. We're close, aren't we?" he asks, and I nod. "Then you drive. Drop me off a few blocks away and tell me the address."

I shake my head. I do *not* like that plan. I'm terrified to walk into the house alone after all this. After everything we've done and the things we'll do in the future. "What am I even supposed to tell him about where I've been?"

"Just tell him the truth. That you were carjacked."

"I don't want to go in alone," I whisper.

"You have to. Have I ever let anything bad happen to you?" he asks.

I cock my head at him because he almost sold me, and I'd say that was something pretty fucking bad. "You offered me as payment for that fake ID."

"I didn't let it happen, rabbit," he says. He gets out of the car, and we swap seats.

I tighten my lips as I sit in the driver's seat. I don't like this idea. I hate it, actually. But he's right. I can't pull into my driveway with Lex in the passenger seat. He needs the element of surprise once I get inside the house.

We creep closer to my home without speaking. My stomach twists in knots, more so than when I first had sex with Lex. I pull over before we get into the upscale neighborhood I used to call home. It doesn't feel like it any longer. It feels like a stranger's street. It *is* a stranger's street.

I'm not the same Selena who last drove on this road.

I cut the engine, but we don't move a muscle. "Give me your house key," he says. He reaches toward me with an outstretched hand, but I hesitate before leaning over and twisting the key from the ring.

I hand it to him and cut my gaze.

He gets out of the car and leans through the open door to look at me once more. His hand digs around in his pocket before revealing a pocketknife. He tosses it on the passenger seat. "I'll be there for you as soon as I can. If anything happens, use that, okay?" His hand grips the door handle. It's as if he doesn't want to leave me, or like he has something more he wants to say.

But he doesn't.

I watch him walk away as I turn the key in the ignition and drive toward my hell. The devil is waiting for me, and I want to vomit from the fear squeezing my stomach.

Will he smell Lex on me? Inside me? Will he know I've become a willing participant? I had so many opportunities to escape, but I didn't. Escape meant running back to the nightmare my husband and I share.

I pull into my driveway and stare at the house that doesn't feel like my home anymore. I feel safer in my car. Safer with Lex. I tuck the pocketknife into my waistband and exit the car. The moment I step onto the first stair, the door whips open. A fog drifts over me as I stare at Bryce. He looks so cold, and his hardened mask shows no emotion, not even concern or excitement at seeing me. This blank nothingness is scarier than his rage.

His face finally twists into a familiar anger—the expression I'm used to. I see it in a renewed light this time, as if there's a bullseye planted in the middle of his forehead now, and it almost makes me laugh. I *enjoy* the idea that this might be his last anger-fueled inhale.

Bryce grabs my arm and rips me inside. The sharp points of his fingers dig into my flesh, painting another bruise on my skin.

"Where the hell have you been, Selena?"

I strain against his grasp. "I got carjacked," I say through gritted teeth.

"Bullshit. Stop fucking lying to me."

My eyes well with tears. "I'm not lying to you. I swear."

I'm not lying, but I'm not telling the truth, either. Yes, I got carjacked, but then this whole road trip became something else entirely, something that made me see life in a different way, and I welcomed Lex into my home to get rid of my problems.

"It's been days. Who did you run off with? Have you been fucking around on me?"

"I didn't run off!" I take a deep breath, trying to push away the stampede of guilt that seeks to trample my voice. "I haven't done anything."

"Fucking whore," he says with a curl of his lip.

"Bryce, please . . ." I plead. Such a familiar sound, yet it never made him stop. Pleading only angers him. He hates the weakness.

He silently broods, which is worse than when he yells. His fist pulls back, and before I can react, he punches me in the face. The force knocks me into the wall, and framed pictures fall and shatter at my feet. *Hurry Lex,* I think as the glass spreads along the floor. I don't make a sound, though, because I know he gets off on it. I can't even reach up and baby the stinging heat in my cheek.

He's never hit me in the face like this because it would be too hard to hide. His attacks have always targeted places my clothes could conceal. Everyone probably thought I ran off, and he has no reason to tell them I returned. He can kill me and no one will know any different, and that's what I'm afraid of.

"You want to run off and be a whore? I'll show you how whores get fucked." Bryce grabs me by my hair, leads me to the kitchen, and bends me over the island. A mug falls off the countertop and crashes to the ground as I fight against him. I know what's coming.

It's not the first time.

I slip my hand down and grab the pocketknife from my waistband, concealing it in my balled fist. Cold air bites my skin as he pulls down my pants and works open his fly.

"You don't even have underwear on? My god, Selena. I'm embarrassed to call you my wife." The heat of his cock presses against me, and I pray he doesn't notice the wetness that came from someone other than my husband.

From Lex.

I clench my eyes closed and try to ignore Bryce's harsh grasp as he readies himself. I slip into my mind, where Lex still lives. I try to imagine him behind me. Tears slip past my closed eyes and drip onto the marble countertop. My pelvis rubs painfully against the lip of the island as he pushes his weight against me. I feel guilt, a lot of it, but not for allowing Lex to be inside me. I feel guilty for not fighting harder against Bryce. There's a certain level of acceptance that lets shitty husbands do more than they should to their wives.

Clapping.

The sound forces my eyes to open. Lex stands a few feet away, smacking his hands together in sarcastic applause. Bryce stops and tucks himself back in his pants before zipping them. Only a moment later and he'd have made Lex a liar when he said no one else would get inside me.

Lex draws his pistol and aims it at him. "Don't stop on my account." He circles us, stops across from me, and leans against the island. His eyes meet mine for a moment before returning to Bryce. "She feels fucking amazing, doesn't she?"

"Who the fuck are you?" Spit flies against the back of my arm from the raging force of Bryce's words.

"The one who held your wife against her will," Lex says with a proud, dark smile.

"I told you I wasn't lying," I whisper, though I doubt he hears me over the anger between his ears.

"Is that how you'd fuck her, boss?" Lex asks Bryce. "Come on, show me."

My gaze rises to Lex, but he avoids my eyes as he looks over my head. I drop my forehead to the counter. The shame makes me wish for death all over again. Anger greets me in every direction, and I'm stuck in the middle of a sea of hatred.

"You're pitiful. You can stop or you can fuck her, but mark my words, it'll be the last time you're inside her," Lex says with a disgustingly calm demeanor. I don't know how he's so willing to let Bryce have sex with me, after—

Bryce pulls away from me, and I nearly lose my balance. I go to tug up my pants, but Lex clears his throat.

"Oh no, not yet." The darkness in his eyes makes me tremble. I hardly recognize him. He doesn't look like the man I've let inside me. He looks evil. He's someone else entirely at this moment.

Lex walks up to Bryce and throws him against the wall, and a nauseating *crack* blows through the kitchen when his fist collides with Bryce's face. Blood splatters on the floor, but I can't bring myself to look at the source of it.

With his gun aimed at Bryce, Lex circles behind me and rubs a firm hand down my back. "I thought I'd like watching you fuck her because I've thought about it as I've made her come from my hand, but that was fucking pitiful."

Bryce charges at Lex, but a quick jut of his gun keeps Bryce back.

"If you take another step toward me, I'll blow your brains onto the picture behind you. The one of you and her." Lex goes to unbutton his jeans. Before he goes for the zipper, he turns to Bryce once more. "This stain on my pants? I'm glad you asked. Yeah, it's her come. How often have you worn her like that? Have you even made her come since you fucking married her or is that"—he gestures between me and Bryce—"what she used to get? Some half-assed fuck. I mean, I'm selfish as *fuck* and I still made sure she came."

Lex loops his arm around my hip and puts his hand between my legs. I steal a quick glance at Bryce. His nostrils flare with rage. His face is painted the color of the blood dripping from his nose.

Lex rubs my clit in a way that makes me twitch. "Do you even know how your wife likes to be touched? What makes her do . . . that?" He draws circles around me with the tips of his fingers. "Do you know how many fingers she likes inside her? How about how she likes a tongue on her? God, have you ever tasted her?" He pulls his fingers away from me and licks them. "She's fucking delicious."

"You have no idea who you're fucking with," Bryce snarls.

Lex smirks. "Oh, I do. Someone who doesn't give a shit about his wife. You're a little bitch who beats her even though she's the most—" He swallows hard, as if he has more to say but thinks better of it.

I let the tears fall without restraint. When he takes a step back, I collapse to the floor and press my back against the island. Lex holds an open palm toward me, but he isn't offering me a hand. He wants the knife. He doesn't want to shoot him in this neighborhood—the cops would be called the moment the sound punctuated the serene setting—but I keep the knife pinned to my chest. It makes me feel safer. He looks around for another weapon since my trembling hand refuses to relinquish the pocketknife.

Bryce sees an opportunity and leaps at him. He reaches for the knife attached to a magnet above the island. Lex tucks the pistol behind him before their bodies clash. The sound of flesh on flesh is nauseating. I shut my eyes to hide the view and cover my ears to stop the sound. Blood splashes across me, hitting my face and arms. I'm afraid to look and see who it came from, whose life force has spread across my skin.

I open my eyes.

Bryce stumbles back. Blood runs down his shirt and pants and collects at his feet. He clutches his abdomen, and I scream.

It happened.

It's so fucking real.

Oh god.

Lex clamps a bloody hand over my mouth and tosses the kitchen knife aside. "Shh, bunny," he whispers in that sweet way I recognize as so different from the way he talked before.

"Selena," Bryce whispers. He hits the wall and slides down. "Come here," he says, in a way that is so unlike him.

Lex becomes familiar to me at the same moment Bryce becomes a stranger. It's a desperation I've never seen. It draws me to him. It's a force I can't fight, even if I try. I crawl toward him, shaking off Lex's hand as he tries to grab me. I kneel in front of him, my eyes wide with fear and something else. Something unexpected.

He's dying, I feel it. It nauseates me. It fucking hurts. But . . . it's not pain from the prospect of losing him. It's because the thought of his death doesn't elicit *enough* pain.

I swipe open the blade and stab it into his stomach. All the evilness inside him spills from the wound. I pull it out and stab it through his groin. Lex gasps behind me, and there's a squelching sound as I snatch the knife out and stab him again and again.

"*Fuck you, you fucking asshole!*" I keep stabbing until strong arms wrap around me and pull me away. My arm continues its repeated downward arc toward Bryce, fighting against Lex's grasp as my rage blinds me.

Lex gets control over me, and his hand rides down my arm and grabs the knife. He rubs the handle on his shirt and puts it in his pocket.

"Rabbit, we have to go." He grabs my wrist.

I shake my head. "Fuck me first." I can feel the evil behind my glare when I turn my darkened eyes to him. The need to hurt Bryce one last time. I expect him to fight me on it, but he wastes no time pulling me into him.

His warm breath races across my chilled skin. "You're out of your mind, rabbit. You weren't supposed to get involved. You weren't supposed to touch him." He grabs my bloodied hand and rubs it. "You aren't a killer. You can't be," he whispers. "That's not what was supposed to happen."

"I want this, Lex," I say with more surety than I've ever felt about anything in my life.

He looks at me. "You know I'd do anything for you. If you want me to fuck you, I'll fuck you." Lex turns me around and puts my hands on the counter again. He unzips his pants and pulls out his cock. He pulls down my pants and pushes himself inside me.

I gasp as I drop my head to the marble, and the world disappears again, dripping away like the blood on the floor. He fucks me, hard and selfish, tearing me apart in ways I've never felt. It doesn't matter how wet I am for him; he still makes me ache with the force of his thrusts.

Knowing Bryce is watching, he fucks me differently, and I don't expect anything less. Lex loves control, and nothing screams it more than fucking someone's wife in front of them. He bottoms out inside me and pushes just a fraction further, making me whimper.

"Did he ever fuck you like this?" Lex growls in my ear as he grinds his hips against my ass. "He looked like a disappointing fuck."

"No, he never fucked me like you do," I pant, leaving the fog of my breath on the fancy countertop. Lex groans and runs his arms down mine, leaning his weight into me.

Bryce chokes out a gurgled whimper—a sign of life, albeit a weak one. Lex goes to pull out of me to take care of it, but I grab his shirt. "Don't. I hope he feels it all. I hope he can see us."

"Sadistic fucking rabbit," Lex growls as he pushes himself deep again. "I'm not ready to come yet. Not here." He looks around, eyeing the steps. "Take me to your room."

He pulls out of me and turns me to face him. His hand wipes the blood on my face.

"I want to fuck you in his bed. Your bed," he says, low and smooth, as if we didn't just kill a man.

I bite my lip and tug up my pants as he zips his jeans. With one last glance at Bryce's motionless body, I guide Lex up the stairs. Desire saturates each warm exhale as it leaves his lips and sends pebbles across my skin. The wetness between my legs soaks through my pants.

When my hand grips the doorknob to our bedroom, it feels foreign, like I never belonged here at all. The door drags on the light blue carpet as it opens. It's only through new eyes, gray-colored glasses, that I see how little of myself is in this room. Bryce's suits line the closet, and his drab ties hang on the outside of the closet door. The room is decorated to his liking—black, white, and dark shades of gray. Nothing screams that a wife slept in here except my perfume—his favorite—on the nightstand. My clothes are folded in the drawers, away and out of sight, as he commanded.

Lex walks past me and rubs his blood-soaked hand across the white comforter. A sadistic smile crosses his face as he smears more crimson across the blanket, as if he's painting on a canvas. He lies back with a groan and motions me to him. "Come on, bunny," he whispers. "Get on my lap. I haven't gotten to see you ride my dick outside of a damn car."

I remove my pants and climb over him, straddling his lap as he undoes his zipper again. His warm cock rests against his lower stomach. His hand runs down the front of my thighs, where the worst of my fading bruise remains. The touch unintentionally fills my mind with memories, and I flinch.

"It's over," he says as he brings my face to his to kiss me. "He'll never hurt you again."

"Lex," I whimper.

He wraps his hand around his cock with one hand, lifts my hip with the other, and pushes himself inside me. I lower myself onto his lap, welcoming every inch of him

He's right. I haven't had a chance to look at him quite like this. Looking down, I see a man who looks content to just be within me.

His blue eyes meet mine, dark and hungry. I try to ignore the blood soaking his shirt and saturating mine. My husband's blood. When I lift the shirt and expose his abdomen, I see a long gash. It isn't just Bryce's blood after all.

"Lex!" I put my hand to his wound, blood dripping around my fingers.

He bats me away and smirks. "Let me bleed, rabbit. I'm fine. Just focus on riding my cock."

How is he okay? Doesn't he feel it? I'm not fine, and I'm just looking at his injury, not living with it.

He pulls me closer until my chest rests on his. The warm blood soaks through more of my shirt as he grabs my hips and forces me to move. He shows no reaction to the pain as I move with him. In fact, he looks like he almost enjoys it.

He groans, raising his hips to meet mine. "You look fucking beautiful."

I can't remember the last time Bryce called me anything nice, especially not beautiful. I place my hands on either side of his head and kiss his forehead. I leave my lips there, just feeling his warm breath on my throat.

"I'm going to guess he compliments you about as good as he fucks you," Lex says with a laugh.

"Pretty much." I draw my lips tight, keeping them against his forehead.

Lex lifts his hip and flips me onto my back. I stretch out on the king-sized bed, tie-dyed with blood. I wrap my legs around him, and he leans over and kisses me.

"Bunny, you are the sexiest thing I've ever laid my hands on. Fucking. Perfect. So goddamn smart, too. You deserve so much more than that piece of shit. More than me . . ." His words waver at the end until they cut off completely. His expression grows cold and more focused as he drives me into the mattress. Blood drips from his wet shirt onto mine. "I'm going to come, rabbit," he says in a tone I almost don't recognize. It's robotic and distant. His thrusts slow and he pulls out of me, a string of his come connecting me to him.

Lex goes into the bathroom, leaving me half naked and confused. He comes out with a towel pressed on his cut.

"Are you sure you're okay?" I ask.

"Yeah, it's hardly anything. It'll stop," he says. He uses one hand to zip up his pants. "We have to get going. I'll take care of the cleanup here and your car. Wipe out as much of us as I can."

I lean over and pull a key from the nightstand, tossing it to him. "My old car is in the garage. No one knows about it. Or at least no one who would report him missing right away."

Lex smiles at me, pinched with something I can't recognize.

"I'll grab money, too."

He tosses me a quick nod before heading down the slick wooden staircase.

I pack up some money in a bag. The steps creak beneath my weight as I come back downstairs. I look back once more, inhaling the noxious, metallic scent of blood. With Bryce's spirit heading to hell where it belongs, nothing tethers me to this damn house any longer.

The house that never felt like home.

Chapter Thirteen

Lex

The garage door buzzes and begins to rise. I start to back out, but the door to the house opens. There's no way to avoid her gaze, and she looks more betrayed by the second. I was undecided about leaving her behind until the moment I realized she deserved more than me, so much more than I could ever give her. I knew what I had to do. I *had* to leave her, but I wasn't fast enough. I don't care about the cash or the bloodbath I left behind, but I don't want to see her face. I can't meet her feelings of betrayal.

She's spent too long being betrayed, and I'm doing it to her again.

Selena deserves what Bryce had to offer her, minus him. Now that he's gone, she can go back to normal, a feeling I can never give her.

I hate that I came inside her and left. She deserves so much more than that, but I knew my resolve would weaken if I tried to say goodbye. Now it's too late, and the look of betrayal is even worse than I feared. It makes me feel things that I didn't expect to feel.

She rushes down the steps. Her arms and face are scrubbed, but blood remains on her shirt. She has a change of clothes under one arm and a bag under the other. Her eyes narrow when she tries the door handle and finds it locked. I should have driven away. Put the pedal to the floor and left her. She places her hand against the window, and the broken desperation in her eyes forces me to lower it.

"You were leaving without me?" she asks.

"You can't go, Selena. I can't let you," I tell her, as firmly as I can. I don't want to, but I have to. I can't bring her with me. "Tell the police he assaulted you. Self-defense. You have the bruises. Nothing will happen to you." I've promised her safety, and she'll be safer away from me.

"Really, Lex?" She raises her voice. The garage door is open to the idyllic neighborhood, and she'll draw attention if she keeps this up.

"Lower your fucking voice, rabbit," I snap.

Her lip trembles. "Fuck you! After everything we did! Everything we've been th—"

"For fuck's sake." I unlock the doors. She can't keep yelling like this. "Get in the fucking car."

She stares at me for a moment before dropping into the passenger seat of the SUV. She crouches on the floorboard as we drive away from her old life and into my new one. The new life I don't want to make her a part of, but I have no choice now.

"Get off the fucking floor," I say as I pull her up by her arm. She flinches. "Did he hurt you?" Only once she sits up and allows the sun to touch her skin do I see the bruises forming on her arm and cheek. I fight the urge to reach out and touch them.

I promised her I wouldn't let anything bad happen to her, and she ended up getting beat on and nearly fucked again by that piece of shit. It breaks something inside me. I hear the shattering sound in my chest.

"Bunny," I whisper, "I'd have been there sooner, but your neighbor was putting groceries away and I had to wait for her to close her garage door."

"It's fine."

I shake my head. "It's not."

"I'm more upset that you tried to leave me," she says as she tugs off her shirt, exposing incredible tits that I can't help but stare at as I try to drive.

She puts on a clean shirt and hands me something of Bryce's to wear. I shake my head, but she keeps it held toward me. I grab it and have her hold the wheel as I change. It's too small for me, and my muscles stretch the t-shirt, but it'll work for now.

"You wouldn't understand, Selena, and I'm not getting into it with you. I needed you to listen to me."

"I want to go with you," she whispers.

I raise my voice. "You think I didn't want to take you with me? It's not safe. It's not something we can do together. You weren't supposed to do anything but play the grieving fucking widow." I swallow hard. "And go be fucking happy."

"I want to be with you," she says, a defiant pull in her voice.

I steer to the side of the road and throw the car in park. I turn her face to mine. "I have never felt anything for anyone like I feel for you, and that's why you can't be with me. You need to be free and happy. It took everything in me to let you go. Being with me means prison for you, do you understand that? I carjacked you. I got your address off your ID. I took you back to your house to rob you, and I ended up killing your husband. My fingerprints are everywhere in the car and your house. They were on the kitchen knife." I sigh. "If you don't want to be a victim of domestic violence, be a victim of a botched robbery. I don't care which, just be a goddamn victim, rabbit, please."

As much as it breaks me, she needs to go. Being with me means she's a willing participant in all of it. She'll be as culpable as me. A girl like her wouldn't survive in prison, and we both know that.

If she refuses to be a victim, I'll have to kill her. I'll have no fucking choice.

I wait for her answer, knowing if I'm backed into a corner, I'll give her a humane death before I let her go into the system.

Her eyes narrow. "I stabbed him too."

"I know you fucking did," I say as I brush a hand through my hair.

"We need to get going if we want to make it to the border before he's found." She sits back with a stubborn huff and crosses her arms over her chest. "I don't want to be a victim anymore, Lex." She speaks with such finality, so I don't say another word. I can understand that. At least she has *someone* to look out for her.

Even if that someone is me.

"Toss your shirt out the window," I tell her, and she does. She seems so distant as she sits back and stares out the window. Maybe she realizes the gravity of what we've done. Together. What I tried to save her from.

We drive south, and I almost expect her to tell me to turn around and bring her back home. But that isn't an option any longer. I've stayed long enough in the state I needed to leave the most. The state I left and then returned to.

For her.

I toss out my bloody shirt once we reach the northern tip of Pennsylvania, spreading our evidence across state lines. A stifling silence hangs between us. I don't know what to say to her, and she sure as hell doesn't know what to say to me. I look over, and she's staring at me.

"What's on your mind, rabbit?" I ask. I look at the rearview mirror, pull the rabbit's foot from my pocket, and hang it up. Whether it's lucky or not, it's become an icon of our fucked-up little relationship.

Her eyes narrow. "What happened back there."

"Elaborate." I'm getting annoyed with her evasiveness when I know she wants to talk about it.

"You acted weird." She swallows. "Like you wanted him to have sex with me."

I shake my head. I didn't intend for it to happen, I truly didn't, but when I saw it happening, the sick part of me wanted him to keep going. I watched them at first because I thought I wanted it. I had thought about it enough times to at least learn how it made me feel when I actually saw it, but when I realized how much it broke her, I decided to break him instead.

"I thought I wanted to watch. It's something I've fantasized about," I say.

She chews the inside of her cheeks and drops her gaze.

"Turns out, I didn't. I couldn't."

Her gaze shoots to me. "Why were you saying those things about him, then?"

I knew calling out her husband for being a pitiful lover would hurt his pride and crush him before I could even touch him. When he found out I knew how to touch his wife, how to make her feel good and make her come, I knew it would break him. Showing him the come stain on my jeans forced him to realize she'd been a willing participant. It was physical proof of our affair. I went too far with it, though. I disappeared into the shadow of who I was before I met Selena. I hid from the light she cast on me as she tried to draw me from the darkness. But then she stabbed him, dragging herself into the darkness with me. The moment she pushed that knife through him, I knew I'd caused that. I pushed her to be the woman who was on her knees, stabbing the man who hurt her. I transformed her into me, but I don't want her to be me.

I wanted more for her, and that's when I knew I had feelings for her. That's why I tried to leave her. I don't want her to be a predator. I need her to be Selena, the sweet little rabbit that slept with a wolf.

I grip the steering wheel. "You seem to selectively forget what I am. I'm a killer. I didn't intend to just kill your husband. I wanted him to hurt, really fucking hurt, before I killed him."

"I just don't understand why you would tell him to keep going," she whispers.

"Because that wasn't me in there. That's the person I was before you. I was thinking about inflicting pain instead of thinking about you." I pull to the side of the road again and reach for her, ignoring her flinch of mistrust. I draw her into me. "He needed to know it would be the last time he'd be inside you. It was all mental warfare, and I'm sorry you were collateral damage in that war." I press my forehead against hers. It's such a battle inside me sometimes, and I have no way of explaining that to her. Not really. "The moment I realized how pissed off it made me, there's no way I could let him fuck you, rabbit. Trust me on that."

"Why'd you stop fucking me in the kitchen? Was it because of him?"

"God no." I smirk at the thought of the moment she surpassed me in a way I never expected. She wanted me to fuck her in front of her dying husband. That turned me on more than ever before. Her vengeance was delicious, and I was happy to be a part of it. I gave her what she wanted, but I didn't want it to end there. My balls ached to unload in her, and she felt incredible, but I wanted to fuck her in their marital bed. Even when I was ready to bust, I realized she was better off without me and that I had to push her away. I shouldn't have let myself come then, but I couldn't help it. That sick part of me wanted to leave her dripping with my come.

When I lean into her, I smell the soap she used to clean herself, a variation of the same flowery soap I used to wash away the blood. She'd have gotten rid of all traces of me before she changed her pants. I don't care that she cleaned herself and changed her clothes, but she better not have any panties on. She knows how I feel about them.

When my hand slips down the front of her pants, she whimpers out a moan. There's nothing between my hand and her pussy. *Good girl.* I growl before kissing her. I have plans for her. She's along for the ride now, whether I like it or not, and I intend to claim her as my own—*truly* my own—until death parts us.

"Wait until it gets dark, bunny, because that pussy is mine."

Towering maple trees surround both sides of us, as if the road has cut the woods in half. I pull the car onto the shoulder and park as deep as I can in the brush, trying to conceal the vehicle. Branches scrape the paint until we're in our own little alcove of seclusion.

"Get in the backseat," I say. She wastes no time climbing over the center console and melting into the bench seat's buttery leather. There's no way I'm climbing over shit, so I get out and open the back door.

The overhead light illuminates her, and her eyes are big and tempting. I climb into the roomy backseat, and the light flickers off when I close the door. Darkness surrounds us with a heavy blackness that reminds me of the first night I slept with her in the back of her other car.

"Last chance to back out," I whisper as I lean over her. I can't see more than her silhouette, but I bask in the heat of her beneath me. I'm giving her one more chance to change her mind before I make her pussy mine for good.

"I'm not backing out," she says.

I undo my pants and lower the zipper. I run my hand along her neck and chest by mere memory. When I go to remove her pants, she lifts her hips to help me. I rest my cock against her pussy. She feels so warm and welcoming as she throbs beneath me. I lean down and kiss her.

She's so wet. All it takes is pulling my hips back enough to push inside her. I groan as I go deep from the very first thrust, hitting the end of her. A melodic whimper breaks through the stagnant air.

"God, bunny, you have me by the balls, you know that?" I whisper before nipping her throat.

I'm destined for hell but her pussy is heaven, and I'll be saved as long as I'm inside her. I'm washed of my sins as long as I bathe in her come.

Selena moans as I angle myself just right, rubbing her in all the ways I've learned she likes. I know what makes her moan and sends her body into waves of trembling pleasure. Her nails rake my back and her hips move beneath me, getting me too close too soon. The more I try to prolong it, lengthening and slowing my thrusts, the more her pussy squeezes me for more. I don't know why I feel the need to come, and I sure as hell don't want to do it so soon, but she creates a feeling of euphoria inside me.

She's going to stay by my side—she's *choosing* to stay by my side—and my mind is a hundred percent focused on her right now. I start to imagine an "us." We became a team, after all, a pairing in blood that neither of us can wash away.

"I'm going to come," I tell her. I can't see it, but I know her face is painted with disappointment. As her hips buck into mine, I know she wants more. Shit, I want more, too, but my balls tighten and I'm going to come whether we want it or not. I kiss her as my thrusts slow, and the growl that comes from my throat vibrates the air. It feels so good to spill myself inside her. I don't want it to end, and I won't let it.

I sit back, my cock spent but still hard. "Come here, sweet bunny. I'm not done with you."

Her silhouette crosses the backseat, and she straddles my lap with her bare thighs. I push myself back inside her, past the warm stickiness of my come. I wrap my arms around her and draw her into me. She nestles against my chest.

I begin to soften, losing my erection as I overstay my welcome inside her. I don't care, though. It still feels so good to be within her tight, warm pussy. A warm drop of my come slips from inside her, running down my dick and landing on my pelvis. She leans back, and I take the opportunity to rub her clit. She twitches with pleasure, making the walls of her pussy clench around me.

"I'm going to stay inside you for as long as I can," I tell her as I brush hair from her face. "Until I can fuck you again."

I rub her clit with a side-to-side motion of my thumb, thrumming the hood until she trembles on my lap. Every twitch of her pussy draws blood straight to my dick. She awakens me with the warm heat of her body on my lap.

Selena drops her head to the crook of my neck, her chest rising heavily against mine as I work her toward the edge. The closer she gets to coming, the more she breathes life into my dick. Her incredible moans carry the blood through my veins and toward my cock.

"Come, sweet bunny. Come on my dick and make me hard again so I can fuck you through your orgasm," I growl as she rides my lap, grinding against my fingers.

She moans my name in the throes of her orgasm. It's worth all that I've done to hear that because it led me right to this moment, with Selena coming on my dick.

As her body tenses and tightens, the spasms awaken me until I'm hard again, filling her as I grow. I meet her with a thrust of my hips, and she screams out from the pleasure of riding out her orgasm with my cock stretching her once more.

"Good fucking girl," I growl as I hold her hips and thrust harder. The wet sounds of our mingling come intensifies. It's a sound I'll always remember because it's an audible rendition of how good she makes me feel every time I'm inside her.

My come drips down the length of my dick, smearing across my skin as I thrust into her. I reach between us, swiping two of my fingers through a pool of my come on my pelvis. I see her face, illuminated by the moonlight. Moans roll from her loose lips. I bring my fingers up to them and push my come into her mouth. Her lips close around my fingers, and the look she gives me brings me close to busting all over again.

I grab both sides of her face and kiss her, taking the taste of my come into my mouth. "Do you want me to fill you again?" I ask as I draw away from her.

She whimpers out her answer, her face nodding against my neck as she drops her mouth to my skin.

"Your husband never came inside you, and yet you're on my lap, willing to let me fill you a second time."

She moans against me, her body tensing at the mention of her husband. I lift her to put her on her back once more. I never pull out of her, not for a second. I want to stay buried inside her where I belong.

I reach between us and rub her clit, sticky with my come and her own wetness. Every time I push myself as far as I can inside her, more of the intertwined pleasure slips onto my dick. Her moans are the only other sound I focus on, the growing screams lengthening and becoming hoarse the harder and faster I fuck her. She covers her mouth to keep from crying out, and I lean over and tug her hand away from her face.

"I want to hear those sounds leaving your mouth."

"God, Lex, you're too deep," she whispers, and I realize just how much of my cock I'm making her take. Every fucking inch. I'm deep enough that I feel her still swollen clit against my pelvis.

I draw back, giving her a fraction of relief. "Have you ever been spit on?" I ask.

"What?"

"Has your husband ever spit on your pussy?"

She shakes her head fast enough to make me certain she's never had such a disrespectful thing done to her.

I reach over and push my thumb into her mouth, tugging her lower lip as I pull it out. I lean down and spit on her pussy, the warm wetness dripping down her clit and spreading around my cock. It isn't a disrespectful gesture. Quite the contrary. I respect no one else the way I respect her. She lets out a soft moan that surprises us both.

"Oh, bunny, you liked that?"

Unwilling to face her own shame, she doesn't answer me. I push my thumb back into her mouth and graze her lower lip before raising her chin.

"Open your mouth," I say. My spit on her pussy isn't enough, and I'm sure no one's ever spit in her pretty mouth, either. She hesitates, and I stare at her full lips as I wait for her to do as she's told. "Come on, sweet bunny, open up for me." My voice is low and rich with pleasure.

I hit the overhead light because I want to see it all. She spreads her lips for me, and my cock twitches at the sight. Part of me wants to pull out and put her incredible mouth on my dick, make her taste us both, but I want to be inside her pussy more.

I smirk as I lean over her, my mouth watering with anticipation. Not often do you get to do such an act to a woman so above you. At this moment, it doesn't matter how much more money and power she has. She's below me.

I spit in her mouth. A startled yelp leaves her throat as it hits her tongue. I know she doesn't want to like it, but it's clear her body does as she clenches around me.

"You've taken all I've given you," I groan as I thrust deeper. I'm getting close again, feeling the walls of her pussy tightening around me. The thought of filling her again, giving her another load that claims her as mine, shoves me closer to my edge.

Something about spilling my pleasure into her and keeping her on my dick until I could fuck and fill her again makes me forget about everything around us. It makes me forget about our crimes. I forget that we're running from the law.

I come. A low and gravelly groan vibrates her mouth as I kiss her. I put my hand around the base of my dick as I draw away from her and sit up. When I'm most of the way out, my tip still twitches inside her. A trail of come washes along my dick. There's so much come. She's a fucking mess as I pull out of her. I gather as much as I can with the tips of my fingers and push it back inside her. I graze her clit as I draw my fingers away.

"You look so fucking sexy covered in my come," I growl. She does. She's spread open for me, coated in two loads, and she has my spit on her tongue.

We're from two different worlds, but only a thick layer of our remnants separates us now. We're in a place where pain and suffering can only be cured by pleasure.

A place where there are no rules or laws.

A place where wolves sleep with their prey.

Chapter Fourteen

Selena

I can't believe I let Lex spit on me. I've never had such a degrading thing done to me in my life. But when he was over me, with his lips pouting and his tongue moving to gather his spit, I let him. I'd let him do just about anything to me. Hell, I was even willing to let him kill me. A little spit is nothing in comparison.

The spit didn't bother me as much as the way my body responded to it. The wet warmth made me throb. I watched it fall from his perfect lips and move toward my mouth in slow motion, and my stomach tightened with excitement. I hated that I liked it, but I loved how big and powerful he felt above me as his spit lived on my tongue. I swallowed a piece of him, taking it deep into my stomach while his cock drove upward.

"What's on your mind, rabbit?" Lex asks as I drive. His words rip me from my thoughts. I don't know how to answer him. Everything blurs together and makes it hard for me to focus on any one thing.

Red and blue flashes light up behind us.

"Fuck!" Lex says. He doesn't look scared or panicked. He looks angry—annoyed with me and the situation. I've never seen fear on his face, and I don't think I ever will. He flips down the mirror and brushes his hair over the tattoo along his hairline. He's not panicking, but I am. My breath hitches as I pull to the side of the darkened highway.

Lex reaches over and grabs my chin, forcing me to look at him. "If things go south, put your seat down and get out of my way." He gestures to the pistol tucked into his waistband. "You need to get your shit together, little rabbit. You look like a bunny who's seen movement in the bushes—back straight as an arrow, nose flaring, eyes wide. I need you to be brave, or we're both fucked. Do you understand that?"

"Lex . . ." I whisper with a shake of my head that won't stop. I'm *trying* not to panic, but my nerves are rubbing raw from the inside out. I look so out of place beside Lex, and the guilt I feel from all the murders I've witnessed simmers beneath my skin, ready to ooze from me.

You've lied to the police before, I remind myself, trying to harness the bravery Lex thinks I possess. I seek the confidence that concealed my bruises so many times before.

"You can do it, rabbit," he says as he moves his fingers from my chin to brush the hair off my face, wiping cold sweat from my cheeks. His words make me swell with a strength I didn't have moments before. With his encouragement, I feel like I can do anything.

Including lying to the law.

When I hear the heavy footfalls outside the window, I lower it. The officer leans down to look at me, shining a blinding light in my face. The plastic expression I've used to cover for Bryce paints my face once more. "Good evening, officer," I say, trying to control the tremble in my fingers by gripping the steering wheel.

"Nearly morning, miss," he says as he leans closer to look beyond me. Lex is slumped over, as if he's sleeping.

"Yeah, I guess it is." I smile and gesture to Lex. "I got the crappy shift," I whisper.

The officer tightens his lips. "Do you know why I pulled you over?"

"Not a clue," I tell him, envisioning his sweet features blown off by a bullet if I fuck this up. The thought keeps me calm. I refuse to let this man die tonight because of me.

"You were hitting the lines on the shoulder pretty frequently. Have you had anything to drink tonight?"

I chuckle. "God no. I'm just really tired, and there's not another rest stop for a little ways."

The officer leans in and gets uncomfortably close to my mouth. Satisfied that he doesn't smell any alcohol on my breath, he looks over at Lex. "Can he drive instead?"

"I'm sure he could," I say, but when the officer just keeps staring at me, I prod Lex's arm. "Honey," I whisper, and it feels so weird to call him that. I hope the officer doesn't notice. "Hey?" I say louder, prodding harder.

Lex lifts his head, making a show of a dramatic yawn. "What's going on?" he asks, a believable confused look on his face.

"She was driving a bit reckless. Says she's drowsy. Can you drive the vehicle? I'd prefer to not have it towed."

"Oh, yeah, I can drive. I've been sleeping for . . ." He glances at the clock. "Jesus, like, four hours. Why'd you let me sleep that long, baby?" he asks. Him calling me *baby* feels even weirder than me calling him honey. Of all the things he calls me, baby is *not* one of them.

"Can I have your licenses? Insurance?"

My breath cuts off at my diaphragm, as if it's all sucked out of me with just those few words. I don't know if the insurance is current, and I curse myself for not checking sooner. Bryce didn't want me driving this SUV because it's older, and it wasn't as easy for him to keep tabs on me without all the new gadgets you get in cars these days. I don't know *why* he'd have kept the insurance up to date.

Lex is acutely aware of my panic, and he smiles as he leans forward to pull out the proof of insurance. He puts it in my lap, and I see the end date is current. I hide my relieved breath, exhaling into the empty pockets of my wallet as I rifle through it to find my license. My eyes meet Lex as I reach out and wait for him to produce his fake fucking ID. He remains calm and collected as he pulls it out and hands it over.

The officer cocks his head. "Ben Gurgen Hoffe? That's a unique name."

Lex's calm demeanor breaks as he lets out a small laugh that I see more than I hear. "It's a family name. It's actually pronounced JER-gen." He tightens his lips and sobers. "Here, babe, switch spots. Your turn to nap." He climbs out of the car. Hearing him call me *babe* is even weirder than baby. I hated that he called me rabbit and bunny at first, but now I can't imagine him calling me anything else.

The glint of his pistol winks at me as his shirt rides up, and I can only hope the officer doesn't notice it as well. I undo my seatbelt and open the door, stepping onto the pavement with legs that feel like they'll give out on me. After I sit in the passenger seat, I fasten my seatbelt. I can hardly hear over the whoosh of the blood in my ears. I wipe my sweat-coated palms onto my shirt.

"Krause? Is that of German origin, too?" Lex asks as he leans closer to the officer's nameplate.

The officer looks up at him and smiles. "Yeah, actually. No one notices that."

"Have you visited Germany yet?" Lex leans against the door, looking suave as fuck. Even I forget he's a felon for the moment.

"No, though I always intended to. My remaining grandparents live near Munich."

Lex shakes his head. "Yeah, you need to go. First off, life's too short, and second, it's a beautiful city. You have to go during Oktoberfest if you want to get the full experience. Maybe don't bring grandma, though." A genuine smile crosses Lex's face, and I almost believe he went to Germany.

The officer laughs. "She'd probably outdrink them all." He taps the IDs against his open palm. "You know what? I don't think we need to make this more than it is. As long as someone who is more awake can drive, I'm fine with it." He glances at me with a scolding look. "Here you go, Mr. Gurgen Hoffe. Please drive safe." He returns Lex's ID.

Lex opens the door to get in the car once the officer steps away.

"Hey," the officer calls back as Lex closes the car door.

Lex leans out the window, his hand moving to his hip and wrapping around the pistol's grip.

"Maybe I'll see you at the next Oktoberfest!" the officer calls out with a final nod of his head.

Lex's shoulders drop and his hand releases from the plastic grip. "If you do, I'll buy you a drink," Lex says with a wave. "Have a good night, officer."

With tight lips, he puts on his seatbelt and drives away from the shoulder. He keeps silent until we're a few miles down the road. "Ben Gurgen Hoffe," Lex says with a shake of his head. I stare at him because I don't get it. "Been Jerkin' Off." Lex sighs. "Fucking Rodney. If he wasn't already dead, I'd kill him."

I laugh. It rips through me and feels so foreign that it makes my stomach ache. Tears that aren't from pain or fear fall down my cheeks.

"Stop laughing. That was pure fucking luck. I really thought I'd have a dead cop on my hands. On *our* hands."

I can't stop laughing. I rub the rabbit's foot. "Guess it *is* lucky."

Lex's spine slowly relaxes, and his chest falls forward. He finally lets out a small laugh of his own. When he sobers, the tenor of his voice changes. "You need to be more careful when you drive. We're lucky your pea-brained husband kept insurance on this car. I checked before we left." He draws a sharp breath and slowly exhales, a very methodical set of motions he repeats until his rising chest slows. He clears his throat. "You did a great job, bunny," he says with a reassuring rub of my shoulder. "But you have to be careful when you're driving, because luck like that won't happen twice. Even with that damn thing." He gestures toward the rabbit's foot.

Lex brushes back his hair, exposing his tattoo again. "Gurgen Hoffe," Lex says through an annoyed laugh.

"Let it go, Ben," I tell him, a smile drawing my lips upward.

"Aren't you tired? Go to sleep," he commands.

I shake my head. "I'm not tired at all."

"Then why were you driving like shit?"

"Because I had a lot on my mind. I was hugging the fucking shoulder, not the center line. Not a big deal."

"Kind of a big deal, rabbit." He shakes his head this time. "What were you thinking about?"

I scoff. "Nothing."

"Tell me, Selena."

"I was thinking about when you spit on me . . ."

He groans as if he knew that I would bring it up and was waiting for it. "And? What is there to think about?"

I cross my arms over my chest and stare out the window without saying another word. I don't appreciate his attitude about it. He has no idea what direction I was going to go with it, yet he got defensive from the start. Maybe I was going to tell him I fucking liked it, but now, I'm not telling him shit.

"Oh, stop, rabbit. You didn't like it? Did it hurt your little feelings?"

His words and the way he says them enrage me. A fire smolders in my gut. I already felt bad for liking it, but now he's being a condescending fuck about it. I cut my gaze to him and narrow my eyes. "Fuck. You."

"Don't get pissy with me, little girl, or I'll make you sorry for that mouth."

"You won't do anything."

"I'll pull this car over and choke you with my dick until you see stars. I'm serious, Selena. You do *not* want to tempt me."

I throw my hands up. "Why are we even fighting right now?"

"Because you'd rather fight than admit you liked it when I degraded you. That you liked feeling *used* by me."

"I didn't like it," I lie.

His sadistic smirk rubs me all the wrong ways. I hate his annoying smugness. "Whatever helps you sleep at night, rabbit."

We drive in silence. I'm angry enough that I'm thinking about smacking him, but I'm enamored enough that if he angrily told me to suck his dick, I'd drop to my knees without a second thought.

A sign for a lake draws up on our right. Lex looks twice at it. "Well, that will have to do," he whispers, finally breaking the silence. He turns off at the exit and drives toward the lake, following the signs until we reach the blocked entrance to the park. He pulls ahead and takes a dead-end sideroad. The car dips and sways over each pothole. He pulls over, and we get out of the car.

A thin veil of moonlight casts a dim glow over the world around us, leaving us mostly in shadows. Lex walks toward a rusted chain-link fence covered in overgrown brush. He pries at the metal, rattling it before tugging back a broken section. He slips through, and I grab some of the clothes from the car and follow him.

"Hey, wait up," I whisper. The fence claws at my skin as I try to squeeze through. *Thanks for holding it open, asshole.* He doesn't slow down, so I quicken my strides to catch up.

The clearing opens and reveals the lake. I only hear Lex's breathing over the sound of crickets and croaking frogs. A fish surfaces on the other side of the lake, and I hear the ripples it leaves in its wake. It's *that* quiet.

"Get undressed," he says before leaning against a tree and watching me.

I don't want to cave to his demands, especially when I'm still so heated from his attitude, but he has a way of speaking that influences me like nothing ever has. It makes me *want* to do things he asks of me.

I grip the hem of my shirt and begin to lift it.

"Slower," he tells me.

I do as I'm told, removing my shirt as slowly as I can. The heat of his stare is on me, and he watches as I toss my shirt away. The hunger in his expression makes me throb and forget about my annoyance.

I slip my pants down my thighs, and cool air embraces my body. Lex unbuckles his jeans, and I watch as he slips off his pants. My eyes rove down his body. I lock on to the cut on his stomach, glad to see it's stopped bleeding. I still find myself worrying about him, even though he didn't seem to mind being stabbed.

I walk toward the lake and dip my hand into the water to check the temperature. I desperately want to clean up, and it's the best we'll get at this point. Lex brushes past me and gets in, the water spreading around his strong body as he wades deeper.

"Is it cold?" I ask.

"Very. Come on." He motions me in.

I wade into the water, and my breath catches in my throat when it reaches my chest. The blackness stops at the swells of my breasts, nearly covering them. Lex wraps me up in his arms and holds me in front of him. His expression softens for the first time since the interaction in the car.

"It's not the degradation you liked. That isn't who you are."

Lex pushes me under the water and holds me there. I don't flail until my lungs clench for breath, and even then, it's weak. I reach up and grip his wrist, but I don't push him away. I should be scared—that's a normal reaction—but I'm not. I listen to the black emptiness and the thunder of my heart. I almost feel serene, even as my stomach tightens and my lungs scream for air. I just *know* he'll pull me up. I don't know how I know, but I do. I'm safe within his grasp, even in such an unsafe situation.

Even gazing into the cold face of death.

Just as my body begins to lurch for air against my will, he grabs me beneath my arms and lifts me to the surface. I cough and spit water.

"It's the trust you have in me that makes you wet. Not the act."

I hear the seduction in his voice, though it's muffled by the wet hair sticking to my ears. I spit more water and steady my breathing. "What?" I brush back my hair, hearing the droplets return to the lake and blend with the water.

"When I spit on you. You weren't turned on because you like to be degraded. It's because you trusted me enough to do it to you in the first place. You've let me fuck you, take care of you, shit, even put your life in my hands. It's all trust." He kisses me. "You trust that when I cut off your breath, I'll give it back to you." His mouth finds my clavicle, kissing above my breasts. "You always come because you trust me more than your husband. You trust me more than you trust yourself."

"I-I . . . that's . . ." I try to fight his words, but he's right. I trust him. Everything inside me should mistrust him—he took me at gunpoint, for fuck's sake—but I feel no fear when it comes to him. He holds all of me in his hands, and I never worry he'll drop me.

"You'd let me do anything to you, wouldn't you, bunny?"

I gnaw at the insides of my cheeks and swallow before my eyes rise to meet his. "Yes," I whisper.

"Would you let me fuck your ass?" he asks, so casually.

My mouth drops open, and I let out an unintentional squeak. I'd let him do anything . . .

Except that.

"No!" I have never had anyone inside me that way. Not my husband. Not anyone. Lex has already gotten so many parts of me. He doesn't need that too. I shake my head.

"Rabbit," he says more sternly. "Don't I always make you feel good?"

"No. I can think of a few times you didn't." He's done plenty of things that didn't make me feel good . . . or didn't make me feel good at first.

"What if we play a game? I'll let you run, and if I catch you, I'm taking your ass."

My mind flashes to when he ate my pussy on the hood after he caught me. How hard he made me come. God, I want *that*, but I don't want what he's offering now. I don't want him to fuck my ass.

"No, Lex," I say in a firm voice that won't waver.

"No isn't an answer because it wasn't really a question, Selena." He releases me from his grasp. "But I'll give you a head start."

He kisses me, and it feels like a goodbye. My worry shifts from him taking my ass to him chasing me off to leave me. That idea makes me more scared than being held beneath the water. It makes my stomach clench and my heart gallop.

"When the wolf growls, the bunny runs." Lex leans close to me. Cold water drips from my hair and mingles with his warm breath, creating the perfect storm against my neck. He growls in my ear, sending a vibration through my body. "Run."

I stay planted where I stand, with the lake's rocky bottom beneath my feet.

His eyes narrow and he begins to count. "Ten . . ." He smirks. "Nine . . ."

I draw a sharp breath. He isn't joking. I can see the seriousness all over his face. He ticks down the seconds, giving me less time to get away from him. This is his little hunting game. Well, I guess it was mine first, but it has much higher stakes this time.

This game will hurt.

I turn and head for the shore, but the weight of the water slows every step. It's like moving through a nightmare, only I won't wake up when his fingers grasp my skin. Sharp rocks dig into my feet with each step I take. I ignore the pain. What he has in store for me will make these rocks feel like walking on cotton balls. I'm already winded by the time I reach the bank. He slowly walks behind me, still counting down. His usually pleasant voice becomes ominous as each number leaves his lips.

I scan the terrain, trying to adjust to the foreign surroundings. The only light to be found is from the glow of the sun just breaking the horizon. A path loops around the lake, and I bolt toward it. The soil is wet with dew, and my feet sink into the earth. It's cold mush between my toes. Embedded stones cut at my feet, and I try to ignore the pain. I have to keep going.

I can't hear him behind me anymore. I can only hear my feet pounding against the path. I run toward the trees, using the thick trunks to steady myself as I climb up a hill. I don't have time to think about my nakedness or my healing bruises. I don't even register the branches thwacking against my skin. None of that will matter if his hungry hands catch me.

At the top of the hill, I lean over to catch my breath, scanning the direction I came from. I can't see Lex, and I again worry he's done all this just to leave me, that he's run me off like a dog he doesn't want anymore. This thought hurts more than the sharp stab I feel in my side with each breath I take.

A raindrop splatters on my arm, and I look up at the sky. Lightning cuts the waning darkness above me before the sky opens and the rain falls in a steady downpour. Fantastic. The drops roll over my skin and ice my bones. They travel over my chest and chill my breasts, hardening my nipples. I wrap my arms around myself to warm them.

"Rabbit?" Lex calls out, and I whip my head toward his voice. I spin on my heels and take off again toward a small pond surrounded by large rocks. The rain cuts across my eyes, blinding me. I blow it from my lips as I run. Just as I reach the first large rock, Lex pops up from beside it.

"God, I know you," he growls.

I dodge his grasp and take off around the pond. My lungs burn, and it feels like there's not enough air in the world to satisfy my need for oxygen. My heart races, thumping against my chest almost painfully. A sharp rock cuts my ankle, and I limp a few steps before the adrenaline helps me forget the pain.

My thoughts are wrapped up in Lex.

In my mind's eye he looks like a predator, transforming into an actual wolf in front of me. I imagine his paws moving the earth as he runs after me. I'm the rabbit, using sheer speed to keep ahead of his gnashing jaws.

I stop at the tree line and turn, looking back as I lean against a tree to catch my breath. There is no sound. Nothing but the patter of heavy rain. He can easily hide his steps beneath that sound. I can't see anything through the thick raindrops, and blinking does nothing to clear the haze collecting around my eyelashes.

The rain is relentless, just like Lex.

"I don't want to play anymore, Lex!" I yell to nothingness.

An arm wraps around my waist from behind, and I scream out. A hand covers my mouth.

"Got you," Lex snarls against my ear.

He presses his chilled, wet body against me, and I whimper into his hand. He keeps his arm around my waist and pushes me toward a large rock. He bends me over it, running his hands along my arms until he can grip my wrists and put them out in front of me, dropping my chest to the cold, slick stone.

"I've never let myself be fully selfish with your body," he whispers, "but right now, the wolf is going to be a wolf." He drops his hand from my mouth.

"Lex," I say with a shake of my head.

"Shh, rabbit." He comforts me for a moment by running his hands over my sides. I feel the grit of mud on my skin. "Do you trust me?"

I swallow. His hard cock presses against my ass. "I have to," I whisper.

"Yes, you do."

The rain patters against me and drips down the pebbled skin of my back. I tremble, not only from the cold but from fear of the pain he'll cause me.

He surprises me when he pushes inside my pussy, and I gasp as he presses my pelvis against the rough rock in front of me. He fucks me with the selfishness he promised. Hard and rough. Rougher than I've ever felt. He rips through me. A feral groan leaves his lips, and that sound embeds itself in my pussy as much as his cock does. His fingers dig into the flesh of my hips, and I'm exactly where I need to be. Both of us are. We're living in a moment where rain washes away our sins and makes us pure.

We are one.

With his cock still buried deep inside me, he spreads my ass, rubbing his finger along my skin before pushing it inside me. I clench, and it makes him moan. "Relax," he says as he slips another finger inside me. And a third, working me up to his cock. I kind of like how full it makes me feel to have his fingers inside me while his cock is in my pussy.

Lex pulls his fingers out, spreads me, and spits. I bite my lip as his warm saliva mixes with the cold rain. He leans over me, and my ass nestles against the crook of his pelvis.

"You ready?" he asks.

I didn't expect him to ask. He *knows* I'm not ready. I'll never be ready for this. My body thought it had a choice for a moment, but I tense all over again when I realize this was never the case.

"Lex . . ."

He drops his hands to either side of my head, leaning his weight onto me. "Don't say my name like that. I won fair and square, bunny. Your ass is mine."

I want to give him that part of me, but I'm scared. He pulls out of my pussy and draws his hips back to get a better angle. As he pushes the head of his cock inside me, I tense. It isn't like his fingers. It feels nothing like his fingers.

"Remember what I said to do. Relax," he whispers as he strokes wet hair from my cheek. "Let me inside, bunny."

His smooth words make me melt into the granite. I take a deep breath and try to relax my body. He inches further inside me, and I bite my lower lip. He's hardly the selfish wolf he claimed he'd be, too tender to be a predator.

"Good fucking girl," he groans as he pushes himself inside me. He keeps his hips still, allowing me to adjust to his size and stretch around him. "You take everything I give you, don't you?" His words mimic what he said in the car when I took his spit. Now, with him this deep inside me, I want to take everything he can give me.

To make him proud.

I whimper and nod. His thrusts grow hungrier, and the gentleness dissolves. His left hand grips the rock so he can get more leverage. He fucks me harder, but not as hard as when he was in my pussy. The leaves of the trees melt into the ground along with their big, strong trunks. The pond in front of me spreads and takes over everything, blanketing it in blackness. The world becomes abstract, and the only thing that remains real is Lex and his body against mine.

"You feel so fucking good, bunny. So tight. So goddamn perfect."

His words warm me until I only feel the heat of him. It's a fire burning behind me, erasing the cold rain and brisk air. I get used to the pain of him inside me. It never goes away, but I adapt to the hurt like I did with my marriage.

He fucks me harder and deeper, and I feel his full strength for the first time. I feel the selfish hunger he promised me. He uses me as if this is all I'm good for.

My body remains rigid no matter how hard I try to relax. My muscles ache for release. He finally notices that my clenched jaw isn't from the chattering of my teeth. He becomes aware of the tense tremble of pain in my body and transforms back into the Lex I know. He leans over and kisses my shoulder. It's a tender touch I need so badly at this moment. I need it more than my next breath.

"Sweet bunny," he whispers. "I'll stop."

"No!" I cry out. "I want to take everything you give me."

He chuckles, but it turns into a growl at the end. "You have, Selena. You really fucking have. This was a lot for anyone to take. The chase. The rain and the bloody cuts on your feet and ankles. Taking my cock in your ass with nothing more than my spit and the wetness of your cunt. You're such a good girl. Even when your body isn't willing, your mind is."

"I'm sorry," I say as I fight back tears. The prospect of disappointing him incites more emotion than most anything in my life has.

His hand glides down the curve of my spine. "Don't apologize. I wanted to fuck your ass, and I needed you to let me. And you did." He grips my ass, and the rain makes his fingertips bite harder. "You won't like everything I want to do to you, that I *will* do to you, but I'll always reward you for being the good girl you are. No matter how bad you become from being around me, you're my good fucking girl."

He pulls out of me and lifts me to my feet. His mouth finds mine as he lays me back on the rock and spreads my thighs. His lips trail down my body, and he drops to his knees. They sink into the earth. He parts me, and his tongue finds my clit. I lift myself onto my elbows so I can watch him. He tosses back his wet hair as rainwater drips down his temples. Droplets of rain roll over the muscles in his arms and shoulders.

My eyes wash over his prison-etched tattoos, and I realize he's someone my family wouldn't have allowed me to talk to, let alone fuck. I'm in over my head with him. Way over my head. He's an enigma, a mystery that should be left unsolved and untouched, yet he eats my pussy like the answers to all I need to know are in his mouth. He selfishly fucks me with his tongue, his hands gripping my ass as he holds me at his mercy.

"Lex," I whisper.

"Don't say my name unless the words 'I'm coming' follow it," he growls, giving me a dark look before devouring me again. His commands, like always, make me weak. Make me tremble as his words vibrate my clit.

When he realizes his harsh words made me buck against his mouth, his voice lowers "Come for me, bunny. Get off to the one man you shouldn't."

And I do. I come hard against his mouth, with the rain painting my body and the trees crawling up from the earth and surrounding us once more. I grip his hair as he relentlessly tongues my clit, making my body shudder with a pleasure that morphs into discomfort. He smirks up at me and swipes my clit once more, my body jolting from his touch, before he rises to his feet.

The rock rakes my soft skin as I sit up. "What about you?" I ask, feeling guilty as my orgasm wanes.

His broad frame towers over me, and water cascades down his firm chest and stomach. "What about me?"

"You didn't come." I feel bad that I tapped out before he could get his release, but Lex seems relaxed, satiated almost, despite not coming at all.

He reaches out and helps me to my feet. "It's fine, bunny. I'll fill you up the first chance I get." His eyes scan the horizon. "We'll take another quick dip and then we gotta get going. It's morning."

I nod. I have no idea what will happen to us, but Lex is opening me up to a world I never knew existed. One where the risk of losing my freedom is the most freedom I've ever felt.

Chapter Fifteen

Selena

It feels like it's getting more and more rural the further south we go. There's so much farm country in Tennessee, and I can't help but get lost in the sight. Small homesteads with various livestock line the road on both sides. Cows, goats, and some horses stand in a large paddock, and I press my forehead to the glass to take them all in.

Lex takes a right-hand turn, and we follow along the fancy wooden fences. I don't know what Lex has planned as we drive down yet another secluded dead-end road. The eternity of pavement feels endless. We drove for a long time today, and we're both worn down. He just won't admit it. I will, with a long exhale.

"Where are we going?" I ask.

"We need a new car. When I got gas, I overheard two locals talking about a lonely farmer who lives up this road. Said he was away, and it sounded like a good opportunity. An easy one."

I tighten my lips and rub the cuts on my ankles. "I need to wash these with actual soap." Natural water sources aren't hygienic. Not in the slightest. I *need* a real shower.

"You will." Lex's eyes jump to a rickety farmhouse ahead of us. "There it is, just like they said."

Lex pulls to the side of the road, and we walk the last bit toward the house. My feet ache from my shoes rubbing everywhere the rocks and branches bit my skin.

"What happened to your biological parents?" I ask, trying to distract myself from my pain by hearing his.

Lex doesn't speak at first. I don't expect him to answer my question, but he surprises me when he does. "Never met my father and hardly knew my mother. She liked dope better than me. I've been in and out of the foster system since they found me alone in an apartment surrounded by needles when I was six."

"Lex—"

"Don't, rabbit. I hear the pity in your voice." He shakes his head. "We all can't be as lucky as you were growing up."

I stop mid-step and turn toward him. He doesn't need to attack me because he's hurt. He doesn't have to get so defensive. "You know nothing about how I grew up."

"Don't I?"

I scoff. "No. You don't. I hardly knew my parents, either. They threw money at me to make up for being absent. I had one purpose as their daughter, and it was to marry whoever would better their business. They handed me to the devil even though they knew they were sending me to hell with him. They *knew* he'd burn me. Money has kept me alive while simultaneously killing me. I'd give it all up, and I have. There's no more beyond what I took, and I'm fine with it." My shoulders drop from the weight of the finality of my life before Lex. I still wouldn't take anything back.

"Selena," Lex says as I quicken my steps toward the house.

I ignore him. When he keeps trying, I turn on my heels and narrow my eyes at him. "You think I'm a spoiled little brat, don't you? Fancy fucking show rabbit, right? Too special to get it dirty or allow it to be an animal. I've tried to show you that I'm not some fragile, well-groomed little thing!"

Lex raises his voice in a way I've never heard directed at me. "Selena, you need to calm the hell down. Where is this even coming from?"

It's coming from him. The things he says about my life make me so angry. I see the way he looks at me sometimes, like I'm some spoiled brat who ran away from a perfect life. It's a deep-seated insecurity from always being told my life was fine because I had money and nice things. When I told my mother what Bryce was doing to me, she said, "But he's supporting you, Selena. I know how you can be. Sometimes you just need to change your behavior a bit to make him happy." Because he "supported" me, I had to accept the pain. *I* had to change, not the one inflicting the abuse. Fuck Lex for thinking I was somehow shielded from pain because of fucking money.

No, it was the root of all evil in my family and my marriage.

The weight of it crushes me, and I lose the strength to hold myself up. I fall to my knees. Lex runs to help me up, but I push his hands away. "Let me be for a few minutes. The house is right there. I'll meet you inside."

Lex shakes his head and looks up at the farmhouse. "I'm not leaving you out here alone."

"That's precisely what I need right now. I need to be alone," I whisper. I sit back on my heels and breathe in the heavy farm air. It smells like grain and manure. A tear slips down my cheek, and I wipe it away before he can see it. I don't need him to stay and comfort me. I need to comfort myself.

"Selena," he commands, but for once I don't listen.

"Go!" I yell back, surprising myself with the ferocity.

Lex draws a breath and reaches for the knife in his pocket. "Just in case a different wolf tries to bite." He tosses it toward me and it lands in front of me, flattening the grass. It brings back a rush of memories. The way my hand concealed the intricately carved wooden handle. The way the blade blossomed red as I stabbed Bryce over and over again.

Once Lex leaves to go inside, I drop onto my butt and lie down. A broad-winged bird soars overhead, silent and menacing. Cows moo in the pasture beside the house. It's pretty fucking peaceful, and I need this peace. I wish Lex understood. I don't want to fight with him over our pasts. I don't want to participate in a competition about who had the worst childhood. Clearly he did, but it doesn't negate what happened to me. And I feel negated. We chose different paths—I chose complacency, and he chose violence—but we both chose murder, and that's where our paths cross.

Something crashes inside the house. I wipe a rogue tear from the crease of my eyes and get to my feet. I pluck the knife from the grass and grip it against my palm. When I get to the porch, I creep up the steps and open the door, controlling it as it closes so it doesn't make any noise. The crashing grows louder and more violent. It can't possibly be coming from Lex alone. With quiet footfalls, I follow the loud noises to the living room.

What I see surprises me. A burly farmer has Lex in the same hold Lex held Rodney in, but this fight isn't nearly as one-sided. My mouth gapes because after everything I've witnessed, I would never expect someone to get the upper hand on Lex. The farmer's hat falls off as the men wrestle. Greasy strands of hair fall over the man's face. His overalls are ripped and stained.

When Lex catches my eyes for a moment, he mouths, "*Go,*" to me. I shake my head, never more certain of anything in my life. There's no way I'm leaving him to save myself.

My heart thumps in my ears as Lex tries to stay in the fight. His pistol glints in the back of his jeans, but I'll never be fast enough to get to it, nor would I know what to do with it if I managed to get my hands on it.

In my panic, I forget about the knife in my hand. Its weight against my palm finally reminds me of its presence. I slink along the wall, trying to keep the farmer from seeing me. When I accidentally knock over a can of beer, I hold my breath, expecting him to hear. Thankfully, no one hears a damn thing over the grunting and adrenaline. Once I'm flat against the wall behind the farmer, I open the blade and hold it within a familiar grasp. I have no idea how to stab this man, though. I don't even know if I can. Vengeance propelled my arm when it came to Bryce, but there's no vengeance now. There's only the need to protect Lex, and those are two very different reasons for killing.

Fear freezes me in place. I don't know what to do.

The farmer goes for the gun, and I'm out of time to think. The intense need to protect Lex propels my arm forward as I rush for the farmer and sink the knife into his neck. He lets out a roar, and I squeal as blood streams from beneath the handle.

"Pull it out, Selena! Pull the knife out!" Lex yells, and it sounds like he's miles away.

With my hand still wrapped around the handle, I try to tug it out, but a suction that wasn't there when I put it in holds it in place. I wiggle it and it finally gives way with a disgusting squelching sound. The moment the blade leaves his neck, blood escapes the wound in a waterfall, spurting a geyser of crimson with every beat of his heart. The man wobbles on his feet and reaches for his neck. Lex pulls away and rips his pistol from the farmer's hand, putting it in his waistband where it belongs.

It feels like minutes, but it's merely seconds before the farmer crashes to his knees. Without uttering another sound, he falls onto his face. I've never seen so much blood. Every bit of what was in his body spreads around him on the floor.

"Arterial wound. Very fucking effective, rabbit," Lex pants. He's covered in blood, and my arms are sprayed with it, too.

The bleeding I caused.

I back against the wall, the knife still in my trembling hand. As if Lex forgot what murder feels like to unseasoned killers, he doesn't seem to notice the anguish I'm facing. My stomach churns and I heave, nearly throwing up all over the old hardwood floors. Lex grabs my hair and holds it for me as I fight back the vomit. He rubs my back like he's comforting someone who bowled a bad game. How can he be so cavalier?

It's selective of me to forget who Lex really is. It's too easy to ignore the violent and dangerous side of him that seems as normal as breathing to him.

I stand, feeling the weight of that giant farmer on my shoulders. How will I carry that with me? My eyes widen with fear, not of Lex, but of what I've become because of him.

A killer.

I'm not just a battered wife who got revenge. I'm a full-blown fucking murderer.

"It gets easier," Lex says as he pats my back. He strolls toward the cabinet and starts rooting around. My mouth drops open. He is fucking clinical. Literally sociopathic.

"Easier?" I ask, disgusted.

"Yeah, easier. Meaning you don't get all worked up about it anymore."

I blink at him. "You are fucking insane, Lex."

He closes a cabinet and begins to eat from a bag of chips, bloody hands and all. "Yeah, and?"

Anger courses through me. He's maddening. "You made me do that!" I scream as I point at the dead farmer, quickly cutting my gaze when it lands on his fixed eyes, the life drained from them.

Lex laughs through a mouthful of chips. "I didn't make you do a damn thing," he says with an infuriating calmness. "I told you to go. You had the choice to leave."

He walks closer, pushes me against the wall, and wrangles the knife from my hand. His breath rolls over my heated skin. "I didn't make you fuck me or stab your husband. I didn't make you come with me or stab that man. If you're going to stay with me, you need to start accepting what you are."

"And what the hell am I?"

Lex flashes his darkened eyes at me. "You're no better than me."

I draw a sharp breath, as if he's stabbed me beneath my ribs. The air deflates from my lungs, and I shrink in front of him. "I just wanted to protect you . . ." I whisper.

Lex leans in, and I flinch against his touch as he kisses my forehead. "You already knew I'd kill for you, and now I know you'll kill for me." Lex drops his mouth to mine and kisses me once before running a hot hand up my throat. "And as sexy as it is, don't ever ignore me again when I tell you to leave."

"But—"

"But nothing, rabbit. If I tell you to go, you go. Do you hear me? If he'd killed me, what would he have done to a girl like you, huh? If it were me? Shit. I'd have fucked you half to death out of principle. So I need you to listen to me, Selena. For once in your fucking life."

Lex

Stubborn goddamn rabbit. I breathe in her scent as I scold her. I'm not a piece of shit. I appreciate her saving my life, but not at the risk of her own. A shiver dances up my spine at the thought of what would've happened to her if he shot me and turned to face her.

Beautiful little bunny, ripe for slaughter.

I imagine him fucking her, tearing her apart in ways I couldn't bring myself to do despite *really* wanting to. I force away the intrusive thoughts of his hands on what's mine. I can't handle the thought of his mouth on her plump lips or pale neck. His eyes all over her tits and his fingers touching her perfect cunt.

The thoughts alone make me homicidal.

My hands ride up her neck and grip her face. The weight of the risk of her being with me begins to bury me. To suffocate me. This is why I wanted her to stay back in her idyllic home where she was safe. I can protect her if I'm not gravely injured or dead. I'm certain of that. But what would happen once I can't protect her anymore?

If something happens to me.

If my rabbit becomes prey to someone else.

"If you can't promise you'll listen when I tell you something, I'll leave you at the nearest bus stop," I say as I drop my forehead to hers.

"Lex," she whispers in soft protest.

"Promise me!"

"I promise," she finally whispers.

"Atta girl," I say as I pull her into my chest.

"You're bleeding." She dabs at my shirt. I lift it and see that my cut is oozing again.

"It's nothing. Probably from the fight." I draw away from her and go to the bathroom to find some bandages. After I dress the wound, I return to the living room. Selena has seated herself on the couch after covering the farmer's body with a sheet.

"How are you so unbothered?" she asks without looking back at me.

"I'll let you in on a little secret," I say as I walk up behind her and grip her hair in a fist. "I'm a documented sociopath. A convicted killer." I lean down and kiss her neck as she fights against my touch. She tries to pull away, but I hold her there. She isn't strong enough to escape my hold.

"You aren't making this better," she snaps.

"But I'm not making it worse, either," I say through a smirk against her skin. "I'm a killer and so are you. There's no arguing away the blood on our hands, no rationalizing that it was our upbringing or a lapse in sanity. We made the conscious decision to rip away someone's life. We made our bed, and now we'll fuck in it."

I crane her neck and kiss her throat, completely unbothered by the blood painting her skin. In fact, I like it. I love that she's covered in his blood. That she killed for *me*. I lick at the crimson, enjoying the metallic taste on my tongue, and her body tenses in disgust. As my licking becomes a soft bite on her neck, she relaxes. The softest moan, hardly audible, rolls off her lower lip.

"Speaking of beds, I fucked up the last time we were in one. What do you say we take advantage of the one here? Give me a chance to fuck you right. Like you deserve."

Despite enjoying my touch for a moment, her eyes snap to mine. "No, Lex, absolutely not. There's a dead man on the ground behind us."

"Oh, rabbit, must we make it another game? Something new for me to do to you?"

She narrows her eyes. "No."

"Well, go take a shower while I take care of this, and I'll figure out what game I want to play with you."

The call to shower is too enticing for her, and like a scared animal, she leaves the room without turning her back to me, as if I'll pounce on her if she isn't watching.

Believe me, I'm tempted to. I'd love to fuck her with the farmer's blood still on her skin. Unfortunately, dealing with the body is my job to do.

I turn him over and stare at his vacant eyes. *Poor bastard,* I think as I roll him up in the sheet. He had gotten the rare upper hand on me. I didn't expect him to be home. Like an idiot, I hadn't even considered it. Had I been alone, I would have been done for. And I probably deserved it. Then again, if I'd been alone, I wouldn't have been in the farmer's house, and he wouldn't be dead.

My course of action has shifted with Selena involved. If it had just been me, I'd have taken her car and driven straight to the border. With her in tow, I need to give her a comfortable place to sleep every night and keep her fed, fucked, and happy. I desperately want to keep her safe, which is why I wanted to get a new vehicle for us in the first place. That landed us on this poor sap's doorstep.

I wipe my forehead. My fingers work to tie off the sheet toward his feet, then I drag the body outside. The rickety screen door slams. I haul his body behind the house, near the Bilco doors that open to the basement. I cover him with a tarp and stick the shovel over it as if there's nothing but a pile of mulch beneath it. I'll fully deal with that later—when I'm not so sexually frustrated.

I rub my hand on my jeans, smearing the blood. I enter the house and eye the pool of red on the floor. There's far too much to clean. The wood has sucked it into every crevice, every pore. I look around for a rug instead. When I see the one under the coffee table, I tug it out and lay it over the bloody mess. It hides nearly all of it. Out of sight, out of mind—for Selena, at least. I would have fucked her on that couch with or without his body there. Let his soul watch me make her come.

My shirt sticks to my sweaty skin. I follow the sounds of the shower until I reach a rundown hallway door. When I reach for the knob, it's locked. "Sneaky rabbit," I whisper.

She needs to stop trying to lock me out. Hasn't she learned she can't keep me out of anything? Not the room, her heart, *or* her cunt.

The slit in the lock is easy to turn with just my knife. When I open the door, I stare at her naked body through the shower's dingy glass. Arching her back to wash her hair, she doesn't notice me at first. I adjust the front of my pants and watch her. Knowing the blood washing off her body is the life-force of the man she killed for me makes me hard as fuck. The way she stabbed him and listened to me when I told her to rip it from his flesh . . . God, I have never seen a more beautiful act. In the same breath, I feel more guilt for changing her into something she wasn't before meeting me.

I've never felt guilt, nor true remorse, until I met her. I hate seeing pieces of myself in Selena. Her good pieces mix with my bad.

The water turns off, and when she opens the door, she jumps. "Jesus, how'd you get in here?" she asks. By now she should know that nothing can keep me from her when I want her.

I shake the knife in my hand and set it on the countertop. "Get back in there, rabbit."

She reaches for a raggedy towel, but I yank it across the bar and out of reach. "Why? I'm done."

"Maybe. But I'm not," I tell her with a smirk, unwilling to hide how hard I am from watching her. I slip off my shoes and unzip my jeans. Her gaze rolls downward and locks on my hard cock. I slip off my bloody shirt and let it fall beside my pants.

"Lex, I'm not in the mood," she whispers.

"But I am," I say with a growl. I pull the shower door open the rest of the way and run my gaze over her naked body. Without taking my eyes off her, I turn the shower on again. She looks scared and small, like when I first fucked her. That farmer's gotten to her, which means she's still more human than I can ever be.

Good.

I drag her into the shower with me. I lean back and let the hot water rain down on me, taking the blood with it. When I hear the shower door open again, I reach out and grab her waist. "You aren't leaving like that," I say.

"Like what?"

"Scared."

She scoffs. "I'm not scared of you."

I draw her against my body. "I know you aren't scared of me. You're scared of yourself. Afraid of what you're capable of." I kiss her, but her lips don't welcome me like they usually do. "You're capable of anything, rabbit. You can be the sweet woman who softens me and the unsavory—sometimes homicidal—little rabbit that hardens me."

She draws a sharp breath that leaves me wondering if I offended her. As she tries to pull away from me, I realize I have. I let her out of my grasp to pin her against the shower wall.

"Stop, Selena. Stop fucking running from what you are when you never ran from what I am. You have darkness inside you, whether it's in here"—I graze her chest before lowering my hand to her pussy—"or in here."

Her eyes roll up my chest, and she pushes out her lower lip. The tension in her body melts away, and I step back to finish washing the blood from my skin.

"What's going to happen to us?" she asks. She's so quiet I almost don't hear her over the water.

"Nothing, Selena. I won't let anything happen to us. Do you trust me?"

"Not really." Her lips tick up in a small smile.

"Yes you do, bunny," I say as I drag her into me and kiss her again.

She meets my affection this time. I reach back and pull the showerhead off the holder. I turn it to a more focused stream and run it along her body, sending the warm water against her hardening nipples. I move it over her stomach before lowering it to her inner thighs. She grips the metal and stops my ascent toward her pussy.

"What? Have you never got yourself off in the shower?" I ask.

She stares at me with a trembling lower lip and shakes her head.

"Please tell me you get yourself off." My tone is almost mocking, but I don't mean for it to be. This girl cannot be *that* innocent.

"With my hand," she says as she looks away.

"So you've never used any kind of toy?" I ask.

She shakes her head once more, and I remove the showerhead from her hand. I grab her wrists and pin them above her head. She struggles within my grasp, her back arching as she tries to pull away. I put my knee between her legs and spread them.

"Stay open for me," I tell her. I keep both wrists encased in one hand as I run the showerhead down her body once more and aim it at the soft mound of hair between her legs. Her eyes clench shut, and I let her keep them closed.

I palm the back of the showerhead and slip deeper between her legs. The moment the stream parts her lips and washes over her clit, she lurches forward, nearly ripping her hands from my grasp.

"How does that feel, sweet bunny?" I ask as I hold the pressure between her legs. Every so often I stroke her with the stream, moving it in a small circle.

"It feels good," she whispers. A moan leaves her lips, and she bucks her hips forward.

"Keep your hands against that wall." I release her and wrap my hand around my cock. I stroke myself to her grinding against the showerhead. I focus on my head as she moans and whimpers. "Open your eyes," I command. I want to see her looking up at me. I want to see the pleasure lighting her eyes on fire.

She does, but she doesn't look me in the face. Her eyes drop to my hand on my cock. With a deep, passionate kiss, I stroke my dick against her lower stomach and keep the water aimed at her clit. Her hips curl against me and she moans, getting me too close. I stop myself before I come, taking my hand away from my dick for a moment.

I lift my fingers to her face and trace her jaw. "You have the sweetest face, bunny. Do you know what I want to do to you?"

She shakes her head and swallows.

"I want to paint your skin with my come." My fingers graze her chin and cheeks. "Did your husband ever come on your face?"

She shakes her head. "No." The word comes out with a frustrated buck of her hips.

"Would you let me?" I ask.

I expect an instant no—it's probably too demeaning for a girl like her—but she surprises me with a slow, unsure nod. Her building orgasm must have made her more pliable.

"Tell me with your words, bunny. You know I like to hear it."

She moans and her thighs tremble. "I want you to come on my face, Lex."

The way she says my name at the end makes me twitch against her stomach. I want that so goddamn bad, and hearing her ask is nearly enough to make me come without touching myself.

"Come, sweet bunny," I tell her as I stroke myself again.

She leans back against the wall and closes her eyes. She drops her hands, and as much as I want to scold her for it, they land on my shoulders, digging her pleasure into me through her fingertips. I allow it because I need to feel it too.

"Talk to me. Tell me how it feels."

Selena digs her fingers deeper as she bucks her hips. "I'm gonna come, Lexington," she moans.

I hate my full name . . . except when she says it.

"Come for me so I can put you on your knees, sweet bunny."

I rub my cock, fighting the urge to come as her body ripples with her orgasm. She trembles, screaming out in pleasure and grabbing my hand to pull the showerhead away as she gets too sensitive. I keep my hand there, letting the water wash over her spasming clit.

"Stop," she begs.

I lean in and kiss her. "Ride it out to the end," I groan against her mouth.

And she does. Like the good girl she is, she rides out the earthquakes of pleasure ripping through her. She rides out the pain as I keep the pressure on her clit after she comes.

"Get on your knees," I say, knowing my release is coming. I feel it in the base of my balls, and I try to slow my strokes to hold out for her.

I stare at her, following her with my eyes as she drops to her knees. Her gaze meets mine, her large eyes looking up at me with satiated desire. There's a hint of fear there, too. Fear of something new. Something her husband never did to her.

I release my cock and let it settle in front of her face. I'm so tempted to push it between her full lips, but then I'd come in her mouth. My hand grazes her cheek as the other pushes her dark hair away from her face.

"I want you to keep your eyes on me. I don't want you to close them for even a second, even as I spill my come on your face." I stop stroking her cheek and stroke my cock instead. "Talk to me, bunny."

"I want your come, Lex," she whispers.

I growl. "You're mine, Selena. You know that, right?" My abdomen tightens. She looks so obedient at my feet. Her hands grasp the outsides of my thighs as she keeps her eyes on my face.

"I'm yours," she whispers, and I rub my thumb along her lower lip.

I grab the back of her head, ball her hair in my fist, and crane her neck just a bit more so I can see her pout over my cock. I touch the tip to her mouth, grazing the seam of her lips. I stop stroking my head, only jerking off the shaft so I can see it all. All that I need to give her. Her warm lips rest against the tip of my dick, and it's enough to make me come whether I stroke myself or not.

"I'm gonna come," I growl.

Pearls of white shoot from me, and just like I demanded, she doesn't even blink as my come hits her cheek. It spills over her mouth as I rub it against her soft, warm skin. She looks so fucking beautiful covered in my come.

I help her to her feet and wipe some of my come from her mouth before pushing it past her lips and onto her tongue. "Taste me, bunny."

Her lips tighten around my fingers. She doesn't like the taste, but she still moves her mouth up to my fingertips. I growl. I don't care that I still coat her lips and tongue. I lean in and kiss her. She whimpers against my mouth.

"Goddamn it, rabbit," I whisper as I bite her lower lip, taking in the salty taste mixed with the sweetness of her mouth.

I grab the showerhead again, turn it on a softer setting, and tell her to put her head back. I wash my come from her perfect face, and she wipes at her cheeks beneath the stream. The window above the shower sends a halo of light onto the wall above her head. She looks angelic, and it's the closest I'll ever get to an angel.

Chapter Sixteen

Selena

I feel like we're playing house in some alternate universe where it's perfectly normal that Lex just came in from disposing of a body. With dirt still on his hands, he walks toward me, wraps his hands around my face, and draws me in for a hard kiss. The scents of soil and decay cling to his flesh. His hand moves behind my head, and he pulls me into him as he strokes my hair. I feel like a child against him. His strong, overbearing frame feels safe. No matter how safe he makes me feel in that moment, I still find myself longing for stability again.

Lex's body tenses. Heavy footsteps plod across the old wooden porch.

"Richard?" calls the voice on the other side of the door.

Very different expressions cross our faces. For me, it's wide-eyed fear. For him, it's narrowing anger. We freeze, and my heart races in my chest. Despite the haze of fear descending on my mind, I think of something that might work. It may just save us. Well, save whoever is out there and keep another death from weighing on my conscience.

"I have an idea. Go anywhere else," I tell Lex.

"I don't like this," he says with a shake of his head, posturing toward the door with his pistol clutched in his hand. I'm tempted to let him take care of the unexpected visitor, but my guilt from the farmer's death still lingers in my chest.

"Go," I tell him with a firm rise in my voice.

His eyes narrow before he disappears through the kitchen. I stroke my fingers through my unbrushed hair and go to the door, where a stocky young guy waits on the other side.

"Who're you? And where's Richard?"

"I'm his niece. He's gone for a little while. Told me to stay and watch the farm."

The man raises an eyebrow. "You're Lana? You don't look like no farm girl from Nebraska."

"Well, I am," I snap. I don't intend to, but the accusation on his face rubs me the wrong way, even if he has every reason to be suspicious.

He pulls out his phone. "I'm gonna call Richard. Something doesn't smell right." He's not wrong about that, but I'm certain he can't smell the scent of death because it's all in my head.

I take a subtle breath, trying to remain as calm as I can. I know what happens when men sense my fear. They prey on it. Even Lex.

"If you do that, the stubborn old thing will come right back home. Do you know how hard it was to get him to leave in the first place?"

The man lowers his phone. "Yeah, I guess he needed to get away. He was going crazy all alone out here." He leans in and peers inside, his tone shifting as much as his body. "You all by your lonesome, too? Big ol' house for just one girl." He rubs a thick hand through a scraggly black beard.

My tightening stomach fires a warning shot through my body. It's a familiar feeling.

"Well, I best be going," I tell him as I try to close the door.

He puts his hand out to keep me from closing the door, and I nearly slam it on his thick fingers. "Oh, don't be like that. We're just talking," he says.

With a motion too swift for me to react to, he tugs me out by my arm and puts his big hand over my mouth. He even covers my nose, and soon my lungs beg for air. Unlike every time Lex has done something similar, there's an instant panic that drains the pent-up oxygen and makes my body lurch with need from the start. I feel like I'm suffocating.

Dying.

"You ain't his niece," the man says with a snarl. "His kin don't look like you." He pins my chest against the house, and his hand rides up my thigh over my leggings. "Goddamn, if you were *my* niece, I'd be tempted to put you on my lap."

My stomach clenches until I feel like I'm going to vomit. With his hand covering my nose and mouth, I couldn't, even if I wanted to. I'm trapped in this pervert's predatory grasp.

I should have listened to Lex.

Tears slip down my cheeks. The hand over my face moves down and lets me draw in several panicked breaths through my nose. His other hand goes down the front of my pants. More tears fall.

"Fuck," he groans. "That's a pussy like we ain't have around here." His hot tobacco-laced breath rushes over my neck.

I don't see or hear Lex walking along the side of the house until he's in my vision's periphery. He crouches, holds the pistol, and aims. There's no way he'll miss me if he aims at the man's head when it's so close to mine.

He seems to realize this and lowers the barrel. Lex shoots once, and the sound of squelching flesh erupts behind me as the deafening boom makes my ears ring. The man stumbles back, clutching his side. He looks shocked as he wordlessly holds the wound, blood spreading around his fingers.

Lex takes aim once more and puts a bullet through the man's face, taking him down in a bloody spray of brain matter along the porch. I throw my hands over my ears and fall back against the house. Lex runs to me, but I can't hear what he's saying over the ringing in my ears. He lifts me to my feet and drags me inside.

"Selena!" He smacks my cheek, cupping it the last time. He pulls me into his chest, but that safe feeling is gone.

Completely gone.

My ears begin to clear, the residual ringing becoming quieter until it's nearly gone. I don't register what's happening, but Lex sits on the couch and places me on his lap. I turn my head to nestle into his neck, and he lets me for a moment before making me look at him. His eyes glisten with a show of concern I haven't seen from him before. Not as Rodney tried to do what he did or when Bryce went even further.

"I'm so sorry," he whispers as he brushes back my hair. "That's why I didn't like your idea, rabbit. If something happened, I knew you'd be in the crossfire. I had no choice but to go around the house so I could get a shot off without hitting you, which meant he had you in his grasp longer than I would have ever allowed."

"I just wanted to get rid of him without hurting anyone else," I whisper.

"This is why this life isn't meant for you. You have to put yourself first and anyone else beneath you." He drops his forehead to mine. "Actually, I'm failing at that, too. I put you above me. Can't even take my own fucking advice. You give me the humanity I don't need or want." He sighs. "But I can't turn back now. Not with you here."

Lex

I'm not sure what love is because I've never felt it. My mother never knew what it was, either. I didn't feel a thing when I found my mother dead. I almost felt relieved that she couldn't bring her "friends" over anymore. That I'd stop seeing her railed in front of me.

For my foster parents, love had a price. As long as they kept getting paid, they "loved" me, but only in front of the social workers who checked on me. Jack, an older kid more fucked-up than me, showed me how to survive in the foster system, and it wasn't by feeling things. He showed me how to turn off every part of myself until I was an empty shell, capable of destruction without thought or feelings. People think more about the dirty dish they put in the sink than I do about murdering someone.

Cold. Callous. Deadly.

That's who I was and that's what helped me survive prison.

But Selena is changing that for me. She's reversing conditioning that was perfected long before she was born. I have trauma older than she is.

I hold her close, listening to each ragged breath she takes. My heart breaks for her. That piece of shit violated her, and I couldn't jump right in because I didn't want him to fucking kill her. That's been my fear with bringing her along. She has this look about her—a sweet innocence. When I see that in her, I want to rip her apart and brutalize her. When other men see it, I recognize that same hunger.

Even though I can control that side of me when it comes to her, others can't, and she'll always be at risk of having more of herself stolen away. I can't bring her with me over the border, yet I have no clue how I'll force her to stay back. But I have to. She isn't safe with me, and she wouldn't be safe around the people I would have to put myself around to survive. I'm irrevocably torn between selfishly wanting to keep her or selflessly letting her go to keep her safe.

Her lip pouts and my cock twitches beneath her. I still want to fuck that sweetness out of her and fill her with my darkness. I want to take her until she stops having a heart that beats for anyone but me, until she has no more guilt or regret about the people we kill to keep our hearts beating together.

I grab her chin and kiss her. "How far did he get?" I've been afraid to ask because I don't think I can handle the answer, but I need to know if I'm chopping off the fucker's hands before I bury him.

She shakes her head. "Just got his hand down my pants."

That's one hand I'll chop off and shove in his ass before I put him in the ground for touching her like that.

Her pussy is mine.

I take a deep breath, stopping my barrage of possessive thoughts. I have to let her go. I have to push back my need to own her before we both end up dead or in prison.

"I know you're going to fight me about it, tooth and fucking nail, but you can't stay with me, Selena." I touch her face. "I know you want to, and I want you to as well, but you can't. I thought you had to fear the wolf, but there are bigger predators out there than me. I *have* to keep you safe. It's the one thing I promised myself I'd do, and it's the *one* thing I'm not going back on."

She shakes her head. "Nope, I'm not accepting that bullshit excuse to get rid of me."

"It's not a bullshit excuse, rabbit. Bullshit excuses are what I've been giving myself to justify keeping you with me. None of this is a fucking game. I can't see a scenario with a good end for you, and I don't understand how you can't see that."

I ease her off my lap. Even in my anger, I don't want to hurt her like that. I stand up and tower over her. When I rip my shirt off, I expose a mosaic of mostly prison tattoos—a timeline of violence and hate. I gesture to the bundles of scar tissue on my abdomen and back from the many times I've been stabbed. I'm a mess, not just inside but on the outside.

She can *see* the evil on my body.

"What more of me do you have to see to know you need to run? This isn't safe. I'm not safe." My words bite, but she refuses to recoil.

I grab her by the arm and drag her toward the bedroom. It's old, but at least it has a bed. I sit her down and she looks up at me with those big eyes of hers.

"What do I have to do to make you hate me?"

"There's nothing you can do, Lex," she says in a maddeningly calm tone despite not knowing the full extent of what I'm capable of. She's seen so much, yet she still seems to forget all she's seen.

"You need to," I snarl. I need her to because I can't hate *her*. If I could, none of this would be so difficult. She'd be dropped off or killed like she means nothing, and I'd be alone by now.

But she means everything.

She folds her arms across her chest defiantly. "Well, I won't."

I climb over her and put a hand to her throat. She whimpers as I squeeze. "What if I took your pussy? What if I tear into you like I've wanted to since the moment I saw you?"

She shakes her head. Her lips tighten, and I know I offended her.

I squeeze her throat harder. "What if I fucked your ass and didn't stop when it made you cry from the pain?"

"No." She strains to get the word out.

Anger rises through me, lighting my skin on fire. She's so fucking naïve to think she'd still enjoy being in my presence if I tore through her the way I want to. I give her a final squeeze, cutting off her air. Her cheeks redden as she reaches for my wrists. Flashes of my foster mother replace her face as I keep my hands around her throat. That anger gets out of control, nearly past the point of stopping myself. I only let go of her throat to turn her onto her stomach, and she hardly flails beneath me as I tug down her leggings.

It pisses me off.

"Hate me, rabbit!" I scream as I unzip my jeans and pull out my cock. I lie over her, pressing the heat of my dick against her bare skin. She whimpers. "Fucking. Hate. Me."

"No," she strains out beneath my weight.

I wrestle with control when I need it the most. I slam my fist beside her head. "Fine. I'm done trying to make it harder than it needs to be. It ends for you here. You aren't coming with me. That's it. There's no arguing about it. There's no more trying to make it easier for you to let me go. I'm taking you to a bus stop." I feel the twist of my stomach with each word.

This is it. For her. For me. For us.

It has to be.

I crawl off her and refuse to look in her eyes. "Get ready to go, Selena."

I wish she understood that I don't have a choice. Neither of us does. I don't deserve someone so stubbornly willing to stay by my side. But I can't keep her. I could never keep her.

Chapter Seventeen

Selena

The loud pickup truck idles nearby as I walk down the long road leading away from the house. It only creeps forward when I get too far ahead. I'm sick of being pushed away. I can make my own decisions and suffer the consequences of my own choices. But he can't understand that.

"Come on, Selena, get in the truck."

"I'm not getting in the truck, Lex. You want me gone, and I won't sit beside you while you get rid of me."

"I'm not letting you walk out here alone. Remember what I said about the predators out here?"

I roll my eyes. "Yeah, there are worse predators than you." I scoff. "I think I'll chance it. Maybe I'll get taken by someone who doesn't have commitment problems."

The truck slams to a halt beside me.

"God, your age is showing. I do *not* have commitment problems."

I swivel on my heels to stare at him, the darkness beginning to wrap around us as the sun goes down. "My age? Fuck you." My steps kick up dust again. The headlights illuminate my back and cast a long shadow in front of me.

"I'm not *fine* with it. But this is what has to happen," he calls over the sound of the engine.

"Then let it happen! *Bye!*" I admit this outburst shows my age, but I don't care anymore. None of it matters. "Don't call yourself a predator when you can't handle your prey."

"I can *handle* my prey just fine. When they fucking listen," he snaps, kicking up dust as he slams on the brakes again.

I laugh. "If you want a compliant woman, I'm a poor choice."

"Were you?"

Oh, fuck him. How dare he throw my past in my face when I've never thrown his at him. Until now. "Real low blow, felon."

I hear a heavy exhale from the truck. "I'm telling you one more time, Selena, get in the fucking truck so I can bring you to the bus station."

I turn toward him. "No."

Lex's jaw ticks as if he's controlling every ounce of what's inside him that wants to punish me.

"How fast can a rabbit run? You want to play games? I'll play too." His voice is low and laced with frustration. His eyes roll up to meet mine, and he becomes the fierce predator once more, transforming in front of my very eyes. He throws the truck in park, turns off the ignition, and gets out, leaning against the door. "You may be faster, but I'm stronger. You'll get tired before I even break a sweat."

I look around. We're in the middle of nowhere. Wire livestock fencing rises from every direction and as the darkness blankets the landscape, it blends into the blackness. Dark trees sway against the wind. Their leaves shake, sending an eerie rustling toward us on the breeze. It's not like the chase in the morning, when the sky still hung low in gray light. I could see then, at least.

I don't think Lex will hurt me—even when he gets rough in the bedroom, something holds him back—but his taut muscles ripple, making him look dangerous.

Real fucking mad.

"Ten," he begins to count. "Nine." There is a harshness in his voice that wasn't there last time.

I survey the landscape once more and take off through a field behind me. From memory, I'm trying to recall the wire fencing's location. I don't think it stands in my way in this direction.

"Eight. Seven." His countdown grows fainter as I race away.

Tall grass whips at my ankles. I take a sharp right, heading toward the trees. They beckon with their shaking leaves, inviting me to hide among the foliage and giant trunks. But it's also darker beneath their canopies.

I hear a howl. It's not an animal. No, it's Lex . . . signifying the start of the hunt.

Lex

"Ready or not, rabbit, here I come," I whisper. I take off the way she went. I calculate the moves I know she'll make. I'm not just a hunter, I'm also a tracker. Stealthy and smart.

I pick up my pace and follow her. It's so fucking dark. I don't see traces of her until they're directly in front of me. When the tall grass sinks, ending abruptly, I know she took a right turn that shoved her heels into that very spot. What a stupid game to play. All because she called me what I am.

No, it's because of her smart-ass mouth. It's because of her defiant fucking behavior. If she wants to be a child about everything, I'll make her play hide and seek. I haven't decided what I'll do to her once I catch her. Because I will catch her. I'll make the choice the moment she's in my grasp.

Will I please her or hurt her?

A sharp pain races across my thigh, and I bite back the urge to scream out. I look down and run my hand along a barbed wire fence. A twisted point of connection is the cause of my injury. It tore a nice slit in my jeans and brought warm blood to the surface. A piece of fabric blows in the breeze, attached to another sharp piece of fencing ahead of me. I pick it off the wire and lift it to my nose. It smells like her, mixed with the metallic scent of her blood.

She's hurt.

My eyes scan the tree line, and I spot the faintest clearing of brush ahead. I run along the fence. If it connects to an adjacent paddock, I'll see it before I run into it.

"Rabbit?" I call out as I reach the cleared section. She went in there. I can feel it in my bones. My heartbeat throbs in my cock as the chase gives me a rush of adrenaline I haven't felt since I was younger.

When I became a murderer.

To be clear, I didn't get hard from the killings, but they released all these good hormones that made me wonder why more people didn't kill those they hated. It's the ultimate release. Like an orgasm for my brain. I'm hard now because my body anticipates the moment I'll get my hands on her.

As I barrel through the brush, I knock back branches and make my way through the dark, silent forest. The old me burns beneath my skin. Dark thoughts creep from the deepest recesses of my mind to argue with me. Images of what I'll do once I catch her swirl through my thoughts.

I want to fuck her one last time.

Lexington tells me that our backs are against the wall. I have to get rid of her because she'll never just leave. My thoughts weave through the evil ones. It would be better for her if I just . . . ended it. Quick and painless. For her, not for me. It will gut me and fracture the illusion of happiness I've had since I met her. Well, since I took her.

But can I do it?

I'll figure that out once I catch her.

Branches rustle. It's disorienting and difficult to tell which direction the sound came from. I leave it up to my instinct, which drags me to the left. In the following silence, I wonder if the sound was just an animal after all. Maybe even a real rabbit. But it happens again, louder and closer, with footfalls behind it. It's a rabbit, alright.

Mine.

The toe of my shoe catches beneath a root and sends me forward, my palms landing on a rock. Her footsteps will be quieter on the rocks than on the forest floor littered with brittle twigs and dried leaves. I smirk and look up. The wall of stone nearly blends with the darkness.

"Very wise, little rabbit," I call to the top. As I climb, I realize her smaller stature has given her the advantage here.

Prey 1, Predator 0.

I slide down the rock, scraping my hands into a bloody mess on my way down. "Fuck," I growl.

I follow the wall of rocks, trying to find an easier way up. Just as I expect, there's a trail of mud and pine needles that, as steep as it is, is cake in comparison. I know that sneaky little rabbit is up there, hiding and hoping I don't find her.

Or maybe she hopes I will.

If so, that's not very wise on her part because I have no idea whether I'll devour her, kill her, or release her unscathed.

Ignoring the pain in my hands and the blood dripping down my leg, I reach the top and scan the new landscape. It's less dense than the forest floor, lacking massive trees on all sides of me. A scraping sound draws my attention to the lower rock wall. Selena slides down the last bit of scree and hops to the forest floor once more.

Sneaky fucking rabbit.

Prey 2, Predator 0.

I'm proud of her because she's showing her true wit and strength. She isn't just a *compliant* woman. She isn't just a prim and proper girl in a fancy fucking car. She's keen and willful. She's someone who can get dirty and outrun me. She doesn't seem so weak and vulnerable now. Prey can't survive by being weak. They survive on their cunning.

I dig my fingers into my waistband. As frustrated as I am, I make my way back down the cliff, sliding every few steps along the muddy path. I follow her footprints, neither of us running any longer. We depend on our wits, not speed.

Our tact.

Our instinct.

Her footprints stop, as if she vanished into thin air. As if I had imagined her from the start. I look around, letting my eyes adjust to the new layout.

Where are you, rabbit?

My eyes drop to the tree trunks lining a section of the path. I put my foot against one on the left, the other on the right, and hand over hand, tree over tree, make it to the other side where her footprints resume.

She's fucking resourceful, I'll give her that.

Prey 3, Predator 0.

I nearly call it off, ending the hunt as a predator with an empty belly. But then I see her. She's perched low behind brush, looking in the direction she thinks I'll come from. She probably didn't expect me to continue this way when her footprints vanished. She underestimates me as much as I underestimated her.

My breath quickens, and my heartbeat thunders. Drool forms beneath my tongue. I creep up behind her, every meticulous step avoiding the twigs beneath my feet. Like a jaguar, I skulk among the shadows to sneak up on my next meal.

And I pounce.

I catch her and don't bother to cover her mouth as I knock her onto her back and fight her flailing arms and legs. There's no one to hear the sounds she'll make, so I let her scream. With her body sinking into the mud, I still haven't decided what I'll do with her. Lexington wants to play, and the dark part of me fights the temptation to do more than fuck her. The haunting sounds of my past whisper in my ears. I growl.

"Fuck you, Lex!" she yells as she strains against my grasp on her wrists.

"Sneaky fucking rabbit."

She whimpers as I turn her onto her stomach. I tug down her leggings, exposing her pale ass and thighs.

I unzip my jeans and rip open the button. "Nothing has changed, but I'm going to fuck you how I want one last time because I won your body, fair and square."

"I don't want you to fuck me if it's going to be the last," she says.

I laugh. "After all that, rabbit? I'm going to fuck you. The predator doesn't catch the prey to let it go. Not a good predator, at least."

I pull her hips up, spit in my hand, and rub it along my cock before pushing inside her. She gasps as I fuck her in the rough, hellish way I want, with every thrust forcing my frustration and anger through her. I push the thrill of the hunt inside her, relentlessly fucking her as if every moment she outsmarted me deserves a moment where Lexington—the man I hide from her, even as she whispers his name—can come out and play.

"Lex," she whimpers, turning her head to the side, and I don't know what she wants. I can't care at this moment.

I can't.

I answer her by fisting her hair with a hand coated in blood and mud. When I crane her neck, I go deeper than she can take. I fuck her like her pussy is mine, even while knowing I have to give it back. Her body tenses with the fear I've caused her. *Me.* Not the men I worried would hurt her. Instead, I'm the one hurting her— emotionally and physically.

Which is worse than the men who would just break her body.

A tear rolls down her cheek, and I fight the urge to wipe it away. My hips drive her into the soft ground, and I try to ignore the parts of her that will force back the side of me I *need* to feel to let her go. I ignore the soft waves of her dark hair, sticky with sweat, blood, and dirt. I force my gaze above her head instead of at her clenched eyes. Instead of the whimper of pain that leaves her lips with every thrust, I focus on the leaves rustling around us.

The world goes silent, and a nauseating echo of whimpers projects around me. I can't continue to ignore those sounds in this eerie silence. Lexington can't stand to hear them, either.

I stop thrusting and rest my pelvis against her ass. Even when she isn't so willing, she's warm and inviting. She never cries or begs for me to stop, and I can't help but find respect within her anguish and stoic fear.

My cock twitches inside her, and I want to keep going, but the need to comfort her overcomes that primal urge to feast on my last meal.

"Goddamn it." With a deflated breath, I release her hair. I'm disappointed with myself for the inability to do what I need to do to make her hate me so she'll run.

I pull out of her and turn her onto her back. My hand rubs along her torn shirt, blood drying along a huge gash in her abdomen. Mud spreads over her pale torso. Fear and tears gloss her eyes, but she doesn't tense as I lean over her. I lift her thighs and pull her against me. She's slick with mud, and I paint my handprints along her inner thighs as I spread her and push myself back inside. No matter how scared she may have been, she's still warm and wet for me.

She gasps and digs her fingers into the soft ground. I drive my hips into hers, as deep as I can. She's the only thing in my life that feels right. Safe.

And she can't be.

"I can't keep fighting you on this, Selena," I whisper. The moment I look her in the eyes, I weaken. "I'm sorry I got rough with you, but it doesn't change anything." I lean down and bite the side of her neck. I curl my hips into her and make love to her because I know it's the last time I'll be inside her. I wrap my hand around the back of her neck and bury my face into her as I thrust. "I want you to forget me after tonight."

"No, Lex." She lifts her chest. "I can't forget you. I'll remember you whenever my hands touch cool mud. I'll think of you when the leaves crunch beneath my feet. Whenever I run, I'll always imagine you're behind me."

I sit up and meet her gaze. "Rabbit, don't say that to me." As much as I want to live in her mind forever, I need for her to let me go. The nagging voice in my head returns, threatening her life, telling me that letting her live will hurt her worse. "What can I do to get *you* to let *me* go? How can I make you forget me?"

"You'd have to kill me," she says. The sickeningly calm way she says it sounds like me.

And that makes me feel worse.

I wrap my hand around the front of her throat and squeeze. She doesn't even fight me as her abdomen draws in and her body begs for a breath. She just accepts it. Whatever all this is to her, it's somehow worth dying for.

If I keep my grip on her throat just a few seconds longer, the conflict inside me will die with her. My resolve is weakening, though.

I release her neck, and she pants for air.

"I said I'd do anything for you, but I can't do the one thing I need to do," I whisper. I give her a forceful thrust to draw her full attention to me. "Promise me one thing?"

She nods before she even hears my request.

"If we get caught before we reach the border, tell the police I abducted you. Tell them I abused you, forced my way inside you, and threatened to kill you. Say anything you have to against my name to preserve yours. If the police come and shit hits the fan, don't be the wolf. Be the scared little rabbit and run."

She shakes her head.

"Promise me, rabbit. I'm not playing around with you. You still have a chance at freedom. I don't."

She looks up at me, her eyes rounding with sadness. She pulls me into her and kisses me. "I promise," she whispers.

That's all it takes to silence Lexington and the altruistic way I want to save her from me or any other person who can hurt her.

The chase. The hunt. The catch. Her promise.

Maybe she's precisely where she needs to be: a place where her demons can play freely with mine. Under the watchful eye of the wolf, the rabbit will live another day.

Chapter Eighteen

Selena

Our little game delays our departure. By the time we get back inside, I'm a bloody, muddy mess with an ache between my legs. Lex stopped holding back and fucked me so hard and raw. I felt his strength with every deep thrust that rearranged my insides. When he choked me, I felt what he was capable of. He could kill me, and I truly thought for a few moments that he would, that I would die beneath Lex while his cock was buried inside me. For some reason, that didn't seem as bad as it should have. I still don't know if he'll let me stay with him. He told me I won, but I fear he'll change his mind.

While I shower, he moves the piece of shit's body off the porch. I run my hand over the large cut on my abdomen and rub away the dirt. I wash my hair and get rid of the twigs and leaves tangled within.

When I get out of the shower, Lex stares at me. He's still filthy, caked in dried mud and blood, and I have no clue if it's mine, his, or the man's. He gestures to the folded pile of clothes he set on the counter. Without speaking, he strips naked, and I try to look away as he pushes past me, rubbing against my body as he gets in the shower. I dress to the wordless sound of his shower. The tight feeling in my belly proves I still don't believe him. I still fear he only said what he said because he was inside me.

I grab my bag and the homeowner's key to the old Ford pickup before walking down the long driveway toward where Lex left the car before our game. When I get to the rusty tan truck, I notice Lex left the window open. The ripped driver's seat is wet from a quick rain that just passed. I groan and climb inside to back the truck toward the house.

While Lex showers, I load the truck with food and tools. I grab a hunting rifle and a box of ammo off the mantle above the fireplace and a cozy blanket from the couch. I put them in the bed of the truck. Just as I finish, Lex appears, clean and dressed. His dirty-blond hair is brushed back, still slick and wet. He surveys what I've done with a look of pride.

Actually, I'm not sure if he's proud or just less angry than he was when he first told me I wasn't going with him.

Before I can tell Lex the seat is wet, he gets into the driver's side. He slams his hand on the steering wheel. He's so on edge.

"You left the window open," I say as I get into the dry passenger seat. "Also, I put a sign on the front door saying he was out of town the rest of the week."

Lex turns toward me and nods. "Good idea."

I reach into the glove box and grab the rabbit's foot I took from my old car and hang it on the crooked rearview mirror. The corners of Lex's mouth creep upward, but he sobers. It's been our lucky charm so far, and I sure as hell wouldn't leave it behind now. It swings with the rough movements of the old truck as we pull down the driveway.

"Lex," I say, trying to draw his attention.

His lips tighten, forcing back any response. The silence makes me almost certain he said what he said to get me on the road with him. To shut me up and get me in the car so he can do what he always intended to do: drop me off the first chance he gets.

I don't truly settle in my seat until we drive by the sign for a bus station. I release a breath of relief as we pass it.

I'm confused as much as it seems he is. How can he like to be around me when he's so willing to kill me in the same moment? I try to shake off my insecurity. He was always willing to kill me. It's always been on the table, even when I felt the hesitation every time he threatened it. Even when I worried he'd do it, I knew there was a bigger struggle inside him. So I stayed calm, placing my fate in his hands.

Whatever that would be.

I'd rather him kill me than drop me off at the damn bus station. He's the first person who's gotten to know me. Not even my parents let me open up the way I have with him. They thought I had nothing more going for me than being an unhappy wife in a marriage I never wanted. But Lex saw something else in me. Something I couldn't even see. Lex is someone I should stay far away from, but I see things in him he can't either.

His darkness deserves some light.

"You surprised me, rabbit," he says after a nauseating length of silence.

"When?"

"In the woods. You were so tactful. Resourceful. Almost more than me." He lets a smirk cross his face for a moment.

"I'm not as stupid or weak as you think I am," I tell him while forcing my gaze out the window.

"I never thought you were weak." He takes a moment to gather his thoughts. "I considered you vulnerable."

"And?"

He clears his throat. "My trip to the border is suicide." He refuses to look at me as my gaze snaps to his face.

"What do you mean?"

"My story either ends in a shootout at the checkpoint or I die in the goddamn desert trying to cross on foot."

"Lex," I whisper, shaking my head.

"This is why I needed you to go. I needed you to leave because I realized what a fucking pipe dream this was. You think this is your fairy tale, but it's merely a horror story."

"I'm not accepting that."

Lex laughs. "Sure are stubborn, aren't you? You can't buy your way out of this one, rabbit." He doesn't speak for a while, letting the road noise fill the gap in our conversation. "What was your idea? How did you see this ending?" he finally asks.

"Nope, it doesn't matter."

"Rabbit," he says firmly. "Tell me."

I don't respond, dropping my head to my hand. Lex pulls over and fists my hair, pulling me into him. "Tell me, sweet bunny," he whispers. His words are the heat that melts me and he knows it does. He flashes those blue eyes at me, and my resolve dissolves.

"Fine. We used to have a nanny—"

Lex rolls his eyes.

"You know what? Forget it."

"I'm sorry," he says with a sarcastic tone. "Please, continue. You had a nanny . . ."

"I'm not going to help you if you're going to make fun of how I grew up. Would you like it if I made fun of how you grew up?"

"You're right. I had a nanny, though, for your information. He was the local drug dealer."

I curl my lip. "Anyway, my nanny was from Arkansas, and she always talked about this forest, saying you could get lost in there and no one would ever find you. Wichita? Or something?"

"Ouachita. It's a national forest," he corrects me. When I cock my head at him, he shrugs. "A lot of time to study when you're serving life."

"Yeah, Ouachita. She said people built cabins there and just lived off the grid."

"What's the point of this little tale?"

"The point is, maybe we can find someplace down there to hide out instead of trying to cross the border."

Lex releases my hair and sits back. "That's not . . . a bad idea," he says, as if formulating a new plan in his mind.

We take the exit toward Arkansas. We'd have gone through there anyway, but now we'll make a little pit stop, because what else do we have to lose?

We drive into Ouachita National Park through a utility road entrance, avoiding the front gate. A sign attached to a robust tree trunk warns us to enter the heart of the forest at our own risk. We're fine with the risk.

The narrow trail pulls us into the depths of the park. Dense trees surround us in ways I've never seen. It's so thick. So lush. So green. Aside from the path, this place has been completely left to nature and even then, the truck bounces as we drive over large tree roots trying to reclaim that, too. We take another unmarked road, driving further through winding woodlands. Then we take another—and another—until we have no idea where we are, which means no one else will know, either.

Lex yawns, which makes me yawn. He cuts off the engine.

"Let's get in the back of the truck," he says as he climbs out. He unlocks the gate, climbs inside, and goes right to loading up the rifle with rounds.

I get out of the truck, and my feet land on the soft forest floor. When I close the door, the warm, humid night air wraps around me. The forest roars with nighttime sounds: big insects chirping, mosquitoes buzzing, and trees creaking. I climb into the back and close the tailgate.

Lex lays out the blanket I brought, covering the dirty metal. He pulls another blanket from a bag. He lies down and puts the bag beside him so I can lay my head on it. I lie beside him, and it reminds me of the overlook, when I found myself snuggling a man I shouldn't.

I still shouldn't, but now I need to.

Lex wraps his arms around me, and I lay my head on his chest. The faint smell of soap still clings to his skin. He covers me and rests his head on his other arm.

"It's peaceful here," I whisper.

"I haven't figured out if it's a good idea yet."

"It seems like a good idea for tonight, at least."

I lean up and kiss him. He grabs my chin and tugs me away from his mouth. "Not tonight," he says. He's still on edge.

"What's wrong?" I ask.

"I feel like I have to protect you. We're in the middle of a forest I'm not familiar with, so I have to pay attention to the shit around us," he says as he releases my chin.

"There's nothing around us, Lex. Relax."

He shakes his head. "That's what you don't understand. I haven't dropped my guard since I got in your car that night. Even before I slept with you, I kept my eyes open for the police, your husband, or anyone that could hurt you. You wanted to stay with me, and I let you stay. Now I have to be more vigilant than ever."

I rub my hand down his stomach, inching toward the front of his jeans. He grabs my hand and rubs my palm.

"I said no," he tells me, so firmly that I nearly listen.

I shrink beneath the blanket and work off the button until his pawing protests grow weak.

"Don't do what you're thinking, Selena," he whispers through a frustrated groan. "You know once you put your mouth on me, I'm done."

"That's the point," I say before kissing the warm skin above his pants. I work his jeans open, pull out his cock, and take him into my mouth.

"Naughty fucking rabbit," he growls and takes the blanket off so he can see me. He winds his hand through my hair and groans as I bob on him, taking him as far into my mouth as I can, letting him raise his hips to make me take that last inch. When I pull away and look up at him, I wipe the drool from my lower lip.

"Put your mouth back on me, bunny," he whispers as he pushes my head down.

I love pleasing him. I love the way he melts from my touch, causing him to say my nickname again, so endearing and so seductive. I can't believe I once hated it. I'll be anything he wants me to be when he calls me that now.

Lex wraps his hand around my throat, pulling me toward his mouth and kissing me, hard and driven. I moan against his lips.

"Fuck. Your mouth is incredible. Let me devour you." He pulls away and holds his pants up as he unlocks the tailgate and drags me toward the edge.

I sit up and let my legs dangle over the side. Lex kisses me before removing my shoes and jeans. He lays me back, wraps his arms around my pale thighs, and tugs me toward him. Just like he said he would, he leans down and devours me, licking me in long strokes that make me grip the blanket above my head. I moan as he rakes my inner thighs with rough fingertips.

"Your pussy is like something I've never tasted, bunny, and I could eat you all fucking night," he groans as he strokes himself and licks me. His tongue dips inside me before slowly curling over my clit.

"Lexington," I moan.

He sits up and growls with a sadistic smirk before pushing three fingers inside me. He doesn't even try to work me out, and I whimper.

"Get on your hands and knees."

I swallow before doing as he says. The metal scrapes my knees as I back toward him. I'm vulnerable and open, and my cheeks flush with embarrassment.

Lex bites my inner thighs and makes his way up to my pussy again. He buries his face into me, looping his hands around my legs to keep me from moving away from him. The tips of his fingers burn my hips as he squeezes and draws me closer. I moan and drop my chest. His tongue moves at a whole new angle, running along the hood of my clit instead of against it. He moves his head from side to side, and I tremble.

"Come on my face so I can fuck you while you're still spasming." His warm breath washes over my clit and when he starts moving his tongue again, it makes me shudder. He loves how he makes me feel.

And I love it, too.

The sounds of the forest die, and I hear nothing more than the sloppy sounds of him fucking me with his mouth. I hear the hungry groan between each stroke of his tongue.

"Have you ever squirted?" he asks.

"No," I whimper.

Lex pulls me by my hips, drawing me off the back of the truck. I feel empty without his tongue on me. He bends me over the open tailgate and kicks my legs open. He stands beside me with his body pressed against mine. His hand caresses my ass before his fingers push inside me, stretching me with three fingers as he uses the full strength of his arm. He's so fast. So hard. And I feel the intense urge to bear down on his fingers. I scream out as it grows too intense, vibrating my entire body.

"Lex!" I call out. I don't know what I'm feeling, and I'm not sure I like it.

"Shh, bunny, relax and let it happen," he whispers over the intensifying sounds of wetness between my legs. When I tense, he pulls his fingers out of me, and a quick emptiness follows with a gush of liquid.

Before I can say anything, before I even know if I like it, his fingers are back inside me, fucking me with a hungry strength that tenses my body all over again. When he pulls out, I shudder and come again in a wave of pleasure.

"It's too intense," I say as I reach back and touch his thigh.

"Come like that on my cock, and I'll stop," he says with a smirk.

I nod, and he gets behind me. My chest presses against the open tailgate as he leans his weight into me, gripping the back of my neck with a frustrated groan. He pushes inside me, slick and wet with my come. He fucks me hard and fast, with the same rough momentum that made me saturate the ground with my come. The angle is just right, and every thrust makes my body tremble in noticeable waves. When the pressure becomes too much, he pulls out and keeps his cock against my pussy as I cover him in a gush of come. He grips my ass as I drip around the length of his dick still pressed against my swollen clit.

"Such a good girl," he growls as he strokes himself against me, stroking my clit at the same time. "Messy little bunny. You're fucking soaked." He pushes himself back inside me.

My body tenses as he fucks me, and I realize it's from my body wanting more. More of him. Not just his body, but his heart.

"Do you have feelings for me, Lex?" I ask, and it stops him mid-thrust.

"What a time to ask me that," he says as he leans over me. "If I said no, would you want me to stop fucking you?"

I tense, and he groans as I tighten around him.

Couldn't he just fucking lie while he's inside me? Does he have to be so . . . cold?

"Oh, that made you mad, huh? You can't imagine that I didn't get feelings like you did after all our experiences and time together?"

My heart. I feel the cracks run through it, and I fight back tears. If I speak, he'll know he's upsetting me.

Lex wraps an arm around my chest and lifts me to his. He bites my neck. "Bunny, you have all that's left of my heart. Anything I *can* feel is for you."

Just like that, his words crawl through the cracks in my heart and seal them. I melt into his strong body.

"I don't know if I know what love is, Selena, but I know this is the closest I've felt to another person." He pulls out of me and turns me to face him. He draws me close to his mouth. "I wanted you to leave because I needed to protect the one person who made me feel *something* other than numb or angry. The only person capable of humanizing someone as barbaric as me."

I swallow, his breath mixing with mine. "I don't know what love is either, Lex. I never have. I just know it wasn't what I had with my husband, and that's why I didn't want to leave you. Leaving meant losing the one thing that made me feel . . . safe." The word almost catches in my throat, but I manage to get it out.

Lex buttons his jeans, climbs into the truck bed, and motions to me. I dress and climb up with him. We lie down, and he holds me tight. I feel bad he didn't finish, especially when he made me come the way he did. I slip my hand down his stomach, but he stops me with a firm grip.

"We'll play more once we find a cabin. And I'll give you twice the amount of my come."

I nod and kiss him before rolling onto my back and staring up at the dark, star-filled sky. I've never seen something so beautiful. So peaceful. It feels like home, and I'm surprised how little I miss my family and my old life.

But what can my new life possibly be?

Chapter Nineteen

There it is. A quaint cabin tucked away in the middle of the national park, far away from everyone and everything. The whole outside is natural wood, aging ungracefully. Big solar panels line the moss-covered roof. At least there's electricity, which is more than I expected. Selena cranes her head to see what I see.

It's perfect.

We leave the truck a little ways back and follow an overgrown path on foot. She keeps looking at me as we walk, and I know she wants to know why I stopped us from fucking more last night. Her brain is probably in overdrive, trying to figure out what she did wrong. She didn't do anything wrong. It's all in my head. Even then, I still did what I needed to do to make her come, because that's what matters.

There's no way to explain to her what I felt. In that moment, I realized just how important she was to me. You'd think realizing that would have made me want to keep going. Fuck her better. But the foreign, uncomfortable feeling did the opposite. It made me close up.

I knew what to do with her pussy but not her heart.

I'll make it up to her. I'll make her forget I ever stopped us last night.

"What do we do if someone is home?" I ask, trying to get out of my head because it's not a place I like to stay in.

"Get rid of them," she says without looking away from the cabin in front of us.

There she goes, surprising me again with how dark and dangerous she's become.

"Sadistic fucking rabbit," I say through gritted teeth. I feel guilty that she has no qualms about killing someone else. Decades of coldness froze me. She may have warmed me, but she's also taking my coldness as her own. Now I'm freezing her.

Even thawed, I have no issue killing, and that's how I know just how fucked I am. But she doesn't deserve this.

We stop just outside the yard behind some trees and bushes. We watch and wait, but there aren't signs of anyone having been there in a while. Weeds grow upward and have overtaken a wheelbarrow leaned against the wall of a shed. Its tire has been reduced to a pile of melted rubber beneath it. Tattered curtains line some of the windows, which are dirty and broken in some places.

We head toward the front door, looking over our shoulders. I rub my hand along the rickety wooden door. Humidity has warped its edges. I grab the door-knob, and it turns with a rattle because of a missing screw. The moment I open the door, I smell it. I recognize the scent as if I'm thrown back into my childhood within one breath.

"What's that smell?" she asks as she covers her nose with her hand.

"That, rabbit, is the smell of death."

Her eyes widen. "What do you mean?"

I motion for her to wait here. I don't need to worry about protecting us both, but that smell makes me fairly certain I know what's home, and it's not someone living. "Just stay here for a minute," I tell her as I load a round in the rifle.

The smell intensifies as I walk toward the back of the cabin. When I turn the corner, I see a man in a recliner. He's slumped over, the television's remote still in his mottled hand. His face is gray, but he hasn't been dead all that long.

I'm so used to the smell that I hardly notice it at all. I'm almost completely nose blind to the familiarity. "Well, that's fucking convenient," I say through a laugh.

I can't help but think the luck is from her stupid little rabbit's foot, which is nestled in my pocket.

I go back to the front door and find Selena still covering her nose. "Can't kill what's already dead," I tell her.

"What?" she asks, breathing through her mouth.

"Whoever owns this place is very dead in their room." I start to open the windows, struggling against the years of grime to pry them open.

"We can't stay here. It smells like death. Literally."

I stop and stare at her. What does she mean we can't *stay* here? It's everything we've been searching for. It's more than what we could ever ask for, smell or no smell. "We couldn't be any luckier, and you want to leave because of a little smell?"

"It's not little."

"Once I get the body out, the smell will go away. Mostly."

"I'll wait out here," she says as she waves me off and goes to a wicker rocking chair on the porch.

I enter the room and glance at the sad sap before trying to figure out how best to get rid of him. My fingers are crossed as I head into the backyard through an even ricketier backdoor to check the shed. A dingy blue tarp catches my eye, and I yank it out, knocking over a shovel and rake as it comes free. When I head back inside, I lay out the tarp on the floor in front of him.

"Sorry, buddy," I tell him as I shove him off the chair. I haven't apologized to men I've killed before, but here I am, apologizing to a long-dead corpse. Selena's warmth has thawed me a bit more than I'm willing to admit.

The man hits the tarp with a thud that sounds like a garbage bag filled with congealed pudding and bones. The skin on his left arm has begun to slough away, revealing the sinewy highway beneath. I almost laugh when I realize how much this doesn't disgust me. Not even the dark stain of human decay left behind on the chair elicits more than a shrug of my shoulders.

I wrap up the tarp, tie it off with rope, and drag him out the back door. I walk as far into the woods as I can and leave him there—in the humid heat but out of the sun, at least. I'll come back and bury him later, after I've dealt with the chair.

When I go back inside, it's already smelling better. I grab a half-smoked cigar off the table beside the chair and light it with the old Zippo resting beside it. My cheeks puff at the rich smoke, a strong scent that somehow overpowers the perfume of death. It feels good to have it between my lips. I miss the normalcy of having a smoke.

A legal one, at least.

The recliner is light enough to lift. The fabric smells like old man, piss, and death. Definitely not up to Selena's standards. I carry it outside, letting the cigar mask the scent as I go. I lean it against the back of the shed, which is about all I'm willing to do with it in the stifling heat.

I circle to the front of the house and wipe my hands on my pants as I lean against the railing surrounding the front porch. The doors are wide open to let the stench clear, and flies and other insects buzz in and out.

Selena's eyes roll up and stop at the cigar. "Since when do you smoke?"

I smirk, drawing the cigar from my lips. "Since I was eight."

"Jesus," she says with a shake of her head.

I offer it to her. "Want to try?"

She chews the inside of her cheeks before taking it and putting it between her full lips. If she knew it was half-smoked by the dead man himself, she wouldn't have taken it. She puffs on it and hands it back.

"Since when do *you* smoke?" I ask, a sly smile on my face. From the way her lips wrapped around it, I have the feeling it isn't her first time.

She shrugs. "On and off since I was eighteen. Mostly off. How'd you know?"

I step toward her, lift her chin, and look down at her. "Because you smoke like you've done it before. And it's fucking sexy." I run my thumb along her lower lip.

Her eyes roll back at my touch but then she rips her face away and wipes at her mouth. "Dude, you were just disposing of a dead body."

I let the cigar rest between my lips. I smirk at her and go inside to wash my hands. If she only knew about all the things we touched in prison, and honestly, most were worse than a dead guy.

Coffee mugs and a single plate fill one side of the sink. I wash my hands, turning the knob and realizing there's no hot water. I'm not sure how Selena will feel about this. Actually, I do know. She's going to hate it. But she'll deal with it for me. Which I hate. I still haven't told her the shower is merely a stall outside with a hose attached to a rusty showerhead.

When I turn around, she's behind me, sneaky little prey. At least her hand isn't pressed against her nose any longer, which means the smell is getting better. Or she is getting used to it. Regardless, she still has a scowl on her face. I can't help but chuckle.

"Not good enough for you?" I ask.

"It's just so . . ."

"It's all we have, rabbit. What'd you think would be out here? The Ritz Carlton?"

She blows hair from her forehead. "I know. I know."

"You still have a chance to back out. I can still take you to the bus station."

Her eyes narrow. "No."

"Then enjoy what you won in our little game of hide and seek. You got to stay with me, just like you wanted." I'm struggling to find sympathy for her. While this place is a downgrade for her, it's an upgrade for me.

I turn around and start washing the dishes. Maybe she'll feel better without the memory of a person's dirty life strewn in front of her. My hands redden from the chill of the water.

"Hey, at least he didn't die in the bed," I call to her as she sneaks a peek around the corner. You get used to finding silver linings when everything else in your life is just a different shade of gray.

"I'm not sleeping in there," she says. She strolls through the living room and prods the red couch, ignoring the lumps in the cushions. She pushes her weight down on the springs and rips away the cushions.

I turn around, dry my hands on a towel, and lean back against the sink.

"It's a pull-out couch," she says with a beaming smile that tugs at my lips, too.

"Do they even have those where you came from?"

She drops the old frame and snaps her gaze to me. I raise my hands. I don't know why she gets so mad when I give her shit about being rich. I don't care when she says things about me being poor. It's just what we are and where we differ.

I walk over to her and wipe the sweaty hair from her cheek before nudging her aside and releasing the rickety pull-out. The lumpy mattress is stained with signs of age, but it looks clean enough for a fancy show rabbit.

"I hope the quarters are to your liking, your majesty," I say with a playful bow. She doesn't find the humor in it. I'm not sure what's on her mind, but it's making her pissy.

I lie on the bed and tug her into me. The old mattress coils whine, and Selena lets out a squeal. I guess now is the time to confront the big elephant in the room.

"What's the matter, rabbit? You've been weird since last night."

When she doesn't answer, I roll over her and spread her legs with my knees. I look down at her trembling lower lip. If she's not upset about my denial last night, I'm not sure what it's about. She's probably full of regret for staying with me in this decrepit cabin that still smells like a dead man.

"You can leave, Selena. No one is forcing you to stay here."

She fights back the gloss in her eyes.

"What do you want?" I ask louder and shake her shoulders.

"You wouldn't understand," she says, shaking her head.

She always thinks I don't understand. I understand more than she realizes. "Why? Why the fuck wouldn't I understand? I wasn't born with a golden fucking spoon in my mouth, but I can still understand you."

Her eyes widen. "Fuck you, Lex," she says through a huff and tries to squeeze out from beneath me.

"So goddamn mouthy for such a little thing."

My words strike her harder than any fists could. I can only imagine the things her husband used to say that made her close herself off so tightly and lock her heart away. Until a criminal like me came along and knew how to pick it open.

She flails beneath me, but I pin her wrists and lean over her. "Tell me what's bothering you, rabbit." I lower my voice the way she likes. "Talk to me."

She blinks and finally releases the tears she's been holding back. "I . . . I just . . . I don't want you to be so okay with me leaving. You keep asking me to leave. Telling me to leave. You're pushing me away!" Her voice fills with anger instead of sadness.

"You really think I fucking *want* you to leave?"

She lifts her chin, drumming up confidence from somewhere inside her. "Yeah, I do."

"For once in my goddamn life I was being selfless and thinking about the well-being of someone else. I didn't *want* you to leave. I *needed* you to leave because it was safer for you." I lift my gaze to the wall, staring at a rosary hanging from a hook. I drop my eyes to her once more. "I've never felt guilt. I was born like this. Something not quite right in the head. But I knew if you got in trouble for all this, or killed, I would *never* get past that."

"Let me decide what I'm willing to risk."

"I wanted to let you go so you'd be safe at home. I could imagine a life with you I could never have. I could think about how happy you made me when I've always thought I was incapable of such a *normal* emotion. The only thing that ever made me happier than you was fucking killing. And the part of me that enjoys hurting people? I didn't want him to hurt you, either."

"You wouldn't hurt me," she says with a shake of her head.

I choke back a laugh. "I could. And I almost did, more times than you know. I've been willing to kill you since the day I took you."

"I don't believe that, Lex." The shake of her head intensifies, as if reasoning with herself more than me.

"I pushed you away so you could be with someone *better*. I wanted you to have better than the small life I could ever give you. This? This rundown cabin? It's what I can give you." I inhale a sharp breath. It's not good enough for her, I know that. She knows that. We both do. "People describe love as not being able to be away from that person, that it's such a horrible thing to be apart, but it didn't feel like I loved you when I selfishly wanted to keep you for myself. I may not know what love feels like, but I knew enough to know that loving you meant letting you go." I fight back the heat behind my eyes, which I don't remember ever feeling in my entire life. "Old me would have kept you, fucked you, and killed you when I was done with you. New me, the one you drew out, wanted you to forget me and live the life you deserved."

"Even now, you want me to leave," she whispers, her voice wavering with the tremble of her body.

"Because you look so fucking unhappy," I say as I cut my gaze.

"I'm unhappy because you make me feel unwanted."

I sit back and pull her onto my lap. "I've wanted you since the moment I saw you in that car. I've never not wanted you."

She drops her head to my shoulder, and I hear the breathy sounds of her trying not to cry as I hold her.

"If I wasn't in this situation, bunny, I would never let you go or push you away."

She flashes her eyes up at me. "I'm a killer, too, Lex."

I shake my head. "You wouldn't be if it weren't for me."

"This isn't just *your* situation anymore. It's *ours*. Stop thinking of me as the girl you dragged to hell and realize that maybe I've already been there."

"Fuck, bunny." I grip the back of her neck and kiss her. "If you want this, I'll give you everything I can in this little world of ours." I pull away and touch her cheek with a warm palm.

Chapter Twenty

Selena

We've been living our new life for a few nights now, and it quickly became clear we'd need more money, even while living off-grid. Much like the guy who lived in this cabin before us, Lex has been doing odd jobs for others who have moved off the grid themselves, but it's not enough to keep food on our table. Lex keeps promising to teach me how to hunt, and I need to hold him to that one of these days.

Prey can hunt prey.

"Rabbit," Lex says as he walks in. The screen door slams behind him.

I finish drying the dish in my hand and turn to face him. "What?"

"I have an idea, but I'm not sure I can let you go with me."

"I'm going where you go."

He smirks. "I thought you'd say that. I'm going to do a little robbery. Get some quick cash."

I shake my head. "Wh-what?"

"Don't worry, rabbit, I've done jobs like this in my sleep." He walks over and brushes a dirt-covered hand across my cheek.

"You ended up in prison, Lex!"

"I was in prison for murder, not robberies."

"Who are you thinking about robbing?" I ask. We need money but committing a robbery seems like an unnecessary risk. We've committed enough felonies since the night I met Lex. On the other hand, what's one more?

"There's a small gas station down the road. No cameras. Nothing. I know they won't have much, but they'll have more than we do."

"How do you plan on doing this?"

He reaches back, pulls the pistol from his jeans, and shakes it in front of my face. "Easily." His eyes darken. "Especially with a hot little diversion."

125

I lift one of my eyebrows and cock my head at his statement.

"You'd be bait, little rabbit."

"They'd see our faces."

"We leave the truck, go on foot, and avoid that gas station from now on. There's plenty of others."

"Seems really fucking dumb, Lex."

"Then don't go. I don't need bait to get the job done." He tucks the pistol into his jeans again. "I'll be back later."

The moment he turns to walk away, I feel the tug at my heart. "No, I'll go."

"What's the plan?" I ask as we pull onto a dead-end road about a quarter of a mile from the rustic gas station.

Lex chambers his pistol. "We separate as we get closer to the building. You draw out the clerk. I'll sneak in and take the money in the till and the safe, if there is one."

My mouth gapes. "How the hell am I going to lure the guy away from the register?"

Lex's hungry eyes rove down my body, and my cheeks flush. "You'll figure it out. You're resourceful, remember?"

We abandon the truck, and Lex pockets the keys. The sun has set, and we are ghosts walking along the dark road. Lex wraps his arm around me and drags me to the inside so he's closest to the road. What a gentleman.

The small gas station comes into view ahead. A tall black lamp post illuminates the front door. Bugs swarm around it. There's only a single pump for gas, with nozzles on both sides and enough room for two cars at any given time. This is a small and local community.

People here are way too trusting, and Lex will prey on that trusting nature. I doubt they have much more than a few dollars in the till, let alone anything worth protecting with cameras, so at least he was right about that.

Lex pushes me toward the door and walks ahead of me, looping around the building. I brush my sweaty palms on my jeans and take a deep breath before gripping the door's grimy handle. A bell rings overhead when I enter. The racks inside mostly house essentials and snacks—toothpaste, mouthwash, and deodorant alongside a variety of chips, beef jerky, and pretzels.

A door closes somewhere inside a back hallway, and footsteps draw closer. My heart races, and my eyes fall on the old desk with the even older cash register sitting on top of it. Cigarettes line the wall behind the register, waiting to be chosen beneath a worn age-restriction sign.

A balding man appears in the doorway, and he smiles when he sees me. He looks behind me. "Can I help you?"

I struggle to get out the words I need to say as guilt chokes me. I feel absolutely awful about robbing this man. He hasn't done anything to deserve a visit from us. This is where Lex and I differ. He doesn't see people as human beings. Collateral damage doesn't exist to him. There are no innocents.

"H-Hi, yes." I point toward the darkened road. "My car ran out of gas down the road."

"You walked here all by yourself?" His eyes scan me. There's a hint of suspicion in his words, and I try to pull my shit together for Lex.

"Yeah, it's not far. I'm wondering if I could buy a gallon off you." I pull some bills from my pocket and show him the money.

The man steps from behind the counter, his eyes never leaving mine. "You need a can?" he asks as he guides me toward the door.

I nod.

I follow him outside and trail behind him until we reach the circle of light from the lamp above us. I'm not going back into the darkness with him. He unlocks a door, and I can't see anything until he closes it and appears beneath the light. He's carrying an old metal gas can. "Just drop it off when you come back for more gas," he says as he hands it to me and keeps his hand outstretched for the money.

I hand him four dollars, but I catch a glimpse of Lex's shadow inside. I need to keep the man out here with me for his safety. I don't want any more death on our hands, and I'll do what I can to keep this robbery from becoming a murder. I lift the heavy jerrycan and futz with the top. As he starts to walk away, I increase the sounds of frustration leaving my lips. He finally turns back to me.

"Do you need help, miss?" he asks.

I smile and hand it back to him. He works off the cap and puts the nozzle into it. "There you go," he says, and turns to leave once more.

Fighting through panic, I reach out and graze his arm. My eyelashes flutter as I lean back against the pump. "I *really* appreciate your help, mister."

He looks at his feet, seeming bashful all of a sudden. "That's what we do here, ma'am. It's really nothing." His words make me feel fucking awful. This man will probably never trust another person in need because of me.

The meter ticks past one gallon, and I bend over to remove the nozzle from the can. Shy or not, the man is so focused on me that he doesn't notice Lex leaving. I hang the nozzle back in the pump and smile at him. "I'll bring this back," I say as I shake the can.

He nods and goes back inside. Lights turn on as he returns to the back of the store.

Lex and I hightail it back down the road. The can sloshes in my hand, and he's grinning from ear to ear. "You didn't need to steal his can," he says.

"Well, too late now."

We get to the truck, and Lex puts the can in the bed before climbing inside. The gas on my hands creates an overpowering smell when I close the cab door.

"So?" I ask once we get a little further down the road. I'm torn between hoping there wasn't much to steal from the poor guy and wanting there to be.

"I think that dude lives there. He was watching porn in a room with a rickety bed."

I curl my lip. "Gross."

"I bet he doesn't even know he's been robbed yet. Probably still finishing rubbing one out."

I fight the pang of guilt, forcing it away as I look toward Lex's pocket. "I don't care about what he was doing, Lex. What'd you get?"

"He had way more than I thought. Hardly shit in the cash register, but fat fucking stacks in his masturbation station."

"Jesus Christ," I groan. "You didn't rob him of everything he owned, did you?"

A smirk crosses his face. "Of course not, bunny. I knew that would eat at that little heart of yours. I took enough, though. Should have taken more for the way he fucked you with his eyes," he says through a growl. "You did so fucking good."

When Lex doesn't turn onto the utility road, I gesture toward it.

"We aren't going back yet. Let's go get a little something to eat at the diner. I know you like that place, and I love that no one asks fucking questions. Everyone there looks like they have a past they're running from."

Excitement swells in my gut at the thought of a hearty meal. We've been so frugal. He still hasn't told me how much he took, but I'm too distracted by the thought of good food to ask again right now.

We pull into the hole-in-the-wall diner, and Lex covers the jerrycan in the back with a blanket. "Oh, hey, I grabbed this for you," he says as he reaches into his back pocket and tosses a stick of deodorant at me.

My lips tremble. Lex cut the top layer off the cabin owner's deodorant and has been using that. I politely refused. Now I have my own to use. My heart stumbles over itself at the small but significant gesture.

I set the stick on the dashboard, but Lex shakes his head. "Nothing from the gas station in view. Put it under the seat."

I do as I'm told, and his attention to detail makes me realize why he never got caught. Well, for robberies, at least. I hope his street smarts rub off on me like the rest of him has.

Lex

The waitress acknowledges us with a curt nod when we head inside. Red paint peels off the seat of our chosen booth. Selena goes to get in across from me, but I grab her arm and pull her beside me.

"Hey, you two," the waitress says as she tugs out her pad of paper. "Menus?" We both shake our heads. "What can I get you?"

"A cheeseburger," Selena says with too much excitement at the thought of a greasy burger. She's nearly wiggling at the idea.

"Make it two," I tell the waitress, minus the childish excitement. "And two coffees and waters, please."

The waitress scribbles on her pad and puts it in her apron.

"It's too late for coffee," Selena says after the waitress walks away. "We'll be up all night."

"That's the plan," I say. I don't intend to sleep once we get back. And neither will she.

I look back at the empty diner. My hand rises to her throat, and she whimpers. The sound goes straight to my cock. I've been hard since we left the gas station because of how well she played her part. I lean in and kiss her, tugging at her lower lip as I bite into it. My hand moves to her thigh, and she spreads her legs for me.

"Unzip your jeans for me, bunny," I say without looking at her.

She shakes her head. "Not here."

"I want to reward you," I say, leaving no room for another objection. "Unzip those jeans and keep those thighs spread for me so I can make you come before our dinner is served. The longer you wait, the more likely it is she'll return while my fingers are still buried in your cunt."

She inhales a sharp breath, but her fingers drop to her jeans. I dip my hand beneath the splayed fabric and find her bare pussy with the tips of my fingers. Her cheeks flush the moment I run them along her wet slit. I rub her clit.

The door to the kitchen opens, and she grabs my wrist with her hand. I don't move from between her legs. She leans forward to block the view of her sweet little pussy, and the waitress smiles as she sets down two coffees and two red glasses filled with water.

"Sorry it took so long. I had to brew a new pot. Your meals will be out shortly."

"Thank you." I turn to Selena. "Didn't you want to ask for creamer, babe?" I swirl my fingers around her clit. She leans on her fist, anger radiating from her. For a show rabbit, she sure doesn't like to be shown. "Go on," I tell her.

"Can I h-have creamer?" she asks with a tremble in her voice as I dip my fingers inside her in the middle of her request.

A smirk crosses my lips as the waitress nods and grabs a silver creamer pitcher from another table. She leaves, and Selena's eyes jump to mine. *Fuck you*, she mouths.

"Watch your mouth, rabbit, or I'll put you on your fucking knees beneath this table. See how mouthy you feel like being then."

She knows I will absolutely fuck the brattiness out of her throat, and her pelvis tilts at the thought. She loves being used, even if she doesn't want to admit it.

I keep rubbing her until she grips my thigh beneath the table. I take a casual sip of my coffee, and she struggles to keep her moans at bay beside me. She isn't getting close enough from just my touch, too panicked at the idea of getting caught.

"I want you to come, bunny. You were so *fucking* good tonight, so damn sexy. Such a good little bait rabbit. I don't know a single man that wouldn't go out of their way to help you. All you have to do is give us a look with those big, sweet eyes. Fuck," I tell her with a growl as I lower the coffee mug to the table. Her thighs tremble and her muscles tighten the more they try to close against my touch. "Come for me. Come on my fingers so I can eat my dinner with your scent still on me."

That did it for her. She grips her silverware, the metal scraping against the table as she fights the moans and the shudder of her body. A low sound slips from her and makes me ache.

The waitress returns to our table. Selena straightens her back and leans forward. I keep my hand down her pants. She sets the plates in front of us. "Let me know if you need anything else."

Selena leans back, but I don't take my hand away from the warmth of her pussy. I let the throb of her clit speak to my fingertips before I finally pull my hand away. My fingers are covered in her come, and I twitch at the sight of it. I lift my burger with both hands and bite into it. Her mouth gapes as she watches me.

"Don't look at me like that, rabbit. I told you I'm going to eat my dinner with my fingers covered in your come." I nudge her to eat, and she finally starts to devour her long-anticipated meal. Grease from the burger mixes with the sweetness of her come, and after my last bite, I put my fingers into my mouth and finally lick her off my skin.

I stare at her as she finishes eating.

I love that she's sitting in her come-soaked jeans right now, with nothing between her and the denim. She looks like she's enjoying that burger as much as she enjoyed my fingers. I wanted to give her this normalcy tonight. She deserves it. I asked her to do something very abnormal, and she did it without question. Two things, actually. I asked her to help me commit a robbery, and to come on my fingers in the middle of a diner, and she did both.

Like a good fucking girl.

The waitress comes back and puts the check on the table. When she leaves, I pull out the thick stack of money folded in my pocket and lay out two twenty-dollar bills. Selena's eyes widen. When coupled with what I make from odd jobs, the amount I took is enough to keep us going for a little while. It physically pained me to leave some of the man's money behind, but she's rubbing off on me as much as I'm rubbing off on her. I could use a little of her light. Some of her emotions.

All of her.

Chapter Twenty-One

Selena

Lex got way more money than I expected or hoped for. He wants to provide for us in a situation that hardly allows for it. He can give me a place to live, a bed where I can rest my weary head, and he can give me himself. That's all I really want, but we also *need* a little more than what the odd jobs can give. We aren't trying to be extravagant, but we must survive away from the world that will try to separate us.

Driving back from the diner has me in my feelings. I love and hate that Lex pushes me out of my comfort zone and makes me feel good. It's not just a selfless urge to make me come, though; he wants the control I hand to him at the worst times and places. He loves that I listen when everything inside me says no.

Rain begins to patter against the windshield, then the sky opens up and it starts to pour. It reminds me of the first night I met Lex. Unlike me, he's sure behind the wheel, despite the rain.

I blink heavily as my eyes try to adjust to a figure along the side of the road. Through the blur of rain on the windows, I can make out a man with his pale thumb held in the air. He has a limp, and it tears at heartstrings that should have been snipped when Lex carjacked me.

"There's a guy back there," I say, pointing behind me.

"So what?"

"We can't leave him like that."

Lex shakes his head. "We sure can, rabbit. Have you learned nothing from this whole venture? We've finally gotten our shit together so we don't have to keep running. I won't risk that because of some hitchhiker."

"But you're here with me. He's not going to do anything with you here. You're the biggest predator in these parts." I have no fear of any other man with Lex around. He'll always protect me. I push out my lower lip. "I'll feel really shitty if we leave him out there in the storm."

"Don't look at me like that. I don't like how selfless you are. I love that it put me in the car with you in the first place, but your selflessness is suicidal sometimes."

He has to remember what it was like to need a ride.

"Please," I beg. After what happened to the poor clerk, I feel like I need to make amends to the universe and improve one person's day to account for robbing the gas station.

"Jesus fucking Christ, Selena, fine. But so help me God, if he even thinks about touching you, you're going to wish I never stopped to pick him up. His death will be on your hands."

He slams on the brakes, throws the truck in reverse, and backs toward the man. At first I think I must have imagined him because he seems to have vanished within the darkness, but a knock on the window startles me and throws me right back into the night I met Lex. It feels like déjà vu.

Lex lowers my window a little and speaks over me. "Do you need help?" I'm sure the man can tell how much he doesn't want to ask. He couldn't seem less approachable if he tried.

The man stares at us. Rain plasters his dark hair to his forehead. He looks young, closer to my age, and he's not nearly as intimidating as Lex. "Depends. What kind of help are you offering?"

The rain finds its way through the cracked window and wets my jeans. At least it kind of hides the fact that I came just a little while ago and soaked my pants.

Lex seems annoyed by his evasive response. "A ride or a place to stay for the night."

The man looks ahead at the dark, dreary, wet road. "I could use a place to stay for the night, if it's not too much trouble."

"Hop in," Lex says with an annoyed sigh.

I move over, sidling up to Lex so the man can get in. He has that same smell Lex had—a heavy, earthy aroma that sticks with you long after you dry.

"I'm Jamie," the man says. His wet clothes soak into mine.

"I'm Ben, and this is my wife," Lex says.

"Does she have a name?" Jamie asks.

"It doesn't matter what her name is. She's my wife and that's all you need to know."

Lex is being rude. The guy is only trying to introduce himself to us. He seems innocent enough. I know Lex is mistrustful, and I understand why, but nothing and no one will separate us now. I'm confident of that.

The rest of the drive back to the cabin is heavy and silent, and I fight back my urge to ask why he was walking along the road. The longer he's in the car with us, the more I worry I've made the wrong choice. We worked so hard to find a place where we didn't have to run anymore, and now I'm putting us at risk because of residual guilt from the robbery.

We pull onto the utility road and take the winding path to the cabin. We get out of the truck once we park in the spot where the tires sink into the familiar section of ground. Lex gets out first and opens the passenger door. His lips draw tightly downward as the rain begins to soak his clothing. The man beside me scoots out of the truck and Lex steps aside so he can get down.

"You live out here?" he asks.

"The fewer questions you ask, the better," Lex says.

We walk into the cabin, and the heaviness continues past the threshold. As Jamie looks around, I finally get a good look at him. His eyes are as dark as his unruly hair, which has dried, thanks to the heater in the truck. He brushes a hand over his groomed beard and takes off his black jacket. Damp still clings to his white shirt and holds it against his skin.

Lex clears his throat to stop my staring. I'm not staring because I'm attracted to him—and he *is* attractive—but I want to know more about this strange man from the side of the road. I want to know how his story differs from Lex's . . . and how it's the same.

Lex

I hate this. I fucking hate this. Selena is too good, and it puts her into bad situations. Like the night she met me. She's too trusting. I've spent a fair bit of my life on the run, hitchhiking from one place to another, but I was *always* on the run from *something* when I held my thumb in the wind. Very few choose to walk along the road and hope for the kindness of strangers. That's not to say everyone who does is up to no good. Not everyone is like me. But the risk of this man being somewhat like me is too high, and it's a chance I didn't want to take. I do things for Selena that I wouldn't do myself, like heading back to New York when I'm wanted there or leaving half the money during a robbery.

"Why do you limp?" I ask as I toss him a dry shirt.

Jamie grabs the shirt and removes the wet one. Selena's eyes land on him again, watching his movements. She's not looking at him like she wants him. She's looking at him as if she's curious about him.

"Military," he says.

I'm not sure I believe him. There's something not wholly trustworthy in his eyes. Or maybe I just don't like Selena's eyes on another man. "You can sleep in that bedroom back there."

He takes a few steps toward the room. I clear my throat, and he stops.

"I have a couple rules."

"Anything, man. What's up?"

"Don't touch anything that doesn't belong to you." I tug Selena into me. "Don't even let her cross your mind. If you even *think* about her, I'll kill you. Do we have an understanding?"

The man nods and turns toward the bedroom. I know he's been at this for a while because he shows little emotion upon hearing my threat. When someone threatens to kill you, your natural instinct is to escape the situation—even Selena responded that way at first—but he's worn down that instinct until it's too dull to react. He just went to the room as if I never said anything at all.

The door closes, and I turn my attention to Selena. "He sure has your attention," I say as I turn toward her and raise her chin.

"Are you jealous, Ben?" she asks, a smirk crossing her sweet face.

I'm not jealous. I'm possessive. Seeing his eyes on her makes me want to go in there and kill him while he sleeps.

"Mind your eyes, little rabbit. I'd hate to see someone killed because you couldn't," I snarl. "Eyes on me, always."

"My eyes are only for you, Lexington," she says with a pout.

I growl and lift her up, wrapping her legs around me. Our clothes are damp, but it cools my skin after it heated up from hearing her say my name. She does *not* want Lexington to come out to play with another man in the house. But she says it again, through a moan as she drops her head back and gives me access to her throat. I bite into her and walk forward until her back hits the wall. I put her down so I can lower her jeans. She slips off her wet shoes and kicks her pants away. I lift her again and kiss her as I work down my jeans and pull my cock out.

"I've wanted you since I saw you bent over in front of that clerk. I love how he wanted you." That's Lexington coming out to play. The same side of me who wanted to see Selena fucked by her piece of shit husband. Lexington loves her, but not like I do. Not in the same way. *I* don't want to see that shit, but I *know* that nagging thought in the back of my mind is from him.

I lay my cock against her pussy. She's still coated in her come, so slick and wet for me. I pull my hips back and push inside her. Her arms wrap around my neck as I thrust deeply, and the warmth of her recently pleasured pussy makes me groan. I lean into her and kiss her as I thrust upward, grinding her back into the wooden wall. She whimpers against my lips. When I go to bite her neck, my eyes catch on a shadow in the darkened doorway.

Jamie.

I can't see his eyes, but I know he's staring. How could he not? Instead of getting angry at him, I take it out on her cunt. I stare at the shadowy figure and rub my hand up the back of her thigh, lifting her leg and gripping her ass. Lexington loves that he's staring at us, and that's the winning feeling as I thrust deeper into her, taking the frustration out on her pussy. The picture frames on the wall above her head rattle with every ounce of the strength I push into her.

The good part of me fights for control. Lexington wants him to watch, wants him to come over here and bury his face in her pussy, but the other side of me recoils at the thought. I told him not to think about her, but how could he think of anything else as he sees the pleasure coursing through her body with every thrust?

"You feel so *fucking* good, rabbit," I growl. She goes to turn her head, but I reach up and keep her eyes on me. Her intense gaze brings me close too quickly. It doesn't help that I've been turned on for the last two hours. "I'm going to come," I tell her. Lexington doesn't give a shit if Selena comes, but the silky cream of her earlier orgasm still coats her pussy.

I pull out of her and put her on her feet. Only once I put her down does she realize Jamie has been watching us. She reaches for her jeans, her mouth gaped in panic, but I grab her arm and keep her from covering herself. Her eyes roll up to mine, and she looks at me like she did back in the kitchen of her old home.

"Lex," she says, slow and cautious, like the prey animal she is.

"Don't just stand there. I know you're watching, and I know what you want," I tell Jamie as I take a step back.

"He doesn't—"

"Now, hitchhiker. Get over here." I raise my voice. From the look in Selena's eyes, I know she fears what's about to happen. Will Lexington ask him to fuck her? Will Lex kill him for looking at what belongs to him?

Maybe both.

Jamie walks over, his eyes darting between us. I grab his shoulder and turn him to face Selena, but she won't look at him.

Good fucking girl.

"I told you not to think about what belongs to me, yet I saw you watching us from the doorway. I know you thought about what it would feel like to sink inside her. Didn't you?"

He tries to turn to face me, his tongue trying to wet his dry lips, but I grip his shirt and force him to keep his eyes on Selena.

"Don't stop watching now, hitchhiker," I snarl. "This is what you wanted to see, so get a good fucking eyeful now."

My skin burns hot with anger. White-hot rage blinds me.

Selena looks at me, and her loose lips tighten. She knows. She tries to speak, but it's too late.

I grip both sides of his head and snap his neck. The thunderous *crack* breaks the silence of the cabin. His death is instantaneous.

She releases a scream I've only heard in her most intense moments of fear. It's not from someone trying to assault her or kill her. It's from a fear of me and what I've done.

Well, Lexington, but for all intents and purposes, it was me.

"Lex!" she yells. "What the fuck?"

I want to go to her, but the anger and fear in her eyes hold me back. This is why Selena isn't safe with me. I'm not always in control. Lexington does all the horrible things to people.

I inhale a sharp breath because I know I'm lying to myself. I've done really horrible shit as Lex, too, but not to her.

Again, I'm not being truthful. I've done some shitty things to her, and I can't blame those things on the man I used to be.

The man that I *am*.

"Bunny," I say, but her panicked breaths wash my voice away. She's crying, afraid to even look at the man she invited into the truck.

I finally step into her and fist her hair to force her to look at him. "This is who I am, Selena. Unpredictable. Dangerous. If I was a fucking dog, they'd put me to sleep. The courts would have loved to give me that sentence, but I lived in a state that didn't believe in capital punishment, even though I deserved that. I still deserve that." My darkened eyes bore into hers. "What I don't deserve is you."

"This is all my fault," she says through sobs. "He died because of me."

I should tell her it's not her fault. But it is. "You're right, Selena. But it's *my* fault for letting you talk me into it. I knew the moment he sat in the truck that he wouldn't leave the cabin alive. I refuse to risk anyone else finding out about where we're staying." My words make her cry harder. "But you can't help being who you are just as much as I can't help being who I am. I'm a person capable of punishing someone for even thinking about what's mine." I shake my head. I pull the truck key from my back pocket and throw it on the table beside her. "I'm going to go take care of this. I expect you to be gone when I get back."

"Wh-what?" she stammers.

She has to leave. Everything that has happened to us since I took her has been because of me. The situations *I've* put her in. I can't keep doing this. She's not safe with me.

No one is.

"I can't create a life that is safe enough for you. It's not possible. We *can't* play house anymore, Selena. You have to leave."

"Lex—"

"Now!" I snap, loud enough to startle her. "If you're not gone by the time I get back, you won't like how I get rid of you."

Like a screw twisting into my heart, it hurts to say these things to her, but if I have to take some pain for her to be safe, so be it.

I've been through worse.

I grab the man's arms and drag him toward the back of the cabin. I look at the kid and wonder where he came from and where he was going. I wish I'd asked more about him. Maybe it would have kept me from doing what I did. But a large part of me knows it wouldn't have mattered. I still would have killed him, even if his body had a backstory attached to it. Now it's just a body that I have to get rid of because I let him inside the truck in the first place.

Because I listened to the pleas of a kind little rabbit.

Chapter Twenty-Two

Selena

Nothing about tonight should have surprised me. Lex is unpredictable. He's always been unpredictable, but he surprised me when he let Jamie watch us. It didn't surprise me when he came to his senses and killed him, though. It was a pendulum, a moment of pleasure before a man was murdered.

The back door slams, and I go to the sink to wash everything off me. My come, Lex's come, the guilt. The way I don't even think about the key on the table until I dry myself off and walk back to my discarded jeans. I put on my pants and stare at the Ford keychain.

I grab the key and button up my jeans, remembering the heat of Lex's touch. I want to leave. Well, a part of me wants to leave. The rest of me is torn. My instinct should be to run, get away from him as fast as I can, but I walk slowly, with hesitation in every step.

My instinct is dull.

Go.

Stay.

Go.

I argue within my mind. I play back everything that happened. The initial carjacking, Lex almost selling me for a piece of plastic, and Lex commanding my husband to fuck me. But I also remember when Lex killed the men for laying hands on me. I remember all the times he pushed me outside my comfort zone and made me feel better than I've ever felt. I've been so alive since the moment he got into my car and told me to drive.

I have a decision to make. And I have to make it now. I grip Lex's pistol and grab the door's handle.

Lex

I pat the mound of soil with the shovel and breathe in the humid night air. I carry the shovel back toward the cabin and try to reflect on everything. Do I want Selena to leave? Absolutely not. Do I think she should? Yes. I used to think she wasn't safe from everyone else, the other people who are poised to hurt a woman like her, but those aren't the people who've hurt her.

It's been me. Time and time again.

I abducted her. I tried to trade her for a fucking ID. I ignored every no and pushed her until it became a yes. I've made her kill for me and commit robberies. I've almost killed her on so many occasions while trying to protect her from the monsters of the world . . . but I'm the biggest monster of all.

I need her to go. She needs to escape and be a rabbit—blissful, happy, and running free. She doesn't need to be in my cage any longer. She has what she needs to survive now.

To escape the biggest predators.

I lean the shovel against the back porch and head inside the dark cabin. Before I even get to the living room, I see that the tabletop is empty. I release a breath of pained relief. She finally left. She opened her cage and escaped.

The pain in my relief comes from how fucking lost I am without her. She's been all I've known since I escaped prison. I felt things for the first time in a very long time, maybe even my entire life. I had happiness with her.

But I'm not allowed to stay happy. I don't deserve it.

While I escaped the prison for my body, I couldn't escape the prison in my mind. That's a life sentence, and I'll never have freedom from that, even as the most freeing thing lies beneath me. There's no way to turn off who I am. Even for her.

I send a fist through the wall by the back bedroom, and then another. An animalistic scream laced with the frustration I deserve to feel bursts from my throat. I thought I could let her go. When I told her to hate me in the woods, to leave me, there was a part of me that knew she wouldn't, but now she's gone, and I can't handle it.

The anguish turns into anger. Lexington rears his ugly head, trying to blame Selena for what happened. There's no one to blame but him.

Me.

All I can think about is grabbing my gun. I don't know what I'll do once I have it in my hand, but I don't want to do any of this without her. I can't.

The moment I walk through the living room, I hear the sound of the slide racking on my pistol. I turn toward the sound and see Selena behind the silver barrel, staring at me. There's a sharp breath of relief when I see her, but it's short-lived when I take in all the anger on her face. Her eyes are hard and foreign. Her lips are a tight line.

"What is this, rabbit?" I ask as she puts her finger on the trigger. This girl has never handled a gun, and I don't fear she'll willingly shoot me; I fear she'll *accidentally* shoot me while trying to puff her pretty little chest.

"I'm fucking sick of how you treat me," she snarls.

This is *not* how normal couples have this argument. But we aren't normal.

"You aren't going to shoot me, rabbit."

I go for the barrel, but she aims it away from me and pulls the trigger. I don't jump, but she's not used to hearing gunshots and nearly leaps out of her skin at the sound. Splinters of wood break away from the hole in the wall and flutter to the ground.

"You aren't a killer," I say with a laugh.

Her hands shake as she puts the gun back on me. Her finger trembles on the trigger. This girl is going to fucking shoot me in the head on accident. I can't even grab the barrel because she's so damn shaky.

"Why are you upset, Selena? Are you mad because I killed that man?"

"No!" she yells, blowing hair off her forehead in her frustration. "I'm sick of you telling me to leave! I'm tired of worrying about the next thing that happens that makes you push me away!"

I groan. "Really? You're pointing my gun at me because I told you to leave? I was just giving you the freedom you deserve."

I was willing to get on my knees with my gun because I thought she left. I'd be almost inclined to beg once I got there, if I knew it would make her stay now.

Her finger curls around the trigger, and her eyes narrow. "Do you even care about me?"

Do I? I'd kill *anyone* who hurt her, including myself. I've laid my heart out for her, even if it's not in the way she expects.

I ignore the risk and the anger and deflect the barrel upward as I step into her. I decide to bare my underbelly and try to explain why I'm not always myself.

"I'm sorry for what I did to that man. And to you. There's a battle within me to try to be good for you. It's a whole war inside me. I can't win every battle to be the good guy you sleep with. I'm not even sure which one is the true me, but I'd like to think it's the one who would never lay a hand on your pretty head. But I don't *know*, and that's why I push you away." With a heavy grip on the gun, I wait for her to drop it before I grab it and put it behind my back. I pin her against the wall, lifting her wrists above her head. Her heartbeat crashes against mine. It angered me to no end when she pulled the gun on me. It burned the blood in my veins. But on the same breath, I kind of fucking liked that she did it. She proved her little point.

I lower one of my hands from her wrist and slide it down her body, but she drops her gaze and shakes her head. "No, Lex," she says, and her weakened words prod at Lexington. He loves when she's truly prey. When she's weak. But I keep that side at bay and drop her wrists.

Everything feels so fragile, like a glass balancing on a pin. Forcing her further would knock that glass off its delicate balance.

I lean in and kiss her forehead, tasting the saltiness of her anxious sweat. "You sleep out here, and I'll go sleep in the bedroom."

We need to make this work. Somehow. Giving her space seems like the only way to do that. Everything is so raw that it will rip us both wide open if we push tonight.

Chapter Twenty-Three

Selena

I wake up in bed without Lex. Last night came to an ugly head for both of us. I had the chance to leave, and I *almost* did. I got in the truck, wrestled with the pistol in my lap, and decided to go back inside. But my anger still ripped through me, coursing through every cell in my body, and that's why I pulled his gun on him. I needed to know why he sometimes seemed like two different people. Why was he always so willing to push me away? Only he could answer that for me.

I climb out of bed and hold my sweat-soaked shirt away from my skin. I hear the water sluggishly running outside. The sound beckons me and when I walk outside, the steamy air assaults me. It grows hot so early in the day here. I follow the sound to the shower stall in the back of the house and find Lex. He's turned away from me as he washes his hair beneath the rusty showerhead. I strip my clothes off and come in behind him. He doesn't turn around at first, his demeanor as cold as the water raining down on me.

"Lex?" I whisper. He puts his hands on the grime-coated wall. I reach around his slick body and rub a hand over his healing stab wound.

"I was a mess when I thought you were gone," he says. His words make me shiver more than the cold water. "I didn't want to live without you, bunny." He finally turns toward me. Water drips from his nose and slides past his full lips. "I'll stop pushing you away if you're sure you can deal with the half of me I *try* to keep from you."

I lean into his broad chest. "Maybe you should stop keeping it from me. I can handle all of you, Lex. I'm not afraid of *you*. The person you become when you try to fight yourself is the one I fear. It's this neck-breaking pendulum of emotions. It's even more erratic when you try to make sense of that part of you. Even if there were a hundred dead bodies around us, I'd love you. Yeah, I was upset when you killed that man, and I felt a lot of guilt, but I wasn't surprised. I expect you to kill a man who thinks about touching me. I knew a clock was ticking above his head. What I don't expect is for you to push me away every time. Like you say to me, stop running from what you are. What you're capable of." I look up at him, blinking away the water as it wets my hair. "I accept all of you, Lexington."

"How, Selena?" He tugs me into him. "How do I deserve you after hurting as many people as I have? After all the times I hurt you? That's what I couldn't figure out yesterday. After everything I've done to you, you still *want* to stay with me. Someone like me doesn't deserve someone so fucking forgiving."

Lex

Selena cleans up and gets out of the shower. She hates the cold water. I stay beneath it for a while longer, reflecting on everything that happened. I stay there until it becomes too much to bear.

I turn off the water and step into the sun. Its powerful rays warm my skin almost immediately. I grab the pair of jeans I set out and pull them on, letting the sun kiss my skin a little longer before heading back inside.

Selena is sitting on the couch in front of a fan, dressed in a pair of black shorts and a cami. Sweat beads on her forehead. I smirk. She doesn't like the cold or the heat. She's a picky little rabbit. She gets off the recliner and steps into me. I wrap my arms around her and forget all that happened between us last night. It's as if we never extinguished someone's life.

Selena is fucking insane for wanting to stay with me, but she's not stupid. Of all the things she is—a little spoiled, stubborn, and bratty—she's not dumb. I need to accept that she's crazy enough to risk her life to be mine. She understands I could hurt her one day. I have to accept that she's unconditionally mine, even when I murder a man for thinking of her.

I lean down and kiss her, tasting the salt of sweat on her lips. I brush her nipples through the thin material of her cami. She shivers at my touch. I grip both sides of her head as I kiss her, and there's not a hint of fear in her, even after she's seen what I've done with nothing more than these two hands.

She moans against my mouth.

"Oh, bunny," I growl, stepping deeper into her and gripping her perfect ass. I hook my fingers into the waistband of her shorts and tug them down. The moment I expose her pale skin, I grow rabid. I'm hungry for her in a way this freedom allows me to be. The freedom we worked so fucking hard for. It's been a long time since I've felt free in any way, even before I got locked up.

I pull off her cami. Her perfect tits relax and spread, and my mouth waters for them.

She pushes me down on the bed. Well, I *let* her push me down. She climbs over my lap, straddling my waist. I grip her hips and move her bare skin along my fly, letting her leave a trail of wetness on my jeans. She moans at the friction.

Her hands reach for my zipper, and I love how her hunger comes through the motions of her fingertips. When I met Selena, she wouldn't have put her hand on me like this or taken charge of her pleasure. I like when my little rabbit becomes a predator when it comes to getting what she wants, especially when she wants my cock.

She pulls my cock from my jeans and when she lowers herself, I feel the end of her. Her absolute limit. She gives me all of her body, just like she always has, as if last night never happened. As if I hadn't killed a man and she hadn't pulled my gun on me.

"Good girl, bunny," I groan as I drop my head back and let myself feel the weight of her on my lap. I listen to her growing moans. We've made love and basked in each other's pleasure so few times.

Her body gleams with sweat as she rides me. She forgets how much she hates the heat when it's me that warms her. Her hands drop to my chest, and she grinds on my lap. I grip her nipples and make her whimper as I squeeze. I pull her chest to mine and kiss her. She spasms around me, squeezing the base of my dick. I pull out so she can tense around my swollen head. I groan and let her pleasure please me. She feels incredible, even once her pussy relaxes and stretches around me.

"God, bunny," I growl. "I can't get enough of your pussy. Can't get enough of you."

"Lexington," she groans.

I look up at her and fight the flicker of frustration as she says my full name again. I don't want him to come and change how I'm fucking her. How she's fucking me. I don't want him to come and fuck her selfishly when I want *her* to be selfish as she chases her orgasm.

There's a darkness that creeps over her expression, completing the transformation into my little wolf with my cock deep inside her.

"Have you ever been spit on?" she asks, a sly grin on her face as she leans forward and rocks on my lap.

Oh, rabbit. "Not the way you're thinking," I say.

"Open your mouth."

I consider shaking my head and telling her no. I'm not into that. I'd spit on her pretty face, in her mouth, on her perfect little cunt, but I'd never considered taking her spit.

But I'll do anything for her, and if she wants to spit in my mouth, I'll let her.

I put my hand behind her neck and drag her toward my mouth. Her lips are so close to mine. I spread my lips and wait for her move. Selena pouts and releases a slow and sensual mouthful of spit that hits my tongue.

Fuck. I didn't think I was into that, but the moment her spit lands in my mouth and she raises herself to ride me, I'm done for.

I pull her down and kiss her again, with our spit still mixing together. I grab her hip with one hand as I coach her movement until she makes me come.

"Dirty fucking rabbit," I growl as I come inside her, filling her as deeply as I can. She doesn't climb off me, not even as my come drips down my shaft and pools on my pelvis. Her hips just rock and coat her pussy in it.

I lift my hip and lay her on her back once more. She kisses me. Someone like her shouldn't let someone like me inside her, let alone allow me to fill her up as much as I have. I've made her take every drop of me since the first time I fucked her.

I pull out of her, and my come drips from her, covering every arch of her perfect pussy. I push her legs apart. "Keep them spread for me," I tell her. Her inner thighs shine with silky cream. "God, I love seeing my come dripping from you. Such a sweet-faced little bunny who has no fucking idea what she's gotten herself into." I run my hand up her thigh, cleaning my come off her skin. "Or maybe you know exactly what you got yourself into and you just don't care."

I push my come back inside her as I lean over and kiss her. I fuck her with my fingers, and the wet sound of our come is like music to my ears. When more drips from her, I drop between her legs and give her a long lick to clean her up. She moans and fists my hair as I curl my tongue and catch every drop.

I sit up and fist her hair, tugging her up until her lips part against the pressure. I spit into her mouth, making her take the last bit of us—our spit *and* our come. She moans and swallows with a bite of her lower lip.

She'll always take everything I give her.

"I love you, Lex," she pants against my mouth as I shove my fingers deep inside her. She releases a moan, and I chase her words with the tips of my fingers. Her chest rises to meet mine.

I've never said I love you to anyone. It feels unnatural. Too foreign. It's a concept I can't wrap my mind around. I don't understand the word or how it came from her husband's mouth so easily when he clearly didn't love her. How can it matter so much and so little from one person to another? I pull away from her mouth, and the words stick in my throat. I *want* to say it to her—I'm full of that feeling for her—but it's just not as easy for me to say them. I try to show her how I feel, but for a woman like Selena, that will never be enough. She needs to hear it from me, and I'm trying.

I swallow hard. It's as if I am preparing to speak a new language for the first time in front of a room of people. I'll never understand how natural it is for her, how it just rolls off her tongue without a hint of hesitation, especially after everything I've done to her and everything she's witnessed.

I wrap one hand behind her neck and lift her toward my lips. I pull my fingers out of her and put them in her mouth. She takes my come-coated fingers and swallows them whole. God, if that isn't love, I don't know what is.

"I love you, bunny," I let the words roll from my lips and drip into her mouth.

If anyone had told me the scared young thing I carjacked at gunpoint would be the sexy, strong woman beneath me who just spit in my goddamn mouth, I wouldn't have believed them. Not her. Not the sweet little bunny. Now I know what she really is and that she's right where she needs to be.

With me.

Epilogue

Selena

I get into the shower, tugging the old shower curtain across the rusty metal rod. I'll never get used to showering in cold water outside. No matter how cold the water is, my heart is warm because Lex will come in to heat me up.

The curtain moves across the rod, and he's in front of me. Naked already, moonlight illuminates his bare skin. We've been on our own, living away from the confines of our old lives for almost a year now. No matter how long we've been away from it all, my heart still stumbles the moment I see him.

He steps in the small shower, embracing me in his strong arms. "Little rabbit," he growls. Somehow, he never reacts to the cold water, his expression stoic as the frigid droplets rain down on him. My lungs still tighten, shriveling in my chest until my skin becomes numb to the icy fingertips of the water.

Life with Lex is so different from life with my husband. My ex-husband. Gold woven sheets have become cheap swaths of aged fabric we get from the thrift store. Fancy pantsuits have become cotton shirts and denims on sale. Expensive home-cooked meals have been replaced by whatever we get on our runs to the general store on the outskirts of the park, where the sweet little owner knows us as Mr. and Mrs. Gurgen Hoffe. Instead of dining out at lavish restaurants, we visit my favorite diner, where half the time I leave pleased with more than just the food in my belly.

Lex's hands leave my body and brush the hair from my face. When his eyes drop to mine, they darken, and my skin pebbles from more than just the cold water. I keep still, like the moment a rabbit freezes and hopes the predator doesn't see them.

He leans into me, drawing his lips close to the shell of my ear. Seduction drips off him like the water droplets from above our heads. "I want to chase you, sweet bunny," he says, low and smooth.

I know he does. I can tell from the way his muscles tense in his upper body. Despite her desperate attempts to freeze, he's spotted the rabbit. He'll chase me until I'm covered in dirt, leaves, and sweat. Or in our come.

"Run," he growls, deep and threatening.

I know who's out to play, and I welcome him.

Lexington.

Lex

The rabbit scurries off. I nearly lost her by trying to protect her from the darker side of me, so I force myself to stop holding him back. I give in to the unhinged side she loves as much as me, just in a different way.

Selena isn't afraid of Lexington. Even after all she's seen, all she knows, she still likes to call to him while on her knees, as if he won't come out to fuck her throat until she cries.

This side of me courses through my blood like poison. He likes to tell her to run so we can chase her. Whoever catches her decides how she'll be fucked. If Lexington catches her, she's taken rough and hard. If I catch her, we make love until we're covered in mud, leaves, and come.

Losing control has always been easy for me, and she knows that. There's a trail of a bloody past that proves it. For me, keeping control is much harder. And I do try . . . for her. When I fail and the beast inside me roars for her, she doesn't fear me, even when she should. She always takes everything I give her like the good fucking girl she is.

The way she always has.

She used to tell me I never took her from heaven to implant her in hell. She lived among the flames long before she met me. And it's true. But there's something so goddamn innocent about her. It's in the way she laughs as we fall into a habit of game nights instead of robberies or murders. Or when she asks me to explore more of her body in new and exciting ways. She trusts me with every part of her body and, most importantly, her heart.

I'll always say I don't deserve this. Because I don't. Someone like me doesn't deserve someone like her. From hell or heaven, whether fallen or not, she's an angel. She saved me as much as she saved herself.

I know the life I provide her is so different from what she's used to. It isn't fancy, but it's freedom. I'm free from the confines of prison, and she's free from the hell she once called home.

Studies have shown that sociopaths struggle with attaching to anyone. And I truly never have. I've never *wanted* to. Until her. But they also say that one sociopath could potentially form a bond with a like-minded person. So what does that say about Selena?

She's broken through decades of antisocial and homicidal behavior. She worked her way through the layers of me that psychologists never could. She confronted my past and lived to tell about it. She meets my demons head on with her own, which makes me certain she's so much more than I can ever begin to understand.

Maybe there's not much more to understand.

Maybe she's just as dangerous as me, and my kind of crazy loves hers.

And I wouldn't have it any other way.

I yell into the stiff and silent night. "Ready or not, rabbit, here I come!"

Along for the Ride

M/F/M Why-Choose Dark Romance

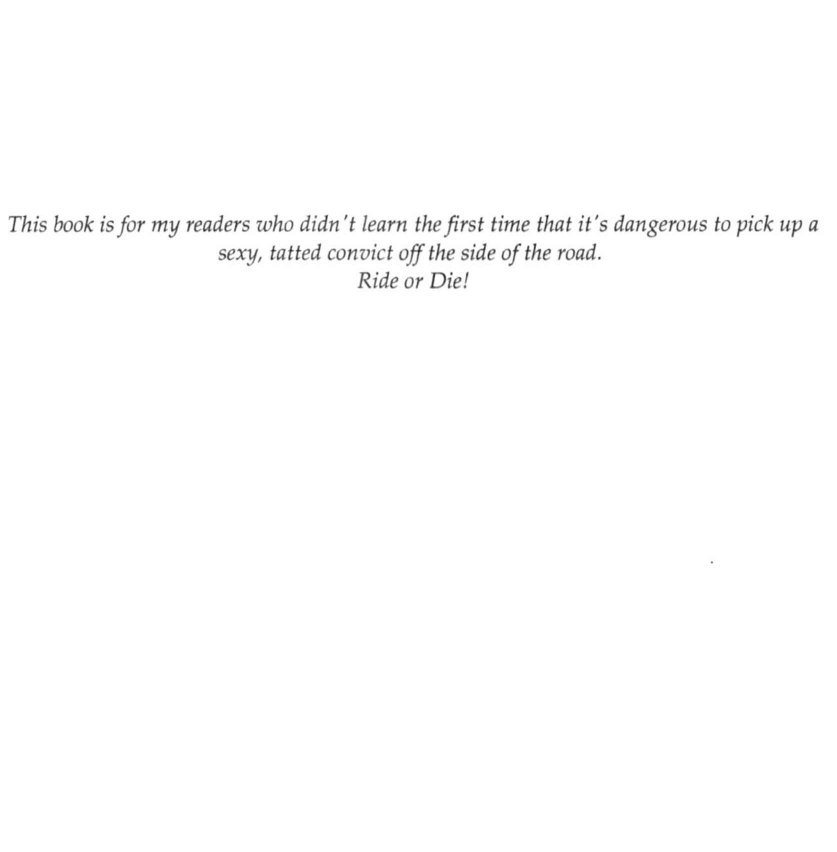

This book is for my readers who didn't learn the first time that it's dangerous to pick up a sexy, tatted convict off the side of the road.
Ride or Die!

Prologue

I trudge toward my front door with blood-covered hands and the whisper of a headache behind my bloodshot eyes. I'm exhausted after this hit, and all I want to do is crawl into bed and sleep for a week. This one was a real fighter.

When I get to the door, I stop at the unlocked knob and my breath catches. In my field of employment, you can't help but worry about bringing your work home. Not figuratively, but literally. Eye for an eye. Life for a life.

I don't have kids to worry about, but I have a wife that I care for at least a little. If she died in a car accident, I'd be a bit sad—I like her enough to possibly even miss her—but if she dies because of a revenge hit, I'd feel fucking guilty.

I draw my gun, wrapping my fingers around the grip as I push open the door. Muffled sounds penetrate the silence, and my mind shifts from murder to torture. If someone is in there torturing what belongs to me, they'll get the same in return. I raise the gun and step from the dark living room. The bright fluorescent lights above the kitchen reveal something far worse than someone torturing my wife.

She's bent over the kitchen table, a man standing behind her and thrusting into her.

Worse?

The man thrusting behind her is my fucking brother.

It's almost like watching myself fucking my wife. If I was a few inches shorter with a lot less muscle, that is. We share the same dark hair, dark eyes, and thirst for blood. We've been partners in the business for years, and while he's always had a screw loose, he's been the only person I could trust with my life.

Until now.

A blaze of red sweeps across my eyes. Never have I seen such a hue. It heats the blood in my veins until I feel like I'm burning. My focus is less on the hard, rhythmic thrusts of Karson's hips and more on the loose moan that leaves her lips. A sound I haven't heard in quite some time.

I holster my gun before I make a loud fucking mistake.

My shadow sweeps over them as I take a step forward, and Karson's eyes widen in surprise. He pulls out of my wife, forcing her forward when his hand leaves her chest.

"G!" he yells. "It's not what it looks like!" He looks down at his dick and zips up his pants. "Well, it is, but it's not what you think!" His tightening throat struggles to push the words through his quivering vocal cords because he knows I'm a fraction of a second away from blowing his head off.

"Honey," my wife says as she pulls her dress down and reaches out for me.

"Fucking don't," I snarl, pushing her to the ground. She hits the tile floor with a squeal and smacks against the cabinets. I throw Karson against the wall, the shelf of spices falling and crashing to my feet. "My wife, Karson? Really?" I lean my weight into him, cutting his oxygen off as my hands wrap around his neck. I envision killing him in twenty different ways, each one more painful than the last.

"Wait, let me explain!" he chokes out as his hand wraps around my wrist. He gasps in front of me. I consider letting him, but what could he possibly say? What could his fucking excuse possibly be? Something darkens his eyes, and I loosen my grip. "She's cheating on you!"

"Clearly," I snap. What a bright observation.

Karson coughs. "No! Well, yes. But I mean before me."

"Explain what the fuck you're talking about, and do it before I lose my fucking temper more than I already have."

"Don't listen to him!" my wife yells from the floor.

"Fuck you," I say toward her. I turn my attention back to my brother. He better have a really good excuse or I'm burying them both in some shallow grave somewhere.

"Paulina has been fucking around on you for months. I was here for one thing." He lifts his shirt to expose his favorite blade on his hip. "To kill her for you."

"Did you trip and fall into her, dick first? What part of killing her involved doing this?" I motion between them with the gun. Paulina lets out a squeal and covers her cheating fucking face. "Do you even have proof that she was cheating, Karson? Do you?"

My eyes narrow on him. The one thing he came for didn't involve bending my wife over my goddamn kitchen table. I don't believe him anyway. Karson will say anything to save his own ass. I tighten my grip on his neck until his face reddens above my grasp. He reaches for his knife, and I let him go long enough to rip it away and shove it down the back of my pants.

"I thought it would be fun to slit her throat while I was fucking her. I swear it was just meant to be payback, Gentry! If you don't believe me, look at her phone!" he pants.

I release him and turn toward the counter. My wife crawls to her knees and leaps for the device, but my arm swings back and rockets toward her face before she can reach it. Maybe she has something to hide after all.

I scroll through her phone, looking through her text messages first. My jaw muscles tighten into writhing knots with each lewd message I read. With each picture exchanged. Nights memorialized in graphic detail. There are even exchanges between her and Karson. In his last message, he tells her he's going to come by and "take care" of her. Maybe he meant to kill her, but he didn't have to fuck her first.

White-hot rage fills me, and I draw his knife from behind me and lift Paulina by her hair.

"Please don't," she begs. "I got lonely, Gentry. Sometimes you're gone for weeks at a time, and I don't hear from you for days."

She doesn't know much about what I do for work, but she knows enough to understand why I can't chat on the goddamn phone when I'm preparing for what I need to do. I've never been the type for goodnight texts or daily check-ins. I'm not a fucking lover boy. I'm a hard ass, and I've been a hard ass since the day she met me. She's the one who said she loved me, regardless of my tough exterior, and I'm not the one who changed. I'm not the one who stepped out of our marriage.

"Fucking whore!" I scream before burying the blade in her chest and twisting.

A look of shocked betrayal crosses her expression, which is ironic since she's the Judas. Right alongside my brother. Her eyes focus ahead of her, somewhere beyond me, and I drop her lifeless body to the floor. I rip the blade from her chest and turn its crimson tip toward my brother. Anger boils over and spills from me in waves.

"Did you have to fuck her first, Karson?"

He shrugs. Just fucking shrugs in the most Karson-esque way.

Deep down in his fucked-up heart, he thought he was helping me. But he's a selfish fucking man. Karson does absolutely nothing unless he gets something out of it.

I step closer and throw my weight into him again. "Fuck you too," I growl. "Fuck both of you."

As much as I want to drive the knife into his chest, I can't do it. We didn't end up as murder-obsessed contract killers because we had happy childhoods filled with family dinners and trauma-free game nights. We've been through hell together, and Karson came out worse than I did. In his fucked-up way, I believe he was trying to do something for his older brother, and that's why I let him live. That's why I push the blade's handle against his chest until he takes it.

Because we're all we have at the end of the day, and nothing will come between us.

Leana

Diesel exhaust fills my lungs. If I cough too hard near an open flame, I'll probably start a wildfire. Bus stops aren't clean places, but they're where girls like me end up.

Girls who flee from broken homes.

Girls whose mothers don't believe them when they say their stepfather does unspeakable things to them.

I couldn't stay in that house. My eighteenth birthday was fast approaching, so they also couldn't make me stay. When I packed a bag and slammed the front door behind me, no one followed. No missing person reports were filed, either. I wasn't missing. I was forgotten. I took one bus after another until I ran out of money and found myself on the other end of the country.

New York. The land of opportunity.

I've been here a week, and so far it's more like the land where dreams go to die. I'm part of a homeless community that sticks near this bus station. Sometimes a few of the workers take pity on us and allow us to clean up in the bathroom, but only if we aren't stumbling drunk or strung out on drugs. I don't touch either.

I won't lie and say I'm not tempted. When I see that faraway look in Greasy Tom's eyes after he snorts a line or the deep sleep Chicken Wing slips into after shooting up, I crave that same escape. For a few hours, they aren't homeless and hungry and dirty and lost. They're gone, exploring some place in their mind that doesn't involve whatever hell brought them here.

Yeah, I'd probably try it if any of them offered.

But they don't. I've stayed clean and enjoyed the bathroom privileges a few times this week. It's a fair exchange, I guess, but it's still not enough. Something has to change.

I've thought about becoming a sex worker, but I haven't even been propositioned since arriving. I'm no blonde goddess, but I'm somewhat offended that no one has asked how much for a handy or a quick trip to the Red Room Inn down the street. I'd probably blow the first guy who asked if it meant spending an entire night in a bed. I wouldn't even mind getting roughed up a bit. It would beat the fuck out of the sweet love making all the high school boys wanted to do. Bonus points if it's consensual.

"You need help, miss?" says a dark, smooth voice beside me. I turn my head and lock eyes with a handsome man. He's tall, broad, and his tousled brown hair gives him a messy no-fucks-given look. He sits beside me, reaches toward my face, and tucks a strand of my blonde hair behind my ear, licking his lips as he meets my blue eyes again. "Too pretty of a girl to be out here on the streets," he whispers.

What does a pretty boy like him know about life out here?

He unzips his jacket, and his hand disappears into an interior pocket. When he pulls out a little baggie with a round pill, I can look at nothing else. It's as if he read my inner thoughts, as if he knows how much I'm craving an escape. My fingers move toward the bag, but he pulls it just out of reach.

"Ah, ah," he scolds. "What would you do for something to take the edge off?"

Anything. I'd do fucking anything.

"What do you want?" I ask, but I find the answer by looking down at the mass straining against his zipper.

"Come to my car and show me what you're willing to trade for a fix." He leans into me and runs his thumb along my jaw. "Show me how little you respect yourself."

I've spent my whole life respecting myself. Hell, my self-respect is what caused such a rift between me and my mother. But I can let that go. It hasn't gotten me anywhere good so far.

I lean on him as we walk toward the parking lot. He pulls his keys from his pocket when we reach a black Mercedes, and my eyes go wide. This car, with its black leather interior and the perfume of opulence, is the most expensive thing I've ever touched. It's about to be the most expensive place I've ever fucked, because he opens the back door and lets me get inside. When he follows me, I abandon what little dignity I have left as he takes the pill out and puts it into his mouth. He leans in and kisses me, slipping it onto my tongue. The moment I swallow, his hand loops behind my head, fists my hair, and pulls me down to his lap.

"Maybe I'll take you off these streets, baby," he says through a frustrated groan. "Make you my pretty little project. But first, show me what you can do with your mouth."

Maybe New York won't be so bad after all.

Chapter One

Six Years Later

Gentry

I've been a free man for one week, but I thought about my brother every day during my prison stay. It wasn't my wife's murder that put me away. We called in a favor from George, our handler, and he had his clean-up crew take care of the mess. With no one to miss her—aside from the men who'd been dicking her down—we got away clean. What landed me in prison was a case of bad timing and empty pockets.

Hitmen are usually paid well for their services, but my brother and I weren't typical hitmen. Instead of working for a large payout, we worked for a gamble. The buyer paid George, George gave us the details, and we got to take whatever we wanted from the scene. Leaving out the bank transfers meant no paper trail, and George had a team that scrubbed scenes for us, so it usually felt like a fair trade. We got to kill—which we thoroughly enjoyed—and didn't have to worry about what happened later. This arrangement didn't always work in our favor, though. Our last two hits had been cash poor, which meant we were cash poor as well. We needed money, so Karson and I thought we'd harken back to our teenage years and do a quick robbery.

That quick robbery turned into six long years in a cell for me.

I can still hear the sound of Karson's voice as he sat in a wooden box and sang like a canary to cover his own ass. I encouraged him to do it, but it still fucking sucked. He's never been right in the head, and serving time in a cage would have resulted in an implosion of his mind. I still hadn't forgiven him for fucking my wife, but I had to protect him.

We'd been killing together long before it became a job, when it was just for sport and didn't matter who got caught in the crossfire. We were called the "Kursed" brothers. It was a play on our last name—Kursicki—coupled with the fact that the people around us always seemed to disappear.

We used to actually enjoy each other's company.

Before.

Before I walked in on him fucking my wife and we split our business. I didn't trust him, and trust was imperative in a business such as ours. I never thought there'd be a day when we had to go on separate paths. Or a day when I began to hate the work I was born to do. *Everything* began to piss me off, and it all centered on Karson and his shit behavior. He'd drag anyone to hell with him as long as he had someone to keep him company. That's why we no longer spoke, and I planned to keep it that way.

Most men in our business lived lonely lives, anyway. A duo was unheard of. Like grizzlies in the forest, we make contact to get laid or make a kill. You don't see us until it's too late.

Our way of thinking is unique, and I've only met one man whose brain worked like mine and Karson's. He was my brief cellmate, Lexington Rowe. Big, but not quite as wide as me, with prison tattoos covering his body. Ten tally marks in his flesh counted every year he was inside, but he'd have a lot more by the time he was done serving his lifetimes in prison. The first night I bunked with him, he broke my hand for touching his bed, and I went out of my way to break his nose in retaliation. We were *almost* friends after that, or as close to friends as people with our mindset can get. I remember when he came back to the cell after he committed an inter-prison homicide.

"What'd you do, Lex?" I asked when he returned from solitary.

"Good old-fashioned payback," he said.

"Violence isn't the answer."

He dropped onto the mattress beneath my bunk and grunted. "Violence is always the answer."

I've never felt such a close understanding like that with anyone besides my brother. Someone who understood that murder is as mundane as brushing your teeth in the morning. It's just something you did.

Then he escaped, and I had to serve the rest of my time with people who had mild homicidal tendencies, not a constant propensity for it. That's why it hurts that Karson and I are so estranged. Because no one knows evil like someone possessed by the same devil. But someone that close can hurt you more than anyone else, and I won't give him the opportunity to shit on me again.

My phone vibrates in my pocket. I pull it out and see a familiar name on the screen.

"Hello?"

"Gentry, you ready for a job, or are you still settling in?" George asks.

I've been living on stashed cash since I got out, and the small stack has dwindled to nearly nothing. Work sounds pretty good right about now. "I'm ready," I say, "but I need a guaranteed payout."

"How about several?"

I run my hand through my beard and consider this. Multiple close-to-home hits right after getting out of jail? Doesn't seem smart. "I can do one, but not several. I don't think it's a good idea to work too close to home right now."

"I don't pay you to think," George says with a dry laugh. He should lay off the cigarettes.

"You don't pay me at all," I say.

"Fair enough, but leave the thinking to me all the same. I've already got it planned out. You and your brother are gonna take a little road trip. You'll find a van and your gear at—"

"I don't work with Karson anymore."

George laughs, and the sound rakes across every raw nerve in my body. "You don't have a choice. He botched a hit, Gentry. It happened a few weeks before you got out, but it's not looking good for him."

"He got himself into this, and he'll have to get himself out of it." I won't go out of my way for a man who pushed me out of his.

"I don't think you understand. Either you take him with you and keep him on a short leash or we'll hang him from one."

George's tone has sobered, so he means business. Karson's in deep shit, and now I have to let him sink or wade through it and pull him out. Fuck.

"Fine, I'll take him with me." What could go fucking wrong?

We could end up on the wrong side of a hit list because of Karson, that's what. And I'll have no one to blame but myself for letting him worm back into my life. I don't have a choice, though. He's an asshole, a liability, a snake, and a major piece of shit.

But he's also my brother.

I get the details for the first hit and finish up the conversation. With a sigh and a death grip on my phone, I dial Karson's number. He answers on the first ring.

"Hey, G," he says. "Since we still aren't speaking, I can only assume you're calling about my impending demise." He follows his sentence with laughter, then crunching as he snacks on whatever the fuck he's eating.

"You heard?"

"Nah, but I know it's coming. It cost George a lot of money to fix that job. I shouldn't have played so much, but I just couldn't help myself." *Crunch.* The sound makes my eye twitch. How can he discuss his death so coolly while eating the loudest snack known to man? I don't think Karson will ever take anything seriously. Not my life and not his own. "What will you say at my funeral, G? You'll probably need a closed casket for what they plan to do to my face."

"For fuck's sake, Karson. I'm calling to offer you an out."

Aside from the non-stop chewing, he's silent.

"Come work with me, and they'll let you live . . . probably."

"Work for you? *Under* you? No thanks. I'll turn myself in to his firing squad before I work under you again. I've been doing fine on my own."

"Clearly. Have a good life, or what's left of it." I pull the phone away from my ear to hang up.

"Wait, *wait!*" he screams, loud enough for it to sound like he's on speakerphone. I put the phone to my ear. "Fine, I'll do it." Somehow he says it like he's agreeing to do *me* a favor. How he twists shit around in his mind is beyond me. Trust me, he is doing me no favors.

I give him the details and tell him to meet at my place in a few days.

The Kursed brothers are back in business.

Leana

I throw clothes into a bag, but before I slide the strap over my shoulder, I freeze. Just like the time before this and the time before that, I can't complete the motions. I can't leave. My body rebels, begging for more drugs before my most recent hit has even left my system. Mickey is a fucking asshole, but he deals narcotics like candy, and those are my friends.

I rub a hand down old track marks on my arm and think about when Mickey met me for the first time outside that bus station. He took me in. Fed me. Drugged me up and made me his. The chains on my wrists and ankles are invisible, but they still bind me in place.

My hand goes to other marks on my skin. Bruises that are still tender beneath my shaking fingertips. A scar near the base of my skull from the first time I told Mickey no. If I leave and the withdrawal doesn't kill me, he will.

I abandon the bag and kick it beneath the bed, going to the dresser instead. Tucked inside the top drawer is my meager stash of pills. I obsessively count them out. The dwindling number gives me anxiety, but asking for more will ensure another beating. The drugs are worth it, though. And besides, there's no pain they don't ease.

I dry swallow one of the pills and await the liftoff I crave. When it kicks in, each cell in my body will become weightless until I float above everything. I lie down, waiting for the release to set in. Just as I'm drifting toward peace, the bedroom door opens with a creak that tightens my stomach. I don't bother opening my eyes. I know who's stepping closer. I know who's standing over me, probably looking down at me like I'm an inconvenient shit stain on the sole of his shoe.

"You look like shit," he says as he rips off his grease-covered clothes.

I open my eyes as he tosses them at me, but I'm too far gone to catch them before they collide with my face. The powerful scent of sweat, gasoline, and oil suffocates me.

He scoffs and shakes his head. "High, too, I see."

His words mock me, but I'm the monster he created, chained to him by an addiction that freezes me in place at the thought of escape.

I've thought about contacting my mother and begging for help, but I'd rather remain in my current situation than apologize for telling the truth about what her pedo husband did to me. Though I've packed a bag and tried to gather the courage to brave the streets on my own, that isn't an option either. I don't have a car, and Mickey would find me if I'm on foot. He has connections all over this city, and the homeless are some of his best clients. Most of them would rat me out for a fix without thinking twice.

"Wash my fucking clothes," Mickey says as he pulls a cigarette from his discarded jeans. He lights it and the smoke sends another craving crawling through my bones.

"Can I have one?" I ask.

His hand strikes out like a coiled snake and winds into my hair, pulling the roots until I whimper. He forces my face into the pile of dirty clothes, and I keep as still as I can. "You lay in the fucking house all day and get high, and you want a fucking smoke? You have to earn it. Wash my fucking clothes, cook my fucking dinner, suck my fucking dick, and don't ask for a goddamn thing until it's done."

When he releases my hair, I gather his clothes from the bed and the bathroom and head for the laundry room downstairs. I know what sort of mood he's in today, and I need to stay out of his way. Even if I do everything he's commanded, there will be no cigarette. I'll be grateful if he allows me to eat any of the dinner I'll prepare.

On my way down the hall, one of his dealer buddies grips my arm and stops my one-track journey. "When you gonna come hang with us instead, Lee," he says, his eyes darting from bruise to bruise like a silver ball in a pinball machine. This act is meant to show he's sympathetic to my situation, but he's no better than Mickey. In some ways, he's worse. His girls don't have bruises on their skin, but that's only because he doesn't want to damage the merchandise.

I pull my hand from his grasp. "No thank you," I whisper.

Even if I somehow wanted to belong in some weird, doped-up harem, Mickey would find me and make sure the saying "if I can't have you, no one can" rings true. Being the sole recipient of someone's affection isn't much better, but better the devil I know than the devil I don't know.

I reach the laundry room and warm air rushes toward me when I open the glass door. I close my eyes and suck in a deep breath of dryer-sheet-scented air. If I block out the sound of a crying child and a woman yelling for it to shut up, I can almost imagine myself back in my childhood. Back when my mother would wash clothes every Monday and I would help her fold the towels. Back before she married a sick fuck. But those are distant memories that feel like they happened to someone else. I feel as if I've been a beaten junkie far longer than I was a child.

I throw his dirty clothes in the wash and slam the lid. Even through the haze of my high, my emotions are stirring and I can't hold them back. I drop to the ground, press my back against the machine, and cry.

I hate crying. It's seen as a sign of weakness, but this is me trying to be strong when I don't have the courage to face my fears and leave. I swipe the tears from my cheeks and make a promise to myself.

I'll get out. I'll get away.

Maybe not today, but soon.

Chapter Two

Karson

I'm not happy about this. Working alongside my brother is not what I had in mind. We agreed to go our separate ways, and I did fine while he was in prison. Well, until I got a little overzealous during a kill and made a mess. Our boss doesn't like any messes.

Gentry didn't need to swoop in and save me from the repercussions of fucking up so royally, though. He's not my hero. I'd have figured it out or died like the fuck up I am. Death doesn't seem like such a terrible outcome for me. I'd probably come before my last breath.

He must feel like he owes me for that one time I saved his ass when we were much younger. He made a rookie mistake and the cops came knocking, asking him where he was that night. He hesitated, but before a guilty look could cross his face, I told them he'd been with me all night and there was absolutely no way he threw some dude in a ravine after stabbing him twenty-five times with a dull knife. Maybe he doesn't realize I did it to keep the cops from finding *my* bodies. I was covering my ass as much as his, so he doesn't owe me shit.

But here we are, back to a joint business. No other job lets people like us do the things we like to do. That we have an inherent need to do. A genetic propensity toward murder that can't be sated while working a typical nine-to-five job.

Things feel different this time, though, and it's not a good change. Gentry's never been a friendly guy, but now he's a miserable prick who answers in grunts and nods instead of speaking to me. No one is as tightly wound as he is, with an asshole so puckered that it changes his gait when he walks, but it's worse than ever now. At least I can still enjoy one of my favorite pastimes—annoying the piss out of him. Bugging him gives me great joy.

What doesn't give me great joy is having to work under him again. Before he went to prison, I didn't mind it so much, but that was before I had a taste of doing things my way. He wants clean kills, in and out without much fuss or fanfare, and I want to play. The muzzle he slaps over my face stops me from getting too out of hand. I can't toy with my prey when Gentry's holding my leash. I'm a wild and unhinged thing, and like any wild thing, he has to cut me loose sometimes.

Maybe I'll remind him of that after we finish this hit. For now, I'll let him take the lead.

Gentry

A squelch echoes in the silent room as I pull out the knife. I decided to go old school with this jackass. Karson sits on the balcony railing, digging at his nails with his pocketknife.

"A little help?" I call to him as I wipe the blade of my knife on a rag before pocketing it.

"You're doing great all on your own," he says with a quick tilt of his head.

I wipe my brow. "Get your ass out here before I push you off that balcony. *Lazy piece of shit.*" I whisper the last bit. My little brother is a pain in the ass. He's always been a risk I stuck my neck out for, but I'm beginning to regret taking him under my wing to try to keep his stupid ass alive.

Karson slides off the smooth metal railing, letting his boots hit the concrete with a dramatic thud. He puts out the cigarette in the palm of his hand and pockets it. His dark eyes match mine as he shoulders me when he walks by.

"I can denounce responsibility for you at any time, you know," I remind him.

He scoffs at me and slips a pair of black leather gloves over his hands so we can hunt for our payday. Our official job is to kill our target, but the unofficial job is to take any cash or valuables we can find before their bratty little relatives get their grimy hands on it. Skim off some of the generational wealth for ourselves since we sure as fuck never had any.

Karson and I were poor as shit growing up, but it made us better killers. It was either take what you want or do without, and we got sick of doing without real quick. We're also a match made in mental health hell. I'm the psychopath with the antisocial personality, and Karson is more the sociopath. Or do I have it reversed? It's been two decades since we received our official diagnoses, so I don't remember. Either way, we're both exponentially fucked in the head.

We search drawers, cabinets, and safes, taking as much as we can and stuffing it into a duffel bag. While we're mostly searching for untraceable cash, we'll nab the occasional jewelry box to toss over the side of a bridge in the next town over because we're assholes like that. Selling shit on the street or in a pawnshop isn't an option. That's how idiots get caught, and I refuse to go back to prison. I'm fairly certain my brother shares the sentiment.

Karson comes out of the bedroom with a fat wad of bills fanned between his hands. "This dude's got enough to make it rain," he says as he flicks the bills in my face like I'm his personal dancer. As they spin in the air and fall to the ground, I swear to god he'll be the next dead man if he doesn't quit it.

"Are you being serious right now?" I snarl as I rip the money from his hands and throw it in my bag.

"As serious as murder."

I hate him.

He turns and walks beside the wall, his hand dragging along the cold marble until he stops in front of a row of pictures. "Look at his little grandkids," Karson coos. He smirks and flicks his fingers toward the frame, sending it to the floor in a puddle of broken glass and bent metal. He continues his path of destruction, knocking every frame off one by one and humming a cheery tune. When he reaches an intricate, very expensive-looking vase, he stops and goes silent. He picks it up, rubbing a finger along the blue paisley pattern before unzipping his jeans and tugging his limp dick from his boxers. As he strokes himself until he's hard, he tosses a devilish smile my way.

I should turn away, but he's a goddamn car crash and my eyes are glued to the scene. "Jesus, must you?" I ask.

Karson leans back on the balls of his feet, his hand working faster until he comes in the vase with a satisfied groan.

"Is this how you've been operating since I've been gone? It's a wonder you haven't been caught. They'll get your DNA off that, dumbass."

He goes to put it down.

"Ah, ah, you gotta bring your jizz jug with us."

Karson's lips pull into a frown as he shoves the vase beneath his arm, and I'm struck by how similar we look. Aside from the eight-year age gap and the height and build difference, we could almost be twins. I'm taller and better muscled, but we have the same jet-black hair, dark eyes, and thick facial hair.

His fingers drum against the side of the vase, and a smirk crosses his face. "This is the second most valuable thing I've ever come in." A playful spark lights his eyes, and I know where he's going with this.

"Don't," I warn.

"First thing was your wife."

Yup. There's about to be a second homicide in this swanky mansion. I try really hard to forget about the fact that he fucked my wife. My ex-wife.

My now very dead ex-wife.

I fight the urge to knock that vase out of his arms and let his felonious jizz spread over the Persian rug beneath his boots, but doing that would mean I'd have to worry about his stupid ass folding on me. And it's a valid concern. Karson will do whatever it takes to remain a free man.

I stuff the bills into my pockets and scan the room to be sure we haven't left anything behind. Karson has already left the building, and I wouldn't be surprised to find him beating his dick into the vase again. Murder is his aphrodisiac, after all. For me it's a means to an end. I want something, they have it, so I take it. I won't lie and pretend I don't enjoy it, but it's more like a schedule one drug than a dose of Viagra for me. I get a high from it, and that's the only way I'll get high because I don't fuck with real drugs.

Not after what I've seen them do to a person.

We never knew our mother because she died when we were young, so we grew up with our father as our . . . I don't know what to call him. He wasn't a parent or a guardian. I was forced into that role for both Karson and our father. When he was too strung out to provide food, I'd work odd jobs around the neighborhood to make sure we had something to eat. I needed a better solution, though, so my first kill was my father's dealer. I figured if I cut off the head of the snake, that would be the end of it. My dad could get off drugs and start taking care of us. But there were more snakes waiting to strike, and my dad never got clean.

That kill taught me something, though. When I looted his limp corpse and came home with more money than I could make doing honest work for a week, I learned how easy it was to take a life.

And I learned that I liked it.

Chapter Three

Leana

The hand around my throat tightens until a black haze creeps across my eyes. The bitter scents of bile and alcohol wash over me, and I fight back the urge to gag. I grip Mickey's wrists and stare at the ring he placed on my finger when he proposed to me. What a bunch of fucking lies. And I was stupid enough to believe him.

This isn't how I wanted to wake up today.

My gaze rises to the angry furrow of his brows as his glassy eyes narrow in anger. I don't know what I did to deserve it this time. Not that I ever did anything to deserve the hell he puts me through. My existence seems like enough to throw him into a mindless rage at any given moment.

I can't imagine living with so much anger in my heart. Actually, I can imagine. The love I had for him has long warped into a bitterness as sour as his breath, and I have a building rage of my own.

"You sleeping around on me, Lee?" he asks.

There it is. Today's reason for the onslaught of abuse is an accusation of cheating. Yesterday it was because he thought I'd stolen some of his stash, which was unfortunately false. What new joys will tomorrow bring?

"Answer me, bitch! Are you cheating?"

I shake my head. *His* friends try to get me away from him, but I've never approached them or taken them up on their offers. One of his dealer buddies probably got sick of my constant rejections and decided to make me pay for it.

"Fucking slut," he snarls, squeezing off the last of my air. I push at his chest as everything inside me tightens to chase the oxygen.

Just when I think I'm about to die, he releases me. Somehow he always knows the moment before he takes it too far. I pant, trying to overfill my lungs with air. I imagine them swelling instead of feeling like shriveled up kidney beans in there.

169

I rip out of his grasp and run for the door. I reach for my purse hanging from a standing mirror, halting when I catch sight of my reflection. I'm no longer a vibrant young woman. Weathered and beaten down, I more closely resemble the way my lungs felt only moments ago. Tears matt my unruly blonde hair to my cheeks, and my blue eyes are bloodshot from his choke hold.

"If you leave, Leana, I will find you. Do you hear me?" he screams, the alcohol tainting his words. "I will find you and I'll fucking kill you!"

He takes a stumbling step toward me, then leans against the wall as the liquor tries to take out his legs. Based on the way his eyes dart back and forth, I can safely assume the room feels like it's spinning beneath his feet. His threats are real, but this is the best opportunity I'll have to escape. He won't be sober enough to find anything but the liquor cabinet anytime soon.

Before he can find his feet again, I leave and slam the door, taking only my purse with me. Nothing in that apartment is worth going back for. I have a few pills stashed in my purse, so I'll have to ration them to keep myself from getting sick. As hopeful as I am, it won't be enough to stave off withdrawal forever. It's something I'll have to deal with, but first I need to put ground between myself and my keeper. I have no clue what's in store for me outside of his home, but it's gotta be better than this.

Anything has to be better than this.

Gravel crunches beneath my feet as I walk beneath an overpass bridge. Black and blue graffiti covers the peeling green pillars that support the concrete. It supplies a nice stretch of shade where I can escape the sun for a few hours during the day, and it's a great place to catch a nap on a night like tonight. It's a popular spot for those living on the street, but I'm happy to find myself alone for the moment. The straps of my backpack rub against my sunburn. I had just enough money to get the bag and some clothes, leaving very little for food. The situation isn't dire enough to send me face first into a trashcan in search of food scraps, but it's getting to that point.

I've been on the run for several days now. If Mickey has been searching for me, he hasn't found me yet. It's only a matter of time if I don't get out of this city, though. I keep my head low when I walk the sidewalks, and I avoid other people as much as I can. Mickey has eyes everywhere.

I pull the backpack off my tender shoulders and try to get it open, but the zipper snags because my hands are so shaky. The immediate panic of such a simple malfunction reminds me why I'm so anxious right now. The skin-crawling feeling that leaves my body pebbled with goose bumps in the summer heat. The nausea that twists my stomach. I'm missing my high and I need a fix. I finally get the piece of fabric out of the way so the zipper can move freely, and I dig around for the mint container.

This tiny tin houses the last of my dwindling stash. When I run out, I'm fucked. Maybe that's what Mickey is waiting for. My eyes dart from shadow to shadow, making sure I'm really alone before I pull open the metal lid. Sure of my safety once more, I take a pill from the container and place it under my tongue to work up enough saliva to swallow it. As it finally slides down my parched throat, the core anxiety washes away, and I wait for the actual drug to take care of the rest.

Now I need a place to ride out my high. A few scraggly bushes at the edge of the gravel should conceal me if I lie behind them, so I trudge toward them and set down my bag. I fluff it up and drop to the ground. The moment my head hits the nylon, my body releases the tension I've been holding. The sound of traffic above me would drive most people nuts, but I'm not most people. I like it. It's soothing. And it's better than being killed by the person who says they love me and want me dead in the same breath.

Yeah. I'll take the brisk air and road noise any day.

I just wish I hadn't waited so long to leave. I touch the fading bruise on my cheek and the handprint around my neck. I wish I'd left the first time he put his hands on me. Better yet, I wish I'd never met him. I try to imagine where I'd be today if he'd never found me at that bus station, but my brain is too fuzzy to conjure up that sort of fantasy. My thoughts circle the drain, touching on things that happened instead of things that could have happened.

I am forever running from abusers.

But that's the past, and I can taste the freedom on my tongue now. Or maybe that's just the drugs. Either way, I'm lighter. If I keep the bad parts of traveling from happening again, I'll be okay. Nothing can be done about the complete vulnerability that comes from being a lone female in a world that doesn't follow society's rules, but if I can steer clear of Mickey—and men like Mickey—I'll make it.

Lights flash around me as the headlights from the cars and trucks break through the cracks in the concrete. Every so often, a rogue headlight drifts from the road beside me and filters through the bushes. It's as relaxing to me as a mobile spinning idly over a baby's bassinet.

I have no clue what I'll do or where I'll go, but this is enough for now. It has to be because I have no other choice. I've tried to get money by offering to work, but people take one look at me and turn me away. Not that I blame them. With all the bruises and the dark bags under my eyes, I look like a typical junkie. Turning tricks isn't an option because Mickey's friend could catch wind of a new girl working in his area, and then I'd really be in trouble. Taking a bus out of this shithole seems like the smartest option, but I don't have enough cash to travel ten feet, let alone ten miles. And I definitely don't have enough to score more pills once these last few are gone.

No wonder people resort to being a criminal. It's fucking easier. And faster.

Between the periodic honking above my head, the leaves rustle against the wind. The drugs drift through my system and slice the edge off my withdrawal, but it's not enough. I draw my sweater closer to my body, trying to keep the heat inside me. I curl up and tuck my knees toward my chest.

It's still better than home, I remind myself.

And it is. Sleeping under an overpass that smells like piss and asphalt after a heavy rain is exponentially better than being beaten and used.

I shiver until I feel warm and my eyes are too heavy to keep open a moment longer. With the city's lullaby thrumming around me, I welcome the comforting embrace of a much-needed sleep.

Chapter Four

Karson

George needed us to do one more hit near the city before we set off on our road trip, and Gentry was pissed about it. Not me. I fucking love doing hits. If I were stuck at a day job, I'd probably hang myself and be real dramatic about it before I do.

I just love killing. Was born to do it. Just like an artist or musician has a drive to draw or play music, I have an innate desire to slice throats and practice macrame with intestines. Going against it would be so . . . unnatural.

I unthread the silencer and holster my pistol. We've finished the hit, but it feels incomplete. Sometimes a gun just isn't enough. It lacks the thrill because it's so quick. So effortless. A pull of a trigger and *bam*, they're gone.

Boring.

I like to play with my victims. A nice mix of psychological torture and physical torment is usually enough to satisfy me, but sometimes I keep going after they're dead. Sometimes killing them just isn't enough.

Gentry *hates* when I play. He's way too serious. He sees it as a means to an end, and while he enjoys the thrill of it as well, he doesn't understand my need to drag it out. It's *supposed* to titillate you. If it wasn't so much fun, people wouldn't do it serially. If you love your job, you'll never have to work a day in your life, right? Well, I fucking love my job when I'm allowed to do it my way.

I let Gentry take the lead on our last hit, but now I'm crawling out of my skin to have a little fun with this one. I skim the room and listen. Drawers open and close behind me on near-silent rollers—rich fuck furniture never squeaks and squeals. Gentry's rifling through shit, looking for some cash, so I turn back to the man slumped on the floor in front of me. His pale hand presses against his abdomen, fighting to hold his blood inside his body. It's a losing battle. A red stain is already spreading across his jeans. His lips part in an open-mouthed pant as he tries to get more air. Nothing is wrong with his lungs, but he doesn't have enough blood to push the oxygen to his brain and probably feels like he's drowning.

Lovely.

I grab my knife from my pocket and flick it open. The moment he sees the shiny metal blade, his eyes widen and he opens his mouth to scream. I leap toward him and cover his mouth with a gloved hand before the initial sound erupts from his lungs. He strains against my grasp, but I refuse to let him alert my brother to my game. I'm not in the mood to be knife-blocked.

"Shh, rich boy. You need to conserve your energy for dying," I whisper with a laugh. I tease his neck with the blade, running the shining silver against the faintly pulsing skin.

Tears fall from his eyes, but I feel no pity. I particularly dislike his kind—well-off people who are younger than me. This fuck can't be older than twenty-five and he has more money than God.

Fuck him.

With a sharp jerk of my wrist, I nick the sensitive skin just beneath his ear. His eyes widen again, and he squeals behind my hand. That sheer display of instinctual panic gets me hard. No matter who they are, their fear goes right to my dick.

I feel for the pocket of emptiness by his right shoulder and plunge the knife into him. His eyes bulge out of his head and his feet push against the floor, but he's losing steam. I pull the knife from his flesh. *Pop.* I fucking live for that momentary feeling of suction as the steel battles to remain buried where I've placed it. It almost makes me giddy.

A weak trickle of blood oozes from the new wound, and this guy doesn't know what to do with himself. He removes his hand from the bullet hole in his gut and clamps it on his shoulder. Life is full of decisions, and I suppose death is as well. He's just made a terrible one.

I reach down and plunge the knife into his gunshot wound, twisting it within the valley of his already grievous injury. The flood gates open and create a crimson pool around his lap. Each breath he takes grows smaller until they're little more than quick gasps through flared nostrils.

Satisfied he no longer has the strength to scream, I remove my hand from his mouth and dip my gloved finger into his gut wound. It comes away soaked and slick. Leaning forward on my knees, I create a little artwork above his lolling head. My fingers swirl along as I write, and I keep having to dip my finger in to add more paint. His mouth just opens and closes like a fish stuck on land each time I dip back into the inkwell. He can't even keep his eyes open now, and they've become tiny slits as his life force drains from him.

Above his head is a message, dripping downward in an eerie pattern. It looks like something out of a horror movie or some shit, but instead of something cryptic like *REDRUM*, it says "Kiddie didler."

I snap a picture and turn the phone screen toward him, but he doesn't even react to my fucking art. Rude.

When I've grown bored, I finish him off by slicing his throat and letting him bleed like the rich little piggy he is. The sound of a knife going through neck flesh actually gets to me a little. Real squelchy.

"Much better," I whisper.

I wipe my blade on a rag and pocket it as I stand up.

"It's spelled diddler, dumbass," Gentry says behind me. Judgmental prick. "Sure doesn't look like the gunshot killed him, Karson. How will we explain that to George?"

"All I did was shoot him. I swear."

Gentry lifts the man's slumped head, which is nearly disconnected from his neck. "Real sharp bullet."

I shrug. "I helped him along. The train was coming too slowly and he was suffering."

"Aren't you a fucking saint." He lets the head slump forward again. "You complicate things when you use multiple weapons. We get in, eliminate, rob, and get out."

"You know, pre-prison Gentry was way more fun. We used to play 'how many weapons can we use before they die,' remember?"

Gentry's lips tighten.

"You remember," I continue. "You were the running champion. What was it? Bullet, blade, claw hammer, screwdriver, and not one but *two* nails to the eyes before he finally died." I sigh. "Good times."

Gentry turns to walk away. "It was three nails. Two in the eyes, one in the ear."

"We have such fond childhood memories," I say with a shake of my head and a longing look toward the window.

"Let's go," Gentry yells from the mudroom area. Foyer? Whatever the snobs call it.

"I'm coming."

We climb into the van and peel off our gloves. It's the first thing we do after a hit because those fucking things are constricting. Safety first, though.

"How much did we get?" I ask as Gentry steers the van down the winding driveway.

He shakes his head and sighs. "Not enough."

"We gotta get out from under George's thumb. We do all the hard work, and he gets all the pay. Yeah, he throws us some scraps, but we should be living like kings instead of goddamn peasants."

"That's the plan," he says, and I wish he'd say more. I'm getting sick of his short sentences.

I decide to press him. "What plan? Care to share with your partner?"

"No. Not really."

Before I can ask anything else, Gentry's phone rings. I lean closer, trying to hear the conversation once he answers, but he only pushes me away.

"All that way? There's no one else—" Gentry is silenced by a rising tone on the other end. "How much . . . Alright. Alright. Fine." He ends the call and cracks his neck after rolling his shoulders.

I lean back and throw my feet onto the dash. "What's up?"

"We have to go to fucking Hollywood for a hit."

"Like . . . drive?"

"Can't get our guns on a plane, now, can we? So yeah, driving. George said we'd need to take a road trip, but I didn't realize he meant we'd have to trek across the country."

"Oh man, that's like thirty-six hours on the road. With me." I laugh. "Good fucking luck, brother."

"I will beat my list of murder items in one body if you don't behave yourself."

"When do I ever misbehave?"

"Every day that ends in Y." He pulls onto the main road and aims the van for the highway. "Let's get this over with."

"Who's the hit?" I ask.

"Some actor that got into shit they shouldn't have. Someone who can buy a new Lambo but not pay their debts. But he's also someone with *a lot* of security."

"Harder job means better pay, right?"

Gentry shrugs and looks out the window. "He says we'll make more on this job than we ever have. If he's telling the truth, maybe we can branch out on our own again. Cut the middleman."

I never liked having a handler, so this plan sounds like a great idea to me. As long as I can survive this road trip, things are looking up.

The engine light comes on, blaring bright orange on the dashboard. A sickening sweet smell fills the front of the van, and a rush of steam rises from the hood. Gentry slams his hands on the wheel. We barely made a dent in our drive. We're still tucked inside wooded hills, miles from the main highway. He's going to be so fucking mad. And insufferable. Great.

He pulls onto the shoulder, and we climb out of the van. Gentry pops the hood, speaking every foul word he knows under his breath, and I drop to my knees. A dark, wet trail runs from where we were on the road to where we rolled to a stop. I place the sweet smell and rise to my feet.

"Cracked radiator," I tell Gentry, lifting my eyes to a face so twisted with anger I don't think it's possible to untwist it at this point.

"Are you fucking kidding me?" He brushes his hand through his hair. "We *have* to get this done."

I whip out my phone to call a tow. What else can we do? Gentry rips the cell from my hand and holds it away from me. "Chill out. I'm just trying to call for a tow."

"And what? Have them tow away the van full of weapons and stolen money? I'm sure they won't even notice the blood on your gloves. Fuck, Karson. Think with your head for once in your life."

I lean against the steaming van and pull a cigarette from the pack in my pocket. I light it, which enrages Gentry to no end. He looks like his head might combust and throw his brain matter all over the grass, and I should feel bad for bringing him to this level of pissed off.

But I don't.

"So we hitchhike?" I ask, bringing the smoke into my lungs.

"Another stupid suggestion. Who the fuck would pick up two men like us?" Gentry throws his hands down on the hood as he slams it closed.

I shrug. "It will look like one man until I pop out and get a gun on them."

"That's—" Gentry starts, his voice curt and ready to rip me a new asshole. "Actually not a bad idea."

Did my brother give me a fucking compliment? Am I dead? Where are the flames and heat of hell?

"But you need to be the face," he says. "No one is going to stop for a a man my size. They still may not stop since you're a man too, but you're slightly less imposing."

"Sorry I didn't have access to the prison workout system for the past six years," I say with another drag on my cigarette, and that almost sends Gentry off the deep end. It's not a good time to poke the bear, but I can't help myself.

"Just get the goddamn bags. We'll keep the pistols, but I'll ditch the long guns in the woods. I'll wait there while you *try* to flag down some chump."

I won't just try. I'll show Gentry my ideas can be as good—if not better—than his.

Chapter Five

Leana

I'm fucking tired. I've been on the streets for a week, but it feels like much longer. It feels like an eternity. This was easier when I traveled as a ballsy teen. Back before I was hooked on pills and looked like death warmed over. Back when my blue eyes were still filled with hope.

I stand with my sign, waiting for the bright glint of a few measly coins to land in the small cardboard box at my feet. If I'm lucky, someone will toss in a half-eaten meal or a flat soda. Mostly I get men yelling, "Show me your tits!" as they wait for the light to change. Shit, I'm so desperate, I've considered it on more than one occasion.

Sweat collects on my brow and trickles toward my eyes. I wipe it away before it can reach my lashes. My sunburned skin heats my fingertips, and I'm not sure how much more I can take. The heat is killing me. What little water I take in is converted to sweat in my body's desperate effort to cool down. Running back to Mickey with my tail between my legs seems like a terrible idea, but it's growing more tempting by the day.

I lift my hand to my forehead and shield my eyes from the harsh glare as I look at the motel across the road. They would have water. They might even let me use the lobby bathroom so I can cool my face and rinse the grit from my skin. If I ask nicely enough, maybe I can score a Tylenol for this pounding headache as well. I've come toward the end of my stash of drugs, and what little I use is only enough to keep the shakes away.

I fold the cardboard sign and tuck it under my arm. My cardboard box netted little more than a wad of trash from a bratty kid in an SUV, so I leave it behind. When the coast is clear, I walk across the road and work my way through the parking lot. Despite the glorious rush of cool air kissing my skin, I feel as if I might pass out by the time I walk through the sluggish automatic doors. Black ink spots

179

dance in front of my eyes and obscure my vision. I reach for a display of travel brochures to steady myself, careful to keep it from crashing down.

"Are you okay, ma'am?" the woman behind the desk asks.

I stumble forward and lean against the lobby counter, my chest feeling heavy with every inhale. "I just really need some water. Do you have any?"

The woman looks around before reaching beneath the desk and handing me two bottles. "They're for guests, so don't tell me if you aren't one," she says with a tight smile.

I nod and rip the top from one of the bottles. Even though the liquid is room temperature, it soothes my cracked lips and coats my parched throat. I chug until I think I might puke, forcing myself to stop as my stomach begs for one more sip. It flows from the sides of my mouth, and I'm wearing half of it by the time I lower the bottle. The woman reaches beneath the desk once more and passes another bottle to me before motioning toward the automatic door with her chin.

I get the message. She's done her good deed for the day and now I need to make myself scarce. The homeless are unwelcome by everyone, even those who feel the slightest twinge of pity for our sorry situation. We're looked down upon, but only when someone takes the time to look at all. Most won't even meet our gaze, as if they think we harbor some contagious disease they might catch by acknowledging our existence.

"Thanks," I tell her, wiping the back of my hand along my mouth. I sigh as I leave the comfort of A/C and brave the heat once more.

The sun is taking no prisoners today.

I force my legs to carry me across the parking lot, my eyes focusing on a huge tree whose canopy would lend me some delicious shade if I can only muster the strength to reach it.

I've nearly made it to the edge of the lot when I spot a dark SUV idling with no one inside it. Black smoke chugs from the old exhaust, and sun rays glint from the sections of paint that haven't peeled away. I reroute my steps until I'm standing beside the driver's door. My head swivels in all directions as I search for an owner, but there's no one nearby. It probably belongs to a guest at the motel.

My fingers graze the hot metal door handle, and my mouth drops open as I discover it's unlocked. *Don't do something illegal,* I try to tell myself, but the legal way hasn't worked so far and I'm fucking exhausted. I'm desperate to make it out of New York. It's only a matter of time before Mickey comes to claim me, and I've pressed my luck enough.

It's their fault for leaving the key in the ignition, I rationalize.

I whip open the door and selfishly sit in the seat. My eyes gloss over the ripped interior, cigarette butts in the cup holders, and bottles of half-empty drinks. The gas tank is full, and that's all that really matters if I plan to do this.

Do I plan to do this?

My body answers the question for me, and I throw the SUV in reverse and ease out of the parking space. As I back up, I watch the rows of doors and windows for movement. I expect someone to rush from the building and teach me a lesson for trying to take what isn't mine.

But it doesn't happen.

No one notices me as I exit the parking lot and pull onto the road. I blend into the light traffic and crank the air as high as it will go, not even daring a glance in the rearview mirror as I put miles between myself and hell.

It's getting dark by the time I near the highway that will lead me to the next state. The occasional oncoming headlights on this back road hurt my eyes, and my vision is already sensitive from the headache knocking at the base of my skull. The stress of stealing a car hasn't helped. Neither has the withdrawal. It's like steam in my veins, building and building with nowhere to go without the release valve.

I spot something ahead on the side of the road and slow the SUV so I can get a better look. It's a white van with its hood cranked open. A man with his pale thumb in the air stands beside it. The tug to pull over draws me toward him. I know what it means to rely on the help of others, and I know the feeling of helplessness as every car rushes by you without so much as slowing for your safety.

Don't do it, Leana.

It's not wise. I know it's not. This man could be a serial killer for all I know, and the whole reason I stole this piece of shit was to get myself to safety. Now I'm considering placing myself in danger once again. I can't.

My foot eases off the brake and moves toward the gas pedal. I roll past the van . . .

Against my better judgment, I pull to the side of the road. If I keep going, I'm no better than the hundreds of people who passed me by today. I also wouldn't mind handing the keys to someone in a better state of mind to drive, especially with this nagging headache biting at the backs of my eyes.

The man approaches my window with a smile, and I feel a little more at ease. He looks like he might be in his late thirties. His dark, unruly hair waves a bit in the breeze. I can't see the color of his eyes against the shadows, which means they're probably dark too. Scruff lines his strong jaw, and though he's not a broad man, I can see the strength in his toned arms. He's attractive, in a wild sort of way, and I find myself ashamed of my haggard appearance for the first time in a while.

"Hey," he says as he adjusts a duffle bag strap on his shoulder.

"What's wrong with your van?" I ask.

"Busted radiator. I need a ride to the shop a few miles from here. They have a loaner car waiting for me, but they can't pick up my piece of shit until later." He motions toward his van.

Everything seems okay so far, and my defenses begin to lower. If he's lying about any of this, he's doing a pretty convincing job. Besides, it's only for a few miles. Then I'll be on my own again.

"Get in," I tell him, pulling my purse off the passenger seat.

The man loops around the SUV, tapping the hood as he walks by. He climbs into the seat, but instead of closing the door so we can get moving, he stares into the trees lining the side of the road. I'm about to change my mind and ask him to get out when he turns to me and . . . just stares.

As his eyes harden, the hair on my neck stands at attention. I reach for the shifter, thinking I can fling him from the car if I drive off fast enough, but a metallic click stops my hands from doing anything at all. My stomach twists into a knot as I turn my head and find the barrel of a pistol aimed at my face.

"I don't want trouble," I say, keeping my voice steady.

"Unfortunately, trouble is exactly what you've got," he says, motioning toward the trees.

A lead curtain of silence weighs down the vehicle, only broken when I hear the crunch of heavy boots emerging from the woods. My heart crawls into my throat and I choke on it.

Another man approaches the SUV, this one much bigger than the man sitting beside me. His full, dark beard obscures the lower half of his face, but I can see his eyes and they're just as dark. His hair is much neater than the other man's, but they look as if they were cut from the same cloth.

My stomach twists, and it's not only from the sheer horror of the shit sandwich I've found myself wedged inside. I'm dope sick, and the water from earlier isn't happy where it's at.

The larger man gets in the seat behind the one holding his gun on me. "Thanks for the ride," he says as they close their doors.

"I didn't really have much of a choice, did I?" I snap. They might kill me, but I refuse to go out like a simpering child. I spent the last six years begging Mickey to go easy on me. I refuse to spend another second begging a man to lay off.

"Mouthy," the man beside me says with a laugh. "I like them with some fire. Then again, we could get rid of you and just take your car." He whips a knife from somewhere in the darkness and puts the metal to my throat.

When I swallow, my skin tenses beneath the blade. "It's not even my ride. I took it."

The man cocks his head, and a low growl leaves his throat. He turns toward the man in the back seat. "What do we have here, G? Seems like we caught a little thief."

I'm not in the mood. My insides are about to become my outsides, my skin is crawling, chills are setting in, and now I have to deal with *this*. I only wanted to get away from my abuser, and now I've landed myself with two psychos who will probably gut me. Or worse.

The thought of what they may do to me is enough to send my stomach into a full roll, and I get the door open in time to puke all over the pavement. The man beside me lets out a disgusted groan, but the big one in back seems more pissed than grossed out. He opens his door, comes around the vehicle, and lifts me by the back of my shirt like a momma cat carrying a kitten. With minimal effort, he tosses me into the back seat.

He gets in the driver's seat, and I lean back to gain control of the waves of nausea threatening to drown me.

The passenger's attention rushes back to me with a sharp turn of his head. "Do you know what we do to thieves?"

"Kill them?" I say.

The driver's deep voice echoes through the SUV, feeling louder with my eyes closed. His words are silky smooth. "No. We take them along for the ride."

Chapter Six

Gentry

"Pull over!" she says from the back seat. The desperate edge to her voice tells me there's no questioning the validity of this urgent demand. I pull to the shoulder, and she nearly leaps from the car to vomit in the grass.

I get out and walk to the hunched form. She's fallen to her knees from the sheer force of her squeezing stomach, but she's brought up little more than bile. When I squat down, she drops her gaze.

"What's the matter with you?" I ask. "Are you knocked up or something?"

"You never ask a woman if she's pregnant, asshole," she snarls, wiping at a line of drool hanging from her lower lip. "But no. I'm not pregnant."

It's night, but the headlights cast enough glare to make the goose bumps visible on her skin. Sweat collects at the small of her back, where her shirt has risen enough to reveal a patch of pale skin.

I reach for her forehead, and she's too shaky and weak to fight my unwanted touch. My fingertips connect with clammy skin. "Are you sick?"

"A kind of sickness, I guess," she says, turning her head to vomit once more.

My eyebrows furrow. She looks rough—clearly homeless, but not entirely like a dope head. Even so, I've seen someone in her state before and I can't deny the similarity. Our father was a junkie, and I spent many hours of my childhood beside him as he shivered and puked. When an addict goes without their addiction, they're reduced to what I see before me now: a helpless, quivering husk.

"Are you dope sick?" I ask, hoping she has an alternative reason for her current state.

She drops to her back, careful not to land in her vomit. "Yes, and I think I just purged my soul from my body."

Fuck. The last thing we need right now is to care for someone going through withdrawal. "Do you have any more drugs on you?" I ask, hoping she does. When my father would get sick, only a fix would stop the downward spiral.

She shakes her head, and her messy blonde hair rustles against the grass. "Negatory."

That's unfortunate. It means we'll have to tend to her while she rides out the withdrawal.

What the fuck am I thinking? It would be better to end her life. She's a liability at this point—has been since she saw our faces—and we have a long way to go before we reach our final destination. What do I plan to do with her at the end of the road? Even if she were well, there's only one answer to that question.

My hand goes to the pistol on my hip. *It's no different than putting down a dying deer on the side of the road,* I tell myself.

But I can't do it.

I feel a bit of sympathy for her. As stupid as it was, she stopped when she saw a broken-down van, and now she'll have to pay the ultimate price for an act of kindness. It doesn't seem fair to end her life now. Right now, she looks broken. And I recognize brokenness like that. I've seen enough of her snark to know she'll be a fighter when she's better, so maybe we can wait until she gives us a reason to kill her.

I scoop her trembling body into my arms and carry her to the back seat. Her head lolls to the side, but she doesn't fight me. Surrounded by my massive frame, she seems so small and fragile, like I could break her if I squeezed too hard. Despite the sickness infecting her mind and ravaging her body, I can see the low glint of a dying fire in her blue eyes.

I force myself to look away. After what happened with my wife, I refused to get sucked in by a woman again. This helpless girl in my arms won't change that. She's beautiful and I admire her attitude, but I won't let her shake my resolve. I'll let Karson end her once she's better, but she deserves to die when she isn't strung out and miserable. That's how I'll repay her kindness.

I place her into the back seat, and she raises her arm over her eyes to shield her pinpoint pupils from the dome light. Her tongue moves over her lips to wet them, and my body tenses, immediately regretting the decision to keep her around. She's a danger to me in more ways than one.

I return to the driver's seat before I do something stupid. Pushing away visions of what I could do to a girl like her, I turn the ignition and pull onto the road again.

"We should kill her, you know," Karson says, making no attempt to lower his voice. "At this point, it might be merciful."

The girl turns her head, her eyes firmly closed. "Fuck you," she whispers.

It almost makes me smile, but it enrages Karson. He whips his knife from his belt and turns in his seat, but I take a hand off the wheel and grab his wrist to block his motion toward her.

"Don't," I say.

"Fucking why not?" he snaps.

"Because I'm the boss and you listen to what I say. Don't forget that I'm saving your ass." It's a better answer than the truth. I have no clue why I can't let him carve her like a Christmas ham. Maybe I pity her because I found our father dead after a particularly gnarly bout of withdrawal. Maybe saving her means I've made up for not saving him. Either way, he can't finish her off . . . yet.

This isn't the smartest thing we've done, I know—generally speaking, taking anyone outside of our pairing is fucking dumb—but I'm intrigued by this stray we've picked up.

Karson scoffs. "She's fucked up on drugs, isn't she?"

I shake my head. "Fucked up because she's *off* drugs."

Karson's back thumps against his seat and his head drops to his balled fist. "I didn't sign up for a babysitting gig."

"I said the same thing."

He can't argue with that, so we continue into the night in blessed silence.

Leana

When the passenger said they should kill me, I had no strength to argue beyond the two words I said. I don't want to die, but I'm too sick to stop them if that's what they plan to do, and it seems likely at this point. The muscles beneath my skin hurt. The twist of my intestines chokes me. My neck is a tight bundle of pain, and I consider pulling my eyes from their sockets to end the painful throb behind them. Every bump and jostle in the road sends my stomach into my mouth.

Someone lights a cigarette, and the heady aroma is both tempting and nauseating. The thick smoke wraps around me, comforting the tremble of my body in a familiar blanket. Maybe a little nicotine would take the edge off, but it might send me to the side of the road again, puking the emptiness from my stomach. I'm also reminded of Mickey's common reaction when I would ask for a cigarette, and asking for one might only get me killed quicker. I shouldn't press my luck.

Then again, I've never considered myself lucky.

Life has dealt me multiple shitty hands, but I'm forced to sit at the table and keep betting. A happy childhood ruined by my father's death. My mother's marriage to a predatory animal. An escape to a hell that was just as horrific. And now I'm stuck as a hostage, too sick to make a run for it.

I groan and sit up to look out the window. We've left the highway again, and dark trees tower against a star-filled sky. I don't know where we are or how far we've traveled, but at least we're moving away from Mickey and toward some unknown destination. Asking where we're headed would be pointless. They haven't offered their names, so I doubt they'll disclose anything else.

I lean against the window's cool glass and stare at the back of the passenger's head. I've come to see him as the dangerous one. His short temper and complete disregard for my life have been put on display more than once, and I need to be careful around him. My eyes shift to the driver. He's shown me an iota of sympathy, which is nice, but I still can't trust him. I'm about ninety percent sure the massive hands clutching the steering wheel will end up wrapped around my throat at some point, and not in a good way.

I laugh at the thought.

"What's funny back there?" the passenger asks.

"Just this situation," I say. "Two weirdos and a dope-sick girl on a road trip."

The passenger whips his head around, glaring at me with pitch-black eyes. "You're the fucking weird one, girl."

"Because you two are the crème de la crème of normalcy, right? Two big dudes playing around in the woods together in the middle of the night." My caution regarding the wild one goes right out the window because my head hurts and it's making me bitchy. I've held my tongue for most of my life, and now that my days are numbered, I can finally say whatever I want. It feels amazing.

"Just one little slice and I could end you, thief," he says. He raises his knife again, and the dash lights reflect off the blade with an eerie green glow.

"Do it then," I snarl, a strange laugh lifting the end of my demand. "Fucki—"

"Enough!" the driver shouts, silencing me mid curse. It's just one word, but it projects and runs along every nerve in my body. It lingers. This man sure can make someone listen up. Even his friend has gone silent, though I can tell what a struggle that is because the muscles ripple in his arms with the effort. It looks like it's taking everything in him not to beat my ass.

It wouldn't be the first time a man's fists rained down on me. I've learned how much of a beating the human body can take, and it's so much more than I once believed. Knowing this, I decide to take my chances. I can't stand the passenger, and I want to poke him a bit. Besides, the big one seems like he'd pull him off me before he killed me.

Probably.

I gather my waning energy and use it to send my knee into the back of the passenger's seat. His chest rises as his back arches to escape the sudden pressure behind him. Before I can react, he's over the center console and in tussling—or killing—range. Black eyes glare at me, yet I don't regret what I've done. Maybe I have a death wish. I smirk, and this sends him off the deep end. His blade flashes for a millisecond before the driver whips his arm away.

The SUV swerves and bounces along the shoulder as the driver wrenches the blade from his friend's hand. Instead of de-escalating the situation, I bring my leg under the passenger's twig and berries with a solid thud. He roars with anger, tumbling against the dash as the driver brings the SUV to a jarring halt. I stifle a laugh because fuck that guy. He deserved it.

"Karson! You're driving," the driver says as he tugs off his seat belt and charges around the front of the SUV. I worry he'll rip the passenger door off the hinges when he whips it open.

"What? Why me?" Karson asks, his hand still holding his crotch.

"Because both of you are acting like fucking children. I can't keep the car on the road *and* play goddamn referee at the same time. She's clearly too sick to drive, so that leaves you. Now get in the driver's seat before I lose my shit."

"Oh, fuck you, Gentry," Karson mumbles before crawling over the center console and dropping behind the steering wheel. "I'm going to kill that bitch, first chance I get." He whispers this last bit, but it's loud enough for me to hear.

It's a warning I should take seriously, but I'm too sick to give a shit right now. If he kills me, at least I got a piece of him before I went. That's more than I can say for my situation with Mickey. I'll never have the chance to get my revenge on that piece of shit. From the way Karson reacted to me, I'm more certain than ever.

Wherever they're headed, I won't be alive when they reach their destination.

Chapter Seven

Karson

We don't talk for the rest of the drive, and I eventually pull the vehicle into a hotel parking lot. George instructed us to drive toward Hollywood, but he'd better line up more hits along the way to make this worth our while. It isn't cheap to bed down in a hotel every night, but we have to sleep sometimes. Gentry seems to think this run of hits will be our last under George, that the payout will be more than we've ever seen, but I don't have the same confidence in our sneaky asshole handler. If he shortchanges us, it won't be the first time.

Gentry always makes sure I know how stupid I am, but my brother is the one being fucking stupid. I'm not only talking about his belief that George will make good on his promises, either. This girl is a problem. We don't bring people along on road trips like this. Involving others is a risk we don't need, and she could blow our cover at any point. She could escape. She could rat us out to the first person she sees, an opportunity she'll have when we book this room. There's no way I'm going back to prison for some doped out whore Gentry seems to have adopted like a sick little puppy from the side of the road. But I can't say that to Gentry. He thinks he knows *everything*.

He'll learn how little he knows soon enough. When that puppy feels better, it will turn and bite the hand that fed it. She's already a snappy little bitch.

I don't care to see Gentry babying his new pet, so I grab my duffle bag, throw it over my shoulder, and head toward the hotel's entryway. It's not the Hilton, but it's not a roach motel either. The lobby is small but clean, with a few chairs and a couch circled around a low table. A coffee maker stands on a counter nearby, and a muted TV hangs above it. Subtitles flash along the bottom of the screen.

I bypass the seating area and head straight for the older woman sitting behind the lobby desk. "Two rooms, please," I say. I refuse to room with those two.

Gentry's show of kindness makes me physically ill, and I can't sleep in the same room as that thief anyhow. It would be smarter if we took turns keeping watch over her, but she's still sick enough that I doubt she'll make a run for it.

The woman at the front desk taps away on her keyboard without looking up at me. When she gives me the total, we exchange cash for key cards, and I return to the entrance to wait for my brother and his baggage. They start across the parking lot, and my jaw clenches at the sight of them. She's leaning against him for support, her useless, unsteady legs wobbling beneath her hips. He looks like a man leading his drunk date to the fuck palace after a night at the bar. It's a good cover, actually, but it still makes me want to gouge out my eyes with a dull stick. I don't like how cozy they look.

I toss Gentry his key when they near me. "You're in three-oh-five," I say. "I'm in the room next to yours." Before he can respond, I turn and head toward the elevator.

The short ride to our floor makes the thief sick again. She leans her blonde head against him and moans, clutching her stomach and nearly collapsing. His arm curls around her, a protective gesture that sends my eyes rolling. This isn't the brother I've known all my life. Sure, he's not as stabby as me, but he's never been caring. Not like this.

This is going to be a fucking problem.

We exit the elevator and I push past them to get to my room. I can't take another second of this shit.

"Karson," Gentry says before I can get the key card into the slot.

I grit my teeth and turn to face him. Whatever he has to say, I'm not in the mood to hear it.

Gentry tells the girl to go into their room, helping her inside as if she's some invalid who didn't kick me in the dick earlier. He closes the door behind her and joins me in front of my room.

"What are we doing?" I ask. I don't give him a chance to speak first. "How do you think this is going to end, Gentry?"

"I know how it ends."

Does he? I'm not convinced. "Then why prolong the inevitable? We should have killed her on the side of the road when she was sick. Now you're taking care of her like you plan to keep her. Tell me I'm wrong. Please."

His lips tighten. "When it's time, I'll get rid of her."

I shake my head. "If you don't, I'll kill both of you and then myself."

Gentry's eyebrows furrow. "Just let me handle it."

"Sure thing, Gentry. You're the boss," I say, and he doesn't miss the sarcastic bite to my words.

I leave him standing in the hall and retreat to my room. Gentry has always been the boss to an extent, but I'm sick of being on a leash. The moment I get loose, I'm getting rid of the excess baggage. The little thief isn't the only dog with teeth.

Gentry

I stand in front of my room in the ghostly quiet hall. Karson doesn't understand. To be fair, neither do I, but this is my show and I'll run it how I damn well please. If he doesn't like it, he can take his chances with George.

The key card reader flashes green and I push open the heavy metal door. The girl is stretched out on the bed, her chest heaving as if the walk to our room was more of a monumental task than I could ever imagine. A lamp on the bedside table casts a dim yellow light over her face, and the shadows under her eyes stand out like two dark valleys on either side of her slender nose. Her scent comes toward me, and I wish she hadn't dropped onto the comforter while reeking of vomit.

"Go on and shower," I tell her. I want her cleaned up because I'll never get to sleep if I have to smell that rancid perfume all night, but I worry what she'll look like when that thin layer of grime and sweat isn't coating her skin. I'm already fighting a strange attraction to her when she looks a mess, so I don't know how I'll react when she's soft and clean.

She climbs out of bed like she's fighting against a body that weighs a thousand pounds. It's a familiar, struggling action my father made so many times. Maybe that's why I'm so intrigued by her. Maybe I need to see if she'll die like our father or find the will to live.

But then how can I kill her?

Because you have no choice.

She enters the bathroom, and the sound of running water silences my thoughts. I slip off my shoes at the door, flop onto the bed, and flip on the television. Watching TV is a really mundane luxury most people don't think twice about. We didn't have one growing up. Well, we *technically* had one, but the big boxy piece of shit was just a giant paperweight. I have no memory of its screen ever lighting up. Karson entertained himself by pulling the legs off of bugs in the weed-filled yard, and I preferred to spend my childhood trying to make a few dollars so we could eat something more than peanut butter sandwiches and stale saltine crackers.

The shower turns off and the girl emerges from the bathroom doorway in a puff of steam. I swallow hard because she looks more than half pretty when she's clean. She's wearing a bathrobe, the belt tied tight around her slender waist. She probably doesn't have shit for clothes to wear, and she sure as hell can't put on the vomit-soaked clothes she had on before.

But there's another problem more present on her mind. I'm lying on the only bed in the room, and I have no intention of giving up my spot.

"No clothes?" I ask.

"My bad. I didn't expect to travel across the country when I left my cardboard box this morning."

I shake my head and pull off my shirt, fighting off a laugh. Her wit annoys the piss out of Karson, but I like it. "Here, take this," I say, tossing the shirt into her lap. It'll be big on her, but it's better than that scratchy bathrobe.

"I have one other outfit in my backpack, but it stinks worse than the vomit ensemble. It's not easy to wash clothes when you're on the street," she says.

I gather her discarded clothes and find the backpack just inside the bathroom door. As I dig around for her extra outfit, my hand hits something small and square. It's a wallet. I pull it out and flip it open, reading the name on her license.

Tucked behind it is another license. It's expired by several years, but that's definitely her picture.

Leana Moore.

At least I now know the name of the intriguing little stranger. I return the wallet to the backpack and leave the bathroom before she sees me snooping.

"I'll go launder these," I say as I pass the bed.

As I reach for the door handle, her soft voice stops me. "Why are you being so nice to me?"

Really weird fucking question. I'm not being overly nice by giving her clothes to wear and not killing her . . . yet.

Instead of answering her, I slip on my shoes and leave the room.

I don't think she has the energy to make a run for it, but I still need to be cautious. I stop by Karson's room on my way down the hall and ask him to listen out for her. He's pissed, but he does as he's told and sits beside my door.

The on-site laundry room isn't hard to find. It's on the first floor, tucked away in an alcove off the lobby area. From the look of the dated machines, they cared more about the appearance of their entrance than the client amenities. I drop her clothes into a washer and spot a stain on my jeans. I don't need to sniff it to know what it is. I strip off my pants and toss them in as well, leaving me in nothing but my boxers. I don't worry that anyone will say something to me about it, because I don't have the most approachable face. Besides, it's late and the hotel seems fairly empty.

When I reach our hall, Karson is no longer seated by the door. He's either deserted his post or . . .

My breath catches in my throat. I was worried she might escape, but I hadn't considered what Karson might do to her if I wasn't there to stop him. I shouldn't care, but I do. I practically handed her to my brother on a silver fucking platter.

I pull the room key from the waistband of my boxer briefs and slide it into the slot. The light turns red, and I realize I've held it the wrong way in my panic. I turn it and the light blazes green. When I rush through the door, I'm able to breathe again. Leana is lying in the same position on the bed, wearing my black shirt instead of the robe. Her wet hair sticks to her skin and dampens the collar of my shirt. Her bright blue eyes stare at the television.

She turns her head and her brows furrow when she sees me in nothing more than underwear.

I answer her question before she can ask. "Decided to wash my jeans too."

She nods and her attention returns to the television.

I knew my shirt would be big on her, but it practically swallows her whole. I'm struck again by how small she is. "How has a girl like you survived on the street?"

She shrugs. "I had no choice."

She shifts onto her side and the collar of the T-shirt droops as her hair falls away from her neck. Greenish-yellow bruises stand out on her skin, wrapping around her throat like a fading noose. Someone has put this girl through hell.

"What are you running from?" I ask.

Her eyes drop and she readjusts, covering the bruises once more. "I don't want to talk about it."

I walk to the edge of the bed and pull back the covers, too tired to pry information from her sealed lips.

Her eyes go wide, and she shifts to look at me. "Aren't you sleeping on the floor?"

I can't hold back my laugh this time. Fuck no, I won't sleep on the floor. I did enough of that growing up. We only had one bed in the house, and I let Karson have it. My dad had a permanent spot on the couch when he was home. When he wasn't, I didn't sleep there because it always smelled like sweat and piss.

"Not a chance," I tell her as I get into bed. She tries to get out from beneath the covers, but I grab her arm and pull her down again. "No one is sleeping on the floor."

"I'm not sleeping in bed with you!" She struggles in my grasp, but she doesn't stand a chance against me.

I wrap my arm around her waist and haul her backward before forcing her down. She doesn't realize what effect she has on me, and this struggle has only made it worse. If she knows what's good for her, she'll stop.

Because soon, I won't be able to.

"You're not leaving this bed, Leana."

She quiets at the sound of her name, the will to fight evaporating from her eyes. "How do you know my name?"

I release her from my hold and turn onto my side, facing away from her so I won't be tempted. She won't try to leave again. "Go to sleep, wanderer."

She moves a bit, then places a pillow between us. A smile forces its way onto my face. If I wanted to take her, does she really think a pillow would stop me? I won't take her, though. I won't even touch her. She might feel too good or taste too sweet, and then I really won't be able to get rid of her. As tempting as she is, I refuse to give in.

I stay awake until she's snoring softly, then I allow myself to fall asleep.

Chapter Eight

I wake up in bed with him. The tall one. The brick shithouse of a man. I don't even know how I fell asleep beside this hulking stranger. Probably because my body was so in need of sleep that it didn't matter if I was lying beside the devil himself, as long as I was in a fucking bed.

After getting a solid six hours on a memory foam mattress, I'm feeling a lot better too. The nausea has quieted to a whisper, so I can ignore it. I still have a slight headache, but it probably has more to do with dehydration than withdrawal. I still feel like shit, but less shitty. Functional, at least.

Which means I need to get the hell out of here.

I peer over the pillow separating my skin from his. He's on his back with his face turned toward me, and even though he's fast asleep, he's still imposing as hell. His muscles have been carved from marble, and I'm pretty sure his abs have abs. I picture him shirtless with an ax in his hand, hauling it over his shoulder and sending it into a block of wood with the ease of a hot knife through butter. Sweat slipping through the curves surrounding his pecs and . . .

And what the fuck is wrong with me?

He's not a sexy lumberjack making thirst traps for social media. He's the man holding me hostage, and I need to get the fuck away from him.

I quietly slip out of bed, careful not to wake the sleeping giant beside me. When I look around, I realize how fucked I am. My clothes—including the spare set in my bookbag—are in a laundry room somewhere in this hotel. I can't go out of the room like this, wearing only his oversized T-shirt and a skimpy pair of panties. I can't call for help, either. Not when I was the idiot who stole the SUV that brought us here.

Jail isn't an alternative for me. Being crammed into a room with women who have done unspeakable things—and who might do unspeakable things to me—is just as bad as living with Mickey.

I'm stuck.

Instead of making my escape now, I'll have to wait for an opportune moment. One where I'm better prepared. And clothed. It's probably for the best, because as I reach the bathroom door, my legs threaten to buckle when a massive wave of nausea crashes over me. Lights spin in front of my eyes, and I grab the doorframe to stop my body from landing on the tile floor. A high whine pierces my ears.

Just as my grip loosens and I begin to fall forward, I'm wrapped in warmth and power. My head dips back and I see his face. His lips move within his beard, but I can't hear what he's saying. I blink until the fog begins to recede.

"You need to lie down." His voice comes from miles away, but it's getting closer.

He carries me to the bed and places me on top of the comforter before walking away. Moments later, he returns with a cool wash rag and places it on my forehead. I try to push his hands away. I don't want his help. This was a lesson I learned the hard way many years ago. Men don't help.

They hurt.

"Get the fuck off me," I mutter.

He walks away again and I close my eyes, thinking he's gotten the message, but he returns with a bottle of water from the mini fridge in the room. He sits on the edge of the bed and holds it out to me, and I take it because my body's needs outweigh my pride. I sit up and rip off the cap before guzzling the cold liquid.

His hand lurches forward and pulls the bottle from my grasp.

"What the fuck?" I say. "First you force feed me help, and now you're snatching it away. Make up your fucking mind."

"You'll just puke it up if you inhale it like that." He holds it toward me again but pulls it away when I reach for it. "Sip it."

I lean forward and snatch it from his hand, hating that he's probably right. Goddamn him.

Taking small gulps of water is a monumental task, but I manage to muster enough willpower to make it happen. Each icy gulp slides down my throat like a cold stone dropping into the empty well of my stomach. After a few sips, I force myself to stop, glad that I'm able to keep it down.

"How do you know so much about what I'm going through?" I ask as I screw the cap onto the bottle. "Are you a recovering addict or something?"

He shakes his head, opens his mouth, then decides to keep his secrets. It's probably best. The less we learn about each other, the better. I don't even know why I asked. I certainly don't give a shit.

When he gets to his feet again, I swallow hard. Against my will, my eyes glide to the massive erection at my eye level. It points toward his navel and nearly pokes from the top of his boxer briefs, but the thickness is what holds my attention. Disgustingly thick. Horrifyingly big. Fuck an ax. He could probably chop wood with *that* thing.

It would certainly split me *in half,* I think, and my cheeks blaze hot.

"Don't act like you've never seen a cock before," he says with a smirk, and I finally look away from his bulging crotch, embarrassed I've been caught staring.

"Most strangers don't make a habit of shoving their morning wood in my face, so you'll have to excuse my fucking surprise," I say. "Where are my clothes? I'd like to get dressed now."

He goes to the dresser against the wall and opens the top drawer. He pulls my clothes from inside and tosses them to me. I pull the fabric against my face and breathe in the fresh scent. Bright floral notes soothe my senses. A person can't understand the simple joy of clean clothes until they've gone without them, and I've been dirty for far too long.

"When did you get these from the laundry room?" I ask.

"I've been up for a couple of hours now."

Bullshit. I'm a light sleeper. If he'd left the room, I'd have heard it. "You were still sleeping when I got out of bed," I say.

"No, I was pretending to sleep when you got out of bed. I wanted to see what you'd do." He steps into his pants and buttons them, finally hiding the third leg. "I need that shirt."

I motion for him to turn around, but he only shakes his head. If he won't turn around and give me some privacy, I'll go to the bathroom. I put my feet on the floor, but before I can stand, his hands grip the hem of the shirt and he lifts it over my head. As my arms lower to cover my breasts, the shirt comes off and I'm completely bare.

"What the hell?" I scream as I scramble to find my shirt. It's inside out, so I have to spend another mortifying thirty seconds righting it before I can cover my body. All while he's standing behind me, watching and laughing. I don't find any of this funny.

"If I wanted to see your tits, I'd have seen them by now," he says.

"Is that a threat?"

His shoulders lift in a shrug. "Maybe." He pulls his shirt over his torso, but it doesn't hide the muscles underneath. If anything, it accentuates them. "You need to learn to trust me a little."

I reach for my shorts, stand, and slide them over my ass. Fuck it. If he wants to look, he can look. I'm not playing games with him. "You're doing a piss-poor job of earning my trust if that's been your goal so far."

He grabs my backpack from the bathroom and tosses it onto the bed. I stuff my spare clothes inside and throw in the half-empty water bottle for good measure. I need to keep my strength up, and the first step will be hydrating my drug-hungry body.

He pulls his cell from his pocket, reads something, types a reply, and looks at me. "We need to get on the road, so do whatever you need to do in the bathroom and let's get out of here."

He's flipped a switch and he's back to being Mister Serious again. Joy.

"Where are we going, anyway?" I ask.

"Me and Karson are headed to California. You won't have to stick with us for the whole ride, though."

"Because you'll kill me before then?"

I'm not stupid. I've seen faces. I know at least one name. Now I know where they're going. I don't know what these men are up to, but it's probably illegal. I'm a risk to their operation.

He walks out the door without answering me, but that's all the answer I need.

Chapter Nine

Gentry

The calm we had in the hotel disappears the moment we meet Karson in the lobby. His scoff rubs us both the wrong way. My patience for Karson's antics wane by the day. Hell, by the minute.

My cock isn't hard anymore, but my balls still ache. I wanted to fuck the ever-loving hell out of her back at the hotel. I *still* do. But it would take more than a beautiful face and a nice pair of tits to get me to break my abstinence streak. The day I found my brother balls deep in my wife was the day I vowed to keep away from lying women.

My fucking hand is faithful, at least.

But I was tempted by her—*am* tempted—and the side-eyed glare she keeps throwing my way as we reach the SUV isn't helping. She's curious about me. I saw that lustful look in her eyes back in the room, and I see it again now. But let's not complicate things.

Karson tosses the keys to Leana, and she looks at me.

"Ass in seat, little thief," Karson says before I can respond.

As she gets in the driver's seat and pulls onto the road, I regret allowing her behind the wheel. My stomach knots up because of how she rides the damn shoulder, and it doesn't help that I chose to sit in the back seat. My eyes remain locked on my brother, though. Every time he gives her a side glance, I prepare to get between them. He wouldn't try to kill her while she's driving, though. He's not that stupid. Maybe it's a good thing her ass is behind the wheel.

Karson pulls his pistol from his waistband and starts flipping it in the air, catching it by the barrel or the grip as it somersaults into his palm. Leana eyes him, and every time her throat bobs when she swallows, I know she wants to say something. She shouldn't worry so much. In all the years Karson has played "catch" with his pistols, they've only gone off twice.

197

We were teens the first time it happened, and the bullet went through *my* fucking foot. Not the twerp spinning the damn thing. Mine. The second time he was playing his solo game of catch while we waited for my wife to finish dinner. He shattered the kitchen window. Even though she witnessed his regular displays of dumbassery, she still slept with him. I don't choose women very wisely, I guess.

Poor judgment on my part for forgiving him for all of his bullshit, too.

Forgiving him for fucking my wife was hard. I'm still not sure I believe he planned to kill her, but it makes more sense than the alternative. And I've had a long time to sit and think about it. I've also never known Karson to *like* anyone, including me.

"Can you stop?" Leana screeches, breaking me from my thoughts. She flinches as the pistol twists in the air and the barrel gets a bit too close for comfort.

"Nope." He sends it into the air again.

The smug satisfaction on his face pisses me off, so I lean over and snatch it away before it reaches his hands again. Unfortunately, this brings the barrel close to Leana's head again. She jerks the wheel with a squeal and sends the SUV bumping along the shoulder before straightening it out again.

"We're done playing around!" I yell, leaving no room for either of them to argue.

"Did your father not play catch with a ball like a normal person?" she says toward Karson, and I fight back a smirk.

I shake my head and meet her gaze in the rearview mirror. "No, *our* father didn't."

Her eyes dart between us as realization washes over her. "You're brothers?"

"Blood," Karson quips, tugging another pistol from his waistband and beginning his game again. A deep laugh rumbles from his chest and erupts from his mouth as he grabs the grip on his last throw and turns the barrel toward Leana. His finger glides to the trigger and pulls it back before I can stop him.

Click.

The sound is almost lost beneath her scream. Her chest rises and falls with each ragged breath as fear grips her body in a chokehold. Karson's laughter grows louder and gains an edge that sets my hair on end.

Her eyes narrow and she whips the car to the side of the road, nearly sending me into the front seat when the tires grind to a stop. "Get out," she says. When we don't move, she raises her voice. "Get the *fuck* out!"

Her tone is potent enough to choke off Karson's laughter, and his mouth falls open from shock. No woman has yelled at us like that. Well, none that are still alive to talk about it.

Now I'm the one laughing. It's a low rumble of sound that I can't contain thanks to the sheer audacity of this girl. Her balls might be bigger than mine.

"You know what?" She snatches the keys from the ignition and throws them toward me. "Take the car. It's not even mine. Have a good life, Brothers Grimm." Her hand goes for the door handle.

I raise the pistol in my hand—the one that is very much loaded—and put it to the back of her soft blonde hair. "The Brothers Grimm were fucking scholars, so thanks." I push the barrel until her golden locks envelop the metal tip. "Now get your hand off the handle."

"Just kill her and get it over with," Karson says.

Her chest falls as the bravado fizzles out at the feel of my gun. The fear creeps back into her at my brother's words.

"I'd rather not," I say, "and if little miss here can behave herself, I won't have to."

"Fuck off," she mumbles, but I can still hear the bite in her voice. She's afraid, but she's also pissed. The hostility takes a detour to my dick.

I get out of the car, looping around the back and coming to a stop at the driver's side door. I whip it open and pull her from the seat. She writhes and tries to break free from my grasp, but I hold her against me until she's still.

"Watch your mouth," I growl in her ear. "Unless you're going to open your mouth and do something more useful with it, I'm kindly asking you to shut the fuck up and stop making this more complicated than it has to be."

The sweet scent of her panic rises to my nose, and I want nothing more than to press her against the side of the SUV and make something louder than some muttered curses flow from her full lips. I turn her and pin her against the metal. My hand goes toward her throat, and she flinches at my touch. Holding her like this sends sunlight against the bruises on her neck. Bruises that look like a shadow crawling along her skin. The shadow of a hand. She doesn't need to tell me what she's running from now. I have a pretty good idea.

I drop my hand to her arm and open the back door, flicking the child locks before putting her onto the back seat and locking her inside. I'm disgusted by the way my stomach twists with a hint of sympathy for what she's been through. Assholes like me don't feel bad for others. We look out for ourselves, and that's it. I remind myself of that and swallow with gritted teeth, squashing the feelings like the meaningless bugs they are.

"I'm not in the mood for either of you," I growl as I sit in the driver's seat and throw the car in drive. We really don't have time for this bullshit.

Karson leans forward and turns on the radio. Music blares through the shitty speakers and for the fifth time, I reach over and silence them.

"The radio was literally invented for road trips," Karson snaps as he throws his back against the seat.

"This isn't a road trip, Karson. Road trips take you somewhere fun. It's business."

"You'd rather just listen to silence? That's fun for you?"

I shake my head before letting my gaze rise to the rearview mirror. Leana's blue eyes stare out the window, the rest of the car seemingly unworthy of her stark glare. Her hair clings to the thin sheen of sweat on her cheek. She doesn't need to sit there looking so bitchy. We've been more than fair with her. We took her car— correction, not even *her* car—and that's it. Well, we took her too, but we haven't hurt her. I've enjoyed our little distraction for the most part, and I plan to keep her with us until we get closer to a place I never thought I'd visit. Hollywood. Puke. A real rich place for two men who despise rich people.

I grip the steering wheel and sigh. "We need to find another car soon. We've been driving this one for a few days, and the cops are probably looking for it."

"Way ahead of you," Karson says with a satisfied smirk. "I found a matching SUV in the last hotel parking lot and swapped the plates. If any tag readers lock on, it won't show as stolen. This is a common car in a common color, so as long as we do that every few days, we'll stay ahead of them. I guarantee the cops aren't hunting too hard for this hunk of junk anyway."

"What part of California are you heading to?" Leana asks, her eyes snapping to mine in the mirror.

Karson's head whips in my direction. "You told her where we're going? Are you fucking stupid, Gentry?"

"Hollywood," I tell her, ignoring Karson. "Where were you going? You were filthy and a thief, so you weren't heading home to visit Mommy and Daddy."

She scoffs. "Out of New York."

"What're you running from?" I ask again. I already know the answer, but I want to hear her say it.

"Nothing," she snaps, crossing her arms over her chest.

"Who the fuck *cares*, G?" Karson fiddles with his window, rolling it up and down in quick succession. Each time the glass leaves the seal at the top of the window, a roar of air vibrates the inside of the car. I use the controls beside me to raise his window and lock it. He mashes the button, getting more aggressive with every push. That incessant *click, click, click* begins to drive me nuts, and he knows it. He does shit just to make noise, I swear.

"Can you just fucking stop doing things?" I snap.

"I'm bored," Karson whines, drawing out the last word.

He sits up and looks behind his seat at Leana, and I regret taking away his toy when a feral smile crosses his lips. He unclips his seatbelt and climbs over the center console, something I could never do. I remain watchful as he drops onto the seat beside her. Karson's kind of a fucking pervert, and if I'm not touching her, I sure as fuck don't want him to lay a hand on her either.

She tugs her arms closer to her body and keeps her eyes pinned to the window. Karson stares at her. When that doesn't get the reaction he craves, he leans toward her and inhales a deep breath. It's really fucking creepy, and I don't fault Leana for what she does next.

Her arm pulls back, and she sends her palm into his nose with all the force she can muster. A crunch preludes a flurry of curse words roaring from Karson's mouth. I tighten my lips to keep from laughing. She did what I've wanted to do since our last gig.

"Fucking bitch," he snarls, yanking her toward him by her hair. He draws back a clenched fist, but she meets his gaze without flinching. She's way too fucking calm about what he's going to do.

"Karson!" I shout, and the rage in my voice is enough to lower his arm.

"She fucking hit me! My nose is bleeding, for fuck's sake! I should shoot her in the face." Karson's hands fumble around his waistband, but I have both his pistols up front. He springs from the back seat and reaches for the gun on the dashboard, but I snatch it away.

"We're not doing this," I say as I tuck the pistol between my legs. "You deserved that for being a creep."

"You think that was creepy? I'll show you both what creepy really is." He grinds out the words through gritted teeth as he rips down the zipper of his fly. He's likely preparing to jerk off in the back seat.

"Wanderer, you have my permission to rip his dick off if it's out," I goad.

The sound of his zipper struggling back into place pierces the silence. "Wanderer? Nice nickname he gave you, thief," he snarls toward her as he leans over and grips her chin. "You're his good little pet, huh?" He throws her away from him and climbs into the front. "Fuck you, G. I'm your family. Is this how you treat family?"

I lift my chin. "Really going there, brother? Do you actually want me to answer that?" Karson didn't care about us being family when he gave me up for a slightly better deal, and he sure as fuck didn't care when he fucked my wife. He continues to show his lack of care as he recklessly bulldozes over every one of my hits.

Leana sits back and shakes out her hand, unfazed by the entire ordeal. Karson lifts his arm and uses the sleeve of his jacket to comfort his bleeding nose. Despite the anger radiating from beside and behind me, at least everyone is fucking silent for once. Maybe we can actually get some miles under our belt now.

I return my entire focus to the road and keep driving.

Chapter Ten

Leana

I don't utter a single word for the rest of the drive. My hand aches from the impact with Karson's stupid face, but it was worth it. They have a really weird relationship, and I have no interest in being in the middle of such hostility. They don't even seem like they like each other. How the hell do they travel together without someone winding up dead?

Gentry pulls into the parking lot of a hotel. It's slightly more run down than the one from last night, but it's still better than curling up beneath an overpass. They grab their duffle bags and start walking inside, and I'm left to press my face to the glass because the child locks are still engaged. Karson turns back and waves at me like an immature fucking child. Gentry turns around and takes a few long strides back to me. How kind of him to remember.

He opens the door, and I nearly face-plant onto the pavement. His powerful arms encase my body, saving me before I end up with road rash on my nose. He lifts me onto my unsteady feet and keeps his hand on my arm for longer than I'd like. I tug out of his grasp.

"You're welcome," he snaps.

Despite making it clear that I don't want him to touch me, his arm winds around my waist and guides me toward the automatic doors in front of the hotel. The glass parts as we approach, and an overpowering flowery scent rushes toward us. It smells like a Glade PlugIn exploded in here. Gentry motions to Karson, who heads to the front desk to secure our rooms. Hopefully three, because I don't want to room with either of them.

Karson returns with two sets of key cards in his hands.

Fuck.

We take the elevator to the fourth floor. Crusty flakes of dried blood flicker beneath Karson's nose with every exhale, and the stain on his sleeve has darkened to a rusty brown. He catches me eyeing it and throws a silent snarl my way that reads like a promise of retaliation.

We exit the elevator and find our side-by-side rooms. Karson turns to us with the key cards in his hand. "There were only single queen-sized beds available," he says.

"Enjoy sleeping together, boys." I reach for a card, hoping those two jackasses will room together, but Karson raises it above my head.

"We aren't leaving you alone, *thief*." He snarls the word with such veracity it becomes literal venom. "Pick who you'd rather shack up with for the night. Hint: don't pick me, because I will kill you and fuck your corpse." Karson releases a laugh that makes the hair on the back of my neck lift away from my skin.

Even if he hadn't just threatened me, there's no way I'd share a room with him. I take a step closer to Gentry, choosing the man who showed at least a hint of normalcy by caring for me when I was at my weakest. While I don't care for either of them, at least this one hesitates to take me out. Maybe earning his trust wouldn't be such a bad thing. It might even make escape easier.

Karson scoffs and tosses one of the keys to Gentry before unlocking his door and going into the room alone. If I'm lucky, he'll pull a David Carradine and hang himself while beating his dick in the closet. He seems like he'd be into some shit like that. I shouldn't wish death upon someone, but he's just so goddamn unlikable. He's as outwardly attractive as his brother, but his attitude turns him into a bridge troll with leprosy.

Gentry and I enter our generic three-star hotel room to a stiffness that makes me think the ghosts of businessmen past probably haunt the room. Gentry throws his bag onto the white comforter that covers the white sheets and white pillowcases. The only darkness comes from the mahogany headboard, screwed into the wall behind the mattress and reaching nearly to the floor. A single chair stands near the bed, but it looks uncomfortable, as if it's only there for show and isn't meant to be sat on. There isn't a couch in sight.

My shoulders drop. "I'm guessing there's no way to get you to sleep on the floor, huh?"

"Not a chance." He tugs off his shoes and walks to the bathroom.

I follow him to the door, and a low buzz breaks the stale silence as he flips on the overhead light. Instead of a shower-tub combo, there's only a shower. Its glass door stands ajar, and my mouth waters at the prospect of cleaning myself two days in a row. Lathering my body with hotel soap when I don't feel like I'm on death's door is a luxury I crave.

"Go on," he says, waving me toward the shower. He must have seen me salivating over it.

I slip past him and ease the door closed, dropping articles of clothing as I near the glass partition. When I turn the tap to hot, steam claws up the glass and fills the room. An exhaust fan sluggishly runs overhead, unable to keep up with the forming humidity. I close my eyes and suck in a breath of thick air. This is as close as I'll ever get to a spa day, so I plan to make the most of it.

I step inside the shower and sigh as the hot water rushes over my skin. Despite the hotel's lackluster accommodations, this showerhead puts out incredible pressure. As I tilt my head beneath the stream, the tiny jets massage my scalp and send a pleasurable shiver up my spine. It's too bad it doesn't come off the wall. I can't remember the last time I made myself come, and this bad boy would have been nice to hold between my legs.

I can't deny that I'm sexually frustrated, and as precarious as my situation is, having to look at a double dose of eye candy for days hasn't helped. One is certifiable and the other is an enigma, but they're both attractive as fuck.

I push away the rising ache between my legs and focus on washing my hair and body. My imagination isn't my friend right now, and letting either man touch me isn't an option. I can't let my guard down.

I soak in the scalding stream of water for a little while longer before I get out and dry off with a scratchy towel. A robe hangs on the back of the door. I grab it, wrapping it around my body and tying it at the waist. My eyes roll to the back of my head at the thought of walking out in this. He's seen me in less, but I don't want to tempt him.

Or myself.

I don't really have a choice, so I exit the bathroom and try to avoid his gaze as I cross to the bed. I don't have to see his eyes to know they're on me, though. His dogged stare burns through the cheap terry cloth and sets my skin on fire. Before I'm reduced to ash, I need to get dressed. I reach for my bookbag, which I placed on the floor beside the bed, but it's not there.

"Looking for this?" He lifts my bag and jiggles it in the air. "I need to get a shower, but I don't trust you to stay put. You can stay in that robe until I get out, then I'll give your clothes back to you."

Running off while he showered hadn't crossed my mind, and I silently berate myself for allowing him to keep one step ahead of me. I don't argue with him, though. If I want to get on his good side, I'll need to be a little more compliant. This isn't the same as submitting out of fear—the way I survived under Mickey—so it doesn't bother me to give in a little for now.

He peels his eyes off me and goes to the bathroom to get ready for bed. I lie back on the mattress. The robe scratches at the backs of my thighs, and I wish I could take it off. I shouldn't complain—there are worse things out there than a shitty three-star robe—but I'm complaining.

I've nearly dozed off by the time Gentry emerges from the bathroom, but I'm wide awake when I see a massive statue of chiseled muscle standing shirtless in front of me again. His well-defined Adonis belt peeks from his waistband, and I consider using the tie from the robe to keep my jaw from hitting the floor. He tosses my bookbag at me, and it nearly collides with my face because I'm too busy gawking at perfection to catch it.

Forcing my eyes away from his body, I pull my spare clothes from the bag and start toward the bathroom. Before I can reach for the doorknob, his hand encircles my wrist, stopping me. Warmth radiates from his freshly showered body, and he smells like soap and sin.

"Get dressed in front of me," he says. "I liked it."

His low, sultry tone shoots straight to my pussy, and my panties would have melted if I had any on.

But I shake my head. My compliance has a limit.

"You gave Karson shit for being a creep and *that* is creepy," I say.

He chuckles, but he doesn't release my wrist. "Then I'm a creep."

I must be a creep too—or at least out of my mind—because I'm seriously considering offering an even trade. We can both get naked and dress in front of each other. Hell, maybe we can dress each other. With our teeth.

My vagina and I will need to have a talk later, because she is putting some really shitty ideas in my head. If I know what's good for me, I'll move away from him before I accidentally put his dick in my mouth.

Before I can move, he grips the tail of the tie around my waist and pulls. The scratchy fabric falls open, fully exposing my entire storefront. I grasp at the robe and pull it around me, dropping my bag in the process. With red cheeks, I scramble to snatch up my things and hurry into the bathroom, but he's on me before I can cover myself. He steps into me, and I flinch as he lifts my chin and examines my throat. The bruises are only whispers now, but they're still visible.

"Is this what you're running from?" His fingers leave my chin, and he engulfs the handprint with his grasp. "Who did this to you?"

I look away. "It's none of your business."

"It is my business when it could affect *my* business. I should know if it's someone I need to worry about."

I shiver when I remember Mickey's promise to find me. To kill me. But Gentry isn't asking because he's worried about *me*; his concern is for himself. If I want to earn his trust, this might not be a bad way to do that. Maybe it won't hurt to tell him.

"It's my fiancé," I whisper.

His hand drops from my throat and he takes the clothes from my hands and places them on the TV stand. "The only marks that should be on a woman are those made in a moment of pleasure. Did you like it when he wrapped his hand around your throat?"

I shake my head.

"Then he doesn't fucking deserve you." He grips my hand and pulls my ring from my finger. Instead of pocketing it or throwing it across the room, he slides it past his lips and swallows.

My eyes widen. "Did you really just do that? You couldn't toss it away like a normal person?"

"I'm the farthest thing from normal, wanderer." He pauses and shakes his head. "Actually, Karson is probably the farthest, but I'm just behind him."

"Karson didn't eat my ring," I mumble.

With a smirk, he slides the robe tie into my hand and starts toward the door. "Let's go wash our clothes."

"Like this?" I motion to my nearly naked body. "Can't I get dressed first?"

His eyes rove down my body and light my cheeks on fire. "Yes, like that, and no, you can't get dressed."

I scoff. "I'm not running around this hotel in a robe."

His big hand wraps around my waist and pulls my back against his body. A hard, thick mass presses against me, and I don't need to look down to know what it is. I clench my thighs together. With a low chuckle, he puts a hand against my back and pushes me toward the door.

We exit the room and the flush in my cheeks creeps to my chest as we walk by a housekeeper. Her eyes widen and she pretends she doesn't notice the shirtless man and the half-naked woman meandering the halls in the middle of the night. She doesn't say anything, but I'm not sure I'd say jack shit to a man like Gentry, either.

We take the elevator to the first floor and find the laundry room near the fitness room. Gentry pulls me inside, and an automatic light flicks on. A chill runs through me, and my nipples poke against the thin fabric. I fold my arms over my chest to hide the diamond points before he notices. Thankfully, he's busy putting the clothes into the washer.

"These shouldn't take long," he says as he starts the machine.

Great, what are we supposed to do until they're done? Probably go back to the room. When I grip the handle to head back, he sneaks up behind me and puts his hand over mine.

"Where do you think you're going?"

"Back to the room?"

"There's no point in going upstairs to come back in thirty minutes. I know you want to get out of that uncomfortable robe, but you could always take it off here." He teases me by raising the robe's hem up my thighs. The rough way his massive hands brush against my skin makes my stomach clench with need.

I slam my hands over his. "No, I just want my own clothes."

His eyes fall to the washer, and the smirk that crosses his face goes right to the juncture between my legs. He places his hands at my waist and lifts me as if I'm made of air. I try to stop him, but each thrash is pointless. It's like hitting a cement wall. He sets me on the washer, and the cold metal nips at the backs of my thighs because the robe has ridden up in the back.

"Fuck . . . off," I say.

Instead of listening to my demand, he steps closer and spreads my legs with his body. His hands grip the robe and pull it away from my ass, and my bare lower half presses against the metal. The cool temperature begins to warm from the contact with my heat. He reaches behind me, adjusts something on the machine, and pulls me forward when he leans back. My swelling clit meets the metal as the vibrating machine trembles beneath me.

"How does that feel, wanderer?" he asks as I dig my nails into his bare shoulders.

The vibrations beneath me feel amazing, but the man pressed against me takes it to another level. I want to feel his skin against mine instead of this shitty robe.

As if reading my mind, he slips his hand between us and pulls the tie away. He parts the robe before pulling me against him again.

"*Fuck*," I moan.

His hand snakes between us, and his fingers find my nipple. With an expert touch, he pinches, rubs, and twists the hardened point. His other hand moves to my ass, and he rocks me on the corner of the washer. Each movement teases my clit, adding and removing pressure and vibrations until my thighs quiver. His fingers squeeze my ass in time with his hand working my nipple, and the multitude of differing sensations spins my mind in a whirlwind of pleasure. I'm unable to think about how wrong this is when everything he does to me feels so good.

"Come, little wanderer," he growls as my nails bury themselves in his muscles. He lowers his mouth to my neck, his teeth teasing my skin.

My hips rock on their own, my pussy gliding with ease through the wetness he's brought out of me. His rock-hard dick brushes against the side of my calf. I imagine sliding that inside me, and it's almost enough to push me over the edge.

But I can't. It's not enough. I'm desperate for release at this point, desperate enough to lower my walls and throw all caution to the wind, but the vibrations just aren't strong enough. "I need more," I pant. "Help me come."

His fingers move toward my clit, and I lean back a little, giving him just enough room to touch me. The machine's vibrations travel through his fingertips, and he creates the pressure and movement I need. I lean back more, bracing myself by putting my arms behind me. He leans forward and captures my nipple in his mouth, nipping and sucking and swirling his tongue.

I spot the housekeeper outside the glass doors, and our eyes meet. Instead of feeling ashamed, I feel a sense of pride. This insanely massive and attractive man is currently working to get me off, and I'm almost glad someone was here to witness it. It's real. This moment is real.

I come.

Hard.

The orgasm rips through me, and I have to bury my mouth against his sweat-coated skin to keep from drawing attention to us as I cry out. My hands tighten their hold as every muscle in my body sings with relief, and he doesn't stop until he's sure he's drawn out every ounce of pleasure.

When the wave recedes, he lifts me from the washer and sets me on shaking legs. I've left a large wet spot on the machine, but I don't care. I'm not ashamed of the proof of what I've just experienced. His erection strains against his fly, and I expect him to take me.

At this point, I would let him.

Instead, he takes the robe tie and fastens it around my waist, concealing my body once more. With a sinful smirk, he looks down at me, and I almost rip off my robe and climb him like a tree.

But I take a deep breath and try to remember my morals. The man did abduct me, after all. I let him make me come, but I don't have to return the favor.

"Let's get back to the room so you can get dressed, wanderer," he says.

As I follow him to the elevator, I make a decision I'm sure I'll regret.

Instead of trying to escape, I'll stick with them a while longer.

Karson wants to kill me, but Gentry won't let that happen. I know that for certain after what just happened between us. If I remain under his protective wing, I'm untouchable.

Chapter Eleven

Getting into bed with a hard-on that just wouldn't go down was tough, and trying to sleep with her curled up on her side beside me seems like a monumental task. She relaxed the moment her head hit the pillow, and she didn't even place a barrier between us. I almost wish she had.

Her soft, repetitive snores should make my skin crawl, but I like hearing them because it means she's sleeping well. Her smile should piss me off, but I like seeing it because it means she's content. Not even my wife affected me this way. This has to stop.

While I didn't break my vow of abstinence by making her come, it was too fucking close for comfort. I'm really trying to behave myself because I don't want this to become a thing. I'm on a mission. My focus has to remain on making enough money to get out from under George, and nothing should distract me from that. And that's exactly what Leana is. A walking, breathing, long-legged distraction who makes me do things—makes me hunger for things—that are better left alone.

Maybe I just need to rub one out and get it out of my system.

I turn onto my side and pull the covers away from her body so I can see every curve. The bathroom light reflects off her soft blonde hair. Her lips part as she breathes through her mouth. Her back isn't warmer than any other part of her body, but it's so close that it burns me.

I get ballsy and rub my hand up the back of her thigh with a ghost of my usual touch. She stirs and nestles into me, the warmth of her pussy pressing against my leg. My feathery touch rises upward and grips her ass. A moan leaves her parted lips, and she opens her eyes, her lids heavy with sleep.

"Are you watching me?" she mutters. "Creepy."

I move my hand over her hip and pull her against me, expecting her to jerk away when she feels my erection against her ass. She doesn't. Instead, she creates a slight arch in her back and pushes against it.

I'm fucked.

I need her to tell me no because then I can stop. If she gives in, if she welcomes me inside her, I won't have the strength to turn her down. I have to put distance between us, and I know which topic will do exactly that.

"Tell me about this shit-bag fiancé of yours," I say.

Her body stiffens, and I almost sigh with relief. Now she'll shut me out again. Now she'll move away from me and put a pillow between us.

She relaxes. "Odd thing to talk about when you've got your hard dick pressed into my ass, but okay. Though there's not much to tell. I ran away from home when I was eighteen, and he found me at a bus station. Once he got me hooked on opiates, I was trapped."

Well, that backfired. I didn't expect her to open up like this.

"I'd wanted to leave for a long time," she continues, "but taking that first step was hard. The bruises you saw were the last straw. He'd beaten me plenty of times, but that was the first time I thought he'd kill me."

Knowing a man put hands on her was enough to piss me off, but I see red when I think about some asshole repeatedly abusing her. Instead of pushing her away as I intended, I wrap my arm around her and bring her closer.

"I'm sorry you went through that," I say against the back of her head.

"My turn," she says through a yawn. "How did you know I was going through withdrawal?"

I've begun a game I have no desire to play. I've never shared my upbringing with anyone, and I don't like the idea of peeling back the curtain and giving her a glimpse of my pain. My father's struggle with addiction and his subsequent death aren't tokens I freely hand out, even if they could buy my way between her legs.

When I don't answer, she huffs like a moody teenager and tries to pull away. I tighten my hold until she settles.

"How old are you, wanderer?" I ask.

"Twenty-four."

She's so fucking young. "I'm forty-six. Old enough to be your damn father."

She scoffs. "My daddy doesn't look like you, sir."

Pushed forward by the sass on her tongue, the word "sir" rolls past her sweet lips and travels straight to my dick. People have called me that while begging for their lives, but it never had any effect on me. When she says it, all hope of behaving goes out the window.

I roll her onto her back and push her legs apart so I can get between them. When I lean over her, she wraps her legs around my waist. Her blue eyes stare up at me as I raise her shirt and grip her stunning breasts with my hands. I like the idea of closing my lips around her pink nipples, so I lower my head and take one of the stiff peaks into my mouth. She moans as I nip the sensitive skin and tease it with my tongue. I'm lost in the sound of her voice.

I snake my hand between us and rub her clit. Her eyes roll back, her back arches, and I can't wait another moment to feel how wet she is. My fingers slide backward and plunge into her, and a whimper leaves her throat as I explore such a tight space.

"If you can't handle my fingers, you won't be able to handle my cock." I put a third finger inside her and her back raises from the bed, her chest colliding with mine. "You sure you want to try this?"

I don't know why I ask. I haven't cared about the pain my dick caused other women. When they consented to me, they consented to the pain that comes from someone as big as me. Like everything else, I'm learning that my little wanderer is new territory.

And I want to explore.

My mouth waters for her, and while I won't force myself inside her pussy, I'll probably beg her to put her pretty mouth on my cock to ease the ache I feel for her.

She nods, but I need to hear it. I need to hear that she knows what I'll do to her pussy and that she wants it. I grip her chin, forcing her to meet my eyes.

"Tell me. You haven't been shy about using your words so far, so tell me you want me to rip you in two."

"I want it," she whispers.

"Good girl."

That's all the answer I need, but I'll have to work her up to it first. I lean weight onto my arm and pin her to the bed so I can fuck her with my fingers. When her back rests on the mattress and stays there, when she writhes from pleasure instead of pain, I know she's almost ready for me.

Her whimpers shift to moans, rising to a volume that can probably be heard on the adjacent floors. I throw my hand over her mouth, silencing her. I don't need shit from Karson tomorrow. If he hears these sounds, he'll know what I've been up to and his desire to get rid of her will become a much bigger problem.

"Shh, wanderer."

Her nostrils flare above my hand, her eyes widening with fear. She reacts like someone who's been silenced like this before. I take my hand from her mouth and stick my fingers inside instead. The moans escape through the gaps, but they're muffled. Her tongue slides against my fingertips, and my cock twitches against my boxers.

I pull my fingers from her mouth and pussy, and her body responds to the emptiness by curling against my dick. I tug down the front of my boxers and rest my cock against her wet slit.

Even though I've worked her up to it and she's dripping for me, I still worry I'll be too much for her. I lean down and spit on her pussy.

"Oh, wanderer, this is going to hurt," I growl, "but you can handle me, can't you?"

After she nods, I grip myself and lean back to line myself up with her entrance, then I push my head inside her. She whimpers as her pussy grips my cock, sucking me inside the small space.

I'm not the type to make love to a woman, but I'll give her a few gentle strokes before I show her the full extent of my strength. I pull back and ease in, pushing until I reach her end. She screams out when I pull back and plunge into her once more, and I'll be forced to cover her mouth again if she can't keep quiet.

I stop thrusting, leaving myself buried inside her. I fist her hair and crane her neck. "If you can't keep quiet, I won't make you come."

She nods her understanding.

"Now call me sir."

"Yes, sir," she pants as I push into her again.

Yeah, I fucking like that.

I lean over her and fuck her with the selfishness that's pent up inside me. The selfishness that makes me who I am. I widen my stance, which spreads her open and stretches the muscles in her hips. She whimpers as I wrap my arm around her body and press her flush against my skin. I fuck her mercilessly. Her hands grip the sheets for support as I drill her pussy until I can't tell if her sounds hold more pleasure or pain. They're a package deal with a cock like mine.

So I don't stop.

"You feel so fucking good. I feel the flinch of your body every time I bottom out inside you. I'm hurting you, aren't I?"

Her fingers dig into my lower arm, raking my skin and causing pain of her own making. "Yes, sir."

"I told you I'd rip you in half, didn't I, wanderer?" I growl as I grip her hip bones so I can hold her in place and fuck her harder. She screams out, but I don't silence her this time. I'm lost in the feeling of her swollen clit against my pelvis. Between every thrust, I grind against her until she tightens around me, clamping down with so much force that I'm sure my cock will bear bruises tomorrow.

"Good fucking girl. Come for me. Come with my cock buried in your little pussy."

An orgasm rushes through her in a wave of pleasure that surrounds my dick. I tighten my grip on her hips to steady her core so I can fuck her through it.

"I'm coming, sir," she says through a fading moan, and it's enough to bring me to the edge of release.

"I'm going to fill you, and when I do, I'm going to keep my come inside you all night. Do you understand?"

"Yes, sir," she pants.

I empty myself inside her, coming harder than I have in years. I don't care if she's on birth control. The thought of breeding her, of keeping her bred for eternity, squeezes every drop from my balls. When I've finished, she looks at me as if she expects me to let her go, but I don't. I keep my cock inside her, with her throbbing clit resting against my pelvis. I like the warm squeeze of her come-filled pussy. Before my dick can soften, I turn her onto her side, lie beside her, and pull her against me. I stuff myself inside her, preventing even a drop of come from slipping out of her.

"You look so beautiful filled with my come." I brush the sweat-coated hair from her cheek. "But now we have a problem."

Confusion flashes across her face.

"If you have any fantasies about running off the first chance you get, get them out of your head. I'm real overprotective of what belongs to me." I turn her face and look into her eyes. She needs to understand the weight of what I say next. "For the remainder of this night, keep my cock inside you. And for the remainder of this trip, you and your pussy are mine."

Chapter Twelve

Karson

I heard everything. The *tap, tap, tap* of the mattress slamming against the wall. Her moans. How the fuck did that even happen? Since when has Gentry ever been more fuckable than *me*? He's a miserable grouch, for fuck's sake. She's already caused problems, but now she's a serious threat to our operation. I need to talk to Gentry about this and make sure his mind is still in the game.

I knock on their door as I pass it and hope it annoys them as much as their late-night fuck fest annoyed me.

Dicks.

The lobby welcomes me with that god-awful flowery scent the moment I get off the elevator. My bag's strap digs into my shoulder, and I swap it to my other arm as I make my way to the sad breakfast on offer—crumbling muffins, dry-ass cookies, and coffee. Very nutritious. I make myself a cup of coffee and take a sip. At least it tastes okay.

I carry the foam cup to the SUV, whip open the passenger side door, and plop down, waiting for them to appear. He'll lie to my face. I already feel it.

And what about her? Who the hell has a consensual fuck with their abductor, anyway? Those sounds were definitely fucking consensual. I might have a few screws loose, but she's not rocking with a full toolkit, either. Gentry's fucking her because she's attractive—mouthy, obnoxious, and a total bitch, but she's beautiful despite her circumstances. But what does she see in him?

I don't know why I give a fuck—I didn't stake a claim on her or anything—but I still bubble with rage at the thought of him sinking into her. Maybe I should take a piece of her for myself. After all, Gentry didn't stake a claim, either. Yeah, he fucked her, but unless he says she belongs to him, she's fair fucking game.

I scoff and sit back, setting my bag at my feet. The whir of the automatic door breaks the stifling silence, and I look back and see them emerging from the hotel.

She's dressed in some really lame clothes she must have bought at the gift shop. Correction, my brother would have bought them. The sweatpants say "Pennsylvania" down the leg, and "Pursue Your Happiness" blazes across the chest of her T-shirt. Guess they found the time to do a little shopping between all the gross fucking.

My eyes drop to the tense movement in her hips. She's almost limping. Did this mother fucker really . . . Heat creeps into my cheeks. I don't want him to see me react, so I try to let it go, even as she gets in the back seat with an obvious flinch when she sits.

Gentry slides into the driver's seat. "Sleep well?" he asks me.

If I had my gun, I'd have shot him for the casual line of questioning. No. I did not sleep at all while listening to their zoo noises. "Fine. You?" I lie.

"Yeah, slept fine."

That's it. That's all he says. I'm already pissed that some pussy is fucking up our job, but I'm irate that he's also lying to me now. His own flesh and blood! We don't betray each other.

The moment the thought floats across my mind, I taste the bitter sting of hypocrisy on my tongue. I betrayed Gentry in the worst ways. I fucked his wife. I gave him up for less prison time. In my defense, I planned to kill his wife while I was inside her, but he showed up before I could finish the job. And at least one of us had to do prison time, and he knew he could handle it better than me. I mean, look at him.

Gentry puts the car in drive, and I pull a some chips from my bag. I eat with my mouth open because I know it grinds his gears. His fingers wind around the steering wheel a little tighter with each satisfying crunch and smack. As his muscles flex in his lower arm, I notice the claw marks and shake my head.

"What the hell is the matter with you?" Gentry asks.

"You two fucked."

He readjusts in his seat and tries to lie. "We did not."

I scoff. "Yeah, I suppose she tore up your forearms while you two were jumping on the bed. That would also explain the headboard banging against the wall, right? And then she fell and hurt herself, which is why she was moaning."

"Shut the fuck up," he mutters.

"What was that song we learned when we were kids?" I bounce two fingers near his face. "Two little monkeys jumping on the bed. One fell off and—"

"I said shut the fuck up!" He swats my hand away and clenches his jaw. "Hate to tell you, Karson, but what I do—or *who* I do—is none of your fucking business."

"It's my business when we're supposed to be working."

The little thief leans forward and sticks her pretty nose where it doesn't belong. "What is it that you guys do, exactly?"

"Don't ask that," my brother and I say in near unison. At least we're on the same page about *something*.

"You can't keep it from me forever," she says. "How do you plan to do your super-secret job when I'm with you everywhere you go?"

"Yeah, how?" I turn to G, and his lips tighten. "You gonna leave her in the car like a dog?"

"Fuck off, Karson!" His voice rises to an explosive level for such an enclosed area, and it silences both me and the girl.

While he's still riled up, I reach out and flip on the radio. He roars out an inhuman sound before smashing the off button, leaving only the remnants of his scream behind.

I turn to the girl. "You know, thief, I have no clue what part of this made you spread your legs." I gesture toward Gentry.

She shrugs and sits back, dropping her gaze. I hate how easily she gives up today. I'm about to hop into the back and see how long it takes to make her squirm when Gentry's phone rings. The ringtone lets us know who's calling, and I see the hesitation in Gentry's muscles. He doesn't want to answer it, but we always have to answer it. We're *always* on call.

"Fuck," he says under his breath before tugging his cell from his pocket and accepting the call. "Hey."

I lean closer and try to listen in, but he hits the volume button down so I can't. Or maybe it's so she can't. Either way, I'm left out of the loop.

"We're still heading to the other gig," Gentry says into the phone. "You sure you want us to take a . . . detour?" He's making this call sound the least homicidal as possible and it's tripping him up. "We're almost in Ohio." Gentry nods as he listens to our boss. "Alright. We'll be there." He hangs up and sighs.

"Still think you can 'figure it out'?" I quip.

He glances in the rearview mirror and tightens his grip on the wheel.

"I don't care what you two do," the thief says from the back. "There's no need to try to shield me. I'm not an innocent little girl, you know. In case you forgot how I got this vehicle."

"Theft isn't even on the same playing field as what we do," I say, and it's almost laughable that she thinks she's reached our level. If she saw what we do for a living, she'd probably shit her panties.

"Do you deal drugs? Guns? Fucking organs?"

Growing tired of her stupid guessing game, I give an exasperated sigh and ignore her.

"You really aren't going to tell me what you guys do?" she continues. She's like a yappy little dog, and it's wearing on my last nerve. "What are you guys like . . . hitmen or something?" She lets out a chuckle, and I've had enough.

My head whips toward her and my lip curls. "You'd be wise to stop asking questions, thief."

"My name's Leana," she says with an inflated puff of her ample chest.

"Okay, thief."

Gentry throws us both a stare—first me, and then her through the mirror—and we both shut up. His dark eyes are as lifeless as his personality, and this motherfucker *still* got inside her. I hate that my brain keeps harping on it, but it bugs the piss out of me that Gentry is getting laid and I'm not. We'll have to change that, whether they like it or not.

Lauren Biel

Leana

Hearing them talk about a detour fills me with nervous energy that makes my leg shake, but a twinge of pain zaps my insides with every movement. I ache from the inside out, and I burn where he ripped through me when he first pushed inside me. I feel the pain in every movement of my hips from where his hands left bruises and the strain in the muscles as he spread me. My insides feel rearranged, like he pushed my uterus into my fucking chest. I've never been fucked like that.

And I hate how much I liked it.

I don't know what came over me last night. First I let him make me come in the laundry room, then I let him fuck me. I want to blame it entirely on my urge to get off, but I can't. The first orgasm should have cleared my head. Instead, it only made me want more. It can't happen again, though. Especially not when he still plans to get rid of me.

He said he would "figure it out" when Karson asked how they'd do their job while I'm tagging along. That can only mean one thing, and I didn't escape Mickey so I could fuck my future murderer. No matter how hard Gentry made me come, no matter how good he felt inside me, I have to keep my legs closed. If he fucks me like that again, I won't be able to run straight. I thought maybe he'd changed his mind about killing me, but I guess men never change.

Before I take off, I need to know what these men do for work. The not knowing will keep me up at night, even though it's probably best to keep my nose out of it. Whatever it is, I'm certain it's illegal. As long as it doesn't involve children, I can probably look past it, but they don't seem to care that I don't give a fuck if they rob or rip people off. Who am I to judge? Maybe if I can convince them I'm not the straight-and-narrow type, they'll rethink murdering me and I won't have to leave. I don't exactly look forward to struggling on the street again after spending a few nights in a bed—and having multiple mind-blowing orgasms.

We take the next exit, making what seems like more than a little detour.

Karson whips out his knife and drags the tip down the length of his finger. A bright line of blood springs to the surface. He rolls down the window and moves his fingers in the wind with an innocent playfulness. Crimson beads strike the glass and spread along the length of the window beside my head as the wind blows it toward the back of the car. When he tugs his hand back inside, he lifts it above his head and sends a few drops into his mouth before putting his finger up to his lips. He sucks, his cheeks hollowing as he holds pressure to his wound with his tongue.

What the fuck is wrong with this dude? His brother seems so normal.

Normal people don't carjack and abduct strangers, I remind myself.

Gentry doesn't acknowledge his brother's behavior. Maybe Karson's one of those people who stops their attention-seeking behaviors if you don't react. Unfortunately, I struggle to keep my mouth closed as I watch his sadistic enjoyment of his own blood. I mean, he's really going to town on that finger. Total fucking weirdo.

We drive until we get off the highway in the middle of Nowheresville, Ohio, and there isn't a motel or hotel in sight. Gentry pulls to the side of the road and punches something into his phone, and Karson busies himself by pressing his nails into the cut on his finger, opening it again.

"We'll have to camp out until it gets later in the evening," Gentry says.

So much for enjoying a bed every night.

He drives to a campground and parks in the back of the lot, then he takes a hundred out of his wallet and hands it to me. "Go get a site," he says.

"Yes, sir," I say, and the corners of his lips tremble as he tries to avoid smiling at me.

"Buy a bundle of wood too!" Karson yells as he gets out and loops around the SUV.

I make my way to the tiny building, and a bell chimes overhead as I enter. A young woman sits behind the desk, a visor holding back her blonde hair.

"Checking in?"

"Well, no. I'm hoping there might be a site available for a walk-in tonight?"

The woman types on a yellowed keyboard that sounds sticky with every press of the keys. "Tuesdays are usually good for walk-ins," she says as her eyes scan the screen. "We have availability. Let me just get the paperwork." She leans over and pulls out a paper with three identical segments. She marks the areas for me to fill out my information, and marks three X's, one on the bottom of each.

After I fill the paper with false info, I slide it back to her.

She tears the top one off, writes D34, and marks tomorrow's date in bold marker. "Place this on the dash." She hands it to me. "That will be thirty-five dollars."

Karson passes the building's window with a bundle of wood in his arms. "Oh, and a bundle of wood, please."

"That will be forty dollars, then."

I hand over the cash and she pulls out a money box to make change. She's short five dollars. She looks around, the cash curling in her hand as my foot taps with growing nerves. "Just keep it, thank you!" I tell her, taking what change she has.

I walk back to the car and hand Gentry the paper for the dashboard. Karson loads the wood into the back as I walk by him. "Useful for something, at least," he mumbles as I pass.

I get in the back seat, and Karson slams the back hatch and gets in the passenger seat. We pull onto maintained dirt roads that loop around lines of campsites. Gentry pulls to a stop in section D at pole thirty-four, and I glance around at the campers and tents surrounding our spot.

"We don't have camping gear," I say.

"It's just a place to chill until late tonight." Gentry gets out, grabs the wood from the back, and lights his cigarette before stacking the wood in the firepit.

As I sit against the rock on the outskirts of the site and watch them work, a heavy tunnel of dread surrounds me. Mickey's words echo in my mind. I've put a lot of ground between us, but he swore he'd find me. I still feel the heaviness of his anger, even from this far away, the thread tethering me to our history trying to dissolve in front of me. He likely knows I've skipped town by now. Waiting for me to come crawling on my hands and knees has backfired, and he's not one to lick his wounds. If he manages to track me down, he'll have no chance against Gentry, but Karson would probably hand me over on a silver platter.

Fucking Karson.

"Wanderer!" Gentry raises his voice. "Did you hear anything I said?"

I shake my head.

He steps away from the fire and stands in front of me, dropping his voice. "What's on your mind?"

My head keeps shaking until my eyes drop to the grass.

"Is it about what you're running from?"

I scoff. "I'll tell you what I was thinking about when you tell me what you guys do for work."

"Fair."

Karson appears beside me like some psychotically ill ghost. He puffs on a cigarette before drawing it from his lips and offering it to me.

I want to say no because I shouldn't accept anything he offers me, but the temptation overpowers me. I take the cigarette from his fingers and bring it to my mouth, inhaling a deep cloud of nicotine. My throat tightens, and I cough as I exhale.

"A criminal should be able to handle a cigarette, don't you think?" he quips, and the way he says it makes me want to stab the lit end into his eye.

"You don't know anything about me."

"Enlighten me, thief. You sure love to ask *us* questions."

"And you don't answer them either."

Karson graces me with a sadistic smile and rubs a hand down his face. "Mouthy. Real mouthy." He steps in front of me, and my glare rides up to his crazed eyes. His fingers twitch at his side, and I can see what he's thinking. And I don't like it.

"Karson!" Gentry shouts, stepping between us.

"He can't protect you forever, thief," he says over Gentry's shoulder before stepping away.

The fire casts an orange glow on Gentry's face, accentuating each curve of his muscles and dancing in his dark eyes. A cigarette dangles from his lips as he maneuvers the logs, sending sparks and crackles from the wood. He stands upright and wipes his hands on his jeans.

"Come with me," he says, juggling the cigarette between his lips as he speaks.

"Of course," Karson clips.

I push off the rock and follow Gentry into the woods. For all I know, he could be leading me to my death, so why am I so unafraid? How have I put so much blind trust into this handsome stranger? Maybe he's about to tell me to get lost, and that strikes more fear into my heart than the thought of his hands wrapping around my throat. It seems more possible, at least.

Once we're far enough away from the campsite, Gentry stops and turns to face me. "Be careful with my brother," he says. I meet his eyes in the darkness. "He's dangerous. Well, I'm dangerous too, but not like him. Watch your pretty mouth with him before you end up without a tongue."

"You sound afraid of him."

Gentry shakes his head and looks back toward our campsite. "I'm not scared of Karson. Being aware doesn't mean I'm fearful. I'm just being smart. Karson is like a rabid dog. And he's as predictable as one too. He's the type of person who can greet you with one hand while stabbing you in the neck with the other."

The words leaving his lips carry a heavy truth, and I can barely nod under that weight.

"Brave to call me sir earlier," he adds. A grin crosses his face, and I'm struck by the realization that he only really smiles when we're alone.

He steps toward me, and the look in his eyes makes me take a step back. My back hits a towering oak, but he keeps moving forward until I feel like I'm sandwiched between two trees. He leans closer and my breath catches in my chest.

"It makes me want to fuck your mouth when that word rolls across your tongue," he says near my lips. "As soon as you say 'yes, sir,' I want to drop you to your knees and bury my cock in your throat until I feel you beg for a breath."

He leans closer and kisses me. His tongue finds mine, and a soft whimper leaves my throat. Alarm bells spring to life in my gut, but they're silenced by the overpowering beat of my galloping heart.

Gentry feels so incredibly wrong. I've let him inside me and despite knowing it's a terrible idea, despite promising myself the last time was the last time, I want nothing more than to let him inside me again.

"Yes, *sir*," I whisper against his mouth.

He pushes me to my knees, and his hand works open his jeans until his cock stands in front of my face. His hand winds through my hair, gripping my head to hold it where he wants it as he lines himself up at my lips and shoves past them. I feel like a snake who has to unhinge its jaw to take its next meal. He drives his hips forward, pushing until he's filled my throat completely.

I suck air through my nostrils as his cock plugs my airway. I can't move away from him because my back still presses against the trunk of the oak tree. My hands grip the front of his jeans, smacking at his thigh as I think about the poor medical examiner discovering the trauma to my fucking throat. I never in my life thought I would actually die in the face of my own insult and choke on a dick, but here I am, choking away.

I'm fucking stupid for wanting this, but the feral groan that leaves his lips creates a deep, wet heat between my legs.

"You have no idea the beast you tempt, wanderer," he growls. "It takes so much restraint to let you draw a breath when I only want to feel your throat clamping down on my dick."

He finally pulls back so I can breathe, and I pant and wipe the drool from my chin.

"Still want to test my willpower?" he asks, balling my hair in his fist again. His fingertips graze my neck and send a pleasurable shiver through my core. "It takes me longer to come than you can hold your breath."

The way he looks down at me with such dominance is enough to make me pliable mush in his powerful hands. "Yes . . sir . . ." I choke out.

Before I even finish the last word, he's back in my mouth, fucking my throat with renewed energy. My throat tenses around him as he gives a final push toward the farthest depths of my mouth.

"Ah, ah," he says, twirling my hair in his hand. "Feeling you squeeze around me like that gets me too close, and I don't want to come down that pretty throat of yours. I want to fill you." He tugs me to my feet and pulls me into him. His mouth moves to my ear, and his beard caresses the side of my neck. "I like you stuffed with my come. I like the thought of breeding you."

He lifts my arms and pins me against the bark of the tree. My chest rises to meet his as my pulse quickens. With a swift and powerful motion, he spins me around, tucking my ass into the curve of his pelvis. He grips my wrists with one hand and presses my palms against the rough bark as his other hand rides down my body. He hooks the waistband of my sweatpants and yanks them down.

"I can't take you again," I whimper as his cock heats the skin of my ass.

"Of course you can. Don't you want to be a good girl and take my cock?" Encouragement and seduction collide and saturate his words. Not even the painful reminder between my legs can overpower the persuasion in that dark, gravelly voice. He sounds like he knows what's best for me, and I want to listen.

"Yes, sir," I whimper.

The moment the words leave my lips, he pushes inside me, sliding his way to my core. I grip the wood, sending chunks of flaky bark to our feet. He's firm but gentle, selfish as he grips my bruised hip but kind as he eases forward until he bottoms out inside me. His mouth drops toward my ear and praises me with a pleasure-laced growl.

"That's my good girl."

His hand leaves my hip and detours to the growing heat between my legs. He rubs along my slick slit, his touch battling the pain, rivaling it with brute strength and tenacity. It sends pleasure through my entire body, blanketing my skin with warmth against the cool night air. His fingertips stroke my clit, back and forth, and each swipe leaves me clenching the tree for dear life.

"You're going to come, aren't you?" he asks.

"Yes, sir," I whimper.

"I want to fill you. I want to breed you. I'm going to come deep inside you, coat every inch of you," he says with a groan, "but first, I want to feel you coming around my dick."

His words speak directly to my clit, and I come. My body drops against the wood, and my moans gain a mind of their own as they erupt from my mouth and blend with the sounds of the forest.

"I'm coming, wanderer," he groans as his hips dig into my ass and he buries himself deeper inside me. He twitches within me as he unloads his pleasure with a low rumble that vibrates my chest.

He stays inside me until he finally softens, then he pulls out of me and turns me to face him. A growl leaves his throat at the sight of his come dripping down my thigh. His fingers glide up my pale skin, gathering his come and pushing it back inside me.

"If you're on birth control, don't tell me. Let me imagine that every load I fill you with carries the risk of breeding you."

Thank fuck I'm on the implant, because I have no interest in bringing a child into my shitty situation. I've kicked my addiction to opiates, but it seems I'm doomed to always find myself hooked on something that isn't good for me. This time, his name is Gentry.

Chapter Thirteen

Gentry

We're back on the road a few hours later, on our way to a hit. Karson was in a mood when we returned to the campsite. I told him he could take the lead on this hit to try to cheer him up, and it seems to have worked. He's keeping quiet and has stopped his brooding and glaring. It's a short-term solution to a bigger problem, and I need to find the permanent fix. Logically, that's getting rid of Leana.

There has to be a way to keep her that doesn't piss off Karson. I just haven't figured it out yet.

I debated telling Leana what we do so she'd understand why it's so important to stay in the car while we work, but I don't know how she'll take it. Probably not as well as she takes my dick.

We reach the bottom of the driveway and tuck the car into the woods. The man in the house on top of the hill betrayed our boss in the worst kind of way. He acted as an informant to cover his own ass, and now George wants him to pay in blood. Because George wants him to suffer as much as possible, he also gave the go ahead to let Karson off his leash. A professional crew will come in to clean up our mess.

I'm more interested in getting the job done and securing a payday. I don't enjoy murdering as much as I used to. It lost its shine when I turned it into a full-time job, which is often what happens when someone shifts their hobby into a business. Karson still enjoys it, but he gets so carried away. His reckless abandon is a risk. He doesn't consider how his actions might get us caught, so I have to do the thinking for the both of us. It's exhausting.

I turn to Leana before we exit the car. She's asleep in the back, curled up on her side, and I consider letting her stay that way in the hopes that she'll remain knocked out while we do our job. I decide against it. Part of me hopes she might try to escape while we're occupied. That would get rid of so many problems.

"Hey," I say as I shake her awake.

Her eyes blink open, and she sits up and looks around.

"We've gotta take care of something. I need you to stay in the car."

She nods her head and closes her eyes again. She seems more than happy to go back to sleep, so maybe I'm worrying for nothing.

Karson pulls me aside, and he doesn't look as sure about this plan. "Do you really think she'll stay put?"

I shrug my shoulders and start toward the house.

"What's gotten into you, G?" he asks when he catches up. "You know we need to get rid of her, and you know it should have happened before we took her to a fucking job with us. You're not only gambling with your freedom. You're gambling with mine."

I stop and turn to face him. How fucking dare he be such a raging hypocrite. "You gamble with our freedom every time we do a fucking job, so I don't want to hear it. Or have you forgotten about the jizz jar?"

He rolls his eyes and throws his hands in the air. "It's not the same thing, and you know it. I don't like this, and I want you to promise me something. If she doesn't stay put in that car, if she sticks her nose where it doesn't belong, I get to handle her."

I don't like this, but I don't see another way to shut him up. "Fine. If she's dumb enough to let her curiosity get the better of her, you can do whatever you want with her."

He nods and turns for the house, but I don't like the smug smile that springs onto his face.

I grab his arm and turn him to face me. "I have one condition. If she's gone when we get back, we consider it settled and we don't go after her."

"You don't get it, do you?" he says. "She's not going anywhere. Maybe you don't see the way she looks at you now, but I do. She's got it bad for you, G. And I'm starting to think you might have it bad for her too."

"Bullshit."

"Oh, really? So you wouldn't mind if I borrowed her for a night? Hell, that might make it worth keeping her around." Karson waits for my answer, knowing he's called my bluff. Of course I don't want to share her, but if he knows that, it will only paint a bigger target on her back.

"Do whatever you want. Good luck getting her to agree to spending a night with you, though."

"Who said she had to agree?"

I've had enough of this conversation, so I walk away before my fist finds its way to his mouth. We have a job to do, and I'm ready to get it over with.

Getting into the house is easy enough. The only security camera on the property faces the front. It's easy to skirt, and we find the back door unlocked. What a moron. It's not a large house, and Karson finds the target fast asleep in his king-size bed.

While he handles the asshole, I start my search for payment. I find a safe in the study, tucked away in a closet behind a stack of classical music records. What a pretentious fucking collection.

Screams echo from the room across the hall. "Ask him what the code is before you kill him!" I yell.

My brother repeats the question, but the man merely wails in response. I slam my fist against the safe and go to the bedroom to see what type of torture Karson has cooked up today. The man is in a pile on the ground, and both Achilles tendons have been severed. Karson stands over him, flipping the knife and catching the handle. The man's hands claw forward as he struggles to drag himself toward the door, but Karson halts his progress by placing his boot on his limp foot. He looks like a cat toying with a mouse by stepping on its tail.

"What's the safe code?" I ask again, leaning toward the man's bruised face.

"Fuck you," he snarls.

I bring my foot down on his hand, grinding the heel of my boot until I hear the satisfying cracks. He screams as his only remaining useful limb paws at my leg.

"Goddamn it!" he squeals. "Your boss knows why I did what I did. He acts like he wouldn't do what he could to keep his ass out of prison too!"

"It doesn't matter what our boss would or wouldn't do because he's not the one who was dumb enough to get caught," I say. "Now, what's the code to your fucking safe?"

His wide eyes rise to mine with a ridiculous amount of defiance for a man in this predicament. "You're going to kill me anyway. Why would I give you anything more than my fucking life?"

Karson leaps onto the man's back and straddles him. He grips a fistful of hair and pulls back his head. "Because if you tell us, I'll leave you looking good *enough* that your family can have an open casket at your service. Don't you want them to see this ugly mug one last time?" he asks through a laugh.

The man strains to hold himself up with his good hand. "I'm not . . . giving . . . you anything," he grinds out.

"Alright," Karson says with a sweet lilt to his words.

Which means he's going to—

A visceral scream cuts the air as Karson puts the knife to the man's cheek and skins him from his mouth to his eye. The flap comes off with a squelch, and he holds it in front of him. Red, raw muscle glistens beneath his eye socket, and I'll admit it brings back good memories.

The man pants out the code, and I have to give it to Karson. He has a way with these idiots.

"See how easy that was?" Karson asks. He balls up the flap of skin and shoves it into the man's mouth.

I turn to leave but the rip of flesh behind me stops my feet from moving. When I face them again, I find that Karson has slit his throat. "Goddamn it, Karson! Let me try the fucking code first!"

"You don't have to yell," he says, but he uses the gaping neck like a puppet as he speaks. The gasping, gurgling man doesn't have long, and that's a mercy I'm surprised Karson afforded him.

All in all, the hit has gone well. And I didn't even have to make good on my promise to Karson.

Leana

I should have stayed in the car. When I heard the screams as I approached the house, I regretted my decision to be a nosy bitch, but I still crept closer. Now I'm inside the house. I'm almost certain they've murdered someone, but I can't stop my feet from taking me toward the source of those screams.

I reach the doorway, and my wide eyes lock on Karson as he releases a man's head and it thumps to the ground. A greedy excitement casts a shadow over his eyes, and the snarl of his lip freezes my soul. The mutilated body doesn't affect me. The blood doesn't bother me. But that look on Karson's face when he sees me is enough to make me regret my curiosity.

"I told you she wouldn't stay in the car," Karson says to Gentry as he rises to his feet. He doesn't seem angry, which unsettles me. He should be pissed, but he seems almost happy that I've fucked up so royally. He licks up the length of the blade and turns his attention back to me. "Now the fun can really begin."

Gentry curses under his breath. "Run!" he says as Karson rushes for me.

My heart thumps a painful rhythm against my chest as I rip open the front door and take off into the night. My head whips from side to side as I try to gather the lay of the land, but aside from the woods, I see nowhere to run.

"Little thief?" Karson's voice calls behind me. The high, taunting sound breaks through my fear and spurs me forward.

My feet stomp with a muted thud across the grass until I reach the edge of the forest. Running over twigs and leaf litter will be anything but quiet, but I don't have another choice. Branches whip at my face, sides, and ankles. I risk a glance over my shoulder, and my heart stops beating when my eyes land on the ominous black shadow on my heels. He almost dances as he pursues me, as if this is all one big game to him. My near-exploding heart doesn't think it's a game.

The toe of my shoe snags on a root snaking across the path, and I fly forward. As the ground comes toward me, I push my arms forward and bear the brunt of the impact in my wrists. I try to kick off the ground, digging the toes of my shoes into the earth to gain traction, but arms wrap around me before I can find my feet.

Karson has me.

He's over me, pressing his weight into me. No matter how much I flail, I can't move him. My lungs beg for air, but I can't draw a full breath beneath him. I'm drowning.

"Naughty little thief," he whispers near my ear. "When we say stay in the car, it's because we're doing something you can't unsee. You've always been a liability, but now you're a goddamn threat. Do you know what that means?"

"Please, Karson. I won't say anything!" Tears stream down my face because I know exactly what that means, and Gentry is nowhere in sight. There's nothing to stop him from ending me right here.

"Only the dead don't speak," he says. He brings his knife to my throat, and each panicked beat of my heart pushes my pulse against the cold steel. "But I want to feel what my brother has felt. What's made him so . . . weak. Lower your pants."

With the knife keeping me under his control, I don't have a choice. I search for a reason to deter him from what he plans to do as I pull my pants past my ass. "Gentry had sex with me at the camp! He came inside me."

Karson's sadistic laugh rattles me to my core. "I don't care whose come is inside you as long as mine follows. Besides, nothing turns me on more than a kill, and filled or not, your cunt is much better than my hand."

I drop my chest to the grass again and give up. Maybe he'll let me live if I don't fight him.

Karson pushes inside me with a groan. He has some kind of piercing that rips through me with different sensations I've never felt. I dig my hands into the ground, gripping the soft earth as he fucks me like a man who still fully intends to kill me after. My tears don't derail him in the slightest. If anything, they seem to fuel him.

"Fuck, little thief. Now I know why my brother likes you." He fucks me harder, faster, removing the knife from my throat so he can place his hands on the ground for leverage. A groan leaves his mouth, and I can tell he's getting closer.

"Please, Karson, Gentry is going to be pissed."

"I don't give a fuck what Gentry will do or think when I'm balls deep in a cunt like yours." He grinds me into the ground.

Something catches my eye—the glint of moonlight reflecting from the blade beneath his palm. I rip it from his grasp and blindly stab behind me, jabbing until he finally lets out a scream. The sound he makes turns my blood to ice. It isn't a sound born of pain.

It's a sound born of intense pleasure.

He comes with the tip of the blade in his fucking thigh. An animalistic groan claws from deep in his gut as he sits back, and I scurry out from beneath him.

Gentry's heavy footfalls sound behind me. When he sees that I'm alive, his chest falls with a moment of relief, but then he takes in the rest of the situation.

My pants past my ass.

His brother on his knees, wiggling the blade of his knife in an almost pleasurable way.

The tears cutting a track through the dirt on my face.

Gentry is on me in a moment. The heat of his anger emanates from his skin and pours into me. He pulls me against him, pulling my pants up with his free hand.

"You didn't?" He snarls the question at Karson.

"Sure fucking did. Decided to give her a chance to convince me to keep her alive." He tugs the knife tip from his thigh. "Then she fucking stabbed me."

"You didn't," he says to me, soft and low.

I nod and rest my head on his chest.

"I decided to let her ass live." He gets to his feet. "For now."

I don't understand him. And I don't trust him.

Gentry steadies me on my feet before walking to Karson. With little effort, he lands a disgustingly hard punch in Karson's gut. "I told you not to touch her," he snarls before ramming another punch beneath his ribcage. I can taste the earthy tone of his anger on my tongue.

Karson smirks. "No, you told me to do what I want. And that was what I fucking wanted."

"Get out of my sight," Gentry commands, shaking out his fist.

"I'm not—"

"Now!" Gentry shouts, raising a pistol from behind his back and aiming it at Karson.

Karson throws his hands up. "Fine, don't get your panties in a wad," he says as he holds a hand to his thigh and takes off for the car.

Gentry turns his attention to me. His hands brush my wet, dirty hair from my face. His fingers sweep over my body, and I feel him everywhere. He's trying to see if I'm okay. He sits on the ground and drags me onto his lap. His strong arms wrap around me. "I didn't think he'd—I thought I'd find you dead. Not beneath him." He raises my chin. "I can't believe you stabbed him, wanderer. My brave girl."

His buttery-soft words push away the fear and pain coursing through my body. I drop into him, smelling the familiar scent of his shirt.

"You're okay," he soothes, his big hand rubbing up and down my back until I stop crying.

Until I stop feeling the guilt from his brother's assault.

I hate that I enjoyed the feeling of his piercing, because I hate *him*. I hate that I enjoyed the thrill of being hunted. I hate that I didn't fight harder because it started to feel good. What the fuck is wrong with me?

"Why didn't you wait in the car?" Gentry asks. "When a man like me tells you to stay in the car, you stay in the fucking car."

"I'm sorry," I whisper.

"You walked into something you can't walk out of. And I *know* I need to get rid of you, I do. But I can't. I don't know if Karson will, and that's even more of a reason for *me* to take you out, because *he* enjoys the pain and punishment. He'd enjoy killing you. But against everything I believe in, against all the rules I've laid out, I can't get rid of you, wanderer. I don't want to." He takes a deep breath. "Welcome to the fucking business."

I sense the lack of permanence in his voice. There's no finality. "For now?" I ask.

He leans in and kisses me, but he doesn't answer the question. Instead, he grips my arm with one hand and the waistband of my pants with the other. "I don't want his come inside you." He slips my pants down to my thighs and brings his lips close to mine. "Push it out."

I don't argue, because I also don't want Karson's come inside me. I lean back on my heels and squat, using Gentry's arm for support. I bear down as if I'm going to pee, and Karson's come drips onto the ground. When I've voided every drop, I stand, pull up my pants, and follow Gentry to the car.

What a horrible fucking night. I learned more about myself than I ever wanted to. A deep seed of disgust takes root in my stomach and branches into my veins. I should be more bothered by the gory murder scene and Karson's following assault. My legs should itch to beat a path away from these psychopaths. Instead, I want to run toward them. With them.

When Gentry welcomed me to the business, I didn't feel an ounce of fear or trepidation. For the first time in a long time, I only felt like I belonged.

What does this say about me?

Chapter Fourteen

I understand what has Gentry wound so tightly now. Sinking inside her certainly changed my outlook on things. I find myself looking for reasons to keep her as we drive through the night and put some road between us and the mess we left behind.

Slitting her throat is still a viable option, but maybe I don't have to do it immediately.

My abdomen hurts, and a wave of pain races through my core with every inhale. The pain in my gut is hardly a deterrent. I like it, and even though I should feel bad for what I've done, I don't. I've never felt bad about the pain I inflict on others. It's part of my diagnosis. I *wish* I felt some semblance of guilt so I wouldn't do it again, though.

We pull into a hotel parking lot, and Gentry ushers the little thief inside to get our rooms. He won't leave her alone with me. Not now that I've tasted the delicious haze of panic as I forced my way inside her. Just thinking about it gets me excited for the next time, and there will be a next time.

She hasn't spoken to me since we started driving again. Not a single word. But I get it. I took her against her will when I couldn't quiet the ache in my cock after such a glorious murder. Homicide sends a rush of hormones through my body, and coming after such an act gives me an indescribable release. Usually it's in my hand, but her cunt presented a much better prospect.

Yeah, I understand why Gentry acts like a stupid fuck because of her. I could lose myself inside her too, so I have to be careful to keep my mind on the prize. We can't both be dumb now, can we?

I suck in a deep breath and enjoy the sharp sear of pain rising into my chest. It should piss me off that he got in a few punches because I did what we agreed to, but I can't find the fucks to give. And he *did* agree to it. He even said he didn't care if I used her a little, but I guess we both know that's a lie now. The anguish was written all over his face when he saw that I'd played with his new toy. He'll need to build a bridge and get the fuck over it. Our piece of shit father didn't teach us much, but he always told us to share our toys.

My hand goes to the center console, and I pull out the pack of smokes tucked inside. I light one and watch the hotel entrance. I understand why they left me in the car while they went to secure the rooms—I'm the one covered in blood—but that doesn't mean I have to like it. This isn't a tricycle and I'm not the third goddamn wheel.

Gentry knocks on the car window and motions for me to follow them. I put out my cigarette, throw both duffle bags onto my shoulders, and head toward the back entrance. When we get to our floor and the elevator opens, Gentry throws the key card at me.

"Your room is on the next floor up, because fuck you," he says.

I drop his bag on the floor, and they leave me to ride up to the next floor alone. I don't miss the backward glance the thief gives me, though. I have a feeling that sexy piece of ass is going to rip us apart if we're not careful.

Gentry

They had three rooms—two of them on the same floor—but I made the decision that was best for everyone. I need to keep Leana close, and she didn't argue when I chose two rooms, so I feel better about that. There was no way I wanted to be anywhere near Karson, though. Not after what I walked up on.

Guilt eats away at me because I didn't get to them sooner. I can't run as fast as Karson, and a knee injury from my time in prison slowed me down further. But that's not entirely true. Guilt mostly eats away at me because I was relieved he'd fucked her instead of killing her. I expected to find her dead, and my red-hot anger cooled to a simmer when I saw she was alive. Used, yeah, but fucking alive.

I pull her toward me when we get inside our hotel room, but she flinches at my touch. She probably fears me after learning what we are. What we do. I loved how she looked at me before learning why the Kursicki brothers are "Kursed."

I replay the look I saw on her face when she spotted the dead man—eyes wide with shock—but her reaction wasn't what I expected from someone who just walked in on a grisly murder. Her head had cocked with an almost curious tilt.

I replay my galloping heart when I heard Karson's pleasure-laced scream—a sound I feared had come from a kill. She wasn't as freaked out about his assault as I thought she would be, either.

This girl glows with a gray hue around her.

And I'm fucking obsessed.

What switch is broken in her little head? She might be more like us than she realizes.

"I wish you had stayed in the car," I say.

She swallows. "I needed to know what you guys did, and you wouldn't tell me." Her voice is a low whisper, and I almost can't make out the words.

"I wasn't hiding it from you for *my* safety. I wanted to let you go in the end, but I knew there'd be no hope for you if you knew what we did. Now I have to figure out how to argue my point with Karson."

At the mention of his name, she looks away from me.

"Did he hurt you?" I ask.

She shakes her head. "No, not like I expected him to."

He's so fucking lucky he didn't hurt her, because I'd have to hurt him much worse if he had. But Karson will want her again after this. She's got a target between her legs.

I fist her hair and bring her lips close to mine. "Even if he fucks you, you're still mine, wanderer."

"Yes, sir," she says, and it hardens my dick in an instant. I don't want to intrude on her body any more than she's already experienced, though. She's been through enough. I turn for the bed, but she grips my arm and holds me in place.

"I'm not a piece of glass," she whispers. "Do you think your brother was the first person to take that from me? I didn't shatter then, and I won't shatter now."

"Your fiancé?" I ask.

"It doesn't matter who it was. I just don't want you to treat me like something fragile."

If she doesn't want me to handle her with kid gloves, I won't. "Get in the shower, wanderer."

She doesn't argue because I'm sure she wants to rid herself of the memory between her legs. The steam welcomes me inside, and I strip off my clothes and join her. Hot water flows down my neck and back, soothing my tense muscles.

I brush the water-darkened strands of blonde hair from her face and pull her naked body against mine. I'll admit, I'm feeling some kind of way toward her, and I hate that she's become an obsession for me. As much as I'd love to push inside her right now, I'd rather put her above myself. "I want to make you feel good," I growl against her mouth. "My good girl."

I lift her, and her legs wrap around my waist. My cock moves through her slit, but I don't push inside her. I remove the showerhead from its cradle, and her eyes fall to the gleaming mass of silver in my hand. I put space between us, leaning her against the wall so the water can rain down in a direct stream on her swollen clit.

"Gentry," she begs. "Please."

"Tell me. Tell me what you want. Use that mouth I love."

"I want to come, sir." She knows I'll do just about anything if she calls me that.

I draw the stream closer to her clit and her fingers dig into my flesh. She throws her head back, those sexy lips spreading as she lets out a deep moan that draws her abdomen tight. Her heels dig into my back as she comes.

Screams of pain have always been music to my ears. The only songs I enjoyed. But now my favorite songs come in the form of those sounds that erupt from her mouth as she comes for me. It's fucking beautiful.

But as selfless as I am about wanting to make her come without fucking her, I selfishly need to fill her. This intense, animalistic desire to overpower Karson's come by filling her with mine won't be denied.

I carry her to the bed, grabbing a towel on the way, which I lay beneath her before I drop her onto it. "I need to come, and you know where I want to spill my load, don't you?"

"Yes, sir," she says with a nod.

I scoot closer and tilt her hips upward, and she keeps herself in that position, with her thighs hooked around mine. I stroke myself against her warm, slick slit. She moans as my fingers graze her clit with every pass over my dick. The thought of filling her little pussy at this angle pushes me closer. I lift her hips a little more and put the head of my cock to her entrance.

"I'm going to come," I groan. I stroke myself until I explode, unleashing my load directly inside her. I lean over her with a growl, keeping her hips raised. "Stay like this, my wanderer. Let my come drip to the back of your pussy and coat your cervix. Let me breed you, even when I can't bury myself inside you."

"Gentry," she moans as she keeps her hips tilted against my spent dick.

She'd have let me fuck her, let me bury myself inside her, but I wanted to show her I have more restraint than my psycho brother. That I can be her safe space. She may not be fragile, but if she needs to break, she can do so in my arms.

I lay beside her, finally releasing her hips and tugging her thigh over my legs as I brush my hand through her hair. "I'll always protect you, but you'll have to accept me for the killer I am. The man who can make you feel so fucking good after causing the ultimate pain to someone else. Can you do that, wanderer?"

"Yes," she whispers as she cozies up to my body.

It feels so foreign to me. I didn't even cuddle with my wife like this. I get the feeling this girl will rip me open and rearrange my insides until she finds some semblance of a heart.

And I'll let her.

Chapter Fifteen

Leana

We're on the way to California for all of two hours before Gentry's phone rings again. He sighs and pulls it out. The stern voice screaming into his ear is loud enough to rise above the road noise, but I can't make out what the caller says. Whatever it is, it has Gentry's hand tightening on the wheel.

"You heard what?" Gentry says, his tone remaining stern as his eyes leap to Karson's. "No, I—"

The voice rises to a higher octave, and the words that slip through send a bolt of ice water through my veins.

Get rid of her.

Job to do.

I feel it in my bones. I'm fucked. Instead of convincing them to let me live, it's now in the hands of a faceless entity.

"I'll fucking handle it," Gentry says. He ends the call, and his angry eyes leap to his brother, completely ignoring the road. "Did you tell George about Leana?"

Karson scoffs and throws his foot onto the dash. "Why does it matter how George found out? We never should have kept her this long, anyway."

My heart gallops in my chest. Did Karson really turn me in? What kind of dick move is that? I'm the one who should have turned their fucking asses in, particularly that royal cunt in the passenger seat who assaulted me and murdered a man in front of my eyes.

Gentry pulls into the lot of an abandoned gas station. Woods have nearly overtaken the building, and the sign above the front door has rusted to unreadability. Gentry reaches down and removes his pistol from his waistband.

Karson looks back at me with a devilish grin. "If you're going to do it, you shouldn't do it in here. Let's chase her first."

Gentry aims down the sights, pointing the barrel on his brother instead of me.

A normal person would panic at this point, but Karson merely rolls his eyes and tosses his hands in the air. "Really?" he asks. "You'd kill me over a piece of ass? A dope whore?"

Gentry growls and leans into Karson, grabbing him by the collar of his shirt and pressing the barrel against his temple. I rub the back of my head, remembering that feeling against my scalp.

"I'm going to kill you because you went above my head," Gentry says through gritted teeth. "You're fucking with *my* business. He's *my* boss, not yours. He gives the orders, but I run shit the way I want to, not how *you* want to run it. You want to run things again? Go face the executioner on your own."

"Fuck you, G," Karson sneers, ripping his shirt to tug out of Gentry's grasp.

"I should have killed you after the stunt you pulled last night."

"What? The little assault on your pet?" A gross smile crosses Karson's lips. "She fucking liked it."

Shame blooms in my gut because he's not entirely wrong.

Gentry scoffs. "I know what she likes, and what I do to her doesn't get me stabbed in the thigh."

Karson puts his hand to his chin. "It's kind of like how your wife liked how I fucked her too."

Gentry punches the gun butt into the side of Karson's head. In the same motion, he pulls Karson's knife from his belt and holds it to Karson's throat. "I should have let them kill you."

"Why didn't you?" Karson laughs and leans into the blade until a slender trickle of blood slithers down his neck.

Gentry shakes his head and lowers the knife. "Fix this," he snarls, throwing the phone into Karson's lap. "You fucked it up, so you can fix it. Tell him it's done."

"He'll find out it's not and then we'll all be in a load of shit."

"If anyone tries to kill her, they'll have to go through me. That includes you."

Something swells in my chest as he chooses me over his piece of shit brother. The choice can't be that difficult, though. I'd choose syphilis over Karson.

"You really think you can handle George? Not just him, but his men too?" Karson sits up taller. "You've always been the level-headed one between the two of us, always the responsible, cautious killer, so why the fuck are you throwing it all out the window for her?"

I don't know if I'm ready to hear the answer.

Gentry

My eyes hyper-focus on the heartbeat pounding a steady rhythm in the artery in his neck. It would be so easy to end him. I just need to send the blade across that jumpy bit of skin, and then life would be better. He betrayed me, yet again, and I shouldn't even be surprised by it anymore. It's so fucking normal for him.

He's not wrong, though, which infuriates me. I've always been the responsible one. Even when we were younger, I made sure we picked targets that wouldn't draw too much attention. I made sure not a bit of evidence was left at the scenes. Leana is making me throw away the saying I coined when we were kids. *No one's Kursed but us.* Bringing a third person into a business like this triples our risk of getting caught. That's just basic mathematics.

But I want the risk.

She is *my* responsibility. She's *mine.*

And now she's marked for death. Offic:ally. Fucking Karson.

I get out of the SUV and get into the back seat with her. Her big eyes look up at me, and I try my damndest to keep a brave face. Karson twists in his seat and stares, and I can almost hear him wishing for a bowl of popcorn.

"Easiest way would be asphyxiation, but if you can't bear to drain the breath from her body, try her blood." He tosses me his knife, and I catch it.

She shakes her head, scooting backward until her spine connects with the door. I don't want to do this, but I don't see another option. If George gets his hands on her, he'll torture her, then he'll kill me when I try to stop him. I can offer her a swift death.

I grab her ankles and rip her toward me so I can lean over her. She's crying, hands pushing at me as I flip open the blade and push it against her throat.

"Why'd you let us in the car?" I ask. It's the same pleading tone I used when I asked her why she got out of the car at the last hit.

"Gentry, don't," she pleads.

"Don't," I snarl. "Don't try to plead with me because you think I have a heart." Despite my words, her voice has reached the bit of beating tissue in my chest. If I don't hurry and silence her, I won't have the willpower to finish the job.

With the blade against her throat, I lose sight of myself.

Some people lose themselves inside a mental labyrinth when they need to escape a situation that is too painful to experience, but that's not what I do. I follow a red mist of rage into the depths, going until I find myself hovering over a scene that feeds my inner demons. I watch the murder unfold in front of my mind's eye like a movie, committing it to memory so I can replay it as many times as I want. The playback moves past the boring parts and slows to a near standstill when it gets good. Like the moment their last breath arcs from their lips.

This is what I can offer Leana—a place where she can live in my mind forever.

"Please, sir," she whispers as the pressure on her neck increases. The moment she says that, the cold killer thaws.

I can't do it.

I sit up on my knees and toss the knife to Karson. "Tell them it's done and make it believable," I say, pointing at the phone. He better, because that cold killer will happily come for him instead.

"You want me to call George and lie?" Karson says. "That's a death sentence."

I lean back and look him in the eye. "If anything happens to Leana, it's a death sentence, so you're fucked either way. You can run from George, or you can run from me. Pick your goddamn poison and drink up."

Karson grips the phone and exits the car. Instead of making the call, he paces back and forth, scratching his head and muttering to himself. He's flustered, and I'm glad. He deserves every ounce of hell he brought on himself when he ran his big mouth.

I scoot closer to Leana and wrap my arm around her, and I'm surprised when she doesn't pull away. "I'm sorry, wanderer," I say.

"Why are you apologizing?" she whispers against my chest. "You didn't kill me."

That's exactly why I'm apologizing.

Chapter Sixteen

I look around the wooded area and cram the phone into my pocket. "Fuck, fuck, fuck."

Gentry and Leana have been listening from the open door, but now that I've failed to make the call, Gentry decides to get out of the SUV and rub it in. "That doesn't sound like you're fixing the problem you caused."

"We need to kill her," I say.

"I told you. You'll have to go through me to—"

"Stop posturing. We won't really kill her. We just have to make her look dead."

"There's no way that will work," she says.

Gravel scatters beneath my feet with every step I take toward the mouthy thief. I lean into her face and grit my teeth. "Make it work."

She doesn't even bat an eye. She just shrugs her shoulders and says, "I failed theater courses two years in a row. It. Won't. Work."

I flip open my blade and go for her throat, but Gentry rushes between us. I've had enough of this bullshit. "Gentry, we have no fucking choice. George will want proof of the little thief's demise. If she doesn't want to play dead, we have to do what we have to do."

Gentry looks between us. The smug, self-assured look on her face has my hands itching to wrap around her throat and squeeze until something pops. She enjoys a blissful ignorance we've never known. She doesn't understand that Gentry and I live in a kill-or-be-killed world. We've broken the code of our universe by allowing her to stick with us for as long as she has, and now it's time to set things right. If she won't give in and go with my scheme, I'll have to fix this shit myself, Gentry be damned.

"What's it going to be, you two? Fake or real death?"

Leana drops to the ground with a dramatic huff. "Get it over with," she says before lying back with her tongue sticking out and eyes rolling back in her head. It's the least convincing fake death I've ever fucking seen, and now I understand why she failed theater class.

I climb on top of her. If we're going to do this, it has to be believable.

"Get off her, Karson," Gentry says as he grabs my arms.

I rip out of his grasp. "No, Gentry. You'd pose her all nice, as if you just strangled the life out of her, but I plan to do this shit right." I pin her arms beneath my legs and look up at Gentry. "Get down here and choke out your sweet little 'wanderer.'"

"Excuse me, what?" she asks, trying to wiggle free.

"Fuck no!" Gentry shouts.

"Now, Gentry. I need you to trust me."

"I haven't trusted you in a very long time," he says as he drops to his knees. "You just keep fucking shit up."

I smirk at him. He may not trust me, but he doesn't have a choice right now.

"No, no, wait!" Leana says before Gentry's big fucking hands wrap around her throat and squeeze. She flails beneath me, bucking her hips against my crotch as she struggles. It gets me hard, and as red spreads from her throat to her face, it feels like I've got a rebar rod in my pants. Spit gathers on her lips in a foamy spew of panic at the prospect of death. Her hands claw at his. He looks down at her with a glassy stare that I know too well. He's enjoying it, even if he doesn't want to do it.

Even if he'd never admit it.

She strains more violently beneath me, and I groan as she grazes my dick. Her lashes flutter, her struggle wanes to a flop, and Gentry rips his hands away from her.

"What . . . the . . . fuck," she pants. "And why is your dick hard?" she asks me. Her gaze shifts to Gentry, and she lets out a weak groan. "Jesus Christ, yours too?"

I laugh because who the fuck comes out of a choking like that? Unfazed by the near-death experience, but totally offended by the stiff cocks.

"That was the easy part," I say.

"Wh-what do you mean?"

Gentry's head pivots toward me. "Yeah, what do you mean?"

I grip the collar of her shirt and snatch down, ripping the thin fabric and fully exposing her left breast.

"What the fuck?" Gentry and Leana snarl in unison.

"Trust my process." With a feral grin, I revel in the beautiful sight before me. Her breast is so round, and the nipple has peaked against the coolness. Seeing just one of her tits makes me want to see the rest of her. All of her. I reach down and trace the cupid's arrow tattoo on the outside of her breast, wrapping around the curve. Gentry growls a warning, and I pull my hand away.

"What'd you get this for?" I ask.

"Don't answer that," Gentry commands, his body trembling.

"It's from when I used to believe in love," she says.

My stomach gives the slightest squeeze in my gut. I remember when I thought love was something to look forward to. I found a woman I liked a lot when I was eighteen. Gave her flowers and shit. Walked her home from school. Well, I walked behind her while she walked home from school. I thought we were heading toward fucking marriage until she rejected me. I had no choice but to kill her after that. Regardless, I also got it tattooed on my body. The word *bitch* down my forearm.

My open blade sits beside me. I grab it and bring it to her breast.

"Don't you hurt her," Gentry says.

"It's a fucking knife, Gentry. It's going to hurt her."

"No! No!" she screams.

"If it's blood you need, use mine." He thrusts his arm forward. What a white fucking knight.

My dark eyes rise to his. "It needs to be hers. It needs to be perfect if you want her to live so badly."

I cut into her, careful not to ruin her lame tattoo. She screams and I throw a hand over her mouth. Crimson rises to the surface. It pools for a moment before it drips under her breast, down her side, and onto her ripped shirt. Another line forms and gathers in the hollow of her neck. The cut looks deeper than it is, but the amount of blood it produces is fucking artistic beauty. I adjust the frayed fabric so it kind of looks like a fatal stab wound. The outside of her tit still hangs out, wet and bloody.

God, I'm so fucking hard.

"Fuck you," she snarls as I rip my hand away from her mouth.

"Swear all you want, thief, just don't fucking move." I look up at Gentry, who's furiously pacing at this point. "Now we need to do something with this," I say, waving my hand above her face. "Give me your best dead face."

She drops her head to the side and her jaw gapes. I sigh and smack her cheek. "I have killed so many people, and none of them died with their mouths hanging open like a yutz."

"Fine, since you're the professional, show me the death face."

I lie on the grass beside her, turn my head—she was pretty accurate about that —and keep my mouth fucking closed. I relax my jaw, fix my eyes on the SUV's tire, and hold my breath for good measure.

"Gentry, get a stick and poke him to see if he's dead," she says through a laugh, and even Gentry chuckles for a moment.

"Stop fucking around, thief. Look at me. Mirror what I'm doing."

She turns her head toward me, but now her lips are pressed together too tightly.

"Relax your jaw. You want it somewhere between gaping like before and . . . whatever the fuck you're doing now." I look over at Gentry. "Real death would have been a lot less labor intensive, you know."

"Yeah, yeah," he says, throwing me a dismissive wave.

I turn back to Leana. "Now your eyes. Look at something beyond me. Focus on it. Count the ridges in the bark for all I care, but keep those eyes open and fixed."

Her sexy lower lip is loose and relaxed. Coupled with the vacant stare, the blood, and the fresh marks on her neck, she looks pretty fucking dead. She's a fucking masterpiece.

And I'm hard again.

Jesus. *Calm down, boy.*

Is this a new kink for me? Why's my dick aching like this?

"Give me that phone," I tell Gentry.

He hands it to me, and I snap a picture for . . . personal reasons. I look down at her once more, my hand across my chin. I kneel beside her, and she flinches from my touch as I grind her hair in the dirt, making it all messy. Yes, now she's perfect.

I lean down to the shell of her ear. "Don't breathe, little thief," I whisper. When I stand, I bring up the camera and count her down from three so she can hold her breath. For all intents and purposes, she looks dead, so I start recording. "Here's your proof, Georgie." I zoom in on her neck as I narrate. "Gentry's a little bitch who couldn't finish strangling her, but don't you worry your ugly head about it, boss. I took care of her." I move the camera to the cut in her breast and mentally tell her to keep still. If she moves now, this was all for nothing.

A light breeze kicks sand toward her face, and I'm certain she'll flinch when the grit collides with her glassy eyes. She doesn't, and I breathe a silent sigh of relief. Her acting isn't so bad after all. She just needed the right teacher. Someone who has seen enough dead people to know how they should look. Someone like me.

Leana

I don't dare move or breathe until Karson pockets the phone. I sit up on my elbows, and the sticky film of blood makes my skin feel tingly. The wind sends a draft across my bare breast. Remembering how exposed I am, I turn the shirt around backward to cover myself. "I appreciate the help, but was this really necessary?"

Karson shrugs.

"Let me see it," I say, putting my hand out for the phone. He hands it to me, and I watch the clip. I look dead. Really fucking dead. Dirt and twigs decorate my blonde hair as it fans around my head. I don't even recognize my blue eyes. I touch the fresh marks on my throat. "Did you really have to do this?"

Karson squats down, and a terrifying darkness slides across his eyes. "It was either that or be killed in ways I couldn't conjure." He leans down and licks the blood from the pool that formed at the base of my throat. His warm tongue brushes across my skin and sends flutters through me that shouldn't exist. "God, you taste like the thing that made the angel that became the devil fall."

I push him away. "Poetic."

"Don't be a dick, thief." He stands up and wipes his hands on his jeans, smearing dirt down the denim.

Gentry comes over and lends me his hand so he can help me to my feet. He pulls me into his chest, not caring about the blood covering me. "I'm sorry," he whispers, tracing the handprint he left on my neck. "I'll make up for every moment of hurt with twice the pleasure."

"You didn't have a choice."

Gentry's harsh glare lands on his brother. "None of this would have happened if someone had kept his big fucking mouth shut."

Karson lifts his chest. "You know, if the roles were reversed, this wouldn't . . . No, you know what? This would never happen to me. This isn't take-your-whore-to-work week. I never would have brought her along."

"Call her a whore again and I'll castrate you," Gentry says.

"It's fine," I say, and it is. His words don't offend me. I've been called worse.

Gentry shakes his head. "No, it's not fine. You're an extension of me, which means he's coming at me when he calls you names. If anyone is going to call you that, it's me, and the word 'good' will come before it because you're my good little whore." He points his glare at Karson. "*Mine.*"

My heart thunders in my chest at his words. It also shuts down Karson, which is a major pro. But now, covered in blood and dirt, all I can think about is a hot shower.

Gentry stomps toward the SUV, but I turn to Karson before I follow him. I have a question, and I need the answer before I climb into the car with them again. "Did you tell your boss about me?"

Karson shoves his hands in his pockets and rams the toe of his shoe against the grass. He looks into the distance and shakes his head. "What does it matter? That's the conclusion Gentry immediately jumped to, so it must be true. He's always right, isn't he?"

Before I can press him further, he joins Gentry in the SUV. I'm not convinced he was the one who ratted me out, but that's an unsettling thought. If Karson didn't tell their boss . . . who did?

Chapter Seventeen

Gentry

We don't get a response to our video. I'm not sure my boss believed it, but we tried our best. Well, she tried her best. I look over at her and swell with pride. She did so fucking good. Even though I almost choked her to the point of unconsciousness, she held no ill feelings toward either of us once it was finished.

Guilt taps on my shoulder when I remember how delicate her throat felt in my grasp. How much I enjoyed that fragility beneath my fingertips. It was hard for me to pull away when all those sweet endorphins fired off in my brain, but Karson's groan ripped all those feel-good hormones away from me. It also didn't help when I realized she was running from a man who'd done something similar to her. She seems to understand the difference, but it still concerns me. Especially since she knows how much it turned me on to choke her like that. It's one thing to fuck a killer, but it's another to fuck a killer who got hard at the thought of killing *you*.

I like this girl more than I've liked anyone else before—including my wife—yet the primitive urges to end her sometimes bubble beneath the surface. I can't cherish her without thinking about how her death at my hands would feel. Good, probably. So fucking good. But the aftermath, after the high wore off, would break me. The act would be self-sabotage of the highest level.

A heavy silence presses down on us as we pull into a motel parking lot. There aren't any hotels where we are, but I don't think Leana minds as long as there's a bed. I wish I could guarantee it would be a clean one, but we're in the middle of nowhere and I don't have high hopes.

I throw my jacket to Leana so she can hide her blood-stained shirt before we head toward the front desk. A young girl mans this family-owned shithole, and she hardly looks old enough to drive, let alone run a business.

"Two rooms, please," I say.

She nods, hands over two keys, and has us sign a paper as she marks off two rooms with a dry-erase marker. What an archaic method. It's discreet, though, and I like that. I pay her and she shoves the cash into a box beneath the desk.

"Thanks," I tell her before we head down the hallway.

We head outside and walk toward our rooms. Duct tape and cardboard cover window damage to one of the rooms along the way. Rust has eaten through the metal roofing over the walkway, giving us a glimpse of the night sky through the many holes. The scent of piss overpowers my nose as we pass the vending machines, and I make a mental note to ignore my growling stomach. The place is an absolute dump, but what can you expect for fifty dollars a night?

I toss Karson his key, and we part ways at the metal stairwell. His room is on the upper story, and I can only hope the floor doesn't collapse and send his bed on top of us as we sleep.

Leana and I enter our room to the high-pitched squeal of aged hinges that have never seen WD-40 in all the years of their existence. When I flick the light switch, the bulbs send out a fluttering strobe before staying on with an obnoxious hum.

She slips off my leather jacket and hands it to me, her lips tight. I reach out for her, but she ducks away from my arm. "I'm still processing what happened earlier," she says. "I understand you and Karson did what was needed to keep me safe, but it was still . . . a lot. I didn't expect you to enjoy choking me so much." Her gaze falls to the crotch of my jeans before flitting away again.

"I'm a killer. I like to hold life in my hands before watching it crumble in front of my eyes."

Her eyes rise to mine and burn through me. "You fantasize about killing me? Is that what you're saying? Should I be concerned?"

I laugh. "Aside from my brother, I don't usually keep things around that I want to kill. He likes to toy with his prey, but that's not my M.O."

Her chest and chin rise in unison, and her little show of courage is adorable. "What if I don't want to be kept? What if I want to leave?"

I step into her, forcing her back against the wall as I lean into her. "You're mine, wanderer."

"You can't make someone stay with you."

My hand rises and twirls strands of her blonde hair between my fingers. "I can when that *someone* saw what you did. There's no going back after what you witnessed."

"So I'm stuck?"

"There's worse people to be stuck with."

"Worse than two fucking contract killers? And I think it's more than that. Hitmen don't get turned on by hits. By killing. You two are sick."

I saw the lack of shock on her face when she walked in on Karson with a nearly severed head in his hand. We might be sick, but she's got a little touch of the illness herself. "We are sick. Very fucking sick. We're horrible, vile men who will stop at nothing to get what we want. And wanderer? You're what I want."

"Well, I don't want you!" She looks away, her body language betraying the lie she tells.

"Have you ever fantasized about killing someone?"

"What? No." She tries to meet my gaze, but she looks away again. Another lie.

"Tell me your fantasy. Who have you thought about killing, and how did you want to do it?"

"I don't want to play this game," she says. She tries to move past me, but I push closer and hold her in place. "What part of 'I don't want you' don't you understand?"

I put my knee between her legs and spread them. My hand leaves her hair and dips down the front of her jeans. She strains against my hold, her hands wrapping around my wrist to stop my descent, but I can already feel what I suspected. She's wet. Soaked.

"Yeah, you don't want me at all." I push my fingers inside her. "You don't like that I could kill you, but you *love* that I'm too fucking obsessed with you to do so." I kneel before her, taking her pants down with me. "It turns you on to know you made a big, selfish killer weak enough to drop to his knees. Even though I have a taste for blood, you want my tongue on your pussy."

She shakes her head but scoops her pelvis closer to my face. I help her out of her jeans, throwing them aside. I don't normally go down on women, and I can't say I've ever wanted to be in this inferior position, but she's fighting me on it. By taking it, I'm still superior. In control. The moment I put my tongue on this girl, she'll melt into me and become a taste I would kill for.

I blow a warm breath on her slit and swipe my tongue through her. She shudders, falling forward to grip my shoulders for support. She curls her hips to give me more access to her pretty little pussy, showing me how badly she wants my mouth to devour her.

But I want to hear her say it.

"Tell me you want to come on a killer's face," I say.

She closes her eyes and leans her head against the wall. I fucking love her internal struggle. I can feel it. Her pussy wants one thing, but her mind tells her it's wrong. She should listen to her mind, but if she wants to feel good, she'll spread her legs a little wider and let me devour her until she comes on my face.

I put my hand on her clit, and her excited pulse throbs against my touch. The twitch of desire.

Her shoulders drop. "I want to come on your face."

I smirk. "That's not what I want to hear." I pull my hand away and blow another hot breath on her swollen clit. "Tell me."

"I want to come . . . on a killer's face." Shame drips from her words, and I guzzle it down.

With a rough grasp on her inner thighs, I spread her lips. Her body trembles with anticipation, and I've hardly touched her. I can't wait another moment to feel the explosion of pleasure against my mouth when I finally lick her, so I dip my tongue inside her pussy and put my mouth around her clit. I tongue the most sensitive part of her with quick lashings that turn her trembles to shudders.

"Fuck," she groans, as her hands grip my hair.

I lick her harder, faster, eating her until her thighs clench together and she ends up riding my face.

"You're . . . fucking . . . evil." She pants each word with every forward rock of her hips.

I pull away, eliciting a frustrated growl from her. "And yet you ride my face like I'm a saint."

I bury myself in her pussy once more and lick her until her clit twitches with a strong pulse against my tongue. With a long, thorough lick, I gather every ounce of wetness I brought out of her. I stand up, look down at this vulnerable, satiated girl, and drag my thumb across her bottom lip.

"Open your mouth, wanderer. I want you to taste yourself. I want you to swallow what I've done to you."

She spreads her lips as if she expects my fingers to slip inside her mouth, but I tip her chin, ball up my spit and her come, and drip it into her waiting mouth.

I expect her to spit it out, but she doesn't. "Good girl. Now swallow."

Her throat bobs as she takes every drop. When her tongue flicks out to catch the bit that slipped onto her lip, I almost want to drop to my knees and worship her pussy again.

But I won't. Not tonight.

"Go get cleaned up, and let's get some sleep," I say. "We have a lot of driving to do tomorrow."

As she showers, I lie in bed and try to think of anything aside from the increasing risk we're taking by keeping her with us. But I can't let her go. As long as Karson keeps his mouth shut—and as long as our piss-poor snuff film works—I can only hope that George won't be a problem for her anymore.

When she climbs into bed after her shower, she doesn't put any space between us. She snuggles up to me, throws her leg over my thigh, and presses her pussy against my leg. My favorite sleeping position. I listen as each breath slows to a drowsy cadence, and when I'm sure she's asleep, I cut off the lamp beside the bed.

"I fantasize about killing the man who sexually assaulted me throughout my childhood," she whispers, and her voice nearly makes me jump.

What she says enrages me. There aren't many lines a man like me won't cross, but nobody should fuck with a kid. Knowing she was assaulted by someone sick enough to cross that boundary . . . There are no words to describe the anger I feel.

"Who?" I ask.

She doesn't speak for a long time, but when she finally does, her voice is almost a whimper. "My stepfather."

She hasn't given me a name, but I'll get it out of her eventually. And when I do, we'll make her fantasy a reality.

Chapter Eighteen

Leana

We've hardly pulled out of the motel parking lot when Gentry's phone rings. I'm beginning to dread that generic ringtone. Why do I get the feeling we'll never reach California? From what I can gather from the call, they've just been given another job. I don't hear any mention of my death video, which could be a good thing.

Or a very bad thing.

I can't dwell on it. Whatever happens is out of my hands.

Karson drives all day, and my stomach is a grumbling mess once dinner time rolls around. We've lived mostly on convenience-store fare since our journey began, and I could really go for a burger right about now.

"Any chance we could grab some fast food this time?" I ask.

Gentry glances at the time on the dash clock. "Yeah, as long as we eat in the car. Where do you want to go?"

I shrug my shoulders. "It doesn't matter to me."

"That's not how this works," Karson says. He turns to Gentry. "Why do chicks always do this shit? They say it doesn't matter, but the moment you name a place, they aren't in the mood for it. I'm not playing this game."

Gentry turns in his seat and looks at me. "Name the spot."

"It really doesn't matter," I say. "Anything will be better than a crusty hot dog from the gas station."

With a sigh, Gentry looks at the interstate. We near a sign that names off fast-food places, and he assesses it as we pass. "Get off at this exit," he says to Karson. "We'll grab something from Taco Bell."

"My stomach will be upset for days," I say.

Karson's head twists toward Gentry. "See? I fucking told you!" He glances in

"

the rearview mirror and meets my gaze. "Pick what you want or go hungry, thief. Your choice."

"Fine," I mutter. "Just pick a burger place."

Gentry turns to Karson with a smug grin. "There, problem solved. We'll grab Wendy's."

"I don't like their fries," I say, and I regret even asking for food at this point because Karson looks as if his head might explode. The exit is quickly approaching, and Karson makes no indication that he plans to turn off. Golden arches gleam in the distance. "McDonald's!" I shout before it's too late.

He flicks on the turn signal and whips the SUV off the interstate. "Was that so fucking hard?"

We order our food and continue down back roads for a few miles. I've finished my fries by the time Karson pulls into the woods near the start of a driveway. He looks back at me, his dark eyes menacing. "Did we learn our lesson from last time?"

"What lesson?" I ask through a mouthful of burger.

"Don't play dumb. We have something to take care of inside that house. You're going to wait right where you are."

I stuff another bite of burger into my mouth and toss him a casual nod. "Mmhm."

"Why don't I believe you?" Karson asks as he threads a silencer onto his pistol.

"If she knows what's good for her, she'll stay put," Gentry says.

"If she knew what was good for her, she wouldn't have pulled over for us in the first place."

I scoff, sit back, and fold my arms across my chest.

They go inside and I try to stay put. I really try. But pretty soon my leg is shaking and I'm wondering what the heck is taking so long. What if something happened to them? What if their victim turned the tables and now they're in trouble?

I shake my head. What the fuck would I even do if they needed help? If it's something two big-ass psychos can't handle, I'd be up shit creek without a paddle *and* I'd have a hole in my boat.

In the end, my curiosity gets the better of me. Even if I can't help them, I can at least figure out what I should do if they're dead. I get out of the SUV, make my way across the front lawn, and ascend the marble steps. My eyes rise up the Victorian home's dramatic arches and I'm intimidated by the age and grace of the building.

I round the house and reach for the back door, but I catch myself. If they're doing what I think they're doing, I don't want my fingerprints on the scene. I tug my sleeve over my hand before I open it. It slides open with an eerie creak, which is what I would expect from a door from the eighteen fucking hundreds. But it announces my presence much more than I'd have liked. Cursing beneath my breath, I look around, but I don't see or hear anything.

What if everyone's dead?

What if they ditched me?

Would that last one really be so bad?

I take a left, careful not to touch anything as I pass by delicate vases and intricate busts sitting atop pedestals. These knickknacks are probably worth more than my life.

My eyes widen as soon as I cross the threshold into the kitchen. Lying on top of the island is a balding older man with his cuffed hands held over his head by Karson. Duct tape seals off each scream he makes. When his wide, pained eyes turn to me, a look of relief flashes across his features. He talks beneath the tape, pleading with me to help him, before his eyes rush to the ceiling and his nostrils flare. My vision pans to the blade moving over his abdomen . . . to the large hands holding the knife that's carving something into the man's flesh.

"Goddamn it, wanderer," Gentry snarls. Before his face twisted with anger, I saw the enjoyment in his expression. It reminded me of Karson. That divide between them has lessened, becoming a blurred line in my mind.

"Don't you stop," Karson says to Gentry. "She needs to see the *real* you before she spreads her thighs again."

Gentry's mouth opens and closes, but he shakes his head and goes back to his task. Disgusted curiosity makes me take a step closer. He's not just slicing the man's stomach. He's etching words into his skin.

The younger they are, the—

He starts cutting into the man again.

B-e-t-t-e-r.

Gentry stares at me as he tugs down the man's sweatpants, exposing a thin, limp dick. A muffled scream pushes against the duct tape, and I can almost hear the words.

No. Please.

"Our friend here is a pedo," Gentry says as he grips the man's dick with a gloved hand.

"And a stupid one at that," Karson adds. "He stopped paying the man who kept all his dirty little secrets."

"We take extra pains with the fuckers who hurt kids," Gentry says as he slices the man's balls clean off. The sack hits the floor with a smack, followed by a freshet of blood.

The man's screams begin to fade, and his head drops heavily to the table as he passes out from the pain.

I can almost taste the blood on my tongue, and I fight back a gag. I'm not disgusted by what I see. I'm disgusted by the fact that I'm not terrified by what I've just witnessed. I'm disgusted that I'm glad the sick fuck is getting exactly what he deserves.

"Don't just stand there and gawk, thief," Karson says with a wild look in his eyes. "This is the part where you're supposed to run. So run."

"No, Karson! No. Goddamn it!" Gentry shouts.

I race out the door, choking on adrenaline as I dart toward the woods. My body remembers this chase before I even hear Karson's steps trailing after me. A burst of fear rips through my body. A nervous energy is breathed into my lungs. Anticipation tightens my throat, cutting off my breath.

"You know I like the chase!" Karson yells behind me. "The harder you make me work to catch you, the more I'll take it out on your cunt."

His words make my heart thud against my sternum. I put my hand against my chest, and I swear I can feel it protruding from the skin with every beat. I'm terrified of what will happen when Karson catches me.

But I kind of want to be caught.

Chapter Nineteen

I follow her scent through the trees, and it's strong enough to overpower the smell of Mother Nature's cunt. Chasing is fun for me, especially that final moment when I catch them—the moment they're snagged in my grasp and they falter like an animal whose leg just got snapped in a trap. The best part? That split second when I feel the hope dissipate in their chest when they realize they've been caught. That last breath of freedom they exhale.

It's fucking euphoric.

When I was younger, I made a habit of letting my prey escape. They'd gather bits of hope as they ran, each step propelling them toward perceived freedom. It made it that much sweeter when I caught them a second time.

I won't have time for a catch and release today, but I'll have more time to play than I did after our last game of chase. Gentry has to finish the job before he can catch up and stop me.

As the little thief runs from me, her shoes kick up dirt. We've played this game already, and she ended up on her hands and knees instead of in a fucking grave, so why is she bolting away as if her life depends on it? She wouldn't have to run if she'd stayed in the fucking car.

Girl doesn't listen.

"Fuck you," she shouts back. "Go back to your brother."

"Here's my proposition, thief," I say, trying to catch my breath between words. I can't run like I used to. "If you stop right here, right now, I'll just fuck your cunt. For every additional ten feet, that's another hole I'll take. You have thirty feet and three holes. If you go beyond that, I'll stab this knife into you and fuck every new hole I make."

She stops, and disappointment smothers my excitement.

"Only one hole? Really? I expected more from you." I catch up to her and spear her to the ground, straddling her waist as her back hits the grass and a pained breath escapes her lips.

"Karson, don't," she squeals, her hands reaching for fistfuls of nothing above her head.

"I could take more, but what kind of man would I be if I went back on my word?" I say against her sweat-coated skin.

"You're a fucking psycho!" Her leg wiggles loose and she sends her knee right into my nuts.

I wish it numbed the ache I feel for her, but the sharp pain that shoots into my stomach only fuels my hunger.

"You aren't right in the head, Karson."

"Neither of us is right in the head. Why let one in so willingly but fight the other?"

Her cheeks puff as she struggles to get free. "Because you're an asshole!"

I sit up and look down at her, and she stops squirming. I love her fight, but I love when she stops and gives in to me more. I like watching the desperation seep from her. There is so much beauty in her defeat.

"Are you going to take off your jeans, little thief?"

"Probably not."

I whip out my knife and spin it in my hand. "Fair enough." I unbutton her jeans and unzip them until I can reach in with my knife and cut the crotch. That's all I'll need, anyway.

"No, no! Wait," she says, her hands gripping my wrist. "I'll take them off!"

She cares more about the damage to her only pair of jeans than she does about me stretching her around my cock. Hilarious.

"Atta girl," I tell her as I adjust my weight and sit over her abdomen instead.

"Asshole," she mumbles.

I pull out a cigarette and light it while I wait for her to finish undressing. She clenches her jaw, her lips tight. I'm sure it's agonizing to know what's coming while I take my sweet time to get there. Whether she wants it or not, it's agony either way.

Her hands work down her jeans, and she kicks out of them like a flailing fish once she slides off her shoes. I put the cigarette between my lips and work off my belt. When I pull my cock from my boxers and place it between her perky tits, her eyes widen. Their eyes always widen when they get a good look at my dick. I'm pierced. Twice, to be exact, with a nice ball on all four sides of my head. A magic cross.

"What the fuck is that?" she squeals, straining beneath me.

I press the lit end of the cigarette against my wrist until it's out, then I tuck it behind my ear. "Stop being a baby. You've already had me inside you. You've felt these before."

"Not like this! It's different now that I've seen them."

Pinning her arms at her sides, I adjust myself until I get my legs between hers. "Then you don't need to see them. I'll do a fun little magic trick and make them disappear. Now you see it . . ." I smirk and throw her thighs over mine while pulling her into me. "Now you don't."

I push inside her without inhibition and growl as I sink to the depths of her. Her mouth gapes as the silver balls rake her tight cunt. There's no escaping the feeling, and she could enjoy it if she'd just fucking relax.

When I thrust into her again, the force sends a whimper out of her throat. She's squeezing around me, and I'm reminded again why my brother is so fucking obsessed. To have someone like her give herself so willingly to him must be nice. She hates my guts, but the hatred cools when I'm buried inside her. I pull my hips back so my piercings tease the most sensitive part of her, the ball at the top rubbing along her exposed clit. Her back arches off the ground, yet she holds back her moan.

"It's okay to enjoy it." I lean into her and bury myself inside her once more.

"The fuck it is," she says.

I ball her shirt in my fist and use it for leverage as I sit up and fuck her harder. Her tits wiggle beneath the raised hem with every thrust, and I'm mesmerized by the cut above her left breast. The only thing that draws my attention away is a bubble of blood that swells on her lower lip because she's bitten it hard enough to break the skin. All of that to hold back the sounds of pleasure. So fucking defiant.

"Give me your mouth."

"No," she says. She reaches up to wipe the blood away, but I grip her wrist and pin it to the ground.

"Then I'll take it." I lean over her, open my mouth, and absorb the crimson droplet with my tongue. The sweet metallic taste bathes my brain in ecstasy.

But it's not enough.

I snatch the knife from my belt and cut a shallow line along her collarbone. Blood springs into the channel and ignites a fuse inside me. Ignoring her subtle protest, I drop my mouth to her porcelain skin and suck her life force into me. A line of blood drips toward her shirt collar, but I stop it with my tongue. I fist her hair and whip her head back until her mouth parts from the strain on her neck.

"Taste what I taste," I say.

Before she can register what's happening, I spit at her parted lips. It hits her mouth and some of it dribbles out the side. I lean over and lick up the remnants with a deep groan, grazing her lower lip before leaning in and kissing her as hard as I can. I've never kissed anyone like this, and the way our breaths become one makes me dizzy.

Fucking weird.

I rip my mouth away from hers and bury whatever I just felt inside her cunt. I spread my knees, grab her by the back of her neck, and pound into her with deep, fast thrusts that finally force a moan out of her.

"Admit you like when I fuck you. How I take you. Use you. Admit that your sweet little cunt is clenching around me."

"No," she says. "I hate you."

"Fine, I'll make you love me." I pull out of her but keep hold of her neck as I drop my other hand between her legs. Pushing three fingers inside her, I fuck her with more force than I can with my cock. As I pull her curved abdomen into me, putting all the pressure I need on her lower belly, she gushes on my fingers and saturates the grass. A feral moan pours from her gut, and I bite my lip.

As soon as she takes a breath, I pound her cunt with a relentless barrage that leaves her whimpering and moaning. The sinful tone makes my dick twitch against her thigh. She squirts again, coating the front of my jeans. As soon as her come splashes onto the fabric, I know Gentry will be pissed.

"Jesus," she whimpers as I pull my hand from her. It makes me the slightest bit proud that her frigid ass warmed right up with my hand inside her.

"If you were afraid of my piercings in your cunt, wait till you feel them in your throat," I say as I rise to my feet and pull her onto her knees.

"I thought you said one hole," she pants.

"I'm a liar."

She settles heavily in front of me, like she doesn't want to be there. Which is fine. I don't need her to be enthusiastic.

"Make the sign of the cross," I say, "but with your tongue."

"I'm not—"

I grip the back of her head and bring her mouth to the head of my dick. "Now," I command.

She looks up at me before she touches the top ball with the tip of her tongue. "In the name of the Father." She goes for the underside of my dick. "And of the Son." Her tongue moves from the left ball to the right. "And of the Holy Spirit."

I shove my dick into her mouth and complete the prayer. "A-fucking-men."

I keep hold of her chin as I push to the back of her throat. The metal balls clack against her teeth, but I know to be careful. I'm not stupid. If I break Gentry's toy, he'll break me.

"I'm going to come," I growl, feeling the sudden tightness in my balls. "When I fill your mouth, do not fucking swallow." I pull my hips back a bit, wanting my come to pool around her tongue instead of slipping down her throat. With a feral groan I don't recognize, I unload inside her mouth before easing out. "Now show me what I gave you."

She sits back on her heels and slowly parts her lips. Her throat tightens. She better not throw up so close to a crime scene.

"Tongue out."

She sticks out her tongue, but her chest lurches forward with another violent heave.

"Fine, come give me what you don't want."

She tries to ask me what I mean, but that sends a dribble of come onto her lip. I pull her to her feet and wipe it away, bringing it to her forehead and anointing her with a cross. Her nostrils flare.

"Sorry, I'm getting carried away. Gentry and I grew up catholic. You know, real religious and shit until we started killing regularly. Then the hypocrisy of kneeling in front of God became comical." I kneel in front of her and open my mouth. "Spit it back in my mouth."

She *happily* does as I ask. It's so aggressive. So fucking hot.

"Show me," she says, and fuck does it almost harden my dick again.

I stick out my tongue, waggling it around without a hint of protest from my tastebuds, then I swallow it. God, I'm starting to like her, and I fucking hate that for me.

My little thief. His wanderer.

Whoever the fuck she is, she's getting under my skin.

Chapter Twenty

Gentry

Why can't this girl do as she's told? I asked nothing more than for her to stay put. A third person means more risk. With her long hair, it would be too easy to leave DNA behind, and she doesn't even have gloves, for fuck's sake. I also didn't want her to see who I am. What I do. She already knew enough, but she didn't know everything. Now? Now she knows I'm just as crazy as my brother.

After finishing off the child predator and finding a nice stash of cash in his sock drawer, I walk out the back door of the house and listen for Leana and Karson. I take off the way they ran. I hate that I couldn't go after them sooner—especially when I know what Karson is likely doing to her right now—but I had my hands a bit full at the time.

When I get to them, I expect to see her trapped beneath him like last time. Instead, she's standing there, bare from the waist down. Karson's kneeling on the ground in front of her, with his head tilted back and his mouth gaped open. And she's . . . spitting in his mouth?

Jesus fuck.

"What the hell happened?" I ask.

Karson rises to his feet and tucks his dick away. "We played around, is all," he says. The casual way he speaks is like nails on a goddamn chalkboard.

"She consented to that?"

Karson buckles his belt. "Ish."

I go to Leana's side and check her body for marks. Not seeing any, I pull her into me and kiss her, thankful she's okay. The salty bite of her tears burns my tongue. She reaches for her pants when I step away, but I don't want his come inside her. "Squat and push it out before you dress."

Her eyes go to Karson, and realization hits me.

"She didn't catch it with her cunt," Karson says with a laugh.

I pull away from her, tasting the salt of his come—not her fucking tears—on my lips. Cool. That's what I wanted to experience today. I assess her face again and spot a glob of come on her forehead. I pull my sleeve over my hand and wipe it away.

"Wait . . ." I stop myself, sidetracked by the image of him on his knees in front of her. "Did you have her spit your shit back into your mouth? Is that what you were doing when I walked up?"

Karson smirks. "Don't act like you've never done that."

"I can say with utmost certainty I have not."

"You kiss women after they suck your dick, no?"

I scoff. "It's not the same."

"Don't kink shame me, Gentry. I'm not the one who gets off by having their hair shampooed. Now *that's* fucking weird."

This motherfucker. Clearly my ex-wife had a big mouth. Yeah, I'm a tripso-lagniac. For me, the hair salon has always been the equivalent of going to a massage parlor for a rub and tug. After coming in my pants in the middle of a wash when I was younger, I started cutting my own hair.

"Need me to wash the dirt out of your hair when we get back to the hotel?" Leana asks with a giggle. "If you stop by the store and buy the supplies, I can even do a conditioning treatment. So fucking hot."

I do *not* need this judgmental shit. "See you back at the car," I say, turning away from them and heading toward the SUV. Fuck those two. If they want to sit back there and cackle about kinks, by all means, go nuts. At least I don't guzzle my own jizz like it's hors d'oeuvres.

I whip open the driver's seat, sit down, and wait with the door open. My fingers tap on the steering wheel. They eventually emerge from the woods, and Leana climbs into the back seat.

"Gentry," she begins.

"Can we just not talk?" I snap. I'll deal with them when I'm not so pissed off. When I'm less annoyed. When I don't want to ring both their necks, because I'm liable to do exactly that if they keep going.

Karson hops into the passenger seat and throws his foot onto the dash. "Sorry I exposed your kink. If it makes you feel any better, I almost came in my pants when the thief played dead. That kink is much worse than a little sudsy one."

Jesus Henry Christ. What did our mother take when she was pregnant with us? Just when I think we can't get any worse, now one of us is a pseudo-necrophiliac?

"Excuse me?" Leana says.

Karson turns toward her. "When I saw you playing dead, it got my dick hard. I don't think I can break it down into simpler terms."

"For fuck's sake," she says as she sits back with her arms crossed. I can't help but smirk at her reaction, mostly because it's not enough of a reaction when Karson just admitted he wants to fuck her corpse.

I love that about her.

"Let's just drive and stop talking about this. We've got a long drive to California, and I'm ready to finish this shit." I close my door, and they follow suit.

As we continue on our journey of destruction, I glance in the rearview mirror at Leana. For not being a Kursicki by birth, she's fucked up enough to be one of us. Instead of kicking and screaming and trying to escape, she's just resigned herself to the fate of one serial killer who wants to breed her and another who wants to fuck her dead body.

What a trio.

The sun sets as we inch closer to our final destination, but we have to keep going. Karson is already napping in the passenger seat, and Leana's eyelids hang heavy over her blue eyes. We're taking too long to get where we're going, so I plan to keep driving and let them nap. I'd like to change out of my bloody clothes, though, and Leana's last shirt has seen better days. We'll have to make a pit stop.

I pull into a strip mall and wake Karson. "I need you two to get us some clothes." I turn to Leana and place a wad of cash into her hand. "I need a shirt and some jeans. Do *not* let him pick anything out for me." I glare at Karson.

The last time I let him buy an outfit for me, I had to commit a double fucking homicide with the word "vagitarian" on the front of my shirt. I don't think he'll find anything like that in this little strip of outlet stores, but I refuse to risk it.

As they head inside, I'm left to sit and contemplate my life choices. What will we do with Leana when we're done with this trip? She's too much of a liability to release, but I can't kill her. I can't. I also haven't fully wrapped my head around this whole sharing thing. At least I know about it and Karson isn't doing it behind my back.

After a little while, the doors open and the dome light brightens Karson's beaming smile. He grips a shirt in his hand as he sits down. Here we fucking go. I glare at Leana, and she gives me a sorry-filled shrug. Karson spreads the gray shirt open and laughs. It says "Cereal Killer" right across the front. A playful skull smiles below the lettering, complete with crossed spoons instead of crossbones.

I scowl.

"Oh, come on. It's punny." He looks at the shirt proudly. It could be worse, I guess. Silver linings and shit.

I look into the back seat and pin Leana with a pleading glare. "Please tell me you also got something I can actually wear."

"Of course." Leana nods and shakes a bag beside her. "But if you don't do our next hit with a cereal killer shirt, what are we even doing?"

My eyes narrow on her. "It's not our hit. It's *our* hit." I gesture between me and Karson.

She tightens her lips. "You know what I mean."

No, I don't know what she means. She can't be a part of this. She can't even follow simple directions when I tell her to stay in the fucking car.

"Give me the goddamn shirt," I say.

Karson hands the monstrosity to me, and I rip off the blood-stained shirt and shove it beneath the seat. I'll discard it when we're back on the road. "I hate you. You know that, right?"

"Cute," he says, and I fight the urge to strangle him.

We take turns driving for the next twenty-nine hours, sleeping in shifts as we travel the road. When we finally reach Nevada, it's time for a break.

I eventually find a suitable hotel. It's much nicer than anywhere we've stayed before, and I'm more than ready to crawl beneath some clean sheets and get some shuteye when we enter the lobby.

A wheedling little man in thick-framed glasses sits behind the lobby desk. When he spots us and offers a plastic smile, I fantasize about knocking his big teeth down his throat and watching him choke on them. My rage only intensifies when I ask for two rooms.

"Sorry, sir, but we're nearly full tonight. There's a big book signing in town, and we only have one room left."

I groan. "A room with two beds, right?"

"Nope, only one. But it is a king!"

As if that makes it better.

I turn to Karson and Leana. "Next hotel it is."

The little man raises his finger. "You won't find a hotel with vacancies until the next town over, and that's at least an hour away. This group of authors is very popular."

I glare at the man. We're all too tired to drive, and I won't risk getting pulled over.

"Fine," I growl, handing over a fake ID and cash.

After we receive the room keys, we begrudgingly head to the elevator.

"When was the last time we shared a bed together?" Karson asks. The pep in his step makes me want to stab him in the knee.

"When we were kids, Karson," I deadpan. "Someone will have to sleep on the floor, but it won't be me or her."

We step inside our room and inhale the fresh scent of clean sheets and proper housekeeping. It's a step up from our usual hotels. It's fucking nice. My first stop is the bathroom because I've had to piss for the last two hours.

When I return to the main room, Karson is laid out on the white bed with his boots all over the pristine comforter. Leana perches on the other side.

"Get your shoes off my bed." I go to the mini fridge and tug out a tiny bottle of vodka. "Want one?" I ask Leana.

"Yes, thanks for asking," Karson interjects.

"Vodka is fine," she says.

I toss the small bottle of vodka to her and fish out a bottle of bourbon for Karson. I walk to the side of the bed, where Leana is swigging her drink like it's water. "Floor," I tell Karson as I point to the carpet.

He just stares at me. "Or, hear me out . . ." He pulls Leana closer. "She can be our buffer, and I get to sleep in the bed."

"Fuck off, Karson. Also, don't think I didn't notice it looked like you pissed your pants earlier. Take a fucking shower."

"Oh yeah, no. I'm housebroken. That was just her come. A whole lot of it."

I don't know why I thought Karson was incapable of making someone come. I always imagined he was as selfish a lover as he was a person. I hate knowing he made her come. Even worse, he made her squirt hard enough to saturate his jeans like that.

"If this is going to be a thing, we need fucking ground rules," I say. I don't *want* this to be a thing, but Karson has been less adamant about killing her since he started playing with her. I don't like the idea of her being his little plaything because he always breaks his things—and by break, I mean accidentally murders them—but I also feel like I don't have a choice in the matter. "First, I know you have a thing for blood. If she lets you cut her, fine, but you better control yourself. If I need to stop the bleeding, you'll become the bloody one. Second, her pussy is mine to fill. Come anywhere else. Third, don't do shit in front of me. I don't want to see it."

The last rule will be hard for him to follow, but I don't know that I can watch them and not feel the need to break his neck.

"What?" Karson says. "That means no sportsmanlike competition."

He slides his hand between her thighs and drops it down the front of her pants. Her breath hitches, and she doesn't know how to react. I can't breathe either, because I don't know how *I'll* react. Jealousy-fueled anger lights a time bomb inside me, and I can hear the *tick, tick, tick* of the clock. I can feel the heat of the fuse. Her eyes roll back just a bit, and it's enough to detonate my rage. I explode, reaching past Leana to grab Karson by the throat and pin him against the headboard. Even as I put dangerous pressure against his airway, he keeps moving his hand beneath her jeans.

"Get your hand off her, Karson."

"Don't I have a say in this?" Leana's soft voice says beneath me.

"No," I say.

Karson's face darkens to a red hue, but that still doesn't stop his hand from moving against her pussy. I swear to god, this dude's death dream is to piss me off as he dies.

"I want one," she says, her voice slightly raised.

I lower my gaze to her and loosen my hold on Karson's throat. "What?"

"I want a choice."

"I heard you. What's your choice?"

I know what's coming. I know because she hasn't pulled his hand away from her. I don't want to hear it.

But I need to.

"I want you to let him touch me," she says as she sits up.

What game is she playing? I don't know, but I don't like it. I pull my hand from Karson's throat, and he gasps for air. "He already had you once today, wanderer. He can't have you again tonight." I grip Karson's wrist. "If you don't take your hand off her right now, I'll break your goddamn arm."

He rips his hand away. "Fine, but only because that's my good knifing arm."

I get into bed beside her, turning her on her side and nestling her ass against my pelvis. And putting more space between her and Karson. I bring my mouth to her ear. "Don't ever side with him again." I drop my hand to her abdomen and slip it down the front of her pants. My hand soaks up her heat, and I leave my fingers wrapped around the curve of her mound. "This pussy is mine. Don't forget it. Even if he touches you, even when he's inside you, remember who you belong to."

She gasps against my touch.

"You're mine, and I will *always* be the last man to mark you." My hand remains firmly planted on her pussy.

My pussy.

"Goodnight, wanderer."

Chapter Twenty-One

Leana

I slept all night between two madmen, and Gentry's hand is still down my pants when I wake the next morning. The sinful thoughts I had during the night coat his fingertips. Gentry stirs, tugs his hand away, and puts his fingers into his mouth, tasting me. It lights a fire between my legs, as if his hand was the only thing that had smothered the eternal flames. He effortlessly pulls me over his lap, drawing me in for a kiss. He inhales all of me, as if he's taking my soul inside him. It'd probably be alone in there.

I grind my pelvis into his, rocking my hips and sliding my slit along his ridiculously huge dick. It feels like I'm grinding on a log. Un-fucking-necessary. I'm fanning the flame his hand created. I look over at Karson, curled up on his side, fast asleep.

"Just grind your sweet little pussy against me, wanderer. After my touch all night, you're aching for release, aren't you?"

I ride the inseam of my jeans against his zipper, back and forth, until my motions grow ragged. Until I'm digging my knees into the mattress and trying to hold down every moan to keep from waking Karson. Gentry drops his head back as he grips my hips and guides me along his shaft. I feel like I'm being unfair, chasing my pleasure while he can only sit there and feel mine.

My thoughts wander to last night and the sexy show of possession from Gentry. Then Karson kept rubbing my clit, even as he was being choked out. Imagine dying and the last thing you did was stroke the clit of your brother's girl.

Wait.

Am I Gentry's? Just his? Or has this transformed into something else entirely? A thrupple I never imagined or asked for. One where two psychopaths want to sandwich me between them and fuck me in different ways. Maybe fuck me together?

These thoughts fill me with the intense urge to come. I want to get off. I *need* a release.

"Bite me," Gentry whispers. "Moan your pleasure into my flesh."

I listen because I have no other choice. I'm about to scream through the intense orgasm cresting like a wave between my legs. I lean into Gentry, inhaling the scent of murder and cigarettes. My mouth opens and I sink my teeth into his shoulder. My moans slip past, so I bear down with my teeth until his hips rise and his hands press me tight against his lap.

"Fuck," Gentry says, and I release my grip on his shoulder.

Karson turns over, his eyes narrow. "What the fuck kind of junior-high bullshit is this?"

"How long have you been awake?" Gentry asks as he pushes me off his lap.

"Long enough to hear you two acting like horned-up teenagers in the back of your mom's borrowed minivan," he says with a curl of his lip. He gets out of bed and heads for the bathroom. "You two are lame, and I need a shower. Thief, if you want a real fucking, you know where I'll be." He slams the bathroom door behind him.

I hate that they talk about me like I'm an object. Like I'm a lamp and they're arguing about who has to get up and turn it off. I don't mind being used in the heat of the moment, but I expect to be treated like a fucking person at the end of the day.

"What is this?" I ask Gentry.

He tugs off his shirt and balls it in his fist. "What's what?"

I gesture from him to the bathroom. "This. You two. Me."

"A goddamn predicament, that's what it is." He sighs. "You really want us both? I mean, can your soul be any more damned after allowing two serial killers inside you? You have a chance at salvation, wanderer. We don't."

"If there's a god, I think he'd forgive me. I mean, he's the one who wants you on your knees, right?"

He rolls his eyes.

There's a bigger problem here than just sharing me, though. I see it in the way Gentry and Karson interact, and it goes beyond a simple annoyance born of Karson's antics. "Why do you hate him so much?"

Gentry chokes out a sarcastic laugh. "You've met him, right? Heard him speak? Heard him fucking eat? He does that shit on purpose, by the way."

"What's the real reason, Gentry?"

He sits on the bed. "Fine, you want me to spill my secrets?"

I nod.

"First, Karson fucked my wife. I came home from a hit and found him pounding her in the kitchen."

That's fucking gross of Karson. No wonder Gentry isn't too keen on sharing. "You said first, which means there's more."

Gentry rubs a hand through his beard. "Shortly after that, he sold me out for less prison time when we got caught on a botched job. Granted, I'm the one who told him to take the deal, but I sat behind bars for ten years longer than I should have so his ass could be free, and he never once acknowledged the sacrifice I made. He's a fucking piece of shit."

I crawl over to Gentry and sit in his lap. My arms wrap around him in some kind of weird, comforting, sorry-your-brother's-a-dick embrace. His arms remain at his sides, clearly unaccustomed to comfort. I grab his arms and wrap them around my waist, and he finally leans into me. "You two need a mediation," I whisper.

"No thanks. Karson and I talk enough."

"Me and you talk about what?" Karson asks as he emerges from the bathroom. He brushes a towel through his dark hair and looks at us.

There's really no delicate way to do this, so I just go for it. "Did you really fuck Gentry's wife?"

Karson

What the fuck do these two talk about when I'm gone? "Excuse me?"

"Did you or did you not fuck his wife?" She stands and her hand lands on her hip.

"Why bring up something that happened forever ago? I don't even remember her."

I do remember her. I remember the day she dropped to her knees while Gentry was working late. She gargled my balls like a whore chugs mouthwash after a gnarly John. Frankly, I was impressed. I gripped my knife to slit her throat, to let her go out on a swan song achievement, but then she wanted more. I'd never killed someone while fucking them, so I figured I could cross that off my bucket list and end her cheating ass in one fell swoop.

"Why can't you just admit you did something wrong?" she asks. "Don't you see that's why he doesn't want to share me?"

I swallow. I don't really have these feely conversations. If I had feelings, I wouldn't be such a phenomenal serial murderer. "Gentry doesn't share. Even before he got married and I fucked up his unhappy little home, he's always been selfish. But if you think I should apologize, fine." I turn to Gentry. "I'm sorry I made your wife moan my name."

Gentry jumps to his feet, but Leana gets between us before he can charge.

"Fucking stop, Karson!" she shouts. "You walk around with this obnoxious persona so everyone will dislike you. Why? Because if you push people away, they can't reject you first?"

Ouch. As much as she's pissing me off. I'm feeling a certain type of way about what she's saying. And I don't like it. I step into her, fist her hair, and pull her against me. "You don't know me, thief. Just because I've been inside you doesn't mean you've been inside *me*."

"Get your hands off her," Gentry says.

"She wants my hands on her. Isn't that what this little come-to-Jesus meeting is about? Trying to make amends so we can all participate in a fucked-up circle jerk?" I release her hair with a sigh and meet Gentry's eyes. Maybe she's right. Maybe I should try a little harder here. "I'm sorry I fucked your wife, Gentry. I'm sorry I testified against you. And I'm kinda sorry about shooting you in the foot." I sit on the edge of the bed.

"Was that so fucking hard?" she asks as she sits beside me.

"I just find it funny that you think this will make a difference," I say.

"Actually, I think it did. As mad as he is right now, he hasn't turned you inside out yet." She reaches out and places her hand on Gentry's arm. "Now it's your turn. You need to let go of the past, Gentry."

"I can't," he says, a low, deflated growl leaving his lips as he sits beside her.

"Everyone here is being honest. I'm not your wife, and sharing me with Karson isn't the same as the betrayal you experienced before."

Gentry brushes his hair back. "You think I don't know that?"

"Then try," she says. "Try to let go of the past and the anger."

He won't even look at her as she speaks, and it's enough to piss me off. I took a step forward by apologizing to his burly ass, and now it's his turn. If he won't take that step on his own, I'll give him a fucking push.

I stand and rip down Leana's jeans. Tension wracks Gentry's body with every inch the fabric falls, and it's wrecking him.

But at least he's still sitting. At least he hasn't killed me yet.

I drop the towel from my waist, leaving it in a bundle at my feet as I tug her toward the edge of the bed. My attention is glued to her, but her blue eyes are glued to Gentry, seeking his approval. I don't think we'll get it, but I'm not ready to give up yet.

My cock rests against her absolutely soaked cunt. Her little humping session left her a sloppy mess, and the proof glistens on her pale thighs.

"Kiss me," she whispers, but the demand isn't directed at me. She's speaking to him.

He shakes his head but leans toward her, as if he's drawn by a rope that she's tightening around her little finger.

"Please," she begs. "Please, sir."

The moment she calls him sir, the entire expression on his face changes, morphing from cold and angry to something fucking starved. He leans into her and captures her mouth, his hand burrowing into her hair. God, it's sweet. I've never seen Gentry look comfortable, but he looks at home when he's touching her like that. That one word turned a giant fucking serial killer into a little puppy.

As sweet as it is, my cock twitches for her, and I'm willing to risk his wrath to sink inside her. I run the length of my dick along her slit, drawing my hips back until I'm lined up with her opening. I push into her, and she inhales Gentry's breath as the barbells rake against her insides.

He stops kissing her, and the corners of his lips twitch. That's a face I've seen too many times. He's trying to stay in control. It's a look that preludes the ultimate demolition of everything around him. It masks an untouchable anger that bubbles just beneath the surface until he rediscovers his control.

I still inside her. At this moment, we're all in danger. That's not me being a sarcastic asshole. Our lives literally teeter on the edge of a knife. Gentry is Zen as fuck for a serial killer. Centered as hell. Until he's not. And when that happens, it's fucking terrifying.

Her cunt squeezes around me, begging me to keep thrusting inside her, and all caution goes out the window. It feels too good to care. Too good to stop. If he wraps his hands around my throat and throttles the life from my body, I'll happily die inside her. I push into her with a long, deep stroke, and a moan rolls across her tongue. That sound may seal my fate.

"I hate that I want this," Gentry growls as he unbuttons his jeans and whips out his dick.

It's been a long time since I've seen my brother's junk, and I can't figure out why his wife wanted me when she had *that* to fuck. Like everything else on him, it's massive. Talk about insecurity inducing.

"Put her on her hands and knees," Gentry says as he runs his hand up his dick.

I pull out of her, and her pussy clenches and tugs at me. I can hardly resist telling Gentry to fuck off, but I *really* don't want to ruin this kinky therapy session.

I use her hips to turn her onto her belly, then pull her ass toward my pelvis. She leans over Gentry's lap, knowing exactly what she should do in this position. She takes him into her mouth, moaning on his cock as I push inside her, and she feels fucking incredible from behind.

He refuses to look at me, but I can't take my eyes off them. The way her head bobs and coats him in her spit. The way his hips rise every time my cock makes her moan. I enjoy seeing something other than bitterness on his face. Something that mimics happiness.

As she rides down his length with her mouth, Gentry buries his hand in her hair and pushes her down with his massive fingers. "Wanderer," he growls, spearing her throat with a thrust of his hips.

Her slick, warm walls tighten around me as she chokes on his dick. It's too much for me, and I come inside her with a groan I couldn't hide if I wanted to. I've already fucked up rule number two *and* three.

Gentry's eyes snap to mine, and the familiar haze of anger returns to his face. He starts to get up, but she keeps him down with a hand across his lap. Nothing has ever held him back when he was angry, yet he's become this pliable wad of muscle from nothing more than her arm and her perfect fucking mouth.

"I told you her pussy is mine," he says.

"I know, dude. I didn't mean to. She started choking on your dick, then she tightened on mine, and . . . and I'll take care of it." I pull out of her and drop to my knees. "Give back what you stole from me, little thief." My tongue grazes her clit as I curl it around her entrance, and I love the way she jerks forward from nothing more than that tiny touch. My come emerges from her in creamy white ropes. She tilts her pelvis, and it drops onto my tongue. The salty mixture of semen and her pleasure dances on my taste buds, and I stick my tongue inside her so I can swallow every delicious drop.

"Come here," Gentry says, and she's tugged away from me and brought onto his lap.

I wipe the come from my lips and back away to put on my jeans. By the time I tuck my spent cock away, I'm blessed with a pretty sight. I may not know enough to appreciate fine art or understand the intricacies of a symphony, but I can grasp the beauty of what's happening before me. She rocks on his lap as she rides him, her round ass bouncing on his thighs, and musical moans spring from her throat with every curl of her hips. Fucking magnificent.

And then Gentry's phone breaks the magical moment. The ominous ringing that signals another hit. I stare as the phone vibrates on the desk beside Gentry. He's never missed a call from George, and for good reason.

I step toward the nightstand.

"Don't," he says. "Not with the noise she's about to make." He holds her hips and punctuates every word with a firm upward thrust. The strangled scream she releases would sound pained if I didn't see the pleasure woven through her eyes. He's right not to answer. Dead women don't scream like that.

Gentry's hips stall beneath her, and he grunts as he fills her. He leans into the crook of her neck, but his eyes meet mine. "My pussy, wanderer. Mine."

Two steps forward, one step back. I'll take it.

Chapter Twenty-Two

I return George's missed call, and I'm shocked to find him in a pleasant mood. He's lined up one more hit before we reach the end of the line. The target is a man who likes to play the ponies but doesn't like to pay up when he loses. And he loses a lot, apparently. I get the details in the hall, then return to the hotel room. It's almost time to check out, but I need to speak with Leana before we push on.

Not wanting to have this discussion near Karson, I tell him we're walking to the lobby for food and that we'll bring something back for him. He's engrossed in a true-crime documentary on the flatscreen, so he's more than happy to hang back. He loves watching that shit and laughing at all the stupid mistakes the killers make, not realizing he'd be the star on one of those shows if I didn't always clean up after him.

Down in the lobby, Leana and I enter the attached restaurant and convince them to swap out the breakfast menu a little early by greasing their palms with some extra cash. I'm not in the mood for fluffy pancakes and crepes, and Leana had her heart set on spaghetti. We order everything to go, then step onto the veranda while we wait for our food. I don't want anyone to hear our conversation. I'm not even sure Leana will talk about it with me, but she'll definitely clam up if we're in front of strangers.

The hotel is attached to a winery, and a light breeze brushes over the fields below and shakes the grapevines. It's the sort of place where rich people go for brunch and mimosas, but we're alone for now. I glance at Leana as another puff of wind plays with the strands of blonde hair framing her face. She looks so content. So serene. I hate to ruin it, but this conversation can't wait.

"Wanderer," I whisper as I lean against the balcony railing overlooking the sprawling vineyard. "What did your stepfather do to you?"

"Don't ask me that," she whispers, her head shaking. "It doesn't matter what he did. It was wrong, and that's all you need to know."

"Are you afraid I won't feel the same about you if you tell me? Because nothing you tell me would change the fact that I want to *live* inside you." I smirk, but I'm not sure she notices. My smile fades when she doesn't speak. "I don't think you're dirty or used or broken because someone took advantage of you. What happened to you wasn't your fault."

She scoffs and blinks away a thin veil of tears. "That's rich coming from someone whose brother forces himself on me regularly."

"I'm sorry." I grit my teeth as the truth of her words binds my chest with barbed wire. "I'll talk to him about it. He's not really capable of caring for someone, but I think he comes as close as he can with you. I think he'd stop if he knew it bothers you. He thinks you like it."

Her hands tighten around the railing, and she meets my gaze. "But that's the problem, Gentry. I don't want him to stop. I do like it. What the fuck does that say about me?"

I try to pull her against my chest, to comfort her the way she comforted me, but she pushes away. I let her have her physical space, but I won't back down. She made Karson and me work through our shit last night, and now it's her turn. "Let me in, wanderer. Let me give back what your stepfather took away when he hurt you."

"Hurt me? That's the understatement of the fucking year. More like he emotionally wrecked me, ruined my life, and shit on my soul," she says. "Do you really want to know what he did to me? What he did to a terrified child for *years*?"

I swallow and nod. I'm not certain I want to hear any of it, but it might help her if she finally tells someone what she went through.

She swipes her eyes, her chin shaking beneath her lower lip. "It started shortly after he married my mom, but I didn't realize it began there until years later. He'd buy clothes for me and ask me to model them while my mom was at work. I thought we were just playing dress up." She scoffs and stops speaking. I don't think she'll continue, but she takes a deep breath and presses on. "It only escalated from there, but slowly at first. Coming into my room at night. Telling me he could make me feel good, but we had to keep it a secret." She turns to me, her eyes hard and cold. "It never felt good. It felt scary and wrong."

"Did you tell your mom?"

She laughs and folds her arms over her chest. "Yeah, eventually. It went further than touching when I was sixteen. Just before my eighteenth birthday, I decided I couldn't take it anymore. I went to her and told her everything. I expected her to be angry, and she was, but her anger was directed at the wrong person. She called me a liar and said I was cruel to make up such terrible stories about a man who worked so hard to provide for us. That's when I left."

"And that's when you met your fiancé?"

"Yeah, after traveling across the fucking country."

Realization dawns on me. "We're heading back the way you came."

She nods. "Yep. All this time, we've been headed toward my origin point. California. We lived a few hours from LA. That's why it scared me when you asked if I'd ever fantasized about killing someone. Because I have, Gentry. I've fantasized about what I'd do to him for years. I imagined all the ways I could hurt him every time he touched me."

"What was his name?"

She looks at me, and I can see the wheels turning behind her blue eyes. She knows why I'm asking, and part of her wants to tell me everything I want to know.

But she turns away. "Please leave my past in the past, Gentry. Please."

She knows better than to ask that of a man who held a grudge against his brother for six years. The past never stays in the past. "You can't let him get away with this. He has to pay, and I plan to collect his debt."

Before I can press her further, a waiter pops onto the veranda and tells us our food is ready. I drop it for now, but she taught me something last night that's just as powerful as a grudge. When you have someone in your corner, fighting for your sanity, healing is possible.

And I plan to fight for her.

Karson

When they get back to the room, they both look absolutely miserable. We eat without speaking, but Leana only picks at her plate. Which is fucking odd considering how she's been bitching about eating some "real" food. After she chokes down little more than half her meal, she rises from the bed and says she wants to shower before we take off. I take the opportunity to talk to Gentry about the odd vibe.

"What's got you so upset this early in the morning? You and the thief get in a fight?" I ask.

"She's mentioned that someone assaulted her in the past, and I got more info on that today. I want to slit the fucker's throat, but she won't give me a name."

I'm surprised when my stomach tightens at hearing this. My stomach hasn't tightened when I've disemboweled people, fileted them while they were still alive, or used my condom-clad dick to fuck the holes my beloved knife created. I don't give a fuck. Ever.

"How far in the past are we talking?" I ask. "Is it me? Not that I would stop, but is it?"

"No, you unfeeling dumbass. I talked to her about that too, and she likes your sick little games." He shakes his head, his fist clenching into a ball. "This happened when she was just a goddamn kid."

My stomach unclenches and blossoms with red rage. I've done some supremely fucked-up shit in my life, but I have a line, and it's a hard stop at children. That's why I take so much joy in torturing the pedos of the world. Child predators and junkies are the fucking worst. Gentry hates dealers more than junkies because he still can't lay all the blame on our father, but I have no problem doing that. I carry a lot of hatred for dear old Dad, and I take it out on every addict I can. But we share our hatred for the sick fucks who touch kids. We may not have much in the way of a moral compass, but it points due north at those deplorables.

"What are you thinking, G?"

"I don't know yet. She said she wants to leave the past in the past, but I think she'll change her mind if we put her in front of him and give her the upper hand she deserves."

"Or she'll hate you for it," I say. She'd expect *me* to disobey her wishes, but she expects so much more from Gentry. "You've seen it too, though?"

"What are you talking about?"

"You said you think she'll do what needs to be done if we give her the chance. You think she'd murder someone, which means you've noticed the same things I have. That she might be just a little fucked in the head. Like us."

He nods and sighs. "But none of that matters if we can't get a name."

"Bullshit. We don't need his name when we have hers."

"What the fuck are you on about, Karson?"

"You know her full legal name, right?" I smile when he gives me another nod. "And how did you get that?"

His eyes widen and his spine straightens because he's finally picking up on what I've already realized. One day he'll have to admit I'm not as stupid as he makes me out to be.

"Bingo," I say. "Her old address is probably still on that expired driver's license." When Gentry mentioned those licenses after our first night in a hotel, I tucked the info away. I figured we'd need it to track her down when she eventually bolted, but I like this outcome so much better.

Gentry goes to her bag and pulls the wallet from inside. He opens the camera on his phone, pulls the expired license from behind the current one, and snaps a picture of the address. After he tucks everything away, he looks at me and nods. We can't let her know our plan. We can see the shadow lurking in her eyes, but it's not the same shade of midnight as ours. She's not as black as us. If she catches on, if she figures out where we're headed before she's in the car, she'll fight us on it.

"This doesn't guarantee the guy still lives there," Gentry says as he sits on the edge of the bed. "We also need to figure out how to deal with the mother. Leana might be okay with carving a new eye socket into her stepfather's forehead, but I doubt she'll turn on her mom."

"Did her mom know about this?"

The bathroom door opens, and we stop speaking. I'll deal with the mom if Gentry and the thief are too weak to do what needs to be done. Even if she's an innocent bystander in all this, it doesn't matter to me.

As Leana dresses in front of us, I'm tempted to see if she and Gentry want to go for round two. But I'll save it. If my little thief takes a life in front of me, it'll be worth the wait.

"Grab your things and get ready to hit the road," Gentry says as he heads toward the bathroom. He stops in front of her and kisses her before he disappears behind the door.

Wearing nothing more than her shirt and a thin pair of panties, she stares at the door. I'm a bit jealous of the relationship between those two. He softens for her, and she melts like ice cream on a hot day. A girl like her will never like someone like me the same way. I'm unapologetically myself and I won't change for a woman, even one as perfect as her. But I'll make *changes*.

I walk over to her, cornering her against the dresser. Her breath hitches as mine washes over her, and she gasps as I drop my hand between her legs, sinking beneath the waistband of her panties. My eyes catch on the closed bathroom door. She's lucky I don't need much time to make her gush for me. A soft moan leaves her lips as I palm her and push my fingers inside her. I place my hand on her throat, and it bobs beneath my palm as she fights louder moans.

"Come for me," I whisper. "Before Gentry comes back, I want you to come on my fucking fingers."

"I can't," she pants, and I kiss her, drinking the sounds sliding from her mouth to mine. When her pussy clenches around me and her stomach draws in, I rip my fingers from her and a warm gush rains down on my palm.

"Fuck, that's a dirty little thief. You'll have to sit in that now."

The toilet flushes, and I pull my hand from her and sink my fingers into her mouth. She closes her lips around them.

"Show me what you taste like," I say, spreading my lips for her. She stands taller, prouder, and spits come-coated saliva into my mouth.

She steps into her pants, not bothering to clean herself up. I glance at the clock. It took three minutes to make her come. Maybe I don't have anything to be jealous about.

Chapter Twenty-Three

Leana

We say goodbye to the hotel, and I'm sad to watch it disappear in the rearview mirror. It's the nicest place I've ever stayed. As we pass through Nevada, I'm grateful Gentry doesn't press me for more information on my stepfather. The piece of shit definitely deserves whatever hellscape those psychos can conjure for him, but it's not something I'm ready to confront. I don't know if I'll ever be ready.

We reach the state border by early afternoon. After stopping long enough to piss and grab a few snacks from a gas station, we take a turn toward familiar town names. I try to swallow my fear that they've discovered my old address, telling myself their next target just happens to live near my mother's house. I don't bring it up, though. If my suspicion is incorrect, they'll know we're close and will likely force the information out of me. If I'm right . . . Well, it won't fucking matter.

I can't stop them.

I pass the time with small talk. Or try to. They're focused on getting ready for the job they have to do and don't have much to offer in the way of conversation. I eventually give up and stare out the window. My stomach rolls at the sight of every familiar landmark.

An hour later, they turn into the neighborhood where I grew up, and I can no longer pretend I don't know where we're going.

"You lied to me," I say from the back seat.

Karson turns to face me, his finger wagging in the air. "No, no. We didn't lie. We said we had a few more hits, and this is one of them."

Gentry turns onto my old street. I can see the house from here, and I don't recognize the car in the driveway. "Just stop! That's not even his car. I don't see my mother's car, either, so they probably moved. Let's just—"

"Let's just wait and see," Gentry says. His eyes meet mine in the rearview mirror, and my lips snap shut. I recognize the dark cast they've taken on. It's the same look I saw when he was carving words into that man.

We pull into the driveway, and my skin is ice. My mouth is a desert. My heart is a bass drum. The engine cuts off, and I can hardly hear the silence over the sound of blood rushing through my ears. I've boarded a train that's barreling toward a dark chasm, but there's nothing I can do to stop its forward momentum. I'm a passenger, taken against my will once more.

"Let's go, thief," Karson says. "We're home."

I shake my head, sending strands of blonde hair across my face. "No. If you guys feel the need to kill someone, go for it. I don't want any part of this. I'll wait in the car."

Gentry's head snaps in my direction. "*Now* you want to wait in the car? Of all the times, you choose now to be a good girl and stay put?"

"That's fine," Karson says. "If she doesn't want to make sure we're killing the right person, we'll just slaughter everyone in the house without verifying their identity first. This house is at the end of the street, and there's no one close enough to hear the screams. I have no problem with any of this." He reaches for the door handle.

"Wait!" I shout. When he puts it like that, I don't really have a choice. He's not bluffing. "If we knock on the door and it's not my stepfather, do you promise you'll let the people inside live?"

Karson looks away and sighs. "Yes, but only because this isn't an official hit. I've never willingly left a hit alive, and I don't plan to start today. But if your evil step-monster opens that door, don't even think about pleading for his mercy. Got it?"

I nod.

We get out of the car and approach the front door. Aside from the car in the driveway, everything else looks the same. Even the curtains in the windows haven't changed after all these years. With Karson and Gentry behind me, I pool my courage, use the hem of my shirt to cover my fingertip, and ring the doorbell.

Silence answers. No footsteps approach. No blinds draw back.

"Well, we tried," I say. I turn for the SUV, but Gentry grips my arm.

"Where do they keep the spare key?" he asks.

My shoulders deflate, and I point to the wreath on the door. "In a metal box behind it. It's magnetized."

Before retrieving the key, they pull gloves from their pockets and slip them on. This singular act makes everything too real. Too final. My throat constricts, and I'm choking on my need for air.

"You can't," I say on a strangled breath.

"Can't what?" Gentry asks, genuinely confused.

"You can't kill him."

Karson and Gentry raise their eyebrows at me.

"We aren't going to," Karson says with a smirk.

"*I* can't kill him. Get that out of your head right now. I'm not one of you."

Karson grits his teeth and struggles to keep his voice down. "How can you not feel homicidal when someone makes your body react so strongly to the thought of them? When they traumatized you to this point? Man up, thief. You have every reason to want him dead. Accept the blazing hatred for someone who hurt you, then embrace it. Let it cleanse you."

I swallow. He's right. But I can't do this. "If you two want to kill him, fine, but I'm not doing it."

"We're gifting you a prize," Gentry says. "You've fantasized about how you'd like to end this fucker's life, and we're making it possible. Sure, we could kill him, but we can't kill him the way he deserves. By your hand." He grips my shoulders with gloved hands. "Wanderer, listen to me. There are two kinds of people in this world: them and us. This is your chance to learn where you stand. Can you do this?"

I look into his dark eyes and finally draw a breath. "Yes, sir."

"Good fucking girl." He fists my hair and pulls me closer. As he kisses me, his length presses against me, and I don't know if it's because his lips are on mine or because we're about to commit murder.

Probably both.

"We can fuck when this is over," Karson says beside us. "My idea of foreplay is waiting inside, so can we get this show on the road?"

When Gentry releases me, I look at Karson, set my jaw, and nod. I'm ready to face the piece of shit.

Karson reaches into the bag on his shoulder, pulls out another pair of gloves, and slides them into my hands. "Put these on. Gentry will bitch and moan if you leave any prints behind."

I slip them on and try not to grimace when I notice what looks like old blood on the fingertips.

We enter the house, and I feel as if I've walked into a time capsule. All pictures of me have been removed, but everything else is exactly how I remember it. We silently search downstairs, but we find no sign of my stepfather in the living room or kitchen. The only other room is my old bedroom. My heart refuses to beat as we near the door.

Memories rush forward. Of the times my childhood was taken from me. Of the times the man who was supposed to protect me chose to hurt me instead. I don't want to cross the threshold before me, but I don't have a choice. With a shaking hand, I reach for the knob and turn it, opening the door just enough to peek inside.

This is no longer my bedroom. It's been converted into an office, complete with a bookshelf, computer desk, and a large leather chair. Someone sits in that chair—a man wearing a pair of headphones as he watches something on the large computer monitor in front of him. I recognize the balding patch on top of his head, though it's grown a bit since I last saw it.

My throat constricts again as I close the door, and I freeze. Heat burns in my chest and crawls up my neck. I struggle to breathe. This reaction is completely out of my control. I never thought I'd see this man again.

I never wanted to.

Gentry turns toward me, a genuine look of concern on his face. "Shh, wanderer," he whispers. I don't think he expected such a visceral reaction from me. *I* didn't even expect this type of response. "It's him, right?"

"Yes," I whisper.

Gentry and Karson look at each other and nod before pushing past me and opening the door. The time for sneaking is over. They each go to one side of the chair and grab an arm, lifting the man before he realizes what's happening. When they turn him to face me, his pants are around his thighs and his dick is out. I peer past him and see what's on the computer screen. Bile rises into my throat.

"Looks like he still has a sick taste for kids," Karson says. He reaches out a fist and shatters the screen. He turns his face toward my stepfather and snatches the headphones from his head. "Don't worry, I didn't damage the hard drive. All your nasty videos are still there for the cops to find."

Gentry socks him in the mouth before he can scream. "What's your name, you piece of shit?"

"M-Martin," he mumbles through a swelling lip. "What are you doing in my house?"

"Where's my mother?" I ask.

He turns and sees me for the first time, and a look of recognition washes across his face. It's fucking priceless. The shock. The horror. The transient moment where he remembers what I felt like beneath him. The buffet of emotions he's laid in front of me is the most gratifying meal I've ever seen, and I intend to eat my fill. My trepidation has fled, scared away by this unfamiliar hunger screaming inside me.

"I see you remember me," I say as I walk up to him and lift his chin with my gloved hand. His green eyes are the same empty, floating orbs that haunted me every night of my childhood.

"What are you doing here, Leana?" he pants as he spits blood onto his T-shirt.

Karson pulls a roll of tape from his bag and begins securing Martin's wrists, who then tries to scream. Gentry's ready for him and sends his fist against his mouth again.

"You don't know when to shut the fuck up, do you?" Gentry says. "Now answer her. Where's her mother?"

He squirms against the tape on his wrists, his eyes darting between the three of us. "She died. About t-two years ago. She had a stroke."

I don't know how to process this information. Maybe part of me hoped my mother and I could make amends, as unrealistic as that sounds. That's been taken away from me now. And he's already taken everything else.

Karson sees the tears welling in my eyes, and darkness rushes over his gaze. He steps behind Martin, wraps his arm around his throat, and strangles the ever-loving hell out of him. My stepfather's face reddens as he fights to suck a single breath past the pressure on his neck. Karson's hold only tightens, and I worry he's going to take the fucker's head off. Just as Martin's eyes roll back, Karson releases him.

Martin pants, trying to gulp every breath he missed out on. As soon as he's breathing normally again, Karson repeats the process. He does this torturous dance three more times, and Martin sobs at every release.

"What did you do to our girl here, Martin?" Gentry asks as he stands in front of him and leans down.

"Fuck you," Martin cries, and Gentry throws another punch to his face. White bone protrudes from the bridge of his nose this time and sends a gush of bright blood over his lips.

"Tell me what you did." Gentry puts a hand up to the shell of his ear.

"I raised her like my fucking daughter. That's all!" he squeals.

"Bullshit!" I scream. "You stole my innocence! You hurt me! You did things no one should ever do to a child!"

Karson unsheathes his knife and hands it to me with a wink. I embrace the handle and hold it at my side.

"That's what you remember?" Martin smirks, spitting a gob of blood onto the floor. "You wanted it!"

His words fuel my arm as I thrust my hand forward and grip his cock. I send the blade through his flesh, slicing it off. Martin releases a hellish, girly scream, and Karson puts a hand to his own mouth to hide his shit-eating smile. Gentry tightens his lips to keep from laughing.

I grip the thinning hair at the back of Martin's head and wrench his head back until I can look into his soulless eyes. "I was a fucking child. I didn't consent to what you did to me. I didn't like it, and it didn't feel good. You took so much of me, and you never cared, did you? Have you ever wondered what you did to my fucking psyche?" I spit in his face. "Fuck you!"

"I didn't hurt you! You were fucking fine!" he screams out, spit and blood flying from his lips.

"Fine? I'm fine? I'm fucking two serial killers for fun!" I shout.

Karson lets out a laugh, and Gentry punches him in the side. "Sorry, I just love her mouth," Karson says through a heave. "Please, continue."

"I have never been okay since you did what you did! I still have nightmares! I still close my eyes and see your ugly face."

Martin lifts his chin and spits blood at me. Gentry brings back his arm to hit him again, but Karson holds him back. "Let her," he whispers.

I bring the knife to Martin's face and drag the blade down his cheek. He screams and tries to move away, but Karson and Gentry have him in a firm grip, holding him in place so I can continue.

And I do. I fucking do.

I carve his face until the flesh spreads and he becomes more and more unrecognizable. With every pass of the blade, I scream out the pain I've held inside for most of my life. I grip the handle and prepare to drive the blade into his gut, to finally slay the demon who has haunted my mind.

But my hand won't move.

It was one thing to carve him up and slice off his dick like I've imagined doing, but ending a life . . . That's something else. My hand shakes, and the knife falls to the carpet. My eyes dart between Gentry and Karson, pleading for them to step in and finish this. "I can't do it. He deserves it, but I can't!"

Karson steps behind Martin and keeps him standing so Gentry can come to me. Gentry leans down, grabs the knife, and places it against my quivering fingers. When I don't grip it, he stands behind me and wraps his hand around mine, forcing my fingers to close. His other hand goes to my arm, rubbing it, comforting me.

I'm not alone. I'm not weak. That's what his touch tells me.

We step forward and plunge the knife beneath Martin's ribcage. I expect it to take more force, but the blade glides in, only stuttering a bit as it rubs against bone. I also expect to feel sickened by this act, by these sounds, by the horrific scream from Martin. Instead, I feel a rush. A dizzying wave courses through me, and I'm like a bird flying from a cage. I'm free.

Karson groans. "That is so fucking hot, thief."

"Good girl, wanderer," Gentry growls in my ear. "My little killer."

I melt into his touch as his words rush straight to my pelvis. Gentry eases our hands away from the knife handle, and he rubs my sides. Karson releases Martin, who falls to the ground in a gasping heap. Blood sputters from his lips, and he's stopped screaming.

Gentry hooks his gloved thumbs into my pants and tugs them to my thighs. When he pushes me down by the back of my neck, my hands land on the dying man's knees. Gentry unzips his jeans and pushes inside me. Martin shakes with each thrust, blood falling from his lips in heavy drops as his breathing grows more and more irregular. He blinks at me as if he wants to speak, but he can't. We've silenced him forever, and I hope he enjoys the show.

Gentry reaches between my legs and rubs me. "I want you to come for me, with your hands on his fucking knees as he bleeds out in front of you."

Karson walks over, unzips his pants, and pulls out his hard cock. His hand strokes his length as he brushes the hair away from my face. "Suck it, thief," he growls, and I turn my head toward him. "Not me," he says as he guides my chin toward the handle sticking out of Martin's abdomen. "Suck my favorite knife."

I stare at the bird's-head grip and take the weapon's handle into my mouth, my tongue rolling over the finger grooves along the bottom. The tangy taste of metal, blood, and leather fill my mouth. Karson strokes faster as I suck off his knife.

"Like that, thief," Karson growls as he strokes himself above my head. Martin coughs, sending a spattering of blood across my face and Karson's dick, but we don't stop.

Karson's strokes oddly turn me on, and I find myself biting into the grip as Gentry's fingers bring me that much closer. I want to come before Martin dies. I want him to see what it looks like when a man makes a woman feel good. Gentry's thrusts knock me forward onto the handle, sending it deeper into Martin's gut. Each breath my stepfather takes grows shallower, more irregular.

I pull my mouth away from the handle of the knife and bear down on Gentry as he makes me come. Karson strokes himself harder and faster as each moan leaves my mouth. My entire body shudders in front of the man who hurt me. My pleasure overpowers any pain he caused, and his current pain only fuels my pleasure. As he dies, I find life—an undeniable and explosive dichotomy.

"I'm going to fill your perfect pussy," Gentry growls as his hips stutter against my ass. His thrusts grow ragged as he comes inside me. "Don't let a single drop fall out of you."

As he pulls away, I sit up so that my pussy hovers over my jeans, then I pull them up so I don't lose a drop of Gentry's precious come.

"We have to finish him off," Karson says. He turns to me, still stroking his dick. "May I?" He asks this with a childish excitement, and I don't have the heart to tell him no.

"Please do," I say. I've more than fulfilled my fantasy at this point.

I stand up and find myself wanting to put my hand on Karson as he steps between me and Martin. I stand behind him, reach around, and grip his dick. Karson lets me take over, leaning forward and ripping the knife from Martin's abdomen. He groans, and I'm not sure if it's from the squelching sound the blade makes as it pulls free or the movement of my hand or all of the above.

Karson lifts Martin by his blood-soaked hair and stabs the blade into his throat. Arterial blood sprays across my face as he removes the knife, and Martin finally stops breathing.

"Fuck, thief, you're going to make me come. Squeeze my base," he says through clenched teeth.

I do as he says. The last thing we want is for anyone's come to be left at the scene of a homicide. Karson secures the knife on his hip, grabs my shoulders, and pushes me to my knees. He shoves his cock in my mouth, and the metal piercings clack against my teeth in his haste to be inside me. He pushes to the back of my throat three times before easing back and filling my mouth.

"Show me," he says through a growl.

I spread my lips and show him what he gave me, then he rips off one of his gloves and smears his finger through the blood on my face before pushing it into my mouth. The metallic taste mixes with his salty come.

"Now swallow."

I take the unpleasant mixture to the back of my throat and do as he commands. He pulls me to my feet and kisses me, his tongue exploring my mouth to taste what I tasted. He grips my chin and pulls away to lap at my cheek, licking my abuser's blood from my skin. Gentry comes up behind me and buries his face in my shoulder. I love when both their hands are on me.

"You did such a good job, my dirty little killer," Gentry whispers. "No one who hurts you will be allowed to draw breath. I promise you that."

"*We* promise you that," Karson clarifies as his tongue swipes my lips once more.

Gentry turns my face toward his and kisses me. With a low and loving voice, he says, "You got the revenge you deserve. Now you're one of us."

Chapter Twenty-Four

I stare at Leana in the rearview mirror as we travel to our next hit, but I force my eyes back to the road so we don't end up in a ditch. Darkness blankets the earth, and an overcast sky silences the stars. A heaviness hangs in the air. I am so incredibly proud of her for facing her abuser and silencing him, but I'm still struggling with what's happening between the three of us.

My eyes rise to her once more.

How did years of bitterness sweeten up enough to let us share someone? Not just someone, *my someone*. My wanderer. How did knowing she was being fucked by him send an undeniable ache through me?

My brother and I used to be so connected, so close that it felt like we were twins instead of years apart. We shared so many things, like the hunger we felt before a kill and the satisfied elation after a job was finished. When he hurt, I hurt. When he was angry or happy, I felt those emotions as well. But the moment I saw him with my wife, our connection severed. Tore apart in an instant. Broke in ways I always thought were irreparable. Then she changed that. When he was inside Leana, I felt all of it. The desire and excitement. The need for her. And it made me need her too. She was the glue that reconnected the loose ends.

I don't know if Karson and I are capable of love, but our need to protect her comes pretty close. After the way she stepped into her role earlier, she's more than earned her place by our side. Hell, beginning to mend the years of hurt between us was probably enough, but it helps to know she's got a touch of darkness inside her. Darkness that was there before we put more inside her, that is.

I pull into an alcove of trees and peer at the colonial home on the dead-end road. It looks so plain. So inexpensive. Our typical hits live in mansions, complete with wads of cash to pilfer after we've finished a job. I don't expect to leave with much money from this one, and I don't like that. This feels like a waste of fucking time. Regardless, it's a job, so I tuck my pistol down the back of my pants and climb out of the SUV. I go to the back door and open it.

"Stay," I command, though I know she won't listen. That's her thing—being a beautiful problem. Her eyes flash up at me, and I rub my finger along her lower lip before leaning down and capturing her mouth.

"Haven't I proved I can handle myself?" she asks.

She's not wrong, but I'm not sure she can handle just how depraved we become. Back at her house, she fed on her rage and pain. She might struggle more when she's faced with taking the life of someone who hasn't wronged her, and I don't need a voice of reason in my ear when I'm trying to work.

"Come on, G," Karson says.

"Stay," I tell her once more.

She sits back with a scoff, and I shut the door.

We walk through the trees, then along the side of the house until we reach the back door. Karson uses a gloved hand to check windows as we pass, but they're all locked. When we reach the door, it's locked as well. Karson pulls a lock-picking kit from his pocket and gets to work. He's always been a wizard with locks. He learned the trade when we were kids. Instead of collecting action figures or baseball cards—which we never had the money for anyway—he learned how to disengage every lock known to man.

His tongue peeks from between his lips as he faces a challenge with this one. He tries a few techniques and tools before he's greeted by a satisfying click, then he opens the door with a sinister smirk.

As we creep through the house, I draw my knife and ready my grip on the handle. We know nothing about this man other than his name and the reason for the hit—poor Allan owes a lot of money to a lot of people—which is unusual. We normally get more info than this, but George said he didn't have time for specifics. He was probably pissed that I missed his call and figured he could annoy me by withholding info. It worked. I'm definitely annoyed. Karson and I like to know about our hits so we can tailor their death to their personality. Kind of like a personalized service. We should really charge more.

After searching the house, we find the man on his stomach, sprawled across his bed with one knee toward his chest. He's fast asleep, snoring away. I stay in the doorway, but Karson moves closer, leans down, and clears his throat in the man's ear. He wants to see the fear on his face when he emerges from his dreamy slumber and comes face to face with a nightmare.

The man slowly rolls over, his eyes widening as he takes in the confusing scene above him. He leaps from the bed and runs right into me as soon as he crosses the threshold. A single punch is all it takes to put him right back to sleep.

We grab a dining room chair and set it in the middle of the living room. Once we've hauled his body into the seat of honor, we duct tape his hands behind his back, threading the tape through the wooden slats. I go for his ankles next, wrapping the tape around each chair leg and connecting it to his skin. His head flops forward, his mouth gaped, blood dripping from his nose.

Karson goes to the kitchen and begins rifling through the drawers. There are tons of murder weapons right out in the open, but that's not what he's looking for. This is another Karson specialty. He finds random shit around the target's house and uses it to torture them. Bags, nail guns, walking sticks—you name it, he's used it on a hit.

He plucks a roll of plastic wrap from a drawer and holds it up with a grin. Happy to have found what he needs, he comes behind the man and tries to hold up his head while securing the plastic around his face. Unfortunately, the wrap sticks to itself and doesn't create the effect he's going for. He's an artist, after all, and he needs his masterpiece to mimic his vision.

"Little help?" he asks, shaking the man by the hair. "I can't hold his head and line this up."

I roll my eyes and walk over, replacing his hand with mine. Karson winds the plastic around the man's face, keeping the sheet flat to create the perfect viewing window. It sucks into the man's mouth with every attempted breath. I have to admit . . . it's beautiful. Unlike a bag, which would have given him a few good breaths before the oxygen started to disappear, the wrap just instantly traps his face and obstructs all air.

The man's eyes widen as his brain kicks him awake. Within a haze of palpable panic, he jerks against the restraints, his chest heaving with every gasp. Fucking delicious. It will be over too soon like this, though. He needs more time to really feel the fear, to let it soak into his bones and leave it etched on his face, even after death.

I grab a fork from a drawer and use it to poke a pinhole into the plastic over his mouth. The air makes a whistling sound as he breathes. "Do you have any cash?" I ask.

He shakes his head.

Karson steps in front of the man and assesses his handiwork. "He's a gambling addict. If he had cash, it's probably gone by now."

"Even losers win sometimes," I say. "Keep him alive while I go look for a safe."

Karson scoffs. "Waste of time."

I turn around and head toward the bedroom. I rummage through the closet, but I don't find a safe or money or anything of value. Worthless sentimental shit clutters the shelves, and simple clothes hang from the racks. I go for the dresser drawers next, but they're just as disappointing as the closet. A wallet rests on the bedside table beside a half-empty glass of water. I snatch it up and flip it open, finding only a ten and some ones. When my eyes fall on the driver's license, my stomach sinks.

I rush back to the living room and slash my blade across the plastic over his mouth, slicing his skin in the process. Blood drips down his chin and stains his shirt. "What's your name?" I snarl.

"Roger!" he screams out.

"We've got the wrong fucking guy!" I yell.

Karson looks down at the trembling man. "He's not a target?"

I flip through the wallet again and find a business card. "He's a goddamn pastor."

"Have we ever killed a holy man?" Karson asks, cocking his head. His eyes rise back to mine. "I mean, we don't really have a choice now. We have to—" He swipes his finger across his own throat.

Unlike Karson, I feel things. I'm not totally on board with killing innocents, but sometimes it can't be helped. This is one of those times.

"If we confess now, do you think it absolves us of our sins?" Karson asks as he leans closer to the man.

Pastor Roger furiously shakes his head.

Karson smiles. "I think it does. I think that's how this works. I tell you my sins, I do three or four Hail Marys, and then I go to heaven, right?" He leans closer and whispers something that makes the poor old pastor see the devil before his eyes, then Karson starts reciting the prayer.

Once.

Twice.

The third time, he stabs his knife into the pastor's gut. "Hail Mary, full of grace, the Lord is with thee. Blessed art thou amongst women, and blessed is the fruit of thy womb, Jesus." He twists the blade. "Holy Mary, Mother of God, pray for us sinners, now and at the hour of death." He drives the knife upward. "In the name of the Father." He rips it downward. "And of the Son." He pulls the blade sideways to finish the cross. "And of the Holy Spirit." With a wide grin, he removes the blade and flicks a splash of blood onto Pastor Roger's forehead. "Amen."

My lips tighten. What the ever-loving fuck is wrong with him? "Are we done?" I ask.

"Yeah, yeah." He wipes his blade on the inside of his jacket and slides the knife into its sheath.

"Actually," I say, "find a Ziploc bag." I pull out my knife and hack the pastor's right hand from his limp body.

The fact that he doesn't question me is one of the *few* reasons I like my brother. Chopping off a hand and asking for a bag usually begs for questions, but he just rolls with it and begins searching cabinets and drawers.

"Oh my god, this man has a vacuum seal machine! And bags!" he shouts.

I meet him in the kitchen and toss the hand into the bag. Karson slides the bag's open edge into the machine and it sucks out the air, leaving the hand looking like a bloody chicken breast. The machine clamps off the end with a mechanical click.

"What do you plan to do with it?" Karson asks, his eyes lighting up with anticipation.

"We have one more hit. One final job to do. I figure we can find some use for it and really go out in a blaze of glory."

Karson gives a slow nod. "I like it."

"Let's get out of here." I start toward the door. "We need to call George and figure out where the wires were crossed. He's never fucked up like this before."

"I'm surprised the thief is actually waiting in the car," Karson says behind me.

Yeah, it *is* fucking surprising. She usually comes barging in when her morbid curiosity gets the better of her. A shitty feeling squeezes my gut, but I try to push it away. She probably had her fill of murder after what we did just hours ago. Considering she didn't put up too much of a fight when I told her to stay put in the car, I'm going with that.

Even as I try to reassure myself, my feet pick up their pace toward the SUV. I step off the porch, seeing only what's directly in front of me. Karson's boots crunch against the earth as he tries to keep up when I break into a run. When I see the car, my stomach drops.

The back door is open, and the dome light reveals an empty SUV. I blindly hope she's just run off, that she wants us to chase her, but that hope evaporates when I reach the open door. A track of drying blood streaks the seat, and claw marks run through it. My wanderer didn't run off. She put up one hell of a fight to stay.

Someone took her.

My eyes dart around. I see only trees, smell nothing more than nature and blood. Blazing anger sears my insides until I'm a boiling kettle of rage. I've never felt such an insurmountable sense of loss. Of emptiness. This is the exact fucking reason I've always been so guarded. I shouldn't be allowed to feel such strong emotions because it makes me fucking homicidal when I'm *already* homicidal.

Karson's feral smile fades when he reaches the car. "What's the matter?" he asks.

"Leana is gone."

"She probably ran—"

My glare hardens. "No, Karson. She's fucking gone."

"Wait, what?"

"There's blood. They pulled her out of the car!"

"Who's they, G?" he asks as he takes a cautious step toward me.

"You fucking know who. And it's your fault."

I whip out my pistol, and Karson takes several steps backward.

He raises his hands. "Gentry, wait!"

The terrified gleam in his eyes almost makes me laugh because Karson has *never* feared me. My rage usually inspires him to poke and prod and make me angrier. But not this time. I can only imagine what I must look like for him to step back like a scared little animal. Like the things we catch and kill.

I level my barrel at his face. My finger wraps around the trigger, and everything in me tells me to do it. To kill him. His finger has depressed the detonator on every single fucking thing in my life that's blown up on me. This is all his doing.

"You did this, Karson! You! If you hadn't called George and told him Leana was with us, none of this would be happening right now!"

"G, it wasn't me! I swear."

"Who else knew she was with us, Karson? Who else would have called George?"

He licks his lips, the wheels spinning in his mind as they struggle to gain traction on an answer that will lower my hand. "The guy she was with," he says, his eyes widening. "The guy before us. She was dope sick when we picked her up, so maybe that guy has connections to George's druggie side jobs. Maybe they're working together on this."

His words almost make sense. I can understand her ex going to great lengths to get her back.

"Think about it. This hit wasn't a mistake. It was a fucking setup. And I know where they might be," Karson adds. "George has a warehouse about an hour from here. I've only been there once, but I think I can find it again. Let's go there and get the truth. If I'm lying, you can kill me then."

I lower the gun. "Get in the fucking car."

We load into the SUV, and Karson just stares at me as we turn onto the road. "Are you going to kill me if we don't find her?"

My fingers tighten around the steering wheel. "Yes, and there's a good chance I'll kill you even *if* we find her."

He throws himself backward like a child. "Then why should I bother helping?"

"Because if you don't, I'll cut off both of your hands, put them in a prayer position, and shove them so far up your ass you'll be shitting Hail Marys for a goddamn year."

That's enough to shut him up, and aside from offering some directions, he doesn't speak again. That's a good thing. If I discover he's lying, I'll be forced to silence him permanently.

Chapter Twenty-Five

Leana

Tape strangles my wrists, and I breathe used air beneath the heavy black sack on my head. I'm in the back seat of some luxury car that smells like expensive cigars, money, and warm leather. A hand lands on my thigh, and I jerk my leg away with a growl.

"Vicious one," someone says beside me.

I recognize that voice. It carries the same low, authoritative tone that told Gentry to get rid of me. Well. Fuck.

George's phone rings again, and I can only assume Gentry or Karson have been blowing it up. Probably before they come and actually blow shit up. If they can find me.

"They're going to kill you," I say through the hood.

He hears my muffled words and smacks my cheek hard enough to make my ear ring. "I hope they do. I want them to find you so I can kill them after I kill their little toy in front of them."

"You need home-turf advantage because you *know* what they'll do to you on a level playing field. You knew you couldn't take them out at that target's house."

"Target? What have they been teaching you? You haven't taken the prerequisite courses on living a life of hardship to get into this class."

"You don't know anything about me."

He lets out a hollow laugh and holds my thigh in a grip I can't shake off. "I know enough."

A sharp tingle runs through my arms and hands, and I shift my weight to relieve the building pressure. The vehicle eases to a stop, and so does my heart. The dozens of unknowns rush through my head and drown out any rational thought.

The door to my left opens, and hands wrap around my arms and haul me out of the car. I spew curse words beneath the hood and kick my legs until my feet connect with concrete. A garage door rises in front of me, clicking and clacking on its track as the motor whirs, so I'm probably at a house. I consider screaming, but if they're brazen enough to bring a hooded woman through the garage, I doubt there's anyone around to hear my cries for help. Doing so would only piss them off, so I keep my mouth shut as they lead me forward.

"Stairs," a gruff voice says behind me.

My foot searches for the first tread, and I clumsily climb a staircase that seems to go on forever. When we reach the top, I'm ushered through another doorway and my feet connect with the familiar thud of hardwood floors. The man behind me grips my shoulders, turns me to face him, and eases me backward until my spine touches something cold and tall. He slices through the tape on my wrist and secures something else in its place. I feel around with my fingertips until my mind can piece a picture together: I'm handcuffed to a fucking pole.

The hood lifts from my head, and I squint against the room's bright light. As my eyes adjust, my mouth falls open. I'm tethered in a spacious living room, dwarfed by the tallest ceilings I've ever seen and windows that would fill the room with sunlight if it wasn't late at night. The slick hardwoods gleam, and plush red couches and chairs surround a giant fireplace.

My eyes move to the men. George—wearing a three-piece suit in an ostentatious shade of baby blue—stands between four muscular men. He isn't at all what I expected. He's much older than he sounded, and he's kind of short. But I guess he doesn't need to be big when he has Vin Diesel's body-doubles for friends.

"So you're the reason my best men have been acting fucking suicidal?" George asks. He takes a step toward me, and his men mirror each move. He lifts a strand of my hair, screws up his mouth, then drops his hand. "Kind of plain if you ask me. Don't you think?" He turns to his men.

"She looks better than she did when she was high." That voice crawls up my spine and raises the hair on the back of my neck. I refuse to believe it until he steps into the room, and then I can't deny what's right in front of my face.

"Mickey?" I breathe.

"What? You didn't believe me when I said I'd find you if you ever left me?" He steps closer, and his cologne sends a million terrible memories rushing to the surface of my mind. "I had a tail on you the whole time you were on the street. I lost you for a bit when you stole that car, but when I found out George's boys were riding in a similar make and model, I put two and two together."

"So Karson really didn't tell George?" I ask. "It was you?"

"I wasn't certain at first, but when I saw that little video, there was no denying it. Your tattoo gave you away." He drags his finger along the curve of my breast, and I wiggle away. "Great acting, by the way. He asked me if I thought it was real, but I know you. I said, 'That's my Lee, but she ain't dead.'" He circles me.

"I'm not yours anymore, Mickey."

"You're damn right you're not. Not after you've been all used up. I expected you to hop on the first dick you saw, but the Kursickis? You got yourself involved with some real bad people. Way worse than me."

"How do you know them?" I ask, my eyes narrowing.

"We all work in the same circus, but we perform in different rings. I'm one of George's dealers, but I'm well aware of George's star acts. His deadly, daring duo."

Go fucking figure. Just my luck.

He brushes a firm hand through my hair. "You're looking good. Healthy," he whispers in my ear, and I rip away from his words, straining against the handcuffs. His hand rides down my neck and grazes the scabby cut on my left breast. He rips my shirt, exposing my nipple. "Since you like to show your tits to random men."

Refusing to give him the satisfaction of a reaction, I suck my lower lip into my mouth to stop the tremble. I curl my toes, letting the tension run through my calves so I don't kick him. If he knows how much he's hurting me, he'll do more. Worse.

Mickey reaches into his pocket and tugs out a pill. The sight of it makes my mouth water. Makes my toes uncurl. It would help ease some of the pain in my head from where they hit me when they took me.

I shouldn't want that pill.

But I do.

I stick out my tongue and allow Mickey to place the pill into my mouth, then I dry swallow and wash it down with immediate regret and guilt.

"Good girl, Lee. You're always more pliable when you're high."

George lets out a laugh and slaps a hand on Mickey's shoulder, then they all exit the room. As my head begins to swim a few minutes later, I can only think of Gentry and Karson. When I was with them, I no longer craved pills or escapes. I was happy. I found freedom. Now I'm caged again.

I sink to the floor. "Please hurry," I whisper before I close my eyes and slip beneath the waves.

Gentry. Karson. I want them. I trust them. I need them to save me again, to set me free.

My eyes crack open as an immense weight presses down on my body. So heavy. I turn my head and glance out the window. It's still dark outside, but the moon has hardly moved across the sky. I haven't been out for very long, but enough time has passed to leave me feeling incredibly disoriented and confused. What did Mickey give me? Something stronger than I'm used to, that's for sure.

Metal digs into my wrists as my arms strain backward. I try to jiggle them against the pole, but everything happens in slow motion—a disconnect between my movements and my brain.

A rough grasp pulls my chin downward. The weight above me is George, and my thighs are spread around him. As if trying to scream underwater, my mouth opens and produces a silent cry. His fingers dig into my thighs as I try to kick at him.

"Morning," he says as he leans over and squeezes my cheeks, forcing me to close my mouth.

I can't even feel him between my legs. I'm either too high or he's too small. I only feel the thump of his hips slamming into me. The familiarity is too much. My stepfather is dead, but George is a reincarnation of the worst kind. Just like Martin, he has stolen my voice. He has silenced me.

I'm so fucking tired. Every breath takes too much out of me. I gather enough strength to pull my face away from his grasp, but my head only lolls to the side. A lamp across the room catches my eye, and the light blurs as I try to focus on its tasseled shade. I move my gaze to the mahogany desk beneath it, but it all blurs until it's just an array of colors and shapes in the distance.

Am I going to die? Am I about to overdose with this bag of old bones inside me?

When I think my situation can't get any worse, words come from somewhere far away from me. "Your turn," George says as he climbs off me.

One of the guards kneels and brings his face close to mine. I shrink away from his warm breath, but my disgust doesn't deter him. He lifts my thighs and hooks them over his knees.

And it starts again.

Chapter Twenty-Six

Karson

I'm not showing it like Gentry, but I *am* upset about this. It's fucked up. We tried to keep her in the car to protect her from us. Protect her from our job. If we'd taken her with us, she'd be safe right now.

"G?"

"Don't, Karson. Don't speak unless you're giving directions to George's place."

I open my mouth and close it again. I'd normally push him a little further, annoy him a little more, but he's beyond the point of no return. If I even opened that bag of chips between us, he'd slice my jugular with his knife.

I don't know what else to say. I can't fix it. Even though it's not my fault, I can't make him believe me. I can only help get her back and let Gentry learn the truth so he can stop being so pissed off. He has no choice but to work with me in ways we haven't worked together in years. We used to know the exact move the other would make, like a fucked-up dance. Serial synchronization. For once in a very long time, he needs my help, and as much as it sucks, it's a chance to prove I'm not *as much* of a fuck up as he thinks.

My stomach grumbles and sends a hunger pang through my insides. "Do you think we should stop to eat?" I ask.

He glances at me.

I'm not being annoying, I'm starving.

"No. I won't stop for a single fucking thing until we get there. Every extra minute she's with George—" His hands tighten around the wheel in a death grip. The thing fucking squeals, and I worry he's about to snap it in half.

"Alright." I take the risk and pluck the bag of chips from the center console. The cellophane screams like a jet engine in this silent space, so I snatch the bag open and bring a single chip to my mouth.

But Gentry reaches over and smacks it out of my hand.

"Dude, chill!" I say. "I want to find her too. She's grown on me, believe it or not, but I'm still a human being and I need to eat. And piss."

"We can't."

"The little thief is tough, G. She'll be okay." Trying to relate to or comfort someone isn't my strength, but I'm fucking trying. I can kill someone, but fuck off if I have to connect with someone on a personal level.

Except Leana.

Aside from my brother, the weird dynamic between me and the thief is the closest I've ever felt to caring for a person. I let her steal a part of whatever heart I have.

"George is a man even *we* fear, so how do you expect Leana to survive his wrath?" Gentry says. "We've always been on borrowed time with him, and that's why I wanted this run to be our last."

My eyes snap up to him. "I am *not* afraid of that sack of shit. I've been ready to turn on his ass for ages. Don't forget that I gave zero fucks when he wanted to kill me."

"What are you going to do, Karson? What do you really think you'll be able to do when you face him?"

I grip my pistol in one hand, my knife in the other, and wave them in the air. "I'm going to find his old ass and humble him. Or die trying. You just worry about getting our girl while I'm busy."

Gentry's lips tighten but draw up at the corners. "If they touched her, you won't be the only one doing some humbling."

He pulls the SUV to a stop in front of a large building. The warehouse is beyond massive—even bigger than I remember—but my stomach twists when I spot the empty parking lot. George is in one of three places, but I've made the wrong choice. He's not here.

We get out of the SUV, and the first thing I do is take a piss in the bushes. Gentry sighs and unzips his fly to do the same. The short time it takes to pee unnerves him and sets him on edge. A snarky comment lurks beneath my tongue, but I let it pass. He feels like every second matters, but George doesn't want *her*. He wants *us*. Well, he wants to kill all of us, no doubt, but he'll keep her alive until we get there. That's the sort of sick shit I would do, anyway.

I walk along the outside of the building with Gentry. We peer into windows scabbed over with dirt. When I check the only two entrances, there's a layer of scum on the knobs. No one has been here in a while.

"He's not here, G." My words aren't enough to get him to stop searching, and I have to physically pull his giant ass toward the car. "Come on, dude. You can't handle seven seconds to piss, but you'll wallow around an empty building for an eternity?"

"Fuck you!" he roars before turning back and socking me in the face.

He's punched me many times over the years—probably more times than I can count—but I've never felt so much hatred within his balled fist. My arms go behind me to brace myself for a collision, and I crash to the busted concrete. Even though he sucker punched me, I won't fight back. He's hurting more than I am right now.

"I'm sorry, Gentry."

Something in this apology seems to resonate with him more than the apologies in the hotel. This one sinks in. Maybe because I meant this one.

He shakes out his hand and groans before helping me to my feet. "Where to next?"

"His club," I say.

Gentry cocks his head. "You really think he'd bring her to a club?"

"There's a whole sketchy basement with soundproof walls and a side entrance. You don't have something like that unless you plan to bring some people down there who don't want to be there."

"Get in the car," he snaps.

We drive through the city until we reach the nightclub. A shitload of vehicles clutters the parking lot here, but I don't know if any belong to George and his men. I can only hope I'm right this time.

Gentry parks, wipes at his eyes, and gets out of the car, then we conceal our weapons and head toward the entrance. As soon as we step inside, music bumps in my chest and I'm mesmerized by the strobe lights flashing over the shadowed bodies in the next room. The bouncer stares at us, as if we have "I'm going to ass fuck your boss before slitting his throat" written on our foreheads. He stands up and steps toward us.

Gentry rushes forward and pushes him against the wall before he can draw his gun, knocking into his shitty podium on the way. I whip out my knife and hold it against his throat, and suddenly the big, scary bouncer is nearly pissing his pants.

"Where's your boss?" Gentry asks.

"Joe is inside," he says through a tensed jaw.

"Not Joe. Your real boss. Where's George?" He shakes him, which scrapes my blade over his skin.

"He's been gone since last night," the bouncer nearly whimpers. "We don't know where. He doesn't tell us anything."

Gentry pats the man's cheek. "If I find out you're protecting him, I'll come back here, cut off your dick, stuff it in your mouth, and choke you with it. Are we clear?"

I pocket my knife and stare him down.

"Crystal," he says.

Gentry rams him into the wall once more before releasing him, then unholsters his pistol and pockets it. "I'm taking this for my inconvenience." He backs away and motions for me to follow.

"Got any more bright ideas?" Gentry says through gritted teeth as we jog back to the SUV.

Before I can answer, his phone buzzes for the first time since Leana was taken. I rip it from his hands and open the message before he has a chance. I have a feeling I know who's reaching out on this fine evening, and Gentry won't be able to handle what I suspect will be embedded in this message. My shoulders fall when I open it.

"What is it?" he asks.

I don't answer him, which is probably pretty alarming, considering I never shut the fuck up.

"What is it, goddamn it!"

My mouth falls open before I can stop it. He's seen me fuck a knife wound before. *Nothing* makes my mouth gape. Which means it's really something. And it is.

"Give it to me," he commands.

I shake my head. "Trust me when I say no. You don't want to see this. If it's making *me* this upset, it will break you."

He grips my wrist and bends it backward, but I hang on to the phone, even when I feel my bones strain to a breaking point.

"Stop, stop! You can watch it, but not now. Wait until just before you go in at the next stop. The video shows where they are. I know where to go, but we'll never make it there if you look at that video."

He releases my arm. "Where are they?"

"It's a bad fucking idea to go there like this. They'll overpower us."

"We have four pistols, several knives, and a vendetta. What more do we need? Now tell me."

"It's his home, Gentry. He has guards, trained attack dogs, and who the fuck knows what else?"

Gentry sets his jaw and shakes his head. "We can't leave her. We have to try. She wouldn't be in this mess if we hadn't taken her along on this messy goddamn ride. If we hadn't climbed in her car and brought her into this fucked up world where she doesn't belong."

"We'll figure it the fuck out," I say.

I'm entirely unsure how we will, but we don't have another choice.

Chapter Twenty-Seven

Gentry

Any chance of getting out alive means working hand in hand with my brother and trusting him in ways I haven't in a very long time. I don't even know if I'm capable of this. I will have to trust him as if he didn't betray me so many fucking times. I'll have to lay my well-being in his lap and trust that he has my back.

Alone, we can't win.

Together? We might just stand a chance.

Karson silently broods beside me as we travel on winding back roads toward George's house. His nails dig into his thighs every so often, as if he's reliving the video in his mind. I squeeze the wheel. Was she being tortured? Touched? Fucked? I growl at the thought. He's right to withhold that video until we get there.

The man beside him right now is controlled.

Leashed.

Repressed.

When I see that video, I will become the old me, and the old me coupled with the current Karson might just be enough.

We turn onto a tree-lined road that snakes up a hill. As we near the top, the massive mansion comes into view, illuminated against the stark black sky. Floodlights perch on the perimeter like mechanical sentries with tall black bodies and brightly glowing heads. There's also a fucking guard post. Two, actually.

This will be fun.

We're hitmen, not fucking assassins, but if you get us mad enough, we might just change our line of work. And George has taken this too fucking far.

I kill the headlights and pull the SUV into the woods. An embankment blocks the view of the mansion, which means they can't see us, either. I gesture for the phone, and Karson places it against my palm and turns away. When I turn on the screen and run my finger over the giant crack in the glass, George's message pops into view.

I'm only looking at the cover image, but it's enough to make my blood heat to a simmer beneath my skin. Leana lies on a hardwood floor, her blonde hair fanned around her head. Her eyes are closed, and she looks like she's sleeping. I click the video and an icon swirls around on the black screen before it begins. The camera operator zooms in on Leana. Her face is toward the camera, but she doesn't move, even as the cameraman puts his dick in her mouth. Then her eyes flutter, and she gives a weak groan.

She's drugged up.

The camera pans downward and focuses on the ripped shirt and her bare chest. It moves lower and I don't want to watch, but I can't look away. It stops on her pale thighs, which hook around the legs of someone in black slacks.

Then, the cameraman speaks.

It's George.

"You want your girl, Gentry? Come and get her. We've come for her several times already."

It's the first time Karson has heard the audio, and his hands clench into fists when he hears the laughter from the other men in the room. He was wholly correct when he chose to keep this from me.

I crack my neck, then my knuckles, and expand my chest with a deep inhale to send another rush of snaps down my spine. "Get the fucking hand."

"What?" Karson asks, his eyes wide.

"The pastor's hand. Get. It."

He keeps his eyes on me as he reaches back and grabs the vacuum-sealed appendage. I lay the pistols and knives on the dash, then pick up my pistol and rack it to ensure it's loaded. I stuff my spare magazine in my pocket. I don't carry more than that because I've never needed to. If I run out of ammo in one magazine, I use my hands. Or my blade. I check the Glock I pulled off the bouncer. Ten rounds. California "legal."

Lame, but that's ten more than I had.

I pocket the Glock, affix my blade to my hip, and tuck my larger pistol down the back of my pants as I get out of the car. I stuff the hand into my free pocket, but the baggy sticks out a bit, brushing the bottom of my arm. It's annoying, but I need it. Karson follows me, racking one of his pistols and letting a bullet land in his open hand. He drops it into his pocket.

I stare at him. "Why?"

He slides his gun into the holster on his hip. "I always stash a bullet before a hit. Have since we started." He shrugs. "It's lucky."

I shake my head. "If you were lucky, you wouldn't have been a marked man yourself not too long ago. It sounds like a bad omen if you ask me."

"You have your hand. I have my bullet. Don't judge what I carry into battle," he says with a scoff.

Touché.

We crest the embankment and I squat down. The view of the mansion is enough to shift my blood from a simmer to a boil. It's a grand display of exquisite architecture and impressive craftsmanship, with intricate carvings and ornate details adorning the sprawling facade of brick and stone. All of it paid for with blood and drugs. My eyes focus on the entrance, which is framed by two towering pillars, each with a wrought iron lantern that casts a warm glow over the entryway. The double doors are made of heavy, dark wood, and feature intricate carvings of vines and leaves, giving the impression of a hidden garden. There's a lot hidden beyond those doors, and it's not a fucking garden. I scan the manicured lawns and spot the guard stations.

"Get that one," I whisper to Karson as I jerk my chin toward the farthest booth. He likes to run, so I'll let him run. "I'll get this one." I motion to the closer booth, and he nods and takes off.

I skulk along the perimeter, trying to avoid the spotlight swinging across the grass. It runs on a pattern, scanning each section before going to the next. I wait until it makes a pass before I walk among the shadows and end up beside the booth. When I take a quick look inside, a young man is fumbling with the CCTV. Based on the way his fingers jerk and move and reach for the walkie on his shoulder, I can only assume he's spotted Karson. I lean inside and wrap a hand around the man's mouth before he can depress the button on his mic. He throws his body backward, trying to slam me into the wall. With a quick jut of my knife, I sink the blade into the base of his skull and push until I hear a satisfying pop. His arms still. I could have just broken his neck, but I want George to see the blood on my clothes. The blood of his men.

I grip the man's mic and tug the radio off his belt. I clip it on, lower the volume, and take off toward the other box to see if Karson needs help. When I lean in, I see a very dead man with a very determined Karson standing over him, stabbing his chest and abdomen with a very determined purpose. I don't stop him. He's taking out his anger the only way he knows how. Finally, a sigh leaves his lips, and he drops back with a glassy high to his eyes.

The radio makes a noise before a muddled voice breaks through the static. "Me and Roy are heading to the back of the house to have a smoke. It's just us, so don't release the dogs."

Karson was right. They have fucking dogs.

We look at each other and nod. Two men alone at the back of the property? It's the prime situation for us. Just as we're about to leave the booth, a deep growl rumbles from the tree line. Before I can even react, the sound of paws slamming against the ground draws closer. I step through the doorway and face the massive fur missile barreling toward me. A chain collar rattles an eerie tune with every movement the German Shepherd makes.

"I don't want to kill a dog," I say. I will, but I don't want to. My brother was the one who brought home dead animals, not me.

Karson takes a step in front of me, but the dog is focused on me. Just as his form comes into the spotlight, I move Karson out of my way and stare down the dog. His paws dig into the ground as he slows to a stop in front of me, his brown eyes trained on me as his head cocks. He comes to my feet and sits beside me, looking up at me with a drool covered maw.

Killers recognize killers, I guess.

Karson draws his blade, and I grab his wrist to keep him from stabbing the dog. "Leave him," I say.

"Remember what you're here for, Gentry. This dog can be used against us later."

He's right. But if there is a god, and if he's watching, we need all the karma we can get. I rub the dog's head, grab his collar, and look at Karson. This dog can be used against someone . . .

But it won't be us.

"Fass!" I say, and the dog lunges forward to get to Karson, his paws kicking up dirt as I keep him in place.

"Hope you know the 'off' command too," Karson says as he takes a step back.

"Fuss!" I say, and the dog goes from grizzly to teddy in a near instant, though his focus remains on Karson.

"When the fuck did you learn German commands?"

"I was looking into getting my own trained dog for my business before I had to take on a different kind of dog." We start toward the back of the house, and the dog remains at my side, his collar jangling with every step.

"Bring the murder mutt. What could go wrong?" Karson quips.

I remove the collar and drop it to the grass.

We lurk in shadows as we crawl the perimeter of the unmanned front yard. When we reach the back of the house, the thick scent of cigarette smoke hangs in the air, and three men stand beneath a light, not two. Only one of them has a radio, though.

I look at Karson. "If you can avoid it, don't use the guns, and don't let them get to the radio."

Karson throws his blade up and catches it. "No problem."

"Fass," I snarl toward the dog. He races toward the men.

"Goddamn it, I told him it was just us!" a man screams, and the group scatters.

The dog latches on to the man in the middle. Another runs right into us and before he can do anything, Karson sends his blade through his eye socket. He pulls it out and shoves it into the soft space below the man's jaw, using so much force that it emerges from the bridge of his nose.

"Fass!" the man on the ground yells, which only continues to fuel the dog. Idiot. The murder mutt releases his leg and goes for his throat.

I grip the scruff of his neck. "Fuss!"

He releases the man, and I reroute him toward the dark figure running away. I give the command and release him. The man with the throat wound goes for his radio. He hits the button, sending a squeal over my own receiver, but I straddle him and use my knife to finish off what the dog couldn't. My blade cuts along his neck like butter, spreading the tissue until it creates a gaping hole as his head separates from his neck. He paws at my hands for a few seconds, then he stills.

Snarls come from around the corner, and I follow the sounds. When I turn the corner, the guard's gun is aimed at the dog with a death grip on his calf. Karson flips his knife, catches it, and sends it through the air. The blade sinks between the man's eyes, and his upper body falls backward. True to his name, the murder mutt refuses to let go, even once the fight has been won.

"Fuss!" I command, gripping his scruff until he releases the man. I back up with him and pat his bloody head. I recognize that bloodlust in his eyes. We're not too different. Someone had to train him to do what I was born to do, but we're pretty much the same. "Platz." His belly hits the ground at my command. "Bleib." I turn to Karson. "When did you learn to throw knives?"

"How do you think I killed all those squirrels and shit when we were kids?" Karson says with a shrug. "Couldn't buy myself a gun at ten. Thank god." He leans down and rips his knife from the man's forehead. "If people didn't hear any of the barking, I'd be shocked. Gun time?"

I remove my pistol from its holster, and Karson does the same. We keep our weapons at our sides as we walk toward the wall of windows with a heavy-duty door beside it. I peer through the glass and look around the mansion's interior, but it's empty. These windows are a really stupid feature. Give up safety to overlook the hills behind this place? Wise.

Karson comes up behind me, smoking the dead man's cigarette.

"Really?" I ask.

"Shame to let it go to waste." He looks back toward the dog. "What about him?"

"He'll stay put until someone releases him. He'll be safer out here than in there."

We expose ourselves as we walk along the windows and rip open the back door, tracking mud across the expensive rugs as we enter. Fancy art pieces line the walls, and marble everything greets me everywhere I look. George is literally everything we hate. Taking Leana only elevated that hatred to a personal level.

As we reach the end of the hall, I glance up and spot a security camera. "Fuck," I mumble.

"Wh—" Karson looks up. "Oh." He gives the camera a smile and his middle finger.

Boots pound down the hall, and I can see their owner's reflections in the fancy fucking walls. Karson and I aim our pistols and take the first couple of men off guard. Their stunned comrades nearly fall over them as they gather their bearings and shift their rifles.

I want one of *those*.

Karson and I work in unison, clearing out the wave of men as we go. Bullets ricochet and shatter walls and vases, sending glass, ceramic, and marble everywhere. I get to one of the men with a rifle and rip it out of his cold hands. Just as I do, an unarmed man grabs Karson from behind—the idiot probably dropped his gun in a panic—and the two go hand to hand.

Karson is so much more muscular and rugged than the suited man in front of him. It's hardly a fair fight. With his calloused hands clenched, Karson lunges forward with a powerful punch, but the agile suit dodges the blow with a sidestep. Karson growls before retaliating with a swift kick to the man's knee, causing him to stumble. Then he charges forward, throwing a flurry of punches at his rival.

Someone comes around the corner with a pistol drawn, and I aim the rifle and drop him before turning my attention back to the violent dance in front of me. Karson and I used to fight when we were younger, and I'm pleased to see the level of skill that probably came from going hand to hand with someone as big as me. But this is different from the way we fight. He loves to hurt people, but with each heavy strike, it looks like he's fighting for *her*.

"Finish him, brother," I tell him, and I can't help but call him brother. At this moment, as he fights for a reason other than his own selfish regard for death, I see myself in him for the first time in a while. He becomes the brother to me that he was before it all. Before I hated him.

Karson nods, sweat dripping down his forehead. He lands blow after blow, his fists raining down with the brutality I know and love. The man tries to fight back, but no one can match Karson when he's that homicidal. So determined to kill. He throws himself forward, landing on the man as he falls backward. He digs his gloved thumbs into the eye sockets, and his eyeballs eventually deflate with a squelch beneath his weight. He bites his lower lip at the sound, loving it way too fucking much.

We're definitely related.

That sound would disgust my little wanderer, but it's a symphony played over the silence of death for me. For Karson, it's a moan being whispered in his ear. We're so fucked up.

Karson rises to his feet with a satisfied sigh, and we continue down the hall. I've abandoned my pistol for the rifle, and I sweep the rooms with the barrel. There's a room at the end of the hall, tucked behind dark wooden doors. I take a deep breath before wrapping my hand around the doorknob, because it may be the last breath I take.

As long as I save Leana, I don't fucking care.

Chapter Twenty-Eight

I wake up to the sounds of gunfire. At least, I think that's what I hear. I take inventory of myself as I try to sit up. I'm sore between my legs, and dry, sticky come clings to my thighs. And my chest. And my cheek. I gag when I remember blips of what they've done to me and the way they've taken turns with my body.

The guards draw their guns, and now I'm certain I heard gunshots. I get the energy to sit up at the prospect of my men barging through those doors, but I'm absolutely horrified by how I'll look when they see me.

Dirty. Used. Covered in the come of other men.

The doors whip open and like two weird, blood-covered, psychopathic guardian angels, Gentry and Karson charge in with guns blazing. Bullets buzz around me, and I can't dodge or do anything to defend my ears from each deafening blast.

"I want George alive!" Gentry screams, his voice straining as if he's in pain. The blood oozing from the tear in his sleeve confirms my fears. I can hardly see much of anything through the smoke and shattering glass, but I focus on that trail of crimson leaking from him.

"Over here, Gentry!" Karson yells. "Everyone else is down. Get Leana!" It's the first time I've heard him speak my name, and it's one of the sweetest sounds to grace my ringing ears.

Gentry makes it over to me. After assessing my body, he wipes at the come on my cheek, smearing blood on me in his attempt to clean me. "Oh, wanderer," he says. His body trembles as an earthquake of emotions ripples through him.

He reaches back and touches the handcuffs, then pulls a small keyring from his pocket. He finds a generic handcuff key on the ring and frees my wrists. I rub at my raw skin the moment I'm free. Gentry removes his shirt and helps me put it on, covering my bare chest. I don't know where my pants are.

"Where is he?" I yell.

"George is over here," Karson says from across the room.

"No, where is Mickey?" I ask. I don't see him among the bodies.

"Who's Mickey?" Gentry asks, clearly confused by how I could be on a first name basis with any of these fuckers.

My eyes narrow. "My ex, the one who put the bruises on me. He knows George. Works with him. Was here. He's the one who told George I was with you. It was never Karson."

"Told you!" Karson shouts from his side of the room before he sends a bullet through the head of a still-moving body.

A look of relief passes across Gentry's face before he turns back to me. "What does he look like?"

"A fucking dumbass."

His lips twitch upward. "We'll find him, but we need to take care of our friend over there."

I follow Gentry, who looks like a Greek fucking god as his muscled, shirtless form stomps through the destruction. Karson has George pinned on his stomach, a cigarette dangling from his lips as he holds him in place. Gentry's body continues to tremble as he kneels and stops George's flailing legs. He rips down the prone man's slacks and boxers, leaving his bare ass out for everyone to see.

"What the fuck?" George screams, flailing more violently. Gentry takes out his knife and cuts a deep gash into his ass cheek, sending a slick of blood into his crack, then he pulls something from his pocket. A bag with . . . something inside. He rips through the plastic with his knife, and I get a good look at it.

"Why does he have a hand, Karson?" I ask, my mouth hanging open.

He shrugs. "For this, I guess."

"For what?"

"No, no, wait!" George screams.

"Shh, George," Gentry coos. "It will only hurt a lot." Gentry's muscles flex as he shoves the hand—fingers first—inside George's asshole.

George releases a horrified scream. "Oh god, stop!" he wails.

I have no clue what I'm looking at, but Gentry is so fucking beautiful in his predatory anger. "The Pastor sends his regards," he snarls as he pushes the hand until it disappears completely.

George sure has a lot of tears for someone who didn't care about mine.

I walk over and drop to my knees in front of him. "Sexual assault sucks, doesn't it, George?" I pull the cigarette from Karson's lips and put it between mine. I inhale, long and deep, then blow the smoke into George's face before pressing the blazing cherry against his cheek. I don't pull away, not even when he screams for me to stop.

Karson hardens as he witnesses my depravity, and the feral smile on his face makes my cheeks flush.

"Kill him," Gentry says as he climbs off him. He doesn't worry George will try to get up, because his legs are stuck straight behind him from the intrusion in his ass. Karson whips out his blade and stabs it into George's neck, finally silencing his screams.

"We have to find Mickey," I say to Gentry.

He looks across the room, at a door that looks like a coat closet, and lets intuition guide him. Someone screams as Gentry nearly rips the door off the hinges, then he reaches into the darkness and pulls someone out by their hair.

It's Mickey.

"This him?" Gentry asks, shaking him by his scalp.

"Yeah."

"You're the one who hurt my girl," Gentry says as he lifts him to his feet.

Mickey flails. "She's not *your* girl. She's mine."

"What an absolutely suicidal thing to say," Gentry says. He turns to me. "He fucked you too, didn't he, wanderer?"

When I nod, he shoves his fist into Mickey's gut and sends him to his knees before kicking him onto his side.

Karson joins them and leans down until his breath is close enough to ruffle Mickey's hair. "She's not yours. She's *ours*," he growls.

"Hang on to him," Gentry says as he crosses the room and guides me back to Karson and Mickey. He pulls me in and kisses me despite everything that's been done to me. His hand rides up my thigh and grips my ass. "Let me fuck you in front of him, wanderer."

"Why ask? Just take," Karson quips, his murder-induced sexual frustration taking over.

Gentry's hand wraps around my chin and lifts it. "She's had enough taken from her already," he growls.

"Fair point," Karson agrees.

"Don't you say yes to him, Lee," Mickey says as he tries to pull out of Karson's steadfast grasp.

"Fuck you, Mickey. You don't own me anymore. But for the record, I didn't plan on saying yes to him." I turn to Gentry. "I planned to say yes, sir."

"I got an idea," Gentry says, his eyes lighting up like sadistic Christmas lights. "Bring him to the pole and handcuff him. Just like they had her."

Karson does as he's told, dragging a flailing Mickey across the bloody hardwoods. The metallic click of the handcuffs sends an eerie shiver up my spine.

"Keep his legs pinned," Gentry adds.

Karson holds him by the legs, getting obnoxiously overzealous about whatever he thinks Gentry has planned. He's a jumping bean of dark excitement. Gentry drags me to Mickey and steps on his right leg, moving Karson's hand away. Gentry pushes me down on my knees between Mickey's thrashing legs.

"If he kicks her, slice him from throat to asshole," Gentry says as he drops to his knees and leans over to replace his hold on Mickey's leg.

I hope he doesn't plan for me to suck Mickey's dick. I'm in the precise position for that, and I'm not fucking interested. I open my mouth to protest, but Gentry hands me his knife.

"Carve something into his fucking gut," he says.

Karson rips open Mickey's shirt, and he furiously kicks and bucks in front of me. "Lee, this isn't you!" he pleads. "Look what they're making you do!"

My hold tightens around the handle. "They aren't *making* me do anything."

"Come on, I love you! Remember all the things I did for you? You wouldn't even be alive right now if it weren't for me."

Gentry growls behind me, and I aim the blade's tip at Mickey's skin. He draws his hairy abdomen in, trying to avoid the cold steel. I want to do it. I want to make him hurt like he made me hurt. But just like before, I'm stuck in place. Even after everything he did to me, I can't do what I want to do. My morals draw swords and charge at the shadows in my soul, and I'm cemented in place as I wait to learn my fate.

Karson puts his hand over mine and depresses the knife into Mickey's flesh. "The first cut is the hardest. Not for me, but for most." He draws his hand away to control Mickey's renewed fight.

Mickey releases a scream, and I can almost hear a violin song woven somewhere in that sound. I kind of like hearing his pain.

Without any more help from Karson, I finish the first letter. The channel fills with blood as his skin spreads, and I move on to the next. As I transfer years of pain into the knife's handle, Gentry's free hand rides up my thigh and moves over my ass. He lifts my shirt, bunching it at my hips.

Mickey starts to slip in and out of consciousness from the pain, but I keep carving.

"Stay awake," Gentry says as he leans forward and smacks Mickey's cheek. "I want you to see me set free what you thought you could own."

Gentry's warm cock presses against me as I begin another letter. He leans me forward, nearly pushing my face into Mickey's blood so he can spit warm saliva onto my pussy. My eyes meet Mickey's for the first time—truly meet—and I see anguish on his face. It's so much more than the physical pain I'm causing.

And I love it.

Gentry pulls my hips toward him and pushes inside me with an unstifled hunger. His hard thrust makes me gasp, and I blow a pleasure-soaked breath across the gouges in Mickey's skin.

"You are all so fucked up," Mickey gathers the strength to say.

"Affirmative," Karson says.

"Cut him while I fuck you, wanderer," Gentry says. "Keep getting your vengeance."

I try to do as he tells me, but every thrust pushes me forward and smears the letter I'm working on. But I keep going. Mickey releases pained groans in front of me, Gentry utters pleasurable ones behind me, and I'm swept into a vortex of conflicting emotions around and inside me.

I don't need Karson's help with the next letter, but I look over at him. He's nearly frothing at the mouth over what he's witnessing: Gentry fucking me while I carve my feelings into my ex's belly.

"Keep going," Gentry says. "I won't last much longer like this. Your pussy needs to be claimed by me again. By someone who will kill anyone who tries to take you away from me."

"Or me," Karson whispers in a voice so low I almost don't hear it. It makes my heart swell until I think it might cut off the next breath to my lungs.

I finish the last letter just as Gentry slams his hips into me a final time. He holds himself inside me, savoring me as he fills me, then he leans over to look at what I wrote. In haphazard chicken scratch, I have scrawled a single word in all caps.

CUNT

Gentry wraps his arm around my chest and squeezes me to his. "Good fucking girl. Welcome to the dark side."

"Not yet," Karson says, handing me his larger blade. He sits up, holds Mickey's leg beneath his knee, and leans over, beaming at me with a sadistic pride. "You have to kill him, thief." He rubs his hand over the left side of his chest. "Stab here if you want him to die quickly." His hand lowers to Mickey's gut, beneath my writing. "Or here if you want him to suffer."

I bring the blade to both spots, trying to decide what feels right. Memories flash in front of my mind, and I'm forced to relive everything Mickey has done to me. The things that put the bruises on my body. And on my soul. The drugs he filled me with, the way he kept me sick so I couldn't leave. Yeah, I suffered plenty at his hands.

I drive the knife into his gut, and he lurches forward, his eyes wide. His body puts pressure on the blade as he squirms, and I'm thrilled to imagine all the ways it must be tearing up his insides. Blood sputters from his mouth, and I pull the blade from Mickey's flesh and run my fingers over the slick crimson marking the steel.

Karson stands up, unzipping his pants in front of me. "I know Gentry says we can't take, but if I don't get inside your mouth, thief, I'm going to burst. I've never been so fucking turned on in my life." He gathers the hair at the base of my neck, and I raise my chest and grip his thigh as his cock springs from the fabric. "Let me feel your lips around me."

Too weak to move, Mickey stares at the scene playing out above him with glassy eyes. "Lee," he murmurs.

"Surprised she lets two men like us inside her, yet she hated every moment with you?" Karson says with a laugh. His hand wraps around my throat and tugs me into his pelvis, and I take his cock into my mouth. The barbells tap my teeth as he pushes to the back of my throat with a feral groan. He thrusts against my face, but I feel his heightened excitement with every pulse of his hips. "I'm going to come," he growls, and he draws his cock back to fill my mouth fully. "Don't swallow," he says as he pulls out of my mouth.

I fucking hate holding come in my mouth, but I do as he says because I'm curious to see what he's planned.

Karson cranes Mickey's head, holds his jaws open, and gives me a sick smirk. "Spit my come in his fucking mouth," he commands.

Gentry pulls out of me. "Keep your thighs together, wanderer, and don't leave a drop of me behind on his body."

I squeeze my legs together as I scoot forward and lean over Mickey's open mouth. His eyes are fixed on me, his breath coming in ragged, gulping gasps as death tightens its hold. I move closer, until our lips nearly touch, and I spit Karson's come into his mouth.

Karson rubs Mickey's throat with a gloved hand as if he's trying to make a cat swallow a pill. "Gulp it down," Karson says. "Be a good boy and swallow my come. I want my taste to be on your tongue when you meet the devil for what you did to her."

Instead of swallowing, Mickey takes another heaving breath and sucks the come into his windpipe. His body moves on autopilot and tries to expel it with a weak cough, but that only pushes more blood from the wound in his abdomen. After a few more garbled gasps, he stills.

Karson shakes his head. "Tsk, tsk. If you had swallowed it, you wouldn't have choked to death. What a shame."

I climb off Mickey, and Gentry zips up his jeans and takes a step toward me. He puts his hand between my legs, gathers the come that dripped down my thighs, and pushes it back inside me. He pulls me into him, with his fingers buried deep within me.

"No matter who touched you or who came inside you, you're still ours. And we'll show you that." His arm wraps around me and he pulls me against his chest. "I'd do anything for you."

"*We'd* do anything for you," Karson adds as he fetches my jeans from the coat closet.

The fact that these men get so turned on by homicide is incredibly alarming. There's a sick excitement that riddles them with joy as it maps its way through their veins. It's sick. It's disgusting.

But I'm beginning to understand that carnal desire.

Chapter Twenty-Nine

When we get outside, the dog is still waiting in a down position. Its hind legs wiggle as it watches Gentry, waiting for the release command. Gentry says another German word, and the dog rushes toward him and sits at his leg, looking up expectantly.

"Did Gentry befriend an attack dog?" Leana asks.

"I know. It's embarrassing," I say.

She shakes her head. "No, it's cute."

When Gentry gives the dog a quick pat, she thinks she can do the same. I grab her by the waist and pull her into me. "He can pet the murder mutt, but that doesn't mean you should," I scold. I can't have her getting mauled after all we went through to get her back.

I refuse to be as open and vulnerable as Gentry, but I *am* really glad we rescued her. Not just because she lets us do fucked-up things to her or because she doesn't react the way others do around us. But because I *like* her. I like the person I can be around her. The way I can be around Gentry because of her. She brings out something warm in two very cold killers.

"You destroyed the cameras, right?" Gentry asks as he turns toward us.

"Not only did I destroy the hard drive, but I also took it with me," I tell him as I pull the mangled plastic from my pocket. "Can't recover what isn't there."

Gentry fights a smile. "Why is that one of the most intelligent things you've ever done?"

"I don't tell you everything I do, and I'm not as stupid as you think."

"Are we going to the hospital for your gunshot wound?" Leana asks.

So naïve.

"We don't go to hospitals," Gentry says with a laugh. "We'll take care of it. It's through and through, anyway." He winces as he rubs his finger through the coagulated blood surrounding the hole.

Gentry and I have always dealt with the injuries that come from taking someone's life. Or in this case, battling with the people trying to keep us from saving one. There's nothing you can't learn on the internet.

We start toward the SUV, and the dog remains at Gentry's side, keeping pace with him.

I stop walking. "We cannot keep the murder mutt," I say to Gentry. Judging by the softness in his eyes, that's exactly what he's considering.

Leana stops and turns to face me. "Why not? Look at all the dried blood in his fur. He's one of us."

"Absolutely not!" I say. "We've already taken in a stray thief. We don't need to add another complication to our lives."

Leana takes up a defiant stance, crossing her arms over her chest. "Aren't we done with the murder spree? Your boss is dead, so it's not as if another job is about to roll in."

I match her stance and throw in a smirk for good measure. "No, we still have one more job, and the payout is too good to pass up."

Gentry doesn't hear either of us. He's already continued toward the SUV . . . with the fucking dog.

I jog to catch up with him. "Hey, didn't you hear me? We aren't taking this dog."

He stops and faces me, and the fucking canine does the same. It's starting to creep me out. "George may be dead, and we may be working on our last lucrative hit, but I'm still the boss of *my* business, Karson. Don't forget that."

With a sigh, I give up. If he wants to keep the dog, that's on him. He can work out the logistics.

When we reach the SUV, I climb into the driver's seat. Gentry is happy to let me drive, and the thief and the furry baggage climb into the back seat. We can't go to a hotel like this, so I search the phone for a campground and head that way. After a twenty-mile journey on some back roads, we drive into the park as if we belong there and park at an empty site.

"Put this on the dash," Leana says as she hands a crinkled pass to me. Smart. It's the pass from the last campground, and if no one looks at the date, it appears official enough. As long as no one else comes for this site.

A few leftover logs of wood from our last camping trip sit in the back of the SUV. I grab them and toss them into the fire pit. I draw a cigarette out of my pack and light it, then I scrounge up some kindling and ignite the wood. It finally catches and I pocket the lighter. Smoke gathers and orange flames singe the logs. Gentry steps closer and strips off his shirt, exposing the gunshot. A trickle of blood rushes from the wound any time he moves. We'll need to take care of that.

I pull my knife from its sheath and hold the blade over the fire. The metal shifts from a cold gray to a slight glow, and I pull it away before it gets too hot.

"What are you doing?" Leana asks as she eyes the fire, eyes wide.

"Cauterizing," Gentry says, pulling her into him with his good arm.

"But—"

"Just be with me," he says.

"This is going to hurt," I tell Gentry with a smirk.

"Yeah, I know, and you're going to love it," he snaps as he pulls her closer. Instead of biting down on something, he's bracing against the one thing that brings him comfort. The dog comes over and flops down at Gentry's feet with a yawn. It's like a fucked-up Norman Rockwell painting.

I grab Gentry's shoulder and pull him forward as I push the blade flat against his skin. The flesh sizzles, and he bites his lip to keep from screaming out. He's so stoic when he feels pain. I swear he does it just to ruin my fun.

With a slow inhale, I revel in the scent of burning flesh the way someone might breathe a little deeper when they walk by a bakery. Delicious. "Now the back." I dip the blade into the fire once more.

Sweat gathers on Gentry's forehead, and the thief looks fucking queasy, which I'm enjoying. I put the blade to the exit wound, and it smokes and sizzles just like the front. His back curves, but he does little else to indicate how the pain rakes his spine.

"You guys are so fucked," Leana says through a gag as the smell reaches her.

"Yep," Gentry and I say in unison.

The bleeding stopped, Gentry assesses the wound care and nods. "I'm going to shower," he says, looking over at the building across the road. He drops his gaze to Leana. "You look like you could use one, too."

She does. Dark splotches of dried blood mark the pale canvas of her skin. It reminds me of the night she played dead for us, and my cock hardens at this thought.

I reach out and pull her into me. "I have a different idea," I say.

Gentry postures, raising his huge chest toward me.

Before he can tell me why I can't have her right now, I tell him why I can. "You always get her how you want her, G. Praise her and please her. Be all sweet to her." I brush the blonde hair away from her face. "I want to fuck her my way. I want to play with my fantasy." I want her to play dead for me again. But this time, I want to spread her thighs as she lies lifeless before me. I turn to Leana. "You'd let me play with you, wouldn't you? Let me fuck your dead body?"

What a fucking question to ask a person. But she's not just any person. She's *our* person, and she's not normal.

She swallows hard, as if she's choking on a golf ball, then she glances between us, torn but not scared. She looks to Gentry for permission, but I don't need permission from either of them. Regardless of what they feel, I *will* have her lifeless body beneath me.

He steps into her, sandwiching her between us. "Do you want this, wanderer?" I can't see the look she gives him, but it produces a scowl on his face. He leans in and kisses her before his dark eyes rise to mine and bore through me. "Fine, Karson, but don't fucking hurt her and *do not* actually kill her." He turns away. "Fucking freak."

Instead of heading for the showers, he plops in front of the fire with the dog. He really needs to clean up, but at least he's leaving me alone to do what I need to do with Leana. I won't press him.

I lead her toward the nearby lake, and a plan forms in my mind. As the water comes into view, so does the full moon. It hangs low in the sky—a big, bright orb of light that will allow me to see everything and etch it into my memory. The rippling water catches each moonbeam, and it's really pretty.

But not as pretty as my thief will look when I'm through with her.

"Take off your pants," I say as I begin to strip off mine.

"Are you really going to do this?"

"Absolutely. I want to fuck you while you pretend to be dead. Honestly, if I didn't like you, I'd fuck you actually dead."

Her eyes widen but her expression flattens. "This is insane."

"Well, *I'm* insane."

She doesn't argue. Instead, she licks her lips, takes a deep breath, and removes her pants. Her hands go for her shirt, but I reach out and stop her.

"Leave it on."

I guide her toward the water, and the sandy bottom caresses our feet. Staying in the shallows, I push her to her knees before easing her onto her back. She isn't fully submerged, but each time the water reaches toward the shore, it covers more of her. Her breasts rise above the waterline, the nipples forming tight peaks at the top of each mound. The gentle waves pull at her hair, darkening the blonde strands as they sink beneath her head. Yeah, she looks fucking hot.

"This is so fucked up, Karson," she says, but I don't miss that excited glint to her eye. She might not be entirely okay with this, but she's curious.

"Even when I do some shit you won't like, I need you to trust me. Just keep still." I know she likes praise, but I can't bring myself to say some cringey shit and call her my good girl like Gentry does. I reach for the next best thing—the only thing I can bring myself to say. "Be my dead girl."

I hook her thighs over mine as I drop to my knees and sink a bit into the sandy bottom. The cool water goes up to my balls, tightening them, but I lean over and push inside her. I let her gasp, let her live a little longer while I push deeper.

"Trust me, and don't move," I remind her as I lean over her. "Keep your eyes closed. Part those pretty lips like you did when we played dead before." I put my palm against her cheek. "I'm going to drown you now."

Before she can say anything, I turn her head and push her mouth and nose beneath the water. Her hands grip my wrists, and she flails. Her cunt tightens around me as she struggles. I let out a groan of pleasure, and as her body writhes, I draw back my hips so I can fuck her harder. I love her fight. I love how her cunt squeezes my dick.

Her hands fall away from my wrists, and she goes limp. I hold her there for a few more thrusts, then I grip her cheeks and bring her mouth above water. Her lips are perfectly parted, eyes closed, and she's motionless. Water laps over her stomach and chest, and I can't tell if she's breathing. For all intents and purposes, she looks dead—a drowned woman on my dick. Lifeless and beautiful.

The water ebbs and flows as I drop my hand from her face and dip it into the water. Silk strands of hair wrestle with my fingers, but I pull free and put them on her shoulder. No matter how hard I fuck her, she keeps those eyes closed. Those lips parted. She remains silent through every rough thrust. The only indication of life is the subtle twitch of her cunt around me and the slight, nearly negligible tilt of her pelvis. A dead woman most definitely wouldn't do that, but I can't fault her for enjoying this as much as I am.

I lean over her. "You're so fucking sexy like this, thief. Cold. Dead. Beautiful." I swear I see the corners of her lips twitch, but she doesn't break character. If her theater teacher could only see her now . . . Well, they'd probably have me arrested, but they'd also be pretty fucking impressed.

I dig my fingers into her skin as I fuck her harder, and the sand beneath us spreads with the strength of every thrust. I lift her upper body out of the water, and her head lolls to the side. Drops of water dribble down her chilled skin, and her full chest doesn't rise or fall. It's enough to make my balls tighten.

I reach up and grip her throat, drawing her to me and kissing her. Only once her lips meet mine do I feel the escape of breath in her gasp, but her lids remain closed.

"Open your eyes," I say.

They flutter open, and I've never felt more for a person. Who lets someone like me play out a sick fantasy like this?

My little thief, that's who.

I fill her cunt, burying myself inside her. I know Gentry doesn't want me to come in her pussy like this, but the water will wash away my sin. I smirk against her mouth when I imagine explaining my transgressions to the guard at the pearly gates. I murder for a living, but I also enjoy it, and I fuck the pseudo-dead body of my brother's girl. I imagine the shock and horror across St. Peter's face before the clouds blacken, open up, and swallow me to hell.

Worth it. Worth every fucking second of it.

Chapter Thirty

Leana

When we return to the campsite, Gentry is still seated in front of the fire. His eyes move to mine after they burn through Karson. My soaked shirt saturates my jeans, and my damp hair clings to my cheeks.

"Did you two go for a swim?" he asks, and I don't miss the jealousy woven tightly within his voice. I like it. His ownership is my weakness.

"Something like that," Karson says as he walks to the SUV to get a change of clothes.

Gentry steps into me, inhaling the scent of sex and nature. His warm hand hooks around the back of my neck and tugs me into him. "What'd he do to you, wanderer?"

I don't know what to say. How do I even describe what happened? More importantly, how do I explain that I liked it?

"Can we talk about it later?" I ask in a whisper. By that I mean when I've had more time to process it. Or not at all.

Karson pops up behind Gentry, his shirt half on. "I put her face beneath the water until she stopped squirming, then I fucked her as she played dead for me." He pulls his shirt over his stomach.

Then Gentry asks the dreaded question as his eyes darken. "Where'd he come?"

"Inside me," I whisper, dropping my gaze from his heated stare.

Gentry turns toward Karson, giving him a shove that I'm surprised doesn't send him into the next site over. "What did I tell you about coming inside her pussy? I let you enjoy her body, which is very much mine. Stop fucking betraying the grain of trust I've given back to you. Spill your load anywhere else, but her pussy is mine. I'm the only one who can breed her."

His words, his possessive display of force—it makes my skin heat and my thighs clench. His body goes from stressed and tense to crumbling as he steps into me. He grips my chin and raises my eyes to his, then he leans down and kisses me.

He pulls away and speaks to Karson, but he keeps his gaze pinned on me. "Stay with the dog. I still need to shower." He lowers his voice so that only I can hear him. "And claim what belongs to me."

Karson mutters something about babysitting the four-legged weapon of mass destruction, but he stays put as Gentry leads me toward the showers. He already has my bag in his hand, so he's been thinking of this while Karson and I were gone.

A light buzzes to life when we enter the small shower area, and a pale yellow glow washes over us. The place is well cared for, and it smells clean enough. I strip off my wet clothes and head for the shower stall, pushing a button in the wall several times so I can wet my hair with something warmer than lake water. The trickle from the showerhead strengthens, and I stick my head beneath the stream.

Gentry steps into the stall doorway, a sexy smirk drawing his lips upward at the corners. He holds a small bottle of travel shampoo in his hand, which he passes to me. He steps out of his clothes and gets in beside me. His body heat warms me instantly. The water slows, reminding me to pump the button again.

I motion for Gentry to get beneath the water. As he wipes at his skin and sends a rush of red toward the drain, I squirt some shampoo into my hands and lean into him.

"What are you doing?" he asks.

"I helped Karson with his fantasy. What about yours?"

He scoffs. "My fantasy would involve your belly swelling with my child," he whispers, running a hand from my lower abdomen to my pussy.

"That's not something I can take care of right now, but what about your other thing?"

"What Karson told you? Don't listen to—"

I interrupt him by pressing my breasts against his chest and rubbing my hands through his hair. The moment my fingertips meet his scalp, his hard cock twitches against my stomach. He drops his head forward so I don't have to strain as hard to wash his hair. His lips part, and soft groans ease past them.

"Fuck, wanderer," he growls.

I scrub his silky strands, swirling my fingertips in circles as I move from the crown of his head to the nape of his neck. His head snaps up and he grips the base of his cock. Can he really come so fast from this?

His other hand drags mine from his hair to the back of his neck, and he speaks through ragged, frustrated breaths. "You know I don't want to waste a drop of my come," he says with raised eyebrows.

He lifts me and wraps my legs around him, lowering me until his warm cock presses against my entrance. He grips my ass and pushes inside me. I gasp as he stretches me. It burns, like I'm being impaled by a torch. Instead of thrusting, he eases his cock deeper until he can't fit another centimeter of flesh inside me. He motions toward his hair, and I happily oblige.

I brush the dark, graying strands back as I scrub them. I dig my fingertips into his scalp, raking them against his skin. He groans and twitches inside me. Throbs. His fingers bruise my ass as he squeezes. His eyes are closed, like the most euphoric moment he's ever known is right now, with my hands in his hair and his cock in my pussy.

He pulls me deeper into him as he gets close, each harsh breath more ragged than the last. I drag my fingers down and rub the hair behind his ears, and he lets out the most seductive moan I've ever heard. If my legs weren't already wrapped around him, I wouldn't be able to hold myself up.

"I'm coming," he growls.

I yelp as he grips my ass and spills his come inside me. My fingers clench from the pain, going from washing his hair to gripping it in a tight hold. He groans, puts his arm beneath me, and lifts me off his dick before putting my feet onto the slick tiles. My legs shake, and I'm so sore, even without a single thrust from him. But it leaves me wanting more. He pulls me under the shower stream and kisses me as the shampoo falls from his hair in a sudsy veil.

"You want to come, don't you, my wanderer? My girl?"

I nod because I've never wanted anything more. "Yes, sir."

He reaches between my legs, but the moment he brushes my clit, Karson whips open the bathroom door and whistles.

"We gotta go. Now," Karson says before slamming the door.

Gentry groans. "I'll make it up to you."

I nod, disappointed but understanding. When Karson says it's time to go, it's probably for a reason. We dress in a rush and meet the sun's early rays as we walk outside the dark building. A van idles beside our site . . . which must be *their* site. Gentry throws them an apologetic wave, and we climb into the SUV. Karson mans the steering wheel and points us toward the park's exit. We make our escape before anyone is the wiser.

"How long were they waiting?" Gentry asks.

"Just a few minutes. I told them we stopped to shower and didn't realize the spot was taken. And then I went and got you two."

"Did they seem suspicious of anything?"

Karson shakes his head. "Not really. Karen seemed annoyed, but that's probably because her little brats were screaming in the back. No clue why breeding is your fetish." Karson fakes a gag.

Gentry shrugs. "I like the idea of getting my sweet little wanderer pregnant. But actually dealing with the product of that? No thanks."

"What if I got pregnant?" I ask as I lean forward, putting my head between them.

"We'd deal with it," Gentry says.

"Deal with it how you deal with things?" I ask, swiping my finger across my throat.

Gentry laughs. "No, we'd somehow raise a kid in a world of homicide, I guess. They'd become like us, though, which is why I'm not the dad type, even if I love the risk I take each time I fill you."

Karson clears his throat. "I once had a dream that I had a baby. I picked up the little thing and ate it." My mouth drops open, and he tosses me his Karson smile. "So I'm going to say I'm probably not dad material, either."

Thank fuck I'm on birth control. That's all I'm saying. I enjoy Gentry's breeding fetish and love being filled by him, but I refuse to bring a baby into a world where it will either become a serial killer or get fucking eaten.

Even though I'm in a world where I'm faced with those options myself.

Chapter Thirty-One

I t's odd to look at the phone on the dash and know it won't ring anymore. George is dead, with a pastor's hand so far up his ass not even the funeral home will find it. I hope he's fisted for all eternity. Even so, we won't waste the last mark on our list.

Leana leans into the front seat, her hand idly scratching the dog's head. "Where are we headed now?"

"The last hit on our magical murder tour," Karson says.

She frowns. "We're still doing that?"

"Yes, we are. We're counting on a big payout so we can lie low for a while," I explain. "It's not like there's a hitman classifieds section. We'll have trickling work after this, but it won't be like it is now. The wife who hates her husband. The businessman with too much money and hatred for a competitor."

I'm a little nervous that the gigs are ending, and it's not only because of the financial aspect. What will happen to Karson and me when we don't have an outlet for our murderous tendencies? We've been killing since we were kids, and I don't think we can just turn it off. I'm more concerned we might funnel that aggression toward Leana.

I'd like to think we wouldn't turn on her, but when that blood lust hits, we forget who matters to us. Who's been there for us. As much as I want to keep her around, it might not be safe for her. Letting her go after this hit might be the best thing we can do for her, even if it sucks for us.

She sits back, but I keep glancing at her through the rearview mirror. Just the sight of her gives me an erection. Remembering how it felt when she washed my hair. How the tips of her fingers raked my spine as they rode along my scalp. She wanted to please me by fulfilling my fantasy. My wife never even indulged me like Leana did. She poked fun at me. But who am I kidding? It's a funny fetish.

But at least my fetish doesn't involve dead girls.

Jealousy warms my chest at the thought of her pleasing Karson as well as she pleases me. I imagine him fucking her, her eyes fixed in front of her. Her body cold from the water. She was probably such a good fucking girl for him.

The way she always is for me.

"Did he make you come?" I ask Leana.

She nearly spits out the water she's just placed to her lips. "What?"

"In the lake. Did he make you come?" It's the only thing I can think about. I need to ensure I please her better than Karson can, and I didn't have a chance to please her at all in the shower. I don't mean to get so jealous at the thought of them, but it's an ugly monster I can't seem to shake off my shoulder.

"No," Leana says. "I didn't get off in the lake."

Karson glances at me. "I may not have pleased her then, but I made her come in the three minutes while you were in the bathroom at the fancy hotel. Had her gushing all over my hand. Then she sat in a puddle for the drive to the next hit." He licks his lips as he looks at her in the rearview mirror.

The ugly monster on my shoulder roars.

"I can do it faster," I snarl toward Karson.

Sensing the rising tension, the dog rumbles with a low growl in the back seat. Karson closes his mouth. Whatever he considered saying, he thinks better of it.

"Please stop fighting," Leana says with a groan. "I thought we were past this."

Karson and I have gotten past a lot, but sharing my wanderer is proving increasingly difficult. And she *is* mine. I don't know how to quiet this possessive need to keep her to myself. Breeding her after Karson touches her should be enough, but it's not.

"Three minutes," Karson mumbles with a smirk.

It takes every ounce of strength to keep from reaching out and strangling him.

Leana

The competitiveness between those two is growing, and the increasing push and pull intimidates me. It would be any girl's dream to have two sexy brothers pining over her, but that's when the brothers are normal. I worry these two will turn on each other over me. A fight would likely end in a fatality—me or one of them—and I don't want that.

What *do* I want?

I don't want to think about it. I've been awake for too long, and I'm tired. Now that they've stopped arguing, I enjoy the silence, especially since we no longer need to worry about that godforsaken generic ringtone.

The dog groans and stretches out beside me. His head drops onto my lap, and I play with his ears. "We need to give this guy a name."

"He already has a name," Karson says. "It's Murder Mutt."

I roll my eyes. "Could you imagine walking him in the park and calling his name? We'd get so many stares."

"Could you imagine walking in the fucking park?" Karson asks.

Fair.

"Well, we're all murderers. He needs a name that fits." I think back on my serial killer knowledge. "I've got it! We'll call him Sam!"

Gentry turns to look at me, his face screwed up in disgust. "Sam? What kind of lame ass name is that for a murderous fur missile like him?"

"David Berkowitz," Karson says as he turns in at a cheap motel. "When he got caught, he told the cops a dog named Sam orchestrated the whole thing and dictated who he should kill."

"Yeah," I say, genuinely confused. "How did you know that?"

Gentry shakes his head. "He loves watching true-crime shit."

Odd, but okay. "So can we call him Sam?"

"Is that what you want, wanderer?"

I nod my head and smile.

"Then his name is Sam," Gentry says with a sigh.

"Jesus fucking Christ on a cross. You two make me sick," Karson says as he exits the SUV.

Karson goes inside to get a room so we can nap until nightfall. We're all exhausted and need some sleep before we head on. Driving and killing and fucking for almost twenty-four hours straight will do that to a person. The place isn't the nicest, but I couldn't care less. I just want to lie down. We sneak the dog to our room and pile onto the bed. I close my eyes and begin to doze.

"Have we thought this through?" Karson's voice breaks through my pre-sleep haze, but I keep my eyes shut and listen.

"We kind of committed to this. And besides, we need the money. Remember, it all stops for us after this hit. At least for a while."

"Yeah, but this is a risky final target, G. I don't exactly like the idea of taking down Ralph Weeks right after we—"

My eyes snap open. "Ralph Weeks? The actor?"

Gentry waves me off. "Don't get excited. You know what happens when we pay people a visit. But if you're a really good girl, before we slit his throat, we'll get you an autograph."

"In blood," Karson adds.

"He just finished that movie, *The Glass,*" I say. "He's really hot right now and should have tons of money. Why would he stop paying George?"

Karson looks at me and shrugs. "Rich people do stupid shit. Think they're untouchable. We're about to prove just how touchable they are."

This seems so much worse than the other hits. I don't *know* the guy, but I know *of* the guy. It's not just some nameless person or shitbag human being.

"What'd he do?" I ask, hoping he's done something to deserve whatever these guys have in store for him.

"He's a goddamn junkie, for starters," Gentry says as he looks at the ceiling. "He got a bunch of drugs on credit, and now he doesn't want to pay." He shifts and looks down at me. "Will you be okay with this?"

I tighten my lips. No. I won't be. I know what it's like to need drugs so desperately that you'll go through hell to get them. My habit forced these men to take care of me when I was at my lowest, and I find it unfair that the same habit will cost someone else their life at their hands.

I rub the hem of my shirt between my fingers, locked in a prison of guilt they don't share. It's isolating to be the only one with normal human feelings. I drop my gaze and focus on the soft fabric.

"Wanderer?" Gentry says. "Will you be okay?"

I shake my head. "If I asked you to skip this hit, would you listen?"

Karson chuckles, and it makes me want to backhand him. Gentry's lips tighten. He looks torn between what he wants to say and what he thinks he should say.

"I guess if—"

Karson's voice hardens. "Speak for yourself. You'd let her stop a hit like this, knowing we have no job afterward? I'll do this hit with or without you, G." His eyes meet mine. "I like you, thief. More than I care to admit. But you're wrong for putting your guilt on us. We're felons, remember? We can't put our skill set on a resume. This is the life we've chosen since we were kids. Violence has always been the only thing we're qualified for."

Gentry narrows his eyes at Karson. "What Karson means, I think, is that if you want this life with us, you have to accept certain things. I can't provide for you without money from this hit."

"And the goddamn dog, G! Don't forget that." Karson shakes his head. "And no, I meant that she can't be a little bitch about what we've already been doing."

"Enough, Karson!" Gentry snaps.

"I'm just saying. She needs to learn to be a little selfish if she wants to be with us."

I know they're right, but it still conflicts with my humanity. I can't help that it feels wrong. Even so, I don't want to lose them, because being with them is the only thing that feels right in our fucked-up little world.

"Let's just get some sleep," Gentry says. He turns on his side and pulls me into him. "We have to do this hit, and we need clear heads when it goes down."

Sleep might clear my head, but it won't do shit for the smog surrounding my heart.

Chapter Thirty-Two

We sleep until nightfall can safely conceal us from prying eyes, then we drive toward our final target. We park near the woods and conceal the SUV behind some heavy scrub. We left Sam back at the motel, but I almost wish we'd brought him now. He's an extra weapon we might need.

I get out of the car and open Leana's door. "I need you to wait—"

She silences me with the glare from hell.

"Will you let me finish? You need to wait outside the door when we get to the building. Let us get the lay of the land, then you can walk in like you always do."

"You still want to keep me from seeing parts of you." She shakes her head. "I've seen you shove a disembodied hand up another man's ass. There isn't much more to see."

Good point.

I ease away from her door and let her out.

I expect a heavy security detail, but we walk through the woods without any issues. We spot what appears to be a security box tucked away behind a huge marble pillar, but it's empty. I shake my head. The point of security is for them to be present. Obvious. Not hidden behind rich ass marble.

"There's a fucking pond," Karson says as we cross the expansive lawn behind Ralph's gloriously excessive mansion. He squats down, his finger hovering above the water. A massive koi surfaces, its mouth gaping at him. "And there's a big ass fish." He scoffs. "So dramatic."

"Will you stop fucking around?" I snarl

"You know," Karson says as he matches my step, "I saw our last murder on the news at the motel."

"Fuck," I curse. The con to George being dead is the lack of a clean-up crew. Bodies we leave behind will be found so much quicker. That ups the chance of getting caught. I'm not too worried, though. Karson and I didn't have anyone to clean up shit when we were kids, and we did just fine.

Leana makes a small noise but says nothing. She wouldn't stay in the car, and now she's dragging her heels as we walk. I grab her arm and place a pair of gloves into her hand, then brush her hair from her face. "Are you sure you'll be okay?" I ask. She absolutely doesn't look okay.

"She'll never be okay with it, G. That's what separates her from you and me. But she'll get over it, and that's where she blends with us," Karson says. So confident. So sure.

She blows out a breath because she knows it's true. "What if the police come?" she asks as she slips on her gloves and pulls her hair into a ponytail.

I grip her chin. "I'll put a bullet through your pretty head before Karson and I go out in a blaze of glory," I tell her with a smirk.

"Stop. I'm serious."

"So am I." I will absolutely put her out of her misery before I let her go to jail, and we sure as fuck won't willingly return to a cell. "Hopefully they don't come."

When we get to the driveway in front of the mansion, I'm struck by its size. Such an unnecessary expense for a single man and his part-time kid. The extravagant masterpiece of architectural design boasts towering columns, balconies along the entire second floor, and floor-to-ceiling windows. The security booth near the front is also empty. I expected more of a challenge.

When we get to the big arching door—probably meant to look historical—Karson gets to work on the locks. Once I hear the click and we get it open, we step into a dark, empty foyer. There's no way this dude is here.

An alarm light flashes beside us. At least the guy was smart enough to keep his system on. This is a silent alarm, meant to get police here before we even know what happened. Typically that means we have about a minute to disarm the thing.

I rub my gloved finger on the outside of the pin pad and shine my flashlight over it.

"Better guess right, G," Karson says behind me.

"Shut up, Karson," I snarl, trying to focus.

I try Ralph's birthday: 0417. *Invalid pin.* Next, I try his ex-wife's birthday. *Invalid.* My research was for nothing. Sweat gathers on my forehead. We have three to five tries before it locks us out, then we're fucked. I lift my finger to try the son's birthday, but Leana's small hand wraps around my wrist. She grabs the flashlight, leans close to the pin pad, and punches in four numbers before I can stop her. The alarm flashes green and deactivates.

"How?" I ask her.

She shrugs. "I saw the slightest bit of wear on the buttons. One, two, three, four. I assumed they were in order and that the guy is an idiot. And voilà!"

I grab her face and pull her into me for a kiss. My smart little wanderer. I should have noticed that first, but my mind was on too many other things. I take the flashlight from her and find the light switch.

We flip on the lights, and pristine marble floors gleam up at us. A grand staircase leads up to the second floor, and a chandelier over the dining room table reflects the foyer light. Chandeliers are such a douchey requirement for these people. Have you even made it if you don't have one?

"What now, G?" Karson asks. "That piano is covered, and so is some of the artwork. If he's been staying somewhere else, he's probably stashed his cash somewhere else."

I shrug my shoulders and shut off the flashlight. "We'll have a look around. He's definitely still living here. The couch is uncovered and the remote for the television is on the table beside it. Plus, this is the address George gave us long before shit went sideways. This is the right house."

We go upstairs, sweeping the place for the master bedroom. When we find it at the end of the echoing hallway, it's bigger than my entire apartment. Intricate patterns line the wallpaper, sectioned off by wood trim. A fireplace dominates the room, only rivaled by the massive king-size bed that faces it. How fucking romantic.

Karson and I open closet doors and scrounge through the clothes. These people have so many fucking closets. Karson moves aside a mirror and exposes a safe. Our payday.

I try his birthday again, his wife's, the kid's, and finally, the simple numerical pin that he stupidly used to safeguard his entire fucking home. The green flashing light shows that our dear friend Ralph is not only predictable but extremely dumb. I hold my breath as I open the safe. We *really* need this. For her. For us.

Stacks of money stare back at us, standing tall like the pillars outside of this place. I release a sigh of relief. It's more than we expected. The anxiety about our future evaporates and leaves me feeling a few pounds lighter.

"Fill the bags," I tell Karson before stepping out of the closet.

"Did you find anything?" Leana asks.

"All of it," I growl as I pull her into me. I kiss her. For once, because of her, everything is going exactly right. I release her once Karson exits the closet, and the moment I do, she flops onto the bed with a contended sigh.

Goddamn it.

"You're leaving your fucking DNA all over that blanket," I snap, gripping her arm and yanking her into a sitting position.

Karson drops down beside her with a smirk.

"Really?" I ask.

"She's already on it. Might as well make the best of it. We'll just take the fancy fucking blanket with us," Karson says, leaning onto his elbow.

He's not wrong. We've already fucked it up.

His hand snakes around Leana and draws her into him, and a low growl leaves my throat. "Come on, G. I only need three minutes, remember?"

"We aren't playing here," I tell them. He's lucky I don't want to get caught. Otherwise I'd paint the fucking walls a gaudy shade of Karson red.

Leana grips my pants and pulls me closer. "Why don't we play a little and then get out of here? You got the money, so there's no need to kill him."

Before I can respond, Karson sits up and shakes his head. "Fuck that. As much as I'd love to fuck your brains out on this rich asshole's bed, we have a hit to do. I'm not leaving a job unfinished, and I'm sure as fuck not passing up the chance to murder a celebrity."

Tears fill Leana's eyes. She really thought she could make a difference. She believed she could change Karson's mind at the last second and save this man from his fate. Not even I could stop Karson from doing what he was made to do. That's like trying to teach a tiger to live a vegan lifestyle. Ain't happening.

"Are you crying, thief?" Karson asks. "Don't fucking cry. This guy is a piece-of-shit junkie. He's not worth your tears."

She looks at him, unashamed of the visible pain in her eyes. "I was a piece-of-shit junkie too. When you two found me, I was so hooked on that shit that I wanted to die. If you hadn't saved me, I would probably be six feet under. People can change, Karson. They can clean their shit up and find . . ." She stops, her voice breaking. "They can find something to live for."

I can't stand to see her like this. If he's too stupid to comfort her, I'll have to do it. I might suck at it, but I'm learning. I go against my better judgement and sit on the bed. When I pull her into me, she doesn't fight it and just leans against my chest.

I look at Karson over her head, and he only looks away. I'm about to try to help Leana understand when a door slams downstairs. The time for reasoning has ended.

"Showtime," Karson says with a gleeful laugh.

Leaving Leana on the bed, I go to Karson's side. If he can't see my wanderer's point of view, it can't be helped. I won't leave him to do this job alone.

Karson

"Karson," Leana pleads, her voice a mere whisper.

"Save it, thief. We're doing what we came here to do, which is kill this fucker."

Gentry looks back at her, and the pained expression on his face disgusts me. Mostly because I feel it too. I want to give Leana what she wants because she's given so much to me, but we can't back out of this now. It's too late. The fucker's home, for Christ's sake. We don't run from hits with our tails between our legs, and we sure as fuck won't start today. I will smother him like I'm smothering the flicker of guilt in my gut.

Her hand grazes my arm before I pull it out of her grasp and leave her and Gentry behind. Gentry will follow me, though. The only thing that feels better than Leana's cunt is cold-blooded murder. She needs to understand that while we hold her higher than we've ever held another person, including each other, she can't transform our hearts from two lifeless stones to beating flesh. It's just who we are.

No amount of love can change that.

Gentry's heavy steps follow mine as we descend the stairs and come face to face with the man of the hour. Ralph's eyes widen the moment he sees us.

"Guys, wait," he begins. He's never seen our faces before. Most of them haven't, but they always seem to know who we are, as if we're wearing cloaks and carrying fucking scythes. They know we're coming. It's just the matter of when. And where. They also know there's no escaping once we get there.

"Ralphie boy," I say. He turns to run, but I draw my pistol. "I wouldn't. I *really* don't feel like chasing you."

He stops mid-step and slowly turns to face me. Gentry walks around me, and his overbearing stature makes Ralph swallow.

"Did you snort all your payment, Ralph?" Gentry lifts the bag. "Well, all of it except this."

"Come on, guys! You got the money. Give it to George and call it even!" he pleads. His eyes round as he looks behind us, which means—

Goddamn it, thief.

She looks like a little girl as she slips beside my brother. I pull my attention away from her and return it to the task at hand. Specifically, Ralph's hands, which need to be chopped the fuck off, pronto. My eyes clench closed for a moment as the embers of guilt catch hold of my insides and burn a little brighter. I shake my head and drop my hand to the blade on my hip, but then my eyes land on her instead of my target. How the fuck can I kill Ralph when I can't even kill the gross feelings in my gut that tell me what I'm doing will hurt the one person I don't want to hurt?

I draw my knife and step into Ralph, who recoils from my touch and pisses his pants. I've never wanted to get a killing done faster, and that thought terrifies me. I like to go slow and savor every moment before their heart ceases to beat and the fun *mostly* goes away for me.

"Karson!" she pleads, and the anguish in her voice reaches inside and chips away the stone surrounding my heart.

No, this can't happen. This is a terrible time to get a conscience. If I get one afterward, fine, but not when Ralph has seen our faces. He has to die. Period. End of story.

Yet . . . I fucking can't.

I release a long, drawn-out breath. Anger gnashes its teeth against my lungs, and my chest burns with the building rage. None of it's directed at her, though. Or the rich piece of shit in front of me. It's all aimed at myself.

I throw Ralph against the wall and hold the knife to his throat. He flails in front of me. "Please," he begs, tears falling down his cheeks. "My son. My son needs me."

Instead of increasing my guilt, his words smother it. Gentry and I didn't have a father to give a shit about us, and Leana had it even worse. If this prick dies, he at least leaves his child with a fuck ton of money to live on. Our father left us with a mess to clean up.

I press the blade against his skin.

"Please," Leana begs behind me. "Don't let him live for his kid. Let him live for me. Show me that you believe in me, because that's what you're doing if you give him a second chance."

My hand slams through the wall beside his head.

"You deserve to die, Ralph," I say into his face. "You should be dead. I should torture you until your very last breath, especially when you use your kid as a bargaining chip when you can't even stay clean long enough to spend any quality fucking time with him."

He trembles, his throat knocking into my blade with every swallow.

"But I won't kill you. Because of her." I gesture toward Leana. "Because she's walked in shoes like yours. Not the rich, expensive leather you wear, but the cement blocks that cling to your feet when you're high off your face." I take a sharp breath. "She wants us to show you a fraction of the sympathy we showed her, which is so incredibly gross. But this matters to her, so it matters to me."

He tries to blubber out his thanks, but I press the knife against his Adam's apple, and he closes his lips.

"I'm not fucking finished. Here's what's going to happen. We'll take the money and leave your ass alive, and you won't call the police. If you do, I'll send someone from fucking prison to find you *and* your son. Don't make me do that." I tap the tip of the knife on his nose. "Next, you're going to get off the drugs. I know all your dealers, Ralphie boy, and it would take a whole lot of nothing to get them to lace your next hit with some fentanyl so you can take a nice dirt nap. You wouldn't be the first celeb we took down."

His eyes widen with fear, and he almost looks more terrified to live without drugs than to die by my knife. "I can't go through withdrawal. It will kill me!"

"If she can do it, you can fucking figure it out. These are my terms."

He closes his eyes and tries to swallow again, but the blade won't allow it. "Okay, okay," he chokes out.

I grab him by the back of the neck and lead him to Leana. Shock fills her big blue eyes. Same, girl. "Thank the thief for saving your ass."

"Thank you! Thank y-you!" he cries.

I roll my eyes.

"Promise you'll get help," she says to him.

He nods. "I promise."

Against everything in my nature, I let him go and he falls to the floor. I can't even look at Gentry because I have no clue what his expression is. Whether he's happy or upset, I'll end up annoyed with him. As we walk toward the door, Gentry calls out a parting shot.

"And change your security code. Jesus, a toddler could have guessed that," he yells over his shoulder. I fight a smirk because he didn't guess it.

My good little thief did.

Chapter Thirty-Three

I feel like the world has imploded. The ground beneath us shattered, and everything we knew washed away as it broke apart. Karson turned down a kill. He's gotta be ill. Actually sick. Maybe even dying. "Come here. Let me check your forehead." I lean over and reach toward his face, but he smacks my hand away.

"Fuck you," he says. "It's her fault."

"My fault?" Leana asks, genuine surprise coloring her tone. She knows damn well it's her fault. Neither of us would leave a target alive like that.

But she would.

"Yeah, you had to walk over and look all fucking sad." Karson waves us off as he quickens his steps to pull ahead of us. It's a long walk across this damn yard.

"Since when do you care if anyone is sad?" she asks, and I let the retort lift the corners of my mouth.

So mouthy. I love it.

Karson stops and turns around. "*Your* sadness is the *only* one that bothers me. Not his. Not mine. Yours." He looks away. "And I hate it. I don't know how Gentry juggles feelings and homicidal thoughts in the same body. The same mind. How are you a killer with a conscience, G? It makes no fucking sense to me. I don't like how it feels, and I don't *want* those feelings. I was doing fine as I was!"

I cock my head at him. He has never been *doing fine*. He has never been fine a day in his life.

"Fine-ish!" he snaps before turning away from us again.

I pull Leana into me as we walk. "You know that was incredibly dumb, right?"

She knows. It doesn't take someone who kills for a living to know that was dumb. That piece of shit might call the police before we even reach our car.

"Then why didn't you stop it?" she snaps, and I squeeze her sides.

"For one, I was too shocked to stop it. But also, I wouldn't have let him kill Ralph, anyway. So fucking stupid to do, but it was for you. If we get caught, we fall back on the plan. I'll put a bullet through your head"—I lean over and kiss her forehead—"and then go out in an exchange of gunfire."

She pulls away from me just as we get to the SUV.

"We forgot the blanket," she says as she gets into the back seat.

"He won't do shit," Karson says as he climbs into the passenger seat. "He's probably still cleaning himself up. Dude pissed his pants. Besides, you don't come face to face with reapers twice. He won't like what happens to him if I have to pay him another visit. Not even you could save him, thief." Karson punches the dash and looks out the window. "I hate that I don't feel like much of a killer now."

"Trust me, you're a killer," she says. "Just not this time."

"Don't get used to it," Karson says. "I won't always be selfless. Actually, I probably rarely will be, so just remember this moment when you think I'm a selfish dick."

That sounds more like Karson.

We return to the motel parking lot, and Leana and Karson seem more than happy to crash here for the rest of the night, but I have something else in mind. I tell them to grab their things and walk Sam before we hit the road again.

Leana

When Gentry pulls up at the expensive hotel attached to the winery, I can almost forgive him for the long drive. He has to grease the wheels with a little cash to get them to allow the dog in with us, but we eventually take the elevator to a fancier room than we stayed in before, complete with a lounge area and club-room access. I'm only surprised by one thing.

One king-size bed waits in the room.

"Three minutes?" Gentry says as soon as we've placed our bags on the floor.

Karson rolls his eyes. "Not this again."

"I can get her off in two." He captures my mouth and pulls my lower lip between his teeth. When he releases me, he tosses me onto the bed and lowers my pants until he can pull them off. He flips me over and raises my hips until I'm ass-up for him. "Time it."

Before I know what's happening, he buries his face in my pussy. Jealousy fuels his tongue, and he finds my swollen clit with ease. My moans gain in intensity as he hooks his hands around my thighs and pulls me against his face. Sounds of pleasure leave my lips, harder and faster, until my thighs tremble against his lips. He digs his fingertips into my skin to steady me.

I'm so close, and I'm sure he can feel it. He sinks a finger inside me to send me over the edge, and I gasp at the sudden addition to the pleasure coursing between my legs. He pushes his fingers deeper, searching for the next moan and bringing it out of me with ease.

He wants to make me come harder and faster than Karson could, and that's something Karson will never understand. He will never know what it's like to need to please me so desperately.

And that's okay.

Gentry will never know what it means to take me selfishly and use my body to fulfill his own hungry need. He can't understand what it means to take from me because he's too busy giving.

And that's okay.

They are the two opposing forces that somehow hold me together.

I can't control the orgasm as it rips through me. I clench around his fingers and cry out, shuddering and gripping the comforter to keep myself upright. I don't want to move away from his mouth. I don't want this feeling to stop.

When he pulls out of me, I turn my head and see that Karson's eyes are locked on us. Knowing that he watched his brother get me off makes me want more. I've just been fed, but I'm still so hungry.

"Two minutes and thirty-five seconds," Karson says as he turns his phone toward us, displaying the stopwatch.

Gentry sits on the bed and pulls me onto his lap. His hard cock presses against my bare ass, and I'm glad to know I'm not the only one who wants more. "I know your body, sweet wanderer," he says. "I know it better than my brother."

"Who did it better, thief?" Karson asks.

I shake my head. I can't compare Gentry and Karson. They almost become one when it comes to killing, but when it comes to caring about or loving someone, they're a world apart.

"Please don't ask me to pick between you guys," I say. "There's no way to choose. I need both of you. I need your selfishness, Karson." I turn to Gentry. "But I also need your selflessness."

Karson moves closer and leans in to kiss me. His hand wraps around the back of my neck as he draws me closer to his mouth. I kiss him, expecting Gentry to pull me away at any moment, but he doesn't. I'm pressed between them, and I've never been so turned on.

When Karson releases me, I turn to Gentry. "Are you okay with this?"

He leans in and kisses me. "I will never be okay with sharing you, but Karson isn't the only one willing to make a change for you. This is what you want, isn't it?"

"Yes, sir," I say.

He growls against my mouth and kisses me once more. "Just remember who you belong to, wanderer."

Karson turns my head toward him again. "Thief," he whispers against my mouth, "I want my brother to stretch your cunt while I sink inside your perfect ass."

I've never done that before, but I don't think that will matter to Karson.

"Come here," Gentry says, low and soft as he lies on his back. He drags me over him, and I straddle his wide hips, feeling the length of his hard dick through his jeans. There's something so erotic about riding his zipper, but I want more. I *need* more. He reaches down and unfastens his jeans, releasing his cock. He's so turned on that the bare skin burns hot as I lower myself against it. "I can't wait a moment longer to stretch your sweet pussy," he growls before burying his face into my neck and biting my flesh.

"Please, sir," I beg. "Can I have your cock?" Whimpers punctuate my words as his teeth sink deeper.

"You know I love when you call me that," he whispers. "I can't tell you no when you're such a good girl."

I whimper as he slides his hand between us and glides the throbbing head of his cock toward my entrance. When he pulls my hips down, I'm impaled with pleasure and pain, mercilessly ripped in two. I cry out and he muffles my screams with his shoulder as he pulls me against his chest.

"Sorry, wanderer." He brushes my hair away from my sweaty cheek. "Selfish of me to take your pussy like that, I know, but I needed to feel you around me."

The burning subsides between my legs and leaves me feeling warm and full, but hair rises on the back of my neck as hands grip my waist, just below Gentry's. Karson's body heat warms me from behind. He leans closer and bites my shoulder before pushing my chest down to his brother's. His hands grope my ass, pushing his fingertips into my flesh with a low growl.

"Gentry may own your pussy, little thief, but your ass is mine," he says as his hands spread me. The moment he does, my body tenses and tightens, and Gentry jolts with this renewed pressure.

"Wait, Karson," Gentry says. He lifts my chin, forcing my eyes to meet his. "Is this what you want?"

I hate that he asks, because I'm not sure. Based on how my body responded, it certainly seems like I don't want this, but I *want* to want it. I'm just scared.

"I won't hurt her, G," Karson says. "Not any more than what comes with taking my pierced dick in such a tight hole."

His words make me tense further. "You aren't helping."

Karson leans over, puts a hand to the front of my neck, and lifts me toward him, bringing my ear close to his mouth. "Let me inside you, thief. I'll show you that Gentry isn't the only giving lover."

I sigh, exhaling a long breath as he releases my neck. Sweat rolls down my back, and I need to get out of this shirt. I peel it off and lean forward, putting my bare chest against Gentry's shirt. I bury my face in the fabric as Karson's hands wander to my ass again. He unzips his jeans and spreads me again. Warm saliva drips between my ass cheeks and coats me.

I'm fucking terrified.

Karson puts his cock up to me, and I brace myself for his intrusion. Instead of pushing inside me, he rests it between my cheeks as his hands soothe my lower back with a soft, caring caress. Dare I say . . . loving?

I relax a bit, and he doesn't seek out permission as one hand leaves my back and guides his cock inside me. I bite Gentry's shirt as his head spreads me, the piercings clicking past my opening. He pushes further inside me, slower than I expect, then he waits until I stretch around him before pushing further.

His fingertips dig into the small of my back. "Don't get used to my kindness, thief," he growls. "I plan to drill your ass the moment you stop fighting me."

I'm not fighting him. I'm just so full of his brother's cock, and there's only so much room inside my body. Just when I think I can't take another inch of Karson, he pushes until I feel the soft hairs of his pelvis against my ass. There's too much friction as he tries to ease back, so he spits again, coating his cock. When he pushes forward again, he glides inside me. I'm so fucking full.

"Fuck, thief," Karson grits out, his words laced with feral pleasure.

Gentry can't move much beneath us, but he remains buried so deep that I can feel it in my lower abdomen. He pulls my face toward him so he can kiss me, and his lips make me forget about everything as Karson rips away the glimpse of humanity and mercilessly fucks my ass. I cry out into Gentry's mouth, and he swallows all the pain.

"Good girl," he whispers.

Karson's hand winds through my hair, and he cranes my neck as he fucks me. "She's not a good girl," he growls. "She's a dirty little thief."

There's a competitive edge to his words, and it goes right to my pelvis and buries itself between them. I'm pulled from Gentry's soft sensuality and thrust into Karson's rough, passionate grasp. I feel so fucking alive, spared by the hands of death that grip parts of my body. My hips. My shoulders. My chest. I feel them everywhere.

Gentry lifts his hips, keeping pace with his brother so that I remain thoroughly and uncomfortably stuffed. I move my hips with Karson's thrusts. I like how it feels. How dirty and raw it is.

Gentry pulls me into him, wrapping his arms around me. "I'm going to come, wanderer," he groans, letting Karson's motions and my throbbing pussy work the come from him. His hips rise to meet mine as he fills me.

"Good. Now she can be mine," Karson says.

"Not a chance. I'll keep her stuffed with my cock so she doesn't lose a single drop of my come."

"Selfish," Karson clips.

"Yeah, sometimes." Gentry's fingertips brush the hair from my cheek as he looks into my eyes. "She's my breedable little wanderer," he says, and fuck if it doesn't make me throb. "Mine."

"Ours," Karson corrects as he smacks my ass. "There's a reason she won't choose between us. You like how we *both* use you, huh, little thief? You like how Gentry fucks you like he loves you and I fuck you like I hate you."

"Yes," I whimper.

It's true. Karson is fucked beyond comprehension, and yet my body still craves his harsh, feral touch. Almost as much as I crave the protective, loving hand that belongs to Gentry. And I won't choose. Not now. Not after we've clawed our way to this moment.

"Do you want both holes filled?" Karson asks as he puts one hand on my hip and the other on my shoulder, but he doesn't wait for my response. It was never a question.

He fucks me harder and faster, the hollow pain of his dick pulsing through me. I moan, loving the friction as their cocks collide within me. It's sick and twisted, but that's what I've become.

And what they've always been.

Karson slows the hard thrusts that pound against the backs of my thighs.

"I'm going to fill you, thief. Officially claim this tight little ass of yours," he growls as his hips stutter, and with a groan that sends shivers up my spine, he comes.

Sweat slicks my body as Gentry's hands rove over me, playing with my nipples as we all gasp for air. I'm fucked and filled, and they're empty and satiated. The heat of their bodies presses against me until I feel like we're one. I'm sore and used, yet I'm more content than I've ever been. More free than I've ever felt.

I lean down and kiss Gentry, the man who will protect what's his at any cost. Karson grips my hair and pulls me toward him, and I kiss him too. The man who will take what he wants, regardless of the repercussions.

And then there's me. Right in the middle, where I belong.

Epilogue

One Year Later

Gentry

The smell of blood is nearly overbearing. Not in an unpleasant way, but the way something too sweet can almost make you feel sick. Tonight was such a sloppy kill—bloody as fuck, with the perfect amount of torture for Karson. Even though Leana still hasn't taken the kill shot since her ex, she takes part in the torture when she feels like the victim deserves it. Which is cute because she was once so insistent that no one deserves death. Plenty of people deserve death, but fewer deserve life. I certainly don't. Especially not *this* life with her and my fucking brother.

And Sam. He greets us at the door as we enter the apartment, happy to sniff at the blood on our bodies. We take him along on the kills sometimes—the murder mutt is a Kursicki, through and through—but we left him to guard the apartment tonight.

The only downside to this life is having to share Leana. I hate handing her off to Karson because I want her for myself, but *she* wants both of us, and she gets whatever she wants. If she doesn't want to choose between us, I won't make her. Neither of us will.

As we shed our clothes, Karson turns to me with a grin. "I heard about a way we might make a little side money," he says. "There's this fighter named Ambrose not far from here, and he's making waves in the ring. We can fight on the weekends when we aren't busy. There's good money if we win."

"I'm not kicking your ass for money," I say as I pull off my shirt. "I'll do that for free."

Leana stands naked in front of the bathroom door and waves us toward her. "Stop the competitive shit and let's get clean."

We shed the rest of our clothes, and all three of us are naked by the time we get to the shower. High on the endorphins from the kill, we drag her in and close the door. The spray sends blood-tinged water toward the drain, cleansing us of our sins.

Until next time, that is.

"My thief," Karson whispers as he kisses the back of her neck.

"Will you ever stop calling me that?" she asks. "I stole one car."

So mouthy. As usual.

"You've stolen more than that," Karson says through a laugh.

I cock my head at him. If he says some Hallmark shit like, "She stole my heart," I will shoot him in it. Even if it's kinda true. I call her wanderer because she's taken me to places within me that I'd never have gone into alone, and she's definitely a thief for stealing both of our hearts. She's also force-fed humanity down our throats. But the sweet shit? That's my half of the fucked-up equation. I'm the sap. I would put a knife through my own chest for her. I love her more than I love killing, and I never thought that would be a thing for me. She even makes me love my brother again, as an extension of her.

"I love you, wanderer," I say as I pull her into me and kiss her.

"I love you too." Her gaze bounces between us. "Both of you."

Karson—because he's still a mega douche—pulls her against his chest and whispers something into her ear. I've learned to harness the jealousy. Instead of allowing it to create hatred, I let it fuel my desire and need. I always want her more when I know my brother wants her too. I want to make her come harder, faster, and better than him.

Karson and I look at each other before we each pin one of her arms above her head. My free hand trails over the curve of her breast, where a new tattoo rests just below the arrow—the word "Kursed," written in a mixture of our blood. She's ours, completely and fully.

And she is Kursed.

We all are.

"Who can make you come faster, thief?" Karson asks, baiting me with the words as much as her. "Me or my brother?"

I drop my hand from her chest and bring it between her legs with a smirk. "Time it."

Driving My Obsession

M/F Stalker Dark Romance

It's not that we haven't learned our lesson about jumping into a car with a morally-black stranger. It's that we just really like them. To any reader who agrees, this one's for you.

Chapter One

Ambrose

Club lights strobe above me, their pinkish-purple array casting a warm glow on what little skin I've left exposed. My leather jacket covers my arms, but the scars on my head and face are still on display. The place smells like sweat, like the walls have been painted with the stuff. They probably have been.

A woman with raven hair stumbles onto the stage. Black panties hug her hips, and a black-and-white sequined bra covers her tits. I can't help but think of my mother as her hips begin to sway. As she gyrates along with the beat. She climbs the pole and hangs on by her thighs as she reaches back and unclips her bra, exposing one of the worst boob jobs I've ever seen. Puckered skin surrounds two huge bags of saline.

A topless blonde catches my eye, and she dons a soft, sweet look as she starts toward me. That expression fades when the lights flash and catch on my disfigurement. Disgust has a unique look to it. It's so hard to hide.

I take out a stack of money and wave it in front of her as she tries to sashay past me.

Her throat constricts as she gulps, probably swallowing the bile that rose into her mouth at the thought of grinding against someone who looks like me. "I would, but I'm on my way to another private dance," she says, looking toward the back rooms.

I lower my cash to my lap and allow her to think she's fooled me. As she nears the back room, I look away, knowing she'll glance back to see if I'm watching. Then the dirty little whore has the audacity to stroll to the bar and casually order a drink and sit down to talk to her coworkers. I hate liars. I'd rather you admit to my face that you don't want to dance for me because of how I look. Don't lie. Lying hurts worse.

She'd make a good target. That's why I'm in this shithole, after all. To find the vessel to receive all the anger that pours from me like a never-ending fountain. I don't get hard when I see these women with their goods on display. If anything, the opposite occurs and my dick tries to invert itself to get away from their filthy bodies.

The blonde walks by me again, as if I forgot about her lie. I pull her into me and she whimpers, but no one will hear it over the loud music.

I lean toward her ear. "I got these scars from surviving what should have killed me, you judgmental bitch."

I release her and she scurries away, looking back at me with wide eyes as she runs toward the back room. She probably plans to tattle on me, so it's time I make my exit.

I leave the club and get in my Jeep. I have somewhere I need to be, and I should have been there sooner, but my desire for revenge has been eating away at me recently. If I could resurrect the person who hurt me, I'd do what I should have done and pour my wrath into her. Since she's no longer an option, another whore will have to do.

When I pull up to the warehouse, I struggle to find a parking spot amongst the tightly packed cars. Stifling warm air engulfs me as I leave my Jeep behind and head inside.

I walk into a roaring crowd. Fists fly toward the stage as a fight rages on in the center of the room. Blood splatters across the makeshift ring's concrete floor, and bodies collide with the filthy ropes marking its perimeter.

I recognize one of the fighters. Boris is a Slavic beast. Despite his tiny stature comparatively, he's a monster in the ring. Had I been here earlier, I'd have had time to play the crowd for this fight. The fresh faces almost always bet against him, not realizing the power contained in that smaller body. They also don't realize he fights dirty. Darby, the club's owner, doesn't have any rules to break, probably because he thinks it makes for a more interesting experience when someone's fucking ear gets ripped off and spat onto the concrete.

It kinda does.

The bell rings, signifying the end of the fight, and Boris charges off the stage. His wide smile peeks through the blood coating his face like a gory mask.

He spots me in the crowd and heads toward me. "Beautiful fight," he says, a thick Slavic accent coating his words.

"Looked good."

"Felt good, too." He gives me a rough pat on the back before heading toward the locker rooms.

The sharp scents of blood and sweat fill my nose as I suck in a breath and weave through the crowd. They're focused on the two men readying to fight the next match, and that's fine with me. It gives me a chance to study their faces and find my mark. I don't want to screw up and swindle the same fucker twice.

I spot a new face in the crowd, his dirty fist gripping a wad of bills as he counts out what he's just won. The idiot might as well be waving a sign with my name on it. Judging by the smile on his face, he's already won a few others tonight. Sure would be a shame if he lost while he was on a streak.

"You got a bet on this fight?" I shout over the roar around us.

He offers a glance my way, then returns his gaze to the men.

I pull out a wad of money to rival his, and that gets his attention. "I'm willing to put everything on the underdog," I say. "If I lose, you'll get twice what you put in. You game?"

His eyes go to his winnings. He's weighing it up in his mind, and the bait is too tempting to pass by. The underdog in this fight hasn't won since he joined our little club eight weeks ago, but he's due for a win tonight. This guy doesn't know that, though. Only I know.

I set it up, after all.

"Tell you what," I shout. "I'll give you till the end of the first round to decide."

The man nibbles his lower lip and turns his attention to the ring. The fighters circle each other a few times before the bigger guy takes a swing and sends the underdog against the ropes. The one-sided beating continues for a few more minutes before the schmuck to my left eyes the fighters once more and shakes my hand.

"Pretty stupid bet to make. This guy is barely staying on his feet," he says.

I shrug and fold my arms over my chest as I catch the underdog's eye and wink. He turns back to his opponent and grips him in what looks like a hug. In fighting, this is known as a clinch. They use this move for a multitude of reasons, but this time it's so he can let his opponent know the deal has been struck and it's time to take a dive.

The underdog sends forth an uppercut when their bodies part, and the other guy takes it and goes down. The upset sends the crowd into a frenzy, and I take a moment to enjoy the look of shock on the man's face.

Ah, yes. Victory.

His gaze runs over my muscles, as if he's considering backing out on our deal and he wants to figure out if he can take me. He can't. Realizing this, he shoves his money into my hand, tucks his tail, and pushes toward the exit.

As much as I'd love to hang around and add a few more twenties to my stack, I won't be able to watch the main event. Especially since I *am* the main event.

I head to the back to prepare myself. I spend my time street fighting and ripping people off. Sometimes both at the same time. Well, it's less "street" and more "dilapidated building," but still. I bare-knuckle box, which is a fancy term for those of us that fight raw and dirty, without gloves between us. It's the most brutal way to fight, and it suits me well.

Before I leave the locker room, I check the roster. I like to know who my opponent is before I see his face. My finger scrolls down the chicken scratched list, and I release a sigh of relief because I'm not against one of the "Kursed" brothers. Gentry and Karson recently got back into the game after years away. Those two fight like bona fide psychopaths, and I'm not in the mood to earn a few more scars tonight. I heard they were hitmen before they became fighters, and while I don't usually put much stock in rumors, I believe this one. The bigger one is built for homicide, and the other looks crazed enough to do it for fun.

When I finish taping my wrists, I cut through the crowd and step into the ring to a wave of murmurs rippling through the room. Those disgruntled voices probably belong to the morons who just realized they were taken for a ride when I parted them from their money last night. If my boss paid me half a living wage, I wouldn't need to swindle people. If he didn't keep most of the money from those of us balls deep in the blood sport, I wouldn't have to work the crowd and my fellow fighters wouldn't be so willing to take a dive for a little extra cash.

The crowd transforms into a churning sea of screaming, chanting, roaring faces. Their fists pump the air as they demand more brutality. The audience is alive. I can feel the strength of it in my bones as I approach the ring. A woman in a bikini lifts a sign, panning it over the crowd. It's tacky. Putting someone pretty beside the ugly doesn't make these fights less ugly.

As we ready ourselves to begin the match, the roar of the crowd voices their disdain for the space between us. Makeshift stage lights and neon signs flicker above us and illuminate their red faces. Time to give them the show they came for.

I take the first swing, and blood slips from a split in my opponent's lip. He opens his mouth, turns his head, and spits out a tooth, which causes a roar of laughter and catcalls from the crowd. With a dazed look in his glassy eyes, he falls back into the corner, trying to recover. In a normal fight, this is where a ref would step in and call for a medical team to give us the go ahead to continue, but this isn't a normal fight. There is no medical team.

I charge toward him again, and he catches my jaw with a surprise right hook. My teeth click together on the side of my tongue. The pain fuels me to hit him harder. His blood splatters on my cheeks and forehead like war paint.

My scarred body crashes into his as we take turns searching for soft spots. We're evenly matched in body size, but he doesn't have the years of experience I've gained. Or the anger. I don't have enough time to collect myself before he throws a punch to my face that sends me stumbling backward a step. Blood flows from my nose, and it hurts like hell, but it doesn't hinder me; it fuels me.

Thin scarlet ribbons drip from my chin, leaving little red stains all over the cracked floor. I lick the blood beads rolling down my lips so they fill my mouth with their iron tang. Nothing tastes better than blood drawn from pain—and there's something about tasting that pain.

The lights warm my sweat-slicked muscles, and I send my cut fist into his face. His scream echoes in my ears, and I revel in the power and violence. It's my love language. The crowd roars in approval, growing louder with each blow.

When he finally falls to his knees and clutches what must be a broken jaw, I let out a sadistic laugh. An audible crunch rings out over the cries from the blood-thirsty crowd as I prey upon that weakness and knock his head back once more. Blood sprays from his mouth and stains the concrete, and he doesn't rise to his feet again.

I win.

Nothing in my life feels right, but this? This feels right. When I'm surrounded by cheering crowds while covered in someone else's blood, knowing it will never be my life essence leaking onto the ground, I feel normal. And that's saying something. Not even the skin I wear feels normal. It's a tattered costume I can't take off.

I run a hand through my dark blonde hair. A few strands fall into my eyes, and it looks almost brown from the amount of sweat woven through it. Red lights catch on my scars—tough strips of tissue lacing my body. I can hide the worst of them with clothing, especially the deep gouges I received on my abdomen, but I'm forced to show them to the world when I fight. It doesn't matter here, though. It adds to my persona and makes me seem like I've been through some shit.

They have no fucking idea what I've been through.

While I can hide the scars on my body outside of this place, I can't do shit for those on my face and neck. I keep the sides of my head shaved because it's patchy as shit if I let it grow. These marks keep me from blending into society, so I've given up on trying.

Who needs a fucking society that set free the monster who did this to me?

I look down at my beaten opponent and smile. Yeah, I win. It's what I do. Every time I step into that ring, I win. But I never feel like I've won as I leave—my body battered and bruised, my heart beating hollowly against my chest. On the outside, I'm un-fucking-defeated, but inside, I'm fighting to feel something more than numb. It's a place to push my constant anger.

But winning doesn't feel as good with no one in your corner.

The crowd quiets and begins filing out of the building. Everyone loves the scary, scarred-up fighter in the ring, but I'm dogshit on the soles of their shoes once it's over. Their eyes are no longer glued to me. Now they just want to look away. They cower from me or shield the eyes of their curious kids. Some of them know about my past. Some people even think I'm immortal. No little boy should have survived the damage flashed all over the paper and the six o'clock news. I'm the living embodiment of their worst nightmares.

I throw my shirt over my shoulder and head toward the makeshift locker room. The stench of men and unwashed towels fill the space, and I fling my shirt onto a metal bench against the wall. I stroll past a line of warped lockers and a dirty, cracked mirror, then groan as I run my hands beneath the sink's cold tap. Before I can even dry my hands, my "boss" storms in, his face contorted with anger. He raises his hand and sends his palm against the back of my head. The red rage spilling from his veins has now infected mine. I exhale, trying to keep from killing him.

"Why the fuck are you working the crowd like that, scar?" he shouts.

"It's none of your business," I say. I hate when he calls me that. I am not just my scars.

Darby's eyes narrow. "It *is* my business when you're doing it under my name. This whole thing is my business."

Darby lords over the fighters like a king, but I'm no one's property. He masquerades this business as legitimate when it's anything but. These fights are not only illegal but the last resort for those of us too desperate and broken to do anything else. We're the forgotten, abandoned by society and by the law. It's a shame that our only hope lies in this depraved, violent world he created.

He shoves his hand into my face. "Give me what you swindled off people or lose your spot next week, Mr. Sinclair."

My muscles tense as I fight the overwhelming urge to snap this man in half and leave him in a shallow, unmarked grave. But I know if I do, I'll have no future. Without this gig, there's nothing for me. With an animalistic growl, I reach into my pocket and fling the money near his feet. The cash flies into the putrid mix of pooling water, sweat, and urine.

"Oops, sorry," I say, though I'm not the least bit sorry. If I could whip down my jeans and add to the piss leaching into those bills, I would.

Darby reaches up to put a hand on my shoulder. "You know, scar, you're one of my best fighters. Piss-poor attitude, though." His voice lowers as he squeezes, and I'm about three seconds away from sending him across the locker room.

I shrug out of his grasp. "My attitude is what makes me a good fighter."

"You won't go far in this industry with it. Learn to be good without it."

The corners of my vision blur. He's hitting every last nerve I have. Does he see what I do to people's faces? He's coming dangerously close to being next.

Holding back is not my strength. It never has been.

"Get out of my face, Darby. Unless you want me to rearrange yours."

He juts a finger at my chest. "Thin fuckin' ice, scar."

The thinnest.

Chapter Two

Oaklyn

Nerves flutter in my stomach, spreading their wings and taking flight with every quiet moment. Once the music begins, it will pass. I'll find the tempo and move with it. I'll forget the people in the audience for a moment as the bass beats in time with my heart. The raised eyebrows and pursed lips will disappear as the song pulses through the speaker, and it's just me and the stage.

My body remembers this feeling all too well. It longs for it. Dance is so natural for me. It was the most important thing in my life before my life changed forever. My body remembers how to accentuate each note with a movement and make the most of every beat. As I step onto the stage, it doesn't matter what the patrons think of me. All that matters is what I think of myself. I may shed my clothes, but in my mind, I'm wearing the familiar outfits that gave me life.

I close my eyes, and the tacky neon lights shift into elegant spotlights that shine down on me. I'm not half naked, dancing for a bunch of men. I'm in a costume, preparing for my debut on a stage.

The song starts, and I begin my show. The men throw money instead of roses. They demand a private dance instead of an encore. But I'm dancing, and that is all that matters at this moment. I lose myself to the song, which is better than what most of the other girls lose themselves to.

When the song ends, I'm brought back to my sweaty, half-dressed reality. No longer in top condition from hours of rehearsals, I'm winded and sore. The ache in my leg reminds me I'm not the person I used to be. That I'll never be that person again.

My skin itches from the sweat and glitter, and I fight back the urge to run off the stage and wipe away the icky feeling as I scoop the money from the floor. I avoid looking at the crowd as I lean over to pick up the last bill. Dancing isn't the most demeaning part of this job; it's the scrounging up the cash at the end that makes me uncomfortable. I can avoid their eyes, but I can't avoid their hoots and whistles and greedy hands. They reach for me as if they're owed a pound of my flesh for every dollar they tossed my way. My ankles wobble in my clear heels when I stand upright again. They always do by the end of the night, and the blisters between my toes don't help.

I hold the money to my chest and race off the stage to the safety and solitude of the dressing room. I lay the cash on my little desk in the back and slip off my shoes before I start to count it. No matter how much I make, I feel as if I'll never have enough for the car I so desperately need. Everything comes with a price in this life, and the cost of a ride is more than I'm willing to pay.

A deep groan comes from behind me. He'll notice the look of disgust in the mirror if I react, so I keep my face stony and continue counting the bills. Jake's arms wrap around my waist, and I swallow the clawing urge to push him away and scream for him to never touch me again. He's the club owner, and he's taken a liking to me, as much as I wish he hadn't. His favoritism comes with the burden of unwanted advances instead of the perks of preferential treatment.

His fat hand rises to my chest and squeezes my nipple. My cheeks flush, not from arousal but discomfort.

"How's my girl?" he whispers in my ear. Alcohol dances on his sour breath, and my stomach twists.

"Tired," I say. I try to step away from him, but he's determined to hold me in place.

"You've been working so hard." He brushes back my red hair with his other hand. "If you give in to my offer, I'll give you a little something that will help you with your car situation. You'll make as much as a whole night, if you let me inside you."

My spine tightens. Even a shiny new Mercedes wouldn't be enough to get me to agree to sleeping with him. I may not have much left to my name, but I still have my dignity. People may think that removing my clothes for money makes me less than dignified, but they're wrong. I still have limits, and Jake is a hard no.

"Maybe another night," I tell him.

He gives my cheek a light smack. "Then you'll need another ride tonight."

"Really?" My heart sinks to my aching feet.

"You can't get something for nothing." He growls as he reaches down and squeezes my ass until it hurts.

Oh, fuck you, I think. I shrug away from his touch and wrap my long jacket around me, then stuff the money into my pocket and slip my feet into the flats I keep below the desk. "See you tomorrow, Jake," I say with the fakest pleasantry I can muster. I brush past him, but he stops me, reaches into my pocket, and takes out a large chunk of my money. I ball my hand into a fist at my side to keep myself from snatching back what belongs to me. "What's that for?"

"My cut. Now get going, sweet cheeks."

I can't respond, not because I can't think of something to say—I have *plenty* to say—but because I don't want to give him a reason to put me in a more precarious situation than I'm already in. Until I can afford a car, I'm stuck here. Each day chipping away more of my soul than the last.

He waves me off, and I head out the back door. I try to snag an Uber, but there aren't any available. Probably because of the sports game that's ending right around now. I consider going back inside and sucking Jake's dick for a ride home, but I can't.

Another dancer steps outside to smoke a cigarette in her car. She's almost done for the evening, so maybe she can give me a lift to my house if I wait around until her last dance. I shuffle toward her car and tap on the window.

When she looks up at me, her face shifts from friendly to disgusted. "What do you need?"

The other girls don't like me, and I wish I could say it's a problem of my own making. That would be easier than the truth. If I had some horrible character flaw, I could work to improve myself, but I can't fix the disdain they feel because Jake hovers over me like a fly on shit. They probably think I make more money, which would be a valid reason to hate me as much as they do, but that isn't the case. I probably make less than they do, especially on nights like tonight when I've pissed off Jake.

"Any chance you could give me a lift home when you get off?" I ask. "I can give you a few bucks to cover the gas if it's out of your way." I happen to know it's not out of her way by much, but I hope my offer will sweeten the deal.

"Sorry, can't do it," she says with a flick of her cigarette. "My man is home with the kids, and I don't have time to travel all over town if I want to get back before they drive him insane."

Her shitty apartment is less than a mile from my trailer. That's hardly driving "all over town." But I don't argue. What's the point? "Oh, okay. Thanks anyway," I say.

I return to the road and throw my thumb into the air to flag someone down. Hitchhiking was surprisingly normal where I grew up. If someone needed a ride, you gave them a ride in the spirit of helping your neighbor. Here in New York, it's a different story. The cars just whiz by as if I don't exist at all.

A cool breeze bites at my thighs, and I pull my jacket tighter. When no one stops after fifteen minutes, I decide to wait a bit and see if the buzz from the game dies down. I walk back to the side of the building and slide down the wall. I watch as men and couples enter and leave.

With a deep sigh, I check the app once more and find no sign of a ride option anytime soon. The back door slams and Jake walks out, counting his money and pretending I don't exist. He's my only option, and I hate that he is.

When I don't speak, he finally looks down at me. "What? You couldn't find a ride?"

My cheeks burn. "No. Can you please take me home?" I hate begging. I'd walk, but my feet are so mangled, and it's far enough that I'd never make it. Not before I had to hitch another ride just to come back here.

"What will you give me for a ride? How desperate are you?"

I take some cash from my pocket and wave it near him. He understands the language of money, but it's not the language he wants to speak tonight. My eyes ease down his body until I land on the hard mass pressing against his jeans. I shiver.

"Can't you just be nice for once?" I ask. Nothing about his undersized palm-tree t-shirt and gold chains screams "nice guy," but a girl can dream.

"Here's the deal, sweets. A hand job will get you halfway home. Put your mouth on me, and I'll take you all the way."

He's just as desperate as I am, but he has the bargaining chip I lack: his fucking car. I refuse to put my mouth on him, but a hand job beats walking the entire way.

"Take me halfway," I say with a drop of my gaze.

He leads me to his BMW, and I get inside. The fancy leather sticks to the backs of my legs. The moment he sits down, his hands go for the button on his pants. He's not wasting any time, but I'm frozen in place, unable to move my hand toward his exposed dick.

"Well, come on. I want payment in full before we pull out of this parking lot."

I shake my head. "Not here, Jake." Not where we work. I don't want any of the other girls to get wind of this. It's bad enough they already think I've fucked him. That he favors me. I don't *want* that attention from him. I don't want *him*.

"Put your hand on my dick, baby, or get the fuck out of my car." The tone of his voice shifts, and the second half comes out aggressive and raw, as if the choice to leave isn't really a choice any longer.

I glance at the parking lot once more before I reach over and put my hand on his dick. The flesh there is warm and sweaty, like an armpit. A similar smell wafts toward my nose, and I nearly swallow my tongue as my stomach lurches. God, he's vile.

The moment I touch him, he groans as if he's been waiting for this. For any kind of touch from me. I stare at the rotating light tracing each letter in the Purple Lounge sign. My hand moves on his lap until he thrusts his hips up into my hand and calls me baby on repeat. Warm beads of come squirt from his head and dribble down my hand, and I look away. If I puke, he'll definitely fire me. I swallow the vomit creeping up my throat.

His sweaty hand winds through my hair. "Let's get you home, baby," he says, a satiated lilt to his voice. He has a more giving attitude once he comes, it seems.

I wipe my hand on a napkin I find on the floorboard and put my hands in my lap. Degrading acts are just something I need to get used to. For now.

Chapter Three

Oaklyn

I struggle at work the next night. As I wrap my hand around the pole climbing from the center of one of the smaller stages, I can't help but imagine Jake's skinny dick within my grasp. The hot skin burned my flesh and left a scar on my mind. At least he took me all the way home, though.

When I lower myself to the floor and arch my back, the men around the stage reach out to me, their sweaty hands accosting my chest. Fingers slide over my exposed skin, groping and squeezing things they have no business seeing, let alone touching. As they assault me, I have to smile. If the disgust shows on my face, I'll never make enough money to buy a car and begin to salvage my life. Thankfully, the dream I once had of dancing and acting in a theater has prepared me for this nightmare, and they aren't wise to the fake look of seduction on my face.

Without making it obvious, I raise my chest and rise to my feet. Their greedy hands recede like waves of toxic sludge, but no shower can last long enough or burn hot enough to wash away this film of dirt on my skin. It's inside me now. For feeling up my breasts, some of the men toss a compulsory bill onto the stage. It doesn't feel good. They might as well scream, "Here's your money, bitch!"

The song ends, and mumbles of conversation fill the silence before generic club music rushes into the gap. Sweat drips between my breasts as I lean over and pick up the money. The bills stick to my skin as I clutch them to my chest and scurry behind the curtain.

Back at my station, I stack the cash. I drag some of the crumpled rectangles along the edge of the desk to smooth them out, but it's pointless. They've been shoved in someone's pocket for too long, awaiting their chance to be thrown at my feet.

Speaking of my feet, they need a break. I slide off my heels and rub at my aching ankle. The bane of my existence. The sole reason I will never dance on any stage with clothes on again. I can handle a three-minute song, but anything longer than that and I'd probably fall on my face. Or worse.

I bend over to put on my sneakers, and the tough, tight fabric rubs against my blisters. My second shoe is half on as Jake's cologne wafts over me and turns my stomach. Before I can straighten my spine, his length presses against my ass and his hands move to my hips. This is the last thing I want at the end of a shift.

"Hey, baby," he says. He grinds against my panty-clad ass, and I try to step out of his grasp. "Don't be like that. You want a ride home tonight, don't you?"

I'm fucking sick of having a ride held over my head like this. Being down on my luck shouldn't equate to being down on my knees. And that's what he'll expect tonight. A hand job was enough to get by last time, but he'll up the ante.

One of the other girls enters the dressing room and clears her throat. Jake releases me, and I fall forward onto the desk. My cheeks burn red, and I'm sure the other girl thinks I look like a naughty schoolgirl who got caught bending over her teacher's desk for a good grade. That couldn't be further from the truth. His unwanted advances make me sick, and I don't keep quiet about them to get a leg up in this business. I'm not trying to one-up these other women. I'm just trying to survive.

Through my mirror, I glance at the other woman. She's at her station, busying herself with her outfit for her next dance. I can't be the only one he sexually harasses. There's no way.

Without waiting for Jake to solicit me for sex again, I throw on a cami and shorts and top it off with my long black jacket. He realizes he's not getting anything from me, so he snatches the stack of cash from my hand and strips half my money before walking away. My heart sinks. He didn't earn that money. His breasts didn't get fondled. But there's no arguing with him. Instead, I throw my leftover cash into my pocket and head out the back door.

As I step into the night air, I count the money he's been nice enough to leave in my possession. An Uber will take an even larger chunk out of my meager earnings, so I trudge toward the bus stop with anger-fueled steps. A chill wind bites at my bare ankles and legs as I get to the bench and check the time on my phone. I missed the last bus of the night by five minutes. Fabulous.

With no other option, I throw my thumb into the air as the rare car drives by. Their headlights glide over my skin, but they keep driving. I'm tired. I'm cold. I'm angry. My rage only grows with each passing vehicle.

How can an entire city of people be so blind to the needs of their neighbors? I'm not some scary man mumbling to himself on a street corner. I'm a woman with aching feet and a sharp pain in my leg. I pose zero risk.

I raise my thumb again as headlights peek around the bend. Instead of speeding by, the Jeep slows and pulls to the side of the road. I've accomplished the first task, which is getting someone to stop. Now I just have to hope the driver doesn't harbor the same expectations as my shitty boss.

If I walk to the driver's side, I'll be standing in the middle of the street, so I step up to the passenger-side window. It lowers, but I can't see the driver's face in the shadows. "Can I get a ride home?" I ask. I should feel ashamed for begging like this, but when the alternative means fucking Jake inside the building, I feel little more than grateful for the opportunity to beg at all.

"Where about?" the low voice says from the driver's seat.

"Just outside the city. Off Jones Avenue."

He flicks on the dome light and dips his head as he moves a duffle bag off the passenger seat. When he sits up and the light lands on his face, I nearly gasp at the sight of him. Scars cross his face and neck, and even more occupy his right arm. My eyes land on a dark patch of blood on his knuckles, and I gulp back my discomfort.

"Sure, get in. But judging by the way you're looking at me, I'm guessing you won't."

I take a step back and pull my coat tighter around me. "I don't usually get in cars with strangers, especially not when they have—"

"Scars?"

"No," I say, shaking my head. "You look like you've . . . been in a fight." I almost said he looks like he's murdered someone—or a bunch of someone's—but I caught myself.

The man looks at his hand. "You aren't wrong. I *was* in a fight, but not the sort of fight you're thinking of. I do bare-knuckle boxing down at the warehouse off Jensen Avenue. And this is nothing."

I look back at the club. At the empty bus stop. Getting into this Jeep with this stranger is better than returning to the club and begging Jake for a ride. I can't afford his fee.

I open the passenger-side door and take a seat in the car. The man eyes me as my jacket spreads a bit in the front, his gaze crawling over my fishnet stockings and the glitter-covered shorts that ride up my thighs. He looks at the club, putting two and two together.

The man throws the Jeep in drive. "You work at the club?" he asks.

"Yeah."

He scoffs. "You're too pretty to be a whore."

I don't even know how to respond to that. This backhanded compliment is borderline offensive. I'm not a whore. If I was, I'd have fucked Jake for the money by now.

I cover myself with the skirt of my jacket. "I'm guessing you won?" I ask, pointing toward his hand.

"I always win."

"I see you're quite modest." I fidget with my jacket. "What's your name?"

He swallows, as if this question is wholly unexpected. I suppose most hitch-hikers don't reach for pleasantries. "Ambrose," he says. "What's yours?"

I consider lying, but I'm too tired to fabricate something on the spot. "Oaklyn."

"Is that your real name or your stage name?"

"My real name." God, he's a dick. "You're being kind of rude," I tell him.

A hauntingly handsome smirk slides onto his face and twists the thin scar beside his mouth. I should ask him about his face. It's only fair. But I push the question down in my gut and leave it alone. It's none of my business, and I don't want to piss him off, even if he's bordering on that with me.

Like a ship drawn to a lighthouse on a rocky shore, his dark eyes keep drifting to me. He looks at me as if he's imagining how my shift went. In his version, I'm probably bouncing on dicks all night. He couldn't be more wrong, so he should keep his eyes to himself.

He turns onto my street, and I sit up taller. "You can drop me off here," I say. I'm not a complete idiot. If he doesn't know where I live, he can't storm into my house and murder me.

"Don't be ridiculous. If I want to know which place is yours, I can just sit here and watch which home you enter."

He has a point.

I take a deep breath. "It's that gray trailer on the right, just past the house with the basketball hoop in the driveway."

He pulls against the curb in front of my trailer and puts the Jeep in park.

"Thanks for the ride," I say.

He doesn't respond. When I've closed the car door behind me, he throws the Jeep in reverse and leaves me in front of my trailer without waiting to see if I go inside. But at least he didn't kill me and put my skin on a blow-up doll, so that's a plus. As his taillights fade and disappear, I wonder if I'll ever see him again.

Probably not.

Chapter Four

Ambrose

Anger simmers, boiling within my veins. I shouldn't have picked up a girl like her outside of a place like that. I let her out and hightailed it out of there before I did something I'd regret. Or that I wouldn't regret at all. She seemed like the perfect victim for my plan, but I haven't thought through all the details yet. I need more time to come up with the perfect way to exact my revenge. That's why I let her live tonight. I'm not yet ready to unleash this black monster inside me.

I don't know why it has to be her, but it does. It's not her fault the other dancers ignored and avoided me as if my skin imperfections were contagious. She wasn't the one who pushed my money back toward me like it was soiled. But she still wears skimpy little outfits and dances for men much worse than me who just look more normal. Close enough.

Fucking. Whores. Just like the woman who carved me up with a butcher knife.

I drive toward home, stewing in my frustration with every mile marker I pass. I rub at my cut knuckles and anticipate a hot shower to wash away the dry, sticky blood. When I pull into the apartment parking lot, I take a deep breath before getting out of my Jeep. The late-night stragglers milling about outside turn and stare. Their judgmental eyes go from my face to my hands and back to my face again. I bark at them as I pass, and they look away. They didn't care if they made me uncomfortable, but the moment the shoe slid onto the other foot, they got to feel that pointy rock of discomfort grinding against their sensitive skin.

I begin pulling off clothes the moment I step inside my silent apartment. My leather jacket. My shirt. My shoes. The undershirt I put on after my fights. My fingers work open my jeans, and I step out of them without missing a beat. By the time I reach the bathroom, I'm down to my boxers. Such simple tasks seem so monumental when my body is racked with this much tension. I'm always tense after a fight, but that girl made it so much worse. The familiar scent she emitted sent a lead weight into the pit of my stomach. Like sweat and old liquor. Stale.

They all have that smell.

I turn on the shower as high as it goes and climb beneath the spray. The hot water attacks my skin and matches the heat in my veins. The caked blood dissolves from my hand and circles the drain, but I wish there was so much more. I stare at the white porcelain until I can almost see a rush of red instead of the pale pink tinge. I imagine rinsing off my body after picking up a woman like Oaklyn. My brain conjures up fantasies of what I'd have to do to her to coat myself in that much blood. It lands on my favorite imagining: a butcher knife carving up skin. She would beg for me to stop, but I wouldn't. My attacker didn't stop, either.

Then I see Oaklyn's face in my mind. Terrified, tear-filled eyes. Mouth moving as she asks why. I only have one answer for her.

Because someone has to pay.

She seemed different, though, and that gives me a moment of pause. It doesn't derail my desires, but it slows the train to a crawl. I rationalize that it's not *me* who would commit such a heinous act. It's the big, black, ominous creature lurking inside me. One that my mother recognized in me so long ago.

One that I'm forced to silence now.

I close my eyes and wash the sweat from my hair, and flashes of that girl pass behind my eyelids like pictures in a photo album. Dark red hair flows over her shoulders, and the familiar lifelessness dims her big green eyes. The pictures begin to move, and I see her in a grocery store or a bank instead of twirling on a pole. Something about her seems to belong to those places more than a club.

Then my mind's eye roves lower, and I catch a glimpse of the scars on her thigh as her jacket spread. My fingers graze similar ridges of pink flesh on my inner thigh, and I drop my head back and let the water drown me for a moment.

The moment I turn off the shower, steam rises from my reddened skin. I wrap a towel around myself and head toward my bedroom. Beside my bed, I lift the towel from around my waist and run it through my hair before dropping it to my feet. Too tired to worry about my clothes strewn through the apartment, I crawl into bed and cover myself with the sheet.

Every time I close my eyes, I think of that girl again. This isn't ideal. I don't need anything more stirring up my shitty brain.

But I can't stop myself. I think of her and the way she looked when she had her thumb in the wind and the defeated glint to her eyes as she asked a stranger for a ride and sealed her unfortunate fate. Though I try to keep that image of her in my mind, my brain would rather fabricate other images. Now she's topless, coming off the stage after a dance, and she's walking toward me instead of avoiding me. When I offer money to her, she doesn't recoil in disgust. She smiles and takes my hand, leading me toward the back.

My cock hardens to these dirty thoughts, and I rub my hand along the length of my dick, toying with the piercings on the underside of my shaft. My fingers graze the barbell in my frenum piercing, then stroke down to the lorum barbell at the base. Apparently I wasn't scarred enough and needed to add more.

I crush my cock in my grasp, sending a shot of pain through my groin. This is wrong. I shouldn't beat my dick to thoughts of her. I release my cock and put my hands above the sheet.

Don't even think about doing that. Whores are not worth my pleasure.

Ashamed of myself, I roll onto my side and force my mind back to thoughts of revenge. The whore doesn't deserve my come. She only deserves my wrath.

And I'll make sure she takes all of it.

Oaklyn

A crack runs through the center of the full-length mirror hanging from my bedroom door. The placement splits my reflection in half. In more ways than one, this is a fitting way to see myself. A broken woman stares back at me, the two halves not quite matching up.

I strip off my jacket and hang it on a hook in my barren closet. The cami comes off next, and my breasts relax as my arms lower to my sides. The tight, sweat-coated shorts cling to my skin, and I breathe a sigh of relief as I peel them away. After removing my stockings, I'm finally naked. It feels good to be exposed within the safety of my home, where no one can grope me with their hands or eyes. When I'm naked at home, I don't look like the woman at the club. I look like the person I am—a sad creature who misses her old life.

That's not entirely true. There are many parts of my old life that I wouldn't return to, even if someone held a gun to my head and tried to force me through a door to the past. My parents weren't supportive when I chose to pursue a career as a professional dancer, and I wouldn't want to relive any of the moments when they tried to talk me out of it. Soon the talking turned to a personal attack on my character. They couldn't understand the joy I felt when I prepared for a show and took the stage. They refused to support my dream of broadway lights and cheering crowds. Unable to see the merit in being part of an ensemble of talented individuals, they told me to call them when I failed.

Instead, a doctor called them to let them know their daughter's life hung in the balance. It was all downhill from there.

I push those memories from my mind, unable to relive them right now. Their vicious words still bite at me, even after all this time, and the man who drove me home didn't help matters. His attitude toward my current profession reopened those festering wounds. Despite what he said in the car, I'm not a whore. I haven't had sex with *anyone* since I started working at the club six months ago, and I've made a special point to sidestep all advances, especially those from Jake. If I could let go of my dignity and fuck him, I'd probably have a car by now. A few times with Jake and I could probably afford a better place to live, too.

I shouldn't say that.

The trailer was my grandma's, and she was the only person who still accepted me when she found out how I earned a living after my accident. She even let me move in. She died shortly after and left the trailer to me, much to my surprise. It's nothing fancy but it was hers, and now it's mine. I should be grateful I have a place to live at all, even if the power is finicky and the roof leaks every time it rains. My parents wanted nothing to do with me, though they viewed me as a failure long before I stepped into a pair of platforms and grabbed a pole.

My hands graze my thigh, rubbing over raised scar tissue. I started cutting long before my career ended, but I slashed shallow gashes into my hip instead of these deeper gouges on my thigh. The cuts on my hip hid behind my costumes, but when I had to change the sort of stage I danced on, I didn't care who saw my pain anymore.

I pull a razor from the nightstand and sit on the edge of the bed, rolling the glinting metal between my fingers. This will give me the release I need. Instead of turning to drugs or heavy drinking, I find comfort in creating an outlet for my pain.

It's been a while since I've cut, but as my life spirals out of control, it feels like the only logical thing to do. Maybe Jake will stop wanting to get between my legs if I paint them with blood and scars.

Blood and scars.

That makes me think of the man who gave me a ride home. He said his name was Ambrose, but I just keep thinking of him as "the man." He seemed more concerned about the marks on his skin than I was, and his definitely weren't self-inflicted. His haunting brown eyes appear in my mind, and I almost drop the razor. I recognized the emotion there. The anger. Everyone has a little anger in them, I guess.

I close my eyes and bask in the pain as my skin spreads around the metal. Warm blood rises within the wound and races down my leg in a steady trickle. I rub my hand through the blood and write the word *whore* on my pale skin. Just like the man who dropped me off said. Just like my parents believe.

In a way, I am a whore. Dancing and removing my clothes don't make it so, but I've been a whore for a long time. I sold myself for a dream, only to wind up in a nightmare. I'll wake up eventually, but not today. Tomorrow isn't looking too good either.

Chapter Five

Ambrose

Rain taps against my bedroom window as I sit on the edge of the bed and stare into the darkness. I'm not scheduled to fight tonight. Usually I'll go work the crowd and make some side cash when I'm not slotted for the ring, but my mind is on other things.

Like that girl from the club.

I've tried my best to think of anything other than her red hair and porcelain skin, but she invades my mind like a virus. Thoughts of her multiply at an alarming rate, overtaking rationality and making me feel sick. She's the vessel that will hold all my rage. I can't allow her to consume me. Without even trying, she takes bites of my sanity and spits them at my feet, chewed up and coated in saliva. I have to do something about this. These feelings need an outlet.

I grab my keys and jog through the rain until I reach my Jeep. The parking lot lights make the asphalt glisten like a black canvas with miniscule diamonds tossed across it. I pat my pocket when I sit behind the driver's seat, ensuring I have what I need, and a smile spreads across my face when I feel the little objects rattling against each other. This won't be as satisfying as choking the life out of her and running a blade across her skin until she comes to, but it's close.

After a short drive, I pull into the club's parking lot. When she comes out, I'll use the rain as an excuse. I'll say I just wanted to make sure she had a way home. Then I'll slip my little gift into her pocket or her bag when she isn't paying attention, and the mind fuck can begin.

I've decided it isn't enough to just kill her. Like a cat with an injured mouse, I want to toy with my prey before I rip out its entrails.

The clock on my dashboard marches toward midnight, and I worry I've missed my opportunity. Maybe she isn't working tonight. Maybe she's already gone home.

I don't enjoy the idea of stepping foot in that filthy club again, but my curiosity wins out and propels my feet toward the door.

I enter the dimly lit strip club, struggling to draw a breath when a heavy cloud of alcohol and cigarette smoke descends on me. The haze obscures the patrons and gives the illusion of secrecy. Music pulses in my chest, heightening my senses as I walk through the maze of dark corridors to get to the main floor.

I scan the walls. The vibrant mixture of crimson paint and gold accents creates a seductive glow on everyone inside, including myself. The place reeks of allure and temptation. I hate it. The flashing lights and gaudy colors only veil the evil inside this place. It disguises the flaws of the whores who creep along the floor like cockroaches searching for a crumb. Mirrors line the walls, reflecting fragmented images at me. Naked women writhe and grind, their glittering outfits casting bright rays of light at me. It's infinite. It's sickening.

A diverse cast of characters fills the dirty seats in the main room, from clean-cut businessmen to dirty old men. Actually, they're all dirty old men. Their hushed conversations and smothered laughter blend with the sultry melodies.

The bar along the back wall calls to me like a beacon of light. When the club environment chokes me, a stiff drink is my only source of oxygen. The prospect offers a momentary escape from the pain growing like a disease inside my body, but my sobriety nags at me. Instead of reaching for air, I search for a place to sit down and suffocate. Alcohol almost ended my fighting career, so now I force myself to stay sober.

I choose a seat near the entrance to the private rooms and the back of the building. An electric candle flickers in the center of the table, casting intimate light across my scarred face. I study the little device until I find its off switch, letting darkness wash over me when I snuff it out. I don't want to be seen for multiple reasons.

The stage is mesmerizing, even for someone like me. It's bathed in a spotlight that draws my eyes, and the crimson curtain separating the stage from the back area looks like a waterfall of velvet blood. I fixate on the woman swirling her hips in the middle of the main stage, but I don't watch her the same way as the other men. Hatred fills my gaze, not lust. Each sway raises my blood pressure and increases my heart rate. Plenty of shit stiffens on me as she removes her top and reveals her breasts—my jaw as my teeth clench, my fists as they form tight balls in my lap—but not my dick. Never my dick.

The whore finishes her half-hearted performance and leaves the stage with her money tucked inside her flimsy underwear. Generic rock music fills the silence as she exits through the curtain and by the end of the song, I'm ready to leave. I haven't seen my fire-haired target since I sat down, and I figure I've chosen the wrong night to begin my work.

Another song starts, and the curtain parts. Heads bob like buoys in the sea, all turning toward the woman stepping into the spotlight. She is a goddess among mortals. Oaklyn glides across the stage, her red hair cascading over her shoulders. My eyes lock on the sequined bra pushing her tits to her chin. I'd rather see them relaxed, but the bright, flashy fabric hugs her body and gleams with an ethereal light. She hardly looks real.

A cyclone of emotions tears apart my insides. The round muscles at the hinges of my jaw tighten until I'm certain they'll explode. Instead of titillating me, her beauty ignites a burning rage I struggle to control. She's tearing me apart.

This club is a theater of desire, where fantasies overtake reality. Where you leave your coat of morality at the front door and put it on when you leave, cloaking your naked desires once more. Though Oaklyn stands there in little more than her own skin, something about her doesn't belong. Unlike the other women who work here, she doesn't engage the crowd. I worried she might spot me, even after I shut off that stupid candle, but she doesn't even see us out here. As she grips the pole and leans back, she's lost to something else. We don't exist.

I observe her from my dark corner. The natural seduction that comes from seeing a beautiful woman's nearly naked form contrasts with the dark undercurrents born of my obsessive hatred. Within this intoxicating realm where sexy meets loathing, my obsession thrives, drawing me deeper into a game that blurs the line between sanity and madness.

A man near the stage leans forward and waves a handful of cash at her. With her eyes closed as she moves to the music, she doesn't even notice him. She slides down the pole and removes her top to an onslaught of hungry hands. The men reach for her breasts and thighs, and I envision breaking each finger that nears her body. A low growl rumbles in my chest, but I force my ass to stay planted in this cheap chair. I close my eyes and take a breath. When I open them again, I see my mother on that stage instead of Oaklyn. My fists clench into tight balls and drive my nails into my palm. The pain clears my head, and I can see clearly again.

But the anger and need for revenge have been renewed.

I stop focusing on Oaklyn's looks. Her beauty doesn't negate the rest of the deplorable shit in this place. It can't. I haven't spent most of the last thirty-five years of my life hating this club and the whores within it for something beautiful to come and lighten up the darkness I've shrouded it in. It's ugly and disgusting, and she can't change that.

Oaklyn's song ends. With a curl of my lip, I watch her grab the money from the floor. How degrading. Soon after she disappears into the back, another set of tits replaces her. No shortage of whores, I guess. This one is a haggard ghost, with dark, choppy hair that comes to an abrupt halt near her jawline. Black makeup circles her lids like it's trying to escape her watery eyes. She looks like she could be anywhere between twenty and thirty-five. The lifestyle seems to age them in weird ways.

I drop my gaze when I hear someone come out from the back area. I don't have to turn around to know it's Oaklyn; I can tell from her scent alone. Defeat with a touch of vanilla. When I'm sure she's walked past and won't notice me, I turn to watch her walk away. She's traded her heels for a pair of low tops. Interesting choice of footwear for a woman like her. A cami strap slips down her arm, and her shorts hug her ass. She drifts to the bar as if she has the weight of the club on her shoulders, then plops down on a leather stool. Her hand rises, and she flags down the bartender. I can't hear what she orders, but I know it's a Moscow Mule when the bartender delivers her drink in a copper mug.

Now that I know she's occupied, I can put my plan into place. I slip out the door without her noticing me—hopefully without *any*one noticing me—and look around the parking lot. I'll head to my Jeep and drive back and forth in front of the building until she steps outside and needs a ride, then I'll swoop in and leave her with a parting gift before she exits my car in front of her trailer. I get nearly to my vehicle when I hear a door open near the back of the building.

Curiosity gets the best of me and I turn around, spotting the dancers who were on stage before and after Oaklyn. The women walk with their arms hooked together. How chummy. As they climb into a car together, I wonder why these women never offer Oaklyn a ride home. Can they sense how different she is?

They back out of the parking lot, and my eyes swivel to the door near the back of the building. The door they conveniently left slightly ajar. With no one else in the parking lot to witness it, I walk toward a new plan.

The door creaks as I ease back the thick metal and peer inside. Seeing no movement, I take a step into the small room lined with mirrors, makeup, and lockers. My heart quickens as I imagine my mother back here, getting ready for her moment on the stage. Or getting railed by her manager. I wouldn't be surprised if that was my shitty origin story.

My eyes land on the heels Oaklyn wore on stage. They're tucked beside a desk, between the wall and what I assume is her area. I'm drawn to her property, entirely overcome by an intense desire to get my hands on her stuff.

My hand runs over the tabletop. A brush teeters on the edge, and I lift it and examine the red strands of hair woven through the bristles. A palette of green eyeshadow gleams up at me. Instead of coating her lids in darkness like all the other whores, she chooses a color that accentuates her eyes. I fucking hate how different she is.

Pictures of children and boyfriends adorn the other mirrors in the room, but her spot is devoid of any personal touches. It doesn't seem like anyone would even miss this girl.

Which is good.

A black bra hangs over the back of the chair. The sequins stitched into the stiff cups catch the fluorescent lights and shimmer beneath my fingers as they glide over the material. I lift the heels, dangling them in front of me like I'm holding a dead animal. They're just as disgusting. I hate these excessively tall and needlessly skanky shoes.

After sitting in her chair, I unzip my fly, pull out my cock, and hold it against the soles of her slutty stilts. I look back at the curtain that separates this room from the rest of the building and hope no one comes in as I stroke myself against the same material that's been against her skin. I don't know why I'm scared someone might come in. I probably blend in with the creeps that frequent this place. There's no way I'd be the first masturbating maniac they've had to chase from this room. And that's what I'll go with if someone catches me.

I'm just a crazy, crazy guy.

I stroke myself faster, trying to think about anything other than her full tits straining against that bra. My mind reaches for anything other than the way the light hugs the curve of her ass when she bends over and rocks her hips.

Fuck it.

Just because she's killable doesn't mean she's not fuckable too. I explode to some convoluted thought of squeezing her throat while the walls of her pussy squeeze my dick. Beads of come shoot into her heels, and I love that she'll step all over it the next time she slides her feet inside. I hope it's still wet and sticky. I hope she's disgusted.

I reach into my pocket and pull out one of the little gifts I've collected for her. After I place it on her desk, I zip my fly and make a hasty retreat. I'd give anything to see the look on her face when she discovers what I've done, but I can't risk getting caught. Not when I have so much in store for her.

Chapter Six

Oaklyn

Heads turn toward me when I step onto the bus. Some of the frequent flyers know what I do because they watch me get off at the stop in front of the club several days a week. A few keep their judgments to themselves, but I don't miss the curled lips and avoidance of the others. The old woman who likes to sit up front does her usual thing. She grips her massive carpet bag of a purse and places it beside her on the seat, silently telling me I can't sit with her. I wouldn't want to anyway. Her musty baby-powder perfume assaults me from here, and the tiny whiff makes my head hurt.

I choose an empty seat toward the back and stare through a dirty window. I hate riding the bus, but I wish it ran later at night so I had a reliable way to get home after work. The heavy scent of exhaust creeps into my nose and intensifies my growing headache. My workday is just starting, and I already have visions of crawling into bed and returning to sleep.

The bus pulls to a stop in front of the club, and I make my way down the center aisle without crying. It's a feat. I'm burned out, defeated, and my ankle aches like an absolute bitch. On top of all that, I have to do a walk of shame just to get on and off a bus so I can earn a few measly dollars while avoiding sexual assault for the rest of the night.

I can't take much more.

An invisible cloud of smoke drifts from the main room, and I can't understand why it's so hard for the other girls to remember to put on the goddamn fan when they come in for the early shift. I don't care if people smoke, but I don't want to smell it when I have a jackhammer pounding behind my right eye. It's also as hot as Satan's asshole in this room. I go to the window and flick on the shitty box fan.

As I turn toward my station, I pause. Something small and brown sits on my desk, right on the corner. It's some sort of nut. At least . . . I think it's a nut. I pick it up and look at it.

It's a fucking acorn.

"Ha, ha," I mutter under my breath. "You girls are so funny. How original to mock my name like this." They must have rubbed their two collective brain cells together for a week to come up with this shit.

I drop the acorn, and it rolls across the floor until it hits the wall. It can stay there and rot or grow a tree for all I care. I hope one of those bitches steps on it in bare feet. Better yet, I could slide it into one of their shoes to ensure they step on it.

But I don't. While it would feel good to give those catty bitches what's coming to them, I've never been a mean girl and I don't intend to start today.

I slip off my sneakers and pick up my heels. Something white and flakey coats the inside, and now I've moved from annoyed to pissed. I'm definitely being fucked with. I look around the room, trying to figure out who has whatever goo this is. Hair gel? Fucking glue?

Bitches.

The song before mine ends. I brush off my shoes to remove what I can, but it's really stuck to the material. Without another option, I slip them onto my feet with a grimace and pull off my jacket and sweatpants. I dressed for work before I left the house because the bus schedule conflicted with my call time.

Psh, call time. You can force the girl out of the theater, but you can't force the theater out of the girl.

I rush to the curtain just as my song begins. I chose a slower number today. My ankle has been giving me fits since the rain last night, and I don't want to strain it with a fast song that's loaded with tricks. I'll have to rely on the pole a bit more than usual, but my body needs a break.

Using my arms and thighs, I climb the pole, hook my leg around it, and ride down to the stage. I focus on the music instead of the incessant cat calls. I pretend I'm in the ensemble of a production of *Chicago*, my black silhouette cast upon an opaque wall in front of me as the leads sing about how horrible men are. What a treat for the audience.

I wouldn't have had to remove my top in a production like that, though. This is where the fantasy ends and it becomes harder to pretend I'm living my dream. This is no one's dream.

With my breasts fully exposed, I move closer to the edge of the stage and smile. The smile is fake, but even the ensemble needs to have acting skills. Per Konstantin Stanislavski, there are no small roles, only small actors. I wonder if he ever frequented strip clubs.

Probably not.

I purposely avoid scanning the crowd. What is there to see aside from unhappy husbands and misogynists? At least we get some young couples on the weekends. People who aren't so hard on the eyes. People who are desperate for a new experience, not these perverts who are only here to fill their mental spank banks.

But someone in the corner catches my eye.

The leather jacket looks familiar, and I swear I see bandages on his hands. The shadows shield him from view and the lights flashing over my face make it more difficult to make out details, but I think it might be the guy from a few nights ago.

I mentally shake my head. *Can't be. Can it?*

I spin around the pole and try to get a better look, but a man waves a bill toward me and begs me to focus on him. Needing money more than I need to satisfy my curiosity, I lean toward his outstretched hand and offer him a bright smile as I relieve him of his cash.

It's a twenty. Shit. Jake has rules for us by denomination. The more they pay, the more we must play.

I sit on the stage in front of the guy, spread my thighs, and tuck the twenty into the crotch of my panties. I bring his head down and let him snatch the money with his teeth. It's hard to control the roll of my eyes, but I manage. I lean over and take the edge of the bill between my lips, then spit it onto the floor behind me as I stand up. I don't let it touch my tongue. Not after it's been graced by God knows how many pussies, tits, and assholes.

The song ends and I look toward the dark corner of the club. The mystery man is gone. I must have imagined him or, at the very least, it wasn't the same man who gave me a ride. That guy would never set foot in a place like this.

I gather my money, leave the stage, and head toward the back. After stowing my money in my bag, I throw on my cami—sans bra because my tits need some air—and head out to the floor. We're allowed one drink per shift. Right now, with the taste of dirty money lingering on my lips, I need it.

I go to the bar and sit on one of the stools, and the fake leather grips the backs of my thighs. The bartender, a sweet girl who also dances on occasion, walks over to me. Her black hair wobbles on her head in a high ponytail.

"What can I get you, Oak?" she asks. She's not the usual bartender. If she was, I'm sure she'd know my drink.

"Moscow Mule." I reach toward the bar and touch her hand. "And make it strong, please."

She nods and rushes off. I notice something on the edge of the bar, so I lean toward it and pick it up. It's a fucking acorn. My mind goes back to what I found on my desk.

What the fuck?

Despite being named after the tree that produces them, I've rarely seen the things. Now I've seen two. In one day. In places they shouldn't be. This isn't a family park or a hiking trail; it's a goddamn sin den. I run my fingers along the acorn's rough top, wondering if it's even real. It is, and that's more concerning. Unless there is some weird shop that sells bags of acorns, someone has taken the time to collect these little things so they can leave them around for me to find. Then again, you can buy anything online.

Maybe it wasn't one of the girls after all. It's probably a man who's gotten obsessed after a dance. It happens more often than any of us care to admit.

Sudden realization hits me.

The white substance.

I fucking gag and snatch my heels off my feet. *Fucking pigs!* I toss the stupid acorn into the overflowing garbage can by the bar. I'd throw my heels out too if I could afford another pair. Since I can't, I'll just have to soak them in hand sanitizer.

The bartender places my drink in front of me, and I take a sip. Vodka punches the back of my throat and makes my eyes water. It cleanses my mouth and calms the panic in my chest at the thought of some man obsessing over me enough to come all over my heels. But that's part of the job. They pay me to be their obsession.

I nod my thanks to the bartender and down the drink to drown my disgust in the bottom of the copper mug. By the time the cup is empty, the liquor has worked its way through my body and I feel a little more at ease.

I carry my heels to the sink in the back and run scalding water over them. Each pass of my soap-covered hand over the material makes me see red. I feel fucking violated. What happened to creeps beating off outside your window while you undress? Now they come in people's shoes and leave fucking nuts lying around? Make it make sense.

Jake meanders around the back room, sexually harassing the others for once, and I wonder if he's the culprit who jizzed in my shoes. But that wouldn't explain the acorns. He's not smart enough to know they come from oak trees.

I sneak out the back before he can see me. I'm not in the mood to work the floor or shrug off Jake's advances. Even though I could be walking right into the arms of my weird stalker, I'm calmer once I'm away from the building. No matter what monsters lurk out here, it's better than staying inside to be preyed upon.

Raindrops hit the pavement in front of me, then the night sky opens and it begins to pour. Great. My cloth shoes absorb all of it until I feel like I'm walking on sponges as I head toward the bus stop to call for an Uber. The overhang shields me from the bulk of the rain as I pull my phone out of my jacket pocket. It's soaked too.

"Fuck," I whine.

Painted the color of a storm cloud itself, the silver Jeep slows to a stop in front of me. He rolls down his window, and I swallow at the sight of his face. Not the scars, though. The purple hue to his swollen bottom lip is what takes me by surprise.

"Your fight didn't go as well this time, huh?" I ask as I lean forward.

"This?" He rubs his lower lip. "The other guy looked much worse."

We stare each other down. My stomach tightens at the thought of accepting a ride from him again, but the cash in my pocket slaps back my hesitation. I didn't make very much today—the slower numbers usually don't—and I'm loath to part with any of it.

"Are you getting in or what?" he asks.

I look back at the club before opening the car door and getting into the passenger seat. As soon as I close the door, the air shifts with an electrified tension that isn't entirely uncomfortable. But it *is* weird. Is saving forty-something dollars really worth this risk? The moment when I opened his car door, it was. But now that I'm beside him . . .

I'm not so sure.

Chapter Seven

Ambrose

I can't believe she got into my Jeep again. What part of our previous interaction made that seem like a good idea? I said if I ever saw her again and she was stupid enough to get in my car, then I have no reason to hold back that demon inside me. But my plan disintegrates the moment I see how defeated she looks. She probably wouldn't fight me off if I tried to kill her right now, and that's no fun.

The scent of the club clings to her body and hangs like smog in the Jeep. She smells like sweaty old men and cheap perfume. Now it haunts my car, and no amount of air freshener will exorcize the stink from the upholstery.

My eyes glide over her body. Heavy makeup cakes her face, and the rain and sweat have smeared it in some places. Glitter glimmers on her chest, accentuating the curves of her breasts as they bulge above the neckline of her low-cut camisole. She's not wearing a bra, and her nipples press against the thin fabric and beg for my attention. My eyes roll downward, stopping at the tiny shorts over her fishnet stockings. A vision pops into my head. In it, I'm cutting those slutty, stringy stockings away from her skin.

I force my mind to shift the image to one where I'm cutting away her skin instead of her clothing. That's better.

I look away and throw the Jeep in drive, heading toward her home without saying a word. If I speak, I'll say something that will make her hop out before I can do what I need to do. As we travel in silence, my thoughts wander to how fragile her throat would feel in my powerful hands. Maybe I could cover her red hair with a blonde wig, further elevating my revenge fantasy. Make her look like the victim I need but can't have.

Thinking about her red hair was a mistake. Now I want to know what it feels like when it's wrapped around my fist as I force her pink lips over my cock and fuck her face. That thought hardens me, and I put my arm on my lap to hide it.

Guilt rolls in my gut because of my shameful erection. Despite being the beacon of sexuality, a whore like her shouldn't arouse me.

I hate that I want her. It pisses me off.

"Why do you do what you do?" I ask. My voice spears through the silence, and she's taken off guard by the abrupt question.

Her full lips spread as she tries to formulate an answer. "I need the money, and I was born to dance," she says, toying with the hem of her shirt.

"Born to dance on the laps of disgusting men?"

Her eyes widen, and her chest rises and falls as her breath quickens. "I . . . I . . ."

"No one is born to be a whore," I elaborate.

She scoffs, then finds her voice. "Until six months ago, I danced professionally. Not like this."

"Why'd you change streams? Seems like you'd want to go from a dirty pond to clear waters, not the other way around."

"It wasn't my choice," she says, her eyes staring out the window. "But I choose to dance, even if it's lewd. It's what I was made for."

Her words tempt the corners of my lips to rise, but I sober. No matter what brought her to that club, it doesn't negate the fact she's there. That she's one of them. She's tainted now, and no amount of soap can wash away the dirt and decay.

I force my eyes away from her and remind myself why I picked her up after watching her do her filthy dance. That evil side of me hungers to take my knife and rip her apart. Eviscerate her. Fuck her heart while it's still beating. Cover my imperfections with her skin. Wear her.

A low growl leaves my throat, and I hope she doesn't hear it. My hand drops to the knife between the seat and the center console, and I toy with the metal blade between my fingers. Killing her has become a fantasy—sick, twisted, and erotic as fuck. I'm close enough that one swipe of my arm could plunge the knife into her neck. It's exciting.

My eyes fall on her again. The sweet face attached to the body I want to desecrate gives me pause. I hate that she's a walking contradiction. Her clothes and body advertise her slut status, but that face . . . It makes me weak. I fucking *hate* being weak. Instead of lashing my anger outward, I internalize it. I boil myself alive.

I'm on fire.

I want to kill her. I need to. I never had the chance to make my mother pay for what she did to me, but I have the opportunity to send this whore in her place. The overwhelming desire is becoming harder to resist.

But tonight isn't right.

The buzz of doubt in my gut whips back the beast that wants to rip her apart and feed on her sin. How much longer can I deny its hunger?

Oaklyn

The air shifts between us, seeming to grow hot and stale. I try to ignore the heaviness as I shift in my seat. Why would he offer a ride when he seems to hate me so much? I should have told him no thanks and called an Uber.

Ambrose pulls his Jeep to a stop in front of my house. He doesn't even bother pulling into my driveway. He can't wait to dump me onto the concrete.

"Get out," he says. His taut muscles tense further as his fingers tighten around the steering wheel. The twist in his expression wraps a coil around my chest, squeezing until I can't draw a breath. Sweat beads along my hairline.

"You don't have to be a dick," I say as I pull my bag against my chest.

He scoffs. "Yes I do. Go."

Once I'm out of his Jeep, I slam the door behind me. Fuck him. I smack the passenger window as he slams on the gas and throws a thick spray of rainwater into my face.

"Dickhead," I mutter under my breath.

This shouldn't bother me. I deal with plenty of assholes when I'm at work, and my skin has thickened considerably because of it. But it does bother me. *He* bothers me. Something brews within him, and I certainly don't want to meet it head on. Even without adding his shit to the pile, I have enough darkness in my life.

Like the hands that explore my body despite the "no touch" rule. Or the boss that tries to assault me on a daily basis. Fucking Jake. Then there's the overwhelming sense of failure every night when I come home, and it's only made worse when I have to rely on the kindness of a man like Ambrose.

I won't allow him to take me home again, even if he smiles and asks nicely, I tell myself.

It's a lie. His obvious dislike for me grinds my gears, but I feel a weird pull toward him. Even with the scars on his face, I find him alluring and attractive. What the fuck is wrong with me?

When the spray of water settles, I peer into the darkness surrounding my trailer and throw my bag's strap over my shoulder. Trees tower over either side of the quaint single-wide, illuminated only by my weak-ass porch light. There aren't any streetlights out here. From the corner of my eye, a dark shadow stalks around the side of one of those trees. I'm probably imagining it—a fear unlocked after realizing some creep from the club is stalking me. Though I know it's probably not real, I can't stop the fear from climbing up my throat.

I rush toward my front porch and reach under the little decorative bench by the door, my fingers scrambling blindly for the key tucked beneath the seat cushion. Since I don't have a car, I don't see the need for a keyring. I also don't take it with me because I worry about what would happen if a creep from the club found my house key. Namely Jake. I can't imagine what that fucker would do if he could enter my house. Well, I can, but I don't want to. The thought makes my whole body shiver. I unlock the door and tuck the key beneath the cushion before going inside.

My grandma's small, manufactured home doesn't offer me much, but it's more than what I would have had if she hadn't taken me in. My parents have a sprawling four-bedroom home on several acres, but they pushed me out of their oversized nest when I chose to chase my Broadway dreams and pursue what I loved. Dancing was bad enough, but dancing for men? Too far. They cut off all communication when I made *that* choice.

My grandma loved me, though. She was so proud when I told her I'd aced my audition shortly before my accident. She was my only form of support, but she loved so hard that it was all I ever needed. When I told her my parents wouldn't help me after my accident because I'd chosen to dance at the club, she didn't bat an eye. She just helped me bring my things inside and said she was proud I wanted to keep working after what I'd been through, no matter where I worked.

But now she's gone, and I have no one.

I go to the bathroom, flick on the light, and wipe away the heavy mascara stains around my eyes. I never wear makeup like this because it shrinks my eyes and makes me look much older than I am. But "daddy" Jake wants us to wear our makeup a certain way. I'm his doll, and he wants to dress me up to his liking. It's the last thing I want to be, but what choice do I have? My aspirations become unreachable if I don't play along, and I refuse to give up. Buying a car is such a tiny goal, but it's one that I need for my own sanity. To show myself that I can do it. That I don't need to lie down for Jake to make it in this city.

I have other goals, but those are too lofty to reach for right now. They're hidden deep within my heart, buried so that I can't even see them. I know they're there, but having them at the forefront of my mind would destroy me. Like putting a five-course meal in front of a starving woman, I'd lose my mind if I focused on what I'll probably never have. But these dreams aren't impossible. I'd just have to start over somewhere else.

But to do that, I need a fucking car.

Chapter Eight

Ambrose

I sleep most of the next day and finally pull myself out of bed once the sun goes down. There aren't any fights tonight, so I have nowhere to be. No purpose. What else is new? After scarfing down some leftover Thai food, I sit in front of my computer and turn it on. The screen sends a splash of blue light across my face, illuminating my skin in the darkness. I don't fuck around on the computer often, but I have a very specific mission tonight.

To find out more about the girl from the club.

She made the mistake of giving me enough details to dig a little deeper into her background. While I don't know what I'm looking for just yet, I'm sure I'll figure it out as I go. And then I'll decide how to use it against her. The acorns were just the first step in my rousing game of mental tennis. There are many more heats to go.

I type her first name and our city into the search bar, but I only get articles about how the trees do in our climate. Maybe she hasn't been in this area long enough to draw any results. I'll have to try something else.

Oaklyn dancer.

Results populate, but it's nothing to do with the girl I'm looking for. I try again.

Oaklyn professional dance.

This search brings up a large, blue headline.

```
Professional Dancer's Career-Ending Injury
```

I click it and a news article comes up.

Alcohol contributed to the crash that cost a professional dancer her career this weekend. Jaws of life were needed to extricate Oaklyn Grey from . . .

My eyes move away from the words and fall on the image attached to the article. Stage lights shine on Oaklyn, but they aren't the seedy low-budget lights from the club. She's bathed in an actual spotlight as she's frozen in time with a look of sheer concentration on her face. Her arms lock in a graceful pose, stretching to the side as her torso defies gravity. One leg stands below her, the toe of her shoe the only point making contact with the ground. Her other leg stretches behind her and creates a nearly straight line from her foot to her shoulder. Red hair winds into a tight bun on her head, elongating her neck. A pale pink leotard clings to her skin, every curve of her body visible. While it provides more coverage than what she wears when she strips, it's somehow more alluring. Less isn't always more.

My mind places the image beside the woman I've seen with my own eyes—two distinct versions in two very different situations. The mental depictions merge until she straddles the line between two different worlds.

As I study the picture on the screen, I forget the dirty version of Oaklyn Grey and focus on this clean, beautiful creature before me. I've seen her nipples in person, but seeing the way they cast the slightest shadow beneath the fabric of that pink leotard hardens my dick in a way her straightforward nudity never did.

I look around the empty apartment before I lower my gray sweatpants and pull out my dick. My mind wanders, and I imagine this sweet, green-eyed creature in the crowd as I fight. She cheers me on and likes what she sees because I don't have any scars. In this fantasy, I look normal and she doesn't look like a whore. I stroke my cock to the idea of landing a winning blow and bursting through the crowd. Rushing straight for her, I toss her body over my shoulder and head toward the locker room so I can pound my post-fight energy into her pure cunt.

I run my fingers across the screen as I keep stroking myself with my other hand. I touch the juncture between her legs. The skintight fabric hugs her mound, and I envision spreading that material and using her until I've fucked the fight out of my body.

I tap the keyboard, and the printer beside my desk roars to life. After the wheels spin for what feels like an eternity, her picture slides onto the tray. I grip the warm paper with my free hand and place it below my dick. My hand strokes harder and faster to the person Oaklyn was before she became a whore.

I come, spilling beads of pleasure across her picture and smearing the fresh ink. As soon as I've ridden out the waves of release, anger brews in my gut. Hatred swirls with attraction. A need to kill her collides with a need to make her mine. I'm obsessed with the girl she was before she became what I hate. In more ways than one, her life is such a tragedy.

Now she's my tragedy, and she needs to pay.

Oaklyn

I'm running late for work, but it's not my fault the bus arrived fifteen minutes past its usual time. When I burst through the back door, a whoosh of humid air blankets my face. Would it kill Jake to turn on the air conditioner? He probably likes to see us covered in sweat.

One of the girls enters the dressing area and curls her lip at me. I'm accustomed to their bitchy attitudes, but that doesn't mean I don't get sick of it. I'm Jake's little obsession, and that doesn't sit well with them. They were his prior playthings until he moved on to someone else. Until he moved on to me.

She glances at the wall beside her and rolls her eyes. I follow her gaze to a picture taped to the painted concrete. A picture of . . . me? I step closer and recognize the image depicting the last time I looked happy. I looked alive.

My heart sinks into my stomach. This picture brings horrible memories to the front of my mind; it's the one the local news outlets plastered all over the internet after the accident. My ankle throbs while my heart aches to go back to the time in my life when nothing mattered but pursuing my lofty goals. Now my goals are sad. Pitiful. Pathetic.

Just like me.

I turn toward my station and find more pictures taped to the mirror. Tears threaten to stream down my face as I rip the long-forgotten images from the glass and crumple them in my fists. When crumpling isn't destructive enough, I shred them until I can't see my smile or my lively eyes. My arms and legs ache for the familiarity of those dance moves. They call to me like an old language I can no longer speak. An empty void remains where my heart used to beat as I'm forced to see how much my life has changed. I've been taken from the top of the world and driven beneath the soil. Now I'm rotting, decaying a little more every day. I breathe, eat, and sleep, but I'm dead inside.

The other dancer turns her nose up at me as she wraps her hair into a bun and heads for the floor. How the fuck can I step onto the stage and dance after seeing what my life was before it became what it is? Who the fuck is deranged enough to do something so cruel? One of these girls really wanted to hurt me by rubbing my reality into my old wounds, and I hate that they've won. Tears cloud my eyes, but I wipe them away before they can fall. They may have won, but I refuse to give them the satisfaction of seeing the pain cutting a path through my makeup.

Jake enters the dressing area and pauses at the picture taped to the wall. He's the last person I want to see, and he's definitely the last person I want looking at images of me in my element. He pulls the picture from the wall and runs his fingers over my figure.

"You look like a little Barbie," he says. "How did a Barbie like you end up on a pole?" The way he studies the picture sends a chill up my spine. His gaze shifts to me, and my lungs refuse to draw breath as he steps closer.

I turn away, but he doesn't stop until he's pressed against me with his hard cock grinding into my lower back. "Please, don't," I whisper, not wanting to draw attention from the front of the house by speaking louder and telling him off.

He crumples the picture in his hand. "That isn't you anymore, and it will never be you again. Accept what you are and stop fighting it."

Tears burn the backs of my eyes as his hands raise my skirt. He pushes my chest to the desk and throws the crumpled picture at my head. It bounces off the side of my face and rolls to a stop at my feet as he lowers his fly and pulls his dick from his slacks. Hungry fingers grope for the edge of my panties, then he pulls them aside with a grunt. I go to scream, but his sweaty hand covers my mouth and nose. My tears finally fall, lacing through his ringed fingers as he silences me.

He pushes into me and I drop my full weight onto the flaking black paint. My makeup smears. My vision blurs. I scream into his hand and beg him to stop, but nothing will deter him now. His sweat slips into my mouth and burns my lips. My stomach clenches and I retch. I consider opening my mouth a little wider and sinking my teeth into his hand, but I still need this job. Even after he does this to me, I still need this job.

The metal door behind us crashes shut and fills the room with glorious sound. I watch in the mirror as Jake panics and pulls out of me, rushing to put his cock back inside his cheap pants. His eyes search the room, then he rushes to the door, opens it, and peers outside. He must not see anyone, because he returns to me. I can only hope he's too shaken up to try again.

He leans over and brushes my tear-soaked hair away from my face. "I always knew that's how I'd end up inside you. You had so many chances to give yourself up your own way." He slaps my cheek three times before grabbing his gun from his office and rushing outside to hunt down the source of the interruption.

I lower my skirt and drop into the chair. My chest rises and falls faster than it should, and I'll hyperventilate and pass out if I don't regulate my breathing. I close my eyes and force myself to take controlled breaths. I've never been assaulted like that. Most of my life was spent in a cushy environment that kept me overprotected and far away from villains such as Jake. Now I've been abandoned by those who once shielded me, and I'm doing a piss-poor job of protecting myself.

This job blurs the lines of consent. People can reach out and betray every ounce of your personal space for a fucking dollar. Maybe ten if you're lucky. To people like our patrons and Jake, I'm just a thing to use.

I wipe away the tears and makeup stains, then slide my heels onto my feet. The thought of dancing tonight literally hurts my soul and sends phantom pains throughout my entire body, but if I'm still here when Jake returns, he'll finish what he started.

Whoever slammed the door saw what was happening to me and while I feel so many emotions, the one that prevails is embarrassment. What a stupid emotion to feel right now. Anger lurks somewhere in my mind, but the shame overwhelms it. Regardless, whoever it was, I'm thankful for them. Even though it was probably my nutty—in more ways than one—stalker. If I ever find him, I'll be sure to thank him before I call the police. That's if Jake doesn't find him and kill him first.

Chapter Nine

Ambrose

A cold sweat collects on my brow and slicks my palms as I pull my Jeep around the corner of the building. The back door flies open, but I don't stick around to see who opened it. I slide into traffic, then turn around and head back to the club. Pulling into a parking spot, I chuckle to myself. The greasy fuck who had his hands on Oaklyn stomps through the parking lot and peeks into cars, but he's too dense to realize the source of his outrage sits less than ten feet from him. As far as he knows, I've just arrived.

Emotions cyclone inside me, crashing into each other in a shower of sparks and chaos. The pictures I plastered around the dressing room netted the anguish I hoped for. As she ripped apart those little pieces of paper, her pain enthralled me and left me nearly breathless. Peering through the slender crack between the metal door and concrete wall, I could almost taste the torment, and it was fucking delicious. I wanted to hurt my little tragedy, and I did. I really did. But so did whoever the fuck that was inside that back room.

That's where my emotions and rationality collided, locking into a battle fiercer than any fight I've ever been part of. I loved every moment of the emotional catastrophe I created, but Oaklyn is *mine* to torture. That piece of shit had no right.

So I stopped him.

I shouldn't have, but my hands gripped the door and slammed it shut before my mind could register what was happening. Oaklyn is a whore, and she was getting the whore treatment she deserved. What my *mother* deserved and what I was probably born from. So why did it bother me so much?

Anger swells like a tidal wave inside me. It crashes against the destructive cyclone and turns my emotions into a tornadic waterspout. As much as it pains me to do so, I'm forced to admit that jealousy played a small part in slamming the door, but that wasn't what bothered me most. It was the face I saw in the mirror. It was the way her hands clenched into fists that couldn't fight back. She didn't want him to touch her, and that goes against everything I believe about her. If she isn't a whore, she isn't my target. I'll just need to wait a little longer before I make a decision I can't take back. I have to be sure.

I stare at the club entrance. The black doors call to me even though I never want to set foot in that place again. It's like walking up to a tragic car crash and knowing what I'll find as soon as I pry the doors apart. Deceptive agonal breaths may trick others into believing there are signs of life, but those women are already dead inside. They're martyrs for their chosen profession, willing to die for enough cash.

Pathetic.

I switch off the ignition and head inside, unable to stop myself from complying with the magnetic pull. I have to know the truth. I have to know if Oaklyn is who I believe her to be.

A large crowd packs the main floor, which isn't surprising for a Friday night. I blend in with a sea of other men. We become faceless to the women on stage, I'm sure. These men are an ocean of skin, ebbing and flowing with cash, and the dancer on stage is the moon, pulling them toward her by an unseen gravitational force. I'm not one of them. I'm a goddamn island, and I won't be moved.

The sensual music fades as the dancer ends her show, and generic pop music filters through the rising sound of conversation and drink orders. The whore cleans up the cash littering the stage, then rushes through the curtain with her earnings. A hefty bouncer climbs the riser on the lip of the stage and wipes at the pole with a rag, though I don't see the point. The stained piece of cloth appears just as soiled as the pole itself, if we're being honest here.

I sit up in my seat when I see the signature red hair bobbing through the crowd. I expected her to appear on stage, to dance for me, even though it's not for me at all. She's probably too shaken up by what happened earlier and chose to work the floor instead of performing. If that's the case, she needs to put on her game face. No one will request anything from her with her lips drawn down in a permanent frown. Then again, they aren't paying to stare at her mouth, and a man proves that point when he waves his hand and flags her down.

The frown dissipates and a smile slips into the vacancy it leaves behind. Either she's a very good actress or a very good whore. Maybe she just disliked the guy in the dressing room and this guy is more her speed. A whore can still be choosy, I suppose.

Her full breasts spill from her skimpy top and rest on the man's shoulder as she eases her ear toward his mouth. A renewed rage floods my system.

I regret helping her earlier. I had it right the first time.

She's a whore.

After a nod of her head, she grips his hand and leads him toward the back of the building. The private dance section. The place I've never been led to like that. I stand out of instinct, my feet determined to follow them behind that velvet curtain, but the bouncer standing at the doorway to the promised land makes me think twice. They let people get away with a lot of shady shit around here, but there's no way he'll let me into that area without a whore on my arm.

A strung-out blonde fumbles past me, and I take a step toward her and grab her wrist. Maybe the copious amount of alcohol running through her system will blur my scars. She smells like she bathed in Everclear. If someone lit a match in her vicinity, she'd likely become a human Molotov. The image puts a smile on my face, which is good since I want her to see me as likable enough to take into the private area.

She turns to face me, but her deadened blue eyes seem to glare straight through me.

"I need a private dance," I tell her.

She stumbles and licks her lips, her lids dropping and rising again in the slowest blink I've ever seen. When her eyes pinch together in a tight squint, I know she's finally focused enough to see me because her muscles tense.

Yeah, I know. I *know*. I'm fucked up, but I'm not the worst looking guy in this place.

If I'm being honest, however, she may be the worst looking girl in this place. With her stringy blonde hair and the stink of desperation and one-too-many oozing from every pore, she should be glad I've even asked for her company.

This realization appears to dawn on her as well because she gives a slow nod before taking my hand and leading me toward the curtain over the doorway. The bouncer waves us in, seemingly oblivious to her inability to make safe decisions in her current mental state. Actually, he probably doesn't care. He doesn't get paid extra to be a voice of reason, after all.

The moment we cross the threshold, the ambience shifts. Instead of body odor and aftershave, I'm engulfed in a cloud of vanilla and spun sugar. The floor stops fusing to my shoes in a sticky death grip. Low lights set the mood, and soft music plays overhead as the thumping bass from the main floor becomes a distant memory. This is the money room.

Tall partitions separate the space into four separate sections, probably to keep others from stealing free glances. This is very much a pay-to-play area. Purple curtains drape from brass rods above each doorway. Three are open, but the one on the very end has been pulled shut.

Found you, tragedy.

The woman on my arm guides me to the first booth, but I keep walking toward the one on the end. Too drunk to argue, she follows. We reach the third sex stall and step inside, and she nearly rips the curtain down as she stumbles while closing it. The blonde zombie rights herself, regaining what little composure she has, then stumbles toward me. I have absolutely no interest in a dance. I just needed to get back here. In the same room as *her*.

Because I'm not done hurting her yet.

I want to break Oaklyn's soul before I break her body. It will make my revenge that much sweeter when I finally end her.

The blonde turns around and puts her ass on my lap, doing her best to grind against me in the least graceful fashion I've ever seen. She spins around and her arms flop over my shoulders like two dead fish. When her sour breath infiltrates my nose, I've had enough. I grip her chin between my fingers and squeeze to keep her head from wobbling. She whimpers, taken off guard by my rough touch.

"Get out," I tell her through gritted teeth.

She stops her pathetic grinding and blinks a few times as her eyebrows pull together. "You can't be back here without me." The words come out slurred together, and it takes me a moment to work through the mushy syllables.

"Make up an excuse. Go get me a drink or something."

"But . . . but you told me you'd buy a dance."

I pull out a stack of bills and hand them to her. "You're paid. Now get the fuck out."

That seems to satisfy her need to follow the rules, and she finally climbs off my lap. "What do you want to drink?" She's not the brightest in the bunch, and I don't think she can pin that on the alcohol.

"I don't actually want a drink. I want you to get your drunk ass out of this booth, and I'll be gone before you get to the bar."

"Okay," she whispers, walking out on wobbly legs with the wad of money clutched in her dirty fist.

The moment she closes the curtain behind her, I exit my booth and hover outside of Oaklyn's. Soft moans filter through the purple fabric hanging inches from my face. She's clearly faking her arousal, but the dude beneath her probably believes every fabricated sound that leaves her perfect lips. I need to know what she's doing. I need to see it for myself so I can throw more meat to the angry beast snarling in my gut. Feeding my anger will strengthen my resolve. Seeing her for what she is, what she *truly* is, will banish any doubt from my mind.

I turn on my phone's camera and aim the lens through the crack between the curtain and the doorframe. When I see her pale skin captured within the frame, I look away. I can't watch what she's doing to him. Not right now. If I look at that screen, I won't be able to stop myself from rushing in there and beating them beyond recognition, and that isn't part of the plan. I record for as long as I can before I get the fleeting feeling that I need to get the fuck out of here. I tuck my phone into my leather jacket and rush out of the club.

The moment I slide into the safety of my Jeep, the phone and its secret video begin burning a hole in my pocket. I pull out the device and stare at the dark screen. Unable to wait until I get home, I push play and hope I captured what I need.

Black panties flash before my eyes, the thin material hardly covering her pussy. I must have bent my wrist a bit while recording because the camera angles away from her lower half and focuses on her tits in some dude's face. She swings her deep red hair off her shoulder, giving the camera a glimpse of her face. I pause the video and stare at her. My gaze moves from her half-closed eyes to the seductive way she's biting her lower lip. She almost looks like she's enjoying it. It's seductive and slutty. It's vile.

And it's making me hard.

I'm not aroused by what I see before me, though it's arguably one of the sexiest things I've ever seen. I'm aroused by the idea my mind has conjured while watching Oaklyn whore herself out—a new step in the plan to bring about her demise.

Lost inside a mental maze of nervous energy, I drive home. It's similar to what I feel before a big fight, when all the tension grows inside me and seeks an exit. A release. I've come up with an outlet for this feeling, and the explosion will be euphoric. The destruction will rival goddamn Hiroshima. The drive home is a blur, and I don't even care about the glares and sideways glances as I jog through the parking lot and head for my front door. Let them get a good look tonight. I'm too excited about what I plan to do to give a single fuck about their judgment. Once I'm inside, I connect my phone to the computer and begin porting the video over to my hard drive.

I dabbled in a bit of video editing not long ago when Darby wanted me to cobble together a few promos to draw interest online. Putting my recently acquired skills to work, I craft a clip that shows Oaklyn in all her dirty glory, complete with slowed shots and closeups of her face so there is no denying the veracity of what this video contains. I consider throwing some cliche porno music over the top to really sell it, but I want the recipient of this video to take it seriously. I want them to hear each moan and sigh that comes from Oaklyn's filthy mouth. As a final touch, I throw a clip art acorn into the corner. Like a serial killer, I've developed a signature, and I want my name on my work.

I craft a burner email account, find the recipient's email address, and send the video on its merry way. Energy and anticipation brew and bubble inside me, coming to a rolling boil as I envision the ripple of repercussions this will cause my little tragedy. I rip my pants open, not able to wait a second longer to spill my load to her impending misery and unequivocal embarrassment.

I click on the attachment after I send it, filling my screen with Oaklyn's body. Fantasies of her devastation fuel each stroke. I only wish I could be there to see her face when she gets the call or the text or the email once her dirty little secret has been pushed into the light of day. Disappointment is too weak for what they'll feel when they see it.

I stroke myself faster.

And I come to her misery.

When I finally reach hell one day, what I have done will have me sitting on Satan's lap like he's Santa. But this is just the beginning. I have so much planned, and it's only going to get better from here. Well, better for me. For Oaklyn, it will be much, much worse.

Chapter Ten

Oaklyn

The worst part about being assaulted at work by your own boss? Facing him every day afterward. At least he hasn't tried to proposition me again, which I'm glad about, even if I don't understand what changed. Maybe he's moved on to one of the fresh-faced eighteen-year-olds who doesn't have a care in the world. Those impressionable young girls probably enjoy his attention. Puke.

Speak of the devil, Jake slinks into the dressing room as I'm sliding my arms into my jacket so I can get the fuck out of here. "You had a good night tonight," he says, as if congratulating me on a winning game.

I have nothing to say to him. I don't even want to look in his direction and give him the satisfaction of my undivided attention. He doesn't deserve to breathe the same air, so I grip the door handle.

His hand shoots toward me and wraps around my arm. "No hard feelings, right?"

The casual lilt to his voice ping-pongs inside me, and it takes every ounce of strength to keep my composure. No hard feelings? I have the hardest of fucking feelings. He's lucky I need the job. If I didn't, I'd punch him straight in the throat and then stomp on his dick when he's on the ground. The idea brings a smile to my face, and I guess he takes that as "no hard feelings" because he releases me and leaves.

I throw my bag over my shoulder and escape into the warm night. A truck rumbles by, and a cloud of oil smoke explodes from the exhaust, ruining the clean air. My chest seizes when I try to draw a breath. I'm so sick of this dirty city. Filth greets me everywhere I turn and no matter how many showers I take, I never feel clean. I long for the life I lived before the accident, before I made a stupid decision that upended my soul. If I had a time machine, I would go back to the night of the cast party and beg myself to get a cab or an Uber.

But I can't think about any of that. Time machines aren't real. This miserable life is my reality, and I need to stop wishing for the impossible.

I pull out my phone to call for an Uber, but a glint of silver in the distance catches my eye, and I lower my hand. The familiar Jeep pulls in front of me with perfect timing, and the window begins to lower.

"You need a ride?" he asks.

I nod. I don't know why I keep torturing myself by getting into a vehicle driven by a man who finds my line of work so beneath him, but here we are. Doing it again. Fear of assault is the furthest thing from my mind because I doubt he'd let his dick anywhere near me for fear of picking up all the STDs I don't fucking have. I fear his disappointment more.

What the fuck is wrong with me?

Probably a lot.

I should be more concerned that a stranger would assault me, but I've only been assaulted once in my life, and he wasn't a stranger. He was the most familiar person at my job.

I lean over to fasten the seat belt, and he pulls away from the curb without looking at me. He doesn't even speak. Honestly, I don't mind the silence. I'm embracing it after the deafening din inside the club.

My phone chimes and I pick it up. A name comes across the screen that I haven't seen in a while: Mom. My stomach rolls against my insides, and I grit my teeth to bite back the nausea creeping up my throat. Since I announced my intent to attend a school of dance instead of medical school, she's only texted to let me know when someone has died. I have no grandparents left, so that only leaves my dad. Though we're estranged, he's still my father, and I don't want him to pass away before we've had a chance to reconcile. I've tried in the past. I've reached out. And I've been met with an unending silence.

Moving my dry tongue across my lips, I open the alert and scan the text.

> Do you not have a shred of dignity left in you, Oaklyn?

This message sends me into another sort of panic, denying me the sigh of relief my body craves. She argued her point about the frivolity of dance for months. She spent less than a week cursing the day I was born when she found out I had turned to stripping. What else have I done to earn her disapproval?

> What are you talking about?

> Don't act naïve. I got an email from you.

> I haven't sent you an email.

The furious tap of my fingers across the keyboard and the pings of response fill the silence in the Jeep. I'm so fucking confused. I've made as much effort to contact her as she has made to contact me. I have *not* emailed her.

She sends a screenshot of an email, and I blink a few times when I see the sender's address. That's my name, but that isn't my email.

Another screenshot follows, this time showing a still frame from a video. I can't deny this one.

It's me.

Giving a lap dance.

With my bare breasts shoved into a stranger's face.

My hand flies to my mouth, and I suck air through my nose to calm the explosion of panic inside me. I'm a firework store, and someone has just lit a fuse in the building. I'm imploding. I spot the acorn in the bottom right corner of the screen, and I realize who has struck the match. My stalker. It has to be. He went from coming in my fucking shoes to ripping open old wounds and pouring rubbing alcohol over the raw flesh. He held a flashlight to the keyhole in my closet and exposed my skeletons to my family. Though they know what I do, they've never had to see it firsthand.

An invasion of heat scorches my cheeks. My stomach rolls again, and my abdomen lurches inward. A cold sweat pops onto my brow and lower back. I want Ambrose to pull over so I can vomit what I just saw onto the side of the road, but I don't want him to ask any questions. How would I even explain that my mother just saw me shaking my breasts in some old guy's face? Or the stalker who's hell-bent on destroying what little sanity I have left?

As I dangle on the verge of hyperventilation, the voice from the driver's seat cuts through the darkness.

Ambrose

"What's the matter?" I ask. Bright red patches paint her cheeks and chest, and she dry-heaves behind the hand pressed over her mouth. I pull to the side of the road. Not in my fucking car.

She just shakes her head, her hand glued to her face. The wheezy gasps through her nostrils slow, and she finally speaks. "I got a text from my mother, that's all."

My stomach tightens, and I swallow so hard that I can hear the click of my throat. No fucking way. No. Fucking. Way. "Is everything okay?" I ask.

I know it isn't. Her world is a glass globe that has been flung from a skyscraper, and I'm here to witness the glorious destruction as it collides with the concrete and shatters at my feet. What are the chances her mother would respond to my email while she's in the car with me? Probably about the same as the chances of a baby surviving the onslaught of a psychotic, knife-wielding mother, and I beat the fuck out of those odds. Maybe I'm lucky after all. I should go to goddamn Vegas after this.

Invisible steam rises from her palpable anger, and I take a deep breath and inhale it into my lungs. I would strip to nothing and bathe in her torment if I could, but then I'd never see her again. And I need to see her again. I have so much more planned for her.

She wipes away the tears that have slid down her cheeks and collected on her chin, and that's such a waste. I want to drink them. "It's this fucking asshole from work," she says. "He's doing crazy shit to me."

Not many stalkers get to sit in the car with their stalkee and listen to them bitch about the stalking. They don't get to hear the anger and disgust lacing every heated word. My cup runneth over. "Care to elaborate?" I prod.

I want to hear more.

I want to hear everything.

Give it to me, Oaklyn. Tell me how evil and horrendous I really am. Tell me how my actions made you feel.

She shakes her head. "No."

Way to ruin the fun, tragedy.

She swallows. "I'm just going to go home and hate myself more than I already do."

Do I want her to go home and hate herself for what I've done? Yes. Absolutely. I want her to eat, sleep, and breathe this feeling for the rest of her days. I only wish I could keep watching once she leaves my car. I'll just have to log her look of despair for later.

A seedling of guilt struggles to spread its thready roots in the soil of my heart, but I crush it beneath my heel. Everything that's happening to her is *her* fault. If she hadn't chosen this disgusting profession—the same line of work my mother chose —this wouldn't be happening. I wouldn't be obsessed with a person I want to kill and fuck in equal measure.

Satisfied she won't soil my interior with her puke, I pull away from the curb and continue toward her trailer. I don't rush to get her home, though. I take my time. Every second she's in my car is a second longer I can enjoy her pain.

I get an idea. I want more access to her, and I know how I might achieve that.

"Maybe I should give you my number," I say. "It's probably not a good idea for you to hang around outside that club at night while you wait for a ride. Anytime you need a lift, you can give me a call and I can come get you. Your stalker might think twice if they see a man picking you up. Kind of like how girls do at the club when they pretend they have a boyfriend to get the creeps at the bar to leave them alone."

She nibbles at her bottom lip and stares at the phone in her hand, running her thumb along the screen. "Okay," she finally says.

That was easy. I give her my number, and she punches it into her phone. I expect her to send a text so I have her number as well, but she doesn't. That's okay. The fish has nibbled the bait, and it's only a matter of time before I sink the hook into her jaw.

"Thanks," she mumbles. Her gaze shifts to the window, and I bask in the despondent way she peers into the darkness rushing by outside. Her sadness is like sunshine.

I'm miserable when I see her porch light break through the shadows in the distance. All good things must come to an end, but like a spoiled child who doesn't want to wait in line for another turn on the slide, I'm annoyed. I want more. And I want it now.

As she climbs out of the car and trudges to her front door, I'm struck by another idea. It's incredibly risky and could crash the plane before it even leaves the runway, but I'm on a hot streak. I peel away from her driveway, my courage building inside me at a rapid rate. My dark eyes narrow to slits, not seeing anything through the windshield as I turn the Jeep around. A sly smirk spreads on my face.

Yeah. I'll take my chances.

Chapter Eleven

Oaklyn

I grab the key from beneath the bench cushion and step inside as he drives away. He's such a confusing man. He didn't berate me like he normally does, instead choosing to be almost . . . supportive? But I don't have time to sit and wonder about the bipolar stranger who opted for kindness tonight. I'm still focused on the screenshot my mom sent me as I pull a bottle of vodka from the kitchen cabinet. The events of that lap dance rush through my mind with a clarity that turns my stomach. I know what she witnessed.

My actions.

My sounds.

His sounds.

Oh god.

I need a drink, but I need a shower first. While I usually feel dirty after work, knowing my mother has seen me grinding on a man makes me feel absolutely filthy. A hot shower won't do shit to scrub the feeling away, but I sure as fuck plan to try. I place the vodka on the island in the kitchen and scurry to my room, stripping away my sin-laced fabric at the door. When I kick off the last piece of clothing, I feel a bit better. Until I look at myself in the mirror.

Black mascara and eyeliner ring my eyes, reminding me who I am. Who I can't run from. The girl whose breasts bounced in some old guy's face while a stalker videoed the whole ordeal from the shadows. The girl whose mother saw it all.

God, I'm sickened.

If she didn't hate me before, she definitely does now. I don't know how she could believe I sent it to her. Clearly it's someone out to hurt me. Shouldn't she show an ounce of concern? I'm still her daughter, after all.

But I guess that's not entirely true. Her daughter is dead to her. She buried me when I didn't choose a career she could brag about to her rich friends. Any concern she feels isn't directed toward my safety. She's probably only worried my unautho-rized porno will end up in the hands of someone in her social circle. God forbid I become the topic of the gossip mill during brunch.

I turn on the shower and run my hand beneath the water, ready to wash away the grime of the day. The touches. My shame. Not even scalding water would be hot enough for that. I step over the lip of the tub and shut the curtain. With closed eyes, I tilt back my head and let the heat massage my scalp, then part my lips beneath the stream and let it fill my mouth. I scrub my skin until it's red and raw. After plopping a healthy dollop of shampoo into my palm, I wash a pound of product from my hair and rinse myself off. The water slows to a trickle once I flip the handle, and the pipes rattle within the wall. I get out and towel my hair, then wrap the damp fabric around my body. These mundane tasks don't cleanse me of everything, but they wash away enough to allow me to feel a little different for a while. I'm a little normal, giving me some space from the line that separates me from my life before the incident.

Sometimes after a good shower, I indulge myself and pretend I'm preparing for a big show. I'll wake up in the morning and head to a rehearsal that will last for hours. My fellow cast members will watch as I practice my solo. They'll cheer me on when I land a flawless cabriole.

When I look down at my discarded clothes, it thrusts me back into my reality. My ankle couldn't withstand hours of rehearsal time, let alone a cabriole. I'll never prepare for a show again. Well, not that kind of show. No one cheers me on as I perform. It's just me, myself, and I, and we all hate our life now.

I step into my pajama pants and pull a black cami over my chest. My legs run on autopilot and guide me to the vodka bottle that sits on the island. The cap twists right off, and I pour a hearty dose into an old plastic cup. I tilt back my head and swallow it in one smooth gulp. Some people hate the taste of vodka, but I love it. It's the first alcoholic beverage that my mother let me drink. She always used to say she'd rather I drink responsibly at home than anywhere else.

I hate how right she was.

If I'd stayed home that dreary fall evening, my life would be so different. My fantasy of preparing for a show would be my reality. I'd have gone to bed two hours ago so I could rest up. I'd be happy instead of miserable. My life would still be the one I had molded since I was a little kid.

From the time I was small, I knew I would carve out my future in a pair of dance shoes. If my mother had known what an impact those dance classes would have on me, she wouldn't have ferried me to so many of them. She wouldn't have sat in the audience and beamed with pride during my first solo. When I made a B in sixth grade science, she threatened to take away those dance classes because she thought I was destined for greatness in the medical field. I never made less than an A- after that, but it had nothing to do with a drive to follow in my father's foot-steps. I was more inclined to binge films starring Ginger Rogers than a marathon of *Grey's Anatomy.*

This is called a sign, Mom.

I toss back another shot and wipe my nose. The alcohol opens my sinuses, soothing the inflammation from hours spent in a smoky room. An emptiness fills me as I turn the bottle in my hand. Loneliness creeps up on me like a cat in a dark hallway, weaving around my feet and sending me to the ground. Or maybe it's always there and I just don't acknowledge it. Yeah, that's probably more accurate.

I have no friends. People who I considered friends hung around my hospital bed for a while after the accident. They brought flowers. They offered condolences. Then our paths split. The song didn't end for them. They had a stage to return to while I struggled through rehab and depression. I learned to walk on my busted ankle, but I never got over the unending sadness. Even the girl who I considered a close friend—the girl who walked away from the accident with bruises instead of broken dreams—hasn't reached out for months. I wonder what she's been up to . . .

I pull out my phone as the alcohol nestles into my gut. There's a warm glow inside there, and I find myself feeling drunk after only two shots. It's probably because I haven't eaten since lunchtime.

I flop onto the couch and search for any news about the girl who drove the car that fateful night. A few articles pop into the feed, but they make me feel worse instead of better. She's currently touring with a show. Good for her.

My head drops onto my closed fist, and it feels like I'm holding up a giant stone. My whole body feels heavy, actually. Disconnected. The hand holding the phone trembles under the insignificant weight, and a dizziness overtakes my brain. A rolling blackout barrels toward me.

What. The. Fuck.

Since when have I ever gotten drunk from such a small amount of vodka? Tipsy, sure. But this? This isn't a buzz; it's a clap of thunder on repeat right beside my ears.

I lie back, letting the couch cushion's synthetic fibers caress my back. The moment my head hits the balled-up blanket behind my head, the whole room spins. Hard. My stomach clenches, but the overpowering exhaustion trumps the discomfort. My heavy eyelids refuse to stay open, but my chest is heavier, as if there's a weight above me. Becoming one with me.

I release my body's tension as it fights the desperate need for sleep. Then I give in.

Chapter Twelve

Ambrose

Oaklyn's hand falls from the couch and sends her phone to the floor. I back away from the window, unable to contain the smile on my face because my impromptu plan has gone off without a hitch. Originally, I thought I would just lurk outside her bare windows and watch her sadness unfold, but when she brought out the vodka bottle and left it unattended while she took a shower, I knew she'd be back for it. Using the key she keeps under the bench cushion, I let myself in and dropped a little surprise into the bottle. I would hardly call it breaking in, though. She practically asked for me to come inside when she so blatantly showed me where the key was. Now I can snoop to my heart's content while she sleeps.

An odd silence greets me when I step inside, and I'm shrouded in a sense of unease. When a stranger enters someone's home, a symphony of screams and breaking glass should announce their arrival as the homeowner tries in vain to steer the intruder away from their safe space. It's so quiet in here I could hear a mouse piss on cotton.

Shaking off the eerie feeling, I creep through the attached kitchen and enter the living room. I want to rummage through her closets and drawers to find all her dirty secrets, but I'm drawn to her body. It pulls me with the same magnetism she possesses when she's dancing, but for a different reason. She looks so fucking clean. Innocent. Little cats dot her pajama pants, and the strap of her black cami hangs off her shoulder. Her bright red hair looks almost brown because of the water still clinging to the straight strands. I miss the red waves.

My fingertips move toward her, itching with a need to feel her skin. She'll be soft. So soft . . .

I pull my hand away. I need to do what I came here for.

Her bedroom is at the very back of the house. The bathroom stands right beside it, and its open door allows the mouth-watering scent of her shower to fill the back-side of her home. I peek inside, but continue to her bedroom when I don't see anything of interest.

My lips form a tight line as my gaze falls on her unmade bed. Rumpled blankets and random pillows lie across the mattress. How does she not feel like her mess of a life isn't more so when she climbs into this travesty each night? I roll my eyes.

After scanning the rest of the room, I stop at the closet door. When I open it, it's just as messy as her bed. I flick the racks down the rod and find a few nice shirts, but most of the options are skanky and scandalous. The nauseating amount of sequins and glittering fabrics burns my eyes. And fuck me, they stink. Not even an acid bath could rid them of the stench of that club. I rip down every shirt and bra set that has so clearly been designed to display her body. My knife blade emerges with a flick of my wrist, and I slice through the fabric. Straps, sequins, and clasps fall to my feet in a heap of glorious destruction.

She'll have nothing to dance in tomorrow. I cut the whore off at the head.

I spot a garment bag near the back of the closet and pull it into the light. I unzip the side of the bag and remove its contents: a pale pink leotard and a tutu. The leotard is familiar. It's the same one she wore in the photo attached to that article about her. My hand reaches for the blade I've tucked back on my hip, but I stop myself. Cutting this into pieces would probably hurt her, but I know what would do even more damage to her psyche.

I take a hanger from the closet and use it to attach the leotard to the back of her bedroom door, right over the mirror. She's sure to see it here. When she does, it will be another reminder of her fall from grace.

I toss the empty garment bag on top of the destroyed slut suits and make my way to her dresser. Makeup and hair products litter the smooth wooden top. More mess. Pulling open a drawer, I discover a treasure trove of panties. My fingers run through the river of lace, silk, and mesh in search of something more alluring. I find what I seek near the bottom—a pair of simple cotton panties that are more akin to shorts than the stringy offerings surrounding them. I imagine the way the fabric would hug the curve of her ass, hiding more than it shows. Nothing slutty about these panties. I tuck them into my pocket.

Finding nothing of interest in the remaining drawers, I return to the living room to bid farewell to my target and leave her a parting gift. As I kneel beside the couch, I notice her phone beside my foot. I pick up the device and turn it on. It asks for her fingerprint, which is easy enough. I press her limp thumb against the screen, and it springs to life.

To the gentle sound of each breath rolling past her parted lips, I scroll through her texts, reliving the turmoil she experienced in my car. I swell with pride over the bitter anger woven through her mother's words—venom meant to maim. If she didn't like her daughter before, she probably hates her now.

I close the text message screen and open the internet browser, immediately pulling up an article about a theater production. Scanning the text, I spot a familiar name, though I can't place it. Then it dawns on me. This is the girl who caused the accident that sidelined Oaklyn. It looks like my plan has worked better than expected. She's been digging at her own wounds.

Guilt nibbles at my insides, but I ignore it. I have no reason to feel guilty. She's not worth it.

I read the text messages one more time to remind myself of the joy this brings me, then I place the phone on the coffee table and turn my attention to her. She looks so sweet compared to how she looked in that video. Without the makeup, the deadness in her eyes, and the slutty fucking outfits. When she can't make those whore noises. I breathe in her scent. It's nothing like the club. It's fragrant, almost fruity. My fingers wind through her hair, parting the silky strands. Having dried, they've taken on the red glow again. My cock hardens against my zipper.

I swing her arm over my shoulder and lift her from the couch. She doesn't stir and if it weren't for the gentle rise and fall of her chest, I'd wonder if she were dead. A wobbly bar stool nearly tips over as I carry her toward her bedroom. I catch it with my foot and right it before it hits the floor. When I reach her bedroom, I lay her on the strewn blankets and sit beside her. I don't intend to fuck her, though. I intend to kill her.

Her skin—just as soft as I imagined—presses against my knuckles as I bring the blade to her throat. I could end her so easily right now. But it'd be *too* easy. She wouldn't fight or flail or feel any of the gashes I'd paint on her flesh. She'd be as innocent as I was when my mother attacked me. I thought I'd like the ease of her being asleep, but it's not what my little black heart wants.

It's just not enough.

Or maybe that's just what I'm telling myself.

Ending her shouldn't be this difficult for me, but I find a reason to stay my hand at every turn. Something about her makes me reconsider. What is it?

I study her face and lean over to brush the hair from her cheeks. Warm skin meets my fingertips. Thick lashes frame the seams of her eyelids. If they were open, would I see the dead stare she wears when she's in the club? Or would they come alive?

Every breath raises her chest before letting it fall once more. I'm mesmerized by the motion. Even though I've seen them, I long to pull down the thin cami and expose her breasts. My hand moves on its own and pulls down the neckline. Her tits are even more beautiful when they aren't coated in sweat and glitter. When wandering hands aren't exploring them.

A low growl leaves my throat, and the sound catches me off guard. Why should I care who touches her? I sure as fuck don't want to.

That's a lie. My cock isn't throbbing like this because I don't want to touch her. The naked truth is that I want nothing more than to wrap my hands around the tits I weaponized against her in the video to her mother. I want to touch her. I want to—

Don't, I scold myself. *We don't fuck whores.*

Maybe I can pretend she's not the thing I hate.

Or . . . maybe I'll fuck her exactly like the thing I hate.

I pull my cock from my pants and stand up. Once I've stripped the clothing from the lower half of her body, her perfect pussy makes me forget all about her profession. I toss her pants to the side and hook my hands around her thighs to pull her toward me. My cock twitches against her slit. I lean over her and fill my hands with her tits, reddening the skin as I squeeze. Unwilling to respond to my touch, her nipples remain flaccid. Her nerve endings are as oblivious as she is, unable to register that I'm touching her at all. I drop one hand from her chest and push my fingers inside her pussy. She's not wet, but I don't need her to be. The warmth is enough.

"I should use a condom because you're a whore, huh?" I ask, even though she can't answer. And even though I have no plans to put a barrier between us. I want to know what she feels like. I rub my cock—the only part of my body that is free of scars—along her slit. "With you out like this, you can't judge my scars. You can't judge me at all."

It's been so long since I've fucked someone. Their silent judgment makes it almost impossible, and it's not something I'm imagining. They all want the man in the ring until the man in their bed becomes the grotesque figure they can't look in the eye. But my tragedy can't judge me. She's painfully vulnerable to my carnal desires.

My hatred.

My hands slide over her hips and rake the scars on her thighs. The hum of understanding vibrates through the rough tissue, each mark a permanent memory etched into us.

I draw back my hips and push inside her. Though I'm met with resistance and friction, I don't stop. I tear my tragedy in two, ripping her apart physically this time. A feral groan leaves my lips because I'm wearing the embodiment of my anger on my dick and fucking the painful memories of my past.

And fuck if she doesn't feel like heaven within my mental hell.

I lean forward and wrap my hand around her throat as I pound into her. Pressing harder, I cut off her breath. She still doesn't wake. I could kill her right now, but there'd be absolutely no fun in that. She wouldn't even know what happened or what I'd done to her body while she slept. I loosen my grip and allow her to draw a few breaths before I toy with her some more.

"Such a dirty whore," I growl as her tits bounce against my chest. "Your pussy will be sore tomorrow. Ripped open by me. Your stalker. The man hell-bent on destroying you." My words are met with silence, but it still feels good to spill each anger-soaked syllable.

By doing nothing at all, she's going to make me come. Just by being a receptacle for my pleasure, she'll draw every ounce from me like the whore she swears she isn't. I grip her hips and my fingertips dig into her flesh. I fuck her harder, knowing this would hurt her if she were awake right now. When I pull out to my tip, blood streaks my cock.

I love that she'll think about me tomorrow when she wakes up, sore and used. Well, she'll think of her stalker, but we're one and the same. As she struggles through her shift at work, she'll ache with each movement and remember that someone was inside her. All without knowing who that someone is.

What a mind fuck.

Goddamn.

That's tragic.

The thought tightens my balls with a sudden shock of pleasure that I feel in the base of my spine, but the risk of coming inside her without knowing what kind of protection she's on worries me. I wouldn't want her to have a child from a night she wouldn't want to remember. Breeding a whore means hell for the spawn that is created. Whores like her—whores like my *mother*—aren't good moms.

Even though the risk is high, I can't help myself. An unwavering desire to fill her dirty cunt, her tainted pussy, her whore's hole, overtakes me. I want to use her for what she's meant for. From graceful dancer to desperate cumslut, she has no choice but to take what I desperately need to give her. I fill her, coming deep inside her with a groan that conquers her silence. Like a doll, she remains motionless.

A pretty little fuck doll.

I pull back slowly, watching the white residue of my pleasure mix with the red of her pain. The feelings swirl and blend into a pink hue until I can't tell the difference between the two emotions. A thin line drips from her, and I gather it on my fingers and stuff it back inside her. I don't want her to lose a drop of me. She needs to bask in my come until she wakes up. Before I go, I leave her with a little gift that ensures she'll know exactly who was inside her.

Her stalker.

The unknown man who haunts both her nightmares and her every waking moment.

I zip up my pants and drag her toward the pillows, then throw the blanket over her. A smile tugs at my lips as I admire my handprint around her neck. The marking blazes a bright red across the pale skin. I've accomplished a lot tonight, but it's not enough. I need something more. I lean over her, gather saliva in my mouth, and drop it between her parted lips. The thought of her waking up with an ache in her cunt and my taste on her tongue is almost enough to get me hard again. But I can't stay and play.

On my way out of her room, I look back at her once more before flicking off the light. I fully intend to leave more devastation in my wake before finally ending her suffering. Until then, she's my pretty little tragedy.

See you soon.

Chapter Thirteen

Oaklyn

A hammer pounds behind my forehead and rattles against the base of my skull. I open my gummy eyelids, struggling to recall what I can from last night. I fell asleep on the couch after two measly shots of vodka, but I somehow ended up in my bedroom. My sandpaper tongue scrapes across my lips, and my head swims as I try to fully wake up. I didn't drink that much. Not enough to cause this. I lift my hand to my face, wiping sweat from my overheated skin. When I shift onto my side, I suck in a sharp breath as pain spears through my abdomen and between my legs. It's like nothing I've ever felt—like someone has torn me apart and poured lemon juice inside me. I rip the blanket away and find the lack of pants concerning because I put them on before I went into the kitchen to drink.

I slip my hand between my legs and cup myself. The pain intensifies, but it's not just the burning sensation. A deep ache rushes toward my fingertips whenever they land on my skin, similar to the way a fresh bruise feels. When I try to sit up, a different sensation plagues me. Something moves between my legs. Inside me. A blinding wave of emotions narrows my vision. Ignoring the bruises I've just spotted on my thighs, I turn my attention to the hard object that is definitely *not* supposed to be there.

The torn skin along my opening screams for me to stop as I put my fingers inside myself, but I whimper through the pain and keep going. Something slick and hard meets my fingertips, and I finally get a grip on the foreign body as I fight through the pain and bear down. I bring the object into the light. As I release a scream, the acorn falls from my hand and lands between my legs on the mattress.

I scramble out of bed to get away from it, wincing with every painful twinge of my muscles. The acorn rolls around and drops off the bed as if it's trying to chase me, but I can only stare as it comes to a stop by my toes. I finally gain the strength to pick it up, then freeze again when the slickness coats my palm. It wiggles in my hand, and I realize I'm shaking.

My stalker was inside my room. Worse, he was inside *me*.

My brain can't accept this.

I refuse.

Jake's assault degraded me, but this? This is terrifying. Someone entered my home while I slept and took something from me that I can never get back. Judging by the way my body feels, it was a violent attack. So why didn't I wake up? It was only two shots of—

He drugged me.

My hand releases the acorn as if it sank sharp teeth into my palm. Overcome by a powerful wave of nausea, I race to the bathroom and rid myself of whatever remains in my stomach. All of it. My forehead drops to my arm as it drapes over the toilet seat. Sweat drips from my temples. Vulnerable and half naked, I squat over the tile floor.

I pull myself together because there's nothing else I can do. Reaching out to the police isn't an option. I'm a sex worker. My report would get shoved to the bottom of the stack and eventually forgotten. As far as most of society is concerned, I got exactly what I asked for. That couldn't be further from the truth.

I didn't ask for any of this.

When I stand up, my eyes catch on my reflection and I struggle to breathe. Rows of bruises line my neck on one side, and a single mark stands out on the other. I place my hand over it. Fingers. A thumb. I've been strangled, and I have no recollection of it. And that's the scariest part.

I go back to my room and rush to put on my discarded pajama pants so I can conceal the parts of myself that feel too vulnerable and exposed. That's when I spot the dried blood lingering within the creases of my thighs. Each new discovery leads me further toward insanity as I uncover just how violently I've been attacked. Because I can't remember any of it, it feels like this happened to someone else. But then I feel the pain. See the bruises. Run my fingers over blood. Pull an acorn from *my* fucking body. And I can't deny the truth. This happened to me, and someone wants to hurt me, possibly even kill me.

As I pull my pants into place to cover what I no longer want to look at, my eyes are drawn to the strewn clothes inside my closet. When I look closer, I realize these aren't my clothes. These are *pieces* of my clothes—more specifically, the outfits I wear at work. I kneel beside the pile and lift the tattered rags. They've been ripped to shreds. Glancing at what remains on the racks, I see that none of my everyday wear has been touched.

Then I see it. Hanging from my bedroom mirror, obscuring my face when I stand, is my leotard from my last production. It's a slap in the face. After everything else this psychopath has done to me, it wasn't enough. He had to do more. He had to remind me I will never be more than what I am.

I drop to the bed before I can collapse, then put my head in my hands. I don't know what I did to deserve this. Hasn't enough bad shit happened to me without an unhinged stalker adding to it?

Tears stream down my face, but I raise my eyes to the doorway as a thought crosses my mind. I've been too upset to consider it, but now the alarm bells scream in my ears and rival the sound of my heartbeat.

What if he's still here?

I creep toward the door, looking around my room for a weapon and settling on a broom tucked beside the dresser. I'm not sure how well this flimsy thing will protect me if I find him, but I *need* to know if he's still haunting my home after violating me. I swing the broom against my shoulder and step through the doorway.

The lights are still on in the living room, and the brightness unsettles me because it's another reminder of the break in my nightly routine. I always turn off all the lights before bed. I can't afford the power bill otherwise, and I prefer to let the sunshine do all the work during the day. Sunlight doesn't cost a thing.

Swallowing my unease, I tighten my grip on the broom handle and do my best to clear the house the way I see cops do it on fucking television. I swing the broom around each corner and expect to connect with a body each time. By the time I reach the kitchen, I'm confident I'm alone.

My shoulders fall and a war of emotions rages in my chest. On one hand, I wish he'd been lurking somewhere in my trailer so I could finally put a face to the monster under the bed. I'm also disappointed I can't take a stab at him. On the other hand, I'm relieved as fuck. Sometimes it's better to keep away from the monster and leave it a mystery.

Maybe you already know who it is.

That thought is the most unsettling of all. I've likely seen this person, and they sure as fuck know enough about me. They even made a point of leaving my final costume hanging on my bedroom door. And they knew about that costume because they searched my history online and pasted my past all over the club's dressing room. How did they gain access to the back room at the club? How did no one see him pasting the pictures everywhere?

My blood freezes in my veins.

Jake.

It all makes sense. He has more of a reason to carry such a vicious vendetta against me than anyone else I know. I've turned him down on a nightly basis for months, and his fragile ego probably couldn't take it anymore. He probably stopped trying to sleep with me after his foiled assault attempt the other night because he planned to do much worse to me when the time was right. And who else could get into the private rooms to video the lap dance that ended up seared into my mother's brain? Fucking Jake.

I can't stay here. If I can't go to the police, I have to get the fuck out of town before my stalker comes back. I sure as fuck can't go to work tonight. Even if my muscles didn't feel like pudding, I don't want to be anywhere near the creep who's trying to ruin my life. I don't even want to be in the same city.

I return to my room and toss the broom to the ground as I step onto the worn carpet. I reach beneath my mattress and pull out the money I've been saving for months. The money that was supposed to go to my future and will now have to go toward a momentary escape from my stalker. I have to return eventually, but what do I have to return to? If Jake has taken things this far, I can't return to the club tonight. Maybe not ever. There are other places I can dance, but I have no way to get there. Buses don't run that far out of this city. It's heartbreaking. No, it's worse than heartbreak. This whole situation has done so much more than hurt me. It has destroyed me. Handing over my hard-earned money to escape my deranged stalker is the last straw.

I'll have to figure this shit out later. Once I've gotten to safety.

I pack a bag and stuff the money inside, then grab my phone from the coffee table in the living room. When the screen comes to life, I'm greeted by the volatile text messages from my mom. Which means he looked at my phone. He *enjoyed* reading what he's done to me. Sick fucking psychopath. He's probably so proud of himself.

My stomach tightens and threatens to send me back to the bathroom for another vomit session, but I don't have time for this. The bottle of vodka glares at me from the kitchen island. I'd normally take a swig to quiet my nerves, but I'm almost positive that's how my stalker drugged me. I storm toward the offending vessel of unconsciousness and pour it down the sink. My hand longs to smash the bottle and vent some of my pent up frustration, but I don't want to clean up a mess when I come back.

Speaking of cleaning up messes, I need to let Jake know I won't be in for a few days. If my suspicions prove incorrect, I'll still need a job when I return. Actually, who am I fucking kidding? Even if I find proof that Jake has been sabotaging me at every turn, I'll have to continue working for him. If I want to keep dancing, if I want to continue pursuing my passion, if I want to reach for a dream that seems to be slipping further from my fingertips with every day that passes . . . I don't have a choice.

I send a message saying I need to visit a sick aunt in Florida. I don't have an aunt, in Florida or otherwise, but I can't tell him where I actually plan to go. Without knowing how much he knows about my past, I don't want to give anything away. He doesn't need another bullet for the gun he's aimed at my skull.

With shaking hands, I search for the first bus back to Wisconsin. Just seeing the name of my home state brings back a flood of memories. Most are good, which is the saddest part. My eyes nearly bulge out of my head when I see how much a ticket will cost, and that's just one way. A round trip will eat a significant hole in my savings. As my thumb hovers over the button to confirm an immediate reservation for the first ride out of town, I rack my brain for any other way to get to Wisconsin. But I have no friends. If I call my family, they'll tell me to pay for a ride with my dirty money. Even if I tell them the dire circumstances, I'll be met with, "You wouldn't have had this problem if you'd just gone to medical school." I can think of no other option . . . until one slithers to the front of my mind.

I close the browser on my phone and type out a text message to the only person who might be willing to help me. It's a Hail Mary play, but it's all I have left. What else do I have to lose? Before I can talk myself out of it, I hit send, lock my front door, and grab a butcher knife from the knife block. I don't know how long it might take to get a reply and the sun is already starting to set, so I'll need to be safe while I wait. My stalker could return at any moment. If he does, I'll be ready. He won't get the jump on me again.

Chapter Fourteen

Ambrose

The crowd sings my praises as the ref raises my hand, declaring me the victor in the first fight of the night. I don't usually like being the opening act, but it's the only way Darby will allow me to fight twice in one night, breaking the one-fight rule he imposes on everyone else. And I needed two bouts tonight. Pummeling someone's face keeps my mind off that fucking girl.

Since I sank into her last night, it's all I've thought about. I long to get inside her again, but I need to pace myself. The next time I fuck her will be the last time. There'll be no going back for either of us after that. We'll get the release we deserve. I'll dish out my ultimate revenge, then I'll free her from her tragic life. Like putting down a deer that's still breathing after its entrails have been strewn across a desolate highway, it's the humane thing to do at this point.

I jog back to the locker room and grip the tape around my wrists with my teeth, pulling it away from my hands until they're bare. Once my hands are free, I flex my fingers and allow the blood to rush toward the sore spots. A pleasurable ache greets me with each movement. I towel the sweat off my skin and dress in casual clothes so I can work the crowd until my next fight. Grabbing my phone from my locker, I spot a notification. Someone sent me a text while I was in the ring.

My eyebrows pull together as I read the message.

> I need to get out of town for a few days, and I need to leave as soon as possible. I know this is a huge ask, but is there any way you could drive me to Wisconsin? I can pay for gas and food, and you can stay in the extra room at my family's cabin.

A smile curls the edges of my mouth. Last night produced results I never could have expected. She's decided to run from her stalker, not realizing she's running right into his waiting arms. And we'll be traveling to a cabin? Hopefully that means it's a secluded spot, which would be the ideal location for what I need to do. If everything falls into place, the final act of this tragic play will come sooner than I wanted, but all good things must eventually come to an end. I can't let this golden opportunity pass me by.

I fire back a text and tell her I'm on my way. After slipping into my leather jacket, I grab my bag and throw it over my shoulder. The door whips open as I reach for the handle, and Darby stands on the other side, his eyes widening when he spots the bag.

"What the fuck, scar? You've got another fight tonight. You can't leave."

I shrug my shoulders. "Emergency. Gotta go." I try to push past him, but he sidesteps into my path, his eyes narrowing into dark slits.

"What do you mean? The only thing you *gotta* do is fight."

My frame towers over him as I step closer. "I'm leaving. Call the fight or slide Boris into my slot. I'll be back in a few days. Maybe a week."

"A *week*? What about your—"

"Figure it out." My fists clench into tight balls at my sides. I don't have time for this shit. I have a date with my red-haired destiny.

"I could ruin you, scar. Keep you from ever fighting again!"

I glare down at him and smirk. "But where's the money in that?"

His shoulders deflate and he steps aside. Checkmate. The crowd pays good money to see me fight, and he knows it. That's why his panties are in such a twist. If he strikes me from the schedule for a few nights, he'll lose money until I make my grand return, but firing me means losing his cash cow for good. He'd offer me higher pay before he'd fire me, but I wouldn't accept it. It wouldn't be fair to my fellow fighters.

I push past him, then stop and shout a parting shot over my shoulder. "Call the Kursicki brothers. Maybe if you offer them fair pay for the fights, they'll agree to fill my spot while I'm gone."

Those two would fight for free, but I can't miss an opportunity to take a dig at how underpaid we are.

Satisfied I've made my point, I head toward my Jeep and get into the driver's seat. I feel for my knife between the seats and find the hefty handle. I'm glad I waited for the right moment to take her life, but I worry some semblance of buried morals has kept me from doing what needs to be done. I'll just have to throw more dirt on the pile and bury them deeper. Nothing can stop me from making someone pay for what happened to me, and that someone has to be Oaklyn.

The drive toward her trailer passes by in a blur of trees and street signs. I'm wrapped in a state of euphoria. Anticipation crawls along my spine at the thought of seeing her face, and I allow myself this guilty pleasure because it's almost over now. I can't deny that I find her beautiful, and I won't try to chase away those thoughts any longer. This is as close as I'll allow myself to get, however. If I venture much nearer to admiration, it'll be harder to take her life. I'll be too tempted to keep her around so I can repeatedly take her cunt.

I pull in front of her home, and she rushes from the doorway, looking in every direction as if someone might spring from the trees and drag her to hell. I have no need to drag her. She's stepping into hell on her own.

A tight tank top hugs her curves, and her red ponytail swings over her bare shoulders as she jogs toward the Jeep. I want to wrap that thick tendril of hair around my hand and pull, but am I slitting her throat or fucking her from behind as I reveal her pale neck? My mind struggles with the indecision, but then I smile. It can be both.

She tosses her bag into the backseat and flops onto the passenger seat in a breathless heap. A light sweat glosses her skin, making her shoulders and forehead shine beneath the dome light. Her chest heaves up and down, and she tilts her head as she pulls her ankle into her lap with a sharp wince. The light moves to the marks I left on her neck. She tried to cover them with makeup, but they peer from beneath the translucent smudges. Or maybe I only notice them because I made them. Either way, it hardens me.

"Close the door," I say, wanting the darkness to hide my shame.

She does as she's told, and the light clicks off. "Thanks for helping me," she says. "My stalker broke into my house last night, and I need to get away for a few days while I figure out what to do."

I wish she'd tell me more. I want to hear how my actions have destroyed her—those little details would be a symphony to my ears—but she doesn't offer anything else. That's okay. We have a long drive ahead of us, and I'm sure I can get her to open up along the way.

"I need to know where we're going," I say.

"Oh, right." She rattles off the address, and I punch it into my phone. "It's my family's cabin, but no one should be there. It's a pretty long trek, so we can take turns driving if you want."

I shake my head and pull onto the road. No one drives this Jeep but me. "What do you hope to accomplish while you're away? Your stalker will still be here when you get back."

She shrugs and looks out the window. "Maybe I won't come back."

"Where would you go?"

"I don't know." She picks at the side of her nail and nibbles at her bottom lip. "I don't exactly have a lot of great options. That's why I'm working at the club. To give myself more options."

What a lame-ass excuse. She's working at the club because she's a whore who likes to let men use her body in exchange for cash. I won't let her tell me this lie. "Why not work a normal job like everyone else? You'd be less of a target for stalkers if you worked a desk job."

She turns her head toward me and stops clawing at her finger. "Are you victim blaming right now? Seriously? People don't get stalked because of their profession. People get stalked because there are too many men and women running around with a screw loose."

Shots fired. But she isn't wrong. My mother shook a few screws loose when she sank a knife into me more times than the doctors could count.

"Don't get me wrong," she continues. "If I could go back to the professional dance world, I would, but that just isn't possible. I was in a wreck six months ago that destroyed my ankle, and the professional dance world demands more than what the plates and screws can handle. I can manage a few minutes on stage at the club, but that's about it."

"Do you have to dance?"

She returns her gaze to the window. "Do you have to fight?" When I don't answer, she knows she's made her point. "It's the same thing. Sometimes we're created to do something, and we can't deny the drive to do it. I was meant to dance. It's the one thing that brings me any happiness, and I'm not willing to give up the only shred of joy I have left in life."

A sign marks the interstate, and I ease the Jeep onto the on-ramp and merge with the trickle of vehicles heading the same way. Headlights cut through the darkness and illuminate her face for a moment. A single tear slithers through her makeup.

"Don't you have any aspirations?" I ask. "You aren't happy in your current career, so what's the end goal?"

A soft laugh springs from her throat. "I can't look too far ahead. Whenever I try, things seem impossible. Right now I'm focused on getting a car so I can find work at a nicer club outside of our shithole town."

The speck of sympathy I felt for her blows away on a puff of air. Instead of seeking a way out of her slutty situation, she only desires a nicer place to spread her legs. Which is fine. The last thing I need is for her to give me doubts about ending her life on this trip. Her little admission has only bolstered my conviction. She's the right target, and the right time is just around the bend.

Then she speaks again, and what she says next drives a chasm through my resolve.

Chapter Fifteen

Oaklyn

It's not easy to open up to someone I don't really know, but I'm trying. Since I have to be around him for several days in the middle of nowhere, I might as well be a bit more personable, especially when he's been kind enough to drive me there. Is it the kindness I find myself so drawn to? His good looks certainly help. He's insecure about the scars on his face, but I see more than that when I look at him. Those marks don't affect his strong jawline or the way his tongue runs over his full bottom lip when he's thinking. They certainly don't detract from his dark eyes.

Maybe it wouldn't hurt to tell him about the impossible end goal.

"I have bigger dreams, but I haven't spoken them aloud to anyone because they feel so silly," I finally say.

His hands adjust on the wheel, and his shoulders seem to tense. The shift is nearly imperceptible, so maybe I've only imagined it. "Are you trying to make it to a whorehouse somewhere in the western part of the country? Is that the real reason you need a car?"

"No, but even if that was the goal, who are you to judge me? Who are you to judge anyone? Sex work is still work." I regret even opening my mouth at this point. Maybe I should have stayed behind and taken my chances with the stalker. "Never mind."

His jaw works his muscles into a tight ball, the skin at his temple writhing with every grit of his teeth. "No, go on. What's your big dream?"

I won't give him everything. I haven't spoken of this plan to anyone, and I won't start with him. But I'll give him a taste. "I eventually want to stop stripping. Not because I think it's a dirty profession"—I give him a pointed glare—"but because I just have other aspirations."

He shifts in his seat and clears his throat. "That's . . . admirable."

It pains him to give this compliment. He struggles to speak the word, as if he's just forced a shard of glass from his throat. It doesn't cut me, though. It's the first genuine compliment I've received in months that didn't pertain to my tits or my ass, and I drink it like wine. I'm left with a warm, fuzzy buzz. If he thought the idea was stupid, he would have said as much. He's had no problem offering rude remarks thus far. This gives me hope. Maybe my idea isn't as far out of reach as I imagined. Let the compliment cut him. It's giving me life.

The miles stretch out behind us as we travel in silence, and the gentle hum of the tires rolling over the pavement pulls me toward sleep. I've been drowsy since I woke up. Whatever drug was used on me must have been a powerful one. I rub my thighs together, and the ache between my legs reminds me of the hell I endured while unconscious. Yes. That drug was powerful as fuck. My hand goes to my throat, but I pull my fingers away before they can press into the bruises on my neck. I almost forgot I'd covered them with makeup to avoid any questions. Even though I don't have a reason to feel embarrassed, I can't stop the shame from welling inside me. I wrap my arms around myself, providing the comfort I crave.

"Are you cold?" His voice cuts through the darkness, and he reaches to turn on the heat.

I place my hand over his and shake my head. He recoils from my touch, and my stomach sinks. Does he actually view me as a filthy creature? He probably rubs the seats down with bleach every time I exit his car. How can he go from being concerned about my comfort to disgusted in the blink of an eye? This is torture for both of us. I can't fathom why he'd agree to this when he can't stand the sight of me.

I've had enough.

"Turn the car around," I say. "I'll pay for the gas and your time, but I think it's best if I just go home. This was a terrible idea."

He grits his teeth and cracks his neck, rolling his shoulders to release pent-up tension. He has no reason to be so tense. "No, I'm taking you to the cabin. What's the problem?"

"Since you snatched your hand away like I have the plague, I can only assume I'm the fucking problem. I'm not dirty, Ambrose."

"Sounds like you're projecting," he says with a smirk. "Don't try to pin your insecurities on me."

"Why else would you pull away like that?"

He pushes his hand toward my face, flipping it back and forth in front of my eyes. "Do you see these scars? Did you ever consider that *maybe* I don't want you to see or feel them?"

"Did you ever consider that *maybe* I don't fucking care about them?" I scoff and push his hand away. "Now who's projecting?"

That shuts him up. He tightens his grip on the steering wheel and goes back to grinding his teeth. If he isn't careful, he'll end up with dust for molars.

"How'd you get the scars, anyway?" I ask.

"Story time's over. Take a nap or something."

Fair enough. I guess we all have things we don't want to share. I go back to staring out the window and wondering why his bad attitude hurts my feelings. It's not like I like him or anything. Yeah, he's attractive. Yeah, he's brooding and mysterious.

Yeah, I might have a problem.

Ambrose

She doesn't go to sleep, but at least she's quiet now. It gives me a moment to finish mulling over what she said. It shouldn't have changed anything, but it does. The two opposing sides of my mind grip the rope of indecision and dig in their heels.

She's a whore, which makes her the perfect target.

No. She has dreams. She wants to make something more of her life.

She's still a whore. Now she's just a whore with dreams.

I steal a glance at her. Would this be easier if she wasn't so beautiful? Maybe I should have picked a Tuesday-afternoon stripper. A girl who didn't have such full lips or a perfect nose or a single dimple that pops onto her right cheek when she smiles. I should have picked a girl with the fake tits I can't stand instead of full, natural breasts that make my mouth water.

I need to stop. Thinking about how seductive she is only makes things worse, and by things, I mean the ache in my balls. I need to kill her sooner rather than later, but I have to feel her around me one more time before I do. That's all I'll allow myself. Any more than that and I'll be too tempted to keep her around.

"Oh, can we stop at the next exit?" she asks. "There's a really good diner that makes the best burger I've ever had, and I haven't eaten since yesterday."

I want to say no. We still have a ten-hour drive ahead of us, and I want to finish this play before the sun sets on tomorrow. But maybe it won't hurt to let her have the last meal she wants. Granted, I doubt she'd pick a greasy burger from a roadside flytrap for her last meal if she knew she'd never eat anything again, but this is the best I can do. I ease the car onto the exit ramp and turn to her for directions.

She points and guides me down side streets with an excited gleam to her eyes. It's almost endearing. When we pull up to the building, it's not at all what I expected. From the animated way she directed me, I figured we'd end up somewhere nice, but this place is a dump. Save for the N in the massive DINER sign perched on the roof, the neon lights have abandoned their stations. The busted parking lot looks as if it was paved when asphalt was first invented, then never touched again. Trash tumbleweeds roll past.

"Are you sure this is the right place?" I ask. We're more likely to get a hefty dose of food poisoning than a good burger here.

She nods and opens her door, then leans back into the car when I don't move. "Aren't you coming?"

With raised eyebrows, I stare at her. She can't be serious.

"Suit yourself," she says with a shrug.

Dirty windows line the diner, giving me a clear (enough) view as she waltzes inside and chooses a booth seat right in front of me. Without even sparing a second glance in my direction, she lifts a menu and runs her finger over it. A man at the bar turns on his stool and eyes her with a grin. He whispers something to his burly friend, and that's enough to get me out of the Jeep. I head inside before they can descend on her like vultures.

Despite how decrepit the place looks, the interior has been kept clean. The tables would gleam if their varnish hadn't been worn down to a dull finish. My feet don't stick to the floor, which means they mop the checkered tiles on a regular basis. Maybe it won't hurt to grab a bite.

I drop into the seat in front of her, and the men at the bar turn away, their smiles evaporating from their faces. Mission accomplished.

"So you decided to join me?" she says with a smile as she lowers the menu. Smug satisfaction lights her face and accentuates the dimple in her cheek.

"You said you were paying for the food, and I'm not one to turn down a free meal."

"If you order the most expensive thing on the menu, it's still cheaper than a bus ticket."

"Is that why you picked this place?" I ask. "Because it's cheap?"

The smile drops from her face. "No, I chose this diner because I used to come here with my parents. We'd drive to New York for dance competitions a few times a year, and we'd always stop here on our way home. It was a tradition."

A waitress approaches our table and asks for our drink orders. I order a Coke, but Oaklyn requests some special blackberry concoction from their vintage soda fountain. When the waitress delivers it to our table, I hardly have words. The glass is twice the size of mine, and I don't know where she plans to put all that liquid.

With wide eyes, I motion to her drink. "You don't plan to drink all that, do you? We'll have to stop nine times before we're even out of Pennsylvania."

"I'll use the bathroom before we leave. I have a strong bladder." She pulls the monstrosity toward her and takes a massive sip through her straw. "Besides, when will I have the chance to come here again? Probably not for a very long time."

Probably not ever, I think. Guilt rears its ugly head once more, and I shove it down. It's getting more difficult to deny what I'm feeling for her. How fucking disgusting.

"Let's make this quick," I say. "We need to get back on the road."

We have to reach the cabin so I can finish the job before this girl makes me question my plan. The goal isn't to fall in love and run off into the sunset. Even if I wanted that, she'd never accept me for who I am or what I look like. I don't want her, either. I hate her because she's so much like the woman who took a knife to my body. If I'm not careful, my tragedy will take a knife to my soul. But not if I can strike first.

Chapter Sixteen

Oaklyn

We're almost an hour from the cabin, but I can't hold my bladder any longer. It would be impressive if I'd held it this long, but I've already asked him to stop several times since we left the diner. Four times, to be exact. I squirm in my seat, pressing my thighs together and counting the cars we pass on the interstate to keep my mind from wandering to the pulsing pain in my abdomen. A slight whimper escapes my throat, and Ambrose's head whips toward me.

"Again? Jesus fucking Christ." He aims the Jeep toward the offramp and searches for the nearest gas station. "I told you this would happen."

"I'm sorry for my very normal need to piss," I mutter.

"Pissing is normal, yes, but not every five minutes." He pulls up at a rundown gas station and throws the car into park beside the pumps. "Make it quick."

With a huff, I get out and slam the door behind me. A metal bell rings when I enter the gas station, and the attendant behind the counter leers at me as I head toward the back of the store in search of a place to relieve myself.

"You gotta go around the back of the building," he calls. "You also gotta buy something. We ain't running a charity here."

I snatch the first thing I see from the rack beside me—a bag of chips that are probably as stale as this man's soul—and rush toward the counter. My hand works into my pocket, and I pull out a five. I'm almost desperate enough to leave the change and the chips behind, but every dollar counts right now. It's a good thing I waited, because he slides a key attached to a long stick back to me, along with my change.

"Thanks," I say. I gather everything into my hands and shuffle out of the building.

Late-morning sun beams down on my skin, and cotton clouds hang in the sky. A lone sparrow pecks at a few soggy french fries lying in a puddle on the pavement. I open the bag of chips to toss it a few as I rush past, but it flies off. I dump them near the ground by a trash can and throw away the bag. Hopefully the little bird will come back and enjoy the dry snack I've left it. I'm only sorry I didn't have more time to put them somewhere a bit cleaner.

I round the corner of the building and nearly collide with a couple of drunks hanging out on the sidewalk. For someone who isn't running a charity, the station owner sure doesn't seem to mind the two brown-baggers hanging around the bathroom door. I guess they bought the booze inside. The acrid scent of spilled urine claws toward me as I swing open the door, and I make a mental note to bathe twice when I reach the cabin. I go to lock it behind me, but there's no way to turn the deadbolt on this side.

"Fuck, fuck, fuck," I whisper as I scramble to unbutton my shorts. I'll just have to be quick.

Hovering over the filthy toilet seat, I breathe a sigh of relief as the pressure in my gut lessens. The feeling is only second to a really good orgasm. My eyes drift shut until I've completely emptied everything in the tank, then I reach for the toilet paper in the little silver holder to my right. A cardboard roll brushes against my fingertips. More whispered curses explode from my lips, and I search around the bathroom for something to wipe with. Men have it so easy. They only need to shake the dribble away. I wiggle my ass to see if I can achieve the same effect, but it doesn't work. Not wanting to sit in piss-damp panties for the rest of the drive, I groan and hobble toward the paper-towel dispenser with my shorts around my calves. I don't enjoy the thought of dragging that stiff crap through my crotch, but it beats the fuck out of the alternative.

As soon as I've pulled a few of the rough sheets of brown paper from the dispenser, a sound catches my attention and I freeze. Footsteps. They crunch across the gritty sidewalk outside, and the shuffling gait nears the bathroom door.

"Someone's in here!" I shout as I run the paper towel across my tender skin with a grimace. It feels like sandpaper, especially when it grates against the tears between my legs.

The footsteps stop outside the door, and someone raps against the metal.

"I'm almost done!" I call. I yank up my shorts, flush the paper towel—because fuck this guy's plumbing—and turn on the faucet to wash my hands. I don't know why I expected soap, but I'm still disappointed when I don't see any. The disinfectant spray on the back of the toilet tempts me, but I settle for water alone. As I grip a few of the useless paper towels to dry my hands, my heart refuses to beat.

The door's reflection glares at me from the dirty mirror. It's only open a crack, but an unmistakable eye peers through the tiny opening. Fine hairs rise along the back of my neck. A panicked cramp squeezes my stomach.

The eye blinks, and it's enough to break my frozen state. I move toward the door and put my weight against it, wedging my sneaker at the bottom in a desperate bid to keep the hunk of metal from opening again. I close my eyes and hope I only imagined it; maybe my stalker issue has caused me to see something that wasn't there.

Then the door moves. Whoever is out there is very real, and they want to get inside.

I press my shoulder against the cool metal and scramble to keep my feet planted. I've used my good leg against the door, but my busted ankle cries out any time I'm forced to rely on it as backup. Fear grips my lungs in a chokehold, and I struggle for every breath. I can't keep this up much longer.

"Help!" I scream, but I don't know who I expect to come running. Ambrose is too far away to hear me, and I doubt he'd come to my rescue anyway. But what other option do I have? "Please! Ambrose, help me!"

Each terrified sound only seems to fuel my attacker's need to get to me. The door rocks against me with renewed force. Adrenaline rushes through my veins, leaving me lightheaded and weak. I gasp for air between cries for help. But it's no use. I'll have to make a run for it.

I step away from the door and allow it to open. Then I come face to face with my attacker.

Ambrose

What the fuck is taking so long? Either she has no concept of time or she needed to do more than piss. Whatever the reason, I'm sick of waiting. I lock up my Jeep and jog toward the back of the building, the way I saw her head when she left the gas station with a bathroom key in her hand. As soon as I round the corner, her muffled screams reach me.

I rush past the wino perched on the sidewalk, knocking him onto his back as I barrel by. The brown bag falls from his dirty fist and sends a spray of booze across the pavement. His garbled curses fall on deaf ears. I can only hear the sound of scuffling feet behind the bathroom door. Someone is trying to take what belongs to me, but it sounds like my tragedy is giving them one hell of a fight.

I take a step back and aim my shoulder at the door before ramming against it. The metal hinges squeak, and a thud resounds in the tiny space as the door collides with someone's back. They move away, and I'm able to push it wide open.

Sunlight fills the bathroom, and I spot Oaklyn. She's backed against the wall. Tendrils of red hair fall from her disheveled ponytail, and she grips a long stick in her shaking hand. Her chest rises and falls as she sucks air through gritted teeth. A wild look blazes in her green eyes. I have never seen something more fierce and beautiful in my life.

The man turns to face me, and I'm overjoyed to see the long scratches carved into the side of his stubbled cheek. Beads of blood dot the red lines. His glassy eyes blink slowly as he takes me in, his gaze running over my frame. He can't see the taut muscles beneath my jacket, but he doesn't need to. My size is enough to make him think twice. Too bad he doesn't have a choice. When he touched my tragedy, he lost the right to walk away. He'll be lucky if he can ever walk again when I'm finished with him.

My hand shoots forward and grips the front of his shirt. He tries to argue, the words tangling around his tongue, but I refuse to give him a chance to speak. I raise him up a bit before I bring my other fist around in a jab that rattles his jaw, then I snatch him out of the bathroom. His head clangs against the metal doorframe as I swing his body into the sunlight. A deep groan pours from his mouth, and his eyes roll in his head. I've dazed him, which is a shame. I want him to feel everything I'm about to do to him.

Oaklyn emerges from the bathroom as I continue to pummel his face with my fist. I expect her to run for the Jeep or beg me to stop, but she surprises me when she steps behind him and brings up her shin in a swift kick to the man's groin. My stomach tightens because I've seen how defined her legs are. That had to hurt.

"You fucking creep!" she screams into his face, but I'm pretty sure he doesn't hear her because he's close to passing out at this point.

Blood gushes from his nose and busted lip. His right eye has begun to swell, and I'm almost certain I've freed two of the yellowed teeth from his mouth. But it's not enough. I need more. I release my grip on his shirt, and he collapses to the pavement in a limp heap. His hands rise in a feeble attempt to cover his face, but that's not what I'm going for anyway. I'm a fighter. I know how to work someone over and leave them with something more than a few superficial facial wounds and a concussion.

Like a wild animal, I pounce on him and rain blows to his rib cage until I feel a satisfying crack. Rage flows from my fists in an invisible flood, and I want to drown this fucker in it. As I continue my mindless attack, a mantra plays like a song in my head.

She's mine.

She's mine.

She's mine.

How *dare* he touch her.

Hands close around my arm, and I look up to see who's been stupid enough to stop me from collecting the debt I'm owed. It's Oaklyn, and she's trying to pull me off of him. I snatch my arm away and raise my fist once more, but she pleads for a ceasefire. Her words finally register.

"The station owner is going to call the cops. We have to go."

As much as I would love to keep laying into this piece of absolute shit, I'm not a stupid man. I have no desire to deal with the police. I rise to my feet and send a final kick into the man's rib cage before I turn for the Jeep.

"You don't think they have cameras here, do you?" Oaklyn asks as we pile into the car and pull away from the gas station. She searches the building's roof.

"A dump like this? Doubtful." I eye her as she repairs her ponytail. "He didn't touch you, did he? I mean . . . he didn't—"

"No." She doesn't look at me when she answers.

I don't ask anything else. If she doesn't want to talk about what happened, I won't force it out of her.

Blood darkens the tip of her finger. She broke a nail in the struggle, and it snapped off low enough to expose the quick. I'm struck again by how hard she fought to keep that man away from her. She didn't want him inside her. She didn't want the man from the club either. My brain refuses to admit that she might not be who I've made her out to be in my mind. That she might not be a whore.

Because she *has* to be. For any of this to work, she has to be. The alternative is too horrible.

"Thank you," she says as we pull onto the interstate. "I don't know what would have happened if you hadn't shown up. I didn't think you'd hear me yelling for you, but I guess I'm louder than I thought."

"You called my name?"

She shrugs her shoulders. "Well, yeah. Who else could I call for?"

No one has ever depended on me like this before. What would she think if she knew her protector was also her tormentor? I can't let her find out. Not until the end. If she isn't who I think she is, if she isn't the perfect target I've built her up to be, I'll have to let her go. But if she is . . .

There's only one way to find out. I need to test her.

Chapter Seventeen

Ambrose

A slight thrill runs through my bones when she directs me to turn onto a dirt road ahead—I don't get many chances to test the Jeep's off-road skills in the city—but the feeling is short lived. The red dirt has been packed to smooth perfection without a mudhole in sight. How fucking boring. Even the curves in the narrow path were drawn into the countryside with ease of travel in mind.

We eventually turn off the main strip of dirt and meander down a gravel driveway for nearly a mile. Trees choke out the light, casting dark shadows over the path, even though it's daytime. We're in the middle of nowhere, and it's perfect.

The forest breaks apart, and the house comes into view. Her parents must have an endless store of money if they can afford this property, especially since it sits on the edge of a massive lake. It seems to be the only house in this slough. I've never seen anything like it, which isn't surprising. None of the foster parents I've lived with had enough money to stay in a place like this for a night, let alone owning such a cabin. Well, maybe they had enough money, but I certainly never saw any of it. I was lucky to receive a sliver of the allotment the state paid them for my care.

I park near the wooden front porch and get out of the Jeep, grabbing my bag from the back before following her to the front door. She pulls a key from beneath the doormat, and I roll my eyes internally. No wonder she was dumb enough to keep her house key beneath the bench cushion at her trailer. She inherited the bad habit from her parents.

Judging by the stuffy air when we step into the cabin, this place hasn't seen a visitor in a very long time. After adjusting the thermostat, Oaklyn leads me up a creaky staircase and down a hallway. Instead of family pictures, only works of art line the walls. How goddamn pretentious.

She motions to a door near the end. "You can stay in there," she says. "It's the guest bedroom. We don't have wi-fi or cell service out here, but you can always watch television if you get bored." She looks around. "Well, if my parents still have the satellite connected."

I nod, but I have other plans regarding entertainment while I'm here. And all of them involve her. I don't want her to get too comfortable here. Aside from the test I've planned, I need to remind her that her stalker could be anywhere. She needs to remember she's never safe if I want things to work the way I've pictured. I pull a switchblade from my pocket and push it toward her.

"What's that?" she asks. She turns the handle between her fingers.

"Protection," I say. "If your stalker has a way of tracking you, he might know you're here. We won't be in the same room, so this might buy you some time if he gets to you before I can."

Her eyes widen as she processes what I'm saying, and it takes every ounce of strength in my body to stop the laughter from rising out of my chest. Her stalker didn't need to track her when she literally called him for a ride. It's too perfect.

"Thanks," she mutters. Gripping the blade in shaking hands, she turns for her room.

I step into the bedroom I've been assigned and flick on the light. A lazy ceiling fan churns above the bed. I open a window beside the dresser, but I'm not only interested in getting some fresh air into the room. I need to find a silent way to get to the lower floor, and I'd prefer to avoid those loud-ass stairs. A half roof slopes a few feet below the window. Perfect.

After placing my bag beside the bed, I lie back and wait for nightfall. If I want my plan to have any chance of working, I'll need the darkness. Oaklyn knocks on the door to ask if I want any food from the pantry—dry and canned goods are our only option until we can visit a nearby store—but I tell her no thanks. I'm too excited to eat. Tonight will finally put any doubt to rest. Either she deserves to be the outlet for my long-awaited revenge or she doesn't. And I don't know which one I want it to be.

I have carried this anger for my mother for far too long. It's a bag of bricks on my shoulders, and each time I think about what that woman did to me, I add another to the growing stack. When my mother fashioned her bedcovers into a noose and ended her own life, she piled on a few more and denied me the chance to take the revenge I'm owed. The burden is too much, and I'm ready to shed this weight.

But I'm not ready to say goodbye to Oaklyn.

My stomach sours with this admission. If she hadn't planted this doubt in my mind, I wouldn't find her so alluring. She's a whore. She removes her clothes and allows men to feel her up for money. Her reasons for doing so are compelling, but they aren't good enough. Still, I can't stop this nagging feeling that I've gotten something wrong, and I can't move forward until I know for sure.

I mull these things over until the sun has slipped far below the horizon. By the time it grows dark enough to get started, I'm nearly frothing at the mouth with anticipation.

I ease out of the open window and creep to the edge of the slanted half roof, then drop to the ground. I'll use the ladder I spotted near the matching outbuilding to get back up there if I can't manage it on my own.

Before I enter the downstairs, I go to my Jeep for the little bag of acorns I've stashed beneath the driver's seat. If everything goes how I think it will, I'll need to leave a little souvenir behind for her. I grab my knife and tuck its sheath into my pants. The thought of her panic when she realizes her stalker has followed her all the way to this cabin—when she realizes her stalker is *in* the fucking cabin and he drove her here—sends a rush of adrenaline straight to my brain.

Using the key beneath the mat, I let myself in through the front door and search for the breaker box. I find it in the laundry room and cut the power to the house. Now it's a race against time.

Even if a home seems silent, it's never as quiet as when all power has ceased to flow through its walls. That silence is loud enough to wake even the lightest sleepers. I can only hope she tries to talk herself down from panic before coming into my room to ask for help. I guess I should also hope she comes to me for help. Otherwise, my plan was for nothing. She seems like a pretty independent woman, bound and determined to do things for herself, but she's also in a precarious situation. I've planted enough fear into her heart, so she'll likely be too terrified to search for the source of the problem on her own.

I exit the house and lock the door, then slip the key beneath the mat. As I race around the side of the building, I consider grabbing the ladder but decide to try pulling myself onto the roof via a jump first. My choice is the right one because I reach the roof's edge with ease and pull myself onto the rough shingles with minimal effort. My muscles are good for more than throwing punches.

Back in the bedroom, I stash the bag of acorns within my bag and flop onto the mattress. I try to slow each breath that pours in and out of my lungs. A light sweat slicks my back and forehead, but I can blame that on the temperature. Then again, if I'm so overheated, why would I still be fully dressed? I rip off my shirt and pants and toss them to the floor.

And I wait.

Oaklyn

My eyes spring open. I try to blink away the wave of disorientation, but a wild panic squeezes my chest in a vise grip. Where am I? *The cabin in Wisconsin.* What am I doing here? *Escaping your psycho stalker.* Why is it so quiet?

My inner voice has no answer.

I feel around the side table for the bedside lamp and find the switch, but nothing happens when I click it back and forth. Thinking the bulb has gone bad, I get onto my knees on the mattress and reach for the cord attached to the ceiling fan. I'm met with more darkness. The power is out.

Goosebumps born of fear prickle my skin. I've never been afraid of the dark, even as a child, but having a stalker can certainly change your outlook on things. It can make you feel unsafe in situations you would normally breeze through. This would be one of those situations.

I grab my shorts from the bedside table and slide them over my legs, then feel my way through the dark until I reach the door. I grab the knife from the top of the dresser, but after seeing the way Ambrose beat the living shit out of that man, I don't think I'll need it. He's my weapon, and I need to get to him.

"Ambrose?" I call into the hall. When he doesn't answer, I tiptoe to his door and knock. "Hey, are you up?"

His feet shuffle toward the door, and it swings open. I can't see him, but his masculine scent rushes toward me on a puff of night air breezing through the open window behind his silhouette. Black leather. Some sort of exotic spice. A twinge between my legs replaces my fear for a moment.

"What's going on?" he asks in a husky voice, and I feel awful because I've clearly disturbed his sleep.

My eyes begin to adjust to the darkness, and I look at anything other than the way the moonlight catches on the defined muscles carved into his shirtless chest. "I'm not sure. The power seems to be out. Could you check the breaker box?"

"Maybe Mommy and Daddy forgot to pay the power bill." He starts to close the door, but I wedge my foot in the opening.

"Look, I'm not usually the type to get scared shitless from a power outage, but considering the reason I've come to this cabin, it would be really nice if you could help me. Please?" I place my hand on his, remembering his disdain for my touch only once my fingers graze his slick scars. But he doesn't pull away.

He lets out an exasperated sigh. "Okay, fine." He grips my hand and pulls me into the room, then leads me to the bed and pushes me backward until I'm sitting. "I'll check the breaker box in fifteen minutes if the power hasn't come back, but I'm not risking my neck on those steep-as-fuck stairs unless I have to. Until then, you can stay in here."

That option would be great if a fresh fear hadn't reared its ugly head. I'm less afraid of the power outage than the way I feel now that I've seen the moonlight gliding over his muscles. I consider asking him to close the curtain, but that wouldn't erase the overpowering manly scent or the warmth radiating from his body. He folds his arms over his broad chest, and the shift in his stance highlights the package in his boxers. The moon literally sends a beam of light right along the edge, outlining his bulge in 4K clarity. My mouth waters and my nipples press against my cami. I fold my arms over my chest so the moonlight can't betray me as well.

What the fuck is wrong with me? I'm like a bitch in heat. I should be focused on ensuring my safety, not eye-fucking my chauffeur.

I clear my throat and set the knife on the side table beside the bed. "Sorry it's so hot in here."

He sits beside me, and the mattress sinks from his weight and pushes me closer to him. Our shoulders are nearly touching. "It's not your fault."

His body heat courses over my arm. He's a furnace, and I want to burn alive.

I need to stop. "Maybe I should just go downstairs and check the breaker myself." I get to my feet, but my shitty ankle gives way and sends me sideways . . . right on top of him.

He grips my body with his hands to keep me from rolling to the floor, and I'm draped across his lap like a naughty schoolgirl who's about to get a paddling from the headmaster. Now instead of seeing the outline of his cock, I feel it pressing into my ribs. And it's so much bigger than it looked. And it's hard.

I get to my feet, but he keeps his hands on my waist as I stand in front of him.

His warm grip runs down to my hips, and I don't stop him. I absolutely should, but I don't. I'm too shocked. All this time, I thought he hated me—I thought I hated *him* —but I guess the animosity between us has been some weird form of foreplay. That's the only way I can rationalize the electric heat between us right now.

"What are you doing?" I ask, but it's a stupid fucking question. I know what he's doing, and I want him to do it.

"Shh."

His fingers sink into my sides, and he pulls me closer. After raising the hem of my cami with his teeth, his lips move along my stomach, his tongue spinning warm circles across my skin. I allow my hands to move to his biceps, to feel the taut muscles tensing just beneath the surface. Ridges ripple under my fingertips. I can only assume these are more scars. He's covered in them, but I somehow find them more of a turn on than a turn off. This man has survived something horrific. He has beaten something with his spirit instead of his fist.

A shiver runs through me as his hands explore beneath my shirt. He teases me with his tongue and teeth until he brings a moan from my lips.

Then he stops.

He fucking stops.

"I think it's been fifteen minutes," he whispers against my flesh. Warm breath brushes across the wet lines left behind by his kisses, and I want to melt. But why did he stop? What sort of cruel game is this? I'm ready to pounce on him and ride him like I'm going for the eight-second bell, and *now* he wants to check the breaker box?

He rises to his feet, and it takes everything in me to stop myself from yanking down his boxers and begging him to stay with my mouth. The rustle of fabric fills the silence as he puts on his pants and leaves the room. Once the door closes behind him, I pace beside the bed. No matter how I sort through this weird situation in my mind, it doesn't make any sense. He wanted me—I *felt* how much he wanted me—and even though I don't know why, I wanted him.

My foot collides with something by the bed. Nylon fabric wraps around my ankle. I kick it free, and something hard skitters across the floor. Feeling around, I realize the strap of his bag wound around my foot and I've knocked something out of it. I'll have to clean it up before he gets back so he doesn't think I was snooping. God, how embarrassing.

The ceiling fan whirs to life, and the gentle buzz of electricity fills the house once more. Whatever was wrong, Ambrose has fixed it. Now I just have to figure out how to fix whatever the fuck is wrong with me. I reach for the cord on the ceiling fan and light fills the room. This cabin has been empty for so long that the breakers probably—

Ice fills my veins, turning my blood to sleet. I can't breathe. My heart is the only functioning organ in my body, and it pounds a rapid beat in my chest. My eyes register what I knocked out of his bag, and my brain finally processes the chilling truth.

Ambrose is my stalker.

Chapter Eighteen

Ambrose

My plan didn't go as I expected. Well, it did, but I'm still struggling with doubt. She wanted me, but I wanted her too. I can't deny the way my body reacts to her. I stop at the bottom of the stairs and grip the railing. A crossroads waits before me, and I still don't know which way I should turn.

The risers creak beneath my feet as I climb toward the awaiting juncture. If I go in that room and fuck her the way my body begs me to—the way *her* body begs me to—I don't know if I can live with myself. It goes against everything inside me. She didn't want the man at the club or the dirty vagrant outside the gas station, but she would allow a scarred street fighter to get between her legs. A man other women look at with a disgust they can't hide. She might be a choosy whore, but she's still a whore. She's still too much like my mother.

I reach the top of the stairs and pause. Something thuds inside the bedroom, and the sound of a whimper follows. What is she doing? I rush to the door and open it in time to see her wide green eyes outside the window, her fingers gripping the sill as she dangles above the sloping half roof. Then she drops. I rush toward her, and my foot slams down on something hard. Cursing beneath my breath, I lift my foot and watch as a single acorn rolls beneath the bed.

God. Fucking. Damnit. She knows.

She won't get far in bare feet and on a busted ankle, so I grab my shoes and slip them on, then throw on a sleeveless t-shirt before I follow her. The knife I gave her lies on the small table beside the bed, forgotten. How unfortunate. I tuck it into my pocket so it can't be used against me later. I look out the window and see her running toward the woods. By the time I catch her, I'll be so amped up I won't be able to control myself. But that might be a good thing. I feel for my knife and lean through the open window as her pale skin disappears into the trees. "There's no need to run, Oaklyn!" I yell, but she doesn't even spare a glance behind her.

I drop from the window and land on the half roof with a thud, and I almost worry I'll sink through the shingles and land on the hardwoods covering the floor on the lower level. Instead, my sneakers grip the roof and guide me to the edge. My second descent is a bit more graceful. I sink into the soft ground and turn to face the trees.

"Oaklyn!" I scream into the darkness. "Stop running and face your tormenter. You're braver than this." The sound of bare feet tromping through dry leaves greets my ears, but it's growing more distant. I race into the forest to catch up with her.

Thorny vines scrape my skin, but the marks they leave behind only blend with my scars. These shallow wounds will fade, unlike the deep cuts my mother drove into my skin.

My eyes adjust to the darkness as much as they can. It helps me see the disturbed brush a little better, but not much. The leafy canopy diffuses most of the moonlight. I'm mostly guided by adrenaline and the scent of her fear, but this internal bloodhound serves me well. I rush forward until I spot her ahead, her body puncturing the forest, twisting and contorting through the trees in ways I can't. I'm too big for that. I expected her to be piss-poor prey, but my tragedy has surprised me again. At this rate, there's no way I'll catch up to her, and I desperately need to catch her. If she escapes me, she's sure to turn my ass in to the police. She knows too much now.

My heart races against my chest as I close the gap between us. She's slowing, a limp growing more obvious on her right side. Her injury rears its glorious head to cripple her and give me the advantage. It ruined her life once, and it's fully prepared to do it again. This time more permanently.

"Your ankle is giving you trouble, isn't it?" I shout toward her.

She curses and stumbles against a thin trunk that nearly cracks beneath her insignificant weight. Her gait grows more ragged. The pain coursing through her leg and foot must be terrible, because she's struggling to keep herself between the trees now. She stumbles into them like a pinball thrust into a rectangular box filled with branches and bushes. I slow down a little, enjoying her desperate attempt to escape. The ghosts of her past have wounded her as much as mine have wounded me. Unfortunately for her, my wounds spur me on while hers slow her down.

Even though I'm no longer running, I'm drawing closer because she's fully limping at this point. I'm near enough to hear her strangled whimpers and each gulp of air she fights to take in. As the trees grow thinner and we near the edge of a meadow, I see my opening and rush forward. My shoulder collides with her back, and I wrap my arms around her as I spear her toward the ground. The soft earth spreads beneath us, and her scream punctuates the silent woods.

"Please, don't," she gasps, pleading to any light inside me, but it's too late. This all-consuming darkness has overtaken my eyes, and I see nothing else.

I flip her onto her back, raise my hand to her throat, and enjoy the desperate movement of her skin beneath my palm as she tries to swallow. Her hands wrap around my wrist. Nails claw at my skin, tearing and biting, but I won't be deterred.

"Why did you run from me?" I ask, putting weight into my hand.

"You know why," she chokes out. She kicks her legs, flailing the way I longed for in her bedroom.

"Because I fucked you?" My cock hardens in an instant at the memory of defiling her as she slept.

She squirms beneath me again, gripping my wrist with renewed strength, but she doesn't answer the question.

"You ran because you didn't like what I did to your whore cunt."

She stalls beneath me. "I'm not a whore." That single word weighs her down more than I do. Rage replaces the panic in her eyes, laying a speed bump of doubt beneath the fiery chariot racing toward her.

Some women don't like to be called a whore, even when the ugly shoe fits, but her disdain for the word is . . . different. I still can't decide if she's delusional and wants me to use more politically correct terminology or if she really doesn't believe she's exactly what I say she is. Maybe she needs a refresher.

"Do I need to show you the video, Oaklyn? Show you how much of a whore you are?"

She grits her teeth and stares into my eyes. "Do I need to show you a dictionary? I'm not a fucking whore."

That's enough of that. I adjust my grip on her body and flip her onto her belly, pinning her down with my crotch against her ass. Pulling my knife from my hip, I bring it to her throat and press the flat side against her skin so she can fully grasp what she's up against. Her fingers grip the sparse meadow grass and sink into the earth. It's the only movement she can make with a blade so close to such a vulnerable part of her body. I brush tendrils of sweat-soaked hair from her cheek, and my fingers slide through a river of tears. I absorb the liquid hurt into my skin, letting it live there. With my free hand, I yank down her shorts and rub her tears between her legs.

So soft.

So warm.

She strains against me as I work open my jeans, but she can't free herself from my need. Her thighs clench. It's meant to keep me out, but it only makes it easier to guide myself to the heat between her legs as I push inside her. So deep in her struggle, she feels incredible. So fucking tight.

I lean down so that my mouth hangs just beside her ear, then I curl my hips forward until I feel her end. Turning the blade in my hand, I press the thin edge against her throat. "I'm going to give you your finale, my tragedy."

"No, no, please!" she begs.

I move my free hand to her hip to give myself more leverage, but I stop. My fingers run over something I know all too well. Lines of raised flesh. Several of them. A mosaic of familiar marks.

"What's this?" I ask, tracing the ridges along her hip.

"You aren't the only one with scars," she cries.

It's the first time she's mentioned my scars. How long has she been holding on to her opinion of them? I halt the straining motion of my hips, keeping flush against her ass.

"I don't know if you noticed them before," she pants, "but feel my hips. My thighs."

I saw the scars on her thighs in the car and when I fucked her. But I didn't see her hips.

"Are these from your accident?" I ask.

"Some of them," she says, "but I put most of them there myself."

"Then we aren't the same."

"Someone caused your scars. Someone caused mine too. I just held the blade."

Her words outline a painful story, and that bothers me. I don't want to feel sympathy for her. I don't want her to become a person. I want to use and discard her. That's it.

Unwilling to let her confuse me further, I harness as much anger as I can and push the blade against her neck again. But something stops me. It *can't* stop me. I've gone too far. With my cock buried in her unconsenting cunt, I'm *still* going too far.

"Please don't kill me yet," she begs. "Give me a few days to show you who I am, then you can decide. Please, Ambrose."

When she says my name, doubt sinks its teeth into my gut and rattles my bones in a death roll. And I hate it. I should end her right now. Here in these woods, deep in the middle of nowhere, I could commit the perfect crime and exact my long-awaited revenge. I could finally free myself of these violent thoughts and cleanse these scars with blood.

So why can't I do it?

Her warmth pulses around my cock. Maybe it wouldn't hurt to give her a few more days. A short stay of execution in exchange for something I need just as much as revenge. "You want to live, tragedy?" I ask.

She nods and the blade strains against her neck. "Yes," she whimpers.

I ease the knife away from her and replace it in its sheath. "Then let my come be the only thing that can save you."

I pull back and push into her again. She becomes a small and complacent thing, letting out pained groans as I grind her into the dirt and fuck her harder. Selfishly. Though she tenses and tightens around me, she doesn't try to get free. She consumes every inch I give her and clutches the wispy sprigs of grass in her clenched fists.

"Raise your hips a little. Let me go deeper," I growl.

She does as I command, arching her back so that I can push further inside her. I draw closer to my release with each thrust, but her hair has fallen over her cheek again. I want to see her face. Leaning forward, I grind against her ass and pull back the red curtain to reveal her green eyes. Her full lips. Her fear.

It's enough to send me over the edge.

"Take my come like a good whore," I growl in her ear as I fill her. I bask in her warmth for several more thrusts, then I pull out of her. Her body relaxes, and she doesn't make a move to run as I ease away from her. Good. "You can get up now."

She gets onto her knees and raises her shorts without bothering to clean up the mess between her legs. As she struggles to her feet, I fight the urge to help her. It's her own fault. All of this is her fault.

I fold my arms over my chest and study her. "Don't try to run again. It won't end well for you."

She nods her head without looking at me and rubs her arms with her hands. She must be cold.

I turn and motion for her to follow me, and like a whipped dog, she does. "We should get back to the house. The play is almost over, but I'm willing to see what surprises you have in store for the final act."

And it will be the final act. There will be no encore. When the curtain falls in a few days, this traveling show will come to an end. I refuse to back down next time, no matter how the uncertainty rallies against my purpose. After all, a tragedy can't have a happy ending.

Chapter Nineteen

Oaklyn

I limp through the woods on the way back to the cabin, keeping some distance between me and my attacker. My stalker. What the fuck have I gotten myself into? I nearly fucked him willingly. Had he not stopped to check the breaker box, I would have allowed him between my legs.

The breaker box. He cut it off.

I fight the urge to repeatedly slam my palm against my forehead and rave about what an absolute moron I've been. Though I've never considered myself a genius, I at least counted myself among the intelligent—an egocentric distinction I can no longer claim. It doesn't take Sherlock fucking Holmes to put the pieces together now. The way he always seemed to show up at the club when I finished my shift. The fact that only my stripper clothes were destroyed when my line of work disgusts him. His willingness to drive me, a complete stranger, halfway across the country. It's so obvious.

But not all of it was so clear, I remind myself. How had he recorded the video in the private area? How had he plastered pictures all over the dressing room and left an acorn and some jizz in my shoes without drawing any attention?

Maybe I shouldn't be so hard on myself.

A sharp pain cuts a path from my ankle to my knee, and I stumble against a tree. Rough bark scrapes against my cheek. I try to keep from making a sound, but a whimper squeaks out of me. Ambrose keeps going. He's walking pretty fucking proud of himself while I'm absolutely crippled. He wouldn't have caught me if it wasn't for this damn ankle. Just one more way my injury has affected my life.

"Keep up," he calls over his shoulder.

I stare at the back of his tousled hair. It's not brown. Not blonde. Somewhere in the middle. I've sat beside him several times now, but I haven't really studied him like this. Inching through the forest, I have nowhere else to look.

"My ankle hurts," I say, dropping to the forest floor to rub away the ache in my useless limb.

He stops and turns to face me, his brown eyes narrowing. "Your ankle wouldn't hurt if I had killed you like I was supposed to. Would you like me to remedy that?"

Maybe that would be better at this point. I'm returning to my parents' cabin with a man who plans to use me for several days before ultimately ending me. I stupidly asked for more time because I hoped it would give me a chance to prove my life is worth living. But is it? Now that I've been placed outside the normalcy of everyday life, I can look through the window and see my existence for what it really is. I don't like what I see, so why would he? I'm prolonging my suffering at this point, but the human need to keep sucking air won't allow me to give up just yet.

So I don't answer him.

My silence doesn't seem to sit well with him, because he stalks toward me with clenched fists and a set jaw. I tremble harder with every crunch of the leaf litter beneath his shoes. When he reaches me, I clench my eyelids shut and await the moment he unleashes his frustration on me. Well, I wait for him to do more than he already has. Then his arms wrap around me and . . . I'm rising?

He cradles me against his chest and takes a step forward. While allowing him to carry me would be of benefit to my busted leg, the warmth of his hands on my bare skin makes me uncomfortable. I wriggle in his grasp and try to free myself, but he stops and clutches me tighter, his fingertips digging into my muscles.

"Do you want help or do you want to keep walking on your crippled ankle?" he snaps, his muscles straining to contain me.

I don't want his fucking help. I don't want his hands on me. He's the reason my ankle feels like I've taken a jackhammer to the joint. But I *can't* keep walking on it. The metal plate grinds beneath my flesh and sends a bolt of pain into my hip with each unstable step. So I stop squirming. I relax every muscle in my body, hoping he enjoys carrying my dead weight.

Asshole.

The foliage thickens around us, and we reach the part of the woods where the thorny vines run rampant. They shredded my skin on the way in, and I brace myself for more of the same on the way out. With the way he's holding me, I'll bear the brunt of it.

Seeming to realize this, he stops and sets me on my feet, then gives me his back and squats down. "Climb on."

Allowing him to pick me up was one thing, but willingly draping my body over him and pressing my boobs into his back is another. I go to take a step, determined to do this on my own, but my body refuses to cooperate. My arm flails for a nearby tree trunk, but I only succeed in slicing my palm on a vine. "Fuck, fuck, fuck," I whisper as I pull my hand to my chest.

"Would you stop being so stubborn and just get on my goddamn back? I'd like to make it to the cabin before next week."

"Fuck you," I say under my breath. If he hears me, he doesn't react.

But he's right, as much as I hate to admit it. Getting myself through the tangle of branches, bushes, and vines will take forever. The cabin might only be one hundred yards away, but that's miles on this ankle.

Closing my eyes and heaving a sigh, I step closer and position myself against his back with my arms wrapped around his neck. I'm braless, and I can only hope he doesn't feel the hard points my nipples have tightened into. It has nothing to do with him and everything to do with the chill in the air. He hooks his powerful arms beneath my thighs and rises with little effort, then releases his hold once he's standing.

"You'll need to hook your legs around me," he says. "I can't move shit out of the way without the use of my arms."

I hate the way his deep voice vibrates through his back and sinks into my core, but I grit my teeth and do as he says. As we weave through the compact forest, I duck my head and press my cheek against the back of his neck to shield my face. His leathery scent rushes into my nose. Part of my body recoils with disgust, but the other part—namely my lower half—wants me to keep breathing in that glorious smell. I try to appease the opposing sides of my brain by sniffing, just not as deeply.

Lights glimmer in the distance, filtering through the leaves and dispelling the darkness. We break through the tree line, and he slows to a stop. As he squats again, I ease off his back and steady myself by gripping his shoulders. I go to take a step forward, but pain rockets up my leg and I let out a yelp. Cue an Ambrose eye roll. I want to scream into his face and remind him once more that this is all his fault, but I don't have the chance because I'm swept into his arms again as he carries me toward the house. He brings me in through the back door and sets me on the couch. I bat his hands away the moment my back hits the thick cushion, but he grips my wrists and pins my arms above my head. Leaning down, he places his face against my neck.

And he inhales.

"What are you doing?" I ask, panic climbing up my throat on a wave of bile.

He stops. "The same thing you did to me." His warm breath glides over my skin and brings goosebumps to the surface.

Now I'm just mortified because he knew I was sniffing him the entire time I rode him like a pack mule. I can't get a word out, even if I wanted to. I'm ashamed because of this undeniable attraction I feel for the man who has been tormenting me for weeks. The man who drugged me and took what he wanted. What I would have willingly given him had he asked.

None of it makes sense! He's not unattractive. He's scarred, sure, but there's an undeniable handsomeness beneath those scars. Why the fuck would he need to stalk and assault me?

He releases my hands and goes to the kitchen. He rifles through the cabinets and drawers, finds what he's looking for, and begins filling whatever it is with ice. He wraps it with a dishrag he pulls from a drawer, then brings it to me.

"Put this on your ankle," he says, wiggling it in front of my face. "It'll bring the inflammation down."

I take the baggie of ice from him and apply it to my ankle with a wince. I almost thank him, but then I remind myself that this is. His. Fucking. Fault.

He disappears into the pantry and reemerges with an economy-sized jar of peanut butter. As he bends to look for a spoon, his white undershirt rides up his muscular back and reveals even more scars. My breath hitches. His face, head, arms, and back are covered in them, so I can only imagine where else they mark his skin. What the hell happened to him? I know he fights, but those aren't from fighting. When he turns around, he catches me gawking.

"Want a closer look?" He abandons the peanut butter and spoon on the counter and walks toward me. As he nears the couch, he grips the hem of his t-shirt and lifts it away from him. "Maybe looking isn't enough for you." He grabs my hand and runs it along his abs. Along the scars. There are so many.

I don't try to pull away, and that seems to bother him more than if I struggled to free myself from his skin. If he expects me to be repulsed by these marks, he's setting himself up for disappointment. Am I intrigued? Absolutely. But I'm not disgusted.

He drops my hand and returns to the kitchen for his peanut butter without another word. It's almost as if he's looking for a reason to fly off the handle and attack me, and now he's annoyed that I didn't fulfill my side of the bargain. I won't give him a reason to kill me.

I wrack my brain, trying to figure out why he's chosen me as his target and why he feels like he has to end my life. If he's worried I'll rat him out now that I've seen his face, he doesn't have anything to worry about. No one would believe me. He's not the only one who views me as a worthless whore. If I say he assaulted me, he'll just claim it was consensual. That I asked for it. No one believes the woman.

"You don't have to do any of this, Ambrose. You could leave. I didn't call the police after what you did to me, and I won't call them now. Just go. Please."

He stops the spoon before it reaches his mouth, and he tightens his lips as if he's considering it. The spoon lowers. "Why didn't you?"

I can't answer that. He doesn't need to know why; he just needs to know I didn't. I shake my head and focus on the ceiling. "Why are you doing this to me?"

"That's a complex question with an even more complex answer," he says, then he finally shoves the spoon into his mouth. He has no intention of elaborating any further.

I turn away from him and lie on my side, exhausted after my late night hike through the woods. The chill from the ice burrows into my bones and creates a new ache, but I leave it there. That pain is more tolerable than the alternative. I begin to doze, but I snap awake when I hear him rinsing the spoon in the sink. Then he comes closer.

"Time for bed," he says as he scoops me into his arms.

I push against him and try to free myself, but his hold is too strong. "I'm not sleeping in a bed with you."

A smirk slides across his face as he looks down at me, and a shadow darkens his brown eyes. "Oh, you absolutely are. I won't risk you slipping out the window again. Only one of us will leave here alive, tragedy, and I'm not ready to drop the curtain just yet."

The stark realization stares me in the face, and I can't hide from the truth. I'm going to die. I'm going to be murdered because I got into his Jeep. Because I hitchhiked.

As he climbs the stairs with me in his arms, I can only imagine what I'll have to endure before I draw my last breath. It doesn't help that he's so fucking attractive. If my stalker had been someone like Jake, I would only have to endure situational fear and panic. Now I have to deal with confusion on top of that.

He's a killer, Oaklyn! Think with your head and not your hormones!

"I have to use the bathroom," I blurt.

He lowers me to my feet at the top of the stairs, and I hobble toward the first door on the right. He stays close behind me. I fear he'll demand to watch me relieve myself, but he only wants to check the bathroom to ensure I can't escape. Satisfied with the useless miniature window that only a child could fit through, he leaves and closes the door behind him.

I lower my shorts and sit on the toilet, running through ways to save myself as I piss. There aren't any weapons in here. There aren't even any items that could be repurposed into weapons. The most dangerous item is the seashell soap dish, and that won't do me any good. He looks like he takes harder hits to the head than what I could ever muster. I stupidly left the knife in his room when I panicked and flew out the window. He's probably hidden it now. Without any options—or brilliant ideas—I grab a washcloth from the shelf above the toilet and clean myself as much as I can. As I rub the dirt from my face and rinse it down the drain, I sense him out there.

Listening.

Waiting.

When I exit the bathroom, he's standing there with his arm above his head, resting it against the door frame. That pose would be panty melting if he wasn't such a psycho. He pulls a flask from behind his back and offers it to me.

"For your pain," he says.

How fucking sweet.

I scoff. I'm not taking anything from him. He doesn't have a good track record with mixing drinks.

His hand drops to the handle of his knife and I sigh. I take the flask from him and unscrew the top.

"Good girl," he says with a smirk. "Only take a sip, though. That shit is potent."

With a roll of my eyes, I tilt the flask and let the flavorless liquid wash over my tongue. It tastes like water, and I consider guzzling a bit more. I'm fucking thirsty. I listen to his advice and take the smallest sip I can, though. The memory of the two shots of vodka isn't that far removed from my mind.

I hand over what I can only assume is night-night juice and allow him to lead me to my bedroom. He checks the window as I sit on the edge of the bed, and I hope he'll allow me to sleep alone once he sees no easy way out of this room. He crushes that hope beneath his ass when he walks to the other side of the bed and sits down.

I'm not sleeping with this man. Nope.

I clamber out of bed, leaning my weight on the nightstand as the pain shoots through me again.

A strong hand reaches out, grips my arm, and drags me back to the mattress. "Where do you think you're going, tragedy?"

"Why do you keep calling me that?" I exhale a defeated breath and lie back, scooting as far from him as I can.

He rests his head on his hand. "Because you're going to have an unhappy ending. I knew this from the moment I met you." He turns off the bedside lamp. "Go to sleep. Tomorrow, we begin act three."

Chapter Twenty

Ambrose

She doesn't relax as she lies beside me. Each rigid muscle tightens with tension because she's in bed with the thing of her nightmares. Instead of waking up and escaping the monster in her bad dreams, she'll wake up next to it. And I'm enjoying that way too much. I listen in the dark, and her ragged breathing eventually shifts to something soft and even. It was only a matter of time. She didn't get the heavy dose she took from the vodka bottle, but a sip will be enough to keep her knocked out for a while.

Now that she's asleep, I'm left with my thoughts. I had one goal in mind when I agreed to drive her out here, and that was to end things. The perfect opportunity presented itself in the woods, but it only showed me how weak I truly am. Instead of digging a deep grave to hide my unleashed vengeance, I'm lying beside her to ensure she doesn't run off. I keep coming up with excuses to keep her alive, but I can't continue to do this.

Even though I know how this has to end, I want her around for a few more days. I want to experience more of her. But I'm afraid of what I'll find within her. What if I start to like everything I've hated? I worked too hard and nursed my hatred for too long to let that happen.

It doesn't help that she's trying to find similarities between us. She fails to see that her scars aren't mine. They're hidden in private places, not showcased for the world to see. She doesn't have to wear a leather jacket in the summer heat to keep people from openly staring at her. She may think she understands me, but she has no idea.

The knife on my hip calls to me. I could cut her up and help her understand. Slice her face so she can feel a shred of the shame I've known my entire life. She'd hate who looks back at her in the mirror. Like I do.

I pull the knife from its sheath and shift onto my side. Bringing myself closer to her body, I hold the blade so that it hovers just above her pale skin. I mimic dragging it down her arm and creating a red fissure that would take time to heal. But that flesh would never be as it is now. Pure. Unblemished. A blank canvas. It would become like mine. Ugly. Destroyed. Disgusting. I brush the hair from her face and press the knife against her cheek. The soft skin sinks beneath the weight, and it would only take a little more pressure to bring a line of blood to the surface.

But I can't.

I slide the knife into its sheath and grit my teeth. Why can't I do this?

I reach out and rub my hand down her side, feeling her in ways she won't allow when she's awake. Well, she would have allowed it if she hadn't discovered the acorns. She wanted it. Her soft moan as I kissed her stomach told me so, and that's why I had to stop her. It proves she's the whore I've made her out to be. Only a cumslut would be so willing to sleep with a scarred monster.

Thinking about the soft sound that rolled from her lips hardens me. It shouldn't, but I can't deny the way my body begs to use her again. I band an arm around her waist and pull her against me so that her ass presses into my pelvis. She doesn't stir. Her heat melts into me, and the scent of soil and sweat reaches my nose. She doesn't smell like the club now. She smells like my untamed thing. Mine.

My hand moves to the front of her neck, and heavy thoughts of squeezing her throat creep into my mind. Instead, I move lower and free her breast from her camisole. The natural curves of that soft mound call to me, begging me to touch. To taste. To enjoy. This would be easier if she had those super-fake tits. I wouldn't be so tempted by her. It's a temptation I shouldn't give in to, but my cock aches for her. Once tonight wasn't enough.

I remove her shorts and rush to release myself from my jeans because this girl has occupied every waking thought I've had since the night she got into my car. I put my cock against her, then slide it between her warm thighs. I'm still haunted by the memory of how it felt to slip inside her. I need to feel it again. Selfishly. Her days are numbered, which means I can only relive this moment so many times before I never feel her around me again. A countdown hangs above her head, the seconds ticking down, and I *have* to fuck her until detonation.

I draw my hips back and spit in my hand, then coat my dick with saliva. Gripping her full hip, I push inside her. A muffled whimper sticks in her throat. She stirs against me, but I won't stop. I can't.

"Shh, tragedy. I'm just taking what I decided was mine the moment I set eyes on you. Go back to sleep."

Her face settles against the pillow, but I doubt my words have relaxed her. She's lost to the gentle hum of a dream-inducing cocktail.

I ease out of her and glide through her warm center, my movements controlled and gentle. It's almost as if I don't want to wake her. Because I don't. I just want to use her.

With every pulse of my hips, her wetness grows. She'd never get wet like this if she were awake. I'd probably be forced to listen to fake moans as she pretended to enjoy it, and I don't want that. I want her exactly as she is right now—slippery and compliant. She's fun when she's feisty and full of fire, but I like this just as much. Maybe more.

My hand rises to her chest as I push inside her again, and I find the hardened tip of her nipple. I hold that perfect point between my fingers, rolling it around as my palm fills with her full breast. She stirs again and her back arches. Am I pleasing her? The whimper transforms into a soft moan, and now I'm certain she's enjoying this. I'm also certain she's imagining someone else inside her mind. Someone she likes. Someone who isn't covered in scars. Someone who isn't me.

My hand rises to her throat, and I push into her as I keep time with her pulse against my fingertips. I pull her warm body closer to mine. Everything about her teases my senses. My eyes feast on her slightly parted lips, and I imagine pushing past them with my cock. The scent of her berry shampoo cradles me as I bury my face into her hair and increase the tempo of my hips. I lick the crook of her neck, and her fear-laced sweat dances on my tongue. Each soft whimper and moan elicits a rush of euphoria in my brain. And the touch. Oh god, the touch. She's so soft she doesn't even feel real.

She grows silent, her mind crossing the line between semi-conscious and unconscious. I lower my hand and put it between her legs, exploring until I find her swollen clit. But she doesn't respond.

How very disappointing.

I roll her onto her back and hover above her. A veil of red hair obscures her face, but I want to see those closed eyes. I brush the hair away and am rewarded with a sight that makes my balls ache. Her eyes are closed, her lips moving only when a puff of breath whispers past them. Fuck Sleeping Beauty. My tragedy is a sleeping *goddess*.

I'm overcome with the need to be inside her again. I spread her thighs and rub my thumb against her clit. She's so slick and warm. When I still don't get a reaction, I move closer and push my cock into her until I can't go any further. That brings another moan past her loose lips.

"Shhh. Let me fuck your pretty little pussy while you sleep," I whisper. "Just let me use you. I'll be done once I've given you every last drop of me."

My hands move to her waist. I pull her against me with each forward thrust, driving into her harder and faster. She moans again and the headboard bangs against the wall, overtaking her sensual sounds.

"God, you are *such* a good whore." The last word changes on my tongue. It sheds its cocoon of disgust and undergoes a metamorphosis, shifting into something vestal and precious.

I part her thighs further and push deeper. I can't hold out any longer. I wanted to squeeze her throat and feel her come around me, but I'll have to wait until she's awake. When she's more conscious, I can force her sweet little cunt to spasm for me. Even though she hates me, I'll make those green eyes come to life before they roll to the back of her head. And then I'll rip that life away.

For good.

My hips stall, and a deep groan rolls from my chest as I fill her. She'll be pissed when she wakes up and feels my come between her legs again. When she realizes I took advantage of her once more, that will only add to the anger. But how would she feel if she knew how she'd moaned when I fucked her? Too bad I didn't record it. She'll never believe me if I tell her.

Sated, I climb off her and ease her legs straight, then cover her with the blanket.

I don't bother putting her shorts on because it's not like I'm trying to hide what I've done. On the contrary. I want her to know. When she wakes up tomorrow, I want to watch her face fall when she realizes I've defiled her.

I roll onto my side and close my eyes, refusing to fight with myself over my realization: When she wakes up tomorrow, I want to defile her again.

Chapter Twenty-One

Ambrose

Morning sun fills the room, and I wake to Oaklyn huffing up a storm. She tosses my arm off her with absolute disgust because I somehow turned over and held her while I was asleep. It's a small fucking bed. I'm surprised we didn't wake up on top of each other. Her slender fingers lift the blanket and she peers beneath it, then she reaches down and touches herself. If she didn't realize I fucked her before, her soaked pussy would definitely clue her in now.

Her haunting green eyes meet mine, and she releases the blanket. Instead of panic, a level of brokenness masks her face. It's a look I've never seen on another person . . . besides myself.

"Just get it over with and kill me, Ambrose. You've done enough to me. Stop playing this cat-and-mouse game and just take the final bite already." Tears well in her eyes, and she tries to blink them away. "I can't do this anymore. You act like I had some life I loved before you came and fucked it all up. You think you're causing me so much agony, but I was in agony long before I met you."

I shake my head. "I'm not done with you yet. You don't get to decide when it's time to end the show."

She looks away, her jaw tensing as her teeth clench together, and before I can react, she's on top of me. I don't expect her speed or agility, and that lapse in judgment will be my undoing because she's reaching for my knife. I expect the blade to sink into my skin, so I close my eyes and grit my teeth against the incoming assault. She'll bury it in my flesh, just as my mother did. She'll prove that I've chosen the perfect representation of the woman I hate.

But she doesn't do any of that.

I open my eyes. She's kneeling on the bed, the knife clasped in her shaking hand, but the blade isn't aimed at me. It presses against her own throat.

"If you won't do it, I will," she says through gritted teeth. Her green eyes have taken on a feral glint. She's a cornered animal, fully prepared to gnaw off her own limb to free herself from the hunter's snare. I know this look because I've been there myself.

"Give me that," I say, reaching for the blade.

She leans back, pressing the knife into her skin until a thin line of red appears just below the razor-sharp edge. "My life ended months ago. You can't kill something that's already dead." Her nostrils flare wildly, and something tells me this is much more than an act meant to push me to release her. She's not bluffing.

I spring forward and grip her arm, twisting her around and putting her back against my chest while keeping the knife away from her throat. An inhuman scream erupts from low in her gut. She struggles to break free, slicing my forearm as she bucks and writhes against me.

"Give me the goddamn knife." The words bite out of me, ripping through my throat. I have control of her wrist and I'm not trying to stab her, which is comical considering I had fully intended to do exactly that. It's my entire reason for being here.

She wiggles free and sends a parting kick into my groin. I drop to the floor. Gripping my stomach in a breathless heap, I'm useless to stop what happens next. I can only watch as she retreats to the door, but I don't panic. If she runs, I'll catch her.

But she doesn't run. She stops at the door and turns to face me, an untamed electricity pinging through her eyes. Her chest heaves with each breath she takes. Her nostrils flare. With a scream, she thrusts her arm in my direction and drags the knife down her forearm. Right up and down the road. She looks down at the wound, a haze of disbelief crossing her face as the blood funnels through the gash and drips onto the floor.

Fuck me.

Air rushes into my lungs, and I'm on my feet. I rip the knife out of her grasp and toss it away as she begins to sway against the wall. I wrap my arms around her and carry her to the bed, setting her on the edge and gripping her shoulders to keep her upright. Warmth slaps against my foot, and I look down. A crimson ribbon slides from her and pools against the hardwood. I have to stop the bleeding.

When I release her shoulders, Oaklyn lies back on the bed, her eyelashes fluttering. I tear the shirt from my body and wind it around the wound until I've run out of fabric. It's not enough. Blood crowds the cotton fibers, turning it a deep shade of vermillion.

"Stupid girl," I snarl, even as her eyes shudder closed.

Blood coats my fingers, leaving them tacky as it tries to dry. I have to stop the bleeding, but a hospital isn't an option. I press down on the wound, mentally urging the fucking fountain to shut off before it kills her.

Why?

Why the hell am I doing this?

If she wants to die, I should let her. This ending wouldn't be as beautiful as the one I planned in my head, but it's still a tragic way to go out. If I release her arm, she'll bleed out before long, even if she missed the radial artery. I just need to let go. I loosen my grip, and a trickle of blood snakes down her arm and spreads through the blanket beneath her.

I can't do it.

My hands seize her arm again, applying more pressure than before. "Oaklyn," I shout, lifting one hand long enough to smack her sweat-coated cheek.

She doesn't respond. I want to tell her I'm not ready for her to die. I'm not ready to let her go. Once she's gone, what do I go back to? She gave me something worthwhile to focus on, even if the focus was only harnessed hatred. Now, that hatred has morphed into something foreign. Something I can't explain or understand. The scales stand even, with disdain weighing down one side and admiration on the other.

And I do admire her, especially considering what she's just done. It was something I wanted to do countless times. Hell, I even tried once, but I only ended up adding more scars to my body.

No one was there to beg me to stay, though.

I only survived because I hadn't driven the blade deep enough. She might have accomplished what I couldn't, and the thought terrifies me. No one is exempt from the wake of destruction she's left in the path to her end, and I've been caught in the fallout. Even if I can't explain it, even if I don't yet understand it, I have to save her.

Chapter Twenty-Two

Oaklyn

A thick fog obscures my eyes, and I don't recognize the hard feeling beneath me. This isn't a mattress. It's wood. My fingers move along the surface, gliding until I reach an edge, and I realize I'm on a table. *What the fuck?* I bring a hand to my head, then lower it to my aching wrist. I graze taut, sticky skin and a seam in my flesh.

Memories rush back, and the fog over my eyes begins to dissipate. I'm at the cabin. I ran from my stalker. My stalker is Ambrose. He threatened to kill me, and I . . .

I touch my wrist again, unable to admit what I've done.

A bottle of super glue sits on the shelf beside me. I feel my arm again and note the hard line that runs through the wound. He pushes me to this and then saves me? Why? So I can play more of his little game? The cat has stepped on the mouse's tail and pulled it back toward its teeth.

Footsteps come toward me, and his warm hand grips my wrist. "You're lucky you had super glue here. Otherwise, I was about to have to stitch you with some needle and thread," he says, examining his handiwork. "Superglue is a fighter's best friend."

"Or you could have just let me die."

He shakes his head. "You wouldn't have died. Once the bleeding slowed, I could see that you didn't go deep enough. You nicked some blood vessels, but you missed the important ones. You'll be woozy for a while, but you'll live."

I sit up and immediately regret that decision when the blood rushes from my head and the haze returns. Blinking back the fog, I steady myself and take a deep breath. "I don't understand," I whisper. "You say you want to kill me, but you went out of your way to save me. You should have just let it happen or helped me along."

"You aren't ending this on your terms."

"Let me go or end me, Ambrose." I turn to face him, but he refuses to look me in the eye.

He pats the wound. "It's dry. Go shower," he says, and I realize he already has. Who showers while someone is unconscious on the dining room table? I guess the same person who fucks someone while they're unconscious.

Fucking Ambrose.

"I'm good," I say. If I'm stinking and covered in blood, maybe he won't keep having his way with me.

"Now, tragedy," he says, raising his voice.

My eyes narrow on him. "Or what?"

He fists my hair and draws my lips toward his mouth. "I'll fuck you right now. I know you'd rather die than have my scarred body all over you again." He breathes against my lips. "Right?"

Double A right I would, but it has nothing to do with his scars. I won't explain that to him, though. Let him think whatever he wants. "I'll shower," I say, and I hope my decision drives a dagger through his heart.

As I drop my legs from the side of the table, the weight of the world assaults me. A dizzying buzz knocks me off balance, but a strong arm catches me before my ribs collide with the table.

"Slow down," he says. "You've lost a surprising amount of blood. I wasn't even sure I could get you closed up."

"My hero," I say as I push his hand away.

A smirk creeps onto his lips. I grip the table to balance myself, and my skin sticks to my shirt. I look down. Dried blood cakes my clothes and skin. Yeah, I need a fucking shower, not only to clean up but to rid myself of all traces of Ambrose on my body. In my body. A wild shiver runs through me.

I limp to the downstairs bathroom. He knows I have nowhere to go, so he doesn't follow me. Warm steam rises as I turn on the shower. I undress and step inside, averting my eyes from the rust-colored water circling the drain. A crust clings to the edge of the shampoo bottle from years of sitting on a shelf, and I flick it away so I can squirt some into my hands. I work up a thick lather in my hair, closing my eyes as the sweat eases its grip on my scalp and floats away on the suds. Using a washcloth, I scrub my skin until it's pink. I don't use as much effort around my wrist, only pressing hard enough to release the dried blood. A deep ache claws through my arm. Flaming fingers drag glass nails through the muscles. I really did a number on myself.

Stepping out of the shower, I release a deep sigh. It feels so fucking good to be clean. Renewed. More hell awaits me when I leave the bathroom—more Ambrose—but I can't think about that right now. I wish I was back at the club, bitching about my life. At least I could dance. My ankle sings when I put weight on it, and I'm not sure I'll ever dance again. In any capacity.

I reach for the towel hanging by the sink, and I'm annoyed to find it wet. We usually bring our own towels when we visit because moths always seem to eat up any we've left behind. This one already has holes in it and was probably abandoned because of it. My lip curls as I wrap it around myself. I don't want his body against mine in any way, shape, or form. I also don't like that I enjoy the scent he left behind.

My foot brushes against my shirt on the floor. It's a grotesque reminder of waking up with my shorts off and my pussy full of *him*. Again. I lift the shirt and a groan rises into my throat. The blood will never come out of it. Yet another article of clothing this man has destroyed.

With a sigh, I pull the towel closer and step into the hallway. My ankle cries as I hobble toward the kitchen and look around. I expect to see Ambrose, but he's gone. Maybe he thought better of everything he was doing and left. I'd be forced to limp for miles to the nearest sign of life, but I don't exactly hate the prospect, especially if it means I'm free of him.

But no. He comes through the front door with a plastic bag clutched in his fist. He says nothing as he goes to the fridge and begins placing things inside. Vodka. Ginger beer. Limes? It's everything I'd need to make my favorite drink, but how the hell does he know what I drink?

Realization smacks me and reminds me he's been stalking me, and it's clearly gone on longer and with much more attention to detail than I expected. My brain struggles to wrap around the thought of him sitting in the shadows as I ordered a Moscow Mule and drank it, blissfully unaware.

It's gross.

It's weird.

So why am I the tiniest bit intrigued by it?

He isn't the first man to obsess over me, but I can't remember the last time someone studied things that mattered to me. Usually it's my bra size or how flexible I am, not something so inconsequential as what I order at the bar. A pit forms in my stomach. Instead of being repulsed, I'm bordering on insane because I'm actually a bit touched. Then I think of everything else he's done to me and yep, there it is. The repulsion returns.

I shuffle toward the stairs and grip the railing, but he's at my side before I can take the first step.

His arm winds around my waist, and his warmth presses against my back. "You need to sit down. Those stairs are steep, and you're still weak."

"My clothes are upstairs in my bag."

He guides me to the couch and pushes me onto the cushion, then he heads upstairs. When he returns with my bag, he holds it toward me. "You don't have much in there."

"Yeah, some asshole cut up most of my clothes." I snatch it away, not wanting his hands on my things for a moment longer.

His lips twitch. "Maybe it was an asshole who didn't want you parading around like a whore."

"What's your issue, dude? Whore this. Whore that. Who are you trying to convince? Or are you just struggling with the fact that you're attracted to me?"

A growl leaves his throat, and he's on me before I can blink. He places his hands to either side of my head on the back of the couch, bracketing me between biceps cut from marble. "I'm not attracted to you. I'm not attracted to women *like* you," he snarls. Lies weave between his angry words, tied off with a knot of fallacy. His own voice box doesn't believe the words he speaks.

I look into his dark eyes and steady myself. "Whatever you say."

He leans closer and his warm breath rushes over my cheek. When he speaks, it's all gravel and tempered frustration. "Don't tempt me, tragedy. I'll end the show right now. Break your little neck. Show you just how unattractive and worthless you are to me."

I want to laugh in his face with each new lie he tells. I've struck a nerve, and the way his dick strains against his jeans tells me everything I need to know. He can say he isn't attracted to me all he wants, but his body betrays him. He's very much attracted to me, and I'm far from worthless in his eyes. You don't stop a worthless woman from killing herself.

My body betrays me as well. With each breath that caresses my skin, my core clenches a little tighter. Goosebumps pebble my skin. Confusion overwhelms me as thoughts scrabble for purchase in my mind. I don't want him inside me again, but I don't know if that's because I genuinely don't want it . . .

Or because I'm not *supposed* to want it.

No woman deserves to have her consent stripped away from her, and I'm not advocating for assault here, but what if a woman discovers she doesn't mind if it happens again? I'm sure the first person who voiced their love for being tied up and flogged got some weird looks too. It's not anything I've fantasized about, but now that it's happened, I can't deny that I'm open to being used by him again. I won't lie to myself about that. I won't be like him.

But I won't admit it to his face, either. Admitting it to myself is enough.

I clutch my bag to my chest and duck under his arm. This close proximity is too dangerous for a number of reasons. I'm losing my fucking mind, for starters. Clutching the scratchy towel to my body, I head for the bathroom to change into something comfortable. Once I'm behind the closed door, I dress in a pair of jean shorts and a tank top. My reflection catches my eye. Bruises still stain my neck, and I got some gnarly scratches from running through the woods. An ashen cast to my skin makes me look a bit tired, but I suppose blood loss will do that to a person. I study the gash in my arm—a red wound that will become yet another scar.

Why did I do it?

I don't have a good answer. My mindset at the time wasn't fabulous. He dredged up the sunken ships of my past, and it was hard to look at them lying on the shore. Useless. Destroyed. Decaying. He's forcing me to look at what I've become, and I can't do that without glancing over my shoulder at what I used to be. What I'll never be again.

I close my eyes. I don't want to look anymore.

My line of work doesn't bother me, and I'm not ashamed of what I do. Strippers get slapped with all sorts of unfair labels, but that doesn't mean we're any of those names they call us. It's not the job that I can't bear to think about. It's the daily reminder of my loss. If an up-and-coming neurosurgeon had a horrific accident that disfigured their hands and prevented them from pursuing their dream, they'd be forced to abandon years of study and a lot of work to shift their trajectory toward another line of medicine. This is no different.

Actually, it is. People would pity the neurosurgeon instead of degrading them.

I grab a brush from beside the sink and drag it through my hair. I may feel like a drowned rat, but that doesn't mean I have to look like one. Ambrose will do what he wants whether I look like heaven or hell, so I might as well do something for myself.

Once I've done what I can with my red locks, I turn to face the door. I don't want to go back out there. I don't want to face him again. I don't want to deal with the confusing feelings he stirs inside me. But I must.

I grip the handle with a sweaty palm and open the door.

Chapter Twenty-Three

Ambrose

The bathroom door clicks shut, and her bare feet pad down the hall. I turn to give her a snide remark, but my words tangle in my throat when I see her. I choke on them. She's brushed through the snags in her hair, and that vibrant red color accentuates her green eyes. Her white tank top hugs her body, revealing every delicious curve. Long, toned legs work beneath her in a way that swings her full hips when she walks. I bite my lower lip because what I really want to bite is too far away.

I turn away from my greatest temptation and pull the ingredients for a Moscow Mule from the fridge. There aren't any copper mugs here, so I search for something comparable in the kitchen cabinets. I pick up and put down several old family mugs with pictures of a young Oaklyn plastered along the sides. Pictures of her dancing with a wide, young smile on her face. I'm sure she never expected what she would become. How does a cute little dancer like her become the whore she is now?

I pull one of the picture mugs from the cabinet, knowing it will hurt when she's reminded of her past, but I put it back and choose a plain green one instead. I don't know why, and I'm not in the mood to dig too deep into the meaning of that decision. The answers would probably piss me off.

"When did you have time to go to the store?" she asks as she drops to the couch. "It's miles away."

"You were out for a while. I figured you wouldn't get very far if you woke up while I was gone."

She offers a scoff.

I twist the cap from the vodka bottle, breathing in the strong scent. I miss alcohol. It had a way of numbing the hurt, but the numbness never lasted long enough.

My pain is a needle, driving deeper than the lidocaine can reach. It surpasses the numbness and digs until it finds an awakened nerve ending.

I finish preparing her drink and bring it to her. She's placed the bag of ice onto her ankle again—or what's left of it, since most of the ice has melted by this point—so it must be bothering her. I hold the mug toward her, intending to make up another ice pack once she takes it from me, but she just looks at the drink and turns up her nose.

"I'm not drinking anything from you," she says.

"I literally just opened that bottle, tragedy. Stop." My eyes rove down her body. "And besides, I don't *need* to drug you if I want to have my way with you."

"But you like it that way," she quips.

I shake my head. "I do, but I like it when you fight me, too."

Her eyes narrow. "What's wrong with you?"

I set the mug on the coffee table and sit down on the chair beside it. "How much time you got?" We'd be here for a month if I tried to unload every piece of baggage.

"Not long, I guess," she says, turning her face away from me.

It takes a moment for my brain to register her meaning, and that's a fucking problem. My plan to kill her stays at the forefront of her racing thoughts, but that dark horse has fallen back a few furlongs in mine. I should be more focused than ever on how I'll take my revenge, especially when I've been handed the perfect scenario on a silver platter.

She sighs but she keeps quiet, which is probably a good thing. A headache has been building behind my right eye since her stunt this morning, and I could use some silence. I get these wicked migraines sometimes. Probably from all the head trauma over the years. It feels like a vise has clamped around my skull. Squeezing, squeezing. Usually I sequester myself in a dark room, but I don't have that luxury right now. I don't even want her to know I'm in pain. I can't allow her to see any weakness. As a fighter, weakness makes you prey, and I'm not the one who'll be hunted.

A bullet of nausea pierces my gut, and I adjust in the chair to find a more comfortable position. I have to get a handle on this pain. "Do you keep any ibuprofen here?" I ask. It won't get rid of the migraine, but sometimes it can take the edge off.

"Yeah, in the medicine cabinet upstairs. Why?"

"Just figured it might help your ankle," I say as I rise to my feet. On my way through the living room, I close the blinds and flick off the lights that are driving a nail through my eyes and into my brain.

In the bathroom, I find a bottle of ibuprofen with a faded label, but the pills aren't set to expire for a few more months. I toss back four and sip water from the sink to wash them down. Placing two in my palm, I return to the living room. I hand them to Oaklyn and offer her the mug again, but she shakes her head.

"Thanks, but I'd rather choke while dry-swallowing," she says as she knocks them back.

And I'd rather choke her with my cock, but she doesn't see me spouting off every sarcastic remark that springs into my head.

Gritting my teeth, I head back to the kitchen and prepare another bag of ice for her ungrateful ass. The heat of her skin has reduced the first one to water. When I return to her side, her eyes are closed and her hands are folded over her chest like she's a kitten taking a catnap in the sun. Her shirt has risen a little, revealing a thin strip of skin above her shorts.

That's where I place the bag.

She bolts upright, sending the bag to the floor, then turns to me with a scowl. "Why, Ambrose? Are you insane?"

What more do I have to do to show her just how insane I am? Cut off her face and wear it? Because I will. "My diagnosis or lack thereof is none of your business," I say. I lift the bag of ice and place it on her ankle with a smirk.

Dropping into the chair once more, I try to relax the tense muscles in my neck as I close my eyes. Sweat coats my skin, but I manage to keep a straight face as the migraine rips through my skull. I lift my fingertips to my right temple and press. It eases the pressure in my brain, but only slightly.

A warm rasp of fingertips brushes against my shoulder, and I jump. Oaklyn stands beside me, the bag of ice clutched in her hand. She holds it toward me.

"What's that for?" I ask.

She jiggles the plastic, then places it against my head. "I know a migraine when I see one. You wince every time you walk by a window, and you're sweating like a whore in church."

"You'd know what that's like," I say as I clutch the bag to my scalp.

She's only being nice to me for one reason: freedom. She thinks I'll let her go if she's the magical wonder girl who shows me kindness when no one else has, but this isn't some cheesy Hallmark movie. There are only three options in our scenario: kill, keep, or let go. Letting go is off the table, but I struggle between the other two options. Getting rid of her would be the smart thing. It's easier to get away with murder than kidnapping. Fewer risks involved. This isn't a decision I have to make right now, though, so I don't.

I tip back my head and rest the cold bag over my right eye as she retreats to the couch. "Being nice to me won't get you what you want, you know."

"Probably not, but that's not why I did it. Despite your low opinion of me, being a halfway decent person just comes naturally to some people."

"Halfway decent people don't strip."

She scoffs. "You don't know anything about us. A lot of us are just trying to make ends meet, and some of us even enjoy the work. What makes your career choice different from mine? You're still selling your body for entertainment."

Her words suck because they're partly true, but I'm not selling my body for sexual pleasure. I'm selling it for gory pleasure. For bloody entertainment. I'm not using my assets to titillate grown men. I'm using my strength to tap into their bloodthirst. We are *not* the same.

"Fuck off, tragedy," I say, completely done with the direction of this conversation. I won't allow her to lump us into the same industry in her warped little mind. We're entertainers, sure, but one of us has no dignity. No shame.

I've spent my whole life trying to find something I'm good at and a crowd I fit in with. My mother demolished my dream of a normal life when she sliced and diced me. Oaklyn demolished her own dreams, then danced naked in the ashes.

"I wish you'd stop calling me that," she says.

"Why? Because you don't like being reminded of what an absolute disaster your life has become?"

When she doesn't answer, I turn to look at her. Her chin quivers below her full lips, her eyes locked on the ceiling. A glaze of tears covers her eyes, but she doesn't allow them to fall.

"Yes," she finally says, "but it's not because I strip. It's because I long for things I will never have. It's because no matter what I do, no matter how hard I work or how much I strive, I will never reach my goal. This situation has made me realize that I have been extending my arm toward a brass ring that will forever be out of reach."

The headache begins to ease as the ibuprofen kicks in, and I pull the bag of ice from my face. "All this drama about a car? Yeah, they're fucking expensive these days, and even a used hunk of junk will cost you a fair bit, but it's not that far out of reach."

"It's not about a car, Ambrose." Her voice is barely above a whisper.

"What sort of goals do you have?" I ask, genuinely curious.

She shakes her head. "I've said enough. Probably too much. It doesn't matter."

"I want to know, so I guess it sort of matters," I say.

"No," she says, getting to her feet. "You've used information against me already, and I refuse to give you more boulders to hurl at me. I've never shared my silly pipe dream with anyone, and I don't plan to do so anytime soon, especially not with you. It can be buried alongside me. It's been dead for a long time anyway." She heads for the back door, but she's not exactly a flight risk, so I let her go.

It bugs me that she won't share this secret with me. I'll have a hard time silencing her forever without first hearing about her hidden dream. I don't think it's a ploy, but if it is, it's a damn good one. I haven't exactly built a good rapport with her, though. I would normally just take what I want, but this isn't something that can be manhandled out of her. If I want her to expose this private part of herself, I'll have to earn her trust.

But how?

Chapter Twenty-Four

Oaklyn

Brown water laps at the rusted metal bracings around the dock. Mussels and algae cling to the pilings, only visible when the water eases back to reveal them. I stare across the lake, my chin resting on my knees. So many memories reside in this place. Times when my parents and I played games in the water. Times when we had picnics on the shore. Times when I still had my whole life ahead of me and hadn't yet put a voice to the decision that would prove bigger than our bond.

I blink away a heavy tear and wonder what they're doing right now. Probably blissfully living their lives while I tread water. I'm in my self-loathing era. I've been here for a while.

Footsteps crunch through the grass behind me, but I keep my eyes locked on the glimmers of light in the water. A flash of tan skin slides past, and I venture a glance to the side.

Ambrose walks to the edge of the dock, wearing only a pair of shorts. The sun kisses the light sweat on his skin. I've seen his muscles before, and I've certainly felt their power, but I've never seen them in broad daylight. And never this close. Everything ripples and glistens.

I mentally wipe a runnel of metaphorical drool from the side of my mouth and beat back my hormones with a broom. This man has done horrific things to me. I'm not allowed to admit how insanely attractive he is. I should be locked in a mental health facility for the insane urges rolling through my core.

He rips down his shorts, revealing a perfectly toned ass. I never realized how attractive a man's backside could be until this moment. As he walks closer to the water, his muscles tense and tuck, creating lines that draw my eyes and refuse to let go. He always harps about his scars, but doesn't he realize how his natural physique overshadows them? He's beautiful.

I take a moment and openly study his scars in a way he wouldn't otherwise allow. Unless those street fights involve knife-wielding maniacs, I don't think they came from his fighting career. They're too numerous. I wish I could ask about them, but I don't want to draw his anger. We've kinda hit an impasse. He doesn't seem in a rush to kill me at this point, so that's good, I guess.

He dives into the lake and sends a spray of cold water over me, soaking my white tank top.

"Really?" I yell as I cover my chest.

He pops up at the surface and flicks his head to get his hair out of his face. "Get in here, tragedy," he yells.

That's a hard no. "I don't swim."

"Don't or can't?" he asks. He glides to the edge of the dock and places his forearms on the aged wood. Fuck him for looking like a scarred sculpture as he stares up at me.

He pulls himself onto the dock and kneels in front of me. His cock rests against his thigh, and I steal a glance at his piercings for the first time. My eyes widen. How dare he assault someone with *those* decorating his dick. Ribbed, but not for her pleasure.

He smirks. "So which is it? Can you swim or not?"

My eyes narrow and rise back to his face. "Why does it matter?"

"Fine, don't tell me." He leans forward and drags me into him, lifting me as he stands.

I flail against him. "Don't, Ambrose!"

"Sink or swim, tragedy."

He tosses me into the lake. Cold pressure squeezes me as I sink through the murky water. I stay down for a moment, listening to the quiet. The nothingness. I haven't felt the comforting embrace of open water in a very long time. I'd forgotten just how peaceful it could be to float through silence. Sunlight filters through, breaking into diamonds as the ripples cut through the sunbeams.

A shadow blankets the water, sending a muted crash toward me as it breaks the surface. A muscular arm bands around my body and pulls me upward. Holding me against him, Ambrose brings us toward the dock.

He came to save me.

Not that I needed it. I'm a perfectly good swimmer. I just didn't feel like getting in the water today. I would have resurfaced. Eventually.

His hands grab my sides, and I try to push him away.

"I can swim, dude," I say. He looks so fucking handsome, all heroic and concerned, and it pisses me off. "Get off me!"

He releases me. "I thought you were drowning."

"Maybe I was enjoying the quiet down there. Ever think of that?"

He grips the dock and wipes the water from his face. "Suicidal again, are we?"

"Fuck you!"

I slap him. I hit him so hard I swear the sound crosses the entire lake. He has *no* idea the anguish I've endured since my accident. Since before the accident, if I'm being completely honest. I lost my family. I lost everything. And he's forcing me to face it. He can't see the panicked thump of my heartbeat as the memories swirl around me. Even if he could, would he care?

I go to slap him again, but he catches my wrist and spins me around, pulling me against him. His chest warms my back. "You need to calm the fuck down," he says. His words race across my skin, and I shiver. "You also need to trust me."

"Trust you?" I wiggle against him, trying to break free, but he has all the control. By bracing himself on the dock, he can easily stay afloat and hold me as tightly as he wants. I stop struggling and just allow him to hold me. I'll use my words instead. "Why the fuck would I trust someone who pretended to help me while simultaneously causing me so much pain? Why the fuck would I trust someone who plans to *kill* me, Ambrose?"

He releases me, then turns me again and pulls my body against him. My legs wrap around his waist, and I'm breathless as he stares into my eyes.

"I haven't killed you, have I? I've had enough opportunities, but I haven't done it. You're supposed to use this time to convince me that I shouldn't do it at all, but you're wasting it." His hand goes to the top of my head, then slides down my hair like he's petting me. He leans closer, his lips only a breath away from mine. "Suck me, tragedy."

His hand closes around my hair, and I'm dragged beneath the water. I don't have time to think, let alone stop my descent. His powerful grasp guides my head toward his cock, and I put my hand up to stop my face from colliding with it. My fingertips meet his hard girth. Instead of feeling appalled or afraid, I'm disgustingly turned on. The water dilutes my anger and inhibitions until they dissolve into nothing.

He wants my trust. So I give it to him.

I open my mouth and bring him past my lips. His piercings graze my tongue, and I don't know how I never noticed these inside me.

Probably because I was asleep most of the time.

I push that rational voice from my mind and take his cock fully into my mouth. I swirl my tongue around the tip, and my chest tightens. I need air.

He grips my hair and pulls me to the surface. I pant for a moment, then I'm forced beneath the water again. I take him to the back of my throat, and his piercings wrench a gag from my abdomen. I close off my throat to prevent lake water from sucking into my lungs, but now my organs are screaming for oxygen. I can't surface on my own, and the thought makes me panic. My lungs clench.

But I have to trust him.

I keep going until I feel like I'm about to pass out. Seconds feel like hours, but I don't stop. I suck him, gripping the base of his dick as a black haze crowds my mind. My grip loosens. I'm fading.

He yanks me to the surface.

"No more," I gasp, coughing and spitting water.

He pulls me to him and presses his lips against my ear. "One more," he whispers.

I'm driven down again, and he pushes my head toward his cock. He takes control and moves my mouth along his throbbing length, and I willingly extend my tongue against his heated skin. Moving back my head, he lines himself up and pushes into my mouth, gliding over my tongue until his pulsing head hits my throat. He comes, and I don't know what to do because my mouth is full of water and now his jizz. He snatches me to the surface, then pulls my back against him so he can grip my jaw, holding my mouth closed.

"Swallow all of it," he growls.

Tainted lake water and come slide down my throat. When he's certain I've done as he commanded, he releases me. I scramble up the ladder and race to the grass, where I fall to my knees and retch. Everything comes up, and I'm forced to taste it a second time. I gag again, caught in a wave of dry heaves. I'm so fucking disoriented.

He eventually joins me and kneels beside me, placing his hand on the back of my neck. He's taken the time to put on his shorts again. "I expected a whore to take my come a bit better than that," he says with true disappointment in his tone.

"Maybe it's time to consider the possibility that I'm not a whore, asshole," I snap. I drop to the grass and roll onto my back, my chest heaving as I take in the glorious air.

His fingers trace the outline of my nipple through my shirt. "Until I'm done with you, you're my whore. I own you and every breath you take."

Instead of feeling offended, I feel oddly protected. Safe. The tiny feminist voice inside me shouts that I should buck the ownership of the man, but I'm getting a little sick of these rational thoughts telling me what I *should* or *shouldn't* do. Some-times it's okay to be a little irrational.

I close my eyes and allow myself to let go. I may only have a few more days to live, so I might as well give him what he wants. And what he wants is all of me. If he chooses to kill me at the end of this, I can die knowing I did what I could to save myself.

"Okay, Ambrose. Let's talk."

Chapter Twenty-Five

Ambrose

The sun's rays kiss my shoulders, burning my skin with their fiery lips. This place is beautiful. So vast. The water seems to go on forever. But despite the vastness of the scene in front of me, I can only think of the brooding heat beside me, almost stronger than the sun itself. Oaklyn went from being a whore to being *my* whore—my slutty actress in this fucked-up play I've cast, produced, and directed. And now she's ready to talk.

My trust exercise went better than I anticipated. I figured I'd have to work a little harder to show her she could open up to me, but it only took controlling her need for oxygen while she sucked my cock. Holding her underwater might have been enough, but I couldn't allow her to become complacent or think she was safe from my selfish desires. Best decision ever. I can't begin to explain how it felt to fuck her face beneath the water, where her fear tensed every muscle in her jaw. I lived for it. While my dick was buried in her throat, I wanted her to feel the fear of suffocation before I brought her up for air. She needed to understand the complete way I own her now. I think she does.

"A dance studio," she says, interrupting my thoughts as she sits up.

"What?"

"That's the end goal for me. I want to open a dance studio." She picks at the grass near her thigh, pulling the green strands between her fingers until they snap. Her head turns, and her gaze focuses on something in the distance. "My silly, unattainable dream I've never spoken aloud."

I don't know how to respond to her. Her goal does seem very unattainable, but I don't want to say that.

Why not?

I've gone out of my way to wreck her for weeks, so why do I care about her feelings now? It would hurt her if I said that, which is what I'm supposed to do. I'm supposed to open old wounds and dig until the pain blocks out everything. But I can't, so I say nothing.

"What about you?" she asks. "What's your end goal?"

This isn't about me. I have zero desire to talk about myself or my dreams, so I shift the conversation back to her. "Why can't you just teach at a dance studio in town? Do you have to own it?"

She shrugs and brushes her fingers against the grass to get the dirt from her hands. "There aren't any studios in town. Or anywhere nearby, for that matter. I checked. Despite what you think, stripping wasn't my first choice."

I drop my gaze for a moment, finding the change in her features almost uncomfortable. She's nearly expressionless, aside from an unreadable emotion on her face. It reminds me of burned-out anger. Like when I'm in a fight and I get exhausted to a point where it feels as if I'm punching in slow motion. The anger is still there, crawling inside me, but my body is too tired to feed off of it. My mind can't keep up with the intense emotion worming through my muscles. My body is tired, but my mind is raging. That's what I see on her face now. A tired anger. An exhausted fighter.

"What about your family?" I ask. "They won't help you?"

She looks at me with a deadpan stare. "Even if my family would have helped me before, I doubt they will now that someone sent them a video of me shoving my tits in a stranger's face."

I almost laugh. It's fucking hilarious. But I don't. I keep a straight face and just listen as she continues.

"I'm well aware you feel like I deserve my mother's wrath because of what I do for a living, but she hated me long before I ever shed an article of clothing in a club. She wanted me to be a doctor like my father. She didn't think pursuing a career in dance was worth my time or her money. I put myself through school and honed my craft on my own."

"Your mom hated you because you wanted to dance?"

She doesn't meet my gaze, but she nods.

I look away and toss a nearby twig toward the water. "Well, your mom's a bitch," I tell her. What more can I say? So was mine. We have that in common.

"Do you have parents?" she asks, and it draws my eyes back to hers.

"Everyone has parents."

She scoffs. "You know what I mean."

I do. But I really don't want to talk about this.

Then again, does it matter now? She won't be able to use what I say against me when I leave this place alone. The dead can't speak.

I sigh. "I don't know who my father is. And my mother . . ." Even though it doesn't matter, the words stick in my chest.

Warmth encases my hand, and I look down. Oaklyn has placed her hand over mine. Instead of shying away from the scars on my skin, she's touching them. Willingly. Her gesture gives me the strength I need to continue, but I still can't say it, so I gesture to the scars on my face and chest.

Oaklyn's eyes widen. "Your mom did that to you?"

"I lie and say they're from fights, but a few people in town know how I got my scars. Those that were around back when it was all over the news, anyway." I listen to the waves crash against the dock, hoping what I've said is enough. I don't think I can say much more.

"Why would she do something like that?"

My shoulders lift in a shrug. "I don't know. I was a baby at the time, and I never gave a fuck about the 'why' once I was old enough to question it. Whatever her diagnosis or reasons, it doesn't matter. The institution notified me when she killed herself in their care, and I'm certain it wasn't because she was plagued with guilt for stabbing supposed demons out of her baby. So I didn't ask questions I don't fucking care to know the answers to."

She plays with the hem of her shirt. "And your mom was a dancer?"

I nod.

"Is that why you hate me so much?"

I gnaw the inside of my cheek. I don't hate *her* specifically. I hate all that she represents. She was just the unlucky one to get into my car.

"I hate me too," she whispers, and I almost don't hear it.

Can she not pull on my heartstrings, please? I don't need to be played like that. And she *is* playing me. Her response isn't genuine. She's merely adapting for survival. It's an innate instinct. That's all. Anything else is contrived from that adaptation.

So why don't I believe what I'm telling myself?

"I don't hate you," I murmur.

She lets out a soft laugh. "You don't try to kill people you like."

I shake my head. "Murder happens all the time between people who don't hate each other. Some people even kill those they love."

"Then why haven't you done it?"

That's a great fucking question. Why haven't I?

Because I'm being stupid and weak. The thoughts of killing her were once a constant in my mind, but they've become sporadic at best, overtaken by thoughts of fucking her. Using her. Keeping her. But it can't be that way. It's impossible and impractical.

She wanted to know my pipe dream, and now I have an answer. Keeping her alive is my pipe dream. Ever since I pushed inside her, I sealed our fates and wove our futures together. Now I'm stuck on this road, kicking a can without an end in sight. I want to keep her alive, but I can't.

"How's your ankle?" I ask.

"Don't change the subject, Ambrose. Why haven't you killed me?"

Frustration brews in my gut. Her desire to die almost takes the fun out of killing her. Like handing her a gift instead of a disservice.

"Don't ask me that question, tragedy."

"Why?"

"Because I know you want to die. Or you think you do, at least. When the blade is against your throat, you'll change your mind."

She scoffs again. "Stop acting like you know what's in my head. You have no idea."

I turn toward her and fist her hair, pulling her near my mouth. "Stop acting like a pretentious bitch and I'll think about it."

I inhale every breath she exhales, and fear laces each one. But it tastes . . . different. Now there's a hint of something else. Defiance? Anger? It probably isn't desire, but that might be what I taste on my tongue.

Is she curious about what it would be like to give in and allow me to fuck her? It's human nature to seek pleasure. I don't need to force her every time. She can let me bring her to heaven before I send her to hell.

Her green eyes gloss over, and I can't pull away. Every breath I inhale makes me want to take one more from her lungs. Not just want, but need.

I lean down and kiss her. It's the first time my lips have grazed hers, and I'm lost in the warmth of her mouth. I seek her tongue and—

And she bites the ever loving fuck out of my lower lip.

Pain sears through my face, and a low growl erupts from my chest as I get to my feet. She scoots backward and spits. I run my tongue along my lip, tasting the blood and feeling the bite mark in the tender flesh. Fuck. That's hot. Irritating, but hot. She looks up at me with a doe-eyed stare, probably wondering what my next move will be. Fuck if I know. I can't decide between wrapping my hands around her throat or fucking her absolutely senseless. Maybe both. I stare her down as the battle rages inside me.

"Why the fuck would you do something so incredibly stupid?" I ask.

She licks her lips and shakes her head as she stands. "Because I'm fucking confused! My body wants one thing, but my brain says it's a horrible idea, and I don't know what the fuck is going on anymore. Stop fucking with my head!"

I know exactly what she means. "It's the same for me. I shouldn't want to fuck a whore, but I can't deny how much I want you."

"What? No," she says. "It's not the same because I'm not who you think I am. I'm not a whore, but you are undeniably a stalker-slash-murderer! I can't keep playing this cat-and-mouse game."

Cat and mouse, huh? She should really be more careful with her words.

"You don't know how much fun a cat-and-mouse game can be, but I can show you. Should I show you, tragedy?" I ask, brushing my hair back and spitting blood on the ground.

She shakes her head, but the wild look in her eyes tells me she's waging her own war in her mind. She's curious.

I fold my arms over my chest. "I'll be nice and let you decide. You can go inside the house and we'll continue chatting over drinks if you want." I pause and smirk. "Or you can run. I'll even give you a head start so you can find a good hiding place. If you choose to run and can remain hidden until nightfall, I'll drive you back to New York and let you go. But if I catch you—and I *will* catch you—you're going to spread your whore thighs for me. You're going to *let* me inside your pretty little cunt. When I catch you, you will give yourself to me and fuck me like you like me. Your stalker. Your future killer. Choose wisely."

She looks toward the house, the wheels spinning in her mind. I've placed the deal of a lifetime at her feet. The odds may not be in her favor, but I'm betting on her need to cling to the small chance that she can evade me.

"Do you promise you'll let me go if you don't find me?" she asks, her chest rising and falling.

"Do you promise to let me inside you when I do?"

She closes her eyes and nods.

"Then run," I say.

A fleeting moment of indecision flits across her face before she turns toward the woods and bolts forward. Her hair trails behind her like a red banner in the wind. That—coupled with her white shirt—will make spotting her pretty easy. I walk to the front of the house and flop down in a chair to watch her until she disappears. The head start is the least I can do, especially considering how she's still limping on her right side. The odds are stacked against her in so many ways.

I begin a countdown in my head, working my way backward from one hundred. When I hit zero, the game will truly begin. And I won't be denied my prize.

Chapter Twenty-Six

Oaklyn

This fucking sucks. The woods go on forever, and I'll never find a place to hide. We're in the middle of nowhere, my ankle hurts, and I just need to find a place to lie low. I duck behind a rock and pant as I peek over the edge. I don't see him. I don't hear him either. But I know he's coming, and he'll definitely find me if I stay out in the open like this. Watching the woods with wide eyes, I recall memories from my childhood as I search for a forgotten place to hide. We never played hide-and-seek when I was little. If we were in the woods, it was to—

I mentally snap my fingers. The treehouse.

My legs shake as I take off again. My father built a large tree stand for hunting whitetails in winter. Not a fan of the cold, he included walls on all sides, as well as a roof. When my mother began complaining and saying he needed to be more present for us, he gave up hunting and converted the stand to a treehouse for me to enjoy when we summered here. Ambrose will be searching the ground for me. I can only hope he won't think to look above eye level.

The old treehouse comes into view. Branches snake through the windows, and the camouflage paint has faded from years of neglect. The forest has tried to reclaim it, but it still sits on a sturdy branch, its rear wall securely anchored to the trunk. Well . . . it *looks* secure. If it's not, I'm sure I'll find out when I plummet to the ground.

My fingers grip the wooden blocks my father repurposed into a ladder. The rusted nails poking from the wood don't reassure me. I lift my leg as high as I can, testing the strength with my weight. I hop on my good ankle, trying to gain momentum. It takes all my strength to hoist myself up, and a splinter goes through my finger as I nearly slip. I grit my teeth and look up at the warped floorboards fifteen feet above me. The steps aren't even the sketchiest part of this thing.

When I get to the top, I wiggle the wooden boards and test their strength. They don't give way, so I hoist myself into the death box with a grunt. I freeze, listening for an inevitable creak of wood. The floor holds. Scooting backward until I reach the rear wall, I look around for any weapons, but the only thing left in this treehouse is the table. It's bolted to the wooden beams beneath it, and it looks sturdier than the fucking floor. It won't be of any use to me. With a sigh, I close my eyes.

And I wait.

Bushes eventually rustle outside, the sound somehow so far and too close at the same time. I bite my lip to keep from whimpering. I'm so torn. My mind is split in half. I don't want him to find me, but is that because I fear what he'll do to my body? Or because I fear I'll enjoy it? I don't want to know the answer. He can't find me.

"Tragedy?" Ambrose yells, and I throw my hand over my mouth to stifle the scream that begs to free itself from my lungs. He's near the tree. It sounds as if he's directly beneath it.

Blood rushes in my ears, and I can't hear a thing aside from my pulse pounding away inside my skull. How can I listen for receding footsteps when my eardrums refuse to work properly? Seconds tick by. A cramp ratchets through my leg, and I squeeze my eyes shut. I need to readjust, but what if he's still standing below me?

Enough time has passed. He wouldn't stay in one spot for this long.

I take a risk and lean forward to massage my convulsing calf. The wood groans beneath me.

"Ah, there's my little disaster," he says below me.

Fuck.

My eyes widen with rabid fear as I look around for an escape, and only then do I realize how royally I have fucked myself. I'm trapped.

His steps thump against the ladder, and the sound tells me he felt so confident in his ability to find me that he took the time to put on shoes. I never should have made a deal with the devil.

Fingertips curl over the wooden ledge, and his face rises into view. My heart clenches, struggling to find a steady rhythm as I stand. With minimal effort, he brings his massive form over the edge and sits there, his legs dangling below him.

"Did you miss me, tragedy?" He turns toward me. "You must have, since you picked such an obvious hiding spot. Almost as if you wanted me to find you."

"Fuck you," I grind out through clenched teeth.

He gets to his feet with a devilish smirk. "Yeah, you're gonna fuck me. You lost our little version of hide-and-seek, so that's exactly what you're gonna do. I guess it wasn't a very fair game, though. I expected more from a resourceful whore like you."

"I'm not a whore!" I charge toward him, ready to push him through the opening in the floor and go down with him, but he braces himself and spins me around, pinning my back against his bare chest. He's so goddamn strong.

His mouth lowers to my ear as he takes a few steps forward, moving us away from the only way out. "If you keep fighting me, you won't have the option to give yourself up anymore. I'll take that choice from you." Warm breath slides over my neck. "Now . . . do you want to come?"

His question is so out of place that it puts me into a state of shock. Why would he ask me that when everything feels so hopeless?

"What?" I ask.

He smirks against my head. "I asked if you want to come."

I don't even know how to answer him. I don't even know if I *can* come right now. Shifting in his grasp, I rub my thighs together and sense a wet warmth between my legs.

Okay. Maybe I can.

I relax in his arms, and he releases me. "Get undressed for me," he says, his voice low and deep. "Don't forget our deal. You agreed to fuck me like you like me."

I reach for the hem of my shirt and begin to lift it, but he shakes his head.

"Slower, tragedy. Like I'm paying you for it."

My lip curls. "Do you want me to do it like I like you or like you're paying for it? Because those are *not* the same thing for me."

His lips draw into a smirk. "Like you like me."

I raise my shirt, nice and slow like he wants, and drop it to the floor. A decade of dust rises in a plume around it.

"Yeah, like that," he says.

I step into him. If he wants a believable show, I'll give it to him. I do this for a living. This is no different. Even when I felt sad or hopeless, I flashed a smile that sold the show. The only difference is what I'm hoping to earn this time; instead of money, I want to walk away with my life.

I lift his hands to my chest, and his hungry fingers explore my skin. His calloused touch brushes over my nipples, hardening them and sending a rush of heat between my legs. And I hate that. I shouldn't be so turned on by his touch. He pulls me into him and takes a hardened peak into his mouth. His tongue swirls over the sensitive skin, then he sucks and bites down. I whimper when the bolts of pain and pleasure collide.

"You like that, huh?" he whispers before moving to my other breast and repeating the motions. Lick. Suck. Bite.

I cry out and pull his head against me, unable to split my arousal from my fear.

"Yeah, you like that," he growls. "Take off those shorts. I want to see all of you."

My fingers hook into my shorts, and I peel them away. With a greedy hand, he reaches between my legs and cups my warmth with a groan. I close my eyes, ashamed of the wetness he finds there. He pushes me to my knees, and the dry wood bites at my skin. He doesn't need to tell me what he expects next. I know what he wants. And goddamn me for wanting it too.

Instead of unfastening his pants, he steps away from me. He backs up until he's on the other side of the treehouse, then he stops. His hard glare never leaves my face.

"Crawl to me," he commands.

His voice demands obedience, and I drop my hands to the floor and do as he says. The wood scrapes my knees. Splinters prickle against my palms. But I don't stop. I crawl to him until I'm inches from his legs, then I rest on my knees in front of him.

Without being told, I undo his pants and release his hardened cock. Velvet warmth caresses my palm as I wrap my hand around him and feel his length. With my thumb, I toy with the barbell at the tip, and my mouth waters prematurely as I mentally prepare myself to suck him again. I lick my lips, then spread them to take him inside. The piercing clacks against my teeth, and when I ride down his shaft, my lower lip snags on the piercing right before his balls. He moans, wrapping my hair in one hand and putting his other on the ceiling, bracing against the pleasure.

"Fuck," he whispers. "Such a good whore."

Instead of angering me, his words make my core clench with need.

He grips the base of his dick. His hand guides my head away from him, then he pushes his fingers into my mouth. "You have a great mouth," he growls. "Too good. I want more than just your mouth this time, though."

He grabs the back of my neck and forces me to my feet as he releases the pressure on his cock. His body presses into me, forcing me backward until I hit the rough wooden wall. His hand races to my throat, and the look in his eyes worries me. He's struggling with some internal thought, some mental war, and my life hangs in the balance. I feel it in his tightening hold that only allows me the smallest gasp of air.

He leans against my mouth, and each breath I take belonged to him first. "I hate that I find you sexy, you know that? I fucking *hate* that I want to keep you alive so I can fuck your slutty cunt until it milks every drop of come from me." His grip loosens and slides to my breast.

"You can fuck me all you want. I want you to fill me." I reach out and wrap my hand around his hard cock. "You don't have to threaten me to get that."

His eyes narrow. "I don't believe you, Oaklyn. I don't think there's a single fiber of your being that wants to let me inside you. Now or ever." He takes a sharp breath. "I really hate liars, but even though every motion you make is fake and every word you breathe out is a lie, I still have this urge to make you come before I get rid of you."

His sexy words mix with deep threats, and my stupid body responds to all of it.

He leans down and nips my neck, his fingers twisting my nipples and sending jolts of heat to my throbbing clit. His mouth moves to my ear. "Let me make you come with my mouth," he says, his voice all gravel.

I don't know how to respond. My body wants what he offers, but it feels so wrong. My brain can't let go of everything he's done to me. "You haven't given me a bit of pleasure any time you've been inside me, so why do you think you can get me off now?"

"I can make you come, tragedy, whether you want to or not. Give me your pleasure," he growls, "or I'll take it." He lifts me and sets me on the old wooden table, then grips my knees and parts my legs. "Keep those thighs spread for me."

"Please," I beg.

He shoves two fingers inside me, and I gasp. "Your dirty little cunt is dripping for me. Stop acting like you don't want it. Now come on your *evil* stalker's tongue. Come for the man who ruined you."

He's on me. His tongue swipes across my slit, and he licks me down to his fingers before rising upward again. His tongue spreads my lips until it collides with my swelling clit. An earthquake rips through me, the epicenter putting dangerous pressure on the most sensitive part of me. As much as I hate him, the touch of his tongue blows up the fucking Richter scale. My back lifts from the table as a moan erupts from me.

His lips wrap around my clit, but the intense pleasure is replaced by pain as he bites down. I yelp and try to close my legs, but he pushes them apart. His lips wrap around my clit again, but instead of biting me, he sucks. Intense pressure grows beneath each quick lash of his tongue. His fingers piston inside me, drawing up more pleasure with every thrust. My chest rises and I can't even think about the wood scratching at my ass any longer. I can only think of his violent tongue stroking my clit. I can only think of that warm, wet muscle bringing me dizzying pleasure instead of hurling insults at me.

I'm going to come.

I feel it in every tight muscle in my body. In every jerky movement I make. I'm right there. I'm so close. I couldn't stop it, even if I wanted to. Not as long as he keeps licking me like that and fucking me with his fingers.

Then he stops and sits up, and an emptiness engulfs me.

"I don't want to feel you coming around my fingers," he says. "I want to feel you coming around my cock."

Any inhibitions I would have felt at the thought of allowing him inside me have been thrown to the wind. My orgasm is so close, and I *want* to come.

"Fuck me, Ambrose," I beg.

He notches the head of his cock at my entrance, then he sinks inside me with a wild groan. Each powerful, rhythmic thrust of his hips bolsters my building pleasure. I moan as his cock stretches me. His first piercing rubs against sensitive places inside me, and the second grazes my skin whenever he drives deeper.

"Fuck, I want to come," I pant. No, it's not even a want anymore. It's a need. I'm past the point of no return. I haven't just allowed my pride to jump to its death; I've pushed the mother fucker off the cliff myself.

Ambrose's hand slips between us, and he rubs my clit as he gives me every inch of him, harder and faster. His free hand grips the edge of the table, and both of mine reach back to brace my quivering body as he pounds into me. I squeeze the rough slats of wood as my thighs tremble. It's been so long since I've felt something like this.

"Come, tragedy. Come on your tormentor's cock."

If I wasn't so fucking hard for this orgasm, I would have told him to stop right then. But I can taste it on my tongue. I'll let him say whatever he wants as long as he continues to rub me and fuck me like this.

My body shudders, and I slip into an orgasm that silences my brain. My eyes close, and I cry out. Before I can suck in a single breath, Ambrose's hand wraps around my throat.

"Keep your eyes on me. Don't you look away while I'm balls deep in your cunt."

My eyes roll back in my head as I ride out the waves he's caused inside me, but I keep them open. I don't want this to stop. Apparently, I'm much more pliable after I come. Reckless. Naïve.

"That's my good whore," he groans. "Keep those eyes open."

"Come, Ambrose. Fill me," I whisper over his grip on my throat.

His thrusts grow erratic, and he throbs inside me. His eyes stay on me, never leaving mine until he's sated and ready to pull out of me. This time I *let* him fill me with all that hatred, and I hate that I enjoy that anger dripping from me as he steps back.

"Sexy fucking whore," he growls. His fingers stuff his escaped come back inside me, then he pulls them out, licks them, and draws me toward his face. "Open your mouth for me."

I shake my head. No thanks.

"We're having such a nice moment," he says. "Don't make me hurt you now."

I swallow hard and spread my lips.

He grips my chin, tilts back my head, and gathers spit beneath his tongue. He leans over me. His lips pucker before releasing the warm, come-laced saliva onto my tongue. It startles me, but I keep my eyes on him as I swallow the salty mixture.

"Good fucking girl, tragedy," he growls.

The amount of feral joy on his face from that little gesture makes me feel something I can't explain. He looks almost . . . proud of me? It's been a long time since I've had anyone take pride in anything I've done. It seems I've only managed to produce one disappointment after another in every other aspect of my life. But right now, he's looking at me like I'm a racehorse that's just won the Triple Crown. That look shifts something inside me, and it scares me.

I'm letting him get too close to me. And I don't know how to stop.

Chapter Twenty-Seven

Ambrose

We reach the cabin just as the sun has begun to set through the trees. I want to go inside and rinse off the sticky residue of lake water and sweat, and I figure Oaklyn wants to do the same, especially after having me inside her. She surprises me when she says she wants to sit on the back porch and watch the sun go down.

"Can I trust you to stay put?" I ask. I'll take my keys with me, and I don't think she'll try to make a run for it, but I need to be sure.

"I guess I'm not the only one who needs to build a little trust in someone, hmm?" She shakes her head and looks out at the water. "I won't go anywhere, Ambrose."

Something in the defeated way she speaks tells me she's being honest. If I leave her sitting on the porch, that's where I'll find her when I return from my shower.

A thread inside me pulls tight and snaps. I've wanted nothing more than to break her since this entire ordeal began, but now that I've done it, I'm devoid of joy. A sick urge engulfs me, and I want to grab her and hold her against me until she's whole again. For the first time in weeks, I don't want to hurt her anymore.

I want to be the one who stops the hurt.

Before the urge can overtake me, I turn and go inside. A shower will clear my head and remind me why I'm here and what I have to do.

But it doesn't. As I scrub and rinse my body, I imagine choking her. It only hardens my dick. I envision gripping her hair and pressing a knife to her throat, but the Oaklyn in my mind just smiles and licks her lips, enjoying it. The signals have crossed somewhere in my head. I still want to hurt her, but I want to bring her to the edge of pleasure at the same time.

I still want to hurt her, but I no longer want to break her heart.

My palm slams against the shower wall, but it isn't enough to vent the frustration brewing inside me. I've fucked this up. The universe gave me the vessel for my revenge on a silver platter, and I'd rather play with it than destroy it. I have to kill her. When I leave this shower, I have to end her life before this goes any further. Before I reach a point when I can't bear to say goodbye.

I turn off the shower, dry myself, and walk to the bedroom to dress. Tucking the knife into the sheath on my belt, I steel myself and head downstairs. As I near the back door, I freeze. Voices drift through the wood, muffled but discernible. Oaklyn is speaking to someone.

"I needed some time to think," Oaklyn says, "and I figured you wouldn't mind."

"Who else is here, Oaklyn?" a female voice says.

"Mom, it's just me. I told you."

My fists unclench and I can't breathe. She's been given the perfect opportunity to cry for help, but she hasn't. She's . . . protecting me. She's protecting her stalker, her future killer.

"Then whose car is in the driveway?" her mother continues. "I know you didn't scrounge up enough for one while being a dirty little slut. How much do those men pay to look at your breasts? A dollar per nipple?"

"Mom!"

"Who is here? Tell me now, or I'm going to the police and have you charged with breaking and entering."

Oaklyn pauses. I peer through the gauzy curtain beside the door and watch as she nibbles her lip, thinking. "A friend let me borrow their Jeep."

"What friend? Did you trade your body for a ride? God, you disgust me. I never imagined my daughter would become a whore."

Tears well in Oaklyn's eyes, and her chin wobbles beneath her lips. When I call her a whore, it usually pisses her off—or turns her on—but when her mother says it, a knife sinks into her heart and twists.

I've seen enough. My hand shoots toward the doorknob, and I yank open the door. "I drove her here. I'm her fucking friend, and no, she didn't trade her body for a ride."

The breeze catches her mother's short gray bob and sends strands into her gaping mouth. "Excuse me? You can't talk to me that way on my property. Do you know who I am? I babysit the governor's Shih Tzu!"

I clamp my teeth on my inner cheek to keep from laughing. "Even if you suck the governor's dick every Sunday after tea, lady, I have no fucks to give. What I do give a fuck about is the way you're speaking to her." I point a finger toward Oaklyn.

"Do you know what she does for a living? You must not if you're willing to shack up with her. You might want to get tested for STDs." She turns up her pointy nose, and I clench my fists to quiet the growing need to punch it.

"I know exactly what the fuck she does," I say through gritted teeth. "She dances."

Oaklyn's eyes widen. She stares at me as if my face has changed and she no longer recognizes the man in front of her. Fucking same. I no longer recognize myself. I never thought I'd defend her and her career choice, but I can't stop myself. The look on her face when her mother berated her made me sick.

Her mother throws her hands into the air and starts toward the front of the house. She digs in her purse, then raises her phone in the air as she walks, growing more frustrated by the second when the signal bars don't materialize. "You're all crazy, and I'm driving to town so I can call the police. Dancing isn't a profession. It's a hobby! And taking off your clothes always makes you a whore. As her mother, I just wanted better for my daughter." She tosses her phone back into her purse.

"You're no mother," I seethe.

She stops walking and turns to face me.

Before she can speak, I charge toward her and grip her arm. "You haven't been a mother to that woman since you pushed her out of your life because she refused to live *your* dream. I may not know what a good mother looks like, but you sure as shit ain't it." I snatch the designer purse from her arm, find her flashy phone, and throw it to the ground. The heel of my shoe slams down on it, shattering the case and sending a spider web of colors across the screen.

"What are you doing?" she wails.

"Giving us a head start." I toss the purse to her feet and turn to Oaklyn. "Get your shit and get to the Jeep. Our fun family vacay has come to an end."

Oaklyn rushes inside without a glance behind her. I turn back to her piece of shit mother.

"If you *ever* contact Oaklyn again, I'll smash more than just your phone. You have done more than enough damage to her, and I refuse to let you hurt her any more than you already have. As far as you are concerned, you have no daughter. Don't even think about contacting the police, either," I add. "If you bring any trouble to our fucking doorsteps, I'll bring some to yours. Got it?"

She sucks in a breath to say something stupid, and my hand goes to my knife. Her eyes follow the movement, and she stops.

"Yeah, you got it. Have a nice trip home." I turn and head toward the cabin before she can say anything else.

When I get inside, Oaklyn stands at the foot of the stairs with our bags in her hands. The neck of the vodka bottle peeks from the top of hers, meaning she even took the time to pack up the stuff I bought to make her favorite drink.

Tires rake across the gravel outside, and Oaklyn's attention shifts to the front door. "Is she gone?" she asks.

I nod.

"We'd better hurry," she says, rushing toward the door. "If she gets to town before we're gone, she'll send the cops for sure She'll—"

I grip her arm and stop her, looking down into her frantic face. "She won't call the cops, tragedy."

She struggles, trying to pull away. "You don't know her. She will. We have to leave."

"Come here." I pull her into me, wrapping my arms around her and keeping her still. The bags drop from her arms, and her heartbeat gallops against my skin. My hand goes to my knife, but I stop. I can't kill her here. Not now. Not after her mother saw my face.

A sob bursts from Oaklyn's mouth. She cries against my chest and relaxes in my arms until I have to hold her up. No one has ever leaned on me like this. I've never comforted someone, and no one has ever comforted me. I don't know how to do it. So I just do what feels right and hold her up. I won't let her fall.

We stay like that in the dark room for what feels like hours. When her sobs quiet to sniffles, I let her go and look into her eyes.

"Why didn't you run?" I ask. "Why didn't you tell your mom the truth?"

She swipes at her puffy eyes and shakes her head. "I don't know. I just couldn't."

This woman is just as confused as I am.

I lift the bags to my shoulder and move toward the front door. "We'll head back to New York, but I don't want you to get the wrong idea," I say. "I'm not ready to let you go, and I don't do anything I don't want to do. We'll stay at my place until . . ."

Until what? I almost said until I figured out what to do with her, but I don't want her to realize how undecided I am. So I leave the sentence hanging. Let her think what she wants.

"Until you kill me," she whispers.

I don't answer her. We walk to the car in silence, two paths converging on our way toward the end of the line. One way or another, decisions must be made. Soon.

Chapter Twenty-Eight

Oaklyn

A painful silence wedges between us as we push toward New York. I watch the side mirrors for the glint of blue lights, but I never see them. Whatever Ambrose said to shut my mother's mouth has worked.

I watch him as he drives, remembering the first day I sat in this Jeep and stared at him in a similar manner. It feels like years have passed since that moment. In a way, they have. I'm no longer the same person I was that first night. I'm confused as fuck. I don't understand why my body responds to a monster like him. He should disgust me, but I find myself drawn to him.

"Why do you keep staring at me?" he asks, shifting in his seat.

Because he's so attractive. Because I like his dark eyes and the way the little ball of muscle tenses at the back of his jaw when he's thinking. Because instead of scaring me, his scars excite me.

But I can't say any of that, so I say the only other thing that comes to mind. "Tell me more about what happened to you."

He doesn't look at me. He just shakes his head and keeps his eyes on the dark road.

"It's only fair," I say. "You got to witness my train wreck of a mother firsthand. Thanks for that, by the way."

A deep sigh rolls from his nose, and his grip tightens on the steering wheel. "My mother had some kind of breakdown when I was a few months old. Thought I was possessed or something. Took a knife to . . . Well, she took a knife to all of me. Somehow, I survived, and now I have to look like this for the rest of my life." He glances out the window and lowers his voice to a whisper. "Sometimes I think I'd have been better off if I hadn't survived the attack."

"Why? Because you have scars?" I reach toward his face and run my fingers over the raised flesh.

He yanks his head out of reach. "Don't pretend I don't disgust you. That I didn't have to make a bet to get you to sleep with me."

I guess I'm not the only one in a self-loathing era.

Ambrose is a piece of shit—there's no denying that—but as mentally ill as he is, he isn't ugly. He's a solid sculpture of carved muscle. A slew of cracks run through the exterior, but despite the damage, I still see the beauty in him.

"You aren't ugly, Ambrose," I whisper. I reach for his face again, and he doesn't pull away. Instead, he only flinches as I graze his scars. "Would I have gotten into your car if I thought you were ugly?"

His eyes soften, rounding a pinch. He's trying to figure out if I'm lying. This time, I'm not. I have scars too, so I don't judge him for his. If he had come to the club and bought me my favorite drink, I'd have danced for him for free. If he had asked me out on a date, I'd have said yes. He's the one sabotaging his own self-worth.

My thoughts bring me to another question. "Why'd you pick me? I know your mother was a dancer, so that has something to do with it, but why me specifically? What do you hope to accomplish by killing me?"

"I don't know why it had to be you, but I have to kill you because it's the only way I can make things right. I couldn't end my mother, and someone has to pay for what she did."

I turn to face him, eyes wide. "Do you . . . Do you fucking *hear* yourself? How does ending my life make things right?"

His fist collides with the steering wheel, and the Jeep jerks across the center line. "I don't fucking know, but it does! Don't make me question this shit more than I already do, tragedy."

"Who makes things right for me when I'm gone?" I ask, my voice just above a whisper.

He grits his teeth and doesn't answer me, so I answer myself. No one. Not a single person will fight for me when I'm gone. When my dead body—or body *parts*—are discovered in some desolate area twenty years from now, no one will even know who I am.

The silence answers another question as well. He still plans to kill me. If he didn't, he would have said he'd changed his mind. I thought maybe we'd turned some kind of weird corner when he'd stood up to my mother and defended me, but it seems this was just another level in his fucked-up little game.

"Try to get some rest," he says. "We've got a long drive ahead of us."

My body aches from all the running, and exhaustion weighs me down, but it's pretty hard to close my eyes and drift off to dreamland when my death looms just over the next hill.

My stomach growls, and the silence in the Jeep only amplifies it. I wrap my arms around my stomach to muffle it, but it still draws his attention. He only looks. He doesn't ask if I'm hungry or offer to stop. I guess we're back to Asshole Ambrose. It's probably better this way. It's easier to remember how much I should hate him when he's being a jerk.

He yanks the wheel toward the offramp and sends me into the door. The tires squeal and the rear end fishtails, but he manages to straighten out before we spin into the guardrail.

"What the fuck?" I scream. "Are you trying to kill *both* of us now?"

He sets his jaw and doesn't answer.

I look behind us, expecting to see blue lights or hear the wail of sirens, but it's all darkness and headlights and tires on pavement. What was the big fucking hurry to pull off the interstate?

A few minutes later, he brings the Jeep to a stop in a parking lot, and my anger evaporates. We're at the diner.

"Don't even think about ordering that fucking drink again," he says as he gets out of the car.

We go inside and sit at the same booth we chose last time. The waitress is different, and so is the mood. On our way up to the cabin, I was blissfully unaware of all the surprises fate had in store for me. I thought I was running toward safety when I was really running into the arms of my stalker. Now my brain has been ripped in two directions, with one side wondering how he'll kill me and the other hoping he'll fuck me again before he does it.

Sitting in a diner full of people could be my way out of everything. I only need to call out for help. Ambrose doesn't have a gun, but I have a feeling the long-haul trucker seated at the bar might. That bulge on his hip sure as shit isn't his dick.

But I don't. I keep quiet. The thought of someone hurting the man across from me should fill me with joy, but it only makes me feel sick. I've seen too much of the good in Ambrose to want him taken out, even after falling prey to the dark parts of his soul.

We order our food, and it arrives at our table a few minutes later. As we eat in silence, my mind keeps circling something he said earlier about revenge. It bugs me that I have to be the sacrificial lamb to pay for someone else's sins. I consider asking why he can't just take one of the other girls and let me go, but that isn't fair either. Some of them have kids. Some have families that care about them, even when they don't agree with what they do for a living.

I have nothing.

Maybe he chose correctly after all.

His jaw slows as he studies me, then he stops chewing altogether. "What's bugging you now?" he asks.

I shake my head and slide another fry into my mouth. There's no point in circling the same mountain or asking the same questions.

He slides his plate to the side of the table and leans forward. "You can either tell me what's on your mind or I can take you to the bathroom and force it out of you. Your choice."

God, I hate the way his threat makes my stomach clench with excitement instead of fear. "I don't know. Maybe it's knowing I'll be dead this time tomorrow. Tends to put a damper on things."

He looks around to be sure no one heard what I said, then pulls a twenty from his wallet, slaps it on the table, and slides out of the booth. He stops beside me, leans near my ear, and whispers, "Let's talk about this outside."

I lower the last bite of my burger and leave the booth. As I follow him to the car, I feel like a naughty child being escorted out of a store for screaming in the toy aisle. It was his fault. He pressed me to answer him.

We near the Jeep, but he doesn't go to the driver's side. He turns and pins me between the car door and his body instead. His hands go to either side of my head as he looks into my eyes and leans closer, daring me to move away from him or fight him off.

"Let me try to help you understand." His breath rolls over my lips. "Do you know what it means to be obsessed, tragedy?"

I shake my head. I know the definition of the word, but I don't know how he defines it.

"It means I can't let you go. It means that even if I don't want to kill you, I don't have a choice because the thought of another man touching you sends me into a blind rage. Even if you run to a convent and become a fucking nun, it won't be good enough because I don't even want some *god* to see your naked body if I can't. It means that the only way I can ensure you stay mine until your last breath is to be inside you when you take it."

Words tangle around my tongue. I have so many thoughts, but they fly too fast to catch hold of any of them. Pinned beneath his body and his gaze, I can only listen.

"This started as a way to get revenge on my mother," he continues, "but it has become something bigger than I can control. You are my ultimate obsession. I don't want to kill you, but I don't see another way this can end."

He presses his lips to mine in a rough kiss, and his hand moves to my throat and squeezes. Instead of pushing him away or biting him again, I relent and let him explore my mouth. I give in to the tightening hold around my neck, trusting he'll let me breathe again. Even now, when he's confirmed my definitive end, I want him.

There is no escaping what will eventually happen to me, but if no one can avenge me once I'm gone, maybe I can avenge myself before I leave.

Chapter Twenty-Nine

Ambrose

S he's in my apartment. This moment seems so surreal. Her eyes dart around as if she's expecting plastic curtains draped over my walls and floors for easy cleanup. Her gaze lands on the computer on my desk, and I wonder if she realizes that's where I sat and looked up all the information about her. Where I sent an email to her mother and exposed her in more ways than one.

She lowers her bag to the floor and rubs her hands against her hips as she glances around one more time. "So this is where I die, huh? I mean, it's nice, don't get me wrong, but—"

I grab her bag and walk to the kitchen before she can finish. I feel jilted that she's snatched away the fun of killing her. She ruined my plan by kissing me like I don't disgust her. She sucked all the wind from my sails when she made me *like* her. But I can't show her that, and I can't let her go.

My tragedy has to meet her end, or she was never my very own disaster to begin with.

I set the bag on the counter. All the drink ingredients wait on top, so I pluck them from inside and make a Moscow Mule for Oaklyn. Her favorite drink can be her last drink. It's the last kindness I can show her. She watches every move I make as I mix it and pour it into a coffee mug. I'm not trying to drug her again, if that's what she's worried about. I want her awake for the play's denouement.

I hand the drink to her. She goes to the couch in my humble living room and sinks into the cushions, balancing the mug on her knees. She hasn't looked me in the eye since we kissed.

"What did I do to make you hate me so much?" she asks.

She didn't really do anything. I hate what she does and what it makes her. But I don't hate *her*. Not anymore. Not now that I've glimpsed the sweet dancer inside her.

Her eyes finally rise to meet mine. "I think I deserve to know."

I run my hand through my hair and pace in front of her. Frustration simmers just below my skin. Talking isn't my thing, and working through *feelings* sure as shit isn't either. Whenever I need to let off some steam, I do it in the ring. There's no crowd here, though. No cocky opponent to pour my rage into. It's just me and her.

I stop and face her. "I don't hate you. I hate dancers. Not the dancer you were before, but the one you became. I hate women who flaunt their tits in men's faces in exchange for cash. I hate people who remind me of the woman who ruined my life."

"Sacrificing me won't somehow right your mother's wrongs, Ambrose. You have to see that." Her eyes plead for me to hear her words, and her voice wavers when she speaks again. "Killing me doesn't wipe the scars from your body."

"I have no choice now! I've done far too much to let you live. I barreled past the point of no return when I spread your legs and took your cunt when you didn't want it. Even if I trusted you to keep your mouth shut, I can't let you go because I'm too obsessed with you. I would always be in the shadows, watching and waiting. Is that how you want to live?"

She shakes her head and looks at the mug in her lap.

"There's no other end for you, tragedy. I wouldn't have named you that in the first place if there was."

Her thumb clicks against the mug handle, then stops. "Can I make you a drink at least?"

Her question takes me off guard. "No, I don't drink," I tell her as I sit beside her.

"If you're going to kill me, the least you can do is have a drink with me," she says.

If that's her dying fucking wish, so be it.

"Go on, then. Make me a drink."

She gets to her feet and walks to the kitchen, only slightly favoring her ankle now. A bag of ice is good enough for me after a rough fight, but she needs something softer on her delicate skin. I make a mental note to buy gel ice packs from the store, then scratch through it. She won't be here with me the next time I go to the store.

The thought that once brought me so much excitement makes me feel sick.

I drape my arm over the back of the couch. "Make it strong," I yell toward the kitchen.

She returns after a few minutes and sets a drink in front of me on the coffee table. I stare at it. It's been so long since I've tasted alcohol. She's prepared my drink in a mug identical to hers, and I almost smile. This is the sort of cute couple shit I've never known. That I'll never know. Even once she's gone, she will always be my obsession. No one will ever satisfy me like she does.

I lift the mug and swish the liquid around. The acrid scent of vodka wafts up to me, and the hairs on the back of my neck stand. Drinking this feels more taboo than the murder I intend to commit, but maybe it will drown out the doubt bubbling low in my gut. It's called liquid courage, after all.

I throw back the drink, and the liquor singes my throat. She really took "make it strong" to heart. I look over at her, and she's back to balancing her glass on her knees again. She picks it up and takes a swig before lowering it. She drinks much slower, savoring the flavor. I tip the mug to my lips again and finish mine off. I'll let her take her time. A few more minutes won't hurt anything.

I yawn. The drive has taken more out of me than I realized. "Thanks for the drink," I say.

She nods and takes another sip of hers. "Thanks for drinking with me," she says with a smile.

Oaklyn

Ambrose releases another yawn, this one much heartier than the last. His lids close over his brown eyes in a slow blink, and he shakes his head. I can't help but wonder if he knows he's been drugged. Can he feel the heavy blanket of dysphoria covering his mind like I did when he did the same to me?

I tap my fingers on the mug and hope he doesn't go into the kitchen. I took a big risk by putting his flask of sleepy-time juice in my bag before we left the cabin, and I don't want my plan blown now. My heart had nearly beaten out of my chest while he was making my drink. I'd tucked the flask into a side pocket in my bag, but I wouldn't put it past him to snoop. Thankfully, he only went for the bottles on top.

Another yawn. And another.

It seems to be working pretty quickly. Remembering how a small sip had affected me, I only put a dash into his drink. Unlike Ambrose, I don't have murder on my mind.

"I don't know why I'm so tired," he says, his voice low and groggy. He tries to stand up, but he stumbles backward.

I fight back a smile as he falls onto the couch.

"Shit," he groans. "What did you do, tragedy?" His words meld together. He lifts his hands, but they flop back to the couch before his head follows. Wordless whispers leave his mouth. His eyes close, and the whispers stop.

I peer down at Ambrose as he sleeps. A ribbed sleeveless t-shirt hugs his muscles. Jeans ride low on his hips. I trace my fingers over the scars on his face, then move to the soft pink lines lacing his chest. So much damage to one body. No wonder he's so angry at the world.

He's not the only one dealing with a lot of emotions, though. I'm angry. I'm frustrated. I feel trapped. The unlocked door calls to me, but running isn't the answer. Even if I run to another country, he'll find me.

You're making excuses. Stop lying to yourself.

And it is a lie. I can't run, but it's not only because I know he'll follow. It's because for some insane reason, I have come to care about this man. He's more than his gruff exterior and unhinged decisions. I'm drawn to *him*. I see past the scars, both literal and figurative. If he could just get over this stupid idea that he has to kill me, I could show him what it means to be cared for. We're two untethered ships, attached to nothing and no one as we sail through a storm. If we could only find a way to sail side by side, we could put all of our hurt behind us and weather the waves together.

475

But that's just another pipe dream to add to the list.

I pull the knife from his hip and put the tip of the blade against his neck. For once, I have all the power, and I want to know what it feels like to hold a life in my shaking hands. I freeze in place before I can pierce his skin, as if an invisible barrier stands between me and the unthinkable. It's probably my moral compass—an internal guidance system Ambrose clearly lacks.

"Fuck!" I scream, and even the piercing frustration in my voice doesn't wake him.

Harnessing that anger, I try to push it through the blade. I don't want to kill him. I just want to leave a mark he'll never forget. The wires in my brain are still firmly connected to my conscience, and I can't take the life of this man, even though he plans to take mine.

And he will take my life when he wakes up. I'm pretty sure about that. I just need to think of some way to get my own vengeance before he does. Something that will show him he's not the only one with a score to settle.

My gaze falls to his lap, and I get an idea.

I drop the knife to the coffee table and step out of my shorts. I unfasten his jeans, nearly ripping off the button in my frenzy, then I snatch down the zipper. Without even bothering to warm my cold hand, I sink my fingers beneath his boxers and pull out his limp cock.

"Get hard for me, asshole," I say through gritted teeth. I wrap my hand around him and squeeze. Even though I stroke him with the rough, callous, painful touch he deserves, his cock begins to harden. It swells and grows until he fills my hand. Wetness drips down my thighs at the thought of what I plan to do to him.

I'm going to use him like he used me.

I'm going to pull all my pleasure from his lifeless fucking body. He's my toy, rendered down to nothing more than a doll with a dick.

I straddle his lap and grind my pussy along his length. The piercings send a satisfying shiver up my spine. The memory of the pleasure his cock gave me is not a distant one. I hate that I liked how he made me come, but I love that I'm taking it again—this time, on *my* terms. He can't judge me or my career. He can't call me a whore or a slut. He can't do anything but lie there while I use his cock.

I lean back and bring his head to my entrance, watching for any reaction as my warmth presses against him. He doesn't move, and the power makes me ache. I lower myself to his pelvis, and a moan leaves my lips as I rock on his lap. With my hands on his chest, I ride him hard. Up, down, up, down, with a scoop of my hips between each motion so my sensitive clit can brush against his pelvis as I force his cock to please me. For a moment, I miss the feeling of hands touching me else-where, but then I remember that dolls don't touch you. They just lie there and get fucked.

I moan as I drop back my head and keep driving my hips on his lap. An angry energy surges through me, and I put my weight into my hands again. I hate-fuck the person who ruined what little of a life I'd gotten back. The man who has wrapped an invisible chain around my heart and won't let me go.

I draw back my hand and slap his face hard enough to make my palm sting. "Fuck you!" I scream as I drop my weight onto his lap. "Fuck you for what you've done to me when I've been asleep *and* awake. You evil . . . fucking . . ."

My angry words morph into moans, and my abdomen clenches. Sweat drips down the small of my back as I increase the tempo and pressure in time with my selfish desires. The hairs of his pelvis give me that last bit of friction I need.

With his cock impaling me and every muscle in my body quivering and tense, I come so fucking hard. I cry out and continue to use him until my clenching core begs me to stop. I drop down, lying on my chest with his hard cock still buried inside me. He won't get to reach his climax. This was all about me getting mine for once.

Full and stuffed, I pant against his skin, but I don't want it to end quite yet. I look up at him and bask in the remnants of my orgasm. His head lolls to the side, and my eyes focus on the soft pout of his lower lip.

"I like you, Ambrose," I whisper, "but I *really* like your dick." I grip his hair and turn his face toward me. "You're my little plaything now, aren't you? Useful for nothing more than my pleasure. You can't talk or move, but you can lie there and let me fuck myself with your cock, huh?"

I grip his chin, open his mouth, and gather spit beneath my tongue. Leaning over him, I drip the spit into his mouth. It's my turn to have control and do what has been done to me. He gets to be blissfully unaware of the degrading piece of me I left inside his mouth, but that's okay. This is enough.

Now I know why he did this to me. It's like I own his body. His cock. Like I can use him without having to worry about getting him off or pleasing him. It's intoxicating, and I'm drunk off his helplessness.

But now the fun is over and I have no idea what will happen once he wakes up. I wish he could see this as a fair trade. I wish we could come to some kind of fucked-up truce. You assaulted me. I assaulted you. The playing field is leveled now. Maybe we can play a new sort of game?

I sigh and turn my head toward the door. The only game he'll play is one where he makes the rules. If I knew what was good for me, I'd grab my shit and never look back.

I return my attention to his face. Will he really kill me? Am I the only one who feels this magnetism pulling us together?

Probably yes on both counts.

I close my eyes and drop my head to his shoulder. He'll be out for several hours at least. I still have time to decide what I'll do.

Chapter Thirty

Ambrose

I wake up on the couch, confused as fuck. My heavy lids struggle to rise enough for my glassy eyes to focus on the room. I don't know where I am or what day it is. I feel as if I've slept beneath a two-hundred-pound blanket for a week.

After a quick survey of my body, concern wraps a twine around my heart and squeezes. Wrinkles and stretched fabric mar my sleeveless t-shirt, as if someone gripped the fabric between clenched fists. Was I in some kind of fight? I rub my hand over the front of my pants to make sure I didn't piss myself or anything. My jeans are buttoned but not zipped. Well, they're half zipped. I sit up and look around.

Oaklyn! Shit.

I rise from the couch, then drop back to the cushions. My head spins and the floor rolls beneath my feet. She fucking drugged me.

The empty mug stares up at me from the coffee table, and I curse under my breath. I struggle to remember what happened. I made her a drink in the kitchen, then she asked me to drink with her. She fucking *insisted*. This bitch. She probably drugged me so she could escape.

I reach for the knife on my hip, but it's missing. Glancing around, I spot it on the coffee table and snatch it up. She must have thought about killing me but chickened out before she could go through with it. After everything I've done to her, she still couldn't do what anyone else would have done in her situation. Now she'll pay for her mistake. My fingers curl around the weighted handle, and visions of what I'll do to her flash through my mind.

But first, I have to find her.

I storm toward my bedroom, eager to change into some fresh clothes. As I barrel through the doorway, my feet refuse to take another step. Red hair drapes over the white pillowcase, and the thin sheet rises and falls in a slow pattern. She's right in front of me, asleep on my bed.

Okay, now I'm really fucking confused.

She turns over, still fast asleep, and the sheet falls and wraps around her waist.

"What'd you do, tragedy?" I whisper as I step toward the bed.

Nothing makes any sense. Why drug me if she didn't plan to kill me and escape? Even if she couldn't kill me, she still had a golden opportunity to get away from me, at least for a little while. But she stayed.

I step closer and study her face. Memories flicker in my mind like a strobe light, only granting brief flashes of what happened last night. Her hand on my cock. The weight of her on my lap. She slipped me inside her. She drugged me and rode me like a madwoman.

I rub my hand against my crotch, and a deep ache burrows through my pelvis. She rode me hard enough to leave bruises.

More memories flicker through the haze. She lay on my chest with my cock still buried inside her. I bet she'd come by then. I vaguely remember a few of the words as her tits pressed against me.

"I like you, Ambrose, but I really like your dick *. . . You can't talk or move, but you can lie there and let me fuck myself with your cock, huh?"*

Jesus Christ in hell. I wish I could remember more. I wish I could have felt that whole scene play out. Did I even get off? I undo my jeans and pull out my cock. Remnants of dried come cling to my skin, but I don't think any of it belongs to me. Two bruises mark my junk, probably from her banging up and down on my lap like I was a fucking Hopper Ball.

For a fleeting moment, I feel used. It's just a drop of water in the ocean compared to how I've made her feel, though. It's not even the same, really. Knowing she fucked herself with my cock turns me on to the point of being painful, and I worry I'll bust while just thinking about it.

I grip my hard cock, unable to deny the urge clawing through me. Stroking my dick, I step closer to the bed and ease her head around so she's facing me. My mind clings to those fleeting memories of how she used me, and my balls throb with an ache I need to quell. My erection aims toward her mouth. I stroke harder and faster, keeping my eyes on those full lips that released such hate-filled words as she came on my cock. It's enough to push me over the edge, and I come, shooting ropes of pleasure across her lips and cheeks.

Her eyes fly open as soon as the warm beads hit her skin. She opens her mouth, and some slides onto her tongue. "What the fuck!" she screams.

I lean over and gather the come with my fingers, then push it into her mouth. My fingertips curl at the back of her tongue and she gags, straining against my hand.

"This is for using me last night," I say, fucking the back of her throat with my come-coated fingers. Not wanting her to puke, I pull them out and get into bed with her before she has a chance to run away. I crawl between her legs, and she kicks at me. Avoiding her flailing feet, I hook my arms around the backs of her thighs and draw her knees upward. I pull her shorts aside and expose the pretty little cunt that left the bruises on my dick.

"What are you doing?" she says while trying to pull her legs out of my steadfast grasp.

I growl in response and bury my face in her pussy. She already pleased herself plenty with my dick last night, but she deserves to come again. I like that she stooped to my level and used me the way I used her. It was beautiful. Her need for vengeance spoke to me in a language I understood very well.

Her struggle ceases as I tongue-fuck her pussy, licking upward and teasing her clit. Instead of pushing me away, her hands relax and pull me closer.

"You liked raping me, didn't you, tragedy?" I stuff my come-coated fingers inside her, and she gasps as I sink them up to the knuckles. "You came from it, didn't you? Tell me." I swivel my hand so I can curl my fingers toward the front of her pelvis, dissolving her anger.

Her back arches and her thighs tremble. "I liked . . . using your cock . . . while you were asleep," she pants.

I slam my fingers into her as she admits what she did. "Did you come?" I ask. I want to hear her say it. I want her to tell me that what I found on my dick had been left by her alone.

"I . . . came," she moans, the sound amplifying as I curl my fingers inside her. "I came as I rode your dick, Ambrose, then I told you how much I hated you as I lay on your chest."

She's so pliable when she's on the tip of an orgasm. So much more willing to bend to me. I don't even mind that she's lying about what she said.

"Do you hate me right now, when I have you hanging off the edge of an orgasm?"

"Yes," she pants. "I fucking hate you."

God, I love that. I think I like it more than when she said she liked me. Let her hate me if she needs to. I had no issue coming when I hated her.

Hated.

Why is that past tense? As her slick, wet pussy drips from my touch, I struggle to harness the hatred I once had for her.

I sit up on my knees, keeping my fingers inside her, as I lean over and lick my come from her cheek before kissing her. As I thrust in and out of her cunt, she slowly welcomes me into her mouth.

Kissing her is something else. I sense the need and hunger in every movement of her tongue. She doesn't shy away from the salty taste of my come, and her throat moves as she willingly swallows me. My compliant little whore.

"Come for me, tragedy," I growl against her lips.

She tenses as if she expects me to threaten her life with the next set of words that leave my lips, but I can't find the desire to kill her anymore. I want to make her come for me again and again, and I can't do that if she's dead. Instead of a threat, I let my new truth fall from my lips.

"Be a good girl and come."

She does. I have to pull away from her mouth as her moans grow and rise to a trembling crescendo. Her body quivers beneath me, and her eyes roll to the back of her head. My hand goes to her throat, and I put pressure on her neck as her orgasm wanes. She accepts her fate, ready to die if I don't let her draw air. This would be the perfect moment to take her life, but whatever stayed her hand last night has chosen to affect me as well. I can't do it.

I release her throat and brush the hair from her face as she pants. "I don't want to be without you," I whisper.

"Then don't," she breathes.

She makes it sound so simple. She doesn't understand that I stand to lose her either way. If I kill her, she's gone forever. If I let her live, she'll leave.

"You won't choose to stay with me," I say. "You and I both know that, and I can't be without you."

Her eyes flutter as they rise to meet mine. "Haven't I chosen already?"

I can't deny the veracity of her words. She had every opportunity to take off after she drugged me. When I realized what had happened after I woke up, I expected to have to hunt her down. I was prepared to travel across the country to find her if I had to. When I found her in bed, I was too distracted by what happened while I was drugged to think about what didn't happen. The magnitude of what it means didn't hit me until this moment.

She could have killed me. She could have escaped. She could have turned me in to the police. And she did none of those things. She made a choice, and she chose me. My little tragedy stayed.

But what could we ever be? Enemies born from my obsession couldn't possibly become lovers. Can't she see that?

"How can this work?" I ask. "After everything I've done to you, how can you stay?"

Her hands brush against my cheeks, and her soft touch glides over my scars. I don't pull away. For the first time, I don't feel the need to hide my disfigurement like a dirty secret or wield it like a weapon to induce fear. I allow her to see these marks and touch them in a way no one else has. No one else has even tried.

She licks her lips, and her eyes meet mine. "When you pushed my head below water, I had to trust you to let me up for air. When you give me pain, I have to trust you to follow it with pleasure. Now it's your turn to trust me." She pulls me closer and kisses me, then speaks against my lips. "If I run, just let me run, Ambrose. But if I stay, don't push me away."

I nod. It's the best I can do because I can't make a promise I can't keep, but for her, I'll try.

Chapter Thirty-One

Oaklyn

He posed a good question. How *can* this work? I'm not entirely sure, but I can't walk away. I proved that last night when I had the chance to leave and I chose to stay.

"Having doubts about sticking with me, tragedy?" he asks.

I must look doubtful. I'm not *doubtful*, per se, but I am confused as fuck. Why does my body respond to a monster like him? Why does it betray me when he touches me? His touch should disgust me, but it has the opposite effect. He's an expert with my body, despite having abused it so much. I guess that's what I should expect when fucking my stalker. He knows me in ways no one else has taken the time to notice, like how I like my favorite drink or how to turn me into a quivering mess on his lap by rubbing me a certain way.

His hand rises to my face, and his ginger touch lands on my cheek. "If you expect me to feel remorseful for the things I've done, you'll have to wait forever. I'm not sorry for what I've done to you, because I wouldn't have seen you as more than a whore destined for death at my hands if I hadn't."

I sigh. Threats dilute each compliment that springs from his mouth. Can't he just say something nice without it preceding something about murdering me? And that brings me to another concern.

I'm attracted to Ambrose, scars and all, but I don't feel *safe* with him. While I trust him to protect me from others, I don't know if he can protect me from himself. I'm still unsure he can triumph over his desire to kill me.

My stomach grumbles, and he looks down at it with a smirk. "Looks like I haven't fully satisfied you after all." He rises from the bed and goes to his closet. "We'll have to do some shopping later, but I'll go grab a quick breakfast to hold us over this morning."

I almost laugh at this. A few days ago, I was running through the woods to get away from him. Now we're planning a shopping trip and breakfast. Life has thrown me some hellacious curveballs over the past few years, but this one has beaned me right between the eyes. I'm almost dizzy from all the changes.

His phone rings in the living room, and he goes to answer it once he's dressed. I close my eyes again, happy to sleep a little longer after Ambrose relaxed me, but his voice rises and reaches me from the next room. Wondering what has him so heated, I slip out of the bed and tiptoe to the doorway, keeping myself out of sight should he pace past the hall.

"I fucking told you," he says. "The reason doesn't matter, so stop asking. I'll come back and fight when I'm good and goddamn ready. If you want me in tonight, either pay more or book me for a double."

He's speaking with his boss, which reminds me I have to call Jake and let him know I'm back in town. I haven't even considered how my return to work might affect Ambrose. He doesn't like what I do, but I'm not willing to stop doing it. I want to dance, and I want to earn my own money. I'll need to broach the topic before he leaves, but the thought sends a rock rolling through my gut.

"If you've already blasted promos for tonight, that sounds like a you problem. Either book me twice or pay more for the last fight of the night." He pauses. "I don't give a fuck. Make it happen or find a new headliner."

The phone clatters onto a hard surface. I scurry back to the bed and situate myself beneath the covers before he can return and catch me eavesdropping. He comes toward the bed and sits on the edge with a sigh as tension weighs down every muscle in his body. Leaning forward and placing his elbows on his thighs, his hands curl into tight fists, and the muscle in his jaw contracts and relaxes in a rhythm that scares me. Unable to fight this confusing urge to comfort him, I reach toward him and rub slow circles on his back.

The muscles begin to relax.

"I might have to fight tonight," he finally says. "I don't know how I'll get through the night when I don't know if you'll be here when I get back."

I shrug. "I need to get back to work too. You can pick me up from the club when—"

His attention snaps to me. "I don't fucking think so."

I knew this wouldn't be easy, but I didn't think it would go south quite this fast. The anger raging in his eyes reminds me to choose my words carefully, but I can't just roll over and agree to stop dancing.

"We have to find a way to work through this," I say. "I'm not willing to give up my dance career, even if you don't agree with it."

"I can provide for you, so there's no reason to go back to that shit hole. Yeah, I can't buy you a Tesla or put you in a mansion with a pool, but I'll make sure you have everything you need and as much of your wants as I can afford."

I shake my head. He doesn't get it. "It's not just about the money, Ambrose. You say you'll provide for all of my needs, but I *need* to dance. I'm not asking you to like it, but you'll have to learn to deal with it."

"Fuck no." He gets to his feet and paces at the foot of the bed. When he stops and grips the railing, I fear it will snap in his tightening grasp. His dark eyes meet mine, but I refuse to cower under his glare. "Your body is for my eyes only. Don't you get that? If you want to be mine, you can *only* be mine. You'll have to make a choice."

His words are a slap in the face. Haven't I made enough choices already? "That isn't fair."

"Don't talk to me about fair, tragedy. Don't you fucking dare."

There has to be a solution to this. A compromise lies somewhere, but he has to be willing to see it. "What if I stop doing private dances? I can tell Jake I'm only available for stage time and nothing else. That way, I can keep dancing and you're the only one getting a private show."

"No," he says, leaving no room for compromise.

I fold my arms over my chest and look away, unwilling to continue this conversation. If he can't see how irrational he is, rubbing his nose in it won't help. It's already right in front of his face.

He releases the bed railing and stands upright, his muscles tensing beneath his shirt as he comes toward me. I flinch when he reaches my side, expecting him to grab my throat or fist my hair, but he does neither. He leans forward and kisses me hard. His fingers rake my scalp, and he grips the red tendrils tightly enough to make it hurt while sending a shiver through my core. He made me come only minutes ago, but I'm already hungry for another mind-blowing orgasm only he can provide. When he pulls away, I'm breathless.

"The bus stop is two blocks down," he says against my lips. "If you're gone when I get back, I'll respect your decision. I can't promise you won't see me in the shadows every day for the rest of your life, and I can't promise you won't wake up some days with pain between your legs and the memory of the previous evening erased. I can only promise that if you leave, I will kill you if you ever come looking for me. You can't have it both ways, tragedy, so choose wisely."

He releases my hair and leaves the bedroom. Seconds later, the front door slams and I'm left with an ache between my legs and an impossible decision.

Ambrose

I leave the bagel shop with two orders because I can't stop myself from hoping she'll still be in my bed when I get back to the apartment. Guilt claws at my throat, begging to burst from it in the form of an apology when I return. I'm no better than her shitty family for forcing such a decision on her.

But I won't apologize and I won't change my mind. Sharing her isn't an option.

I meant what I said. I'll let her go if she chooses to keep dancing, but she better not show her face to me again. If I want to see her, I'll find her myself. Probably on a regular fucking basis. I'll continue to take what I want from her, but she'll no longer reap the benefits of an amicable arrangement. Maybe I'm no better than her family, but if she can't choose me, she's no better than my fucking mother.

Pulling into the apartment parking lot, I take a moment to prepare myself for what I might walk into. An empty home never bothered me before, but the thought of it now pulls my stomach to my feet. I want her to be inside when I open the door. I want that more than anything I've ever wanted before, and I don't know how I'll handle the disappointment if she's not there. She came into my life and fucked everything up, and now she holds the final thread of my sanity between her fingers. If she's severed that thread, I don't know what I'll do.

I grab the brown paper bag containing our breakfast and start across the parking lot. Anxiety badgers my brain, and I can't even be bothered to cover my face from the prying eyes that seek out my scars. Let them look. Hell, let them take a fucking picture for all I care. I just need to get inside and learn the answer to the question that's been burning through my mind since I left the house.

Did she stay?

I unlock the front door and step inside. My footsteps brush along the carpet, then shift to a thud as I toss the sack of breakfast on the counter in the kitchen. Her bag no longer sits beside the sink.

Maybe she grabbed it so she could shower and change clothes.

My heart grasps at excuses, but logic shouts the truth over each weak argument. I won't find her in the shower. I won't find her in the bedroom, either. I won't find her anywhere in this apartment because she probably left as soon as I drove out of the parking lot. Silence greets me in every room, and I'm forced to face facts when I reach the bedroom.

She's gone.

My brain tempts me. It tells me I should rush straight to my Jeep and hunt her down so I can put an end to my torment, but that organ fails to realize I'll be tormented either way. She chose to leave, and I have to let her go. Killing her doesn't solve anything anymore. At least if she's alive, I can still watch her. And use her.

I go to the couch and sit down with the breakfast I no longer have the stomach to eat. My tragedy has lived up to her nickname, but not in the way I anticipated when I first coined it. She was supposed to meet her tragic end in the finale, but she turned the tables and brought about my tragic end instead. Fucking plot twists.

My phone chimes, and I roll my eyes when I read the message. Darby caved and scheduled me for two fights. I'll go head to head with Boris for the first bout, then I'll face a newcomer in the final match of the night. I squint at the screen and study the man's name. He must be new to the street fight scene entirely because I've never heard of him, and I know everyone worth knowing. It isn't like Darby to put a rookie in the ring with someone like me, so he must be looking for a bloodbath.

If that's what he wants, that's exactly what he'll get. I have a lot of pent-up frustration to let out.

I try to sit back and get my head in the game. When I have a scheduled fight, I need to warm up my body *and* my mind. The crowd thinks it's all a game of thoughtless jabs and kicks, but there's a lot more to it than that. Sure, all the heavy blows and sprays of blood are fun to watch, but the opponents are playing a different sort of mental chess in the ring. We're searching for weaknesses and exploiting them. We're calculating. It helps when you know your opponent, though, and the unknown elements for the final match are grating on my nerves.

It also doesn't help that my thoughts keep circling back to Oaklyn. I picture her in the crowd, watching me do what I do best. I know what it feels like to hear people cheering me on because they've got money riding on my win, but I've never had someone root for me because they support me. And now I never will.

She made her choice, and it wasn't me.

On top of everything else, my body aches and I'm tired. I'm in no shape to fight tonight, but the money is too good to pass up. My opponent won't care if I'm in top form, though. He won't care that I'm mentally exhausted. He will happily kick my ass with a smile on his face if I can't get my shit together. Most of these fuckers couldn't beat me on my worst day, but I won't risk my winning streak for anything. I have to focus.

I lift my phone and consider telling Darby I can't come in tonight, that I'm sick or hurt or some other fabricated story. But it's no use. Like Oaklyn needs to dance, I need to fight. I just have to make sure I don't lose.

Chapter Thirty-Two

Oaklyn

Dressing for work doesn't feel the same as it did before I met Ambrose. I never considered how much skin I show to the men who watch me dance, but now it's *all* I can think about. Even though I chose to leave, I still feel like I belong to him. It doesn't feel right to give these parts of myself away anymore. They aren't mine to give.

I contemplate tucking my tail between my legs and returning to his apartment. It hasn't even been twelve hours since I last saw him, and I already miss him. That would be suicide, though. He'd make me pay for hurting him, and I'd deserve it. It isn't right to yank around someone's emotions like that, and he was falling just as hard as I was. I'll just have to forget about the devastatingly handsome man who made me come like I never had before. But that task is easier said than done. He hasn't left my mind since I closed his apartment door behind me and shuffled to the bus stop.

Since returning to him isn't an option, I do the only thing I can and apply a little makeup to hide the red, puffy skin around my eyes. I've been crying all day. If I wipe my eyes one more time, the skin is liable to fall right off. Sick of moping around my trailer, I dress in a baggy t-shirt and some sweats to cover my dance outfit—the only work attire left standing because it was in the laundry room when Ambrose went on his rampage in my closet—then I head for the bus stop.

The sun sinks below the city skyline as I board the bus and find a seat near the back. Vibrant oranges and purples stretch behind the buildings. It's the sort of view I would have used to distract myself from the judgmental glares of my fellow travelers, but now I don't even notice their pretentious eyes. Now I use the sunset to distract myself from yet another impossible dream that has been snatched away from my empty hands.

He asked how we could make this work, and I didn't answer him because I didn't know what to say. I still don't have an answer, but I wanted to find out. More than anything, I wanted to try. But once again, I slid on my dancing shoes and arabesqued my way to the exit. My dream was worth more to me than the family who refused to acknowledge it, but was it worth more than what I could have had with Ambrose?

I'm not so sure anymore.

The bus pulls to a stop near the club, and I trudge down the aisle. Maybe I'll feel better when the music starts and I can put my emotions into movement.

When I enter the dressing room, my eyes land on something beneath my station. It's the acorn from the first night Ambrose started leaving me these twisted little gifts. I'm not afraid of it anymore. Like a psychopath, I get on my hands and knees and retrieve the little nut from the shadows. It's all I have left of him. I slide it into my pocket, then head to the front of the house to grab a drink before my shift officially starts.

A few men sit around the stage, paying more attention to each other than the poor girl grinding against the pole for all she's worth. It's pretty dead tonight, which sucks for my finances but bodes well for my psyche. I don't think I can handle a bunch of drunk idiots pawing at me tonight. Or ever again.

The bartender spots me as I slide onto the stool, and she sways toward me. She asks what I'd like, and I'm a bit shocked by her question. I always order the same thing, yet this girl can't remember something as simple as a Moscow Mule.

Ambrose knew it.

The thought is an arrow to my heart.

I can never tell anyone about my feelings for Ambrose and how they came about. I'd get analyzed to hell and back, which is wholly unfair. Doesn't every relationship begin with a little obsession? Yeah, Ambrose needs a little work in the impulse control department, but we all have our flaws. He just refuses to hide his.

The bartender slides the copper mug into my hands, and I take a gulp. God, I miss him, and now that I've tasted this monstrosity, I miss him even more. He never went too heavy with the lime.

A couple of guys enter the club. Muscles bulge from their too-tight t-shirts, though they don't hold a candle to Ambrose's beautiful build. I don't recognize either of them, and when they sit near me at the bar, I wish they'd chosen a different spot. I just want to enjoy my disgusting drink in peace.

"No, that's the beauty of it," the short blond man says to his taller, balding friend. "All Marty has to do is take the guy out. After that, he can catch the next flight back to Florida with his cut of the door fee."

I should really stop myself from eavesdropping on this particular conversation. It sounds like these men are talking about a hit. But I'm a nosy bitch, so I keep my ass planted on the stool.

"I don't know," Baldy says. "He agreed to fight dirty and knock the guy down a peg, but now he wants Marty to kill him?"

Yep. Definitely a hit. I pull out my phone and pretend to be very much engrossed in my inactive Facebook account.

"Shhh, keep it down." Shorty looks around, but he doesn't seem to notice me, even though I'm only one stool away. The perks of being a lowly "whore" in this establishment, I guess.

Baldy shifts in his seat. "Look, I'll get Marty to do it, but have you seen the guy he's supposed to fight tonight? I'm not sure anyone *can* kill him. He's never lost a fight, for starters. Then he's got these scars all over. He's been through some serious shit."

I nearly drop my drink into my lap. My brain puts all the pieces together, and I don't like the picture it shows me. A fighter who never loses. Scars.

They plan to kill Ambrose.

"No one is invincible," Shorty says. "Look, just send Marty the text. Darby says this guy has gotten too big for his goddamn britches. While he was away for a few days, the fights only brought in half the revenue. Now that he's back in town, he's threatening to find somewhere else to fight if Darby doesn't pay more. He's bad for business. If Marty can dethrone him and shed more blood than this place has seen in a while, we'll kill two birds with one stone. The fighters will realize how expendable they are and won't bitch about their pay, and Darby won't need that disfigured fuck anymore. The bills will pay themselves."

Disfigured fuck? I nearly lose it. These assholes don't know what he went through to get those scars. But I can't say anything. I have to let Ambrose know about Darby's plan before it's too late. He's scheduled for two fights tonight, and I don't know if the hit is planned for the early fight or the headline.

I switch to my messaging app and shoot a text to Ambrose.

> Don't fight tonight. Darby plans to have you killed.

While I wait for him to see the message, I listen for any more information, but the men have switched to discussions of football as they enjoy their beers. Minutes tick by, but Ambrose doesn't respond. I'll have to go to the fight myself to warn him. When I break the rule and show my face to him, he might kill me before I have a chance to tell him why I'm there, but at least this Marty guy can avenge me if Ambrose is dumb enough to slit my throat before I can speak.

I hurry to the back of the building to look for Jake. He'll have to do without me for one more night, and I imagine he'll be pretty pissed about it. He already gave me an ass chewing for taking off for several days, and I'm scared he'll fire me altogether if I leave tonight. But I don't have a choice. I can't let these men hurt Ambrose.

I enter Jake's office and wince when he eyes me up and down. Even in a baggy t-shirt and some grungy sweatpants, I still feel naked when he looks at me. An oscillating fan blows across the desk, ruffling the stack of comic books he keeps on one corner. I don't think Jake actually reads them. I'm not even sure he *can* read. He probably just looks at the pictures.

"Hey, I hate to do this," I say, "but I have an emergency and I need to leave. I can come in tomorrow and—"

"Hold up," he says, rising from his desk. He walks past me and closes the door, then turns to face me again. "Wouldn't want the girls to hear this, now, would you?"

I shake my head, but the way he stands between me and the door fills me with an uneasy feeling.

"You've already been gone for several days, and I really can't afford to have you disappear on me again. You're one of my best dancers, but I'll have to find someone to replace you permanently if you keep leaving me in the lurch like this." His eyes flick to my breasts. "But maybe we can come up with an arrangement."

A light sweat slicks my palms. I don't like that he's closed the door and caged me in like this. I'm more concerned about that than his threat to hire someone to take my place. I try to push past him. "Never mind, Jake."

His fist closes around my arm, and he swings me in front of him. The backs of my thighs hit the chair, dropping me into the seat. When I try to rise, he grips my shoulders and holds me in place.

A smirk slides onto his face as he leans closer. "Maybe you should stay right where you are and show me how bad you want to keep your job. Then I'll consider cutting you loose for the night."

A strong garlicky odor clings to his breath, and my stomach clenches as the pungent scent finds its way into my nose. I turn my head to escape the stench, and I'm met with a fist across my lip. Warmth trickles down my chin. I touch my fingers to the heat, and they come away red.

"Don't turn away from me, you bitch." He pulls me to my feet and bends me over his desk, slamming my head against the cheap particle board. Stars dance in front of my eyes. "I've wanted to do this since the first night you came to the club, and no one is going to stop me this time. Now stay still and take this like the whore you are."

I don't have time for this, and I am sick and fucking tired of being labeled as something I'm not. The acorn in my pocket presses against my hip, and I know what I have to do. Instead of giving in and taking it, I'll do what I should have done a long time ago. I'll fucking fight back.

As he's busy unbuckling his belt, my eyes search the top of the desk. A pair of scissors and a pen sit in a cup, but they're just out of reach. If I go for them, he'll notice before I can grab them. His zipper falls, and I turn my head to check the other side of the desk. I'm running out of time, but I still don't see anything useful. Then I spot it. A gaudy letter opener with a woman straddling the top sits inches from my fingertips. I ease my hand forward and grab it as he approaches me from behind.

"Just stay like that," he says. "The more you fight it, the worse it will be for you."

His fingertips curl around my waistband, and he's within striking distance. I spin and drive the letter opener into the first thing I see, which happens to be his pasty, flabby thigh. With a high-pitched scream, he releases his hold on my pants and goes for the metal sticking out of his flesh. I don't stick around to deal with the aftermath. I bolt for the door.

I duck through the back hallway and head straight for the dressing room. While grabbing my bag, I catch a glimpse of myself in the mirror. My lip has swollen on the right side and my tears have smeared my mascara. This isn't how I want Ambrose to see me when I go to him, but I don't exactly have time to fix myself up.

My ankle groans with each step as I run toward the bus stop. The overworked joint begs for me to take it easy, but I can't. The bus is already pulling up to the little booth, and it's the last one for at least an hour. I don't have that sort of time to spare.

A loud hiss comes from the massive vehicle as it prepares to resume its journey.

I raise my bag in the air and flail it around as I cry at the top of my lungs for the driver to wait. I'm almost there, but I won't make it. It's pulling away.

A flash of color rushes past one of the bus windows, and the behemoth comes to a stop before it's too far off the curb. As I near the vehicle, the woman with the massive carpet bag returns to her seat and eyes me through the window. She stopped the bus?

The doors open and I climb inside as Jake barrels from the building. His waving fists and angry words shrink into the distance as the driver pulls away. I turn and start down the aisle, and the old woman slides her bag into the space beside her on the seat. No words pass between us, but I think I have a better understanding of her now. All this time, I've imagined people were judging me because I was so accustomed to receiving criticism from everyone I let near me. Meanwhile, I've been placing my own misguided judgements on others.

The old woman doesn't have anything against me because of what I do for a living. She just likes to sit by herself.

I have been so blind, but I refuse to keep walking through life with my eyes closed. Maybe throwing away my family to chase my dance dream was the right call, but I never should have walked away from Ambrose. I should have stayed and fought for him, even if it meant fighting with him. If he doesn't kill me when he sees me, I'll tell him how I feel. I'll beg if I have to.

But first, I have to save his life.

Chapter Thirty-Three

Ambrose

I slide from the Jeep and shrug out of my leather jacket. A fresh sleeveless t-shirt clings to my sweat-coated body. I haven't even gotten into the ring yet and I'm already dripping with it. Adrenaline rushes through me like a drug. I've been away from the ring for too long, and I'm ready to get that release I feel when a punch lands with a solid crack.

A few people mill around the parking lot, but most of the crowd waits inside. Their animated voices reach me from here, and each step I take raises the noise level another octave. By the time I reach the door, it's a roar. They came for a show. They came to see blood. And I won't disappoint them.

"Scar!" a booming voice calls from my right.

I roll my eyes and turn to face it. "Darby," I deadpan.

"I tried to call," he says.

My shoulders lift in a shrug. "Left my phone at home. Didn't want any distractions."

He motions me up a flight of metal stairs that leads to his office, and I follow because I don't have a choice. As long as I fight in his ring, he's my boss.

He pulls a cigar from a box on a shelf and pops it into his crooked mouth, then offers me one. I shake my head. I don't put anything other than oxygen into my lungs before a fight. He shrugs and returns the box to its spot before dropping into a leather chair and lighting his cigar.

"About time you show your face around here," he says through a haze of smoke. "I was about to come to your door and drag you back to the ring if you didn't make an appearance tonight."

God, I hate him. "Well, I'm here, so fuck off."

"Word around town is you've been shacking up with some hot little redhead. Since when does scar have a pretty thing like that?"

If his goal is to have me throttle him to death in this office, he's dangerously close to succeeding. "I fight for you. That's the extent of what you need to know about me."

He takes a long drag of his cigar, then studies it for a moment. "You seem to forget what you are, scar. You're a fucking product. All my fighters are like livestock to me. When one strays too far from the herd for too long, its business becomes my business. If you don't want me to track you down, don't leave the pen."

"Maybe if you took better care of the herd, we wouldn't feel the need to run off. Ever think of that?"

His shit-eating grin evaporates, and that's enough for me.

"On that note, I've got a fight to win." I turn and leave his office. I've had enough of his shit.

I make my way down the stairs and push through the packed crowd until I reach the locker room. After wrapping my hands and warming up, I'm ready to take on Boris. I exit the locker room and head toward the center of the building. My eyes focus on the ring, and I roll my neck and work out my shoulders, trying to wake up every aching muscle as I head toward the ropes.

Boris stands in his corner, ready to go. I kind of like that little fuck. Men who fight him often underestimate him because of his short stature, but I know what he's capable of and I respect him. Which means this fight isn't ideal. Fighting someone I respect is worse than fighting someone I hate. He's also a tenacious little shit. He'll fight until he can't stand, then keep swinging while he's on the floor. This bout will be brutal because he almost always wins and I never lose. Good thing I'm in the mood for brutality.

I duck beneath the ropes and approach the scrappy brick house that is Boris. He steps into me and grabs my hand, pulling me into his chest.

"You ready, scar?" he asks, his accent thick in my ear.

"Do me a favor, Boris," I say. "Don't be afraid to tap out if things get rough. I've had one hell of a day, and I really don't want to kill you."

He nods and we both separate with an honest agreement to leave the ring alive tonight. I need him to not be so . . . Boris. In exchange, I agree to not be so . . . me. I strip off my shirt and throw it on the ropes.

The bell rings, and our friendship falls away. Boris and I meet in the center of the ring, and our two sweaty, muscular bodies collide with disgusting force. Fists swing with marginal inhibition on both sides. Exhaustion plagues my muscles long before it should, but I push through it.

Boris sends his signature swing right into my face. For such a compact dude, he packs a nauseatingly strong punch. When he goes for his next move, I block it—a perk to our familiarity. Blood drips from my nose and splatters onto the mat.

I see a flash of red from the corner of my eye, and I'm tempted to look into the crowd for a woman who won't be there. She has no reason to come here, especially not when I made that stupid threat. I did it to protect myself, and I've regretted it more with every passing second. I keep my eyes on Boris because looking for a ghost means risking another jab to the face.

I push forward, sending a hook into Boris' face. The blow stuns him, and I take the opportunity to slam my elbow across his jaw. This sends him to the ground. I pounce on top of him and we lock in a grappling stance. Blood drips from a cut above my eye, blurring my vision in a red haze. I try to wipe it away with the back of my hand, and Boris sees his opening. Using his powerful legs, he flips me onto my back and pins me beneath him. His muscles flex as he strikes me, and I deflect with my forearms.

Blood fills my mouth, and I need to spit it out if I want to draw enough air into my lungs. I turn my head and spew a spray of red onto the mat. My eyes land on the crowd, and time stops.

Oaklyn stands at the front of the crowd like a goddamn angel. I blink to clear the blood from my eyes, sure that I've only imagined her, but she's still there when I focus again. Her makeup runs down her face as if she's been crying, and her bottom lip is swollen to twice its normal side on the right side of her face. Dried blood paints the corner of her mouth. When she realizes I've noticed her, she waves her hands and screams something, but I can't hear her over the roar of the crowd. They're building into a frenzy, and she's in the danger zone.

I have to end this fight right now.

Boris readies himself for another punch, and I slam my head forward so that our foreheads collide. Colors flash behind my clenched eyelids. I flip Boris onto his back again, and I see I've done more than stun him. He's barely hanging on to consciousness at this point, but his fists continue to drive into my ribs. This feisty little bastard refuses to give up, and that's a real problem. It means the only way to end this fight right now would be to kill him.

I could take Boris out with one adrenaline-laced punch to his exposed throat. It would crush the delicate bones and obstruct his airway, which would be one shitty way to go out. He would fight until his last breath, but I need to get to Oaklyn before the crowd swallows her whole.

I pull back my fist, but I can't do it. "Boris, you need to tap!" I shout.

He shakes his head and mumbles something, but I can't hear him.

I move my free hand from the mat and press it on his throat. He'll be disqualified if he's unconscious. Choking him out will take longer, but it beats killing him.

The crowd releases a unified cheer of approval as I push my weight into my hand. This is what they paid to see. Like one cohesive, massive monster, they push forward toward the ring. Everyone wants to be on the front lines to witness this. Oaklyn gets jostled to the side, and she loses her balance, sending her to the floor. Her fucking ankle. They'll kill her if I don't get out of this ring.

So I do the only thing I can to save her.

I release my hold on Boris, and he springs forward. His forearm presses against my neck, and I can only look up at him and smile as I extend my right arm and tap the mat with my hand.

I need to lose.

For her.

The bell rings, ending the match, and I don't stick around to answer the look of shock on Boris' face. I slide under the rope and push people away until I find Oaklyn buried beneath a sea of legs. Pulling her to her feet, I guide her to the locker room. She keeps trying to pull away from me as she screams something, but I can't hear her. Frankly, I don't give a fuck what she has to say until I know she's okay. I also need to find out who busted her lip so I know who I need to murder when I leave here.

"Ambrose, please listen to me," she pleads once the door closes behind her. "I know you said not to show my face, but I—"

My hand goes to her throat, and I force her back against the wall. Fear colors her green eyes, but she's not afraid of *me*. Something else has her spooked. She isn't the only one who's afraid, though.

"You could have gotten yourself killed, tragedy. What the fuck were you thinking?"

"Please, Ambrose, you have to listen to me," she pleads. Tears fill her eyes, and she's shaking. I release her throat, and she falls into me. "I thought I was too late. I thought that man was about to kill you."

My eyebrows pull together. "Boris? He's a beast, I'll give him that, but it would take at least three of him to take me out. I know all that blood made it look like I was getting my ass beat, but I was winning until I had to save you from your own stupidity."

"No, no, you don't understand." She's breathless. Frantic. "Your boss planned to have you killed during your fight. I heard two guys talking about it at the club, but the fighter's name is Marty, not Boris. I know you said to stay away, but I couldn't let them kill you. I couldn't let them . . ." Her words devolve into guttural sobs.

I hold her against me as I try to wrap my mind around what she's just told me. I knew Darby was getting sick of my shit, but I didn't think he'd stoop that low. I'll have to handle him, but right now I need to know who hurt Oaklyn.

"How'd you get that busted lip?" I ask, pulling back her head so I can get a better look at her face. Mascara cuts black tracks down her cheeks, and the lip looks even worse up close. Even her delicate jaw has swollen.

Her chin quivers, and she tries to look away.

"Answer me, tragedy. Who fucking hurt you?"

She meets my gaze. "Jake."

This mother fucker.

"When I found out about the hit on you, I tried to send you a text. You didn't respond, so I went to Jake to let him know I had to leave. He tried to . . . He tried to rape me again, but I stabbed him and got away."

I hate the shame I see in her eyes. She has nothing to be ashamed of. I grip her chin between my fingers and tip it upward. She should hold her head high. "Good fucking girl."

"You have to get out of here," she whispers. "I'll take the bus back, and I promise to stay away this time, but you have to get away from Darby before he hurts you."

So this is what she was so afraid of? She risked her life to get to me so she could save me? My entire life, people have tried to run away from me or kill me. My mother. Women. The men I fight in the ring. Now I have someone who wants to run toward me. Someone who wants me on this earth.

"You'll do no such fucking thing," I say. "You're coming with me." She'll stay right by my side so I can protect her the way she just protected me. I grip her hand and try to lead her out of the locker room, but she digs in her heels and won't budge.

"What about the man who wants to kill you? Shouldn't you handle that?"

With a smirk, I turn back to her and lift her into my arms. If she won't walk, I'll carry her. "I'll deal with Darby later. Right now, I need to get you somewhere safe so I can doctor that lip."

I also need to plan a nice little surprise to thank Oaklyn for what she's done for me today. She needs to know just how much she means to me. I'm not exactly a flowers-and-dinner kind of guy, but an idea takes shape, and I think she'll love it.

She struggles in my arms, but I only tighten my hold as we leave the building. "Put me down," she whispers as people turn to look at us.

I laugh and lean close to her ear. "Let them stare. I'm beginning to like it."

Chapter Thirty-Four

Oaklyn

Ambrose has been gone since I woke up this morning. I'm familiar with anxiety. I've felt its sharp nail gliding up my back before a big performance or when I've waited for a callback after an audition. The anticipation I feel right now is different, though. It tears at my mind in an unrelenting way and refuses to give me a moment of peace. I don't know where he is or what he's doing.

By the time lunch rolls around and he comes through the front door of his apartment, I'm ready to explode. "Where have you been? I was so afraid Darby—"

"I have something to give you," Ambrose says as he drops a bag onto the coffee table.

"What?" I ask.

He motions toward the bag, and I look at him for a moment before opening it. Pink tissue paper fills the inside. I move it aside and find a gorgeous set of green lingerie. The color will complement my skin instead of washing it out like the harsh blacks I usually wore at work. The low-cut thong and silky garter skirt will hide absolutely nothing, but I guess that's kind of the point.

"Go shower and get ready, and I'll show you what it's for," he says, and his words leave no room for argument. His excited expression draws a smile from me, despite my confusion.

I put the lingerie into the bag. "What about the Darby situation? Did you handle that?"

"I put in a call to a couple of brothers who . . . handle things. They fight at the club sometimes, so they already know what a piece of shit Darby is. They're probably in his office right about now, having a nice little *talk*."

That's all I want to know about that. If Ambrose says it's handled, that's good enough for me.

I take a quick shower and dress in something comfortable. I don't know what Ambrose has planned, but I can only hope a pair of shorts and a tank top will be suitable. He doesn't seem like the type to dine at a fancy restaurant, so I'm probably fine. Before I leave the bedroom, I tuck the acorn into my pocket. I've come to see it as my little good luck charm, which I realize is weird since it was once used to terrify me. On our way out the door, he grabs the bag containing the lingerie. I eye him, still confused about what a bra and panty set has to do with where we're going.

"Just wait and see," he says with a smirk that makes me want to strip where I stand.

We get in the Jeep and drive until we hit a familiar part of town. My curiosity shifts to discomfort when I realize where we're going.

"Ambrose . . ." I whisper as we drive down the familiar road toward the club. "If you're going to the club, it doesn't open for several hours and I have no way to get in." It's early afternoon. Jake doesn't unlock the doors until five.

He just keeps driving.

I don't like this. It doesn't feel right. He hasn't said anything more about killing me, but that's what I fear he plans to do. The club would be the perfect place to sacrifice me. It's the reason he chose me in the first place, and it's the fountain that spews forth all his hatred for women in my line of work.

He pulls into the empty parking lot, and my hand trembles on the armrest between us.

"Do you trust me?" he asks.

My eyes jump to his.

"I told you I have something to give you," he pushes.

I rattle the bag on my lap. "Yeah, you gave it to me already."

He shakes his head, and a low laugh rattles his chest. "Oh no, that's not for *you*. That's for *me*."

My leg shakes as anxiety courses through me. Now the bag makes sense. He's going to dress me up like the whore he always says I am, then he's going to murder me in the club. I don't want this to be my end. We've come too far in this fucked-up little relationship for him to kill me in a place we both hate.

"Please don't kill me, Ambrose," I whimper as I look into his eyes.

"Kill you?" he says. He gets out of the Jeep and comes to my side, then opens the door. He leans down. "I'm not going to kill you, tragedy. As much as I'd love the meaning behind ending you in the place where my mother used to work, I have no intention of killing you here. Or at all."

He grabs my hand and pulls me toward the back door. It's propped open with a large stone, which is weird for this time of day. We enter the dressing room, and I glance at my station. My makeup and brush are missing, probably stolen by one of the other girls who considered it abandoned. It was, I guess.

Ambrose removes the stone from the door, and it closes. A scream from somewhere in the club permeates the silent air. I recognize the voice. My eyes roll up to Ambrose, and my head starts to shake before I can even process what I'm hearing.

"What did you do?" I ask, though I really, *really* don't want to know. Even so, I have the terrible feeling he'll show me regardless of what I want.

He pushes the bag into my hands. "Put this on. When you're ready, I want to see you on the stage. I want to see you dance for me, tragedy."

I'm too dumbfounded to speak, so I only nod. He leaves the dressing area, and I pull out the lingerie. As I slip off my clothes and dress in this outfit, I worry whatever's about to happen will trigger Ambrose to do more than he's planned. Another scream pierces the silence as I tighten the bra straps so that my breasts rise and pull together. I close my eyes. I have to trust him. He plans to hurt someone, but it won't be me. I run my hand down the garter skirt and check myself in the mirror.

For the first time in this dressing room, I feel beautiful.

My eyes fall to the heels beside my station, and I slide my feet into them. The final touch.

I make my way to the stage and step onto it. With the lights in my eyes, it's hard to see, but I eventually realize what's happening as my vision adjusts.

A single chair sits in front of the main stage, and Jake is tied to it. Ropes wrap around his wrists, and another set binds his abdomen to the back of the chair, keeping him upright. More circle his ankles and hold his feet against the legs. A pair of panties have been fashioned into a gag over his mouth. When he sees me, he wiggles against his restraints and nearly tips over.

Ambrose strides toward him and pulls the fabric from his mouth.

"Girl, what the fuck have you done?" Jake screams, thrashing against the binds so hard I'm not even sure they'll hold him.

My mouth wordlessly opens and closes. I have just as many questions in my mind as he does in his.

Ambrose's dark eyes burn through me as he takes me in. He looks like his jaw might drop to the floor. I wouldn't let it if I were him; these floors are disgusting.

Ambrose grabs Jake's face and forces it toward me. "Remember what you did to her?"

Jake scoffs. "She wanted me."

Ambrose's eyes flash between us. "That's not the way I saw it. How about you?" he turns his attention to me. "Did you want it?"

I shake my head.

"Two versus one, you sleaze."

"What are you, her boyfriend or something?" Jake says with a sadistic laugh. "You dating a whore?"

Ambrose punches Jake with a ferocity I don't expect. The single blow is enough to rock his neck so hard that I fear his head will snap clean off. With a frustrated exhale, he stuffs the panties into Jake's mouth once again. Jake lets out a tirade behind the fabric, but it's a muffled and wordless mess to my ears.

The anger on Ambrose's face softens as he pulls up a chair and places it beside Jake. "Dance for me, tragedy," he says as he takes a seat. "Eyes on me." He bites his lower lip and pulls a remote from his pocket, then aims it at the DJ booth to start the music.

Sound springs to life. Has it always been this loud? Or is he drowning out Jake's screams and thrashing?

I take a deep breath and let the music guide me. My hips begin to sway, and I glide across the stage before I grip the pole and climb. When I hook my leg around and drop myself backward, I fight the urge to look over their heads the way I normally do when I dance. The way I normally do when I want to pretend I'm somewhere else. Ambrose's words ring in my ears.

Eyes on me.

I focus on Ambrose, blocking out the erratic thrashing Jake does beside him. A confusing twist of emotions rushes across his handsome face as I dance. He's battling between anger and admiration, and I can only hope the latter wins out. As my back hits the cool stage, I tuck my legs under me and sit up, giving him a full view of my ass as I sensually stroke the pole before hooking a leg around it once more. I spread my legs and twist around to face him again.

"Crawl to me," he says.

His stern command overpowers the music, and I can't deny my need to obey him. I get on my hands and knees and crawl to the end of the stage. His eyes ride along each sensual curve of my body as I drop to my elbows and look up at him. He bites his lip again and leans toward me.

He turns to Jake. "She's *really* good, but I don't like that you're getting a chub while looking at my girl." He gets to his feet and sends his foot between Jake's legs.

Jake's eyes bulge and he tries to double over, but the ropes hold him in place. His face shifts from red to purple.

Ambrose turns back to me and walks to the stage. There's no one to tell him he's too close. That he can't touch. Not that I think he'd listen, even if there was. His hand glides down my back until he reaches the bra clasp. He unhooks it in one swift motion, and it slips down my shoulders. Despite the numerous times I've bared it all on this stage, a rush of insecurity floods me. Ambrose lifts me to a kneeling position and brings his lips toward mine.

"My tragic little whore," he growls, and instead of recoiling from the word, I lean into it.

His hand goes to my chest. His touch is firm around the flesh of my breast, but it shifts to something tender toward my nipple. His other hand goes to my throat, and he pulls me into him for a passionate kiss that makes me weak. When he pulls away, I'm a wet mess.

He hops onto the stage and squints as he peers into the audience of one. The bright lights burn into his eyes like they do ours. He walks over to the pole and puts his back against it. As his hands work open his jeans, he doesn't need his words to tell me what he wants.

"Crawl," he says, the word drenched with demand.

I crawl over to him and kneel at his feet as my hands ride up his legs. He pulls out his cock, and the metal studs reflect the strong overhead lights. I take him into my mouth. A low growl rumbles from him as soon as my lips wrap around him. I move along his length until I feel the studs at the base. He puts one hand on the pole above his head to steady himself, then he buries the other in my hair as he fucks himself with my mouth. I love the way the head of his dick twitches as I pleasure him.

He wants my eyes on him, but his are on Jake.

Wearing a menacing stare, he pushes my hair to the side so Jake has no choice but to watch me please Ambrose—the man who bound him to that chair. The man who kept me fucking captive until I captivated him.

"Do you want to see me fuck her?" he yells to Jake.

The dude doesn't even say no. He's gone quiet and almost seems to be enjoying it.

Ambrose pushes me back so I land on my ass on the stage. He drops to his knees and spreads my legs. His hands hover at the shoes before he raises them to my thighs. He pulls my panties to the side, and the warmth of the lights sears through the wetness between my legs. I keep looking at Jake, anxiety tensing every muscle in my body.

Ambrose leans over me. "Keep those eyes on me, tragedy," he growls as he tugs me into his pelvis before pushing inside me.

I gasp as he pushes to my depths and his piercings tease different parts of me. I reach back and grab the bar that sits a couple of inches off the stage floor to brace myself as he fucks me harder. He basks in Jake's increasing anger and jealousy, then pours that high into me as he drives me into the stage. My eyes remain on him, and I try not to think of what happens once he's finished fucking me.

Chapter Thirty-Five

Ambrose

I thought she felt incredible when she fought me, but she feels so fucking good when she willingly lets me inside her. She's truly mine now, in a way I never could have imagined. Like anything that belongs to me, I have to protect her. I have to think about what she needs. I've hurt her too many times, and now I have to make sure no one ever hurts again. I'll take out anyone who does.

Her boss squirms and screams, but his weasel eyes don't leave my tragedy's body. I'll let him watch the way her tits bounce with every thrust of my hips. He's going to die, so he might as well enjoy the beautiful fucking view in front of him while he can. I know I am. Even in danger, he can't help but be mesmerized by her. Like me.

The mirrors surrounding everything make it so much better. I can see every angle of her. The pout of her lips between moans. The fat of her ass cheeks as her legs curl around me. That incredible mane of red hair flowing around her beautiful face. It's enough to make me want to bust. But not yet. I want to fuck her on her hands and knees first. I want that ass up in the air for me.

My cock sheens with her wetness as I pull out of her and flip her onto her stomach. I slide my arm beneath her and raise her hips to meet mine. Fisting her hair, I force her eyes on the writhing, screaming asshole sitting in front of her. I want him to see every ounce of pleasure written on her face as I fuck her senseless.

I push inside her and she gasps.

"I want your eyes on him this time, tragedy. I want you to come while he looks at your face. He needs to see what he could never do to you."

"I can't," she whimpers.

I smack her ass, ignoring her denial. My eyes move to the mirrors, and I twitch inside her as I take in the glorious view. Her ass nestles into my pelvis as I slam into her. Her hair falls down her back and to the side. She's stunning. Mind-bendingly beautiful. A goddess like her could completely ruin a man with just one taste of her incredible body.

And she did.

I hook my arm around her thigh and rub her clit. A soft moan struggles to break free, but she holds it back as she stares at the man who wanted what doesn't belong to him. I tried to take that part of her too, but it only began to belong to me when she offered it freely.

I grind my hips against hers between every thrust, trying to draw those moans out of her pretty throat. I rub circles against her before swiping my fingers over her swollen clit. She finally moans, and the sound invigorates everyone. Her boss strains and writhes more with her increasing pleasure, and she pulls a groan from me as well. It's contagious.

"Come, tragedy. Come on my dick so I can kill your fucking boss with your pleasure staining the front of my jeans."

She squeezes me, clenching almost painfully around my dick. Her thighs tremble in front of me, and I have to hold her up as I keep rubbing her clit. "I'm going to come," she pants, and instead of looking at him, her gaze rises to mine in the mirror. Those bright green eyes don't even look the same as when I met her. They eat through me as my hips stutter against her. She's squeezing me so hard, and there's no way I can stop myself from filling her, but I grip the base of my cock as her spasms try to milk me.

"Get your incredible cunt off my dick and go grab one of those copper mugs from the bar," I tell her, trying to keep from spilling my load as she leans forward and pulls away from me.

She gives me a confused look, but she hops off the stage and hurries to the bar. I like her feisty nature, but I'd be a liar if I said her obedience doesn't do anything for me. She hurries back with a copper mug, and just as she hands it to me, I slide it beneath my dick and shoot my load into it. This is a nice start, but it needs something more. I work up some spit in my mouth and add that to the mug, making it even more watery.

With my cock still out, I hop down from the stage, swirling the mug as if the finest wine resides within it. I rip the panties from Jake's mouth, and curse words fly from him the moment he's free to yell—a whole lot of charming, pretentious things revolving around "Do you know who I am?" and "You just wait until I get out of here."

Spoiler alert, Jake. You'll never leave this place.

I hand the copper mug to Oaklyn, and she stands beside me with her perfect chest bared to the world. I'd drink up just about anything if those tits remained in front of me. An intrigued expression crosses her face as she glances into the mug.

"Don't you do what you're thinking of doing. I'll ruin you!" he shouts at her.

I whip back his head by his greasy fucking hair, and he clamps his mouth tight. He's ruining all the fun by fighting.

"You don't get to boss her around anymore," I say. "You also don't get to threaten her anymore. Now open your fucking mouth."

I raise a fist in the air and bring it down on the bridge of his nose. The cartilage gives way, and a gush of blood fills his sinuses. If he wants to breathe, he only has one option. He shakes his head and tries to clear his airway of blood, but it's futile.

He opens his mouth to take a breath.

The moment his lips part, Oaklyn steps forward and tips the mug on its side, pouring my come and spit down his throat. He gags and tosses his head, then turns toward her. Before he can spit it onto her porcelain skin, I shove the panties into his mouth.

More than anything, I want to torture this piece of shit and then snuff out his existence. I want him to pay for all the pain he's caused my tragedy. But it can't be my decision. If she wants to take revenge, it has to be on her terms. I can't do this for her.

I turn to Oaklyn. "If you don't want to be a part of what happens next, you can leave while I finish what has to be done, but I want you to consider what's best for you. You have an opportunity that I will never know. You can take revenge for everything he's put you through. He dies either way, but I'll handle the torture he deserves if you can't do it."

She tosses the mug to the floor and presses the back of her hand to her mouth as she paces in front of her lecherous boss. This would be the sappy moment in a movie when the heroine chooses to walk away instead of sinking to the villain's level. I never liked those endings. I wanted the revenge. I wanted the depravity. But what does Oaklyn want?

She stops pacing and stares at the man in the chair. Her eyes close, and her fingers move to the slender scab on her lip. Taking a deep breath, she opens her eyes and steps toward him. With her teeth bared, she leans into his face.

"Fuck you, Jake!" She harnesses a feral scream, lifts her leg, and stomps down on Jake's dick with her high-heeled foot. I feel the strength behind her kick through my own dick and zip up my shit so it doesn't have to bear witness to any more of this.

Her boss strains forward, and before I can stop her, she stomps down on his crotch again. And again. She lets out a whole lot of anger on that man's genitals.

I couldn't be more proud.

Now that we've really gotten the ball rolling, it's my turn to play. I can't let her have all the fun. "Give me one of your heels," I say, motioning toward her feet.

She slips one off and hands it to me, then tries to avoid stepping onto the sticky club floor with her bare foot.

"What are you—" she begins, but her sentence stops when I place the pointed tip of the heel against his eye socket and push until it gives way.

A desperate scream rushes from behind the fabric in his mouth, and the sheer force almost allows the words to come through unmuffled. Blood spreads around the clear heel and drips down his face as he continues to writhe in unbelievably delicious torment. I pull the heel from his deflated eyeball and motion for Oaklyn to hand over her other shoe, but she's gone.

I look around the empty club and a slight panic takes hold when I worry this was too much for her. Curb stomping his nuts into oblivion was okay, but maybe cramming the heel of her shoe into his eyeball was too far. Just when I turn to finish the job myself, she appears from the back of the club, wearing her shorts and clutching something in her hand. She's traded the lone heel for her sneakers, and the lingerie bag dangles from her arm.

"I really didn't want to stand on this filthy floor," she says as she slides her shirt over her bare torso. "Plus, I had one more thing I wanted to do."

She steps closer to her panting boss, then opens her fist. A single acorn wobbles around on her palm. With a sadistic grin that almost hardens me again, she grips the acorn between her fingers and shoves it into the gaping eye socket. Her thumb pushes it as deep as it will go.

After releasing a weak groan, her boss finally passes out from the pain. Or shock is taking over. Either way, I don't give a fuck. He doesn't need to be awake for this next part, though it would have been nice.

I walk to the bar and grab two bottles of the highest proof liquor I can find, then return to the chair in front of the stage. I hand one to Oaklyn, and we work together to douse him. I pour it on the floor around him, pull a book of matches from my pocket, and light one. I hand it to Oaklyn. This is her party, and she's the guest of honor. Without a second thought, she flicks it to the ground and it combusts. Flames overtake the carpet and engulf Jake's body before crawling away to attack the rest of the building.

"Burn the shoes. You'll never need them again," I say.

She pulls the heel from the bag, grabs its mate, and tosses them beneath the flaming chair. The plastic melts in front of our eyes.

Smoke begins to gather against the ceiling. We have to get out of here before someone reports it. I grab her hand and we run for the back door. Before we step into public view, I peer outside to ensure no one will see us leave. I already checked the outside for cameras this morning, and none of the nearby businesses have any that aim toward this parking lot. Finding no one outside, I grip her hand in mine and we bolt for the Jeep.

Once we're inside the vehicle, I use the back exit to pull onto the street, then circle around to park at the nearby gas station so we can get a better look at our handiwork. As the fire overpowers the club, the bright flames dance in her wide, fearful eyes. She doesn't see what I see, though. Watching fire consume the club where my mother once worked is vindicating. Her tortured soul dances above the fire, sexy and sultry, until her damned spirit releases a howl as it's consumed and rendered to ash.

I look over at Oaklyn. The orange hues burn through the green of her irises, and I think it might be a little vindicating for her too. Bittersweet, I'm sure.

In the end, I didn't kill Oaklyn, and I didn't get the vengeance I planned, but destroying Jake and burning the club still felt good. It still feels like revenge. And that's good enough for me.

Chapter Thirty-Six

Oaklyn

As I lie in bed beside Ambrose, every breath I take tastes like the choking scent of the club mixed with cleansing fire. I turn onto my side and look at the man who killed my boss. The man who very nearly killed *me*. I'm now witness to one and a half homicides—me being the half. My mouth waters at the memory of how he looked today. How his thick muscles flexed. How he could have ended me . . . but didn't.

When I close my eyes, the flames dance in my mind. It's euphoric. But it's also a little sad. Despite all the pain that building caused me, it was all I had. In the toss of a match, my only source of income is gone. And what about Ambrose? He hired a couple of hitmen to take out his boss, so how will he support us now? It's not like I can be a big help. Even if another club existed in this town, it's not like I could dance there. Ambrose wouldn't want me to, but I wouldn't want to either. I still want to dance, but I don't think stripping is for me anymore. One man's obsession is about all I can handle.

I reach toward Ambrose's face and trace the many scars that line his strong jaw. So much pain etched into his handsome features. He's a fractured demigod walking the earth alongside someone so downtrodden and tired.

Alongside me.

He doesn't stir as my fingertips graze the imperfections running along his neck and bare shoulders. I can see which cuts were the deepest and which were shallow and hurried. Some aimed to kill, while others meant to maim. I can't help but wonder how much he remembers of the incident. If he recalls any of the pain, it's probably not from the actual incident but the aftermath of it. The pain of looking at himself in the mirror and being reminded that he's different. That he's half dead because he's only half alive. But if you put us together, we make a whole.

This new life I've chosen won't be easy. It doesn't fix the rift between me and my family, but I'm okay with that. If my mother couldn't love me because I chased a dream, she never loved me to begin with. All I've ever needed was someone in my corner, and Ambrose has taken that position to heart. Now, he's all I need.

Ambrose

My phone rings, and the blaring sound pulls me from sleep. The only person who calls my phone on a regular basis is Darby, and I know it's not him. The Kursickis never miss a mark. Through eyes heavy with sleep, I grab my phone and bring it up to my face. I blink twice to be sure I'm seeing this right, but the name remains on my screen.

It's Darby.

I answer the call. Instead of hearing the grinding voice of the son of a bitch I'm certain should be dead, the dark, heavily accented voice of Boris fills my ear.

"Did you hear?" he asks.

I wipe a hand down my face as I sit up. "Hear what?"

"Darby is dead," he says with the slightest hint of excitement coloring his voice.

Oh, I didn't just hear it. I set it up. But I can't tell him that. "What? How?" I ask, feigning concern. Of which I have none.

Boris scoffs, and even that has an accent. "Someone found him in his office this morning. They said something about his severed pinky shoved inside his dickhole. It didn't have something to do with you throwing the fight last night, did it?"

I sigh. "Is there a point to this call, Boris? Besides telling me the good news that Darby is dead."

"Yes, yes, I'm getting there." He takes a deep breath. "How would you like to do this fight club with me?"

"You're the one who should take over, not me. I'm not undefeated anymore."

He laughs. "Oh no, that was not a win I can be proud of. You still hold that title to me. I see no better fighters to run the show than us."

I swallow hard, and Oaklyn stirs behind me. She sits up, pinning her ear to my shoulder to try to hear what's being said. I look back at her. Running an illegal fight club turned out super well for Darby, obviously. Is that what I want? What I want for us?

For us.

I've never had to think of another person. I've never been so intricately linked to another person for there to *be* an us. I've always made decisions for myself. For me.

Sick of waiting for my answer, Boris pushes. "You either join, or you quit fighting."

"You'd keep me out of the ring?" I ask.

"If you refuse my offer? Yes. As the true better fighter, my matka would rise from the grave just to slap me upside the head if I didn't at least offer. Don't offend me, bratr."

It's not the first time Boris has called me brother in his native tongue, but the annoyed snap in his tone took the endearment right out of the word. Now it sounds like I'm offending his great-great ancestors by declining.

So I don't.

"Fine, *brother*," I say. "I'll meet you at the ring tomorrow. I have some shit to deal with."

When I end the call and turn toward Oaklyn, her big eyes have lost all their sleepy haze. She looks at me, waiting for me to explain, but I don't know what to say to her. This could be enough to ensure Oaklyn never has to work again if she doesn't want to, but it means entrenching myself further into a dangerous sport built on the backs of my enemies. It could be risky.

I stare into her eyes. It may not be the right call, but it could give us a chance at making something good out of something that started so badly. It's a chance I'm willing to take.

For us.

"You and that guy you were fighting are taking over the fight club?" she asks as she curls her legs under her. "You sure that's a good idea?"

I pivot my body and push her onto the bed. I fall between her legs and her eyes slowly rise to meet mine. "There's only *one* thing I've ever done that I'm sure was a good idea."

"And what's that?" she asks with a sly smile.

I lean down and capture her lips with mine. "Letting you live, my beautiful little tragedy."

Epilogue

Six Months Later

Oaklyn

A blindfold presses against my eyes as we travel down the road in the Jeep. I tilt back my head to peer around the fabric, but I can only see blazes of light. Every time I lift my hand to my face, he grabs my wrist and moves it away. "Where the hell are we going, Ambrose?" I ask with a frustrated growl. We've been together long enough that I don't think he's bringing me somewhere to murder me.

"You'll see, tragedy," he says, and I can hear the smile in his voice.

"Stop calling me that!"

We no longer live in a constant state of waiting for the tragic final scene. He doesn't need to call me that anymore. But he's never stopped. Being his disaster morphed into becoming his triumph, but I've remained his tragedy. I've also remained his whore, but only when he's about to fill me.

"Never," he says, dropping a warm hand to the back of my neck as he continues to drive.

We finally stop and the engine cuts off, which is good because my patience was about to do the same. Sitting in a loud Jeep when my sense of sight and touch have been disabled frustrated me to no end. I don't like feeling helpless like that.

"Don't take off your blindfold." He gets out of the Jeep and closes the door, leaving me in a stiff, uncomfortable silence. I swivel my head, trying to home in on any sounds outside this metal box, but I only hear his footsteps as he approaches my door.

The door opens and warm air rushes inside. A rope-like handle brushes my palm as he places a bag in my hand. If he thinks I'm going to get dressed in some more lingerie in the middle of the day, he's got another thing coming. That was a one-time deal. I test the weight of the bag in my hand, and I'm happy to find it feels like it holds something a little heavier than some skimpy lingerie.

Ambrose grabs my wrist and dips it into the bag. I expect to feel something . . . wrong inside, but a familiar texture teases my fingertips. Something that feels like home. Even though I feel it, I still can't believe it.

"Take off your blindfold," he says, and I rip it away before he even finishes his sentence.

Just like I thought, the leotard from my final performance rests on the bottom of the bag. The outfit I kept in my closet as a constant reminder of what my life used to be. The familiarity brings a rush of sorrow with it. It's a reminder of what I'll never have again.

Why the hell would he rub more salt in that very open wound? Why is he being this fucking cruel?

Tears fill my eyes, and I drop the leotard. I don't want to look at it anymore.

His fingers find my chin, and he raises my head so that I have to look at him. "Look around."

My head swivels as I scan the parking lot attached to a small, rundown building. The yellow lines have faded on the cracked pavement beneath my feet, and someone has sent a brick or some other hard object through one of the front windows in the sad storefront.

"What is this?" I demand, the thought of his cruelty sending a crisp, renewed anger searing through my words.

He gives me the smirk that always makes my heart gallop, but right now it makes me want to punch him in the mouth.

"It's yours," he says.

My head shakes. "What?"

"It's your new dance studio." He throws his arms to the side as if to show off some grand prize in a game show. His smile widens when he recognizes my look of disbelief. "I'm not kidding. This is where you'll teach dance."

Even considering the shape it's in, there's no way we could afford this place. We don't ever do without, but we don't exactly have a lot in our savings account. If this is some kind of joke, it's stupid at best and cruel at worst.

"We don't have the money for something like this," I say.

"I do." He puts his arm around me and guides me toward the door, then he pulls out a key and unlocks it.

My eyes dance along the building's interior. The inside isn't in terrible shape, and with a little work, it could be brought to glory. I imagine full-length mirrors surrounding us. I imagine silk outfits and sequins and rehearsals. When I move my feet, I can almost feel the floor's smooth surface and the freedom that every dance move lends my body. I can see how this space could become an excellent dance studio—*my* dance studio—and it's just too much for my brain to handle. It's too good to be true. Things like this don't happen to me anymore.

Ambrose pulls me against his body. "Do you want to know where I got the money?" he asks.

Yeah, I really fucking do, so I nod.

"After my mother attacked me, she ended up in a psych ward. Her parents were too old to take care of me, and since she was an only child, she inherited everything upon their deaths a few years later. That money went into some sort of trust while I rotted in poverty in foster homes. When she met her untimely demise, that trust went to me, her bastard child. I have *never* touched that money because I wanted nothing to do with it. I wanted nothing from *her*." He swallows. "But I know you miss dancing, and I don't mean the way you were dancing when I met you. You miss shit like that." He points to the bag containing my leotard. "I know you can't dance like you did before, on the big stage in front of your permanently disappointed mother, but you can teach others who can one day end up on that stage."

Tears erupt from my eyes, and I cry in ways I haven't in a very long time. This time it's not from the unbearable sadness when the rug is inevitably ripped out from under me. This time it's because for the first time since that accident, I'm able to see a hidden part of myself again. Oaklyn Grey. Me.

Through tear-soaked eyes, I rush forward and wrap my arms around him. His powerful arms encircle me. Arms that do so much damage on a daily basis. They don't hurt me, though. They are my source of comfort.

I wipe my eyes and stand on my tiptoes to kiss him. I'll be sure to thank him properly later. I'll even let him call me his beautiful tragedy while I'm on my knees.

"There's one more thing," he says as he grabs the bag and pushes it toward me. "Put this on. I want you to dance for me."

Across State Lines

M/F(ish) Captivity Dark Romance

*This is for the readers who know they shouldn't take a ride from strangers but hop right in when he has a pierced or tattooed d*ck*

Chapter One

Kane

The thick scent of diesel smoke fills the air as a herd of eighteen-wheelers idles in the truck stop's side lot. Some of the truckers have already bedded down for the night, tucked away in the small compartments in the backs of their cabs. Others—like me—still sit behind the wheel. Watching. Contemplating.

Decrepit lot lizards stroll by, their faces caked with makeup to cover the wrinkles of age or the scabs from drug use. They seem to know only one hairstyle tonight: stringy and greasy. They scuttle from truck to truck, more like insects than lizards. Parasites.

I draw a cigarette from my front pocket and light it. None of these women look interesting enough to pick up, so I lean back and inhale a cloud of cigarette smoke rather than spent diesel fuel. My body begins to relax as the nicotine finds a path to my mind, and I flick the ash out the cracked window. I wouldn't want to dirty my house, and for long-haul truckers like me, that's exactly what my cab is. My home.

"Hey, daddy!" a blonde catcalls from across the lot. She waggles her stubby fingers at me, trying to catch my attention.

I turn my head as if she's not there. I'm not interested. If I see someone I want, she won't need to beg for my attention. It's like a rig this size crashing into me when I see the right woman.

If it seems like I'm being picky, it's because I am. I like a very specific type of woman. Someone who still shines through the filth. Someone who isn't too far gone, unlike all the women skulking through the lot tonight. It's too late for them. The grime sinks to their bones, tainting them.

"You looking for some fun?" the blonde says as she reaches my window and scratches her cheek until blood rises to the surface.

I raise the window, stifling her voice. Cigarette smoke fills my cab, but that's better than having to listen to the lot lizard's attempts at begging. She gets the hint and wanders to the next truck, her metaphorical cup still held outward.

Settling back in my seat, my eyes catch on a raven-haired woman standing on her own. She lacks the brazen confidence the experienced women possess. As she clutches her elbows and peers through a sea of metal and asphalt, she looks so out of place.

I look twice, just to make sure she isn't an apparition born from my desperation. When I'm certain she's real, I roll down my window, lean out, and whistle toward her with a wave of my hand. Greedy, drug-hazed eyes turn toward me from all directions, but I'm only focused on her. I whistle again, struggling to be heard over the rumble of engines, but this time she turns her dark eyes toward me.

She points to her chest, asking a silent question. I nod, and she shuffles toward my truck.

"You need a ride?" I ask when she reaches my window.

Her eyes run the length of my truck before landing on me once more. She licks her lips and says, "Yeah, I do."

We don't discuss the logistics of where she needs to go because she doesn't actually want to go anywhere. She wants me to let her into the back of my cab, fuck her, hand her some money, and let her out again. She'll wait around and do it over and over to make her quota for the night.

"Hop in," I say, a forced smile on my face. I'm naturally gruff and intimidating, with tattoos all over my body and a tall frame packed with muscle. If I don't force a smile, even the most desperate lizard will run off.

She opens the passenger door and climbs inside. My riding companion, a brown mutt I call Pup, barks at her. Pup doesn't like anyone, which is probably why we get along so well. We make an odd couple—a big, burly trucker with a small, furry dog—but she's the only other living being I can trust.

"Quiet down," I say to the dog, and her barks shift to an agitated whine.

I stand up and head toward the back, knowing the girl will follow me. She has one thing on her mind, after all.

And so do I.

Pup tries to follow as well, but she'll only get in the way.

"Stay," I command, and she settles in the seat again.

I motion toward the bed in the rear of the cab, and the woman steps past me. Beneath the filth on her face, I can see glimpses of how pretty she could have been, but then my eyes focus on her neck. Her heartbeat pulses beneath the thin flesh, and I can't look away from it. The whore takes my steadfast gaze as a sign of unbridled attraction, so she leans into me and ghosts her fingertips over my chest.

"What do you want?" she asks.

She wants to know what I want her to do to me, whether I want her to suck my dick or let me put my cock inside her worn-out cunt. I don't want her to do anything to me. I couldn't do anything, even if she tried her best. Physically, I'm broken in that way. Realistically, I'm broken in too many ways.

I gently grip her hands and ease them away from my chest.

"Oh, come on, baby," she says. "You didn't let me into your truck to talk about the weather. What do you want me to do to you?"

"Nothing."

This woman would harden any other man's cock—she's fuckable, even if she's a lot whore—but mine remains limp.

Her hands move toward me again, going lower this time, and I nearly jump out of my skin at the brush of her touch. As she strokes me through my jeans, my ears start ringing. Panic tries to overtake my senses, and I force back the feeling by staring at that rapid flutter of her pulse in her neck.

"You're fucking limp, dude," she says, her voice rising to an annoyed pitch. "What? I don't get you hard?"

She almost sounds offended, and I don't blame her. Women like her measure their worth by how quickly they can get a man to come, and she can't even get me hard. But it isn't her fault. Not really.

She applies more pressure, desperate to prove she can do her job. I rip her hand away. She screams from the pressure I apply as I twist her wrist, but no one can hear anything outside this truck.

"Let go of me, you fucking *freak!*" she screams.

My fingers move to her neck, covering that beating pulse, and I squeeze until it feels as if it's inside me. Her hands fly to my wrists, clawing as she tries to free herself, but she's not strong enough. They never are.

I lift her onto the tips of her toes and squeeze harder. Her shoes scrabble beneath her, and she lands a weak kick against my shin. If she'd tried that when she still had enough oxygen in her brain, it might have stung a little, but she doesn't have the power to do any harm now.

The drumbeat beneath my fingers grows fainter before turning erratic. Then it finally stops. I continue to hold her in place as her eyes fixate forward, looking directly into mine.

Taking her life makes my lifeless heart beat faster. It warms the cold spaces hidden away in the dark crevices of my fractured soul. It's much more fulfilling to kill her than it would be to spend ten minutes fucking her, and best of all, it doesn't cost me a thing—aside from the price of a ticket to hell, but I've had a seat on that black train for a while now.

I drop the whore to the floor and lean back against the galley wall with quick, pleasure-filled breaths. Pup hops down from her seat and ventures over to sniff the dead woman's feet before sitting on her haunches and looking up at me as if she's glad the intruder is dead. I reach down and pet her.

Pup is a fascinating creature because as much as I like to watch the life leave the eyes of living things, I couldn't do that to her. When I found her on the side of the road a couple of years ago, broken and bleeding after being hit by a car, I went against every fiber of my being and saved her instead of ending her. I took her to the vet, and the rest is history. She's a three-legged spitfire with a gnarly little attitude, but she's mine, and she doesn't judge me for all the terrible things I do.

"Come on, Pup," I say as I head toward the front again. "Our night isn't over yet."

I can't exactly keep a dead body in the truck, so we'll need to find a good spot to dispose of the trash. And even though this one isn't cold yet, I'm already thinking about the next time. The high only lasts a few days, and then I'll need another fix. When I'm miles away, I'll pull into another lot like this one so I can repeat the process.

Hopefully it lasts a little longer next time. I prefer to play with my victims before releasing them into the black void, but this whore pushed a button when she called me a freak.

Freak. Psycho. Weirdo.

I've heard it all my life. Anyone who's around me long enough to form an opinion usually comes to the same conclusion. Something isn't right with Kane Hargrave. And even though I don't like when they point it out, they're not wrong.

I start up the truck and pull out of the lot. No one will notice that she's gone missing. New girls like her haven't been around long enough to get dirty yet, but they also haven't been around long enough to become accepted into the old hands' inner circle. She might have a pimp to report to, but he'll just assume she ran off with a trucker. It happens.

A few miles outside of town, I find a wooded area with a dirt service road. It's perfect. I'm not hauling any freight at the moment, so it's easy enough to find a lonely stretch of road with a space big enough to pull my rig to the side without jostling the contents. I can't exactly hide the massive thing, but I'm careful about where I stop.

Pup hops down from the truck as I gather the shovel and the body. After walking into the woods and finding a spot that isn't cluttered with tree roots— they're too hard to punch through, even for a guy my size—I set to work.

"One, two, there's been a few. Three, four, bury the whore," I sing as I dig. The soft soil spreads around the shovel's blade before I pull it up and toss the clump of earth to the side. Darkness shrouds me, hiding me beneath its protective cloak.

As I continue digging, I glance at the woman's lifeless eyes staring into a starry sky. They were such pretty eyes. Too bad they belonged to someone stupid enough to get into my truck.

I take a moment to rest when I'm halfway finished with the digging. Burying these girls is a lot harder than it used to be. I have to go pretty deep to avoid getting caught, but at forty years old, I'm not as young as I used to be. By now I should be married with kids or something so I can pass on all my fucked-up genes. Instead, I'm a prolific serial killer working along the I-90.

Being a long-haul trucker makes it too easy for a guy like me to find and dispose of women, leaving bodies along the interstate like breadcrumbs. No one ever traces it back to me, though. I had a scare once. A pack of coyotes managed to dig up what I'd planted beneath the soil, and they dragged it close enough to the road to catch some attention. That's why I bury them deeper now.

A headache buzzes behind my eyes as I drive the shovel into the ground again. I take a deep breath, trying to stay in control. Those fuckers aren't like me. They aren't damaged and deranged, even though the damage I've endured has forced them into being. They'll try to "help," but that's like sending out a medical resident to perform fucking brain surgery. They aren't cut out for this.

Worst of all, they always try to stop me, and I refuse to be stopped when I'm itching for a kill. Whether I get a chain around her neck or, like tonight, I use my bare hands, I need to feel the girl fight and buck for dear life beneath me. I need to feel her nails clawing at me with the desperation that is so typical of the dying. And like I said, no one ever misses them. They were lost and forgotten girls before I got my hands on them.

But it isn't right to call them forgotten. I never forget them, and maybe that's some consolation for their pathetic lives. The kills live in my mind forever. When I lie on my deathbed, my life won't flash before my eyes, but their deaths will.

I toss her body into the hole and begin shoving the soil over her. I start at the feet, saving the face for last. It's the eyes. I want to see them for as long as possible. When I finally cover them, it's over. Finished.

Until next time.

Once I've patted down the earth and moved some leaf litter, twigs, and a rotting log on top of the grave, I turn and look at my truck. Such a beauty. I call her The Purple Wet Dream. She's stacked. Chrome-plated everything, with a chameleon-painted tractor unit. Its color shifts with the light, oscillating between deeper and brighter shades of purple. I never thought someone like me could afford a machine like her, but I pulled some . . . side jobs . . . to afford her. She's literally what wet dreams are made of for guys like us.

I spent a metric fuck ton of money so I would have a ride that looked better than the ramshackle house I used to own. This truck is my true home, where I eat, sleep, and kill. I want to do all those things in a beautiful place, and she's beautiful. And automatic, which leaves my hands free for other activities. Eating . . . torturing . . . You know, the usual.

This dead girl was beautiful too. What can I say? I like pretty things. Even when they're wrapped in shit, I can see the beauty beneath the initial layer of grime. Those are my kinds of women—tarnished but waiting to be polished to a shine. And once she's nice and shiny, I dirty her all over again.

Well, that's what I usually do. I enjoy cleaning them up and making them look nice before I end them, but I was overtaken by anger with this one and kind of skipped that step. Some might say I spend too much time on these bitches when I just plan to kill them in the end, but I can't keep them. They hate me. They'd run off the moment they could, and that isn't an option. You don't stay out of prison and avoid getting caught by letting them live. They all gotta die.

Whining at my feet draws my attention. Pup's tail thumps against my legs. Her half-curled ears flick back and forth as she listens to the scurry of a nocturnal creature in the bushes. We're far enough away from the road that we can hear the sounds of nature instead of tires humming on asphalt. The muscles beneath her fur tense, and I grab her collar to stop her from going after the fading sounds scuffling through the leaves. I don't want her running off. She's the only thing in my life that has remained consistent.

"Let's get back in the truck, Pup."

Now that I'm done burying that girl, I let the hum in my head intensify. I squint my eyes against the growing buzz in my brain. If he wants to come out now, he can. He can provide a break from my evil thoughts. My ailing mind.

After all, isn't that what I created him for?

Chapter Two

Aurora

I shield my eyes and head toward the building as horns blare at me. Black smoke billows from the tall exhausts attached to the massive trucks. A truck stop isn't exactly the safest place for a girl on her own, but what choice do I have? I'm trying to get across the country.

I was born in New York, but I chose to attend college in California. So many brazen dreams and wild hopes filled my head then, and for the first few semesters, things were fine. I did well in my classes and though I mostly kept to myself, I had a budding social life. Yes, things were just fine.

Until they weren't.

My parents believe I've graduated and am living my best life because that's what I told them the last time we spoke. In reality, I dropped out and have been on a steady decline. I stopped answering their calls, and once my phone was stolen, avoiding them became the least of my worries.

I have no source of steady income, and I'm down to a measly twenty, ten of which I'm about to spend so I can take a hot shower. To make more money, I'll have to go on "dates." What little I earn quickly dwindles away once I pay for food and showers. At least the rides from one truck stop to the next are free. Well, I guess they aren't, since I technically pay for them with my body.

Jazz music floats from the overhead speakers the moment I step through the glass doors and enter the truck stop. I stop and listen to the familiar tune and realize it's a gaudy rendition of "Careless Whisper." Now I feel like I'm in an elevator filled with racks of snacks and coolers of beer and soda.

Gripping the backpack strap digging into my right shoulder, I meander toward the counter, where an elderly woman peers at me beneath a mess of white curls. The way her pinched lips curve inward, I can tell she has no teeth. Or if she does, there aren't enough left to push her mouth into a proper shape.

"I need a shower," I say as I slide a ten across the counter.

She lifts the bill and holds it up to the light, then opens the register drawer and slides the money inside. A receipt prints out, and she hands it to me. "The code's on there. Don't dillydally, and we don't allow men and women in there together."

I normally say thank you because it's just good manners, but this old hag can go choke on her remaining teeth for all I care. Sex work is work, and her judgment isn't needed.

Clutching the short strip of paper in my hand, I head toward the showers so I can wash away the travel grime. I punch the code into the keypad, and the door unlocks. Once I'm inside, I fasten the deadbolt and turn toward the shower without looking in the mirror. I don't want to see myself right now. I don't want to see myself until I'm clean, when my wavy auburn hair isn't slick with grease and my clothes aren't sticky with sweat.

I'm looking forward to this shower way more than anything. If someone gave me the choice between a steak dinner and a ten-minute shower, I'd ignore the growl of my stomach and head straight for the running water.

There's only one downside to showers, which is all the thinking I'll do while I mindlessly wash myself.

I step beneath the water, and thoughts begin to circle my mind like the cloudy mess circling the shower drain. Why am I even heading home? To come face to face with my parents' disapproving looks? They think I'm this very successful twenty-four-year-old political student graduate, but in reality, I'm a whore. There's no other way to describe what I do. When they find out the truth . . .

Warm water slides down my back, gliding over a bruise on my left shoulder. The last trucker got a little too rough, but I've been through worse. Thankfully, not all the men are mean. The super truckers are a whole different breed. They're the kind of men who live and breathe trucking. They take care of themselves, they take care of their trucks, and for the most part, they're very respectful.

The last guy was not a super trucker.

I stick my hand beneath the shampoo dispenser and collect the gel in my palm. Rubbing my hands together, I form a lather and run it through my hair. Grime collects within the suds and flows down my body, taking the weight of the world with it as well.

I feel more human when I'm clean. More like myself. For this moment, I'm alive and healthy, despite the clenching hunger in my gut. I can ignore that gnawing pang, close my eyes, and pretend I'm at home, just taking a normal shower.

I can pretend the incident in my dorm never happened.

I can pretend I have loving and understanding parents.

I can pretend I graduated and became an advisor at the state department or joined some up-and-coming politician's team.

I can pretend I'm safe.

A girl can dream, can't she? It's the least I can do before returning to the nightmare of my harsh reality.

Once I've scrubbed my skin raw and rinsed away all the soap, I step out of the shower and look at myself in the mirror. The light has dimmed in my green eyes, and tiny red veins thread through my sclera. I've lost weight. A little too much, at that. I turn away from the mirror and grab my backpack. I don't want to look anymore.

My fingers dig through fabric until I find a clean jean skirt and a shirt that's a little too big for me now. I miss my fuller figure. Like a typical woman, I see the beauty in myself only after time has passed and changed me once again.

My eyes land on the shirt and shorts I discarded on the floor before my shower, and a decision begs to be made. I have enough money left to buy a little food, or I can wash my dirty clothes. Most people don't have to choose between eating and cleanliness. I wish I were most people.

With a sigh, I gather the clothes and stuff them into the side pocket with the rest of the shirts and shorts and panties that will have to wait until I make enough to clean them. I'm not even sure this truck stop has a laundry area anyway. Not all of them do. But I know they have an attached diner. I smelled the chicken grease as soon as I walked in.

After drying off my body, I dress and exit the shower room. Once I've eaten a cheap meal to stave off the gnawing feeling in my gut, I'll need to scope out the lot for my next patron. And my next ride. I can't stay where I am forever, even if I'm not entirely sure where I'm headed. The plan has always been to travel toward home.

But sometimes plans change.

Chapter Three

Jax

I can only think of one thing as I take a seat at the bar in the truck stop's diner: Kane was—*is*—out of control. There's only so much I can do to stop his homicidal tendencies. He's fucked up and I'll be the first to admit that, but he's gone through things no child should. That's why he created me. Not *just* me, either.

When I can't break through, I try to stop him by derailing his thoughts, which is ultimately an impossibility. He becomes so hyper-focused on his rage that by the time I realize what's happening, by the time I feel the excitement and the dopamine, it's too late. He's already committed yet another homicide. He's done what he's done, and there's no taking it back.

Even if I could somehow stop him, that would mean his victim would live, and that creates a different problem entirely. If they live, they'll turn him in. As his protector, I have an obligation to protect Kane—to protect all three of us—and that means I can't step in once he's gone to a certain point. Which is fine, since I usually don't know what's happening until he's well past the point of no return.

While our system worked well in our youth, it isn't very effective now that he's an adult. I should have more control now, but Kane still holds the reins in a tight grip. And he shouldn't. Not until he gets ahold of himself.

A waitress approaches the counter. A few strands of bleached hair fall over her face, and she blows them away with a frustrated exhale. Dark bags under her eyes showcase just how tired she must be.

"What would you like to drink?" she asks.

"Coffee and water, please," I say.

She offers a curt nod and turns toward the coffee machine sitting atop a grimy counter behind her. If her shuffling gait and the way she keeps rubbing her lower back are any indication, she's probably been on shift all day. She grabs a faded red cup and fills it with water. No ice. Instead of bothering her with another request, I let it go. The poor thing has enough to think about.

As I wait for the coffee—which has to be made, much to the waitress's displeasure—I spin around on the stool and study the pokey diner's sparse decor. Glossy red vinyl covers the bar stools, which are bolted to the floor in front of the counter. Some of the covers have ripped, revealing their yellowed foam innards. The red-plastic booths have seen better days as well. Scuffs and scratches from years of trucker butts scraping across them mark their once shiny surfaces.

Another trucker sits at one of the booths. He's double-fisting coffee mugs, and I understand him. When you work for a company, you have to stick to the hours of service, including mandatory ten-hour breaks. Technically, we're all supposed to stick to that, but when you drive for yourself or a lackadaisical company, there's pressure to fudge your logs and keep driving. That guy looks like he's done more than a bit of fudging.

The waitress brings over my lukewarm water and a mug of fresh coffee. As I pull the glass toward me, I motion her closer before she can speed away. "Can I pay for his meal?" I ask, jerking my head toward the trucker in the booth.

She nods and trudges over to him to let him know. He leans back with an appreciative grunt and raises one of the coffee mugs toward me. I lift my glass of room-temperature water back at him, then continue scanning the diner.

An older couple sits at the other end of the counter, each of them picking away at a plate full of greasy food. I don't see that kind of relationship very often in my line of work, but they're more common these days. Couples who travel together. It would be nice to have someone to share the lonely hours on the road with, but Kane wouldn't let it last very long. His house, his rules.

I'm about to turn back to my coffee when a young woman catches my eye. She sticks out in a place like this. Her legs are crossed, causing her jean skirt to ride up her thighs, and her wet hair hangs over her shoulders, dampening her shirt. One sleeve falls from her shoulder and reveals several small bruises. The way they form a line, it almost looks like fingers gripped her there.

Maybe they did.

She imprints on my memory, and I know Kane can sense my physical attraction to her because he knocks at the mental image. That's how it works for us. He can't see her through my eyes, but he can see the vision I've burned into my brain. Well, *our* brain.

Kane comes through as a burning behind my eyes. An intensity that sears the nerves resting close to my brain. I wish he'd let it go. He just fucking killed a girl. He doesn't need to come out and take another so soon. But the knocking gets harder. As he throws his consciousness against the mental barrier, I know it's only a matter of time before I'm pushed out of the driver's seat. I have no control over this. None of us do.

I just want to sit here and enjoy my coffee.

As I grip the warm mug, I search for something else to focus on. Fractured lines run through the glass, but they don't compromise its integrity. From the looks of things, this place plans to hold on to each aged item until it's broken past the point of usefulness. I continue staring at the cracks in the glass, counting every line branching from the main fracture as I try to will Kane away.

I squint my eyes as I pour creamer and a hint of sugar into my mug. I bring it to my mouth and take a small sip. It's the same trash coffee I've gotten used to at places like this. The same bitter bite. The same hint of something left over from the last twenty unwashed pots that have come before this one.

The burning behind my eyes intensifies, regardless of how I try to pretend it doesn't. Usually we communicate with notes. Very rarely do our thoughts overflow into each other. But this time, on this night, they do.

I need her, he whispers.

It's not his voice, though. It's mine. But it's not my thought. It comes from some nefarious place that isn't part of me, even though it's inside me.

No, Kane. Leave her, I respond in my head. I don't know if he can hear me, but even if he can, he'll likely ignore me.

I guess he doesn't like that answer, because an explosion ricochets through my mind. My heart gallops and my vision blurs until the whole diner becomes abstract. I'm losing control. Kane is taking over. And he'll hurt that poor girl, all because I took a liking to her.

Sweat gathers on my temples as each breath grows sharper. I drop the mug and it spills hot coffee all over my lap before it skitters off the counter and shatters on the diner floor.

Chapter Four

Aurora

Shattering glass draws my attention. The sound is brief, but it's enough to overpower the low clatter and hum of the diner. A man sits at the counter, his lap covered in coffee. The shards of a white mug litter the ground beneath his stool. His eyes scour the counter, likely searching for paper towels or napkins as the liquid sinks into his jeans, but the only napkin holder at the counter is empty, and the rest are spread across the restaurant.

I grab a stack of napkins from the dispenser at my table and bring them to him. He takes the crinkled sheets of tan paper and brings them to his shirt, dabbing at the material before turning his focus to his jeans.

"Thanks," he says, a bit of a southern twang in his deep voice. His dark eyes move up my body before he turns away without saying another word.

He seems completely disinterested in conversation, and I feel pretty awkward just standing here, so I back away. I did my good deed for the day.

I settle back in my seat and stare at the empty tabletop. I've been here for a while without so much as a nod from any staff. The waitress finally spots me now that I've been to the counter and back, and she approaches my table and asks what I'd like.

What I'd like is a steak dinner, complete with a baked potato, side salad, and a glass of Moscato, but I doubt I could even afford the potato at this point. After the cost of my shower, I might have enough for some oil-burned fries and a drink. My stomach growls at the thought of anything edible.

"A small order of fries and a small Coke," I say.

The disappointment in my tone must be really apparent, because Mr. Friendly looks over at me from the counter. "Give her whatever she wants," he calls across the restaurant.

"Excuse me?" I say.

"Order whatever you want. On me."

I shake my head at the waitress despite the utter protest of my stomach. That bitch says I'd drop to my knees for a meal at this point. "The fries are fine."

"Girl, if you want a goddamn steak, get it," the man says.

I swallow. "No, really, I—"

"Consider it my thank you."

The waitress shifts her weight on her white-sneakered feet, clearly growing impatient with our argument. Before I can say anything else, he places a wad of bills on the counter, stands up, and heads for the door.

A bell dings overhead as he exits the diner, and I can't help but stare through the dirt-streaked window as he makes his way across the parking lot. His jeans hang low, and a nice leather belt keeps them from dropping off his waist. Heavy black boots peek beneath his crisp pant legs with each step he takes, and a flannel shirt hugs his muscled arms. He moves like an animal stalking through grass, somehow slow and fast at the same time. Somehow . . . kind of sexy.

The man stops beside the fanciest truck I've ever seen and climbs inside. From the shape of the tractor, I can tell it houses an extended sleeper. I've only been inside one like that, and this one is even bigger. I can't help but wonder what the bed is like inside. I'm sick of low, shitty bunk beds.

I bet it's comfortable.

And clean.

The waitress clears her throat, and I turn toward her. I feel bad for making her wait, but I feel even worse about taking the guy's money. Then again, he's already left the building and it would be a real shame to let that money go to waste.

Fuck it.

"I'd like a steak, please, with a baked potato if you have any."

The waitress walks away.

I go back to staring out the window as I wait for my food. The man helps a little brown dog out of his truck, gripping the thin leash in his hand as he leads the furry creature toward a small patch of grass. A few of the truckers I've met have had pets on the road with them, and most of their personalities match the type of pet they own. I expected someone like him to have a Doberman or some sort of shepherd. But no, this little fluffy dog sticks close to his side as they walk toward the grass. It looks kind of like a Pomeranian mix.

The only Pomeranian I've ever met was this dog a girl in my class brought as an emotional support animal. I don't know how much emotional support he provided. He was a yappy little ankle biter who would quite happily shit on your pillow if you let him into your dorm room. This man's dog is the complete opposite. It seems well-mannered and quiet.

Thoughts of that Pomeranian in the dorms send my mind to dangerous places. I wish I hadn't gone right to college after high school. Then running away from college just brought me to truck stops where I'm forced to get on my knees for a meal. It seems I've been running from things my entire life. Now I have nowhere else to run to.

And nowhere to sleep.

I've usually been asked to go on a date by now, but it's too quiet tonight. There aren't many trucks in the lot, and the guy who bought my dinner didn't seem very interested. Once I've finished my steak, I'll have to get out there and weasel my way into someone's good graces. Hopefully, they'll be as nice as the guy in the purple truck.

Chapter Five

Kane

While she sits inside and eats her meal, I wait in my truck. That girl sure is a pretty little thing. Modest too. She didn't even want to accept the favor. I can see why Jax took a liking to her.

And why he tried so hard to keep me away.

No one can hold me back from something I really want, though, and especially not when what I want looks that good in a tight little jean skirt. Poor Jax really put up a fight to stay in control for her sake, but he's just not strong enough.

I don't really talk much about my alters because I consider them nuisances. They always seem to come knocking when I don't want them to. Though their intentions are usually good, they can fuck right off about this. *This* is my life. My hobby. What I enjoy doing. I'm a forty-year-old man, so I figure they should be used to this by now. What I do. What *we* do. They can try to separate themselves from me all they want, but they are a part of me.

My fucking family. Estranged, but family all the same.

Jax is the sweet brother I needed.

Tobin is the pesky sibling I never wanted.

There are others as well, but Jax and Tobin are the two who come around most often. They're the main contenders fighting for space in my brain. I've gained some and lost some over the years, but those two have remained consistent—consistent pains in my ass.

But I need them.

They hold the keys to the doors I can't open. They hide the things that would hurt me and make me more dangerous than I am now. What could be worse than a highly prolific interstate serial killer? I don't know. But I'd sure figure it out without them.

Some people believe that having alters makes me crazy. This couldn't be further from the truth. My alters strive to keep me sane. They compartmentalize the pain, allowing me to escape it. Well, most of it. Sometimes the pain is too great to be contained behind a door. Sometimes it seeps through the cracks.

Movement catches my attention, and I look toward the truck stop. The girl exits the building, looking satisfied after her meal. My eyes lock on her, and a foggy haze falls over my mind. Someone wants to take over and put this truck in drive. They urge me to leave her behind.

But I focus on my breathing and tell him no.

He can't keep me from her. No one can. Not even the person created to protect me from all the pain can keep me from inflicting so much hurt on someone else.

Pup whines beside me before settling on the seat. I reach over and pat her head while keeping my eyes glued to the girl walking toward the parking lot. Something about her seems broken. Not quite as broken as some of these bitches out here, but she's experienced some amount of damage.

It's not that I care, though. These are just observances. Things I notice. Whatever damaged her in the past will be child's play compared to what I plan to do to her.

The young girl looks around the parking lot. She wraps her arms around herself as the breeze whips her auburn hair behind her. After studying the few trucks lined up on the side of the building, she starts toward the entrance to the highway. Her thumb goes into the air when she reaches the road, but she spares one more glance toward the trucks.

She knows what she's doing. This is her signal, letting men like me know she's open for business.

The nag behind my eyes can fuck off. She's placed herself on a silver platter, and I'm ready to eat. She's the one being stupid, walking around like a prime cut of meat in a market full of starved truckers. I won't even have to abduct this one. She'll willingly climb into my truck, especially after that sweet gesture from me.

I turn the key, and the engine roars to life. The mechanical sound fills the silence as I put it in gear and drive toward the highway entrance. My brakes depressurize as I pull up to a stop beside her, creating a loud hiss. I look into her pretty eyes as I roll down my window.

"You need a ride too?" I yell over the rumble of my truck.

She looks around, unsure whether she should take a ride from me. She has good intuition and every right to be concerned. Hitchhikers are my favorite kind of girl to grab. They typically come from nowhere, and with nowhere to be, they're an excellent target.

The knock in my head recedes to a dull tap. Jax knows it's too late. The trap has been set, and she's already nibbling on the bait.

She bites her bottom lip before answering me. "Yeah, I guess I do."

"Hop in." I move Pup to the floor between the seats.

The girl climbs into my rig, and her skirt rides up her thighs as she situates herself in the passenger seat. Pup stands on her back legs to get to the girl. She has this terrible habit of biting anyone who isn't me, including Tobin. I open my mouth to scold her before she scares the girl off, but I'm stunned to silence when Pup licks her arm instead of sinking her needle teeth into her skin.

"What's her name?" she asks as she strokes the fluff behind Pup's ears.

"Pup."

"Hello, Pup," she coos, her hand disappearing beneath the long fur.

The girl looks toward my sleeper. A small galley stands in the middle, complete with a sink and microwave. Further back, there's a flatscreen TV and a couch seat that turns into a tabletop for dinners. Dark cabinets hovering above the full-sized bed provide storage. I paid for all the bells and whistles, and it's been worth every fucking penny.

"What's your name?" I ask, drawing her gaze back to me.

"Aurora."

"Kane," I say, even though she didn't bother to ask. "Why's a pretty girl like you hanging out with truckers like us?"

Her shoulders lift in a shrug. "I go on dates with them."

My eyebrow rises. "*That* kind of date?"

"Yeah," she whispers.

She's not a lot lizard. She's much too young and pretty to be called that yet, but after a few more years in this line of work, she'll fit right in. I'm glad I've gotten to her before her shiny veneer has been rubbed away.

"How much do you charge?" I ask. And why the fuck not? What else would I ask someone like her?

"The standard. Forty-sixty-eighty."

"I don't usually pick up girls like you, so I'm not sure what the standard means." This is a lie. I pick up girls just like her all the time. And then I bury them. I've heard it all before, but I want to hear her young, sweet little mouth say those filthy words.

"Forty for oral, sixty for sex, or eighty if you want both. If you only want a hand job, I could do twenty."

She speaks so transactionally, like a businesswoman. She's not like the others, though. Instead of pawing at my lap to convince me to buy what she's selling, she knows what she's got and she doesn't need to get pushy. Unfortunately for her, I have no use for her product, even though the outer packaging makes my mouth water. It's like charging a toothless man for a roasted and buttered ear of corn; he'd love to eat it, but he can only slobber all over it and make a mess.

Her green eyes harden on me. "Did you want anything?"

"Nah, not at the moment."

A look of rejection crosses her face. She doesn't understand why I'm turning her down, and I don't have the desire to explain myself. Even if I could get hard, I ain't paying for it. Besides, I need to get a few more miles under my belt before I play with her the way I want to.

Her fingers move toward the door handle. My disinterest in fucking her seems to have made her suspicious. I'll need to lower her guard again.

My head cocks as I eye her. I can't do anything with her myself, but she's pretty enough to sell. Considering I still owe The Nameless for the purchase of this truck, maybe selling her would be better than killing her. She'd fetch a higher price than some of the others I've sold.

Most of the girls I've taken aren't worth The Nameless' time. They're too old or tired or unsightly, like knackered horses at the stockyard. So I get rid of them. On rare occasions, I run across a girl who's still got some light in her eyes. Like this one.

It's a double-edged sword. I'd prefer to kill all of them, but without my truck, I'm useless. I can't work, and I sure as shit can't continue my spree. This girl would knock down a good chunk of my debt, though, so I'll have to make a decision soon. Once I've driven her around a bit, I'll decide whether she'll end up with them or in a hole in the ground.

Honestly, the hole is probably the kinder option. The Nameless aren't cruel—wouldn't want to damage the merchandise—but they send the girls to people who do far worse than what I put them through.

Her fingers tighten on the handle, so I put the truck in gear and head toward the highway. We bounce in the fancy air seats as we hit potholes littering the on-ramp.

"Where you headed?" I ask, trying to get her to release the damn handle and sit the fuck back so I can drive without worrying she'll jump out of my truck. Women have tried before. Sheer desperation has a way of removing the fear of rolling across asphalt at seventy miles per hour.

"New York," she says, and I release a silent sigh of relief as her hand returns to her lap.

I head east, but I don't plan to stay on that course. Like purchasing that meal for her, this is just to lull her into a false sense of security until I get her handcuffed in the back. Until then, I'll go the way she wants and keep her comfortable. I've got a tank full of diesel and all the time in the world.

That's part of my problem. I have too much time on my hands at the moment. I drive a reefer unit, which means I transport temperature-sensitive items in a refrigerated hold, but my supplier bailed at the last minute. A downside to being a private trucker is that I can't just whip up an order out of thin air like the drivers for the bigger companies can, but I sure as fuck couldn't kill while driving a company rig. Not easily, at least. In that way, it's a fair trade.

That huge loss in shipment is also why it would make more sense for me to sell her to The Nameless instead of putting her in the ground.

A group of brothers runs The Nameless, and I grew up with the oldest of the three. I call them The Nameless, but I know each of their names and what they're capable of. I've kept their business at arm's length, but when I had the opportunity to purchase this truck, I couldn't pass it by. I dipped a finger into their world, and I can't pull myself from their dirty dealings until I've paid them off.

I don't want to know any more about what they do than what I know now. I keep them nameless for a reason. Aside from the occasional business transaction, I want nothing to do with them. I bring them a bitch, and they carve a few chunks out of the debt I owe.

I eye the girl again and wonder just how much she'll go for. And if it's really worth it.

Chapter Six

Aurora

I glance at him as his powerful hands clutch the steering wheel. The little dog jumps into my lap and places its paws on the door so it can peer out the window. She's missing one of her front legs, but it doesn't seem to hinder her at all.

Kane and Pup. What an odd combination.

A few miles down the interstate, he pulls off his flannel shirt and tosses it onto the back of his seat. His white t-shirt rides up his taut abdomen. With his torso twisted and his head craned backward, I notice the word "Daddy" scrawled on his skin in traditional tattoo lettering. A tattoo like that would normally make me cringe, but this guy oozes the daddy vibe. Like he'd bend you over his lap and spank you while you call him that.

More tattoos paint his arm, peeking from beneath his shirtsleeves and traveling down to his wrists. I'd probably find him attractive if he weren't so grumpy. And if the hard set of his jaw didn't set off warning bells in my head. Unfortunately, I'm not very good at listening to the warning bells. I have a bad habit of waiting until they've become blaring sirens.

I almost got out of the truck before we took off. When he said he wasn't interested in my services, that was somehow more unsettling than if he'd tried to rip off my clothes. The drivers are usually more than happy to get me underneath them as soon as possible. This one? He seems like he couldn't be less interested.

I suppose he might be a nice person who wants to give me a ride, but that feels highly unlikely. No one is nice just to be nice these days.

Clearing my throat, I try to think of something to talk about to ease the growing tension in my gut. "Which company do you work for?" I ask. "Not a lot of companies let people take pets along or pick up hitchhikers."

"I don't work for a company. I work for myself."

Conversing with him is like fucking myself with a dildo. I'm forced to do all the work. I try to think of a question that would force him to talk a little more. Private drivers aren't very common, and I've never gotten in a truck that didn't belong to a big company, so I decide to stick with that line of questioning.

"Why do you drive private?" I ask.

"I'm a felon," he says without breaking eye contact with the road. But it's still a short answer, and now I'm intrigued.

"What did you do time for?"

"Mind your questions, girl."

The stern way he speaks is exactly what I mean when I say he has a daddy vibe. It's the type of tone that makes you shut the fuck up real quick, but there's also an edge of something sinister to his words. My fingers move toward the door handle again, and I seriously consider leaping from the rig and onto the interstate. It wouldn't be the first time I've leaped from a moving vehicle, though it wasn't moving anywhere near this fast.

I take a deep breath and force myself to calm down and remember the clientele I've chosen to associate with. Most are gruff. Most aren't big on talking. And more are unsavory than not.

So far, they've just gotten a little rough with me, but I've always been able to handle myself. My father was a long-haul trucker for most of my life. Then my mother wanted him to settle down, so he gave it up so he could be home every night.

I liked my father better when he was a trucker than when he was retired. Alcohol became his crutch once he was home every day, and he's a nasty drunk. But because of him, I'm more comfortable around truckers than I am with other random men, so that's why I'm a truck stop whore. Well, that's what other people call me. I call myself a working girl. These are merely my dates—a way to eat, sleep, and eventually go back home.

Eventually.

We're currently in Ohio, and I don't know how far he'll take me. Or how long I'm willing to ride with him. I still don't know what he wants from me, and I'm not sure I could handle the unease for more than a day or two.

Maybe he's not even attracted to me. Maybe he's just a nice guy who will drop me off at the next truck stop and I won't have to think about any of this. But then again, nice guys aren't often felons with *Daddy* tattooed on their necks.

To my left, Kane rubs his eyes with the back of his hand and blinks a few times. I have to do a double take, because he looks . . . different. I can't quite put my finger on what's changed, but something about his face isn't quite the same as it was before. His jaw is still as clenched as ever, and he's the same person, but somehow not.

"Are you okay?" I ask.

He clears his throat and rubs his eyes again. "Just a headache."

Well, I guess I'm imagining things, because his answers are just as short and gruff as before.

I settle in my seat and stroke the dog in my lap as the road signs pass by in a blur of headlights. My eyelids try to close, but I will them to remain open. It's not safe to sleep. Not yet. Not until I know he won't pull over and murder me the first chance he gets. This is the risk I take each time I climb inside a stranger's home. And that's exactly what these trucks are for most of these men.

Even if they have a wife back in a little two-bedroom apartment, they spend too much time in these rigs to not see them as a house on wheels. I think that's why some of them choose this line of work. They can live two lives. Meanwhile, I'm struggling to live *one*.

And I'm doing a piss-poor job.

It wasn't supposed to be this way. I was a girl with dreams once, just like anyone else. Those dreams changed along the way, but I still have them. A desire to belong somewhere. A desire to feel safe. I doubt I'll find either of those things if I continue walking along the path I'm on, so that's why I'm headed home.

Is that even the answer?

I push the thought away as soon as it forms. Now isn't the time to think about that. To keep myself sane, I have to live in the moment and focus on the immediate threat, which is a large man who is mere feet from me. As he rubs his eyes again and keeps his focus on the road, I can't help but wonder if I've made a mistake that may cost me my life.

Chapter Seven

The number combo rolls through my head as I take control. *Forty. Sixty. Eighty.* I can't stop thinking about it. Even when I was behind Kane, listening to her talk through his ears, those three numbers taunted me. Even without seeing her, I knew I wanted all fucking eighty.

Since he picked her up, Kane's thoughts have circled back to all the horrific ways he could kill her. Filet pieces of muscle from bone. Chop off limbs until she stops screaming. Hold her head beneath water until she stops struggling. All after he strangles her first, of course.

But I don't care about the killing. I give zero fucks about that. My mind just keeps repeating those glorious numbers.

Forty. Sixty. Eighty.

He won't kill her, though. It might bring him great joy to end her young life, but he knows damn well he needs to sell this one to The Nameless. The sooner he gets out from under their thumbs, the sooner he can kill whomever he pleases. And if he isn't going to kill her, if she's stuck with us until we deliver her to The Nameless . . .

Forty. Sixty. Eighty.

A sign for a rest stop slides by on the right side of the road, and I inhale. Kane let me drive so easily. Instead of fighting me this time, he just let go so I could take control. It was a smart decision on his part. Until he sells her to The Nameless, she's useless to him.

But she's not useless to me.

Kane was sexually abused as a child, and I hold all those nasty memories for him. The pain. The suffering. The fear. As a result, I'm a hyper-sexualized consciousness born from sexual trauma. I can explore the aspects of lust Kane has become immune to. Though his brain has compartmentalized those painful memories, his body has forgotten nothing, rendering him limp any time he attempts sexual acts. Unlike Kane, I have no trouble getting hard.

Now I realize why he let me take control.

The girl is suspicious, and the only way to ease her mind is to sleep with her. If she tries to manhandle our junk while Kane is in control, she'll learn the truth. It would also send him into a blind rage, and he'd bludgeon her to death before he could sell her off. I suppose a limp dick would make me homicidal too.

I pull onto the off ramp and enter the rest area. Dim lights limn the building in a weak glow, and a few towering streetlamps illuminate the parking lot, but a back corner has been left in darkness. Looks like someone forgot to change the bulbs back here. Their irresponsibility is a benefit to me, and I pull into the darkest spot I can find.

I turn toward the girl and finally get a good look at her. Kane had good taste for this one. Long, unruly auburn hair frames her face. Not too dark, not too light. She's not wearing any makeup, which is good. She doesn't need it. Her full lips are the perfect shade of pink, and her long lashes would look garish if she coated them in mascara.

"Forty, sixty, eighty, right?" I ask.

Her hands stop fidgeting in her lap. "Yeah," she whispers.

"Get in the back."

She takes a breath, unlocks her seatbelt, and climbs out of the seat. She knows the drill. With an air of confidence possessed only by a whore who's ready to lie on her back, she heads right for the bed. Unfortunately for her, it doesn't matter if I take her mouth, pussy, or both. I'll get what I want, and I won't pay for shit.

I unbuckle my seatbelt and stand to follow her. As I stretch, the bratty little dog nips at my ankles with a growl that rattles her tiny body. Mean little mutt. Why Kane wanted this annoying thing is beyond me, but he loves the little shit. He won't outwardly say it, but I feel the warmth for the dog in his heart. It's one of the few fleshy spots left inside the dying organ. The rest is black, decayed, and stinking.

"Fuck off, little dog," I say as I pull the denim from her mouth.

Before I can join the girl, I notice a clutch peeking from a backpack on the seat. I pull it free and pop it open, and a picture of the girl smiles up at me from her driver's license.

Aurora Rivelle. Twenty-four. Albany, New York.

I flip past the ID and find a picture tucked beneath a flap. In it, she stands with a man and a woman—her parents, I presume—beside a truck similar to mine. She's a trucker's daughter? No wonder she's so comfortable getting into the rigs with us.

She'll regret that in the end.

"Are you coming?" she calls from the back.

Soon enough, I think with a smirk as I tuck the clutch into the backpack.

As I enter the back of the rig, she looks at me with sweet fuck-me eyes. That look will fade when I get my hands on her.

"What do you want?" she asks.

She wastes no time waiting for my answer, and her hand goes for my zipper. Her eyes widen as she pulls out my cock and sees my dick. I can't help but wonder if it's because of the length or girth. Maybe it's the black metal piercing or the tattoo etched into that sensitive area. *Cry for me*, it says.

Kane fucking flipped when he saw it. Women aren't able to cry for him when he can't even get hard, so I think it hurt his delicate ego a bit. He shouldn't worry. He might be incapable of sexual intimacy, but I'm primed to provide our body with what it needs.

I grip her chin, and she whimpers. "Your mouth. And your dirty whore cunt," I growl.

"Eighty," she says, squeezing her eyes closed against the pain of my pinching grasp.

"You got a meal for free. A ride. With the price of fuel these days, I'd say we're about even, little girl."

Her eyes open. "You have to pay me. I need the money."

"You won't need anything with us."

"Us?"

"Me," I blurt, trying to correct my mistake.

I sometimes forget that to people like her, to everyone else, we're just Kane. It doesn't matter who's driving at the time. And that's the shitty part of this setup because I'm *not* him. I'm *me*, my own person living inside his fucked-up little mind. I matter too. I have my own desires and wants and needs. I'm my own person.

She tries to scramble away, but I grab her arm and tug her back to me.

"If you cause me any trouble, Ms. Rivelle, I'll personally pay a visit to your family on Carnation Road."

Her widening gaze shifts to the passenger seat as she realizes I've looked at her ID. Girls like her don't typically have caring parents, which also means the girls don't care about the parents. She's a unique one, though. As soon as I saw the picture, I knew I had a whore with a heart. That's a detriment in her line of work, though. It gives me all the ammo I need.

"Fuck you," she says, and I'm surprised by how calm she is.

I smirk. She's something else. And I kind of like it.

I push her onto the bed but turn away and head to the kitchen instead of leaping on her. I pull two bottles of beer from the small fridge, pop them open, and offer one to her.

"Drink," I say.

She eyes the bottle for a moment before tipping it against her lips and emptying it as quickly as I empty mine. A line of escaped alcohol dribbles from the corner of her mouth, and she wipes it away with the back of her hand, her eyes never leaving mine.

I take a step back and lick my lips. "Now fuck yourself with it."

Most girls get weird about using objects, acting as if they never experimented with things when they were younger. Not Aurora, though. She spreads her legs, giving me a view of everything beneath her short skirt as she grips the bottle's base. Her hand moves to her pussy, and as she spreads the full lips, I can't help but harden. It's such a good-looking cunt.

She swirls her tongue around the mouth of the bottle, lubricating the glass before she lowers it to her entrance and pushes it inside. She hooks her arm around her thigh and thrusts in and out, but she doesn't moan or make a sound. Even as she fucks herself harder, she remains silent. When she pulls it out and sucks it into her mouth, I nearly come in my pants.

"Why are you fucking yourself so good for me, little whore?"

"Because I'm not trying to be any trouble," she says with a snarky hiss in her tone.

She changes positions, getting onto her hands and knees as she faces her ass toward me. Resting her head on the bed, she positions the bottle between her thighs and continues to fuck herself. I can't keep my hand off my cock as I watch her. With every push of the bottle, my hand matches the speed and strength. But it's not enough.

"Keep playing with yourself, but give me your mouth," I command.

When she doesn't move, I fist her hair and pull her face to my cock. Her upper lip curls in a snarl before she relents and opens her mouth. My skin sings with pleasure as I push my cock into her warm mouth, and I don't go easy on her. I force myself to the back of her throat because a seasoned whore like her can take every inch of me. She's a goddamn professional.

The writing along my dick disappears and reappears as I fuck her mouth. Her eyes water, and a tear slips down her cheek.

"Yes. Cry for me. Just like my dick says."

Tears stream down her cheeks. I give her a hard smack, yet she hardly reacts to it. I'm confused by her lack of fight, but I don't need it to get off. I'm a deviant, not a rapist. In fact, I love that she isn't fighting me.

It won't save her, though. I don't have that power. I'm just enjoying her while I can.

She pulls away from me, and I allow it. "Are you going to fuck me or what? Just get it over with."

"If you want to skip to the fun part, that's fine with me."

And it is. It doesn't bother me that she's treating this as a transaction. She doesn't have to fight for me to enjoy it, but she doesn't have to be into it either. It might be more pleasant for her if she was, but I don't mind using her body if she's not.

I flip her over, pull the bottle from her pussy, and replace it with my cock. The ink along my dick disappears inside her. I should use a condom with a whore, but I want to feel what the bottle felt. Something inanimate shouldn't get to experience something I can't.

She whimpers as my piercing rakes her pussy walls, and it's the first reaction out of her aside from her mouthy words. I grip her hair and lift her, and she screams out.

"Kane," she whimpers.

I want to tell her Kane isn't here and she should be glad, but I don't. "You were the one who wanted to skip ahead. I'd tell you not to cry, but I like your tears. I like them so much that I inked it into my fucking skin."

I wrap my hand around her throat and feel Kane behind the motions. His desire to kill rivals my desire to fuck, but I knock him back. I'm too close, and I won't let him rob me of this.

I fuck her harder, thrusting into her with as much force as I can muster. She becomes a whimpering, screaming mess in front of me. There's no way she's enjoying this, but I sure as fuck am.

"Where do the other johns come?" I ask, because I know it's coming.

Sweat and tears mingle on her face as she turns her head and answers me. "Inside me. But with a condom."

I chuckle. "Well, I'm not using a condom, but I'll still come inside you."

"Don't!" she cries.

But I do. I come deep inside her, with every word of my tattoo buried within her cunt. But I'm not done with her. I want to savor our mess.

I pull out and press the lip of the bottle to her entrance. "Push it out."

She bears down and the come drips into the bottle. And it's a lot. Her pussy was incredible, so I'm not surprised.

With a flick of my wrist, I swirl the mixture of beer and come around the bottom of the bottle as I go to the fridge and remove the empty ice tray. I've been meaning to fill this, but I'm glad I forgot until now. I put a little water into the bottle and swirl again before filling what few empty rectangles I can. Then I fill the right half of the tray with normal water.

As I slide the tray into the freezer compartment, a thought hits me. If Kane and Jax take any from the left side, they'll kill me. Tobin, back at it again, fucking up our peaceful little system. I hate to tell them, but that ship has sailed. One third of the system is majorly homicidal, the other is a sexual deviant, and the remainder isn't strong enough to bring the peace we need. Besides, with the way Kane kills, the least of our problems is some come-laced ice cubes in the freezer.

As the backs of my eyes begin to burn, I grab a bag of chips and return to the front of the truck. Now that my job is done, someone else wishes to take the helm for a bit. I wonder who she'll have to deal with next. For her sake, I hope it isn't Kane.

Chapter Eight

Aurora

I fix my skirt without shame, lowering the hem to its proper position and turning it the right way around again. Shame isn't really in my vocabulary anymore, though I suppose it should be. How I use my body—or rather, how I allow others to use my body—is certainly deemed as shameful by a large chunk of the population. But I'm willing to bet those individuals haven't been through what I've been through. They judge through rose-colored glasses. I stare through unprotected eyes.

We are not the same.

Though I've had some odd interactions with my clientele since starting this line of work, what just happened wasn't the strangest. Not even close. Fucking myself with a beer bottle was small beans compared to the men who've paid extra for me to piss on their chests or shit on their stomachs. Some have even asked to do the same to me, though I politely declined. We all have our hard limits.

That brings my mind back around to payment, a subject he seems to have no interest in revisiting. The food and the ride aren't payment enough, and he offered those things without mentioning reimbursement. If he'll just pay what he owes, I won't even bother with my kink add-on fee.

As I walk to the front of the truck, I spot a Post-it note on the fridge. I didn't notice it before, but then again, I wasn't exactly admiring the decor when I made my way back here. On the little square piece of paper, a singular sentence has been scrawled in blocky letters.

I FUCKED HER
—TOBIN

Who the fuck is Tobin? Didn't he say his name was Kane?

With more questions than answers—and an increasing sense of unease building in my gut—I muster the courage to press the payment issue. Once I have the cash in my hand, I'm getting out of here. I can hitch a ride to the nearest truck stop. Someone is bound to stop by this rest area.

Eventually.

By the time I reach the front, he's back in the driver's seat, a small bag of chips in his hands. With hungry eyes, Pup watches each triangular morsel travel to his mouth. He tosses her a chip, and I take that to mean he's in a better mood.

"Can I have my money now?" I ask.

Putting the bag of chips between his teeth, he pulls a weathered wallet from his back pocket and eases four twenties from the stack of bills inside.

"Sorry about that," he mumbles past the cellophane as I accept the cash.

Now I'm a bit confused. I expected some pushback, especially after he so brazenly threatened my family, but his willingness to pay up isn't the strangest part. It's his voice.

When I first met him, he'd been gruff. In the back of the truck just now, he'd seemed almost gruffer, if that's even possible. He'd certainly been more demanding. But now? Now he sounds almost nice. His tone isn't as sharp, there isn't as much of an edge to each word, and he seems genuinely apologetic about the whole payment debacle.

Is this guy bipolar?

In college, my roommate struggled with bipolar disorder. When she'd go off her medication for weeks at a time, she'd suffer from personality shifts that were abrupt enough to worry me. One minute she'd be happy as a pig in shit, and the next she'd be screaming about how messy my side of the room was. When she finally broke down and explained her condition, I understood her so much more. But something about this doesn't quite fit.

For starters, her voice, facial expressions, and mannerisms weren't so drastically different. Whether she was manic, depressed, or somewhere in the middle, she was still the same person. This guy is more like night and day. Antarctica and Africa. Soup and steak.

This solidifies my decision. It's time to get the hell out of here.

"I'm going to go now," I say, looking around the front passenger seat for my backpack.

He stands and places a hand on my shoulder. The touch is gentle, not at all forceful, and his eyes radiate a sadness that stops my search. "That's not possible, Aurora. He—" Kane sucks in a breath. "You can't leave."

"Sure I can," I say. "Just give me my things and I'll get out of your hair. You'll never hear from me again. That's a promise."

He shakes his head. "It's not that simple."

"No, it's not that complicated. You paid me. I have no issue with you. If you're concerned about what you had me do back there, don't be. Keeping kinky secrets is part of the job description."

I try to force a smile and appear calm, but it's difficult when my heart is trying to beat out of my chest.

"I wish I could let you leave, sweet girl, but it's out of my hands," he whispers, lowering his gaze. "I never wanted to take you in the first place."

Take me? So it's as bad as I feared.

I make a run for the door handle, which is so stupid because the space is too small to escape his reach. His hand wraps around my arm, and my eyes clench shut as I anticipate the fist that will strike me or the fingers that will cinch around my throat. But he does neither of these things. Instead, he pulls me to his body, holding me against him as I struggle to break free. I'm uselessly expending energy—he could hold me like this all day without tiring, judging by the way his muscles bulge against my skin—so I still.

He tosses the bag of chips onto the dashboard, and his free hand brushes the stray strands of hair from my sweat-coated cheeks. "You're such a pretty girl. I'm so sorry."

I rip away from his touch. "Fuck you! Stop playing these mind games with me!"

"It's not a mind game. You just found yourself in a . . . particular situation."

"How so, Kane?"

He takes a deep breath. "I'm not Kane. My name's Jax."

What. The. Fuck. "I don't understand."

"You got in the truck with Kane, but I'm Jax. And you clearly met Tobin." He gestures toward the note on the fridge.

I sink to the passenger seat, my feet melting into the floor. The strength has been sapped from my body. My feet are lead weights attached to limp noodles. My hands refuse to listen as I scream for them to grip the door handle. My voice seems to be the only cooperative participant.

"Please explain," I say as I stare straight ahead.

He rubs the space between his eyes, shakes his head, then pinches the bridge of his nose before a long, pained exhale rushes past his parted lips. "We're different people with the same brain. I'm sorry," he says. His eyes darken and his tone deepens. "Get your ass in the back. Now."

His eyes seem to change shape as I'm looking at them. His lips draw tight, and his sharp jaw tenses. He's not the same person he was seconds before. I don't know how this is possible, but it is.

Confusion, fear, and adrenaline freeze me in place. I'm unable to follow his order, even if I wanted to. And I don't. If I go back there, it's unlikely I'll ever make it out of this truck alive.

His hand wraps around my arm again, but this time, it isn't a gentle tug. Powerful fingers dig into my muscles, and I'm helpless in his grasp. As he pulls me through the kitchen, his eyes land on the note and he growls at the words etched in black marker.

"Jax?" I whisper.

"Jax? What the fuck is he telling you?" he snaps as he throws me onto the bed. "Stay the hell back here and shut the fuck up. You aren't going anywhere, and you need to forget about whatever I said before."

His heated stare drops to the money in my hand, and he rips it from my grasp. I reach for it, but he pushes my back onto the bed again before leaning over me.

"I don't owe you a goddamn thing, least of all an explanation, so don't ask any more fucking questions. Don't speak at all. Don't even *breathe* too loud. Just stay back here and look pretty." He slaps the side of my cheek, his touch too soft to be considered assault but too rough to call it a love pat.

I don't move as he stands, nor as his heavy bootsteps recede toward the front of the truck. This isn't a conscious choice. It's a learned response. My body has experienced fear before. It's an old friend, though it's paying me an unwelcome visit.

As I lie on this bed, my thoughts run in exhausting circles. He changed. Right in front of me, in the time it took to blink my eyes, he became a different person. This wasn't some act, either.

Time passes in slow motion, but I finally dare to sit up. My gaze darts across the space that seemed so large before. Now I feel more like a grain of sand within the eye of a needle. There are no weapons to speak of, so defending myself is out of the question. The only windows back here are too small to squeeze through, meaning my only exit is through the front.

Past him.

I lick my lips and lean to my right so I can peek at him. He's in the driver's seat, with his arms folded across his broad chest and his hat lowered over his eyes. He's settling in for a nap. How nice of him to give me the bed.

But how rude of him to fucking kidnap me. And that's exactly what this is. I've been kidnapped.

It shouldn't come as a surprise, but I never expected to find myself in this situation. I've tried to be careful. When people choose unregulated sex work, we understand the risks involved. We know we're all just one trick away from having our throats slit and our bodies dumped in an unmarked grave. It's all over the news. A few days ago, it was a girl from Portland. A month before that, it was a runaway teen from Spokane.

Today . . . it's me.

Chapter Nine

Kane

I pull the hat a little lower to block the glare of distant light as I lose myself to my thoughts. I don't know why Jax tried to explain this fucked-up situation we're in. He's got a little thing for the girl, I get it, but it's not his place to make her understand. She *can't* understand. No one ever does.

This goes deeper than trying to make her understand, though. Jax is the protector. The nurturing type. What I choose to do eats away at him, and he would have released that girl if his goal to protect our system didn't override his desire to protect things in general. But if he releases her, it puts all of us at risk. Deep down, he knows he needs to keep her right where she is so I can take care of what he can't.

We can't get caught.

Jax won't survive more prison time. I'd be fine, but he struggled when we were on the inside. Hell, even Tobin struggled, though his main complaint centered on the lack of pussy. From what the other inmates told me, I learned he combatted his desires by loudly jerking off every night. Though I will say, being so open about his sexual deviancy kept a *lot* of people away from us. Win-win. But Jax was a mess. He cried all the time. Imagine being known as the chronic masturbator and crier in one cell block. It wasn't a good look.

"Why are you giving me the bed?" she asks from the rear of the truck, and I don't even lift my hat from my face. I won't move unless she gives me a reason to.

"Go to sleep, dropout," I say. I let her take the bed so I could get a little shut-eye without worrying about her escaping.

"How do you know I'm a dropout?"

"I saw your college ID. I'm guessing a whore like you studied dicks instead of classwork."

When she scoffs and goes silent, I know I'm right.

Fabric scrapes against metal as she pulls the curtain across its track, separating us the only way she can. Is she planning an escape? Will I have to kill her here and now instead of handing her over to The Nameless?

The endless questions grind to a halt when gentle pressure lands against the front of my jeans. My torso jerks forward, and my hat falls to the floor as I escape her touch.

Abso-fucking-lutely not. I can't handle touch like that. Besides, she's just trying to butter me up so I'll lower my defenses and she can run off. That's also not happening.

My cock remains limp as can be, even as her big green eyes look up at me from her knees. Her hand moves toward me again, but I swat it away.

"Don't touch me," I say.

When she put her hand on me, it felt as if she'd wrapped her fingers around my throat instead of my dick. I don't remember why I have such a visceral reaction to touch.

My memories are black boxes in my mind. I know they're there, but there aren't labels or pictures to remind me of what waits beneath the locked lids, and I can't access their contents. Tobin has the keys. But even if my mind can't reach into those dark places and bring those memories into the light, my body recalls something about that touch.

The girl doesn't listen, though. She reaches for me again. Sweat slicks my skin and my heart thunders in my ears as my arm draws back. Before I know what's happening, I've backhanded her in the face. It's a knee-jerk reaction, that's all. If I wanted to hurt her, I'd have hit her with more than my hand.

She flies backward, and her back crashes against the leather passenger seat. "What the fuck!"

I shake my head and try to calm my breathing as I stare at her reddening cheek. I tried to warn her. She was told to stop, but words weren't convincing enough.

The backs of my eyes begin to burn, but I can't lose control right now. I *have* to set up this meeting with The Nameless, and that won't happen if I'm not in the driver's seat. Jax would be too busy hugging her and apologizing, and Tobin would just want to fuck her again.

I stand up and grip her by the hair as I lift her to her feet. "Don't fucking touch me like that. Don't *ever* touch me. Do you understand?"

Her fiery green eyes rise to mine as she struggles within my grasp. "But you can touch me?"

I didn't. I wouldn't. And I don't know how to explain that. There's absolutely no drive for me, and even if there was, it's not like I can perform.

"If I touch you, it's different," I snarl, "but don't initiate shit yourself. If I want to use your whore body, *I* will be the one to start it. If you try that again, the only thing you'll touch are the clods of earth I throw on your dead body."

That seems to drive the point home, and she stops struggling. "I need to pee," she whispers.

I let out a low growl, but I need to piss too. Keeping my hand within her hair, I drag her toward the passenger side door, pull the keyring from my pocket, and unlock the glove box. Within the compartment sits a beautiful 1911 with a wood grain grip. I like pretty things, what can I say?

I grab the gun and hold it in front of her face, keeping the barrel pointed toward the window. Safety first, after all. "If you run, I'll shoot you before you make it six feet from me. Allowing you to piss is a kindness. Do *not* mistake it for weakness. Do you understand?"

"Yes," she says.

I help her down from the truck, and she shifts her weight between her feet as if she's been holding her bladder for ages. This could all be another ploy, but I'll give her the benefit of the doubt for now. If she tries to run, she won't get very far with a bullet in her spine.

We walk toward the brick building squatting beside the parking lot. I keep her close to me as my mind works to sort through what I'm up against. Some rest areas staff attendants around the clock, but this building has already been locked up for the night. I can tell because the lights are off inside. The restrooms are on the outside—the men's room on the left and the women's room on the right. The lack of an attendant is a good thing. She can't scream for help, and I won't have to shoot two people instead of one. The distance between the two restrooms, though? Not great.

"Go in the men's room," I say as I stuff my pistol down the back of my pants. I didn't see any cameras as we approached, but sometimes they're hidden well.

She sighs and walks into the men's room. I follow her until she's inside the stall, then I head to the urinal. When she starts to piss, I finally breathe a sigh of relief. Maybe she wasn't plotting after all.

The metal roll in her stall is already squeaking as she pulls paper from the holder before I've even finished. Before she can flush the toilet, I bear down on my bladder and piss a little faster.

The hinges squeal as the stall door opens, and she licks her lips as I look over my shoulder and meet her gaze. Then her eyes fall to my undone pants. Seeing an opportunity, the little bitch bolts for the restroom door.

"Fuck, fuck," I say beneath my breath. I shake droplets of urine from my cock and put it away so I can chase her. She can't escape. She's seen my truck. My face. And even though I didn't fuck her, I saw the note Tobin left behind, meaning she also has my DNA between her legs. Once it goes through CODIS, the great state of Ohio will issue a warrant.

I race out the door and scan my surroundings. It's dark out here, and even darker toward my truck and the woods just beyond. When footsteps crunch through dead leaves, I know which way she's gone.

And I follow.

"Stop now and I won't blow your brains all over this fucking rest stop, dropout!" I scream as I barrel toward the trees.

"Fuck you!" she yells back. She sounds so far away now, which means she's clearing ground faster than I can. I guess it makes sense. She's running for her life, and girls are so much faster when something that important is at stake.

Warm heat fills my head, and I know it's Tobin. He loves to run—to *chase*—but he likes to catch even more. And when he catches, he does something I can't. He fucks.

Now that I think about it, that isn't such a bad idea. If I catch her, she's dead. She's pissed me off, and I won't be able to stop myself from wrapping my hands around her throat and pressing down until she goes limp. If I let Tobin take over, she might wish for death while he's on top of her, but she'll still be alive.

And sellable.

Tobin

It takes me a moment to gather my bearings as I run through the woods, but the pounding footsteps somewhere in the distance tell me everything I need to know.

She chose to run.

Kane knows he doesn't have the control to stop himself from killing her if he catches her. He also knows the catching and subsequent fucking are right up my alley. That's why he's put me in the driver's seat. That's why I'm weaving through trees and pushing past the limits of my body as I chase her down.

A sharp pain rips through my side with each breath I take. Sweat collects on my forehead and sears my eyes as it drifts past my lashes. But I don't stop. I keep running.

I catch glimpses of her in the distance, her auburn hair gripping shreds of moonlight and casting it back at me. By the way she's beginning to slow, I know she's feeling just as exhausted as I am.

"When I've finished hunting you like the filthy pig you are, I'm going to take your little cunt, do you hear me?" I let my threat wrap around her as the gap between us closes.

She lets out a shriek and stumbles into a spindly tree trunk. Her body bounces off the bark, but she doesn't stop. After a few flailing steps, she finds her feet and pushes onward. The jean skirt has ridden up her waist, giving me a peek of each pale cheek with every step she takes. Like a kick to the side, each glimpse of my prize spurs me forward.

"I can run longer than you because I want it more! Just give up now!" I yell toward her, though I don't need to yell. I'm close enough to see the way her sweat has collected on her back and darkened her shirt.

"Just let me go!"

Absolutely not.

She ducks under a low-hanging branch and cuts right. I realize what she's done too late. She's taken a path through the woods that's too narrow to accommodate my larger size. She's small enough to squeeze through the brambles and vines, but I'll get tangled if I try to follow.

I do the only thing I can and continue tracking her diagonally. I'm still in a mostly open area, so her little plan has put more distance between us, but it's also slowing her down.

I slow to a jog as she struggles through a thick patch of growth. I can hear each strangled breath from her exhausted lungs. Soon, I'll taste her fear.

"You'll wish you were dead when I finish with you! You'll wish he hadn't let me out to play!" I shout.

"He?" she screams over her shoulder. "You're such a fucking freak!"

"I'm not a freak," I say beneath ragged breaths.

She's lucky Kane isn't out to hear that word fall from her lips. He'd snap her neck for it. We've spent our whole lives being called names. Freaks. Weirdos. Anything you'd call someone you don't understand. Someone different. That word preceded Kane's first murder. That word started it all.

And once I catch her, she'll regret that word.

Chapter Ten

Aurora

My heart beats like a drum in my chest. The rhythm increases until I worry it might burst through my skin. Air sears my throat with each breath and my legs have grown weak, but I can't stop. If he catches me, I'm probably dead.

"Whore," he calls from impossibly close behind. I'm surprised he hasn't reached out and grabbed me. It's hard to ignore the urge to turn and see just how close he is, but I have to keep running. Looking behind would mean slowing down, which would mean giving him the fraction of an inch he needs to catch me.

I'm absolutely desperate to keep away from him, so I force myself to keep going. He's older than me. Surely he can't keep this up much longer.

I break through the thick growth and run into a chain-link fence on the edge of the property. The foliage camouflages it, but it gave the familiar rattle when my body careered into it. My fingers grip the metal loops as I run along the length of the fence, hoping to find an opening big enough for me but too small for him. It's too tall for me to climb, and with his muscles, he'd probably clear it with ease.

I'm so focused on finding a break in the fence that I don't realize I've come to the end of this side until I slam into the panel running the other direction. I've run out of room.

I'm cornered.

In a desperate attempt to escape him, I grip the fence and try to climb. Hand over hand, foot over foot, I grip the spaces between the metal and haul myself upward. From sheer fear and willpower, I make it to the top. Tears spring to my eyes as I hoist my leg over the top railing. I only need to get my other leg over, and then—

Firm fingers close around my ankle and rip me downward. My crotch slams onto the top of the fence, and a scream rips from me as the metal meets my pelvic bone. But there's no time to wallow in the anguish because he's pulling me back down. I send my foot into his face, and he groans, seemingly enjoying the pain I'm causing him.

"If you think I like tears, imagine how much I love blood," he growls as a trail of red trickles from his lower lip. "This is all just foreplay, eighty."

My hands bleed from clawing at the fence, which only makes it more difficult to hang on. It's like trying to grip something after smearing your palms with oil. Strength exits my body with each breath, and I have nothing left to give as he wraps his arm around my waist and pulls me to the ground.

His hands pin my arms to the cool grass. When his face nears mine, I spit in it. The moment I do, he spits back, and his blood-tinged saliva lands on my cheek.

"Stop, please!" I scream as I writhe beneath him.

He swipes the spit from his face. "I thought I was pretty fucking nice to you. You weren't hurt by what we did back in the truck, so why'd you have to go and make me chase you, huh?"

"Just let me go. I won't tell anyone. I swear."

"It's a bit late for that. I can't let you go now that I've seen how terrified you are. I drink up fear like it's liquor. Right now, you're a bottle of Everclear." He takes a deep breath before leaning over and licking the spit and blood from my cheek. "And I'm a fucking alcoholic tonight."

"I'm sorry," I say, though I don't regret trying to escape. I'm just sorry I got caught. "Just don't kill me. Please."

"Kill you? I have no plans to kill you. I had something else in mind. Will you be a good little whore and let me play, eighty?"

"Why do you keep calling me that?"

"Because it's the cost to take all of you. Mouth, pussy, ass. Whatever I want. It's how much you charge to let men like me do anything to you." He sits up, keeping his weight on my hips, and draws the money from his pocket before tossing it on my chest. The bills catch a slight breeze and try to flitter away.

If I reach for the money, I'm agreeing to let him do what he wants, and part of me wants to let the money float out of reach. A large part of me. But he'll do whatever he wants, even if I don't take the cash.

I reach for the bills, grabbing all but one of the twenties that's flown just a finger's length out of reach. He leans forward, grips the last bill, and shoves it against my chest.

"Fine," I whisper as I accept the last twenty and tuck the money into my bra.

Kane . . . Tobin—whoever it fucking is—strips off his shirt. A multitude of tattoos covers his torso. I can't make out the individual images beneath the moonlight, but I *can* see the glint of a knife as he pulls it from his waistband. My hands immediately go up, expecting him to attack me, but he lifts the blade and slices into his own chest. A soft groan vibrates his throat as he pulls the knife away from his skin, then fists my hair and pulls me up to his chest.

"Lick my blood," he growls as he pulls my face toward his skin.

My tongue touches the thin red line, and a metallic taste races over my tastebuds. He pushes the back of my head and grinds my face into his cut as if it's not enough for me to taste it. He wants to cover me with it. And he does. Warm liquid coats my face, growing sticky as it dries.

He pushes me onto my back and raises my skirt. Blood splatters on me as he leans over and pulls my underwear away from my body. Using the knife, he cuts through my panties. Warm blood drips onto my pussy, and I'd be lying if I said it doesn't feel good.

But then I feel the stiff metal blade as he grazes my slit.

Panic ratchets through me as he spreads me with one hand and puts the blade inside me with the other. It's not big, but that doesn't matter. If I move a single muscle, I'll cut myself a second vagina.

"Please get that out of me." A tear falls from the corner of my eye.

"When you're wet like you are from my blood, a small blade like this does nothing to you. It goes in and out so smoothly. But when you're dry? That's when it cuts." The blade moves in and out of me again. "As long as you stay still and don't tense up, you'll be just fine."

He fucks me with the blade, and he's much gentler than I expect him to be. Especially after that chase. But then he pulls it out of me, turns it around, and grips the blade in his powerful hand instead. He winces as it sinks into the meat of his palm, but he doesn't seem otherwise fazed.

Then he sinks the handle inside me, and all gentleness evaporates.

I'll admit, the fear and the chase have done a little something to me. The knife adds a whole different element. He sits between my legs and just pounds me with that knife as the blade slices his hand. Like a fucking psychopath, he pulls so much pleasure from the intense pain.

And like a fucking psychopath, I kind of like it, and my hips rise off the grass.

As he pulls out of me, crimson shadows his flesh. "How much of my hand can you fit inside your pretty whore cunt, huh?"

"I don't know!" I whimper. I've never had anyone put more than a few fingers inside me.

"Let's see if my blood helps grease the wheels, eighty."

His bloody fingers push inside me. Two. Then three. He draws back his arm and forces a fourth in. Warmth spreads through my core, and I accidentally moan, which he follows with a rabid groan. I'm so full, but by his estimation, I'm not full enough. He draws back, presses his thumb to his palm, and makes me take that too. He's up to his knuckles inside me, and it's almost more than I can take.

"Such a good whore. So easy to train. Spread your legs a little wider for me."

I do as he asks and part my thighs as far as they can go. He slowly twists his hand and applies firm pressure inside me. Left and right, pushing into me as he does. When he finally pushes past his knuckles, a sharp burning sensation builds around his fingers. I scream out, but once his knuckles are inside me, it feels like the worst is over. It feels like he's pushed the biggest sex toy known to man inside me. Something worthy of being a gag gift at a bachelorette party.

Something that should never actually be inside a person.

He twists his wrist, wriggling more of his hand inside me until I'm certain I can't take another millimeter. And it feels so good. Too good for something I'm being paid for. Instead of fighting the feelings, I close my eyes and lose myself to the motion of his hand inside me. Warmth works its way up my legs and runs a finger up my spine. I bear down on him as the intense pressure builds, and my come washes away the blood as he pounds me with his hand.

"Oh god!" I scream.

His eyebrows rise. "There's no god, eighty. Only me. Christen me with your come."

I have no clue what he means until he pulls out of me, leads me over to a tree, and lies down with his head against the trunk.

"Put your back against the tree for support and squat over my face," he says.

So I do. He grips my ankles and positions my feet on either side of his head, then he pushes his hand back inside me. It's a little more difficult because of the position, but he's too determined to quit. Hovering over his face with his entire hand inside me, I feel like a fucking puppet. And he's the puppet master.

I try to hold back the pressure when it builds again, but honestly, fuck this guy. I let go and squirt all over his face. My come sprays into his open mouth, and he gargles it before swallowing.

Yeah, he's a fucking freak. And not just because he thinks he's three different people.

He pulls his hand from me, unfastens his pants, and pulls out his cock. He pushes me down his body and holds me over his dick. When he pushes me down on his lap, I take him inside me.

"How do you still feel so good after having my entire fist inside you?" he growls, thrusting up to meet my core.

He grips my hair and puts the bloody, come-coated hand that was inside me in my mouth. Salt and copper tangle across my tongue. He fingers my face, and I gag until tears form at the corners of my eyes and slip down my cheeks.

"Good girl, eighty. Cry for me."

His hand pulls back enough to keep me from throwing up before he's back to fucking my throat with his fingers. Tears stream down my face as I struggle to keep from vomiting. Each time I gag, he groans when the added pressure teases his cock.

"I'll give you this. You sure know how to fuck to save your life, don't you?"

I'm not stupid. I know when to give in to a man to survive. I know how to win them over with my body. This is merely a life preserver. If I have to ride his cock for another chance to escape, then I will. Coming was just an added benefit this time.

"Thank you," I whisper.

"Fuck, you squeezing my cock like this is going to make me come."

As his hips buck against mine, I look over at the knife lying in the grass. If I just lean a little to the left—

"Don't even think about it." His grip firms on my hips and completely eliminates any chance of leaping for the knife. "I like that you considered it, though. Would you kill me as I came, whore?"

"Yes," I pant. His thrusts feel better than I wish they did.

His hips stutter against mine as he comes, probably to the thought of me stabbing him. He's such a sexual deviant, my god.

He drops his ass back to the ground. "You're a filthy girl, and I love it," he whispers, his voice all gravel. "Give my come back to me. Drip it into my mouth."

Before I can say no, he drags me up his body and positions me above his mouth again. His request doesn't even bother me, though. Dripping his come directly into his waiting mouth is nothing in the broad scheme of things.

With his hands around my thighs and his eyes closed, he sticks out his tongue and waits for my gift. I bear down, and pearly strands of come drip into his waiting mouth. I figure he'll swallow it, but he doesn't. Instead, he flips me onto my back and smirks over me.

He doesn't have to tell me what he wants me to do now.

I spread my lips, and he spits into my mouth. My come, his come, his saliva—I take all of it.

"Do you have a shred of dignity in your body, eighty? Is there anything I can't do to you?"

I swallow. I've mastered my ability to seem like I'm enjoying everything and anything because that's my job. And I'm fucking good at it. But he's also met his match. Sexual deviant, meet sexual deviant. I can only hope it will save my life in the end. Why would he want to kill a woman who would let him do anything to her?

Anything.

My gaze is drawn to the tattoo across the side of his neck. Was it Tobin who got that "daddy" tattoo? The man from the bathroom didn't seem like he'd want to be called daddy, but this man definitely seems the type. But if I'm thinking like this, does that mean I actually believe the shit he's said? That there's more than one of them? I've seen it in movies, but I didn't think it was real. Could I really be trapped in the truck with three people instead of one?

And if I am, maybe Tobin isn't the one I should be so afraid of.

Chapter Eleven

Tobin hands control to me on the walk through the woods. He's not an aftercare kind of person, and we can't let Kane out. He'll kill her for what she did. I can only hope he'll calm down before he takes control again. He knows killing her isn't the right call, not when she can fetch so much money from The Nameless. But Kane also has very weak impulse control. We can only hold him back for so long, though.

We reach the truck, and I beeline for the sink as soon as we're inside. Blood stains my shirt, my face, my hands, and because it's drying, it's a sticky mess. Using a stiff rag draped over the side of the sink, I begin to scrub.

Tobin loves blood, but it's not a shared interest. I can't wait to get it off my hands. I rub until every inch of my exposed skin is raw and red, being careful around the new cut Tobin has put on our body. It's not very deep, but it still doesn't feel great when the rag's tough fibers scrape across it.

"You really aren't Tobin, are you?" she asks as I continue my furious scrubbing.

I glance at her in the mirror. She's seated on the bed, wringing her scraped hands in front of her. "I tried to tell you that. I'm really not Tobin."

"And you aren't Kane."

"I'm none of them. I'm me. Jax."

"But Kane's the boss?"

I shake my head. "Not exactly. Kane is the main. He's the one who was born in that physical body."

"But you guys are your own people?"

I dry my face with a paper towel. "Yes, we're different personality states sharing one body. We have our own strengths and weaknesses, likes and dislikes."

"And do *you* like holding women captive, Jax?" she asks.

"Of course not. I don't like anything about this situation. But Kane does, and I have an obligation to him. It's nothing against you. We just have to protect ourselves."

I wipe my hand down my face, and my gaze falls on her hands again. Some of the gouges on her palms look pretty filthy. They need to be cleaned and tended, and Kane and Tobin sure as fuck won't bother with it.

I motion her over to the sink. "Wash your hands. You don't want those cuts to get infected."

She stands on shaky legs and approaches the sink, keeping her eyes on me the entire time. She still doubts what I've said, and how she doesn't believe there are three of us is beyond me. We couldn't be more different. Even when we're boiled down to our base desires, we're nothing alike. If I fuck, it's soft and sweet. If Tobin fucks, it's that bloody mess swirling down the drain. And Kane won't fuck at all.

Now that her hands are cleaned of blood, I can see that the cuts aren't too bad after all, which is good because we don't exactly keep a first-aid kit in the truck. Kane isn't in the business of healing wounds. He'd rather create them. I don't know what she'll do about the bloodstains between her legs, though. For tonight, I just have to make sure she's tucked away in bed so we can actually get some rest. Sleep deprivation isn't great for any of us.

Aurora doesn't need help figuring out how to get clean, though. She rinses the rag I used, lifts her skirt, and begins scrubbing between her legs. I turn away.

"You can look, Jax," she whispers.

Instead of responding, I head toward the front of the truck and plop down in the seat. She's trying to bait me, but I can't fall into her trap. As I flip the hat around and lower it over my eyes, I focus on my need for a shower. I want nothing more than to clean the blood from my junk, and that's something I can't do until I figure out where Kane keeps the restraints.

I have to make sure she can't run off. Because she will. The first time the opportunity presents itself, she'll take off again.

The water is still running, so I'm a bit shocked when her hand grazes my shoulder. She walks between the seats and sits on my lap. Her warmth burns me, but I don't shove her away. Instead, I take the time to look at her. Her appearance was the reason I began staring at her in the first place.

She licks her full lips, and I'm tempted to lean forward and kiss her. It's been a long time since I've felt a woman's caress, but I've never been with a woman as stunning as Aurora. Even though she looks a little tired, a little beaten down from what she's been through at our hands, she's still beautiful.

Aurora turns and straddles my lap. Her hand goes for my cheek as she leans in, but I turn away.

"We can't," I say. I speak as firmly as I can muster, but my voice sounds weak to my ears. I don't get to play like this very often. Tobin comes knocking at any chance of sex, and I'm cast aside because my personality isn't as strong as his. But Tobin is spent, and my mind is silent for once.

"There's no one here but us, Jax. Sure we can."

I'm not an idiot. She's only trying to win me over so she can escape. She doesn't actually like me. But someone needs to tell my dick this revelation.

My pierced, tattooed dick.

My god. I look like an idiot with this thing. I think it's trashy, but then I remember who orchestrated the entire thing. Tobin. Need I say more?

"I know what you're trying to do. You're trying to lower my defenses so you can escape again," I say.

She shakes her head and looks away. "I know that's useless now. I can't run from you. But I want to see if it's different when I fuck you."

Oh, it would be very different. For starters, I won't draw any blood.

Even though I know it's a ploy, she tears down my defenses when her eyes meet mine again. When her hands move toward my lap, I don't stop her. When she unzips my pants and reveals my fully erect cock, I allow it.

My eyes remain on hers as she rises and lowers herself onto me. Her warmth envelops me, and I groan and rest the back of my head against the leather seat. I revel in the way she grips my cock with each movement of her hips and thighs. Her breasts bounce slightly with each up-and-down motion, and I long to take them into my mouth. I long to taste her.

I put my hand behind her neck, draw her into me, and kiss her. She returns the kiss, meeting each surge of my tongue with hers. I raise my hips and meet her next motion halfway, thrusting my full length into her, and she moans into my mouth.

She pulls back and continues rocking on my lap. "When was the last time you fucked?"

"Years. Five maybe," I pant against her neck.

"They don't let you out to play?"

"Not like this." I reach around her waist and grip the steering wheel as she fucks me.

"How does it feel?" she whispers.

"So fucking good."

She increases the speed, riding me harder, and if I don't change positions, I'll come too soon. How fucking ridiculous.

"Let's take this to the bed," I say, and she nods.

I ease her off my lap and guide her toward the back of the truck. I don't even care about the blood on us as I lay her down and get between her legs. I only want to feel her again.

I wrap her thighs around me as I push inside her. She looks up at me with those pretty green eyes as her moans drift from her lips, and I fuck her a little harder so I can draw more of that out of her. Tobin already filled her, but I can't be mad about another man's come. Not when I have this perfect woman beneath me. Instead of focusing on the warm stickiness as I thrust into her, I focus on the soft moan she releases or the way her body responds to mine.

My hand moves between us, and I rub tight circles around her clit. When she clenches around me, I know I'm in the right spot.

Or am I? She's a professional at this, and there's a lot more at stake than a stack of cash this time.

"Don't fake it for me, sweet girl. I can always tell," I say.

"I'm not faking anything," she says. "I'm going to come."

If she's really that close, I want her to come on my tongue. I pull out and kneel at the edge of the bed. Gripping her thighs, I pull her toward my face, only taking a moment to admire the beautiful pussy in front of me. Aside from the bloody smears, it's perfection.

Now I need to know if it's as delicious as it looks.

I hook my arms around her thighs and bring my mouth to her slit. I lick, tasting everything from tonight. It's not great, but her taste lies beneath it all. Warm and sweet. I focus on that as I tongue her.

As I gently suck her swollen clit, her moans shift. They're less restrained. Her fingers clutch the sheets, and her hips begin to move. She chases each stroke of my tongue as her thighs begin to quiver in my grasp.

"Holy fuck," she pants.

I push my fingers inside her, and she gasps as she draws closer to her edge. Her breath comes in sharp bursts, matching each flick of my tongue as I tease her and give her a little push. I want her to fall over that edge. I want to taste every drop of her genuine pleasure.

"I'm going to come!" she screams.

"Who's making you come?" I ask.

"Jax," she moans.

Hearing my name fall from her parted lips sends an ache right to the hardened flesh between my legs. She tightens around my fingers, and warm wetness overflows from her. I lean down and scoop up every drop with my tongue. I don't care that Tobin's pleasure has mixed with hers. I don't care that the metallic tang of blood permeates her sweet flavor. I want to drink her like wine, and nothing will stop me from curling my tongue along her clit as her body shudders.

As she begins to come down from her orgasm, I fist my cock and push inside her again. Firm, pleasure-filled spasms squeeze me again and again. I've never felt something so incredible. It's as if my body was made for hers.

I reach forward and grip her breast in my hand. The hard point presses against my palm as she pushes her chest upward. My hand travels down her stomach, reveling in each panting breath she takes. It's too much. I can't hold back any longer.

I pull out of her and stroke myself. Instead of coming inside her, I want to watch my come paint her pretty little pussy. As I feel the pressure build, I squeeze just beneath the base of my cock and send come spurting onto her skin. I empty everything onto her, then I draw my hips back and push inside her again. I'm sensitive after I come, but it's a reminder that I was given the gift of release as my head strokes her walls again.

When I can't take it anymore, I pull out and lie beside her. My hand rubs between her legs, smearing my come into her skin. God, she's incredible. She's—

"You could let me go, Jax," she whispers.

My hand stops moving. As does my heart. I knew this was all part of her game, but I let myself forget for just a moment. I didn't want to think about it, but now she's forcing me to.

"Aurora, you know I can't."

"If you don't let me go, Kane or Tobin will kill me."

I shake my head. "Tobin wouldn't."

She doesn't respond. How can she? We both know what we're up against. We both know I can't say that Kane wouldn't kill her. He would. Even with the plan to give her to The Nameless, he still might.

"I can't let you go. You don't understand how this works."

"So explain it to me. Help me understand."

I'd almost rather let her go than try to explain our situation to her. To explain what it means to be three minds in one body. I've seen the looks before. People either think it's all an act or that we're crazy. Sometimes both. But no one truly understands because no one ever *tries* to understand. They would rather fear and ostracize the unknown than take the time to hear it out.

Considering letting her go only pisses Kane off. I feel him in my mind, lurking just behind a door that he can easily break down. But this girl doesn't get it. How can I make her understand?

I suck in a deep breath. "Fine. You can go."

Fire blazes against the backs of my eyes, and a headache knocks against my skull. I stay on the bed as she rushes to find her backpack. She looks back at me for help, but I can only shrug my shoulders and rub my burning eyes. I don't know where Kane hid it. She finally gives up and heads for the door.

And just as she opens it, the door holding back Kane swings wide.

Chapter Twelve

Kane

These fucking idiots. This is why sex isn't even a thought in my mind. It makes you fucking stupid. With my pants still undone, I run after her. She isn't hard to find. Instead of racing for the woods, I catch a glimpse of her shirt as she bolts toward the bathrooms.

Too slow, dropout.

She's caught off guard as I catch up to her and yank her back by the hair. A scream tears from her chest as her leg lashes toward me, but I have a solution for that. I grab her legs and take out her feet. Her head collides with the grass, and the screaming stops.

Knocking her out wasn't the goal—The Nameless don't like girls with bruises—but she left me no fucking choice. The rest area is empty now, but someone could drive up at any moment. If someone hears her screaming and sees me chasing her and hauling her back to my truck, it's a guaranteed one-way trip to the nearest jail cell. Even if Tobin doesn't give a shit, Jax sure as fuck does. I can't believe he let her go.

I kneel beside her still form and get my arms under her. Getting her to the truck before someone drives by is my first priority. I can check the goods for damage once we're safely inside.

I climb the metal steps and enter the truck with her limp body in my arms. Once we're tucked away from prying eyes, I drop the caring-guy act and drag her toward the bed by her hair. I pull a scuffed set of handcuffs from the cabinet above the bed, then attach one cuff to her arm and the other to the metal hinge connected to my bed.

She isn't going anywhere now.

I grip her face and turn it toward me. A large red welt puffs her cheek outward, but it doesn't look like it will bruise. Or if it does, it won't be too bad. This almost pisses me off more than if she'd been seriously injured. My hands itch with the need to wrap my fingers around her pale neck. She's a pain in my ass, and I'll be glad when I get rid of her.

I'm about to walk away when I notice the mess between her legs. Her skirt has ridden up, exposing her filthy pussy. I grab a few paper towels and begin cleaning her up. With each not-so-tender swipe, my lip curls further.

I have no clue what those boneheads find so appealing about her pussy. I couldn't be more turned off by the used-up slit between her legs. Something inside me heats to a boil when I stare at those puffy folds of skin. A memory thrashes within a locked box inside my head, fighting to break free, and I can't have that. I need to do something, and fast.

I grab a lighter from my pocket, spread her lips, and flick the metal until a flame springs forth. I bring the heat toward the swollen bundle of nerves that brings her so much dirty pleasure. I should burn that sinful clit off. Maybe Jax and Tobin won't be so interested in her if I damage her a little.

As I stare down at her pussy, memories seep from the locked box like invisible gas.

Big, feminine hands reach for my lap. I'm crying. She pulls me onto her naked thighs . . .

Anger roars like a lion inside me. I don't know who that was, but I know it's a woman. She's the reason I hate women now, and I don't need to know from what well that hatred springs. I know that it's poisoned, filthy and black, and I drink from it daily. The source isn't important as long as the water keeps flowing.

I drop the lighter and clench my eyes shut. I don't want to remember. I don't want to know what happened to me. Tobin spoon-feeds little glimpses from time to time, but I don't want that right now.

I lower the girl's skirt and scoot away from her. I need to sell her, so her body isn't mine to permanently damage. If I wasn't giving her to The Nameless, I'd cut off her clit and feed it to her for running away. Twice.

But that isn't a solution.

Maybe I should cut off my own dick to stop Tobin and Jax from using it and becoming complete dumb asses.

I bring the lighter up to my limp cock and flick the metal again. Heat bursts from the opening, and I revel in the flames licking my sensitive skin. The scent of burned flesh wafts up to me, and I release the lighter. I was so lost in the pleasurable pain that I didn't realize I nearly gave myself a second-degree burn. The thought of how the pain would zip straight to my brain if I'd done more damage tempts me to continue, but I don't. I stuff the lighter into my pocket and turn my attention back to the problem at hand.

The girl.

Killing or maiming her would make her less desirable to Jax and Tobin, but it would do me no good. Aside from the fleeting thrill of a kill, I'd get nothing out of it. I have to find a way to remind the others that she doesn't belong to us. She isn't ours to catch and release at will. She's a commodity.

I go to the front of my truck and pull the burner phone from the concealed compartment beneath my seat. After tapping in the number—it's too risky to save it as a contact—I hit the call button. One of The Nameless answers on the second ring.

"Talk."

"I'm hauling a load your way," I say. "Should I come to the usual spot, or—"

"No. Contact me when you reach Houston. I'll give you an address. Where are you coming from?"

I glance at the brick building, then back at the interstate. Headlights push through the trees as someone pulls into the parking lot. "I'm in Ohio right now. Shouldn't take too long to get there."

"Give me the details so I can line up a buyer. We aren't in a position to hold the product for very long right now. Better to move them quickly."

I smirk. I know what sort of men will be buying this product, and it's exactly what she deserves. I give him the code for a pretty redhead, no apparent drug habits, clean and clear.

"I'm not taking it if the packaging is damaged," he says. "I cut you a break last time. Never again."

My eyes close, and I nod as I end the call. It's a warning I must heed, and now that The Nameless have been promised something, it's a warning Jax and Tobin are forced to heed as well.

I zip my pants and return to the cabinet above the bed. After digging around inside, I find the choke collar and metal leash, and I drop them on the counter beside the sink. The girl is too unruly. If she wants to act like a dog and run away at every opportunity, I'll treat her like one. The next time we leave this truck, I plan to keep her on a very short leash.

Chapter Thirteen

Aurora

I blink back my confusion. The hum of tires on asphalt vibrates the truck. We're moving, then. Swimming up from the blackness, I'm left with a headache and a lot of questions. My eyes rise to the small, dirty window. A pale orange glow filters through, telling me the sun has just begun to rise.

I've survived my first night with Kane. Or Jax. Or Tobin. Whoever he's pretending to be today. I'm still not sure I believe him.

When I try to sit up, metal rattles. A handcuff winds around my wrist, securing me to the bed. Memories rush back to me. I remember sleeping with Jax, and then he let me go. I guess Kane didn't agree with that. I growl as I try to free my hand from the shining metal bracelet, but there's no give.

Fucking fuck.

Pup stirs beside me. Her fluffy paws push forward as she stretches, and she opens her mouth in a yawn. I reach out and give her a soothing pat with my free hand. Her brown eyes close again.

I collapse on the bed. My bladder aches, and I can smell myself. I need a shower and a bathroom break.

"Kane!" I yell, but he doesn't answer.

I have to find a way out of this shitty situation I'm in, and escape is my only option. Even though every attempt has failed thus far, I can't give up. I won't die in this fucking truck.

It feels like forever before the truck stops moving. The curtain whips open and his menacing face glares at me. He looks like he's still sick and tired of my shit. Well, I'm sick and tired of his shit, too.

"What, dropout?"

"I have to pee."

He turns to leave.

"And shower!"

Metal rattles, and he shows up again . . . with a chain in his hand. It looks like a collar and leash. Pup raises her head and wags her tail. How she looks at him with such adoration in her big brown eyes is beyond me.

"Really?" I say.

"If you want to act like a dog that's hell-bent on escaping its yard, you'll be treated like one." He moves closer and clasps the collar around my neck, then rips the leash backward. The metal comes together and pinches my skin between the links, and I whimper. "Are you going to behave yourself?"

It's not as if he's given me a choice. "Yes."

He unlocks the handcuff, and I rub the red indentations on my wrist. My entire body aches from all the running and fucking I've done in the past twenty-four hours, but I can only focus on the relief my hand feels at being free again.

"I need to wash my clothes," I say. "I have a few outfits in my backpack, but they're all dirty. And I don't know what you did with my bag."

Instead of responding, he drops the leash and goes toward a row of cabinets. They open and close as he pulls women's clothes from inside. He tucks some under his arm, grips the leash once again, and drags me forward. Do I even want to know why he has women's clothes in here? How many girls came before me?

He catches me staring. "They're from women who didn't need them anymore."

"Did you kill them?"

"What did I say about asking questions? Best you don't."

"Are you going to kill me?"

Instead of answering, he just turns around and pulls the leash. I take a quick step forward, not wanting to feel the collar's bite again.

We get off the truck and I blink against the growing sunlight. We're at a different rest stop, but this one isn't nearly as clean as the last one. Kane drags me toward the building. There's no one else around, and I'm partly grateful no one else can witness this humiliation. Another part of me wouldn't mind if someone saw because it would mean I could yell for help.

But would I yell for help if given the chance?

I don't know.

This guy—or this particular personality, if he's telling the truth—is completely unhinged. If I yell for help, I'm potentially dragging someone else into the danger zone. That's not something I can live with. Then again, I would need to be alive to feel bad about it later.

Kane snatches the leash, dragging me out of my thoughts with a sharp, pain-filled reminder. I hurry and follow him before he can do it again.

Once we're inside the bathroom, he turns to me. "On the ground. Dogs walk on all fours."

I bite my lip as I look at the years of filth coating the floor. The sticky mess clutching the bottoms of my shoes goes beyond mud and mildew. And the smells. It's like the people who used this restroom chose to piss everywhere but in the urinals.

His grip tightens on the leash.

Fuck, I don't want to do this, but he's looking at me like I have no choice.

When I don't move, he wraps the leash around his hand and raises it high above my head. The pain comes first. Instead of a sharp pinch like before, the metal catches the skin at the back of my neck and squeezes it between the links, holding it there. I reach behind my head and try to relieve the tension, but it's no use.

Then I realize the real danger. He's strangling me.

I push my fingers against the collar, trying to give myself room to draw a breath, but there's no space between the thick circles and my skin. My feet begin to rise from the floor, and crawling through the filth doesn't seem so bad now. Stars dance in front of my eyes, and a black curtain begins to close around the edge of my vision.

I nod my head, hoping he'll understand the meaning. I'll do what he wants.

He releases the leash, and I fall to my hands and knees, forcing back a gag as I land in a wet spot. I gasp for air, each breath coated in the scent of stale urine and mold.

"I can't kill you, so I'm going to enjoy myself by degrading the fuck out of you. Do you understand?"

"Why?" I ask, my throat still tight. The single word sends me into a coughing fit.

"Because I fucking *hate* women. Jax and Tobin may be able to have sex with you, but my cock shrivels at the sight of disgusting fucking whores like you."

I swallow hard. Tell me how you really feel, dude.

The ice in his words makes me more certain they aren't the same people at all. Jax, Tobin, and Kane are just too different. Even if I can't understand it, I'm forced to believe it. If he were acting, he'd have broken character at some point.

He pulls me toward the urinal, and I crawl behind him. "Sit," he commands.

I do as I'm told, and the cuffs of my ass rub on the ground as my skirt rides up. I try to lower the stiff fabric, but it's no use.

"Put your head beside the urinal and open your fucking mouth," he says.

I already know where this is going before he unzips his pants, and I don't like it. He wiggles the leash in his hand. A warning. I lick my lips before parting them, and my stomach threatens to cast up everything I've ever eaten.

"Now close your eyes," he says, and I do.

Seconds pass like hours as I sit on the disgusting floor and wait for this man to piss in my mouth. I mentally prepare myself for the salty bite and the acrid perfume of someone else's waste, but how does someone prepare for something like this?

The anticipation is probably worse than the actual act.

I hear the splash of urine before I feel it, but thankfully, I only feel the droplets ricocheting from the urinal and landing on my shoulder. Disgusting, but far better than the alternative. He finishes pissing, shakes it off, and puts it away. I hear this instead of seeing it because my eyes are still closed. I don't dare open them now. I'm starting to figure him out. He likes to play a mental game as well as a physical one.

"Open your eyes, dropout."

I do, and I'm relieved to see his hand reaching for the flush lever instead of the leash. But then he stops.

"No, you know what? Flush it for me."

I reach for the lever above my head, but he rips my hand away and yanks me to my knees.

"Not like that. I want you to use your filthy mouth. Now."

Oh Jesus. No. I imagine the ghosts of every man's filthy hand on the metal lever. Hands that have just touched their junk. Hands that might have scratched an itchy butthole. Hands that have been in numerous dirty places I can't even conjure in my mind. And he wants me to put my mouth on it.

His other hand buries itself in my hair before he forces my face toward the rusted metal lever. He rubs my cheek against it before drawing back my head and placing my pinched lips right on the tip. Maybe it won't be so bad. I can just use my teeth to—

"Suck it."

The color drains from my face, and I lose feeling in my limbs. It's bad enough that he wants me to use my mouth to flush the fucking urinal, but now he wants me to fellate it as well? I glance at him, hoping he's just testing me the way he did moments ago, but his eyes hold no humor. He's serious.

Having no other choice, I spread my lips and take the lever into my mouth. I puff air in and out of my throat, refusing to breathe through my nose. If I have to smell whatever lives on this lever—coupled with the grimy feel of the handle—I'll puke.

"Stop cheating," he says. "Close those lips around it and show me what you can do."

Fuck.

Like the dog I am, I obey. My lips form a seal around the metal rod, and I give the urinal the best blow job it's ever had. I suck and lick until I've worn off at least one coat of rust, but it's still not enough for him. He grips the back of my head and forces the whole thing into my mouth. He fucks my face with it, and I can no longer stop my stomach from clenching. As I gag, my back teeth scrape against the metal, sending a bolt of pain into my skull.

Having had enough fun, he cranes my neck so that my front teeth grip the metal, then he pulls my head down until the urinal flushes. He rips my head away and turns me toward him, his lips only inches from mine.

"I hope that pissy flusher tastes terrible, whore."

"It does," I pant, fighting back the gags wrenching my stomach in an iron fist.

I hate that it doesn't make me vomit. It should. But one time I got paid two hundred dollars to tongue a public toilet seat as a client fucked me from behind. He even slammed my head beneath the thing and put me beneath the water. Yes, I agreed to it. Yes, I hated it. But money is a fierce motivator when you have nothing but your body to give away.

Now I'm performing for something more meaningful than money. I'm performing for my life.

Chapter Fourteen

Kane

Tobin left a note for me. In it, he said the girl is unbreakable, and that only made me want to break her more. When I say I want to break her, I mean in the most final kind of way, but that isn't possible. Especially not now that I've promised her to The Nameless. So I've challenged myself to break her emotionally instead of physically. She's fucking steadfast, I'll give her that. She hasn't shed a single tear during all of this.

And I want her to cry for me.

Unlike Tobin, I don't want tears of shame. I want tears of devastation and destruction. I want tears from heartbreak and hopelessness. I want to lap the proof of her pain from her cheeks.

This girl, though . . . She's proving to be a steel-skinned enigma. Every other woman I've taken would be a begging, blubbering mess by now, annoying the fuck out of me with their pleading. That's half the reason I finally get rid of them. I get sick of the noise.

I will break her eventually. Women are fucking weak. They're an inferior species. Emotionally driven. Physically limited. She might be a tougher nut to crack, but it doesn't mean she's uncrackable.

"You want to clean up?" I ask.

She nods. She probably sees this as a kindness on my part. It's not. When people are scared, their sweat smells different. Worse. That smell triggers something in my brain and agitates what lies in the locked box. I know I smelled like that once, but I don't know why. I only know that I don't want to smell it right now.

Usually I get rid of the stink by dumping it a few feet below ground, but I'm stuck with this girl until I hand her off. I'm allowing her to clean herself for *my* sake.

"Get undressed," I say.

She pulls her shirt over her head and hands it to me so I can feed the leash through the shirt's collar. With that done, I attach the leash to the top of the stall wall. She doesn't have much room to move without tightening the collar around her neck, which is perfect. Maybe she'll slip and hang herself. A man can dream.

After removing her bra and skirt, she stands and shivers in front of me. I love it. I'm also a bit frustrated by it. She's pretty. Nice curves. My eyes drop to her tits, pressed together by her arms as she tries to cover herself. I see why Jax and Tobin are so attracted to her, but the disconnect in my brain doesn't allow that attraction to reach my groin. It's like a theater of people crying at the end of a movie while I sit there and twiddle my fucking thumbs. I know why they're upset, but I feel nothing.

She eyes me as I strip off my clothes and step up to the sink. Using a rag I tucked inside the bundle of clothes, I gather a bit of soap from the dispenser and begin washing my body. This isn't the first time I've taken a whore's bath, and years on the road have taught me how to be quick. Once I've used another wet rag to rinse the soap from my body, I don't dress. I stay naked because her gaze keeps flicking toward my dick as she shifts her weight between her feet. She's uncomfortable, which is just how I want her to feel.

I release the chain a bit so she can move toward the sink, but she has to strain and contort her body to alleviate the pressure on her neck. She cleans off the best she can, her breath coming out in strained gasps as the chain tightens around her throat with every motion. Again, she says nothing. Just takes it all in stride.

And it pisses me off.

I consider foregoing my meeting with The Nameless. Having my debt knocked down would be great, but breaking this girl would be even better. Even a stoic bitch like her would cry for me before I string her intestines around my truck like fucking Christmas lights. Or maybe I could grind the skin from her fucking face with a sander. That thought almost makes me hard.

I release the leash when she's finished cleaning the stink from her skin, then I drag her to the mirror. Grime and fingerprints mar her reflection. I fist her hair, crane her neck, and make her look at herself.

"No matter how much you clean yourself, you're still filthy," I say. "Never forget that."

I expect her to close her eyes or show some sign of shame, but yet again, she's fearless in the face of depravity. My brain pings with ideas as I consider other ways to break her before I have to hand her off. I can't do anything that would leave a lasting mark, which completely rules out cutting and beating. Two of my favorite things. Choking her is fun, but I'm liable to go too far if I keep on.

When I look at her throat again, a light bulb blazes above my head. A few months ago, Tobin bought an industrial-strength shock collar for Pup. I was able to break through and hide it before he could use it on my dog, but now I think I've found a good use for it. He never had the chance to cut the collar to size, so it should be big enough to go around Aurora's neck. It's rated for disobedient creatures with a high pain tolerance, and that pretty much describes the girl.

With a new plan in mind, I help to dress her in black leggings and a dress shirt a previous victim left behind. It's not like she'll need the clothes anymore. The girl looks pretty when she's dressed up like this, and I like pretty things.

I love to kill them once I've dolled them up. When they look their best and feel their worst. I don't need to slather this girl with makeup to make her look nice, though. She only needed to be washed and dressed in something that wasn't so slutty.

Killing is the closest I come to feeling something, and thoughts of spilling blood on that dress shirt almost harden me. Her fear would be my foreplay, and killing her would be the main event. Murder grants the release I crave, but I can't do any of that, so I'll have to make do with torture. With a smile on my face, I lead her back to the truck.

Chapter Fifteen

Aurora

Once we're back in the truck, he removes the collar and leash and hooks me to the bed again. The handcuff digs into my wrist. As I sit here, held captive in a madman's truck, I'm just glad I'm clean. Such a treasured luxury for someone like me. I rub my free hand along my neck, feeling the indents and bruising where he choked me with the collar. Dick.

Psychos like it when you freak out and react to their madness. He'll be sorely disappointed in me. It would take a lot to make me react to him. I'm used to degradation and pain. What I'm not used to is the lack of payment afterward. *That* pisses me off.

My arm strains as I lean over to look at him. His body sways as he pulls things from compartments near the front of the truck. I don't know what he's looking for, and I'm not sure I want to know. I turn my attention to that tiny window again.

Sitting up on my knees and straining my neck, I can make out the sign near the front of the rest stop. A sign that sends my heart to my feet. He's taken us south, not north. We're already in fucking Kentucky! It was stupid of me to think he'd bring me home after all this, but seeing the sign hits me with a hard truth.

"Where are you taking me?" I yell. The chain rattles on my wrist.

"I have business to do."

"Where?"

"South."

I take a sharp breath. "Kane, just let me go. You haven't done anything to me that would make me go to the police. No harm, no foul. We can just go our own way." I try to keep my voice calm and steady so he knows I'm serious. If he lets me go, I won't go to the police. They don't believe whores anyway.

"Shut up, dropout," he says as his back straightens. He holds a box in his hand, and I don't want to find out what waits inside.

"I'm serious. You're safe. The cops wouldn't believe me, even if I ran to them." I don't add that I'm speaking from firsthand experience.

"I've never been safe in my entire life," he says. "And now, neither are you."

"You think I've been safe? People who've known safety don't take all the things you guys have done to me on the fucking chin."

Kane lifts his bandaged hand and examines it. "How did this happen?"

"You . . . Tobin cut his hand when he was fucking me with the handle of a knife."

Kane scoffs. "And you liked it?"

"Maybe not that part, but if you're asking if I came with his entire hand inside me while he used his blood as lubrication? Yeah. That happened."

He shakes his head and comes toward me, the box still clutched in his hand. Panic sends bile into my throat, but I keep still. He pulls something black from the box and steps closer. I can't see what it is.

"Close your eyes," he says. It's the sort of thing you'd expect someone to say with a smile, but he's as serious as a terminal diagnosis.

Most people wouldn't obey him, but I'm beginning to learn his personalities. This one has a short fuse. If I don't want to set him off, I should close my fucking eyes.

So I do.

Something wraps around my throat, and I fight the urge to fling my hand toward my neck and pull it away. Pup licks my hand. I stroke her fur to calm myself while a storm rages in my mind, thundering for me to scream and fight him off. Then he steps away and takes whatever he put around my neck with him.

"Don't open your eyes, dropout."

It's true, what they say. When you're deprived of a sense, your others are heightened. I can't see what he's doing, but I can hear it. He pulls out a drawer, and the wheels squeak. Metal *shicks* against metal as he cuts something with scissors. Whatever he's cut away falls to the floor, landing in an almost imperceptible whisper. Footsteps thud toward me. Warm breath whispers through my hair as his hands position something around my neck.

And this time, I know what it is.

My eyes pop open.

Zap!

My body jerks from the surprise, but it doesn't hurt that bad.

"I didn't say you could open them yet," he says. He zaps me again, but I don't jerk this time. He'll have to try harder if he wants another reaction.

"What's the point of this?" I ask.

As I reach for the shock collar around my throat, he fiddles with something on the remote in his hand.

Zap! Zap!

"Fuck!" I can't hold back the expletive this time. That fucking hurt. "Did you plan to use this on your tiny dog? It's made for something with a much higher—"

Zap!

My mouth slams shut. Is a tool like this even legal?

When I look at him again, he no longer wears the hardened face of the man who handcuffed me to the bed. His expression is soft and sweet. Handsome. He's another person entirely. And when my eyes travel down his body and stop at his erection, I know he's no longer Kane.

"Sorry you're chained," he says.

"Are you going to release me?" I ask.

"No fucking way. You're already chained for me. You tried to escape again, didn't you? Such a bad little whore."

It's Tobin. The sexual alter. I can make this work in my favor.

He steps closer and fingers the collar around my neck. "Hey, I bought that for Pup. I guess Kane found a better use for it. But how did you get these marks on your neck, eighty? The shock collar wouldn't do that."

I swallow against the pulse in his fingertips. "He used another collar. A choke chain. If I wanted to bathe myself, I had to lean against it."

"And you just kept leaning into that pressure? What a sadistic slut."

"You do what you have to do," I whisper.

"You sure do, don't you? Shove a bottle in your cunt. Take a whole fist inside you. Hang like a guilty whore." His hand tightens around the shock collar.

Tobin is a sexual sadist, but I can't deny my attraction to him. Even Kane is attractive with that face, but as Tobin, the attraction multiplies. He's rough and completely unhinged. At this point, I'm giving him things I'd charge others extra for. Not that he'd pay anyway.

And why shouldn't I get a little enjoyment out of this? If I'm doomed to die at his hands, I might as well enjoy a few orgasms from those same hands as well.

"Let's play a little game," he says through a smile. "I'm going to do whatever I want to your body, and you're going to stay completely silent. Each time you make a sound . . ." He wiggles the remote in his hand.

This doesn't sound like a very fun game. Maybe if he turns it down a few notches, I could enjoy it more. I open my mouth to say as much, but his finger depresses the button before I can speak. A dizzying jolt shoots through my neck, tensing the muscles.

"It wasn't a question, and the game has already started," he says. "Better keep quiet."

He pulls off his pants and climbs on top of me, resting his cock against me. Warmth and strength press against the leggings, and I want them off. I wiggle my legs without making a sound.

"Oh, you want these off?" he says. "You should ask me to remove them."

I look up at him, pleading with my eyes, but he only raises his eyebrows. My lips part, but the sound won't come. Is it worth the impending shock?

"I want you to take them—"

The zap cuts off my voice, but it's a small price to pay for the sweet relief of feeling his hands working the fabric away from my body. When I'm bare, he looks between my legs and licks his lips.

"Spread wider. I want to see your dirty pussy."

And god, why do those cruel words send a jolt of pleasure to my core? I part my knees for him, and he swipes a finger through my slit. Pleasure singes my nerve endings before he pulls his touch away.

"You're so wet. Tell me why, eighty."

I shake my head, and his fingers shoot toward my scalp. He winds his hand through my hair, twisting until he has a good grip. Then he snatches back my head and bends closer to my mouth.

His lips move over mine as he speaks again. "Tell me why you're so wet. Don't be shy."

"You made me th—"

He presses the button, and my throat tightens into a whimper. That earns me another shock, but I don't make a sound this time. After releasing my hair, he gives my cheek a light slap.

"Such a good little whore. I like playing with you." A low growl follows his words as he raises my shirt and reaches for my nipple. At first he's gentle, tweaking the tight nub between his fingers. He lowers his mouth to my breast, laving the skin with the flat of his tongue before using his teeth to put pressure on the most sensitive place.

I cry out. It's partly from pleasure and partly from pain, but none of that matters because I've made a sound. He shocks me again.

"Don't be naughty," he whispers against my skin. "I *hate* having to punish you, but you keep forcing my hand."

Sarcasm drips from his voice. He hates none of this. He lives for it. And right now, so do I.

Since I can't speak, I push my chest against his mouth again, begging for more. He cups my breast with his hand and closes his mouth over my nipple, but I'm ready this time. When he bites down, I grit my teeth and allow myself to feel it. The ache. The ecstasy. It melds into one mind-blowing sensation and travels down my spine.

His hand moves to the warm space between my legs, pressing tight circles around my clit as he alternates between teasing and biting my skin. Pleasure-filled whimpers climb my throat, but I swallow each one.

"Fuck, you're so wet. Are you ready for me?" he asks.

I nod my head.

"Tell me."

I open my mouth, but before I can utter a sound, the numbing zap tears across my skin. This game is impossible to win, but I don't mind. Each time I lose, I'm brought closer to my edge.

His hips draw back, and he thrusts inside me. I hold each whimper and moan, refusing to let them out, but I don't know how long I can keep this up. He feels so good inside me. With each thrust, the head of his cock pushes me closer as his girth fills me completely. That barbell is the metal cherry on top.

"This won't do," he says in answer to my silence. His hand goes to the collar, and he unfastens it from my neck. His fingers replace the collar, and he continues thrusting.

As I let out a whimper, his grip tightens. This isn't just playful breath play. I can't draw any air, and he shows no signs of letting up. His thrusts quicken to a hammering tempo, fucking me harder than I've ever been fucked. I'm sucked into a dizzying wave of euphoria, but I'm fading too fast. My vision blackens as my mouth gapes, and I lose consciousness.

When I wake up, he's still fucking me. His grip has moved away from my throat, and something cold presses against my clit.

"Welcome back, eighty," he whispers. "You feel so good, but I know what will make you feel better."

Zzzt!

Lightning shoots through my clit, simultaneously numbing it and leaving it overly sensitive. My pussy reacts by clamping around him and sending an ache through my core. He groans and fucks me harder.

"Again," I whisper.

Why did I fucking like it? Why does this sadistic act bring me so much pleasure? But the answers don't matter as he smiles and looks down at me.

"Again? What's wrong with you?" He laughs. "Actually, what's so fucking *right* with you?"

He presses the button again, and my pussy convulses around him. I cry out, unable to keep quiet with so much happening inside my body. I'm so close, and I want to come.

He leans down and hovers above me with his mouth so close to mine. I want to lean up and kiss him, but something about him tells me he isn't the kissing type.

"Fucking kiss me," I rasp.

"I don't kiss whores."

"Then punish me until I come."

A sinful smirk crosses his lips, and he sits up. He places the shock collar remote in my hand, giving me control of one form of punishment. Holding the collar to my pussy with one hand, his other hand moves to my throat, slowly cutting off my breath.

"Are you going to die for me, whore?" he growls.

I press the button as another wave of darkness closes in. Invisible sparks shoot through my clit, tightening the bundle of nerves, but I lose consciousness just as I feel my orgasm building. When I come to, he's looking down at me with sweat gliding over his temples. How long was I out?

"I thought I went too far that time," he whispers as he leans over me again. His pelvis curves and his thrusts slow. "Can you come before you black out again?"

"Yes," I whisper. I don't know if it's the truth, but I'm happy to keep trying.

He leans back and grips my hips, pulling me against him as he fucks me senseless. I think he's giving me time to build up and crest the waves of pleasure, but then his hand wraps around my throat again. He plays with the sides of my neck, the blood chokes giving me a dizzying wave of pleasure that's different from the breath chokes.

He places the collar over my clit again and I moan, my hips bucking against him because I want more. My fingers scramble to press the button, but I mash the wrong one. A sharp vibration buzzes against my clit. I alternate between zapping myself stupid and those pleasurable vibrations as he increases the tempo of his thrusts.

"I'm close," I pant. "I'm so close. Please don't stop."

I'm plunged into dizzying darkness once more as he squeezes my throat. I focus on the pleasure instead of the silence in my lungs. They start to squeeze, warning me of an impending blackout.

"Come, whore, because I won't let go if you don't. You'll die around my cock."

His buttery-soft words don't hold a threat. They hold a fucked-up promise.

I press the button repeatedly, and I fly. My eyes roll back in my head, my legs quiver, and I lose all control of my hands. The remote slides off the bed, but I don't care. I don't need it anymore. His cock is enough to keep me here, riding this wave of pleasure.

A feral growl precedes his gravelly voice. "Oh, there you go. Good fucking girl."

He loosens his grip as my orgasm wanes, but then his fingers tighten and he keeps his hold on my neck until I pass out again. When I come to, he's leaning over me, his belly pressed against mine. Wetness slides between my legs, and I can only assume it's a mixture of our pleasure.

His hand leaves my throat and hooks around the back of my neck with a softness I don't expect. He leans closer. "I know I said I don't kiss whores, but you're too fucking good."

His lips capture mine in a kiss that takes my breath away again. His tongue explores my mouth, and I whimper from the veracity in his motions. Kane might hate me, but Tobin doesn't.

I bathe in his affection as he wipes the tears from my face—my body's innate response to having the life choked from me. He pushes his tear-coated fingers into his mouth and sucks before making me taste it too. Then he pulls out of me, climbs down my body, and stops between my legs. He catches all the mess on his tongue.

His come.

Mine.

And because he clearly can't end on a nice note—which is fine with me—he fists my hair and pulls me up to meet his mouth. He gestures to my lips with his chin, and my lips part as I accept the remnants of our pleasure onto my tongue. I hold my tongue out and waggle it before swallowing.

"You're such a dirty fucking girl," he says. "I love it."

When a dude fucks you like Tobin does, it's too easy to fall in love with him. It's just hard when that person is inside a person you fucking despise.

As he puts on his pants and slides the leggings over my skin, I have to accept the truth. All doubt is gone. They are three separate men in one body. And one of those men wants me dead.

Chapter Sixteen

Kane

Each rattle of the handcuffs grates against my raw nerves, but I don't trust her to stay put. I even moved her to the front seat so I could keep an eye on her. She has more grit than the girls I usually pick up, and she's a fair bit more intelligent as well. I wouldn't put it past her to figure out how to escape the cuffs if left alone for too long, so I've tethered her to the passenger door. You can't see the glint of metal unless you're looking over her lap.

Pup sits obediently between us, and I reach down and stroke her head. When I was little, I always wanted a dog. Something menacing, like a Doberman. My father never let me have one, and it's comical that I ended up with this little dog. Not the manliest breed, but she's mean as shit. Kinda like me. Why she seems to like the dropout is beyond me, though.

"Do you plan to tell me where we're going?" she asks. "You said south, but where?"

"Texas."

"That's nowhere near New York," she mutters.

"I see you passed geography. Would you like a fucking cookie?"

Thankfully, that shuts her up.

More specifically, we're heading toward Houston, but she doesn't need to know the details. Especially the part where we meet The Nameless.

I didn't keep in touch with the brothers after high school. I happened upon one of them by chance in the produce aisle at a store in our hometown. Even sketchy middlemen need to shop for groceries, I guess. As we were catching up, I disclosed my current profession, and he asked me to move some merchandise for them. I soon found out the merchandise was, in fact, women.

It rubbed me the wrong way at first, but then I found the right motivation. The truck of my dreams. I didn't have enough credit on my own, but The Nameless have connections. And now I owe them.

I think they're Russian, but I've never asked, just like I've never asked the name of their operation. It's better if I don't know. They direct the women to their next destination, often out of this country, and I get a little shaved off my debt.

I can't wait to hand this one off. The few acceptable specimens I've brought to The Nameless sat shivering in fear in the corner, too afraid to take a step out of place. I didn't even have to cuff them. This one? She has too much . . . something. Something that makes her very difficult to break. I want to call it bravery, but it could be stupidity for all I know. Either way, I have to be way too careful around her, and I don't like it.

I'm also sick of tending to her. She has to piss every few miles, and she's always hungry. If she keeps this shit up, I'll hand her a bucket and a pack of crackers and tell her to make it work. There isn't a word to describe how much I can't stand her.

Tobin fucking *loves* her, though. He left a note basically saying as much. *I choked her nearly to death and she came from it.* That's his love language. Choking and fucking.

Jax started simping over her the moment we saw her, so there's no question that he's attached. And that's a fucking problem. His purpose is to protect me, so what happens when we have a conflict of interest?

She's causing dysfunction in my system, and I don't appreciate it.

In the end, both of my alters will have to let go of something they've grown close to. We can't keep her. Even if I could get past my distaste for her, I've already promised her to someone else. Someone who could cause a lot of problems for me if I back out. Jax and Tobin will have to get over it. We have Pup. We don't need another pet.

I've been keeping a close eye on my phone. When they've lined up the buyer, they'll let me know. Then it's only a matter of completing the drive and handing her off. I'll celebrate afterward. I might even pick up another girl. Jax can talk sweet to her, Tobin can fuck her, and then I can kill her. All will be right with the world.

"I've never been to Kentucky before," she says as she looks out the window. "We should try the fried chicken while we're here."

"This isn't a fucking vacation."

"I'm well aware." She wiggles her wrist, and the metal-on-metal sound rakes a nail across my brain. "Still, we have to eat at some point. Don't you ever get hungry?"

I do, but not for anything I can pick up at a roadside establishment.

A sign lights up as we approach. It signals me to turn off at an inspection site a few miles ahead. Fuck. I can't handle people. If they only asked one question, I could manage, but sometimes they hold us up for an hour or more while they nitpick everything about the truck and our logs. When my patience runs thin, I'm not the best at masking it. That's Jax's specialty.

I feel the tap behind my eyes, and I know I need to relinquish control to him. There's only one fucking problem. The last time I let him have control, he let the girl run off. What if she rats us out? How will Jax handle that? Because she absolutely will rat me out.

But maybe not Jax.

The wheels in my brain begin to turn as an idea forms. Sweet son of a bitch that he is, she might have a little sympathy for him. And it might be just enough to keep her pouty lips sealed. I'm taking a risk either way. If I let him have control, he might set her free, but if I don't, she might try to set herself free by blowing the whistle.

Sweat coats my hands as my grip tightens around the steering wheel. I try to control my breathing, but my chest feels like someone is wringing my lungs in their hands. I can't skip the stop. I'm guaranteed a shitstorm if I pass by.

I have no choice but to let him out. No choice but to let him protect us all.

Chapter Seventeen

Aurora

I can't take my eyes off him as he rubs his hands on his jeans, wearing the denim to a lighter shade with each pass Sweat gathers at his temples. I don't know what has him so shaken up, but he's starting to make me a bit antsy as well. When his anxious, hardened expression loosens, I can only assume he's switched.

"Hey, sweet girl," he says, low and soft, and I know exactly who he is now. Jax has taken over.

I haven't seen him since he let me escape. Maybe Kane punished him by keeping him back. A sliver of guilt winds through me, snaking past my heart and settling low in my stomach. It coils there, tightening and writhing until it's a physical thing I can't ignore. Even though it's technically Kane's fault for picking me up and holding me hostage, I'm causing problems for all of them.

I shake my head. Do I actually believe this shit?

I hate to admit I am, but I can't deny the reality in front of my face. Hearing about people with alters is one thing. Seeing someone with this condition for a few minutes on social media or television isn't the same as living with them for days. The differences between the three men are undeniable and wholly total. He is Kane. He is Jax. He is Tobin.

But why?

From what very little I've heard about this condition, its cause is often rooted in trauma. We brushed over it in psychology, and I wrack my mind now for what I learned, but I only come up with questions instead of answers. What sort of hammer smashed his psyche to the point of fracture? Who hurt him?

Kane won't answer these questions, so I make a mental note to try to get information from the other two.

"Jax?" I ask, just to be sure.

"The one and only," he says with a smile.

We pass a blinking sign that signals an inspection station ahead. Is that what had Kane so on edge? If so, Jax doesn't share the same phobia. Once he wipes his forehead, it stays dry, and his hands relax on the steering wheel.

When he finally glances over at me, he sucks in a sharp breath. "Oh shit, is that from . . ." He shakes his head. "I never should have let you run off."

My hand goes to my throat. He must have noticed the marks. "I had to try, Jax. You understand that, right?"

He pulls over on the shoulder and unclips his seatbelt. After rifling through the cabinets in the back, he returns with a lacy scarf. Whose? I probably don't want to know.

Jax leans over. His fingers trace the marks from the choke collar before covering the bruises with the lace. He knots it on the side, and he doesn't need to tell me why. He doesn't want anyone to see the marks and get suspicious.

This creates a problem in my mind. We'll stop at the inspection site, and someone will give the truck a once over. I've been through this before with other truckers, and I won't pretend it doesn't present an opportunity to escape this hell once and for all. But will I take that opportunity?

For Kane's part in this mess, I'm inclined to scream bloody murder the moment the inspector approaches the truck. I can end it all right now. But Kane isn't the only person this would affect. Jax and Tobin are part and parcel, and I'm conflicted. Jax has let me go, and Tobin's only guilty of giving me incredible orgasms. Is it fair to condemn them for the acts of their splintered mind?

And what if I don't rat them out? Perhaps I can play the long game and win Kane's trust.

To scream or not to scream. That is the question.

Jax leans into me. "Do me a favor, sweet girl. Don't blow our cover at this inspection. I . . . did very unwell in prison."

He's laying the guilt on thick, and I'm not immune. I don't believe he deserves to waste away in a cell, and neither does Tobin. But I want to live. Kane hasn't killed me yet, but that's the keyword.

Yet.

Jax places his fingers on my chin and draws me into him. As he kisses me, I'm reminded of the differences between him and Tobin. He's gentle and sweet, giving more than he takes from me. Instead of tongue-fucking my mouth like Tobin, his kiss comforts me. I melt into it against my will. My lip quivers as he pulls away from me. He isn't making this decision any easier.

He grabs the blanket and puts it across my lap, covering my handcuffed wrist before dropping back to his seat and eyeing me with an approving nod. As he buttons his flannel, he looks like a teenager trying to hide his tattoos from his parents. He looks in the mirror and smooths his hair. Satisfied that he appears as respectable as possible, he rolls back onto the road and heads toward the inspection site.

Two DOT vans crouch at the head of the pull off, and I imagine flagging down the people inside. My brain can't fathom what would happen if I acted on this impulse. Would Kane give up, or would a chase ensue?

Jax pulls to a stop, and a DOT officer appears in the window.

"License?" the officer asks.

Jax pulls out his CDL license and hands it over.

"Thanks, Mr. Hargrave," the officer says before leaning closer to Jax, probably trying to smell if he's been drinking. "Triangles and fire extinguisher?"

"Excuse me," Jax says, and the man outside the window hops from the side of the truck, giving him room to open the door.

Jax climbs out and pulls the fire extinguisher from beneath his seat. The officer checks it over to make sure it's charged before putting it back in its rightful place. The safety triangles are kept in a side box behind the door, and Jax has to step away from the truck to access them. The DOT officer remains just outside the door, and I can't tear my eyes away from him. Everything in me screams that this is my chance to signal for help.

If I'm going to do it, I'm running out of time.

Satisfied with the gear, the officer glances at me. "Along for the ride?"

Now's my chance. The words climb up my throat.

I've been kidnapped. He wants to kill me. Well, not this guy, but the other guy that shares the same body and brain. Maybe I'll leave that part out. All I have to do is kick this blanket away and rip off the scarf with my free hand.

But I nod. "Yep, just keeping him company."

The officer's eyes narrow. "You okay, miss?"

"Oh, yeah, I'm fine. Just pretty tired. We've been on the road for a bit."

The officer nods and turns back to Jax. "Can I see your bills and logs?"

Jax leans over and grabs a stack of papers and hands it to him. "Should all be there. We're dead-heading right now. On our way to pick up a load in Texas."

As he settles in his seat, a light sweat pricks my brow.

Jax buckles his seatbelt as the DOT officer disappears around the side of the truck. "You're doing so good," he says.

He wouldn't say that if he knew what was running through my mind. I still have a chance to get away, and I'm not completely sure I won't take it.

Pup jumps into my lap and settles against the blanket. A low growl rumbles in her tiny chest each time the officer speaks. A glint of silver catches my eye, and I realize she's moved the blanket and exposed the handcuff. I could leave it. If the officer sees it, that wouldn't be entirely my fault.

With my free hand, I pull the blanket over my wrist once more.

The man returns to the window and hands the paperwork and the DOT inspection report to Jax. "You're good to go."

"Thank you, officer. Have a great day!" Jax says, and I truly can't imagine Kane saying such a thing.

As the truck begins to pull away, the vars and the people grow smaller in the mirror. For a moment, it's still not too late. I could lower the window and scream. I could save myself. But I don't, and the figures shrink until they're only memories as we pull onto the road once more.

I shift in my seat, and Pup sighs as she settles in for a nap. I stroke her fur and fight back tears. An opportunity just slipped through my fingers, and I don't know that another will grace my path. I don't even know how long my path is. Everything could end in ten miles, or it could continue for eternity. I have to find a way to survive that doesn't involve hurting Jax or Tobin, and maybe that starts with discovering why Kane is the way he is.

"What is Kane hiding?" I say.

"Best not to ask."

I lick my lips and play my cards. "I just did you a huge favor. Instead of blowing the whistle, I kept my mouth shut. Can't you reciprocate a little?"

He shifts in his seat and shakes his head. "It doesn't work like that."

"Then how does it work?" I blow out a breath and look out the window. "If you can't answer the big question, at least explain why you had to handle the inspection. Give me some insight."

He considers this, then deems it safe to answer. "Kane doesn't do well with people. I'm a people person."

Pup hops down and trots to the back of the truck as I stare at him. I throw the blanket off my lap. I'm burning up, mostly from sheer frustration. "Why do you protect him?"

His lips tighten. "That's what I was made for."

"What does that even mean?"

He chews the inside of his lip. "When the main system goes through something so traumatic that they can't mentally handle it, they need someone else to. That's where I came from. I was born to protect Kane."

"Really?" I ask. I'm not trying to sound that way, but it just all seems so far-fetched to me. Like something out of a movie. Except this is real life.

My life.

"You don't have to believe me," Jax says. "A lot of people don't. Not that we tell very many people about us. I think you're the first girl."

My chest rises in defiance. "Because no one else lives long enough to find out?"

Jax smirks. "There's no point telling anyone who wouldn't understand."

"And what makes you so sure I can?"

He shrugs his shoulders. "Trauma recognizes trauma. You aren't fragmented the same way we are, but you're just as broken."

I think back to my childhood. To the dorms at college. And I realize . . . he's right.

Chapter Eighteen

Kane

We drive by the sign for my favorite diner between here and my hometown in Texas. I've taken these interstate systems a million times, and I'll take them a million times more. By now, these highways are as familiar as the veins in my arm. I could drive this route in my sleep.

My eyes harden on the sign. The corners have begun to peel away from the metal, but that doesn't dictate the state of the food, which is always fucking incredible. Mashed potatoes that are just stiff enough to stick to your ribs but soft enough to go down smooth. Steaks seasoned to mouth-watering perfection. And the steamed broccoli. I don't normally enjoy green vegetables—I'm a meat and potatoes kind of guy—but the cheese sauce they slather over the little green stalks is like liquid pleasure. Aside from killing, eating at the diner is the closest I'll ever come to having an orgasm.

I'm fucking starving. That much is clear. I can't remember the last time I sat down and had a good meal without being disturbed, but it's been too long. My head is quiet for once, so I take the turn and head toward the diner.

Dropout rattles the handcuff on her wrist. She stares straight ahead as if she'd like to be anywhere else, which is probably accurate, but she needs to learn her place. She's with me now, and that won't change until I hand her off in Texas.

Meeting The Nameless isn't my only reason for heading back to Texas, and Jax wasn't lying when I spoke to the DOT officer. I managed to broker a load between here and Texas, which means I need to clean out the trailer before we get there. Having a reefer unit means the distributors want proof of a clean trailer before they stock perishables inside. Which means I need to actually *clean* that trailer before I get there. It's dirty in more ways than one.

"You're bringing me back to New York after this, right?" she asks.

"Sure," I say. It's a lie to keep the bitch calm for my sanity. And hers, I guess. Is it wrong to feed her little nibbles of hope for the rest of the trip? I can only see the benefits. It will—hopefully—stop her from running off again, which means I can sleep without keeping one eye open. If she needs to think this is a detour on our way to New York, then so be it.

I pull into the truck stop and stare at the sign for the diner. I can already smell the sizzling meat

"You gonna be good, dropout?"

"Stop calling me that."

I grip her chin. "Are you gonna be good?"

When she doesn't respond, I tighten my grip and nod her head for her. If she isn't good, she should already know what will happen to her. Yeah, I've already sold her to The Nameless, but I have no problem doing what I love if she can't act right. She'd look even prettier dead.

I unchain her wrist, and she rubs the sensitive ring of red skin. I may need to keep her untethered when we're on the road. If she gets an infection or gets too dinged up, The Nameless won't give me enough for her.

We get out of the truck, and I grab her arm to keep her close to my side. "Look like you want to be here," I say, jabbing my fingers into her side.

"I absolutely want to be here, thank you very much. I'm sick of munching on the expired gas station food you've stashed in the cabinets like some sort of psychotic squirrel."

I almost smile at her little jab. She's got spunk, I'll give her that.

We walk inside, and a bell tolls overhead. A familiar waitress scurries around behind the counter. She's nearly always at her station when I visit, almost as if she lives here. Her graying black hair sits in stressed curls on her head, and she glances up as we pass the counter.

"Kane, how long has it been?" she asks, a hint of flirt in her eyes. This poor old hound is baying up the wrong tree. If I have no attraction to Aurora, she doesn't have a chance in hell. I've never been attracted to anyone. Not like that, at least.

"A year? Maybe more," I say as I sit in the booth farthest from the door. Aurora sits across from me. Her hands go into her lap, and she stares out the large window beside our booth.

"Your daughter?" the waitress asks, her eyes falling on Aurora. I kick her beneath the table, and she turns toward the woman with a fake smile.

"Yes, ma'am," Aurora answers, her whore-customer-service voice coming out to play. It's repulsive.

The waitress drops the menus in front of me, and I hand one to Aurora.

"Thanks . . . Daddy," she says with a snarky smile.

I didn't think I looked old enough to be her father, but I guess that's a better answer than trying to explain she's a whore I picked up to potentially sell. Or kill.

The waitress takes her notepad from her raggedy apron and wrestles out the pen that's speared itself through the newest hole. "Mashed potatoes, steamed broccoli with cheese, and a steak, very rare," she spouts before I can open my mouth.

"That's exactly right," I say. I like my meat like I like my women—bloody and raw. When the waitress turns toward Aurora, I speak for her. "Same for her. But make it medium-well."

She seems like a medium-well kind of girl.

The waitress nods and heads toward the back. Aurora and I sit in painful silence while waiting for our meal. I don't usually have to force a conversation with these bitches. Mostly, they just beg for their lives and I mock their final breaths.

"Who's the 'daddy'?" she asks, pointing to the tattoo on my neck.

"What?"

"Who got the daddy tattoo? The one on your neck. Was it Tobin or you? It certainly wasn't Jax."

I don't answer her. I just tap the fork on the cracked tabletop. Her face draws into a tight frown; the sound clearly drives her nuts. I can't kill her, but I sure enjoy irritating her. And degrading her. I just wish she reacted more to the degradation. If she wasn't such a stoic whore, she'd almost be tolerable. Since I'm finally getting a rise out of her, I tap the metal harder.

She slams her eyes shut. "Can you stop?"

I point the fork at her. "You suck off the handle of a urinal without a peep of protest, but this is what bothers you?"

She glances around the diner as a few people stare at her because of what I've just said . . . a little too loudly. Heat flushes her cheeks, and I revel in her embarrassment. It's not as good as choking the life out of her, but it's enjoyable.

"Why are you the way you are?" she clips in a whisper. "Have you ever thought about trying to be even a little pleasant to be around?"

A lot has happened to me to make me the way I am, but I can't answer her question. It's something I've asked myself many times, but that locked box just remains locked. I am walking, talking evil, but the source of that black fountain is buried too deep.

"I'm incapable of pleasantry," I say.

"Bullshit. I've seen exactly what you're capable of."

I laugh, knowing exactly what she's referring to. "Jax and I are *not* the same person. We may share a body, but we couldn't be more different. He's a disgusting little simp, and I'm not."

I couldn't be like Jax, mentally or physically. Despite him holding pieces of my trauma, he's so kind. And he can fuck. He probably likes pleasing a woman and making love. Jax is the light I could never shine on this world.

He and Tobin are capable of emotions I have no desire to feel. Integration is possible for many people with dissociative identity disorder, but it has never been my end goal. Our system works for us, even if it's a little fucked-up to everyone else. But that's the beauty of it. It isn't meant for everyone else. It's a safety plan designed just for us. We compartmentalize in ways most others can't, and that's how we continue to function.

Or it was how we functioned until Aurora came along. Her attitude is like a screwdriver for me. Her pussy is like a drill for Tobin. Her beauty and charisma are a hammer and nails for Jax. Without even trying, she's tinkering with our machine. If we aren't careful, if Jax and Tobin can't get on the same page with me, we're fucked.

Chapter Nineteen

Aurora

Spit gathers beneath my tongue as Kane's eyes darken. I swallow it down. I tried to get him to loosen the fuck up, but having a nice conversation or sharing banter doesn't seem to be in his wheelhouse. Bringing up his alters like that was probably a low blow, but it's not my fault they're more enjoyable than he could ever be. They're the only reason I'm still alive. They're also the only reason I'm not screaming for help right now.

The waitress appears beside our table and sets our plates in front of us. I start to eat, looking away from Kane as he dives into his bloody steak like he hasn't eaten in a month. When he finally slows down, red-tinged grease drips from his lower lip. He stares at me as he sensually licks it away. It's not meant to be a sensual gesture, though. It's meant to be intimidating. It's meant to scare me.

That's just too bad. I don't scare easily.

I reach across, stab my knife and fork into his steak, and cut a piece away. I rip it off the fork, open my mouth, stick out my tongue, and squeeze the hunk of meat until red juice drips into my mouth. A metallic tang hits my tastebuds.

My little act seems to work. He goes back to gnawing on his slab of E. coli, and I return to pushing my fork through the pile of mashed potatoes.

I've always been stubborn, but I've never been quite as bullheaded as I am when I'm going against Kane. He brings it out of me. The more he tries to break me down, the more I refuse to let him. Even if he breaks me on the inside, I'll never show it to him. I'll die with a smile on my face before I give him a glimpse of my discomfort. He'll have to do worse than what he's tried so far if he wants to break someone who's already used to bending.

My stomach churns with each bite I take, but I clean my plate. There's no telling when I'll be treated to another meal like this. We're almost in Tennessee now, and I don't know if he'll drive straight on to Texas from here. Part of me hopes so. The sooner we get to Texas, the closer I am to making my way back to New York.

Thoughts of my parents burrow into my chest and squeeze my heart. These aren't fond thoughts. Fear shrouds my brain. Telling them what I've done—leaving college and becoming a sex worker—isn't possible, but I don't know how to explain what I've been through. Even if I figure out what to say, they won't hear it. And if my father has been drinking—

"I'm going to go pay," he says, his eyes narrowing on me. "Cut what's left of my steak into small pieces and wrap it in a napkin."

I clear my throat and nod as he eases out of the booth. Once I've done as he asked and packed the leftover meat into the napkin, I turn to look at him. He stands at the register, locked in a conversation with the waitress. I could make a run for it, but I probably wouldn't make it across the diner before he stopped me, and something tells me the waitress wouldn't believe anything that would cast her little crush in a bad light.

If I wanted to escape, I should have said something at the inspection site. So what does that say about me? Do I really plan to stick with these guys until my fate is revealed? Because I'm still not sure what happens at the end of the line. He could kill me. He could drive me to New York.

Neither option appeals to me.

With a deep sigh, I slide out of the booth. "Let's go . . . Daddy," I say as I come up behind him.

He fakes a smile, takes the napkin, and stuffs it into his pocket, then wraps an arm around me. His muscles tense as our bodies make contact, which tells me he's not used to close human interaction.

"Come on, sweetie," he says, and it's the most uncomfortable thing I've ever heard leave a man's lips. He isn't meant to say nice fucking things. That much is clear.

He keeps up the act as we walk outside, but his lips tighten and he releases me a few steps onto the asphalt. As he lifts his shoe, a trail of gum tethers him to the concrete.

"Son of a bitch." His gait changes as he guides me to the truck by my hair. Once we're inside, he throws me onto the floor, sits in the driver's seat, and kicks his feet out in front of him. "Clean my boots," he commands.

Jesus fucking Christ. This guy.

I don't move at first. I just stare up at him. He can't be serious.

"Crawl to me and lick my boots clean. If I have to say it again, I'll shove my boot down your goddamn throat."

I crawl over to him. *Just do it,* I pep-talk myself.

He picks up the boot that doesn't have the gum on it and steps on my neck, pushing me to the ground as he grinds the leather sole into my throat. He puts the other boot by my mouth, and I force out my tongue to lick the side of his shoe. The rich scents of leather and polish rush toward my nose. It tastes how it smells, like a natural musk.

His boot hovers over my face as he pulls it back a few inches and releases the other boot from my neck. A glob of blue gum sticks to the bottom. I try not to think about the mouth who chewed this gum. I try not to think about the pavement it was stuck to and all the feet that walked across it. I just arch my neck, lift my mouth to the gum, and rip it from the rubber. It spreads into thin strings, but it eventually lets go and lands on my tongue. A very subtle mint flavor lingers in the glob, and an earthy note from the ground follows it.

I refuse to gag. I won't give him the satisfaction.

"Chew it and swallow it," he says as he leans back.

"You don't want me to blow a bubble too?"

I roll my eyes and do as I'm told. He reaches down, and I cock my head at him before he shakes his wrist, encouraging me to take his hand. Stunned, I allow him to help me to my feet.

He leans closer, and his breath rushes over my ear. "I got the tattoo. I like when you bitches call me daddy."

For some reason, I don't believe him. Maybe he doesn't want to admit that someone like Tobin has more control over what's on his body than he does.

Kane whistles for Pup, and she leaps off the bed, trots to his side, and sits obediently at his feet. Her tail thumps against the floor as he pulls the napkin from his pocket and feeds her his leftovers.

"Good girl," he whispers, trying to keep me from hearing his momentary softness. But I definitely heard it, and I can't pretend I'm not running those gentle words through my mind now.

Good girl.

Kane kicks off his now-clean boots and drags me toward the bed. He pushes me onto the mattress, and I think Tobin has taken over. He still looks like Kane, though. The mannerisms, the way he moves. Then he speaks, and I'm sure he's still Kane.

"Time for bed, dropout," he says as he unbuttons his shirt. I'd be worried he was going to force himself on me if he didn't look so repulsed by our close proximity.

"We're sleeping in bed together?" I ask, surprised.

"I can't sleep in the seat anymore. My back is killing me. So yeah, I guess so."

I get into bed and lie as close to the wall as I can. He crawls in behind me and sighs as he turns away from me. His posture is so rigid and uncomfortable, and at this moment, I'm not sure who the captive is. Me or him.

Chapter Twenty

Tobin

Kane's so dramatic. He couldn't even handle lying beside the girl for five fucking minutes. Instead of sleeping on a mattress, Kane felt as if he were lying on a bed of nails. The moment I heard his thoughts, I was ready to climb into the driver's seat. She may disgust him, but I'm obsessed with everything about her.

Now that I'm here, I don't see what the big deal was. She's turned away from me on her side, and with all this distance between us, I wouldn't even consider this as sleeping in the same bed. I move closer until my chest presses against her back and her ass bumps against my crotch.

"Hi, Tobin," she mumbles, her voice heavy with sleep.

"How'd you know it was me?"

"Because Kane would rather die than touch me, and Jax has too much couth to put his hard dick against my ass."

"Fair," I say with a dark laugh. Jax would be sweeter about it. He'd talk to her, wipe the hair from her pretty cheeks, and ask fucking permission before touching her. But I'm not a wait-for-permission kind of guy when it comes to her. She's a need, not a want.

"I'm glad you're here, though," she says, and my heart pumps harder—no one has ever said they were glad to see me—but my feeling of elation dissipates when she speaks again. "I wanted to talk to you about something. About Kane."

"I'm not really the talking type. I'm the fuck-you-senseless type, remember?"

I put my arm around her, raise my hand to her mouth, and shove my fingers past her lips. Before she even knows what's happening, my fingertips reach the back of her throat and a violent gag rattles her body. Instead of reaching for my wrists and pulling me away, she rolls onto her back and swirls her tongue across my skin.

This is what I mean when I say I'm obsessed. She's like no other woman I've met. This girl will take anything I give her.

I lean over her and finger-fuck her mouth, and she bites down as her big eyes rise to mine. Pain heats my knuckles, but I don't pull them away. She and I both know how much I enjoy pain.

"You have such a good mouth, eighty," I say as I pull my fingers away. "I'd just prefer you use it for something other than talking right now."

She takes the hint and doesn't ask anything else as I get up to go to the freezer. I pull out two of my special ice cubes and put them in a glass.

Sitting up on her elbows, she eyes the milky cubes. "What are you doing with those?"

"You'll find out soon enough," I say with a smirk.

I kneel beside her on the bed and grab the hem of her dress shirt. Like the obedient little slut she is, she raises her arms and allows me to pull it away. I pull away the leggings next, and now only her panties separate me from what I want most.

She whimpers as I grip the thin fabric and rip it away from her body. I grab one of the ice cubes and I trace the outline of her lips, coating them with a glistening layer of come and water. As I drag the ice lower and run it over her breasts, her nipples pull into tight buds. They practically beg for my mouth, so I oblige.

Her legs pull together as my hand trails toward the curve of her lower abdomen. The skin and muscle suck inward, trying to escape the icy chill, but I keep going. Lower. Lower. I release her breast from my mouth and slide down her body so I can put myself between her legs. Her pretty little clit swells for me as the ice cube drifts over it.

She whimpers as I part her legs wider and push her knees toward the mattress, tilting her hips upward. Come-laced water cuts a path through her slit and drips over her tight little asshole. It's the only thing I haven't taken.

I lean back and gather spit beneath my tongue before dripping the saliva onto her hole. I push the ice cube into her pussy, knowing her heat will soon reduce it to a puddle that will slowly seep out of her. She screams out from the cold, and in the same breath, I put a finger in her ass. Then two. A groan leaves my lips as I push a third inside her.

Her body fights the intrusion before relaxing and accepting the pleasure my touch provides. When I'm sure she's ready, I remove my pants, coat my dick tattoo with saliva, and push inside her. My barbell catches on the rim of her ass, and her back arches as pain rips through her, but I fight past her body's noes until they become a unified yes. A well-trained whore like her knows how to take what is given, and it's not like I would stop anyway.

I want her full of me, so I reach over and grab the remaining ice cube, leaving behind a thin layer of cloudy liquid at the bottom of the glass. While continuing to thrust inside her ass, I run the melting cube over her lips again.

"Say my name before I fill your mouth."

"Tobin." She pants through the pain and pleasure rushing through her in equal measure.

"Now open," I command.

She spreads her lips and I drop the ice cube onto her tongue. Her eyes close and her expression twists for a moment before she gathers her composure and sucks on the cube. Her cheeks pull inward as she swirls the ice around in her mouth. She's such a stoic whore, and it's so fucking sexy.

I shove two fingers inside her pussy as I fuck her ass. With each moan that slips past her parted lips, a little of the come-water mixture slips from the side of her mouth and dribbles down her chin. What a good fucking cum-slut.

My thumb grazes her clit as I finger her. I have to stop thrusting because knowing she's so filled with me brings me too close. It's a majestic fucking sight. She curls her abdomen as her orgasm builds, and she tightens around my fingers and cock.

"Are you going to come for me, eighty? With your mouth and cunt filled with my come?"

She nods, her lips puckering as she sucks on the ice cube.

"Good girl," I growl as she shudders around me.

Her muscles clench around my dick, and I can't wait any longer. I lean onto my outstretched arm and fuck her until I spill my load inside her. I stay inside her ass as I pull her mouth to mine and kiss her, regardless of the residue in her mouth. I can't help the desire to mark her.

My hand leaves her cunt and winds through her hair as I pull her into me. When her lips spread, she tongues the mixture into my mouth. The taste is salty and foul, but I happily take what she gives me.

I pull out of her and look down. My gaze oscillates between her wet lips and the dripping mess leaking from her pussy and the thin white ropes gracing her tight asshole. She's fucking stunning.

I drop to my knees, lift her hips, and bring her ass closer to my mouth. Leaning over her creamy, come-filled hole, I let my tongue slip into her ass. She's stretched and used up, and I love it. Eating pussy is a Jax move, but I'll eat her come-filled asshole all day.

A feral groan leaves her lips from having my tongue on such a sensitive part of her body. A part of us all that's so neglected. It creates such a taboo thrill to know you aren't supposed to be buried between someone's ass cheeks, but here you are, doing it and loving it.

I lick her clean of my come. Her come. The melted ice.

"You like when I lick your ass, eighty?"

"Yes," she pants.

She turns over on her hands and knees and backs her ass into me. This dirty fucking girl knows what she wants. I grip her ass cheeks, spread them, and eat her as her fingers work her clit.

"Lick me, Tobin," she moans. She swirls her fingers, and my tongue works her until she comes again.

I pull away from her and look down at perfection. Fuck Kane. He doesn't know what he's missing with her. Fucking her is like sinking into a fallen angel. If he actually fucked her, there'd be no way he could get rid of her. If I had any say, I would never let her go. She'd be my come-filled fuck toy.

She'd be mine.

Aurora rolls onto her back, her chest heaving up and down as she tries to catch her breath. "Now can we talk?"

The sex only derailed her thoughts momentarily. She's already back on track, barreling toward the station at full speed, and I don't know how much longer I can dance around the topic. I sit beside her on the bed, unable to look at her as I speak.

"He's been through some shit. He doesn't know exactly what, because I keep those painful memories locked away from him. I can't risk telling you because I can't risk *you* telling *him*."

I expect a huff of indifference or an argument, but she only places a hand against my back and rubs in comforting circles. "Kane's lucky to have you and Jax," she says. "I wish I had someone to hold my trauma."

"What have you been through?" I ask.

Her hand stops moving. "Some shit," she says, throwing my words back at me.

Fair enough. It wouldn't be right to expect her to spill her secrets when I keep ours locked away.

I rise from the bed and begin to dress. "If you ever change your mind, let me know. I'm pretty good at holding trauma."

"Thanks, Tobin," she whispers.

Looking back at her, I can't imagine letting her go. Kane still has a chance to stop the boulder he's started rolling down a hill, so I walk to the stack of sticky notes and think of what to write that might change his mind. We make plenty of money and we'll have this truck paid off in a couple of years. Selling her would shave off a few months at most. Even if we can't keep her, I'd rather know she's somewhere safe and not beneath the sort of men The Nameless rub elbows with.

Because I'll always see her as mine.

Ours.

But what would possibly convince Kane to see her as Jax and I do? His hatred for women stems from a secret he can't remember, and I can't reveal that secret without risking his mind. If he knew the truth of his hatred, he might understand that Aurora is not a threat to him. If anything, she could be his salvation.

Then my phone vibrates in my pocket and changes everything. It's a text from The Nameless. They've found a buyer.

Chapter Twenty-One

Kane

I wake up beside her, with Pup curled between us. The dropout smells clean, which means Tobin probably took her inside the truck stop and let her shower. That was a terrible idea. I don't trust that he can keep her from running off. Then again, maybe she was too thoroughly fucked to run.

I lift the collar of my shirt and inhale. I smell clean too. What sort of shit did we get into last night that would cause both of us to need a shower? Neither of them better bond too closely with each other, because this little arrangement isn't permanent. Frankly, I can't wait to get rid of her.

A dull ache pulses through the muscles in my back and ass as I climb out of bed. I'm getting too old for Tobin to fuck like we're still in our twenties. That ship has sailed.

I grab a glass and set it on the counter with a loud clink. I refuse to tiptoe around and keep quiet so she can continue drifting through dreamland. Rise and shine, dropout.

I open the fridge and pull out the milk. I pour some into the glass and take a sip. It's not warm, but it's not cold enough for me.

Aurora stirs, turning over and staring at me. Her eyes drop to the glass.

"That's your breakfast?" she asks, stretching.

I nod. I've had a glass of milk every morning for as long as I can remember. I used to wake up before my parents and pour a glass before they got up. It was my moment of calm before heading into a shitstorm each day. I stare at her as I pull out the ice tray and absentmindedly grab the few remaining cubes.

"Um . . ." she says, and I narrow my eyes on her.

"What the fuck's your problem?"

She smirks. "Actually, nothing."

I drop the ice cubes into the milk, swirl the glass, and take a sip. A pungent flavor hits my tongue. Like old beer and something else. I barely make it to the sink before I spit it out.

"Honestly, I struggled to believe this whole multiple personality thing, but this just solidifies it," she says. "No one would willingly consume those."

I study the glass. "What was in the ice cubes?"

"Tobin's jizz," she says with a laugh.

I know it's Tobin's because it sure as shit isn't mine, and Jax wouldn't dream of coming in the ice tray. Despite how annoyed I am, my lips threaten to pull into a smile. It's her infectious laugh.

"I'm glad you find this so funny," I say as I pour out the milk.

"It's kinda hilarious."

Turning away from her, I allow my lips to pull into a smile. It's a foreign feeling, but I can't pretend I don't like the way it feels. People smile every day. People smile all the time. But not me. I haven't had anything to smile about in a very long time. Maybe ever.

I pull out my phone to check the time, and I notice a text from The Nameless. They found a buyer for the girl, which means there's no backing out now. In a few short days, she'll be off my hands and I'll be free to do as I please again.

So why don't I feel good about it?

I blame Tobin and Jax. Though our system is demarcated by deep lines that keep us within our respective places, we sometimes experience emotional bleed-through. They're upset about the finality of this text. They know what it means. Well, fuck them. I'm happy about it, and I remind myself of that as she rises from the bed.

She's wearing one of my t-shirts, and as she bends over to collect her discarded clothes from the floor, I see that the t-shirt is *all* she's wearing. Something far worse than a smile happens within my body as I watch her put on the leggings. There's a tightening in my jeans as I harden for the first time in years.

My lips draw downward. An erection is a sign of weakness for me. It's an innate bodily desire that leaves me feeling sick. Words flash into my mind, though I don't know why.

Don't get hard. If you do, they'll hurt you.

Whatever happened to me all those years ago has been tucked away from my prying mental fingers, but my cock remembers. It became forever limp. A broken body to go with my broken brain.

Until this moment.

Now it has decided that it wants to work, and it strains against my jeans. Aurora turns to say something to me, but her lips clamp shut as her eyes widen. She stares at my erection.

I glare at her neck and allow myself to think the thoughts racing through my mind. Despite my erection, none of these thoughts are sexual. I imagine wrapping my hands around that slender stretch of flesh and squeezing. My fingertips can already feel the way the bones in her throat will collapse beneath the pressure. I can almost see the light leaving her eyes. I can smell the pungent tang of fear as she fights for a breath that won't come.

And still her eyes remain glued to my erection.

"Goddamn it, dropout!" I scream as I rush toward her. My hand winds through her hair, and I use it like a suitcase handle as I drag her across the cab. The truck door creaks open, and I look outside to see if anyone is around. One other truck stands in the lot, but I see no sign of the driver. They're probably still sleeping.

I put my hand around her mouth and pull her into me as I drag her down the steps and toward the back of my trailer. She doesn't fight my hold on her, which both agitates and pleases me. I don't want her to draw any attention, and fighting me would do that, but does she always have to be so unaffected?

My hand closes around the metal handle outside the trailer door, and I whip it open. Cool air rushes toward us. Once we're safely inside, I release her mouth. She turns to me, confusion muddling her eyes.

"Kane, what did I do?"

"You got in my fucking truck."

"Please don't do this," she pleads, and it's the first time genuine fear has shown on her face.

Maybe it's because she knows what will happen if I leave her ass in here. Wearing nothing more than that t-shirt and the thin leggings, she'll freeze to death. But this isn't about that. I have no plans to kill her, especially not now that I know she's destined for greater things. Leaving her back here is a mind game. She'll be so fucking afraid of me that it will alter her brain chemistry. She won't be able to handle being around me after this.

And that's exactly what both of us need.

I flip on the overhead light, exit the truck, and close the door. After securing the latch on the outside, I shake my head. My reaction to seeing her bare legs and ass has left me confused. She has too much power over me, and I can't have that. I have to be in control at all times because I can't trust the other two nitwits. They lose all control whenever she bats her eyelashes at them.

The temptress may have gotten to Tobin and Jax, but I won't allow her to get to me.

Chapter Twenty-Two

Aurora

Freezing air encompasses my body in an icy hug. The leggings give me a little more protection than the thin t-shirt, but not by much. The weird thing about being trapped in the cold is that it almost feels warm sometimes. Maybe it's the incessant shivering. It's violent enough that my muscles begin to ache after only a few minutes.

I try the door. There's a handle on the inside, but he must have a locking mechanism on the outside, because it doesn't budge. I'm not sure why I thought any different. Considering the random stash of women's clothing and Kane's violent tendencies, I'm probably not the first woman he's stuffed back here.

My feet nearly come out from under me when the truck begins to move. Now I'm faced with the reality of my situation. Kane plans to leave me in here until I'm dead, and I don't even know what I did wrong. That's more frustrating than being locked in a freezer on wheels.

I think back to our interaction. He seemed fine until I turned around and noticed he was hard. I thought Tobin had taken over, but then he got really upset and stuffed me back here. And he called me dropout, which means he was definitely still Kane. So how did he have an erection?

The truck turns, sending me to my ass. It also jostles something near the back of the unit. I turn to get a better look at the mound in the back corner. A faded blue blanket drapes over something lumpy and long. Even though I can't make out what lies beneath the blanket, I know exactly what's peeking from beneath it.

Long, dark hair.

My body leaps backward at the realization, and I slide down the icy side wall as I try to wrap my head around what I've seen. Surely it's just my wild imagination. I'm freezing to death and going insane, but I'm definitely not locked in a small space with a deceased person.

Curiosity gets the best of me, and I crawl toward the mound. I verify my fear as I pull back a crisp blanket and find a dead fucking body.

And she's very dead. Though the cold temperatures have mostly preserved her, a foggy glaze covers her unseeing eyes and her skin has begun to change color. A purplish bruise circles her neck, and I don't need more than one guess to figure out who put it there. I brush the hair away from her face. Wrinkles crease her skin, and smears of dark makeup smudge her cheeks.

I'm alone and there's no one to hide my emotions from this time, so I allow the anger and fear to battle inside me. I'm doing everything I can to stay alive, but will Kane let me live after his nice little trip to Texas? Probably not. I'm doomed to meet the same fate as the poor woman in front of me.

Part of me almost accepts this, but the other part thinks I can win him over. Kane is way more guarded than Jax or Tobin, but I'm willing to do whatever it takes to weasel my way into his mind. Judging by what happened earlier, I'm well on my way to success. I got him hard, though he clearly hated it. But it's a reaction.

Unfortunately, it landed me in this freezer, where I'll probably die from exposure.

Like a terrible human being, I take the blanket off the woman's body and wrap it around myself. It's not like she needs it anymore, but I still feel guilty for taking her shroud. It provides little warmth, but it's better than leaving my arms exposed.

I back into the wall and draw my legs to my chest, curling into a ball. Moments of warmth come over my body, which scare me more than the freezing temperatures. Isn't that what happens when you're in the throes of hypothermia? You feel warm?

Am I going to die here?

It almost seems better to just fall asleep in the cold than to be killed by fucking Kane. It's hard to keep my cool when someone is actively trying to murder me, and I want so desperately to seem like the unbreakable bitch he thinks I am.

In truth, I'm very breakable. A group of frat boys proved that.

In a moment of impending death, I think about what made me run from college. Memories come to me in flashes. Being drunk, hardly able to stand. And then the door to my dorm room opened.

I close my eyes and shut out the memories. Time doesn't heal all wounds.

Shortly after that happened, I left school. I couldn't focus on class and instead began to drink my feelings away, though I wasn't old enough to get booze. That created its own set of problems, but I found solutions. To numb the ache and the racing thoughts, I needed the alcohol, but to get the alcohol, I had to do favors. That started it all for me. The barter system that comes from having a female body and a need I can't fulfill on my own.

I clearly have very good coping mechanisms.

After my assault, I should have gone home to my parents and gotten sober. I should have allowed myself to heal properly. Maybe get some fucking therapy. Extensively. But I dug myself into a grave of lies, and I didn't have the courage to return.

Maybe going home has been a pipe dream all along. Some stupid goal I set because it sounded good. I could have been home ages ago. I've been on dozens of trucks that traveled close to home, but I always climbed into the next one and let it carry me away again. I'm a failure at that too, I guess.

And it brought me right to this moment in this fucking freezer.

I scoff and shake my head. This asshole is going to let me wallow in the down-falls of my life before I die. Dick.

My gaze turns toward the woman again, and something beneath her leg catches the light. I crawl closer and realize it's a bottle of whiskey. Since setting out on the road, I haven't really been a drinker anymore. It's not something I want to pick up again . . . but desperate times, right? I mean, if I'm staring death in the face, I might as well share a drink with the bastard.

"I'm sorry," I whisper to the woman before unscrewing the cap and swigging the chilled liquor.

The familiar burn races down my throat and hits my stomach in a blaze of glory. Drinking may not be the answer to any of my many problems, but it sure as fuck is an answer to my pain. As I wait for the alcohol to work its magic, I scoot back to the wall—as far from the dead woman as possible—and drape the blanket over my head.

I take another sip as I shiver my life away. I drink until I feel warm from the inside out. At least something feels warm. And soon enough, I won't feel anything at all.

Chapter Twenty-Three

Every so often I'm thrust into the real world without much notice. There's a weird sense of panic as I find myself face to face with a situation I'm not aware of beforehand. I'm guessing Kane had a panic attack. Was it because of the girl?

Thinking of her and how she may have upset Kane sends a bolt of icy fear through my sternum. I've been too complacent. I thought his deal with The Nameless would stop him from doing anything too drastic, but when it comes to Kane, drastic is his middle name.

"Aurora?" I call toward the back of the truck, but there's no response.

Pup whines and begins pacing between the front and rear of the truck. I dare to look back, unsure if I'll see her lifeless body, but I only see an empty cab.

What the fuck? Did she escape?

Or did Kane do something to her?

A sign for a rest stop pops up, and I nearly turn the truck onto its side as I snatch the wheel and aim for the entrance. Once I bring the truck to a stop, I rush over to the bed and search for signs of a struggle.

The bed has been made, and nothing looks out of place. After pulling back the comforter, I examine every inch of the sheets for a droplet of blood or some indication of what happened. I find nothing. She's just . . . gone. It's as if she was never here in the first place.

I go to the sink next, and my eyes catch on a note stuck to the mirror.

I PUT THE BITCH IN THE TRAILER

Fuck. If she's in the trailer, odds are good that she's no longer alive. Kane likes to use the unit to keep his kills from stinking things up until he can find a safe place to dispose of them. My heart sinks.

"Goddamn it, Kane."

At least he was thoughtful enough to leave a note, I guess, but that does nothing for the pain I feel at the thought of losing her. While keeping her with us was a near guaranteed impossibility, the thought of her no longer existing in this world is almost more than I can stomach. She was special to me and Tobin. I hoped Kane would eventually see what we see in her, but I guess that was just wishful thinking.

I get out of the cab and walk toward the trailer. A cold sweat slicks my palms, and my brain refuses to accept what I'm about to see. And I don't want to see it. Even if she wasn't dead when he placed her back there, saving her is likely out of the question. I have no concept of time when I'm not in control, so that note could have been written an hour or a week ago.

After undoing the outer lock, I wrap my hand around the cold metal handle and close my eyes, steeling myself for what waits beyond the door. It opens with a clunk and a creak. I open my eyes.

"Aurora?" I yell into the freezer. I step inside the dark trailer and head toward the light at the end.

My gaze moves toward the body that I already knew about, then I allow myself to scan for the second one I hope isn't there. But there she is, curled against the wall with a blanket draped over her body.

I watch for signs of life, for the blanket to move up and down with each breath or for her head to turn as my feet clunk against the floor. She remains still, and panic clutches my heart in a vise. I care so much for that girl, even though I'm not allowed to. It's not fucking fair. And now she's gone.

"Oh, sweet girl," I say as I walk up to her frozen body beneath the blanket.

"I'm not dead," she whispers, but her voice is so low I almost don't hear it over the hum of the reefer unit.

I wrap my arms around her and tug her to her feet. The blanket falls away from her head, and the scent of alcohol smacks me in the face. I pick her up and carry her out of the truck and into the warm air. I rip the cold blanket away and take off my shirt so I can wrap it around her. Violent shivers tear through her body, so I draw her as close to my warmth as I can.

"I'm so sorry, sweet girl," I say. And I *am* sorry, even though I didn't do this. But I'm glad I was able to find her before . . .

I don't even want to think about it.

I carry her into the cab of the truck and flip on the bunk warmer as high as it can go. As I wrap her in every blanket I can find, my mind races through a labyrinth of confused thoughts. I don't know if Kane meant to kill her, but he came too close. He's done a lot of terrible shit to women, and he's often very creative with his slaughter skill set, but freezing a girl to death isn't anywhere near his typical MO.

Her teeth clack together, and the shivering hasn't slowed. She needs my warmth. I peel back the blankets and squeeze in beside her. Her head drops to my shoulder, and I let her cold body freeze mine so that she can take my heat. I'll give her all of me if it means she'll survive.

"What happened?" I ask.

"Kane's a fucking dick," she says through clattering teeth.

I stifle a laugh, glad to see her tenacity is still very much intact. "Fair. But why did he do this?"

"I don't know, Jax. One minute I was getting dressed, the next I was getting shoved into the freezer. He got an erection, but that's the only weird thing I can think of."

That would have enraged him, especially if she'd seen it, but I can't think about that right now. I'm just thankful she's alive and that I've been gifted this time with her. Even given the circumstances. Even knowing I can't keep her.

The sinking feeling returns and settles in my gut. She probably would have been better off if she'd died in that trailer. The Nameless will sell her to someone who will use and abuse her until she's no use to them anymore. She may think she's living through hell right now, but she's only standing outside the gates.

The worst part? There's absolutely nothing I can do about her future. I can't change Kane's mind. He nearly killed her just for giving him an erection.

Something clicks inside my mind.

If Kane wanted her dead, why did he write the note that told me where I could find her? If I hadn't seen the note, I would have kept driving and assumed the worst, and she would certainly have frozen to death.

In some weird way—a way Kane himself probably doesn't even realize—*he* saved her. His raw emotions were too powerful to contend with, so he shoved the danger into the freezer. Out of sight, out of mind. But he wrote the note and allowed me to take control, which means he didn't want her to die, even if that lack of want was subconscious.

But Kane is not unselfish. How could he do something from the kindness of his heart when his heart has no kindness? Has she affected him more than we realize?

I lift her chin and bring her eyes to mine. The icy pallor has begun to give way, allowing her cheeks to take on a pink hue. Better yet, the shivering has eased up. She still has a mild tremble to her lips as her jaw clenches and unclenches, but on the whole, she looks so much better.

I lean down and kiss her. She accepts my lips in ways I don't think I could if I was just in a freezer with a dead body. She's like no one we've ever met or anyone we'll ever meet again. She's a multi-faceted gem in a world of soot.

"Jax," she whispers against my lips. "Thank you for saving me."

I pull her into me and clutch her to my chest. "Are we going to talk about what you saw back there?"

"Can we not?" she asks. "Not right now, at least. There's a time and a place for discussions about dead bodies, but this isn't it."

I smile and brush back her damp hair. I wish so badly that he would let her inside him like we've let her in. Maybe he'd find something that could make him happy for once.

Being inside Kane is like living within an abstract painting. I'm surrounded by nonsensical shapes painted in blacks and grays and reds that represent his terrifying desires. I'd love for him to find some happiness so I don't have to feel so dreadful all the time too.

A sob works out of her chest, and I pull her tighter against me. Her tears don't fuel me the way they fuel Tobin or Kane. They destroy me. I never want to be the reason she cries. Technically, I'm not, but because we all share the same body, my hands placed her in that freezer.

"I'm so sorry," I whisper against her head.

"Don't let him out now," she says. "Please. I don't want him to see me cry."

I don't ask if she means Kane or Tobin, but I can only assume she means either of them. We each have our own set of skills, and comforting isn't something they're very good at.

"Do you want to talk about anything aside from what you saw in there?" I ask.

"Yes," she says through a fresh barrage of tears. "Why me?"

"You were just in the wrong diner at the wrong time."

"No, I'm not talking about getting kidnapped by you three. I mean, why did those men . . . ?" Her voice trails off, and she takes a deep breath. "If I tell you something, can the others hear me?"

I shake my head.

"There was a reason I left college, and it wasn't because I couldn't keep my grades up. I'd been at a party, but I got really drunk. Too drunk. When I stumbled back to my dorm room, I didn't realize someone had followed me home."

I already know where this story is going, and I don't like it.

"He was a young jock," she says. "A real party boy around campus. I guess I forgot to lock my door because one minute, I was ready to pass out on the bed, and the next, his hands were scalding every inch of my body. My tits. My ass. My thighs. I asked him to stop. I even tried to move away from him, but my arms and legs were like lead weights."

"Sweet girl, I'm so sorry."

"As fucked up as it sounds, I could have brushed it off if it had just been him. But he wasn't alone, Jax. I don't even know how many of his friends had tagged along, but it wasn't just him."

She buries her face in my chest and cries, and all I can do is hold her. I can't take her pain for her the way I can take Kane's pain. I can't lock her memories in a box so she can function. She has to do this on her own. All by herself.

For the first time, I realize just how lucky Kane, Tobin, and I are.

"It went on for hours," she finally says. "Sometimes I would pass out, only to wake up to someone else assaulting me. Jax, I bled for days."

"Did you report them?"

She shakes her head and sniffles. "I never went to the police because I felt guilty. I'd worn a short skirt and a halter top, and I won't pretend I hadn't flirted with the guy that followed me home."

Rage simmers beneath my skin. How can she blame herself? "It wasn't your fault. You have to understand that. Being flirtatious doesn't equal consent."

"That isn't how some men see it," she says with a bitter laugh. She takes another deep breath and lets it out. "You're the first person I've told. I've been too ashamed to tell anyone else."

I place my palm against her back and rub circles over the thin t-shirt. "You have nothing to be ashamed of. You are so incredibly strong, and I'm honored that you trusted me enough to share this with me."

She snuggles against me, wrapping her arms around my waist. "Can you hold me, Jax? Just for a little while. I know it can't be forever, but just hold me."

I lie back on the bed, pull her into me, and I hold her, all while my brain races with ways I can save her from the path of destruction we've placed her on.

Chapter Twenty-Four

Aurora

After shedding the weight of my secret, I'm so much lighter. I always thought telling someone would make me feel dirty or ashamed, but I feel neither of these things. Maybe I just needed the right person to talk to.

I wipe the lingering tears from my cheeks and revel in Jax's warmth behind me. It's difficult to lie beside a man who saved me from freezing to death in a refrigerated truck when he's stuck inside the body of the man who put me there, but I know they aren't the same. Jax doesn't want to harm me. He protects me in ways no one else has. As strange as it sounds, the same can be said for Tobin. Jax is my safe place to discuss my feelings, and Tobin is my safe place to explore my sexual desires without judgment.

Kane is the only danger.

Jax's arm drapes over my side, his hand resting on my stomach. Cuddling with Jax somehow feels so natural despite this completely unnatural situation. I don't know why he bothered to save me, though. I'm fairly certain I'll end up in that freezer again, especially after seeing the body back there. He can't stop Kane. I got lucky this time, but I've never been a lucky person. If it happens again, I'm fucked.

Pup jumps onto the bed and curls into a fluffy ball by Jax's hand. She whined incessantly when I first returned to the truck, almost as if she could sense just how close to death I'd come. Now that I'm warm and safe, she's content. I close my eyes and run my fingers through her soft fur.

Jax's hand rips away, and he scoots backward. Which means Jax is gone. And since he didn't grind on my ass when he woke up . . . that means he's Kane.

"Jesus fuck," he snarls, putting more space between us. "What the fuck!"

I turn over and try to control my widening eyes as I lock my gaze on him. "Jesus fuck what, Kane? I think I should be the one saying that. And what are you so afraid of? Thinking you're seeing a ghost?"

"I'm not fucking afraid," he says as he sits up.

I don't touch him, but I lean closer. "Your breathing is heavy. Your heart is racing. That's fear."

"I'm not afraid of *you*," he snaps as he goes to push me away, but I grab his wrist. Anger lights up his face. I expect him to hit me or rip out of my grasp, but he only freezes. He can't handle my touch. He's incapable of doing anything but sitting there and panting.

"You're afraid of something I represent," I say. "Do you hate women? *Whores*?"

"You don't know anything about me."

"I'm well aware, but whose fault is that? I know plenty about Jax and Tobin."

"Get your fucking hand off me." Even as he says this, he still makes no effort to remove my hand. As big as he is, he'd only need to move his arm to snatch me loose.

Pup hops off the bed and begins pacing and whining. She stares at us with wide, glistening eyes. Her ears press against her head, and she begins to shiver.

"I'll let you go if you tell me why you put me in that trailer," I say.

He swallows and clenches his teeth. "Because you . . . Because I don't like how you affect us."

"Because I give those two the companionship they crave? Maybe if you let me, I could show you what it means to have a friend."

"I don't want that."

"I think you do. I think you desperately want to connect with another human being, but you're scared."

This breaks him from his frozen state. He throws me onto my back and raises his fist above my head. I don't flinch or cow to him, though. I just raise my chin higher because fuck him. I've nearly had a corpse party with a dead body in the freezer, so this is nothing.

He slams his fist down beside my head, and it sinks into the mattress. "Fuck you, dropout! The only reason I'm keeping you alive . . ."

I don't know what he's chosen to leave out, but I hope he meant to say he's kept me alive because of Jax and Tobin. Something deep inside tells me this is only wishful thinking. He's kept me alive for much more sinister reasons.

Kane leans over me, and his racing heart thumps against mine. "You mean nothing to me. You're lower than nothing. You're lower than the gum you chewed off my fucking shoe. I don't want companionship from you. I don't want *anything* from you. The other two may see something in you, but I see nothing but a flunky whore."

His degrading words should make me recoil, but I play into the hulking mass of madness hovering over me and lift my head a fraction of an inch. His warm breath rolls over mine as I press my lips to his.

Shock and confusion flash across his face as he pulls back, but these emotions are quickly replaced by anger and something else. Embarrassment? Fear? I don't know. But his pupils dilate and instead of hitting me, I lose Kane in front of my eyes.

"You kissed the big, bad Kane, eighty?" He leans forward and bites my bottom lip. "Are you suicidal?"

I scoff. "He put me in the fucking trailer. I almost died."

"And that made you want to kiss him? You're even more fucked up than I thought." He smirks and rubs a hand down my chest. "Your sweet little lips traumatized him so much it forced a change neither of us expected. *Thrust* me right into your lap." He moves his hips against me to punctuate the word.

"I thought I could get through to him," I say with a shake of my head.

"No one has gotten through to Kane. No one." He gets off of me and sits on the edge of the bed.

"Has anyone gotten through to you before, Tobin?"

He offers me a sinner's smirk. "Nah. Just because I haven't connected with someone before you doesn't mean I couldn't, though. But him? He's physically and emotionally incapable."

"Challenge accepted."

He leans over, buries his hand in my hair, and cups my ear. "Don't be stupid, eighty. Just because you've gotten to me doesn't mean you'll get to him. Just drop it."

I wish I could. I wish I didn't care. But I can't and I do.

This desire to connect with Kane goes beyond wanting to save my life. I've gotten close to Tobin and Jax, and while they're their own people, they're also part of Kane. I'm falling for them, and Kane is part of that package. Is it so bad to want him to want me?

Then a little voice pipes up in my head, reminding me that yes, it's pretty bad to want him to want me, especially after seeing that body in the trailer.

"Why does he kill women?" I ask.

A deep laugh rumbles inside Tobin's chest "Because he hates them."

"I've figured out that much, Sherlock. But why? What happened to him?"

Tobin sobers now, the smile sliding from his face. "I've told you it's not anything you need to know. Why are you so stubborn?"

I grip his hand and look into his eyes. "Please, Tobin. Help me understand him."

He shakes his head and looks away. "He's been hurt pretty badly. He endured a lot of abuse from women who were supposed to protect him."

"Sexual abuse?"

"I shouldn't be telling you any of this."

"I understand him more than you realize," I say. "I was assaulted when I was in college."

I tell my story for the second time, and it hurts a little less than it did before. Tobin's jaw clenches and unclenches, and his eyes remain trained to the floor. When I finish, he looks up at me.

"You are so strong," he says, "but telling you what happened to Kane is a risk I can't take. That strong part of you is still embedded in who you are. Kane lacks that. That's where Jax and I come in. If Kane knew what happened to him, if he was forced to face it . . ."

"You're afraid I'll tell him and risk all of you?"

He blows out a breath. "I need a minute." He stands and walks to the front of the truck, then steps outside, leaving me on the bed.

It turns out Kane and I may have more in common than I thought, but I can't do anything with that information. Despite Tobin's fear, despite knowing that breaking

Kane could save me in the end, I won't risk Jax or Tobin. Though I don't fully understand why, I'm unwilling to risk Kane as well.

A few minutes later, the driver's door opens and Tobin takes a seat behind the wheel. Or I think it's Tobin until he turns to me and says, "Buckle up, dropout. We have to take care of that body."

Chapter Twenty-Five

Kane

After checking my GPS, I spot a lonely stretch of road devoid of houses or farmland. Technology has become a double-edged sword; it sometimes catches men like me in a web, but it can also make finding remote areas a breeze. I turn out of the rest area and head toward the spot I've marked on the map.

The rear of the cab is quiet for once, which makes me uncomfortable. I've grown used to the girl's incessant talking, and the lack of that noise unnerves me now. I won't go so far as to say I enjoy it, but it's like running a box fan in your bedroom during the dead of winter. Sometimes the right kind of noise provides a bit of comfort, even if it adds to your discomfort in other ways.

I look over my shoulder and see her on the bed. Rather, I see her legs. The upper half of her body hides behind the partially outstretched curtain. Something about her body language makes my heart sore, and it's a feeling I neither like nor want to feel. Then I realize it's not my emotion. This is something Jax and Tobin feel.

Why?

It doesn't matter why, because you don't care about the whore.

Now I feel stupid for wishing I could hear her voice. It was never my wish to begin with. It's emotional bleed-through, which isn't something that happens very often for us. My inability to realize that—my inability to recognize their emotions as separate from my own—only shows just how damaged our compartments have become. Our ship is sinking, and the water has begun to breach our hull.

I have to get rid of this girl as soon as possible.

"Come on, dropout, let's bury that body," I say as I pull the truck to a stop. "I need to get the old girl cleaned before we pick up that load."

This body should have been buried several state lines ago. Pick up one, hold her until I kill her, bury her a state or two over. That's always been my plan. Taking Aurora fucked up everything, but I have to clean that trailer and provide proof to the distributor before I arrive to pick up the load. No one wants to put their perishables beside a dead fucking body.

I walk toward the back of the truck to retrieve the shovel I keep stashed beneath the bed. The girl hasn't moved. She continues to lie on top of the comforter, her hand lazily running through Pup's fur.

First she ropes in my alters, and now she's going for my dog. I can't with this bitch.

"You can dig one hole, or I can dig two. Your choice," I say. I'm not in the mood to argue with her.

"Why do I have to dig the grave?"

"Because I'm getting too old for this shit."

"Have you ever considered retiring?"

Retire from killing? Never.

My hand finds the shovel, and I pull it out and hold it toward her. "Get out there and dig, dropout."

She rolls her eyes and accepts the wooden handle, then stands up and plods out of the truck. When I step out behind her, I look at the sky and study the clouds as I draw a cigarette from the pack in my pocket. I lean against a tree and light it. Her eyes follow the cigarette as if it's a magic wand.

"What, do you want one?" I ask.

She nods.

"Beg me."

A scoff slips past her lips, and she tightens her grip on the shovel. "I'm not begging you for shit."

"Say, 'Daddy Kane, give me a cigarette because I'm a dropout whore who doesn't care about her body.'"

"*Daddy Kane* can suck my dick," she mumbles under her breath.

A smirk tugs at my lips. Even though her eyes hold so much longing for this little nicotine stick, she turns to head into the woods rather than play my game. I grip her arm and hand her my cigarette, and she looks up with a sneer before taking it from me. With an attitude like that, I'm amazed no one has beaten her to death before now.

I pull out another cigarette for myself and light both. She leans on the shovel and sucks in smoke with her eyes closed. I stare at her lips each time they wrap around the filter, and an uncomfortable feeling spreads through my body like poison.

I turn toward the truck. "I'm gonna let Pup out while we're stopped."

"You aren't worried she'll run off?" she asks as I open the door. "I had a dog once, but he ran away when I took him on a hike. My dad wouldn't let me look for him because our trip was over and he wanted to get home. I don't want that to happen to Pup."

I whistle for the little dog, and she trots to the front of the truck and hops down. "I don't have to worry about Pup running off. We've been doing this for years, and she always sticks close."

Thunder rumbles in the distance, the sound carried on the darkening clouds creeping across the sky. Judging by the sharp, thick scent in the air, rain is on its way. We need to dig this grave and get back onto the road.

Aurora seems to sense the urgency as well, because she throws down her cigarette, snuffs out the cherry, then sinks the shovel into the dirt and pulls up a large clod of grass.

"What the fuck are you doing?" I ask.

"Digging a fucking grave?"

I shake my head and snatch the shovel from her hands. "You can't do it here at the side of the road. It'll be too obvious. We have to go into the woods a little ways."

"You want me to try to dig a grave in that?" She motions toward the forest. "I can't break through all those tree roots."

I wrap my hand around her bicep and drag her into the woods. "Ye of little faith," I mutter.

We walk for a few minutes, Pup scampering at our heels. When we come to a clearing, I push the shovel into her hands and raise an eyebrow. She scoffs and gets to work.

Aurora is much more methodical than I've ever been. I usually dig a hole that's just big enough to shove the body into and just deep enough to keep the wildlife away. She's really mapping this thing out. Using the shovel's blade, she's already drawn a rectangular perimeter. A very *large* rectangular perimeter.

"Are we burying a body or laying the groundwork for an in-ground pool?" I say. "What the fuck are you doing?"

She blows away a strand of hair that's fallen over her eyes. "I'm sorry. I seem to have misplaced my handbook on grave digging. Maybe an expert should show me how it's done?"

I shake my head as she holds the shovel out to me. "No, no. Carry on. It's just a little . . . big."

We could probably bury two bodies side by side in that thing, but I swallow a smile and go back to watching her dig. My eyes fall to the curve of her back. Sweat collects on the dip just above the waistband of her pants. Those soft lines tempt some buried emotion inside me, but I fight it off by imagining filling her mouth with that loose soil until she fucking suffocates. I have to think these thoughts to fight off the feeling that manifests into something deranged.

She wipes sweat from her forehead with the back of her hand when she's nearly halfway done. It leaves a streak of brown behind. Pup paces at the edge of the deepening rectangle, her little head lifting each time the thunder booms a bit closer. She's never been a fan of storms.

I open my mouth to tell Aurora I'm going to put Pup back in the truck, but lightning streaks across the sky and a loud boom swallows my voice. Before I know what's happening, Pup is a blur of brown as she disappears into the woods.

"Pup! No!" I scream, but it's too late. She's gone.

I look between the girl digging the grave and the woods. Leaving her would be stupid, but I can't lose my dog. My hand goes to my chest, my heart galloping against my palm at the thought of losing Pup. My jaw clenches. I'm not used to feeling sentimental feelings like this, but that dog means more to me than she should.

Memories rush back as I recall the way her little teeth sank into my hand as I tried to scoop up her battered body on the side of the road. By the time I carried her into the emergency vet, I was shaking as much as she was. I rented a room in a nearby motel so I could wait to hear if she'd pull through. It was the most human I'd ever felt. That little dog is my only tether to some form of humanity.

"Kane, you have to find her," Aurora says. "You go, and I'll keep digging."

It's a ploy. I'm not stupid. She sees an opening and she plans to take it. The moment I'm far enough away, she'll drop that shovel and disappear. I curse under my breath, torn in half by this decision.

Rain begins to patter onto my broad shoulders, and that makes up my mind. I have to go after my dog. She's too small to survive out here, especially in a storm, and the thought of leaving her behind does something terrible to me. I'll admit I'm attached to the fucking thing. And now she's gone.

"Don't go anywhere," I say, though I have to raise my voice to be heard over the sudden rush of wind tearing through the trees. "If it gets too bad out here, head back to the truck. Do you understand?"

She nods, but I don't believe her. I don't *trust* her. She's a woman, after all, and women have only shown me that they can't ever be trusted. Still, what choice do I have? I look at her for what I assume will be the final time, and then I head into the woods.

The rain falls in sheets now. The thick canopy holds most of it at first, only allowing intermittent drops to glide past the leaves and branches to land on me. Then the canopy can hold no more, and the torrent breaks through in a blinding wash of water. I call for Pup as I struggle through the thickening brush. I look for signs—fur left behind on a spindle of thorns or broken branches—but I see nothing.

Sharp twigs reach for me and scrape across my exposed skin. My voice is lost to a crescendo of rain, wind, and thunder. Lightning cracks nearby, too close for comfort, but I push on. I can't give up on my dog.

As I stumble along through the woods, I look for places where a small animal might seek shelter from this storm. I get on my knees and peer into every overhang, each rocky outcropping, but she isn't there. By the time the weather begins to let up, I'm soaked to the bone and completely hopeless.

I can't find her.

And I have to head back.

With a sigh, I turn around and begin picking my way toward the clearing. If I were capable of tears, I'd allow myself to cry right now. My exhausted body still clings to some frayed sliver of hope, though. Maybe the girl will still be there when I get back. Maybe my dog has returned. Maybe I don't have to be on my own again.

The sun sits low in the sky by the time I reach the clearing. I step toward the edge of the grave and peer into it. From the looks of things, she continued digging once I left, but she didn't hang around for very long. The shovel leans against the side of the empty hole. She's gone.

Maybe she just went to the truck.

Yeah, and maybe I'll wake up tomorrow with a million dollars and perfect mental health. The girl is gone. The dog is gone. And I have to accept it.

I grab the shovel and head to the truck. Even though I know I'll find the cab empty, I have to check. The storm finds renewed strength as I make my way through more branches and thorns, and another ten gallons of rain soak into my skin before I reach the desolate road. My fingers wrap around the door handle, and I haul myself inside.

I call out for the girl and Pup. Silence answers me. I check the cabinet above the bed and find her backpack tucked inside, but that doesn't mean anything. She didn't know where I'd hidden it, and she probably knew better than to come looking for it.

There's no point in stripping off my wet clothes. I still have to get rid of the body in the trailer. I still have to pick up a load in Texas. I still have to call The Nameless and tell them the deal is off.

Picking up my phone, I ready myself to dial their number, but then I stop. A text would work just as well, especially since I don't feel like hearing anyone's voice right now. I just want to be alone. Misery doesn't always love company.

> I lost the package. Deal is off.

> I recommend you find it. Money has already exchanged hands.

With a sigh, I shove my phone into my pocket and head into the rain again. I reach the back of the truck and lean my head against the rear doors. How did everything go so wrong? I never should have picked her up. If it weren't for Aurora, I wouldn't be in this mess. I would still have a dog, The Nameless wouldn't have scrawled my name on their shit list, and the dynamic between me and my alters wouldn't be so damaged.

I reach for the lock and begin to unfasten it when something stops me. A rustling in the bushes. Footsteps.

Turning toward the sound, I ready my hand over the knife attached to my belt, prepared to take out any threat. Then my hand falls to my side as Aurora emerges from the woods with my dog in her arms.

Chapter Twenty-Six

Aurora

I slide a dry shirt over my head and wrap a blanket around my shivering shoulders. Kane busies himself by toweling off the bedraggled ball of fur I rescued from the woods. It was stupid of me to look for the dog and come back. Even after I found Pup, I could have taken her and run, I could have escaped, but some invisible thread pulled me back here.

Well, two invisible threads, and their names are Tobin and Jax.

Having been confronted with an out and choosing to return has told me everything I need to know. Despite my inability to form a bond with Kane—and Kane's inability to form a bond with anything aside from the dog he now lovingly checks over for injuries—I have adhered myself to Tobin and Jax. I care about them, and I care about what happens to them. That's why I haven't pressed Kane about his sexual assault. Integration may be the goal for some people with DID, but it isn't their goal, and I want to respect that.

But how can any of this work?

To be in a relationship with them would mean tying myself to three people, one of whom can't stand me. I'd love to say the feeling is mutual, but my hatred for him has lessened as I've learned more about him from Jax and Tobin. He's a product of severe trauma, and it feels unfair to judge him so harshly now. There has to be some way to break through his walls.

Kane places Pup on the floor and pulls a worn ball from a cabinet. He tosses the ball across the truck, and Pup's paws clatter against the floor as she races to get to it. It slips beneath the bed, and she wedges herself into the small space, only emerging once she realizes she can't reach it. Kane eyes me as I kneel and dig beneath the bed to retrieve the ball as she whines beside me.

"Where did you find Pup?" I ask.

"I was cutting through a small town and saw her on the side of the road. She'd been hit by a car and left for dead."

"You saved her?"

"I guess."

I swallow hard. I always wondered why he had a dog at all, let alone a small, fluffy thing like Pup. I'm surprised he didn't run over her to finish her off instead of saving her. Something about this little dog has wormed into a heart he insists he doesn't have. If the dog could wiggle in there, I'm sure I can get inside too.

I go back up front and sit in the passenger seat. "Do you know why I dropped out of college, Kane?" I ask. Maybe we can connect if he realizes I've been through trauma too. We aren't so different—aside from the fact that I haven't taken to killing people for funsies.

"I don't care why you left college," he says without meeting my gaze. "We still have a body to bury, though. Once the rain lets up, we'll have to get it done."

I push ahead, ignoring his attempt to put me off. "I was assaulted. The pain and humiliation were too much, so I ran."

He swallows but says nothing.

"I know you don't give two shits about what happened to me, but it was pretty fucking traumatic. It shaped my life from that point forward. Brought me . . . Well, it brought me here."

He considers this, then says, "Why become a prostitute?"

"Why become a serial killer?"

A low laugh rattles his chest. "Fair."

"Do you remember what happened to you? Any of it?"

He shakes his head and picks at the side of his thumb. "Tobin holds that information for me in that fucked-up little mind of his."

"If you don't remember what happened, why do you have so much anger?"

His mouth opens and closes. Opens and closes. "I've given you enough about me, dropout. Let it go."

His soul is a door that opens just enough to give me a glimpse of his human side before slamming in my face again.

"We almost had a moment, Kane, you know that?"

He blows out a heavy breath. "I don't connect with people."

"Even after everything that's happened to me, I can still connect with people. I managed to connect with Tobin and—"

"Fucking Tobin isn't connecting. That fucker would connect with anything as long as there was a hole to use."

Now it's my turn to shake my head. "It might be difficult for you to understand, but I connect with both of your alters on very different levels. And not just in sexual ways."

He inhales a sharp breath. "Even if I could connect with someone, I wouldn't waste my time on someone like you."

Ouch. "Someone like me?"

"A whore," he says through gritted teeth, like it pains him to speak that word.

"I think someone's jealous."

He turns and grips the steering wheel. "I'm not fucking jealous."

"Your dick doesn't work. So what? Who fucking cares? I don't want your dick, if that's what you're worried about. I want to connect with you differently. Emotionally."

"Are you suicidal? It's like you want to die."

His words are a warning, but I've never been one to listen to warnings. I keep going.

"Who cares if you talk to me and tell me about yourself? You'll either kill me or let me go in the end, so who the fuck cares what secret parts of you I take with me?"

"You're literally insane. You know that, right? You have absolutely nothing to bargain with, yet you talk with your chest so high. A girl like you. You're too confident for your own good."

"Because I think we can help each other."

He laughs. "Help each other? Okay. Just sit there and shut your mouth. If I wanted to go to a shrink, I'd have abducted one of those instead of a whore."

This is pointless. I stand to go to the bed, but he grabs my hand.

"Meet me outside at the back of the truck. We still have a job to do."

"Yes, *Daddy Kane*," I say. I'm on a roll, clearly.

"That mouth is going to get you killed, dropout!" Kane yells as I open the door.

He's such an asshole. How did I ever think I could break through the multiple layers of steel he's put around himself?

The CB radio goes off as I climb out of the truck. I can't make out the voice coming through the speaker, but I hear Kane's response.

"This is Three Amigos. Everything's fine. Over and out."

Chapter Twenty-Seven

Kane

As she blindly follows me through the woods again, I'm overcome by a cloud of doubt. I can't deny I've begun to like having the dropout around. That much became clear when I thought she had run off. Instead of feeling glad, another emotion swirled inside me. An unfamiliar emotion. It was similar to how I felt when I thought I'd lost Pup.

I shift the frozen dead woman over my shoulder and duck beneath a low-hanging branch. She's heavy as hell. I don't remember her being this difficult to carry when I killed her. Then again, she wasn't an oddly positioned brick of human waste at that point. She'd been more malleable.

That's another layer to this problematic cake I've baked. I miss killing. It's not exactly a fun family activity, so I would have to give it up if I found a way to keep Aurora.

What the fuck am I thinking? I can't keep her. The Nameless have made that abundantly clear. Even so, I find my mind sifting through ways to get out of this. There has to be a way to cancel the arrangement with The Nameless. She saved Pup, for fuck's sake. I can't repay what she's done by handing her over to them.

But I can't save her.

You don't suddenly *change your mind* with The Nameless, not unless you want to be on the chopping block next. When I set everything in motion, I sealed her fate.

We approach the grave, but I avoid looking at Aurora. Despite all the shit I give her, she has helped me a bit. What have I done to help her? Jax and Tobin have put themselves out there for her. They've given her some form of the love she desperately craves. In a way, I guess we all crave that sort of love. Even me, though I won't admit that to anyone.

Maybe she was right. Actually, she was definitely right. I'm jealous of them and the affection she gives them. I can feel it inside me, like a slow spreading disease.

It's a warmth I can't explain any other way. It was stupid of me to think she wouldn't worm into my heart when she wormed into theirs. We share the same fucking organ.

Unable to cope with my widening range of emotions, I drop the corpse-sicle beside the hole in the ground, and then I do what I do best. I make shit uncomfortable.

"Do me a favor, dropout. Lie in that grave."

She sighs and climbs inside, but she doesn't lie down. Instead, she resumes digging.

"Did I fucking stutter?" I ask. "The hole is plenty deep enough, and you made it more than wide enough, so there's no need to keep digging. Lie. Down."

Call it a trust exercise, but I want to see if she'll obey.

And she does. She sighs, tosses the shovel onto the level ground, and drops to her knees before lying back in the soil.

"Play dead," I say.

"What?"

"Did all that rain clog your ears? I hate repeating myself. Just do as I say."

"Whatever you say, *Daddy* Kane."

When she says my name like that, it does something to me. Something it definitely should *not* fucking do, and not just because it's uncomfortable for me. She doesn't realize she's playing with matches in a tinderbox.

Her eyes fixate and she lets her head loll to the side. Seeing her like that takes the discomfort to another level. I just wanted to fuck with her, but I've ended up torturing myself. I have to do something to stop this boulder from picking up speed and hurtling off a cliff.

I pick up the shovel, gather a clump of muddy soil on the blade, and throw it onto her face. She sputters and sits up. Her hands fly to her face as she tries to dislodge the grit from her mouth and eyes.

"Fucking dick!" she screams, spitting out soil as she sits up on her knees again. She stays that way, filthy and angry, and the sight of her in that position hardens me.

How is she having such an effect on me?

Pain knocks behind my eyes. It's Tobin. It has to be. I don't want to relinquish this time to him, but maybe it's best. It's the only way I can keep her safe.

For now.

Tobin

I rise to the surface and eye the beautiful sight before me. Aurora is bent over, spitting and cursing as she tries to clean dirt from her face. I look at the scene around my feet—a massive grave, a body, a shovel—and put two and two together.

"A little dirty, eighty?"

"Oh god, not you," she says before spitting more dirt from her lips.

I hop into the grave and lean over her. "That's not a very nice welcome. Would you rather I let Kane play with you? His version of play is much less fun and a lot more murdery."

"You guys are fucking assholes."

"I never claimed to be anything else. Now turn around so I can bury your face in the dirt as I fuck you."

Her body tenses as I rip open my belt and unzip my jeans. There's a fire in her eyes, and I almost expect her to argue, but she doesn't. She nibbles her lip, thinking about the prospect of fucking in a grave beside a corpse, then turns around and looks at me over her shoulder as she positions herself on her hands and knees.

That's all the invitation I need. I drop to my knees and lower her leggings. I gather spit beneath my tongue and drip it onto the curve of her ass. A fistful of soil follows, and I spread the wet, gritty dirt along her skin.

"Such a dirty girl, eighty," I groan.

My hands race along her body, dipping beneath her shirt to grab her tits. Her nipples press against my palms, begging to be played with, but I have other plans first. I leave a trail of grit behind as my hand travels toward her hair. After lacing my fingers through the strands, I push her face into the soil. Her hands rake my thighs as I hold her against the ground, but she doesn't fight me.

When I let her up again, she gulps air. "A little warning would be nice," she says.

She doesn't tell me to stop, though. That's my girl.

Dried dirt coats her face, and my balls ache when I think of tears cutting a path through that dark layer. Eighty doesn't cry, though. If I want to make this happen, I'll have to push her body to an extreme to bring it out of her. With enough external stimuli, she'll weep.

I pull my belt from the loops, wrap it around her neck, and draw it tight. Her face reddens. Kane is going to be mad at me for marking up his product, but I want those tears to flow. I pull back my hand and slap her cheek. As her mouth opens and closes wordlessly, tears spill from the corners of her eyes. I keep releasing and tightening the belt until her cheeks are soaked.

"Good girl, eighty. Cry for me. You know how I like it."

I push inside her, and she clenches around me with every strangled breath. I hold the tail of the belt, intermittently choking her as I fuck her senseless. She can't even make a sound as her beautiful face reddens above the ligature. I want to hear her moans and whimpers, so I rip the belt from her neck. Her chest drops to the soil as she catches her breath.

"Dirty, filthy whore," I growl as I thrust deep inside her and hold it, savoring her warmth. I place my fingertips over her clit and rub her. "Such a good girl deserves to come, right?"

She nods as I lean down and bite her shoulder. I swirl my fingers around her and pound against her as I fuck her harder. She takes me so well.

Her hands drop to the soil and her fingers curl into the ground. She's getting close. I feel it. Who comes inside a grave? Both of us, I guess, because her impending orgasm is bringing me closer and closer to my own.

Aurora's body rushes forward as she tries to escape the pressure of my cock. She gushes all over the earth and the front of my pants. What a way to christen a gravesite. This is a new one for me.

I pull back her hips and bury myself deeper again. Her walls pulse around me as she comes down from her orgasm. I pull out of her and spill my come on her filthy, muddy flesh. When I'm finished, I push her forward and lick her clean. Earth and sweat glide across my tongue, mixing into a gritty symphony, but I'm not done yet. I fist her hair and lick her fucking tears, adding a bite of salt to the mixture in my mouth. Then I spread her lips, spit the dirt-coated come into her mouth, and follow up by pushing my muddy fingers to the back of her throat.

I stand and circle her, staring at her face. "You're so dirty. Filthy fucking whore."

My hand winds through her hair. My other hand pushes my jeans down my thighs. She lifts her body as if she's preparing to suck my dick, but that's not what I want her to do. Instead, I keep my hand wrapped up in her hair and turn away from her. I lean over the lip of the grave and spread my legs a bit. With a smirk on my face, I drag her toward my ass and bury her face between my cheeks.

"Eat my ass, eighty. Bury that dirty fucking face and eat me like I ate you."

I expect her to fight me, but she leans in. Her tongue slips from her mouth and grazes my asshole, and my fingers sink into the soil. Pleasure rips through me as she tongue-fucks me. With each movement of her warm mouth, I harden more because she's pleasing me in a way so few have.

God, I love this girl.

I wrap my hand around my aching cock and stroke, bathing in the intensity of the sensations behind me. The sounds, the feeling—it's all fucking euphoric. She's sloppy about it too, and that makes me want to fill her filthy mouth. I let her lick me until I'm close, then I rip her away from me and pivot toward her.

"Open your mouth," I command.

She spreads her lips, and I stroke the head of my cock against the tongue that worked me up to this moment. I fill her mouth, grip her hair, lean her back, and spit on her waiting tongue.

"Swallow." I watch her throat as she swallows all of what I've given her. "I love what you do to me, eighty."

She sits back on her ass, eyes wide as she stares up at me. She knows that's as close as I'll come to saying I love her, but the meaning is the same. Somehow, some way, Jax and I have to save her.

Chapter Twenty-Eight

Kane

I'm back behind the wheel of the truck. We've reached Arkansas, which means Tobin or Jax have been with her for a while. I can only assume they eventually dumped the body in the grave. There's no way I'll ask her about it. Not when she looks so satisfied. Like a cat with a saucer of milk, she just sits there with a smile on her face as she stares out the window. Her hand drags lazy strokes through Pup's fur.

Tobin. Jax. Pup. They all adore her. How will they feel about me after I sell her?

I shift in my seat and tighten my grip on the wheel. There's something genuinely wrong with me and I'm surprised I can even recognize the doubtful feelings inside. I just know that it's nagging me to the point of discomfort.

She looks over at me, and the smile drops from her face.

"Hey, Kane," she says.

A feeling stirs inside me, deep within the crater that once housed a heart. She recognizes each of us. She doesn't think we're crazy for having three minds in one body. Instead of being a judgmental asshole, she acknowledges our differences and our situation. Instead of calling us names or accusing us of fabricating what we can't even control, she accepts us as we are.

Well, she accepts Jax and Tobin. She still doesn't care for the things that make me who I am. Or the lack of the things I could never be.

A sign for a truck stop looms in the distance. My bladder could use a little relief, so I turn in. As I pull the truck to a stop, I eye the girl. She must have used a rag to wipe the dirt from her face, but her nails are still filthy. She'd probably appreciate a shower.

"I'm gonna stop here for a piss break and some food. Can I trust you to shower without running off?" I ask.

"I would love to shower, but how the fuck am I supposed to pay for it? You stashed my wallet, along with the rest of my shit."

I ease my wallet from my back pocket and pull out a twenty. Her eyes light up as she reaches for it, but I pull it away before her fingertips can so much as graze the paper.

"Not so fast," I say. "If you try anything, if you so much as *think* of—"

"You'll break my neck or put me in the freezer or both. Got it." She leans forward and takes the money without batting an eye at my implied threat. "Besides, you don't have to worry about me running off anymore. You might be more intolerable than a Kathy Griffin marathon, but I actually like hanging out with Jax and Tobin."

With a smug smirk, she opens the door and exits the truck, leaving me with another mess of confused feelings. Knowing she prefers them to me is beginning to sting.

I stand and stretch my legs before walking to the back of the truck. A magazine rests on the bed, which is odd. It's a vintage *Playboy*—one of Tobin's prized possessions. I sure as fuck don't have any use for it, and I doubt Jax would know what to do with it. He'd probably whine about it being so degrading to the women.

Picking it up, I look at the woman on the cover. She's attractive, but she's also heavily photoshopped, and her tits are lopsided. I laugh and shake my head. Only I would notice the asymmetry instead of getting a boner.

As I go to return the magazine to Tobin's cupboard of pornographic wonderment, a slip of paper falls from inside. I bend down and pick it up.

KANE,

IF YOU HURT ONE HAIR ON THAT GIRL'S HEAD, YOU'LL DESTROY ALL OF US, INCLUDING YOURSELF. CALL OFF THE DEAL AND SAVE HER. IF WE CAN'T KEEP HER, TAKE HER HOME.

—TOBIN

I crumple the note and shove it into my pocket. Against everything I am, I want to save her too. I just have to find a way to satisfy The Nameless. If I can find another girl as beautiful and clean as she is, that might be the answer to all of my problems, but the odds aren't in my favor. They're expecting a girl in the next twenty-four hours. It would take time to source another one.

It's not like I can pull just any girl off the street. I have to play by the same rules I use when choosing a victim. No family. Unwanted. Someone who won't be missed. I walk to the front of the vehicle and look at the parking area for the trucks. One lonely lot lizard crawls across the heated pavement, but she's too used up to serve my purpose.

I've never felt so conflicted in my life.

"Stay put," I say to Pup as I exit the truck. After I get this pressure off my bladder, I might be able to think more clearly.

A blast of cold air and gospel music rushes toward me as I enter through the truck stop's glass doors. A teenage boy sits behind the singular register. He's too busy scrolling on his cell phone to look up and acknowledge me. I walk past him and head for the restroom to the nauseating country rendition of "Amazing Grace."

After relieving myself and buying a few bags of chips and a couple of sodas, I head back to the truck. I'll wait for the dropout before I head into the diner. She's probably famished. Digging a grave is hungry work, and if anyone would know that, it's me.

If I hadn't taken her, I'd be as happy and murdery as always. Now I'm miserable because she's upended everything. Jax and Tobin may have benefited, but I sure as shit haven't, and getting some kind of drive to be around her only hurts me because she'd rather be around anyone else. Women have caused enough hurt in my life, and I'm not exactly eager to experience more of it.

I open the driver's side door and climb inside. Pup is busy pacing back and forth, a low whine shivering out of her with every few steps she takes on her three tiny paws. She does this if I'm gone for too long, but she usually stops once I'm back in the truck. This time, she just keeps pacing and whining.

I pat my leg, and Pup hops into my lap. "No need to worry. She'll be back," I say as I stroke her head. Do I say this to reassure the dog . . . or myself?

I'm not sure.

If I were her, I'd have taken this golden ticket and hopped on the first train to pull into the station. I just made her bury a body, for fuck's sake. And that was *after* locking her in the freezer and treating her like absolute dog shit for days on end. I really didn't think this through.

I look at the time on the dash clock. She's been gone for almost twenty minutes now. That's more than enough time to shower and throw on some clothes. I'm about to head inside and beat down a shower door when my phone buzzes in my pocket. I pull it out, and my chest immediately tightens. It's a text from The Nameless.

> Did you find the girl?

> No, not yet.

The lie rolls so easily from my fingertips. Too easily. These men hold too much power for me to deceive them like this.

> Are you sure about that, Three Amigos?

My mouth goes dry. I've never told them my CB handle. I thought it was a little odd that someone radioed yesterday while we were preparing to bury that body, but I chalked it up to a trucker being nosy about why a reefer unit was turning off at a heavily forested area. Now?

Now I think I need to get the fuck out of here.

I'm about to get out of my truck to find Aurora when my phone vibrates again. Instead of a text message, it's a picture that sends ice barreling through my veins. The image is a bit blurry, but I can make out the duct tape wrapped around the girl's head and the zip ties binding her wrists together in the leather-clad backseat of a sedan.

The Nameless have Aurora.

Chapter Twenty-Nine

Aurora

I never even made it into the truck stop. Just as I reached the door, a man approached me, stuck a gun into my side, and guided me toward a dark car. After taping my head and securing my wrists, we pulled out of the parking lot. The last I saw of Kane, he was exiting his truck. I only hope he'll realize I've gone missing and that I didn't leave of my own free will.

The sun set hours ago, but the car continues down the interstate on a nightmare trip that seems never ending. We crossed into Texas a while back, putting more distance between me and any hope of rescue. I've loosened the duct tape around my mouth by licking the adhesive. I can't do shit about the zip ties biting into my wrists.

Using my tongue and chin, I lower the duct tape and clear my throat. "Can someone please tell me why I'm being kidnapped . . . again?"

The man in the passenger seat turns to face me. "We are simply taking possession of what belongs to us."

A hint of an accent colors each word in a diluted hue of Russian, but that isn't what my brain latches onto. "What belongs to you? I don't belong to anyone."

I expect a retort, a snide comment or an angry brush off, but he simply laughs and faces the front again. I pull back my leg and kick his seat.

That gets his attention.

He turns to face me again, and the anger in his eyes does more to satisfy than scare me. "You little bitch. If you know what's good for you, you'll remember that your legs are meant for spreading, not kicking."

I've never been one to know what's good for me, so I kick his seat again. "Tell me what the fuck is going on!"

He says something in Russian, and the driver pulls the car to the side of the road. Something silver glints in his hand, and then the barrel of a gun levels on my head. "You will shut the fuck up or I will shut you up. Someone paid a very high price for what you have between your legs, and I would hate to lose that money because I had to kill you. If you have a complaint, take it up with Kane. He made the deal." He laughs again as he faces the front. "Not that you will ever see him again."

I do shut up, but not because of the gun in his hand or the threat he made. Not even because he said I'll never see Kane again. I shut up because I can't breathe.

Kane . . . sold me?

He isn't exactly a candidate for an upstanding citizen award, but I never imagined he would do something so horrible. Choke me half to death and stick me in a freezer? Sure. Force me to dig a grave for a woman he murdered? Understandable. But this? It's more than I can take.

I stare out the window as the sedan lurches onto the road again. Trying to catch the attention of passing cars isn't an option. The windows are tinted to hell and back. For the first time in my life, I don't see a way out. I've always been good at running, but now there's nowhere to run. Kane sold me to these men, and they've turned around and sold me to someone else.

"How much?" I ask.

The man turns toward me and raises an eyebrow.

"How much did you pay him?" I clarify.

"For you?" A hellish smile eases onto his face. "He sold you for a partial repayment of his debt to us. The amount is not important."

A sign slides by on the side of the road, and I realize we're nearing Houston. My brain flicks back to the inspection when Jax took control. Didn't he say they had to pick up a load in Texas? Does that mean all three of them were in on this?

My stomach sinks, and if it drops any lower, it will probably fall out of my asshole. If they were all privy to this plan, that means I was used by all of them. *Deceived* by all of them. The men I've been falling for have planned to get rid of me all along, and my heart and vagina were too blinded by need to see it.

I close my eyes and rest my head against the leather. The car turns onto a side road, but I don't look to see where we are or where we're going. What's the point? I have no control. I can't change the ever downward-trending trajectory of my life.

After a few more turns and bumping along a road that's more pothole than asphalt, we pull up at a large house in a small neighborhood. Or what might have been a neighborhood at one time. Now there is only one house on the street. The others have been reduced to weed-ridden foundations.

The men exit the car and come to my door. As they haul me away from the leather interior, I'm surprised by how gentle they are. Their fingers don't dig into my arms. They don't push or hit me. Like guiding a dumbfounded sheep to the slaughter pen, they just move me along with the threat of a gun.

Once we're inside the house, they remove the duct tape from my head and the zip ties from my wrists before looking me over like two pickers examining a grandfather clock at an antique mall. They study my flaws, pointing at the red marks on my wrists and the bruises on my throat as they mutter to each other in a language I can't understand. Then, in clear English, the shorter one tells me to strip.

"Absolutely not," I say, crossing my arms over my chest.

He pulls out the silver pistol and waves a reminder at my head.

I don't move. Maybe it wouldn't be so bad to die. A few moments of pain, and then it will all be over. But the slimmest hope of escaping this mess won't allow me to give up. Damn my drive to survive.

Gripping the hem of my shirt, I close my eyes. I've taken off my clothes for countless men, but something about this situation makes me feel almost shy. Almost dirty. The choice and control have been taken from me, much as it was when I was in my dorm room. Tears gather behind my clenched lids, but I won't let them fall. Tobin will be the last man to have seen me cry.

"Hurry up. We don't want a striptease," the taller man says. "We're simply inspecting the merchandise."

Both men laugh, and the sound makes my skin crawl. I strip off the rest of my clothes so they can walk around and examine me. And they do. They raise my arms, lift my breasts, and spend far too long discussing my ass. When they've finished, they motion for me to dress again. I can't put my clothes on fast enough.

I'm led to a door in the kitchen and ushered down a narrow flight of stairs that drops into darkness. The door closes behind me, followed by the sound of a heavy chain locking me inside. A light clicks on above me seconds later.

I glance around the concrete-lined space. A stained mattress lies on the floor, and they haven't even bothered to offer any sheets. I hope they aren't expecting a five-star Yelp review from me.

I don't let my gaze linger on the stains, choosing instead to focus on the narrow table against another wall. A sandwich wrapped in plastic film sits on top of it. I remove the plastic, fully expecting to find two slices of bread and a piece of cheese, but I'm partially wrong. They've included a glob of mayo and a few slices of what smells like salami. A plastic cup with lukewarm water stands beside it.

If they think I'm eating this shit, they're delusional. I suppose I'm a little delusional as well, because I can only think of how much I miss the gas station food Kane keeps hidden around his truck.

I can only think of how much I miss *them*.

After tossing the sandwich onto the table, I sit on the floor and pull my knees to my chest. No one is here to see me cry, so I let the tears fall. How did I ever think I could get through to Kane? I was starting to see something in him that wasn't even there. Jax and Tobin fooled me first, though. Being in a relationship with three men is all fun and games until all of them betray you and break your heart.

I will never forgive them for what they've done.

Chapter Thirty

Kane

It's well after midnight as I pull my truck into a parking spot at a truck stop just outside of Houston. Pup sits on the seat beside me and whines. She hasn't let up since Arkansas, and the constant sound only adds to my headache.

"What do you want from me? She's gone," I say as I stroke her fur and try to settle her.

What do any of them want from me? We couldn't keep her. She has *never* been something we could keep. Tobin and Jax knew that from the beginning. We've always had two options, and those were killing her or selling her to The Nameless. The choice was made for me, and now we just have to accept it. That's why I'm heading straight to pick up the load in Houston. I have to let things return to normal.

Well, I want them to return to *my* version of normal, and I can start by checking out my prospects in the parking lot.

Nothing cheers me up more than taking a life, so I eye the women floating between the trucks like bugs drawn to light. Ugly bugs, with pock-marked skin from drug-induced flesh picking and eyes as dull as their greasy, unkempt hair. A blonde looks over and smiles at me. The three or four teeth still clinging to her red gums have more tenacity than the tank man of Tiananmen Square.

I stand and go to the back of the cab before she has a chance to come any closer. I'm drawn to the cabinet where I hid Aurora's backpack. After pulling it from its hiding place, I sit on the bed. I remember going through it and finding her old college ID. Her auburn hair was pulled into a high ponytail, and she had such a sweet, genuine smile on her face (which also included a full set of healthy teeth).

That smile is probably very gone now.

I remember her telling me about why she quit school. I may not have seemed like I was listening, but every word came through in painful clarity. She didn't deserve what happened to her then, and she doesn't deserve what's happening to her now.

Despite my half-assed attempts to lie to myself, the truth won't be denied. I didn't drive through the night to reach Houston because of the product I need to pick up. I came to save the girl.

I drop the backpack on the bed, rush to the driver's seat, and start my truck. After spending my entire life only thinking about myself, I'm thinking of someone else now. Pup must sense my heroic shift, because she stops whining and finally settles on the seat.

Even if I die in the process—which is highly likely—I can't let any more harm come to Aurora. Maybe I can talk to them. Maybe I can negotiate a higher interest rate in exchange for her life. Then I scoff because there's no way they'll talk to me about her. When I head into their territory, we're all as good as dead.

I put my truck in drive and head toward the one place I never wanted to go back to: my old neighborhood.

The Nameless have a warehouse, but I doubt they've taken her there. They like to keep the product at their house on my old street. The soundproof basement is the perfect holding pen.

I shudder when I think of Aurora down there.

When I've gone as far as I can go in the truck, I pull into an overnight parking lot and grab my pistols from the lockbox. I stuff one down the back of my pants and cover it with my jacket and latch the other around my ankle. The cuff of my jeans conceals it. Strapped and ready to go, I give Pup what is likely a final scratch behind the ears and tell her to guard the truck.

The little dog looks up at me expectantly. She doesn't realize this may be the last time she ever sees me.

I exit the truck and head toward the neighborhood I grew to hate. There were only three houses on the long, quiet road. No one heard me screaming as a child. Or if they did, they just didn't care. The Nameless lived on the end. I'm really hoping our longstanding acquaintance leverages things in my favor, even though I hardly know anything about them now.

After several blocks, I'm standing at the start of the street that haunts my nightmares. I try to avoid looking at my childhood home, but my gaze pulls toward it. It's just a slab of concrete now, which is probably for the best. I can only recall brief glimpses of the last time I was in that house.

I only know that I murdered my stepmother in a fit of blind rage.

I'd stopped by to see my father, but she had answered the door. She tried to hug me, and I ended up choking the life from her body. Why? I don't know, and I don't want to know.

I lit the house on fire on the way out. Incredibly, I was never caught, but I ended up in prison a few years later after I got drunk and tried to grab some bitch outside of a bar. I never even got her back to my truck. If I had, I would've gotten away with it. I learned my lesson then. Stay away from booze and always get them in the truck first.

I continue toward the house at the end of the street without giving the crumbling foundation a second glance. The corpses of those secrets deserve to stay buried.

I creep to the edge of a window on the side of the house and peer inside. The bedroom is empty, but the open door gives me a straight view into the hallway. Ivan, one of the brothers, stands in the doorway. I see no need to keep them nameless any longer. They've lost their hold on me.

Grass rustles against my boots as I make my way into the backyard. Peering into another window, I see one of the brothers seated at the kitchen table. I can't make out which one, but it doesn't matter. They'll all be dead by dawn.

I'd like to avoid using the pistols if I can. Even though this is the only house left on this street, there are other nearby streets that are likely still very much inhabited, and nothing makes a noise quite like a gunshot. Though I imagine if Victor has been operating here for the last decade or more, there has already been a gunshot or two.

I don't love killing with a pistol, though, and that's another reason I'd rather use my knife. Guns are so impersonal. I'd much rather kill up close and feel their life force leave them. There's something almost serene when someone dies in front of you, and it's even more intoxicating when they die *because* of you.

I haven't changed my stance on murdering women, despite my current situation. Hell, I even still view the girl as killable. But something about her also makes me want to snatch her back and keep her for myself. Well, myself and Jax and Tobin. I swear they're driving my decision to rescue her because this is highly unlike me.

Weighing things out in my head only confuses me further. I could walk away right now and find a girl I could actually kill, or I could rescue one I can't ever kill. The scale leans toward the former, yet here I am.

Jax knocks against my skull as I stand behind the back door. I can't let him out. Not now. He'll only get himself killed by trying to talk his way out of this situation, and that's why I need to stay in control. I can do what needs to be done.

Ivan enters the kitchen, and I duck below the windowsill so he can't see me as I strain to hear their conversation.

"Sacha, where's Vic?" he asks.

"Down in the basement with the girl. You should probably get down there before he does something stupid."

"Or I could go down there and help him do something stupid," Ivan answers, and both men burst into a fit of booming laughter.

"Yeah, go down. I'll join you two shortly."

Ivan's footsteps fade away, and I dare to peek through the window again. I need to make a move soon, before they have a chance to hurt her.

Sacha stands and moves toward the fridge. He opens it and begins digging around. This is my opportunity to eliminate one of them, so I ease the back door open and step inside. He must hear me behind him, because his body tenses and he stands upright.

Before he has a chance to call for his brothers, I wrap my hand around his mouth and drag my knife across his throat. The blade pierces his flesh and the blood pours. The metallic scent sends me into a frenzy. It's like a high I can't explain. I hold the man against my chest until he stops flailing. Then I drop him beside the island, grab the beer bottle he pulled from the fridge, and pop it open. I pour it into my mouth, careful not to let my lips touch the rim.

One down, three to go.

It's hard for me to stay controlled now, with the scent of blood following me through the kitchen. The stuff is potent. I set the beer on the counter and make my way to the basement door.

Pulling the gun from my waistband, I open the door and start down the stairs. Each step sends a loud creak into the air.

"Hurry down, Sacha," Victor calls. "The fun is just beginning."

As I reach the bottom of the stairs, the men don't turn to face me. They expect their brother to join them, but they're in for a big surprise. Aurora sits on Ivan's lap. He's stroking her hair, and she keeps batting his hand away with an annoyance I've grown to like.

Maybe I'm doing this because I actually respect that girl. She's been so stoic and unbreakable since I've taken her, and that has to come from a place of immense inner strength. Breaking her became a challenge for me, but she never stopped being a snarky bitch, even in the face of death. And she hasn't changed. In an unknown place, with unknown men, she's still being bitchy. That takes a certain kind of bravery—or stupidity.

"Who's going to test her out first?" Victor asks. His back faces me, but each word reaches me as if I'm standing right beside him.

My blood begins to boil in my veins. A strong sense of possession overcomes me, but I can't tell if this feeling is mine. Even if it's from Tobin or Jax, I still feel the raging fire in my body.

Right now, none of that matters. Regardless of whose emotions I feel, Ivan's hands on her body are making me absolutely homicidal.

I fight the toxic thoughts swirling in my mind about her—a misdirected barrage of repressed trauma. I silence the voice that says she deserves to be in this place because of who she was before I took her. I rein in the thoughts that encourage me to walk out now, and I take a step forward.

As my broad frame comes into the light, Victor turns to face me. I revel in the shock coloring his pale face. "Kane, what the hell are you doing?" he asks.

"I made a mistake," I say, "and I've come to fix it."

Ivan makes a move for a gun sitting on a nearby shelf, but I raise my pistol and aim at him before he gets more than a few steps. He freezes. My truth is written on my face. If they move a fucking muscle, I'll shoot.

"Hey, dropout. Be a peach and restrain Victor." I nod toward a roll of duct tape on a wooden table.

"Fuck you, Kane," she says.

My eyes widen. "Would you rather hang out with them? Because I could leave."

She scoffs and climbs off Ivan's lap. He tries to hang on to her, probably to use her as a human shield, but she thrashes her heel against his shin until he lets go. She grabs the tape from the table and heads toward Victor, who sneers at her before putting his hands behind his back. With a wide grin, she begins winding the tape around his wrists.

"You're dead, Kane," Ivan says from the chair.

"Tape Ivan too," I say to Aurora, gesturing toward the man with my chin. "And cover his mouth."

When Victor's hands are secured, I step closer to him. He has to look up at me because he's considerably shorter.

"How did you find me?" I whisper.

"Do you think we would be stupid enough to allow you to drive into the sunset with something we purchased before it was paid off? I installed a tracker beneath the driver's step."

I nod and step away from him.

Once she's finished one hell of a tape job, I walk over to Ivan, pocket my pistol, and draw my knife. Gripping his dark hair, I crane his neck and ignore his muffled pleas as I sink the blade into his throat. I begin twisting the handle, and I don't stop until a spray of blood jets across all of us.

"No!" Victor screams. "We've always been good to you, you fucking bastard!"

Unfortunately, that's true, and I'm destroying our little arrangement to save the girl. The one who's looking at me with complete hatred.

I walk up to Victor, a smile on my face because I'm fully intoxicated by all the blood at this point. I tighten my grip on my knife and, with a quick motion, I jab it in the soft space beneath his chin. Blood fills his mouth, and judging by the way he struggles to speak, I can only assume I pushed hard enough to spear his tongue as well. He drops to the floor and begins writhing around.

I thought I had eliminated the risk until a solid punch wrecks my jaw. I shake my head and turn toward Aurora. She's clutching her fist because she really used all her effort to hit me. I push her against the wall.

"Don't ever fucking hit me, dropout."

"I have the right to be mad. You fucking sold me! You asshole!"

"I got you back, didn't I?"

"Fuck you!" she screams.

"We'll talk about this later. Right now, I need to finish this."

I step closer to Victor, jab the knife into his neck, then use my boot to put pressure on the handle until the blade's tip hits the concrete floor. Blood pours from his mouth, and the jerking turns to twitching before he finally stills.

I turn to Aurora and hold out my hand. "Let's get out of here."

She sets her jaw and balls her hands into tight fists at her sides. "I'm not going anywhere with you."

Chapter Thirty-One

Aurora

My chest rises and falls with a blast of panicked anger. A ribbon of blood stands stark across my chest, but it's nothing compared to the river of red washing over Kane. He's covered in the stuff. He takes a step toward me and reaches for my hand, but I pull away. The look of hurt on his face almost makes me want to comfort him, but then I remember what he's done to me.

"Why, Kane?" That's all I can manage to say.

He runs his hand through his hair and shakes his head. "I'll explain everything, but we can't hang around a fucking crime scene. We need to get out of here."

"I'm not going anywhere until you give me a good reason for fucking *selling me!*"

He grabs his knife from Victor's throat and tucks it into his waistband. Then he comes toward me. Before I know what's happening, he's hoisted me over his shoulder and started up the stairs. I pound against his back, but it's like hitting a brick wall. I'm the only one getting hurt. I stop pounding and go limp as we pass another dead body and exit the house through the kitchen.

Once we're outside, he sets me on my feet. "We're covered in blood. We can't wash up here, so we'll have to be careful as we move back to the truck. If anyone sees us—"

"Us? We? What part of what I said didn't make it through your thick skull? Our fun little road trip ended as soon as you decided to sell me to the highest fucking bidder!"

He rushes toward me, turns me around, and pulls me against his chest with his hand over my mouth. "Keep your fucking voice down. I promise I'll take you back to your home in New York, but I want you to hear me out first. Your other option is to beg for a ride somewhere else, and I can guarantee no one is going to help you when you've got someone's blood all over you."

He makes a good point.

I relax in his arms, and he releases me. We spend the next thirty minutes cutting a path through overgrown backyards attached to what appear to be abandoned houses. He chooses our route carefully, analyzing the way forward before taking a step in any direction. We're both winded by the time we reach the truck. He bends near the step beside the driver's side door, fishes around beneath the metal, and pulls a small black box from underneath. He tosses it into the bushes and opens the door. The sun begins to rise as we climb inside.

Kane tosses a rag to me, and we begin cleaning the blood from our skin as Pup scampers around our feet. I don't reach down to pat her until I'm all clean and dressed in a change of clothes.

I sit on the bed and wait for the explanation I'm owed. It doesn't matter in the long run, I guess. I've made up my mind, and I want nothing more to do with any of them. But curiosity gets the better of me, and I want to hear what he has to say, even if it won't change anything.

When he's all clean, he comes and sits beside me on the bed. "I won't deny that I sold you. That part is true. But I tried to call off the deal."

"You didn't try very hard."

"Why do you think they had to come and kidnap you?"

I don't have a good answer for that.

"Exactly. I told them I no longer had the package—you—but they wouldn't listen. They were tracking me."

I turn to face him now. "Did Jax and Tobin know?"

He nods. "They knew, but they couldn't stop it. They have a duty to protect me, and that meant they couldn't do anything that would potentially get me killed. They have autonomy and can make their own choices, but it only goes so far."

"So why did you come for me?" I ask the question even though I'm afraid of the answer.

"For Jax and Tobin."

"Not for yourself?"

He stands and begins pacing. "I don't know, dropout. I'm not exactly fond of you."

For the first time, I see just how difficult it is for this man to discuss his feelings. It's not a matter of want. It's an impossibility.

Kane stops pacing and begins rubbing his eyes. I've seen him do this before when Tobin or Jax try to come through. They're trying to protect him. From what? Feelings?

Despite everything he's done, I can't stop my heart from aching at the sight of his struggle. And even though I want to continue being mad at him—at all of them —I can't. He said he tried to stop the deal, and I believe him. He came after me. He saved me. Now I need to help him.

"Kane, come sit down," I say. "We don't have to talk about anything else if you don't want to. I . . . believe you." Fuck, that was hard to admit, but I have to do what's best for him right now.

"No, you don't understand," he mumbles. "And no matter how much I want to make you understand, I can't, because I don't even understand. I live with so much anger inside me, and I don't even know why. I only know that I don't want to know more. Do you know what that's like? Do you have any idea?"

I shake my head because no, I don't understand. I can't. But I want to.

On shaking legs, I stand and go to him. It's a risky move. He'll probably turn around and beat me to death with his fists, but I have to try. I have to connect with him, and nothing is more powerful than touch. People connect on so many levels, but touch is universal.

It's also the one thing that sends Kane over the edge.

Swallowing my fear, I step closer and wrap my arms around him. My cheek presses against his warm back, and I just hold him. I shove the lingering animosity into my gut, and I close my eyes as I mentally beg him to accept me.

His body relaxes in my arms, and his hand closes over mine. As his breathing begins to slow, I think I've finally gotten through to him. Then he turns and clamps his hand around my throat.

Chapter Thirty-Two

Kane

My panic stems from never having the clear picture of what makes my body respond like this. I feel and see bits and pieces of something I never truly understand, and it causes a rage to grow until it overflows. That's why my hand is around her throat. That's why I'm squeezing.

A blinding pain pierces my head, and for the first time, memories rush to me. Crystal clear. Painfully clear. In an attempt to stop me from strangling Aurora, Tobin opened the box and let my demons loose, and I can see everything my step-mother and her sister did to me.

The touching.

The *fucking*.

The outright abuse of a goddamn child.

I release her and drop to my knees. I'm trapped in my trauma, gasping for air as I'm shoved into some dark place I never wanted to be. I see and feel the abuse as if it's happening right now. Warm hands wrap around me, and I'm too frozen in place to stop them. People who were supposed to care for me. People who were supposed to protect me. They did neither.

Aurora drops to her knees beside me, and her voice penetrates the memories. "Kane, I'm here. I'm here with you and you're going to be okay."

Her voice lacks its usual snark with an edge of mega bitch, and I allow myself to feel the comfort in her words. Her arms wrap around me, and she holds me until the visions recede into my mind and my breathing steadies.

She pulls my head against her chest. After everything I've done to her, after all the hell and torment I've put her through, she's by my side, offering her strength to me. "Not every touch is a bad touch anymore, Kane. You're past that. You're safe now."

You're. Safe. Now.

I latch onto those words as they repeat in my mind. I haven't felt safe in a long time. I've been a victim of my trauma all my life, including this very moment.

Tobin showed me these things to stop me from hurting Aurora. He's supposed to protect *me*, not *her*. But maybe, in some fucked up way, he's protecting me too. Losing Aurora would hurt more than I care to admit. He also recognizes more than I give him credit for. He's forcing me to confront my memories with someone who is willing to comfort me and help me deal with the fallout. I've never accepted comfort. Not once. But her warmth soothes me in ways I never knew were possible.

My vision becomes my own again, and I see her messy auburn hair and bright eyes full of concern. If I were her, I would have taken this freakout as yet another opportunity to run. But here she is, sitting in front of me as she tries to talk me off a ledge.

"Told you I could break through to you," she says with a smirk and a light laugh.

Jesus, this girl doesn't quit trying to irritate me. But a strained laugh comes from my chest. A chest that is still caught in a stranglehold of emotions.

Aurora leans closer, and my body tenses. She brings her hand up to my neck and draws my face toward hers. So much of what's inside me wants to push her away, to hurt her for wanting to get close to me, but some new feeling urges me to let this happen.

Her lips are so near mine now, and as her eyes close and her lips form a perfect pout, I pray to the devil that my body knows what to do with her. Then she closes that last half inch, and her warm lips are on me.

My brain is silenced the moment her lips touch mine. The memories and terror recede to their box as I focus on her scent and how she tastes. She smells like sweat and fear, a scent I usually kill for, but that homicidal rage is nowhere inside me now. Or if it is, it's buried beneath a concrete slab of need. I spread my lips and for the first time in my life, I kiss the girl.

I push her down on her back and kiss her again. She whimpers as she tugs down her pants and throws them to the side. I can only hope she remembers that I'm not Jax or Tobin. I'm surprised I'm even still hard as her hands reach for the front of my jeans and work them down. She pulls out my cock, her warm touch making me groan. I thrust my hips forward into her hand, just wanting to feel more of her. The motion feels so immature, but these feelings, these actions, are so new to me.

I sit up on my knees and spread her legs. The pussy I hated to look at looks different when I have the chance to slip inside it. It's not just something Tobin and Jax get to play with now. At this moment, it's mine.

I draw back my hips. My cock slides along the length of her slit before I thrust forward and push inside her. It's fucking heaven. She's so warm and wet. I can see why Jax and Tobin are so obsessed with her. Something so incredible should be illegal.

Considering my inexperience, I expect to move slowly and be gentle, but my body drives me to fuck her harder. I push deeper, and the soft moan that leaves her lips lets me know this is what she needs too.

"Call me daddy, dropout. Tell me how you like my cock."

"I love your cock, daddy," she pants. This time it's not snarky like at the diner or in the grave. She's saying it with pleasure woven into the word. Pleasure she's getting from me, a man who's been incapable of offering anything but pain.

With a timid hand, I raise her shirt and look at her breasts. As lust rushes over me in a wave, I'm amazed to find no anger in these waters. Only desire. My hands move toward her nipples, and I pinch and twist as she writhes beneath me.

She feels so amazing, and I want to experience her from every angle. Like a man in a desert, I want to drown myself in the oasis that is uniquely hers. I flip her onto her hands and knees, then slip inside her again with an unstifled groan. She feels even better from behind.

My hands race over her ass, squeezing the flesh as it bounces against me. I pound her pussy, my hips ricocheting off her full ass, and she whimpers from the unbridled ferocity unleashed with every thrust. Decades of pent-up frustration push inside her as I grip her hips to keep her from sliding away from me.

My tattoo rushes in and out of her as I fuck her. Keeping her nestled against me as I rail her, I bottom out inside her and force that fraction of length further until she screams. It isn't a plea for me to stop. No. She wants me to keep going.

"Come inside me, daddy!" she screams, and I love every word that leaves her lips. I love that she senses me getting close before I even notice it. A subtle change in my thrusts, I guess.

My hips stall and stutter against her ass as I fill her. I release a feral groan I don't recognize as I unleash myself inside her. It's like nothing I've ever felt.

I drop beside her and roll onto my back. Once our breathing steadies, I turn to her and look at someone I have come to care so deeply for. "It's time to get you home, dropout," I say. "Like the good little whore you are, I want you to keep my come between your legs. Can you do that?"

She leans over and kisses my forehead. "Anything for you, daddy."

I understand why Jax and Tobin want to keep her. She connected with them on multiple levels, and now she's connected with me.

And now I have to let her go.

Chapter Thirty-Three

Aurora

I bury my face in Pup's coat as I hold her. She jumped into my arms the moment we settled in the front of the truck. How she knew I'd been a day away from never being seen or heard from again is beyond me. I breathe in her scent—the outdoors with a hint of diesel.

I still don't like that Kane initially planned to sell me to those assholes, but I kind of love him for saving me and I'm thankful to be back in the truck. These are two things I never thought I'd say.

My mind still reels when I think of all that's happened in the last few hours. I got through to him. And he fucked me. He has sex like a convoluted mix of Tobin and Jax. Part rough, raw need and part passion and unquenched desire.

Kane turns onto another on-ramp, and we're heading northeast again. He's really taking me home. I have mixed feelings about this turn of events. Going home means confronting my parents with the truth, and I don't know how they'll react. Can they accept that I dropped out of college and have no desire to return? Probably not. Even if I explain the circumstances that led me to this decision, they'll turn it around on me.

But I can't stay with Kane.

I've broken through to him, but he and I both know this isn't a safe situation. He's shed some of those walls for me, but what waits behind the rest of the dilapidated exterior is what I need to fear. He's still a serial killer. A deranged man. A psychopath.

This is the textbook definition of being stuck between a rock and a hard place, but I guess the decision is out of my hands. If Kane wants to take me home, I just need to accept that this is probably his way of ensuring my safety, even though it will break my heart.

I shift in my seat. I'm sick of the silence because it only forces me to overthink, so I clear my throat. "Am I the first person you've been with since . . . ?"

"Yes. You broke through to the big, bad serial killer. Can we let it go now? I think I'm all talked out."

I smirk at him, remove Pup from my lap, and unbuckle my seatbelt. If he doesn't want to talk, that's okay by me, but I need to do something to keep my mind from spinning in circles. I drop to my knees beside him as my hand goes for his lap. His body tenses, and my breath hitches as I prepare for him to lose his shit.

"What are you doing?" he says with a tight jaw.

"I want to blow down the last of the walls surrounding the big, bad wolf," I say with a laugh. "Might as well say a proper goodbye. This is a safe space, remember?"

His muscles relax, and he licks his lips. "Get to it then, dropout."

I unbuckle and unzip his jeans. He tilts his pelvis to give me more access as I pull his cock from the fabric. I stare at the tattoo along the length of his dick and run my fingers over the flesh-warmed piercing. It's so familiar yet foreign. I've been with all three of them now, and each experience has been so different.

He *is* different.

I put my mouth on him, and he groans, the low tenor traveling to the growing heat between my legs. The metal grazes my tongue as his hand weaves through my hair, massaging my scalp before he grips the strands and impales my throat. The sheer force brings my nose against his skin. I gag, and tears well in the corners of my eyes.

This would be the point when Tobin revels in my tears or Jax apologizes for being too rough, but Kane does neither. He just tightens his grip on my head and continues using my face like an inanimate object, and fuck if that doesn't turn me on.

"You're too young and pretty to be choking on daddy's cock," he says, balling my hair in his big hand.

Control and power drip from his words. They bleed into me from the force behind his grasp as he selfishly uses my throat. He goes harder and faster, using my hair as a lead as he drives. There's no inhibition as he bucks his hips and fucks my mouth almost to the point where I need to tap out. But I'm not a quitter anymore. Tears flow down my cheeks as I fight back gags and take him the way he wants. The way he clearly needs.

"Once I come down your throat, I'm bringing you home, dropout. You'll be the only woman to leave me alive." He pulls me off his dick. "Do you understand how difficult this is for me?"

"Yes, daddy," I whimper as he cranes my neck. I wipe the drool from my chin.

He impales me on his cock again and fucks my mouth until warm, salty come explodes down my throat. With a gravelly groan, he thrusts his hips upward and makes me take every single centimeter before he pulls out of my mouth. I swallow every drop of him.

I sit in my seat again and look out the window. Questions begin filling my mind almost immediately. Why is this difficult for him? Is it because he's grown attached to me? Or does he simply regret leaving me alive? Maybe if I knew the answers, it would change my mind. Maybe I wouldn't want to go home if he gave me a reason to stay or showed me some sign of his feelings.

But he won't. This isn't his way, and I have to accept that. Loving these three men will have to be done from a distance, and for the safety of my body and mind, I need to go home. I may be the prey who wormed her way into his blackened heart, but he's still a predator.

Chapter Thirty-Four

Jax

The truck is parked at a rest area when I shift into control. I guess Kane needed a break. I turn and look at the closed curtain separating the sleeping area from the rest of the truck. She must be asleep back there. At least, I *hope* she's asleep back there.

I go to stand, and a small note falls off of my leg. As I sit back and read the words, I can only stare in disbelief.

I SLEPT WITH AURORA. TAKE HER BACK TO NY.
KANE

Excuse me, what? There's no way. We've known Kane our whole lives, and that's just not possible. I look at the curtain again. Aurora is special, but I guess Tobin and I didn't realize just *how* special she could be.

Shifting in my seat, my gaze shifts to a pile of bloody clothes crammed inside a garbage bag. My heart stops functioning. Did Kane finally kill her?

"What the hell happened?" I whisper.

"So much," Aurora says, and I jump from my skin at the unexpected sound of her voice. The curtain rattles along the track as she pulls it open, and her big green eyes stare at me. I've never been so glad to see someone.

"Did he sell you?"

Her shoulders rise and fall in a noncommittal shrug. "Yes and no. He tried to call off the deal with those Russian guys, but they tracked his truck and kidnapped me. Kane saved me from them and . . ." She motions toward the bag of bloody clothes.

"How is this possible?"

A vortex of confusion, joy, and sadness overcomes me. I don't understand how she broke through to Kane, but I'm glad she did. I'm also sad that we have to let her go, even though it's probably for the best.

I move toward her and pull her into me. I've never been so happy to see someone, but getting to hold her now doesn't change the fact that Kane has made another decision that I can't do anything about. One that I'm even more surprised about. He's never let anyone go.

"Jax, he's letting me go home," she says, her eyes rising to meet mine.

"I know, sweet girl," I whisper, even though I hate it. But I'd rather she goes home alive than be killed here. She's too good for an unmarked grave beside the interstate. "I'm going to miss you."

She grabs my shirt and pulls me into her for a kiss. "I'll miss you too, Jax. Especially you. I'm just happy that I have a chance to say goodbye."

Tears gloss her eyes, but they disappear when she blinks.

Our last moments shouldn't be colored in a depressing shade of blue, so I enfold her in my arms and carry her to the bed. If this is the last time I'll see her, I have to make it count. There isn't enough time to tell her all the ways I love her, so I'll just have to show her.

I grip the hem of her shirt and raise it over her head. The smile on her face tells me she's more than happy with this sort of goodbye, so I lower her pants next. I trail kisses down her stomach, losing myself to her soft curves. Her scent. Her everything. She is perfection.

She leans back on her elbows and spreads her thighs for me, and the sight of her pussy makes my mouth water. Not wanting to waste a drop of the wetness glistening on her skin, I bury my face in her heat.

Aurora lets out a soft moan as I grab her hips and tilt her pelvis to devour her further. I eat her like it's the last time I'll have my mouth on such a delicacy. Because it probably is. Her fingertips rake against my scalp as I taste her in broad strokes. My lips spread around her swollen clit, and she squirms as I lash the most sensitive part of her with my tongue.

Her screams rip through the truck and her fingertips clench my hair in an iron grip as waves of pleasure course through her. The waves crash closer together with each gentle nibble, suck, and lick.

Something knocks behind my eyes, and I can only assume it's Tobin. He's trying to come out. He wants what I'm getting, but this moment is mine. I close my eyes, blocking out the beautiful vision in front of me. He and Kane are stronger than I am, but I've never wanted anything more than this. I fight to stay here and let her come all over my face.

Aurora. Is. Mine.

Her growing wetness soaks my chin. She's so close, but she needs more. I release her hip and push two fingers inside her. I groan, imagining that her tightening walls are around my cock.

"Jax," she pants, her chest heaving. Her beautiful tits rise and fall with every breath. I can almost feel her intense pleasure as she pulses against my tongue. Faster. Harder.

"Come for me, sweet girl," I say. "Come on my face."

Her thighs tremble beside my head. One hand drops to my shoulder and squeezes my shirt for dear life. Her back arches, and trembles wreck her body as my fingers piston in time with my tongue flicking against her sensitive clit.

"I'm coming!" she screams, and I know. Anyone within a mile would know because they'd hear those cries of pleasure. Melodic sounds like that only mean one thing.

I ride out every shudder of her orgasm until she softly jerks with every full lick of my tongue. When I'm sure she's finished, I lean over her and press my lips to hers, spreading all her pleasure onto her chin. She kisses me back, and it's something I'll never experience again. My desire and need are tethered to her for eternity.

"Good girl, coming so hard on my face. You soaked my chin."

I pull away and wipe her come from my chin with the back of my hand, and then I slide the fingers that were in her pussy into her mouth. She licks them clean without hesitation.

God, I'll miss her.

She has brought out the best parts of all of us. What will we become once she's gone?

Chapter Thirty-Five

Aurora

We've been on the road for what feels like forever. Kane is trying to get me home as soon as possible, probably so that he doesn't change his mind. I'm still lying in bed after my time with Jax, listening to the road noise and trying my best to fall asleep. My mind wanders down well-worn paths, but I'm no closer to the answers.

For starters, what will I say to my parents when I return home after being radio silent for so long? I've gotten close to home before and never actually made it, and it's time to admit that I've been avoiding this reunion. But Kane is encouraging me to go through with it, so I'll try.

It's not like I have another option. If I can't be with Kane, Jax, and Tobin, I can't be with anyone. Turning back to my former sex work would feel like cheating. Even if they can't keep me, I'll always keep a piece of them tucked inside my heart.

The truck pulls into a parking lot, and I turn over and pretend to be asleep. I'm trying so hard to keep my distance now. Saying goodbye to Kane and Jax was already painful enough. If I get closer to any of them, it will be that much harder to leave.

The curtain slides across the track, and a heavy exhale precedes heavy boot steps. The mattress sinks as he sits on the edge of the bed, pushing my back against his. I try not to think about the warmth and comfort this unintentional touch provides because if I do, I'll probably cry. He pulls off each boot, and they thud against the floor as he tosses them down. The blanket draws back, and he gets into bed.

I don't even know who's presenting right now. I can tell by their facial expressions, voice, and sometimes the way they touch me, but I'm staring at the metal wall beside my head, he's silent, and he hasn't reached for me, which makes me think it might be Kane. He isn't the type to cuddle, even after our breakthrough. I wish it was something I could learn to accept, but I haven't been afforded the time.

His warmth is just what I need to fall asleep, and I'm finally dozing off when a heavy arm drapes over me. His hand glides along my hip, and the touch is too gentle to be anyone but my sweet Jax. I back into him, and his heat engulfs me.

"Jax?" I whisper.

"Not Jax, eighty," Tobin says, his warm tenor dripping from each word. "I'm glad to see you."

I roll toward him, a sad smile on my face because this means it's his turn to say goodbye. "Told you I could get through to him," I say.

"I don't know how."

"Don't pretend you didn't unleash those memories. You knew I'd comfort him."

A sinner's smirk slides across his face. "I couldn't let him do what he was about to do."

He wraps his arm around me and pulls me against his chest. I thought he only viewed me as a nice fuck, but he's actually cuddling me. Being tender. I guess this goodbye is affecting him more than I realized.

Tobin places his fingers beneath my chin and tips my face toward his. I swallow before meeting him the rest of the way and taking his mouth. They each give me something I need, and right now, I need Tobin. He's so tactile, using pleasure and pain as instruments for ultimate fulfillment. He's precisely what I need to forget about the fact that I have to go home.

Without them.

"You're really leaving us, eighty?" he whispers against my lips.

"I think this is what Kane wants."

Tobin nods. "It's probably for the best. Kane isn't always in control, even when he is in control. Even if it isn't for the best for all of us, you'll be better off."

Will I be better off? Kane and Tobin worked hard to break me, emotionally and sexually. They shaped me until I was a puzzle piece forced into place in their world. And now? Now I'm being tossed back home because I fit too well. I can handle their fucked-up, confusing puzzle, and they don't know what to do with that.

"I don't think he would hurt me," I say.

"You're so fucking hurtable. Everything about you makes me want to hurt you. But the difference is, to me, you're also so fuckable. I want to please you after I cause you pain. Kane isn't like that."

"I think Kane likes fucking me now," I say.

"You fucked him?"

I nod.

"Tell me about it, eighty. How'd you fuck Kane?"

Tobin rolls me onto my belly and gets above me. His body presses me into the mattress as his hand weaves through my hair and cranes my neck.

"He fucked me after killing the men who took me," I say, straining to get the words out beneath his weight.

Tobin leans off me just enough to rip down my pants, but he keeps my legs pinned together beneath him. He brings a hand to his mouth and spits before wiping it between my legs.

"Did he make you call him daddy?" The warmth of his cock fills the void between my thighs as he waits for me to answer.

"Yes," I whimper. "And then I sucked his dick while he was driving."

He thrusts forward, and I scream out from the sudden intrusion. He feels even bigger like this, like he's impaling me.

"Did his cock make you cry when he forced it down your throat?" He punctuates each word with a hard, driven thrust.

"Yes," I say, fighting back the tremble in my voice.

He keeps ramming into me, each pleasurable jolt intensified by the presence of pain. If he wasn't holding my legs together, I would probably rip in two from the force of his jealousy. The ferocity in his driven motions forces tears past the creases of my lids.

"That's a good girl. Cry for me. I want your eyes as wet as your cunt."

Then his tattooed hand wraps around my throat and squeezes. There's no warning with Tobin. He just cuts off my breath like I never deserved to have any in the first place.

"You're such a good girl for us, eighty. Such a well-trained little slut. Shame to let you go. I'll miss this cunt." He pushes into me again, then leans over until his warm breath whispers over the shell of my ear. "I'll miss *you*."

My heart soars when he says those words. He reinforces the hope that I was more to him than just a good lay. I mean something to a man who values so little.

"We're almost in New York now," he says as he leans back and fucks me hard again. "I want you to go back to your parents with my come between your pretty thighs."

He flips me over, goes to the galley, and comes back with a wooden spoon. The feral glint in his eyes tells me exactly what he plans to do. As he slides inside me again, he brushes the head of the spoon along my slit before slapping it against my sensitive flesh.

I let out a whimper and he does it again, this time spreading my lips so the spoon can come in contact with my clit. Pain and pleasure ricochet through me, and I clench around him as a scream breaks from my throat.

"You like that, eighty? You like the pain?" He does it again as I nod, and another bolt shoots through me. If he keeps this up, I'm going to come.

Sensing this, he tosses the spoon away and flips me onto my stomach again. He wants to tease me.

His hand snakes around my throat, and he cuts off my breath again as the rocking motion of his thrusts grinds my pussy against the mattress. I grip the sheets as he fucks me in the selfish way I've grown to expect with him. With my breath gone and my chest heaving for air, I'm teetering over the edge of an orgasm.

I want him to remember me the way I'll remember him. I want to squeeze his shaft with my pussy as he explodes inside me. I need to give him the best orgasm he's ever had.

I can't scream out, but the pleasure slams into me as stars dance in front of my eyes. My muscles tighten and spasm as I orgasm without my most basic necessity. Oxygen. He releases my neck, and I inhale a sharp breath as he comes with a force I can feel throughout my body. The ripple effect of his pleasure shakes me to my core. With a loud, unrestrained groan, his hand leaves my hair to slam into the metal wall, a byproduct of the intense orgasm I hoped to give him.

Tobin pulls out of me, turns me onto my back, and presses his mouth to mine.

His tongue rips through my lips as he kisses me with a passion I've never seen from him.

He pulls back and brushes my hair away from my face. "You have my heart, eighty. I won't be out for a while, so consider this my goodbye." He leans down and kisses me again.

I never thought I'd see this side of Tobin. He's still so gruff, but I see the sweetness beneath the rough exterior. And it's too much. I don't want to say goodbye. To any of them.

Tears slip down my cheeks, and I lift my hand to wipe them away. He stops me and brings his tongue to my cheek, licking a long line up my skin, cleaning the tears from my face.

"Let me keep those inside me. As a part of me." His lips draw into a smirk. "You know I like it when you cry for me."

Chapter Thirty-Six

Jax

There's no way Kane could meet her parents without making everyone extremely uncomfortable, so I was thrust into the driver's seat as we neared her family's home. It would sound as if she'd been kidnapped if he'd been the one to explain this situation. Kane is so bad at being around other humans.

I pick up the note Kane left on the dashboard and turn it over in my hands. The paper has been folded into a small square. I haven't read it yet. I plan to wait until I'm around Aurora. Then I'll say goodbye to her for the last time.

My heart aches when I glance at her. She's wearing a clean shirt and a new pair of jeans. Kane took her to a store and bought her an outfit because she couldn't go home in what she was wearing when we found her. I offered to stop to let her shower, but she said she made a promise to Tobin and couldn't. I can only imagine.

"Do we have a story?" she asks as she fidgets in the passenger seat. Pup sleeps on her lap. It's her usual spot now, and I'm worried the poor dog may take the loss just as hard as we will.

"You should probably start by telling your parents you dropped out of college."

Her lips tighten. "I guess I have to."

"It won't hurt to dilute the truth a little, though. Just say you've been traveling across the country. We picked you up and brought you back home." I smile at her. "Maybe omit the parts about being a sex worker."

She hits my arm and we both laugh. Damn it, I'm going to miss her.

She gives me directions to her house when we're nearly there. It's the only house on the road, with a thruway running behind it. I can't see it, but I know it's there. I ease the truck up the long driveway, get out of the driver's seat, and go around to open the door for Aurora. She clutches Pup to her chest, giving her a long stroke and a kiss on the top of her head.

679

"No more running off, Pup," she whispers. "I won't be there to save you next time." She swipes the tears from her eyes, places Pup on the floor, and reaches for my hand.

I help her down. Before we even make it to the front steps, the door swings open, showcasing the confused expressions of her parents.

"Jesus Christ, Aurora! We've been trying to get in touch with you for so long!" Her mother's confused anger turns to happiness as she pulls her daughter into her. "Where have you been?"

"Everywhere," Aurora says. Her voice is flat, completely devoid of the life, snark, and lilt I've heard since she's been with us.

Her short-and-stout father peers behind me, his gaze bolting to my truck after gripping Aurora's shoulder. "What a beauty you got."

"You drove trucks too, right?"

"I was regional before I became local. Then I hung up the keys to be with my wife," he says, but there's an intense longing in his eyes as he stares at my truck. Once a trucker, always a trucker. "But my truck never looked like that!"

I draw his attention back to me by clearing my throat. "Well, I'd best get going."

"Nonsense!" her mother says. "Come in and have some dinner!"

Aurora and I look at each other. Yeah, if Kane was here, he'd keel over from the mention of dinner with Aurora's parents. Lucky for him, I'm always down to socialize. I nod, and her parents welcome me inside.

Family pictures adorn every surface of the quaint home. A lot of the pictures are missing the father. Most show a mother alongside her daughter, looking like a piece of their life is missing. He must have been gone a lot. If I had a family, I'm not sure I'd pick this business. The money is good, sure, and if you don't like your family and want to be away from them as much as possible, this job is great. But if you want to spend time with someone you like, it's hard.

Unless you can bring them across state lines like we did with Aurora.

That creates its own problems, though, and I don't just mean the risk Kane poses to her safety. Because three of us live in the same body, I'd never get enough time with her. I'd be away, like a trucker, no matter how close I am.

Her mother leads us into the kitchen, and the scent of home-cooked soup fills the room.

"You're lucky your mother makes enough of her famous chicken noodle soup to feed the whole city," her father says before sitting down at the table. Her mother exits the kitchen, and he turns to Aurora as she and I take a seat. "So you've been riding with this guy?"

"Jax," I say, introducing myself as I hold out my hand.

He takes it and gives it a shake. "Jax, huh?" He turns to Aurora again. "You've been traveling all over with him after college?"

Aurora swallows, and I reach beneath the table to grip her leg and provide the reassurance she needs. She can do this. She can do fucking anything.

"Dad, I have to tell you something."

"If you're pregnant, don't tell me. I don't think my old ticker can handle it," he says, giving me a death glare.

"You're *pregnant*?" Her mom comes around the corner, having only heard the worst part of that conversation.

I shake my head, and Aurora sighs.

"I'm not pregnant, Jesus Christ," she says. "Just let me get this out, please."

Her mom sits down in the chair beside her father.

"Mom, Dad . . . I dropped out of college "

I watch as her parents' lips draw into the tightest frowns I've ever seen. Judging by their sour expressions, maybe unplanned pregnancy would have been the better story.

"What the fuck do you mean you dropped out of school?" her father shouts. His face changes shades until finally settling or red. No wonder she didn't want to tell them. It isn't going great.

I'm very good at peopling, but I'm not as good with conflict. Kane would be better for this moment, but I'm stuck here.

"School isn't for everyone," I say in a weak attempt to calm him down, but it just angers him further.

He turns his glazed gaze to me. "I'd advise you to shut your mouth, son. This is a family matter."

I lean back and shut my mouth. That's when I feel Kane knocking. Maybe he can sense my rising heart rate. My panic. I'm usually cool as a cucumber, but I don't love this situation.

"Don't talk to him like that, Dad!" Aurora snaps. "I chose to leave school, and he had nothing to do with it. I didn't meet him until I'd started traveling."

Her father stands up and walks around the table, heading straight for Aurora. I stand and get between them. As much as I hate conflict, no one will put their hands on her. Even if we can't keep her, she will always be ours.

"Hey, why don't we all relax and have scme dinner," her mother says.

Her father takes a step back and throws his hands up. "Fine, but this discussion isn't over."

I'm sure she'll get an earful when I'm gone, but I'm glad I could be a buffer for now—even if it's making me anxious as hell I'd deal with anything for Aurora.

I sit at the table as her mother serves dinner with a sour scowl. I've hardly tasted the soup when her father turns to me. Though he's looking right into my eyes, his words are aimed squarely at Aurora. "Why don't you say goodbye to your friend now?"

I nod and stand up, pushing the chair beneath the table. "I think that's best. Let's get your stuff out of the truck."

I motion Aurora toward the front door and bring her outside. She walks to the truck and climbs up to grab her backpack from between the seats. When she has both feet on the ground again, she stares at the paper I've pulled from my pocket.

I pull her into me. "First, I want to say goodbye as me. As Jax." The truck shields this moment from prying eyes, so I lean down and kiss her. I hold her, squeezing her until a laugh leaves her lips. That sweet sound is something I want to imprint on my memory. "Goodbye, sweet girl. I love you."

Her lower lip begins to quiver, and I push on before she can start crying. I don't know if I can keep going if I see her tears.

"And now, this is from Kane." I clear my throat and lower my voice to bring forth Kane's tenor the best I can. Then I unfold the paper and begin to read. "Kane here. I can't be there to see you off, so this is the best I can do. I'm not sorry for the things I did to break you when all it did was make you stronger. I'm not sorry for selling you to The Nameless because it made me realize that I couldn't let you go. I *am* sorry for having to let you go now. I can't keep you safe because no one is safe from me and the shit decisions I make. I want you to be happy, no matter how unhappy that makes me. Don't argue about it, because I won't change my mind. You survived the I-90 Killer, and as soon as you hear that name, I know you'll recognize who I am. You survived me and . . . won me over. Just like you wanted. This is goodbye, but that's a good thing for you, even if it doesn't feel like it right now. So . . . goodbye, dropout."

When I lower the letter, my heart breaks into a thousand pieces. She's crying, and it's the sort of sobbing I can't soothe away. Our time is up.

"I love you too, Jax. You cared for me when no one else did." She wipes her face, removing the proof of her pain. "Can I keep that?"

It literally admits who Kane is. As Kane's protector, everything inside me says no. But as Aurora's friend, I'm compelled to hand it over to her.

She takes it and puts it into her pocket, then pulls me into her. "Goodbye, Jax." She places a kiss on my right cheek. "Goodbye, Tobin." Her lips press against my left cheek, accompanied by a slight nibble. Then she kisses my lips and leans closer to my ear. "And you too, Daddy Kane. Goodbye."

Chapter Thirty-Seven

Aurora

I've made it forty-eight hours, but I can't stop feeling like I'm crawling out of my skin. My parents haven't even spoken to me. Instead of sitting down and having a discussion, they mope around the house with scowls on their faces. I left school, and they can't get past that. They probably wish I'd been missing after all. Dead somewhere. At least I wouldn't be their college fucking dropout.

I walk into the living room. Based on the bottles at his feet, my father is already seven beers deep. His glassy eyes never leave the television. My mom's nowhere to be found. The whole house is silent except for the low sounds coming from the TV.

"Well, if it isn't my disappointment," he says with a cheeriness that grates against my nerves. "Come sit down beside your dear old dad."

I hesitate, but he slaps the cushion beside him. I knock into a bottle as I walk over and sit down. The glass hits the hardwood and rolls.

"You know, I left my job, a job I *loved*, to be more of a parent to you." His voice slurs with each word, and the fetid scent of gut-fermented alcohol rolls toward me. "I did that, and then you go and shit on me by dropping out of college."

"Dad, I left because . . ." I can't seem to form the words to tell him what happened to me. He's my father, for fuck's sake. Even if the awkward factor was removed, he'd probably only victim-blame anyway.

His fiery eyes leave the TV and finally land on me. He clambers off the couch and stands over me. "There is no reason you can possibly conjure up that would make up for me leaving my job and turning in life insurance policies to pay for your fucking schooling. Inconsiderate bitch."

He draws back his hand and slaps me across the face. Aside from blinking to clear the sting in my eyes, I don't react. I learned my stoicism at an early age.

Then his words finally reach my ears, and I have to stuff down the anger. I was never the one who wanted him to give up his job, and I sure as shit didn't ask him to fund my schooling. That was all my mother. I'm not sure why she wanted him home to begin with. His temper has always been terrible.

A burning pain blazes beneath my right eye, and I can already sense the bruise forming beneath my skin. This isn't the first mark he's left on me, and it won't be the last if I stay here.

I stand and push past him. He stumbles backward, then tries to follow me, but I'm already in my bedroom. I lock the door and go to the desk beside my bed.

When I was twelve, my dad bought a CB radio and set it up in my room. He taught me how to use it, but I never took much interest in it. Now, I couldn't be more grateful for it.

I turn it on, and a crackle of static punches through the speakers. My fingers shake as I turn to the same frequency Kane used in his truck. Then I grab the microphone and squeeze. The silence tells me I can speak and possibly be heard.

"Three Amigos, are you out there?" I release the button and the static continues again. No one answers. "Three Amigos, this is Dropout. Can you hear me?"

I try for so long I sound desperate. It's been two days, so he's probably too far gone to hear me now. He'd have to be nearby, but he's probably long gone.

"Three Amigos," I say once more. When no one answers, I squeeze the mic one last time. "I'll try again tomorrow."

I unlock my bedroom door and head for the bathroom in the morning. I glance at my face in the mirror and quickly look away. Just like I thought, a nice shiner mars my cheek. It's purple and pink, nice and fresh. Can't wait to explain that to my mother.

Who am I kidding? She'll play dumb when she sees it. She's completely blind to bruises that come from my father's hands.

I thought things would have changed since I've been gone. The last time I spoke to my mother, she said my father had stopped drinking and was a "new man," so either my mother lied or my college status derailed his sobriety that much. Either way, I shouldn't have come home. Kane brought me here because he thought I'd be safe. I'm no safer here than I was in Kane's truck, but at least I had some happiness with them.

Even with Kane.

I go into the kitchen for breakfast. My mother notices my face and gasps, but she doesn't respond to it directly. Instead, she turns back to the vegetables on the cutting board and starts dicing them. I'm so glad to know the breakfast omelet is more important than my well-being.

"I really wish you would have stayed in school," she finally says.

"Well, I didn't, and *I* wish you guys would accept that."

"Your father won't."

"Then what am I doing here?"

"I don't know." She lowers the knife, and her shoulders drop. "I thought it would be different."

"Did you think I'd come home and be super successful, and then you'd love me?"

She turns to face me. "We do love you. Even if you aren't successful."

"Jesus Christ. Forget breakfast. I'm not hungry."

I go back to the bedroom, lock my door, and flip on the radio. Idle chatter breaks through the static, something about nearby construction, but I don't hear any recognizable call signs.

I click the button and speak over the radio. "Three Amigos, this is Dropout. Come in."

"You sound pretty. How old are you, Dropout?" someone says.

"I'm looking for Three Amigos. If you aren't him, fuck off," I say.

"Ooh wee, you got a mouth on you."

"Dropout, this is Three Amigos, and if Jangles doesn't get off this fucking station, I'll cut his balls off the next time I see him."

The other man disappears, though I'm unsure if he's still listening. Either way, I don't care. The prospect of talking to Kane warms me. I know it's him because I recognize that low, annoyed southern twang.

"Three Amigos, I'm having a bad time here. Over." I release the button and rest the mic on my lap.

"Copy that." His rich voice blares from the speakers, and I lower the volume to keep my parents from hearing. I'm too old for this, but I can't let my father take away my one tie to Kane and the boys. "Having trouble adjusting to life, Dropout? I know damn well you can adjust to just about anything."

"No. It's not that. I just want to come home. Over."

"You are home."

"No, this isn't my home anymore. That truck is my home. *You* are my home."

After a long pause, he responds. "Are you out of your mind? This isn't the place for you."

I sigh and click the button again, but my voice breaks before I can say anything else. My parents don't want me, and it's clear he doesn't want me either.

I raise the mic again. "You know what? This was stupid. Roger that. Dropout, over and out."

I'm literally just spewing radio lingo at this point. I throw the microphone onto the desk and climb into bed. My heart aches for them, but I won't beg him. He should know that by now.

I start to doze off as the hours pass by, but I'm startled awake by the sound of the radio.

"Dropout, this is Three Amigos. You there?"

I don't reach for the microphone because I'm petty and still irritated. I slam a pillow over my head.

"I know you're there," Kane says, low and almost sweet. "I'm still here." Which means he pulled over somewhere to stay within radius.

I grab the microphone. "Why are you still here?"

"Because you don't ask for help unless you need it. Shit, even if you need it, you're not likely to ask."

Fair.

"I don't want help," I say. "I just want you."

"Beg for me, Dropout."

"Wh-what? I'm not doing that over the radio."

"Give the other truckers a show, and I'll come pick you up."

Even when he's not here, he wants to degrade me. Am I sure I want to go back to this guy?

My internal thoughts respond with an instantaneous *yes*.

I turn over and bring the microphone close to my mouth. "Please, daddy. I need you," I moan. "I'll do *any*thing if you come get me. Anything. Please."

"Play with yourself," he commands.

Are we really doing this over public radio? Where any trucker in radius can hear me? He's making me feel like a CB whore—the kind you pick up on this damn thing—and I think that's what he wants me to feel like. Typical Kane.

I drop my hand between my legs, click the button, and rub myself as I moan and plead over the radio for him.

"That moaning won't cut it, Dropout. Tell me what you're doing to yourself."

My cheeks flame hot. Considering my profession was sex work for a while, this shouldn't embarrass me like it does, but my jobs were always private. But this? I'm servicing an entire fleet at once.

But if I want Kane, if I want Jax and Tobin, I have to play along.

I clear my throat and press the button. "I'm sliding my fingers through my slit. I'm so wet for you, daddy."

When my finger slips off the button, the excited chatter of other men fills the silence, their desperation dripping from their thirsty words. But I can't stop or Kane won't come get me.

"I'm imagining your cock stretching me so fucking good. Don't you want to come pick me up so you can feel me tightening around you?"

I let go of the button and hope he'll say yes, that I can stop. Instead, a stranger's voice comes through. "Shit, if he won't come pick you up, I sure as fuck will."

My eyes roll. After experiencing what Kane and his alters have to offer, nothing else could ever compare. "No thanks," I say into the mic. "But it sure would be a shame to let all this wetness go to waste, wouldn't it, Three Amigos?"

Keeping the button depressed, I bring my fingers to my lips and suck them.

"I taste so good, daddy. Don't you want to taste?" I pause. "Or would you rather choke me with your cock?"

I release the button and close my eyes as static pours from the speakers. Then I smile when his voice comes over the radio.

"I'm outside your house, Dropout. Get your ass out here."

Chapter Thirty-Eight

Kane

I'm so stupid for driving back here for her, but how could I resist her desperation over the radio? I tried for as long as I could. Instead of going back on route, I hung around because I couldn't stop thinking about her. The truck is really fucking lonely without her, and Pup is driving me batshit with all the whining and pacing.

Aurora knows who I am now. She knows the true me. The I-90 Killer. A man who has been thought to be responsible for so many deaths. A man every police agency desperately wants to catch. She's in love with a murderer. If she wants to come with me, then she's accepted the risk of being with me.

With us.

I sit and wait in her driveway. When the door to her house opens, yelling follows. Someone isn't happy that she plans to leave again. From the note Jax left for me, I learned they weren't happy about her coming home either.

She whips open the passenger side door and climbs into the truck. That's when I see her fucking cheek.

I grab her face and turn it so I can have a better look at the pink and purple bruising all along her face. "Who did this to you?" I ask, though I'm certain I know the answer. Her fucking father—the man standing in the doorway and staring me down. "Did he do this?"

She nods, and it's all the confirmation I need. I undo my seat belt and whip open the door.

Her hand wraps around my arm and squeezes. "Don't hurt him, Kane, please! Promise me!"

I want to do more than hurt him, but I also want to have some kind of fucked-up life with Aurora. That won't be possible if I get put away for assault. Or, in this case, what would surely be murder.

Without promising her anything, I exit the truck and walk toward the doorway. Her father tries to slam the door in my face, but I catch it with my hand, ignore the pain, and push it open.

"I won't fucking hurt you," I say as I push him against the wall. "I won't do that because she asked me not to, even though you clearly deserve it. But if I'm going to leave this house without putting you in a fucking wheelchair, you have to agree that you won't ever contact her again. Don't even try." I turn to her mother. "That goes for you too."

"You can't just take our daughter!" she shrieks. The sound makes me want to commit homicide twelve different ways. It also shows me where Aurora inherited that awful ability to make such a sound.

"I'm not taking her. She's leaving of her own free will because she's an adult. Have a terrible fucking night, you two." I slam the door behind me as I leave without saying another word. I've made my goddamn point.

It takes everything in me to leave her father alive. No one puts a hand on what belongs to me. But her desperate plea to leave him unharmed replays in my mind, and I force myself off the steps. My hands are shaking by the time I climb into the truck. Aurora looks at them to see if there's blood.

"I didn't hurt them, but we have to go before I do. Self-control is not my strong suit."

"Thank you," she whispers.

I nod at her, put the truck in reverse, and drive her far away from the home I thought she needed to be in. I was wrong, and Tobin and Jax are going to be fucking ecstatic about that. Pup is already showing her joy by licking Aurora's face and turning happy circles in her lap.

They aren't the only ones who have a reason to be happy about our turn of events, I guess. I just don't show it the same way they do. I'll never be like them, but that's why she has them. They can give her the love she needs and wants. I can give her my vulnerability. That's all she ever wanted from me anyway.

Epilogue

Aurora

Being with all three of them has been a difficult—but often pleasant—challenge. I don't know who I'll wake up beside at any given moment. I won't know until I can see their expression or hear their voice. I won't know until I hear the nickname they call me. I know by the way they touch me. Or if they even touch me at all. And I always know by the way they love me. Each one cares for me in different ways—with more or less of themselves, but always with all their heart.

Jax loves to love me. He lives to please me and make me laugh.

Tobin loves to hurt me and then make it all better with a touch that none of them can replicate, despite having the same hands.

Kane . . . To love Kane is to hate him too. He can be the most insufferable man to be around. Angry, miserable, bitter about all that life offered him. Except for me. I'm the little bit of what life offered him that wasn't shit. He hates so many things, but he lets me curl up under his arm and call him daddy as he strokes my back until he calms down.

Tobin turns over and wraps his arm around me, then pulls me against his hard body. "Morning, eighty," he says.

I didn't see Tobin for a while after I came back. He must have been upset when I left. When he finally came out, he was so surprised. Once the shock wore off, he fucked me for hours. He wouldn't get off me until he made up for every day we were apart.

"Morning," I whisper, letting his hand race over my body. His touch pulls me away from every thought until I can focus on nothing more than his fingertips on me.

Pup stretches beside me and hops to the floor. She gives herself a good shake, her collar rattling. I lean over the side of the bed and run my hand through her fur.

She looks up at me with her glossy brown eyes and gives a little bark. It's her way of saying good morning.

My life is so different from what it was. I finally feel like I have a purpose that doesn't involve those three numbers. Forty-sixty-eighty. I'm free from so much more than that, though. I no longer have to worry about going home and trying to force myself into a life I don't fit into anymore.

Home is here in this truck.

Home is Kane, Tobin, and Jax.

Home is a little dog who ran away and brought four people together.

I've found something most people can only dream about. I go to sleep in one part of the country and wake up in another. I go to sleep with one man and wake up with another too. Yeah, this life is a little complicated at times.

But clearly, I like it that way.

Each book from this collection:
Hitched: Books2read.com/Hitched
Along for the Ride: Books2read.com/MFMHitchhiker
Driving my Obsession: Books2read.com/DrivingmyObsession
Across State Lines: Books2read.com/AcrossStateLines

Unable to be included in the collection is *Don't Stop*, a related horror romance novella. Read if you dare: Books2read.com/Dont-Stop

If you want to check out DIET Lauren Biel books:
The Slaycation series, a dark romantic comedy series. Start with *Sinners Retreat*:
Books2read.com/SinnersRetreat
Morally Grey: Books2read.com/MorallyGrey
Stranger Session: Books2read.com/StrangerSession
Her Fantasy: Books2read.com/HerFantasy
Last Mistake: Books2read.com/LastMistake
Protect Me: Books2read.com/ProtectMeNovella
Dark Decisions: Books2read.com/DarkDecisions
Frisky the Snowman: Books2read.com/FriskytheSnowman
The Sin Duet: Books2read.com/EdgeofSin
Men of Mayhem and Vengeance: Books2read.com/MOMAV

If you want to read some darker books, check out there!
Karma: Books2read.com/KarmaNovella
Unethical: Books2read.com/UnethicalNovella
Wanted: Books2read.com/WantedNovella
Toxic Duet: Books2read.com/Toxic-Love
Captured: Books2read.com/CapturedBook
Never Let Go: Books2read.com/NLG

Connect with Lauren

Find all of Lauren's books, social media connections, and other important information at: Campsite.bio/LaurenBielAuthor or LaurenBiel.com

Join the group on Facebook to connect with other fans and to discuss the books with the author. Visit http://www.facebook.com/groups/laurenbieltraumances for more!

Lauren is now on Patreon! Get access to even more content and sneak peeks at upcoming novels. Check it out at www.patreon.com/LaurenBielAuthor to learn more!

Also by Lauren Biel

About the Author

Lauren Biel is the author of many dark romance books with several more titles in the works. When she's not working, she's writing. When she's not writing, she's spending time with her husband, her friends, or her pets. You might also find her on a horseback trail ride or sitting beside a waterfall in Upstate New York. When reading her work, expect the unexpected. To be the first to know about her upcoming titles, please visit www.LaurenBiel.com.